Russian Authors

Mayflower Books
New York, New York

Compilation Copyright © 1981 by The Rutledge Press

All rights reserved.

Published by Mayflower Books, A Division of W.H. Smith Publishers Inc.
112 Madison Avenue,
New York, New York 10016

First Printing 1981
Printed in the United States of America

"Vanka", "Peasants", "The Man in a Shell", "Gooseberries", "The Darling",
"The Lady With the Pet Dog", "On Official Business" from THE
PORTABLE CHEKHOV edited by Avrahm Yarmolinsky. Copyright 1947 by
The Viking Press, Inc., © renewed 1975 by Avrahm Yarmolinsky. Reprinted
by permission of Viking Penguin Inc.

ISBN 0-8317-7587-4

Contents

CRIME

AND

PUNISHMENT

FYODOR DOSTOYEVSKY

PART ONE—

1

On an exceptionally hot evening early in July a young man came out of the garret in which he lodged in S. Place and walked slowly, as though in hesitation, towards K. bridge.

He had successfully avoided meeting his landlady on the staircase. His garret was under the roof of a high, five-storied house and was more like a cupboard than a room. The landlady who provided him with garret, dinners, and attendance, lived on the floor below, and every time he went out he was obliged to pass her kitchen, the door of which invariably stood open. And each time he passed, the young man had a sick, frightened feeling, which made him scowl and feel ashamed. He was hopelessly in debt to his landlady, and was afraid of meeting her.

This was not because he was cowardly and abject, quite the contrary; but for some time past he had been in an overstrained irritable condition, verging on hypochondria. He had become so completely absorbed in himself, and isolated from his fellows that he dreaded meeting, not only his landlady, but any one at all. He was crushed by poverty, but the anxieties of his position had of late ceased to weigh upon him. He had given up attending to matters of practical importance; he had lost all desire to do so. Nothing that any landlady could do had a real terror for him. But to be stopped on the stairs, to be forced to listen to her trivial, irrelevant gossip, to pestering demands for payment, threats and complaints, and to rack his brains for excuses, to prevaricate, to lie—no, rather than that, he would creep down the stairs like a cat and slip out unseen.

This evening, however, on coming out into the street, he became acutely aware of his fears.

"I want to attempt a thing *like that* and am frightened by these trifles," he thought, with an odd smile. "Hm . . . yes, all is in a man's hands and he lets it all slip from cowardice, that's an axiom. It would be interesting to know what it is men are most afraid of. Taking a new step, uttering a new word is what they fear most. . . . But I am talking too much. It's because I chatter that I do nothing. Or perhaps it is that I chatter because I do nothing. I've learned to chatter this last month, lying for days together in my den thinking . . . of Jack the Giant-killer. Why am I going there now? Am I capable of *that?* Is *that* serious? It is not serious at all. It's simply a fantasy to amuse myself; a plaything! Yes, maybe it is a plaything."

The heat in the street was terrible: and the airlessness, the bustle and the plaster, scaffolding, bricks, and dust all about him, and that special Petersburg stench, so familiar to all who are unable to get out of town in summer—all worked painfully upon the young man's already overwrought nerves. The insufferable stench from the pot-houses, which are particularly numerous in that part of the town, and the drunken men whom he met continually, although it was a working day, completed the revolting misery of the picture. An expression of the profoundest disgust gleamed for a moment in the young man's refined face. He was, by the way, exceptionally handsome, above the average in height, slim, well-built, with beautiful dark eyes and dark brown hair. Soon he sank into deep thought, or more accurately speaking into a complete blankness of mind; he walked along not observing what was about him and not caring to observe it. From time to time, he would mutter something, from the habit of talking to himself, to which he had just confessed. At these moments he would become conscious that his ideas were sometimes in a tangle and that he was very weak; for two days he had scarcely tasted food.

He was so badly dressed that even a man accustomed to

shabbiness would have been ashamed to be seen in the street in such rags. In that quarter of the town, however, scarcely any shortcoming in dress would have created surprise. Owing to the proximity of the Hay Market, the number of establishments of bad character, the preponderance of the trading and working class population crowded in these streets and alleys in the heart of Petersburg, types so various were to be seen in the streets that no figure, however queer, would have caused surprise. But there was such accumulated bitterness and contempt in the young man's heart, that, in spite of all the fastidiousness of youth, he minded his rags least of all in the street. It was a different matter when he met with acquaintances or with former fellow students, whom, indeed, he disliked meeting at any time. And yet when a drunken man who, for some unknown reason, was being taken somewhere in a huge waggon dragged by a heavy dray horse, suddenly shouted at him as he drove past: "Hey there, German hatter" bawling at the top of his voice and pointing at him—the young man stopped suddenly and clutched tremulously at his hat. It was a tall round hat from Zimmerman's, but completely worn out, rusty with age, all torn and bespattered, brimless and bent on one side in a most unseemly fashion. Not shame, however, but quite another feeling akin to terror had overtaken him.

"I knew it," he muttered in confusion, "I thought so! That's the worst of all! Why, a stupid thing like this, the most trivial detail might spoil the whole plan. Yes, my hat is too noticeable. . . . It looks absurd and that makes it noticeable. . . . With my rags I ought to wear a cap, any sort of old pancake, but not this grotesque thing. Nobody wears such a hat, it would be noticed a mile off, it would be remembered. . . . What matters is that people would remember it, and that would give them a clue. For this business one should be as little conspicuous as possible. . . . Trifles, trifles are what matter! Why, it's just such trifles that always ruin everything. . . ."

He had not far to go; he knew indeed how many steps it was from the gate of his lodging house: exactly seven hundred and thirty. He had counted them once when he had been lost in dreams. At the time he had put no faith in those dreams and was only tantalising himself by their hideous but daring recklessness. Now, a month later, he had begun to look upon them differently, and, in spite of the monologues in which he jeered at his own impotence and indecision, he had involuntarily come to regard this "hideous" dream as an exploit to be attempted, although he still did not realise this himself. He was positively going now for a "rehearsal" of his project, and at every step his excitement grew more and more violent.

With a sinking heart and a nervous tremor, he went up to a huge house which on one side looked on to the canal, and on the other into the street. This house was let out in tiny tenements and was inhabited by working people of all kinds—tailors, locksmiths, cooks, Germans of sorts, girls picking up a living as best they could, petty clerks, &c. There was a continual coming and going through the two gates and in the two courtyards of the house. Three or four door-keepers were employed on the building. The young man was very glad to meet none of them, and at once slipped unnoticed through the door on the right, and up the staircase. It was a back staircase, dark and narrow, but he was familiar with it already, and knew his way, and he liked all these surroundings: in such darkness even the most inquisitive eyes were not to be dreaded.

"If I am so scared now, what would it be if it somehow came to pass that I were really going to do it?" he could not help asking himself as he reached the fourth storey. There his progress was barred by some porters who were engaged in moving furniture out of a flat. He knew that the flat had been occupied by a German clerk in the civil service, and his family. This German was moving out then, and so the fourth floor on this staircase would be untenanted except by the old woman. "That's a good thing anyway," he thought to himself, as he rang the bell of the old woman's flat. The bell gave a faint tinkle as though it were made of tin and not of copper. The little flats in such houses always have bells that ring like that. He had forgotten the note of that bell, and now its peculiar tinkle seemed to remind him of something and to bring it clearly before him. . . . He started, his nerves were terribly overstrained by now. In a little while, the door was opened a tiny crack: the old woman eyed her visitor with evident distrust through the crack, and nothing could be seen but her little eyes, glittering in the darkness. But, seeing a number of people on the landing, she grew bolder, and opened the door wide. The young man stepped into the dark entry, which was partitioned off from the tiny kitchen. The old woman stood facing him in silence and looking inquiringly at him. She was a diminutive, withered up old woman of sixty, with sharp malignant eyes and a sharp little nose. Her colourless, somewhat grizzled hair was thickly smeared with oil, and she wore no kerchief over it. Round her thin long neck, which looked like a hen's leg, was knotted some sort of flannel rag, and, in spite of the heat, there hung flapping on her shoulders, a mangy fur cape, yellow with age. The old woman coughed and groaned at every instant. The young man must have looked at her with a rather peculiar expression, for a gleam of mistrust came into her eyes again.

"Raskolnikov, a student, I came here a month ago," the young man made haste to mutter, with a half bow, remembering that he ought to be more polite.

"I remember, my good sir, I remember quite well your coming here," the old woman said distinctly, still keeping her inquiring eyes on his face.

"And here . . . I am again on the same errand," Raskolnikov continued, a little disconcerted and surprised at the old woman's mistrust. "Perhaps she is always like that though, only I did not notice it the other time," he thought with an uneasy feeling.

The old woman paused, as though hesitating; then stepped on one side, and pointing to the door of the room, she said, letting her visitor pass in front of her:

"Step in, my good sir."

The little room into which the young man walked, with yellow paper on the walls, geraniums and muslin curtains in the windows, was brightly lighted up at that moment by the setting sun.

"So the sun will shine like this *then* too!" flashed as it were by chance through Raskolnikov's mind, and with a rapid glance he scanned everything in the room, trying as far as possible to notice and remember its arrangement. But there was nothing special in the room. The furniture, all very old and of yellow wood, consisted of a sofa with a huge bent wooden back, an oval table in front of the sofa, a dressing-table with a looking-glass fixed on it between the windows, chairs along the walls and two or three half-penny prints in yellow frames, representing German damsels with birds in their hands—that was all. In the corner a light was burning before a small ikon. Everything was very clean; the floor and the furniture were brightly polished; everything shone.

"Lizaveta's work," thought the young man. There was not a speck of dust to be seen in the whole flat.

"It's in the houses of spiteful old widows that one finds such cleanliness," Raskolnikov thought again, and he stole a curious glance at the cotton curtain over the door leading into another tiny room, in which stood the old woman's bed and chest of drawers and into which he had never looked before. These two rooms made up the whole flat.

"What do you want?" the old woman said severely, coming into the room and, as before, standing in front of him so as to look him straight in the face.

"I've brought something to pawn here," and he drew out of his pocket an old-fashioned flat silver watch, on the back of which was engraved a globe; the chain was of steel.

"But the time is up for your last pledge. The month was up the day before yesterday."

"I will bring you the interest for another month; wait a little."

"But that's for me to do as I please, my good sir, to wait or to sell your pledge at once."

"How much will you give me for the watch, Alyona Ivanov-na?"

"You come with such trifles, my good sir, it's scarcely worth anything. I gave you two roubles last time for your ring and one could buy it quite new at a jeweller's for a rouble and a half."

"Give me four roubles for it, I shall redeem it, it was my father's. I shall be getting some money soon."

"A rouble and a half, and interest in advance, if you like!"

"A rouble and a half!" cried the young man.

"Please yourself"—and the old woman handed him back the watch. The young man took it, and was so angry that he was on the point of going away; but checked himself at once, remembering that there was nowhere else he could go, and that he had had another object also in coming.

"Hand it over," he said roughly.

The old woman fumbled in her pocket for her keys, and disappeared behind the curtain into the other room. The young man, left standing alone in the middle of the room, listened inquisitively, thinking. He could hear her unlocking the chest of drawers.

"It must be the top drawer," he reflected. "So she carries the keys in a pocket on the right. All in one bunch on a steel ring. . . . And there's one key there, three times as big as all the others, with deep notches; that can't be the key of the chest of drawers . . . then there must be some other chest or strongbox . . . that's worth knowing. Strong-boxes always have keys like that . . . but how degrading it all is."

The old woman came back.

"Here, sir: as we say ten copecks the rouble a month, so I must take fifteen copecks from a rouble and a half for the month in advance. But for the two roubles I lent you before, you owe me now twenty copecks on the same reckoning in advance. That makes thirty-five copecks altogether. So I must give you a rouble and fifteen copecks for the watch. Here it is."

"What! only a rouble and fifteen copecks now!"

"Just so."

The young man did not dispute it and took the money. He looked at the old woman, and was in no hurry to get away, as though there was still something he wanted to say or to do, but he did not himself quite know what.

"I may be bringing you something else in a day or two, Alyona Ivanovna—a valuable thing—silver—a cigarette box, as soon as I get it back from a friend . . ." he broke off in confusion.

"Well, we will talk about it then, sir."

"Good-bye—are you always at home alone, your sister is not here with you?" He asked her as casually as possible as he went out into the passage.

"What business is she of yours, my good sir?"

"Oh, nothing particular, I simply asked. You are too quick. . . . Good-day, Alyona Ivanovna."

Raskolnikov went out in complete confusion. This confusion became more and more intense. As he went down the stairs, he even stopped short, two or three times, as though suddenly struck by some thought. When he was in the street he cried out, "Oh, God, how loathsome it all is! and can I, can I possibly. . . . No, it's nonsense, it's rubbish!" he added resolutely. "And how could such an atrocious thing come into my head? What filthy things my heart is capable of. Yes, filthy above all, disgusting, loathsome, loathsome!—and for a whole month I've been. . . ." But no words, no exclamations, could express his agitation. The feeling of intense repulsion, which had begun to oppress and torture his heart while he was on his way to the old woman, had by now reached such a pitch and had taken such a definite form that he did not know what to do with himself to escape from his wretchedness. He walked along the pavement like a drunken man, regardless of the passers-by, and jostling against them, and only came to his senses when he was in the next street. Looking round, he noticed that he was standing close to a tavern which was entered by steps leading from the pavement to the basement. At that instant two drunken men came out at the door, and abusing and supporting one another, they mounted the steps. Without stopping to think, Raskolnikov went down the steps at once. Till that moment he had never been into a tavern, but now he felt giddy and was tormented by a burning thirst. He longed for a drink of cold beer, and attributed his sudden weakness to the want of food. He sat down at a sticky little table in a dark and dirty corner; ordered some beer, and eagerly drank off the first glassful. At once he felt easier; and his thoughts became clear.

"All that's nonsense," he said hopefully, "and there is nothing in it all to worry about! It's simply physical derangement. Just a glass of beer, a piece of dry bread—and in one moment the brain is stronger, the mind is clearer and the will is firm! Phew, how utterly petty it all is!"

But in spite of this scornful reflection, he was by now looking cheerful as though he were suddenly set free from a terrible burden: and he gazed round in a friendly way at the people in the room. But even at that moment he had a dim foreboding that this happier frame of mind was also not normal.

There were few people at the time in the tavern. Besides the two drunken men he had met on the steps, a group consisting of about five men and a girl with a concertina had gone out at the same time. Their departure left the room quiet and rather empty. The persons still in the tavern were a man who appeared to be an artisan, drunk, but not extremely so, sitting before a pot of beer, and his companion, a huge, stout man with a grey beard, in a short full-skirted coat. He was very drunk: and had dropped asleep on the bench; every now and then, he began as though in his sleep, cracking his fingers, with his arms wide apart and the upper part of his body bounding about on the bench, while he hummed some meaningless refrain, trying to recall some such lines as these:

> *"His wife a year he fondly loved*
> *His wife a—a year he—fondly loved."*

Or suddenly waking up again:

> *"Walking along the crowded row*
> *He met the one he used to know."*

But no one shared his enjoyment: his silent companion looked with positive hostility and mistrust at all these manifestations. There was another man in the room who looked somewhat like a retired government clerk. He was sitting apart, now and then sipping from his pot and looking round at the company. He, too, appeared to be in some agitation.

2

Raskolnikov was not used to crowds, and, as we said before, he avoided society of every sort, more especially of late. But now all at once he felt a desire to be with other people. Something new seemed to be taking place within him, and with it he felt a sort of thirst for company. He was so weary after a whole month of concentrated wretchedness and gloomy excitement that he longed to rest, if only for a moment, in some other world, whatever it might be; and, in spite of the filthiness of the surroundings, he was glad now to stay in the tavern.

The master of the establishment was in another room, but he frequently came down some steps into the main room, his jaunty, tarred boots with red turn-over tops coming into view each time before the rest of his person. He wore a full coat and a horribly greasy black satin waistcoat, with no cravat, and his whole face seemed smeared with oil like an iron lock. At the counter stood a boy of about fourteen, and there was another boy somewhat younger who handed whatever was wanted. On the counter lay some sliced cucumber, some pieces of dried black bread, and some fish, chopped up small, all smelling very bad. It was insufferably close, and so heavy with the fumes of spirits that five minutes in such an atmosphere might well make a man drunk.

There are chance meetings with strangers that interest us from the first moment, before a word is spoken. Such was the impression made on Raskolnikov by the person sitting a little distance from him, who looked like a retired clerk. The young man often recalled this impression afterwards, and even ascribed it to presentiment. He looked repeatedly at the clerk, partly no doubt because the latter was staring persistently at him, obviously anxious to enter into conversation. At the other persons in the room, including the tavern-keeper, the clerk looked as though he were used to their company, and weary of it, showing a shade of condescending contempt for them as persons of station and culture inferior to his own, with whom it would be useless for him to converse. He was a man over fifty, bald and grizzled, of medium height, and stoutly built. His face, bloated from continual drinking, was of a yellow, even greenish, tinge, with swollen eyelids out of which keen reddish eyes gleamed like little chinks. But there was something very strange in him; there was a light in his eyes as though of intense feeling—perhaps there were even thought and intelligence, but at the same time there was a gleam of something like madness. He was wearing an old and hopelessly ragged black dress coat, with all its buttons missing except one, and that one he had buttoned, evidently clinging to this last trace of respectability. A crumpled shirt front covered with spots and stains, protruded from his canvas waistcoat. Like a clerk, he wore no beard, nor moustache, but had been so long unshaven that his chin looked like a stiff greyish brush. And there was something respectable and like an official about his manner too. But he was restless; he ruffled up his hair and from time to time let his head drop into his hands dejectedly resting his ragged elbows on the stained and sticky table. At last he looked straight at Raskolnikov, and said loudly and resolutely:

"May I venture, honoured sir, to engage you in polite conversation? Forasmuch as, though your exterior would not command respect, my experience admonishes me that you are a man of education and not accustomed to drinking. I have always respected education when in conjunction with genuine sentiments, and I am besides a titular counsellor in rank. Marmeladov—such is my name; titular counsellor. I make bold to inquire—have you been in the service?"

"No, I am studying," answered the young man somewhat surprised at the grandiloquent style of the speaker and also at being so directly addressed. In spite of the momentary desire he had just been feeling for company of any sort, on being actually spoken to he felt immediately his habitual irritable and uneasy aversion for any stranger who approached or attempted to approach him.

"A student then, or formerly a student," cried the clerk. "Just what I thought! I'm a man of experience, immense experience, sir," and he tapped his forehead with his fingers in self-approval. "You've been a student or have attended some learned institution! . . . But allow me. . . ." He got up, staggered, took up his jug and glass, and sat down beside the young man, facing him a little sideways. He was drunk, but spoke fluently and boldly, only occasionally losing the thread of his sentences and drawling his words. He pounced upon Raskolnikov as greedily as though he too had not spoken to a soul for a month.

"Honoured sir," he began almost with solemnity, "poverty is not a vice, that's a true saying. Yet I know too that drunkenness is not a virtue, and that that's even truer. But beggary, honoured sir, beggary is a vice. In poverty you may still retain your innate nobility of soul, but in beggary—never—no one. For beggary a man is not chased out of human society with a stick, he is swept out with a broom, so as to make it as humiliating as possible; and quite right too, forasmuch as in beggary I am ready to be the first to humiliate myself. Hence the pothouse! Honoured sir, a month ago Mr. Lebeziatnikov gave my wife a beating, and my wife is a very different matter from me! Do you understand? Allow me to ask you another question out of simple curiosity: have you ever spent a night on a hay barge, on the Neva?"

"No, I have not happened to," answered Raskolnikov. "What do you mean?"

"Well, I've just come from one and it's the fifth night I've slept so. . . ." He filled his glass, emptied it and paused. Bits of hay were in fact clinging to his clothes and sticking to his hair. It seemed quite probable that he had not undressed or washed for the last five days. His hands, particularly, were filthy. They were fat and red, with black nails.

His conversation seemed to excite a general though languid interest. The boys at the counter fell to sniggering. The innkeeper came down from the upper room, apparently on purpose to listen to the "funny fellow" and sat down at a little distance, yawning lazily, but with dignity. Evidently Marmeladov was a familiar figure here, and he had most likely acquired his weakness for high-flown speeches from the habit of frequently entering into conversation with strangers of all sorts in the tavern. This habit develops into a necessity in some drunkards, and especially in those who are looked after sharply and kept in order at home.

Hence in the company of other drinkers they try to justify themselves and even if possible obtain consideration.

"Funny fellow!" pronounced the innkeeper. "And why don't you work, why aren't you at your duty, if you are in the service?"

"Why am I not at my duty, honoured sir," Marmeladov went on, addressing himself exclusively to Raskolnikov, as though it had been he who put that question to him. "Why am I not at my duty? Does not my heart ache to think what a useless worm I am? A month ago when Mr. Lebeziatnikov beat my wife with his own hands, and I lay drunk, didn't I suffer? Excuse me, young man, has it ever happened to you . . . hm . . . well, to petition hopelessly for a loan?"

"Yes, it has. But what do you mean by hopelessly?"

"Hopelessly in the fullest sense, when you know beforehand that you will get nothing by it. You know, for instance, beforehand with positive certainty that this man, this most reputable and exemplary citizen, will on no consideration give you money; and indeed I ask you why should he? For he knows of course that I shan't pay it back. From compassion? But Mr. Lebeziatnikov who keeps up with modern ideas explained the other day that compassion is forbidden nowadays by science itself, and that that's what is done now in England, where there is political economy. Why, I ask you, should he give it to me? And yet though I know beforehand that he won't, I set off to him and . . ."

"Why do you go?" put in Raskolnikov.

"Well, when one has no one, nowhere else one can go! For every man must have somewhere to go. Since there are times when one absolutely must go somewhere! When my own daughter first went out with a yellow ticket, then I had to go . . . (for my daughter has a yellow passport)," he added in parenthesis, looking with a certain uneasiness at the young man. "No matter, sir, no matter!" he went on hurriedly and with apparent composure when both the boys at the counter guffawed and even the innkeeper smiled—"No matter, I am not confounded by the wagging of their heads; for every one knows everything about it already, and all that is secret is made open. And I accept it all, not with contempt, but with humility. So be it! So be it! 'Behold the man!' Excuse me, young man, you can. . . . No, to put it more strongly and more distinctly; not *can* you but *dare* you, looking upon me, assert that I am not a pig?"

The young man did not answer a word.

"Well," the orator began again stolidly and with even increased dignity, after waiting for the laughter in the room to subside. "Well, so be it, I am a pig, but she is a lady! I have the semblance of a beast, but Katerina Ivanovna, my spouse, is a person of education and an officer's daughter. Granted, granted, I am a scoundrel, but she is a woman of a noble heart, full of sentiments, refined by education. And yet . . . oh, if only she felt for me! Honoured sir, honoured sir, you know every man ought to have at least one place where people feel for him! But Katerina Ivanovna, though she is magnanimous, she is unjust. . . . And yet, although I realise that when she pulls my hair she only does it out of pity—for I repeat without being ashamed, she pulls my hair, young man," he declared with redoubled dignity, hearing the sniggering again—"but, my God, if she would but once. . . . But no, no! It's all in vain and it's no use talking! No use talking! For more than once, my wish did come true and more than once she has felt for me but . . . such is my fate and I am a beast by nature!"

"Rather!" assented the innkeeper yawning. Marmeladov struck his fist resolutely on the table.

"Such is my fate! Do you know, sir, do you know, I have sold her very stockings for drink? Not her shoes—that would be more or less in the order of things, but her stockings, her stockings I have sold for drink! Her mohair shawl I sold for drink, a present to her long ago, her own property, not mine; and we live in a cold room and she caught cold this winter and has begun coughing and spitting blood too. We have three little children and Katerina Ivanovna is at work from morning till night; she is scrubbing and cleaning and washing the children, for she's been used to cleanliness from a child. But her chest is weak and she has a tendency to consumption and I feel it! Do you suppose I don't feel it? And the more I drink the more I feel it. That's why I drink too. I try to find sympathy and feeling in drink. . . . I drink so that I may suffer twice as much!'' And as though in despair he laid his head down on the table.

"Young man,'' he went on, raising his head again, "in your face I seem to read some trouble of mind. When you came in I read it, and that was why I addressed you at once. For in unfolding to you the story of my life, I do not wish to make myself a laughing-stock before these idle listeners, who indeed know all about it already, but I am looking for a man of feeling and education. Know then that my wife was educated in a high-class school for the daughters of noblemen, and on leaving she danced the shawl dance before the governor and other personages for which she was presented with a gold medal and a certificate of merit. The medal . . . well, the medal of course was sold—long ago, hm . . . but the certificate of merit is in her trunk still and not long ago she showed it to our landlady. And although she is most continually on bad terms with the landlady, yet she wanted to tell some one or other of her past honours and of the happy days that are gone. I don't condemn her for it, I don't blame her, for the one thing left her is recollection of the past, and all the rest is dust and ashes. Yes, yes, she is a lady of spirit, proud and determined. She scrubs the floors herself and has nothing but black bread to eat, but won't allow herself to be treated with disrespect. That's why she would not overlook Mr. Lebeziatnikov's rudeness to her, and so when he gave her a beating for it, she took to her bed more from the hurt to her feelings than from the blows. She was a widow when I married her, with three children, one smaller than the other. She married her first husband, an infantry officer, for love, and ran away with him from her father's house. She was exceedingly fond of her husband; but he gave way to cards, got into trouble and with that he died. He used to beat her at the end: and although she paid him back, of which I have authentic documentary evidence, to this day she speaks of him with tears and she throws him up to me; and I am glad, I am glad that, though only in imagination, she should think of herself as having once been happy. . . . And she was left at his death with three children in a wild and remote district where I happened to be at the time; and she was left in such hopeless poverty that, although I have seen many ups and downs of all sort, I don't feel equal to describing it even. Her relations had all thrown her off. And she was proud, too, excessively proud. . . . And then, honoured sir, and then, I, being at the time a widower, with a daughter of fourteen left me by my first wife, offered her my hand, for I could not bear the sight of such suffering. You can judge the extremity of her calamities, that she, a woman of education and culture and distinguished family, should have consented to be my wife. But she did! Weeping and sobbing and wringing her hands, she married me! For she had nowhere to turn! Do you understand, sir, do you understand what it means when you have absolutely nowhere to turn? No, that you don't understand yet. . . . And for a whole year, I performed my duties conscientiously and faithfully, and did not touch this" (he tapped the jug with his finger), "for I have feelings. But even so, I could not please her; and then I lost my place too, and that through no fault of mine but through changes in the office; and then I did touch it! . . . It will be a year and a half ago soon since we found ourselves at last after many wanderings and numerous calamities in this magnificent capital, adorned with innumerable monuments. Here too I obtained a situation. . . . I obtained it and I lost it again. Do you understand? This time it was through my own fault I lost it: for my weakness had come out. . . . We have now part of a room at Amalia Fyodorovna Lippevechsel's; and what we live upon and what we pay our rent with, I could not say. There are a lot of people living there besides ourselves. Dirt and disorder, a perfect Bedlam . . . hm . . . yes . . . And meanwhile my daughter by my first wife has grown up; and what my daughter has had to put up with from her step-mother whilst she was growing up, I won't speak of. For, though Katerina Ivanovna is full of generous feelings, she is a spirited lady, irritable and short-tempered. . . . Yes. But it's no use going over that! Sonia, as you may well fancy, has had no education. I did make an effort four years ago to give her a course of geography and universal history, but as I was not very well up in those subjects myself and we had no suitable books, and what books we had . . . hm, any way we have not even those now, so all our instruction came to an end. We stopped at Cyrus of Persia. Since she has attained years of maturity, she has read other books of romantic tendency and of late she had read with great interest a book she got through Mr. Lebeziatnikov, Lewes' Physiology—do you know it?—and even recounted extracts from it to us: and that's the whole of her education. And now may I venture to address you, honoured sir, on my own account with a private question. Do you suppose that a respectable poor girl can earn much by honest work? Not fifteen farthings a day can she earn, if she is respectable and has no special talent and that without putting her work down for an instant! And what's more, Ivan Ivanitch Klopstock the civil counsellor—have you heard of him?—has not to this day paid her for the half-dozen linen shirts she made him and drove her roughly away, stamping and reviling her, on the pretext that the shirt collars were not made like the pattern and were put in askew. And there are the little ones hungry. . . . And Katerina Ivanovna walking up and down and wringing her hands, her cheeks flushed red, as they always are in that disease: 'Here you live with us,' says she, 'you eat and drink and are kept warm and you do nothing to help.' And much she gets to eat and drink when there is not a crust for the little ones for three days! I was lying at the time . . . well, what of it! I was lying drunk and I heard my Sonia speaking (she is a gentle creature with a soft little voice . . . fair hair and such a pale, thin little face). She said: 'Katerina Ivanovna, am I really to do a thing like that?" And Darya Frantsovna, a woman of evil character and very well known to the police, had two or three times tried to get at her through the landlady. 'And why not?' said Katerina Ivanovna with a jeer, 'you are something mighty precious to be so careful of!' But don't blame her, don't blame her, honoured sir, don't blame her! She was not herself when she spoke, but driven to distraction by her illness and the crying of the hungry children; and it was said more to wound her than anything else. . . . For that's Katerina Ivanovna's character, and when children cry, even from hunger, she falls to beating them at once. At six o'clock I saw Sonia get up, put on her kerchief and her cape, and go out of the room and about nine o'clock she came

back. She walked straight up to Katerina Ivanovna and she laid
thirty roubles on the table before her in silence. She did not utter
a word, she did not even look at her, she simply picked up our
big green *drap de dames shawl* (we have a shawl, made of *drap
de dames*), put it over her head and face and lay down on the
bed with her face to the wall; only her little shoulders and her
body kept shuddering. . . . And I went on lying there, just as
before. . . . And then I saw, young man, I saw Katerina Ivanovna,
in the same silence go up to Sonia's little bed; she was on her
knees all the evening kissing Sonia's feet, and would not get up,
and then they both fell asleep in each other's arms . . . together,
together . . . yes . . . and I . . . lay drunk."

Marmeladov stopped short, as though his voice had failed
him. Then he hurriedly filled his glass, drank, and cleared his
throat.

"Since then, sir," he went on after a brief pause—"Since
then, owing to an unfortunate occurrence and through information given by evil-intentioned persons—in all which Darya Frantsovna took a leading part on the pretext that she had been treated
with want of respect—since then my daughter Sofya Semyonovna
has been forced to take a yellow ticket, and owing to that she is
unable to go on living with us. For our landlady, Amalia Fyodorovna would not hear of it (though she had backed up Darya
Frantsovna before) and Mr. Lebeziatnikov too . . . hm. . . . All
the trouble between him and Katerina Ivanovna was on Sonia's
account. At first he was for making up to Sonia himself and then
all of a sudden he stood on his dignity: 'how,' said he, 'can a
highly educated man like me live in the same rooms with a girl
like that?' And Katerina Ivanovna would not let it pass, she stood
up for her . . . and so that's how it happened. And Sonia comes
to us now, mostly after dark; she comforts Katerina Ivanovna and
gives her all she can. . . . She has a room at the Kapernaumovs,
the tailors, she lodges with them; Kapernaumov is a lame man
with a cleft palate and all of his numerous family have cleft palates
too. And his wife, too, has a cleft palate. They all live in one room,
but Sonia has her own, partitioned off. . . . Hm . . . yes . . . very
poor people and all with cleft palates . . . yes. Then I got up in

the morning, and put on my rags, lifted up my hands to heaven and set off to his excellency Ivan Afanasyevitch. His excellency Ivan Afanasyevitch, do you know him? No? Well, then, it's a man of God you don't know. He is wax . . . wax before the face of the Lord; even as wax melteth! . . . His eyes were dim when he heard my story. 'Marmeladov, once already you have deceived my expectations . . . I'll take you once more on my own responsibility'—that's what he said, 'remember,' he said, 'and now you can go.' I kissed the dust at his feet—in thought only, for in reality he would not have allowed me to do it, being a statesman and a man of modern political and enlightened ideas. I returned home, and when I announced that I'd been taken back into the service and should receive a salary, heavens, what a to-do there was . . .!"

Marmeladov stopped again in violent excitement. At that moment a whole party of revellers already drunk came in from the street, and the sounds of a hired concertina and the cracked piping voice of a child of seven singing "The Hamlet" were heard in the entry. The room was filled with noise. The tavern-keeper and the boys were busy with the new-comers. Marmeladov paying no attention to the new arrivals continued his story. He appeared by now to be extremely weak, but as he became more and more drunk, he became more and more talkative. The recollection of his recent success in getting the situation seemed to revive him, and was positively reflected in a sort of radiance on his face. Raskolnikov listened attentively.

"That was five weeks ago, sir. Yes. . . . As soon as Katerina Ivanovna and Sonia heard of it, mercy on us, it was as though I stepped into the kingdom of Heaven. It used to be: you can lie like a beast, nothing but abuse. Now they were walking on tiptoe, hushing the children. 'Semyon Zaharovitch is tired with his work at the office, he is resting, shh!' They made me coffee before I went to work and boiled cream for me! They began to get real cream for me, do you hear that? And how they managed to get together the money for a decent outfit—eleven roubles, fifty copecks, I can't guess. Boots, cotton shirt-fronts—most magnificent, a uniform, they got up all in splendid style, for eleven roubles and a half. The first morning I came back from the office I found Katerina Ivanovna had cooked two courses for dinner—soup and salt meat with horse radish—which we had never dreamed of till then. She had not any dresses . . . none at all, but she got herself up as though she were going on a visit; and not that she'd anything to do it with, she smartened herself up with nothing at all, she'd done her hair nicely, put on a clean collar of some sort, cuffs, and there she was, quite a different person, she was younger and better looking. Sonia, my little darling, had only helped with money 'for the time,' she said, 'it won't do for me to come and see you too often. After dark maybe when no one can see.' Do you hear, do you hear? I lay down for a nap after dinner and what do you think: though Katerina Ivanovna had quarrelled to the last degree with our landlady Amalia Fyodorovna only a week before, she could not resist then asking her in to coffee. For two hours they were sitting, whispering together. 'Semyon Zaharovitch is in the service again, now, and receiving a salary,' says she, 'and he went himself to his excellency and his excellency himself came out to him, made all the others wait and led Semyon Zaharovitch by the hand before everybody into his study.' Do you hear, do you hear? 'To be sure,' says he, 'Semyon Zaharovitch, remembering your past services,' says he, 'and in spite of your propensity to that foolish weakness, since you promise now and since moreover we've got on badly without you,' (do you hear, do you hear?) 'and so,' says he, 'I rely now on your word as a gentleman.' And all that, let me tell you, she has simply made up for herself, and not simply out of wantonness, for the sake of bragging; no, she believes it all herself, she amuses herself with her own fancies, upon my word she does! And I don't blame her for it, no, I don't blame her! . . . Six days ago when I brought her my first earnings in full—twenty-three roubles forty copecks altogether—she called me her poppet: 'poppet,' said she, 'my little poppet.' And when we were by ourselves, you understand? You would not think me a beauty, you would not think much of me as a husband, would you? . . . Well, she pinched my cheek 'my little poppet,' said she.''

Marmeladov broke off, tried to smile, but suddenly his chin

began to twitch. He controlled himself however. The tavern, the degraded appearance of the man, the five nights in the hay barge, and the pot of spirits, and yet this poignant love for his wife and children bewildered his listener. Raskolnikov listened intently but with a sick sensation. He felt vexed that he had come here.

"Honoured sir, honoured sir," cried Marmeladov recovering himself—"Oh, sir, perhaps all this seems a laughing matter to you, as it does to others, and perhaps I am only worrying you with the stupidity of all the trivial details of my home life, but it is not a laughing matter to me. For I can feel it all. . . . And the whole of that heavenly day of my life and the whole of that evening I passed in fleeting dreams of how I would arrange it all, and how I would dress all the children, and how I should give her rest, and how I should rescue my own daughter from dishonour and restore her to the bosom of her family. . . . And a great deal more. . . . Quite excusable, sir. Well, then, sir (Marmeladov suddenly gave a sort of start, raised his head and gazed intently at his listener) well, on the very next day after all those dreams, that is to say, exactly five days ago, in the evening, by a cunning trick, like a thief in the night, I stole from Katerina Ivanovna the key of her box, took out what was left of my earnings, how much it was I have forgotten, and now look at me, all of you! It's the fifth day since I left home, and they are looking for me there and it's the end of my employment, and my uniform is lying in a tavern on the Egyptian bridge. I exchanged it for the garments I have on . . . and it's the end of everything!"

Marmeladov struck his forehead with his fist, clenched his teeth, closed his eyes and leaned heavily with his elbow on the table. But a minute later his face suddenly changed and with a certain assumed slyness and affectation of bravado, he glanced at Raskolnikov, laughed and said:

"This morning I went to see Sonia, I went to ask her for a pick-me-up! He-he-he!"

"You don't say she gave it to you?" cried one of the newcomers; he shouted the words and went off into a guffaw.

"This very quart was bought with her money," Marmeladov declared, addressing himself exclusively to Raskolnikov. "Thirty copecks she gave me with her own hands, her last, all she had, as I saw. . . . She said nothing, she only looked at me without a word. . . . Not on earth, but up yonder . . . they grieve over men, they weep, but they don't blame them, they don't blame them! But it hurts more, it hurts more when they don't blame! Thirty copecks yes! And maybe she needs them now, eh? What do you think, my dear sir? For now she's got to keep up her appearance. It costs money, that smartness, that special smartness, you know? Do you understand? And there's pomatum, too, you see, she must have things; petticoats, starched ones, shoes too, real jaunty ones to show off her foot when she has to step over a puddle. Do you understand, sir, do you understand what all that smartness means? And here I, her own father, here I took thirty copecks of that money for a drink! And I am drinking it! And I have already drunk it! Come, who will have pity on a man like me, eh? Are you sorry for me, sir, or not? Tell me, sir, are you sorry or not? He-he-he!"

He would have filled his glass, but there was no drink left. The pot was empty.

"What are you to be pitied for?" shouted the tavern-keeper who was again near them.

Shouts of laughter and even oaths followed. The laughter and the oaths came from those who were listening and also from those who had heard nothing but were simply looking at the figure of the discharged government clerk.

"To be pitied! Why am I to be pitied?" Marmeladov suddenly declaimed, standing up with his arm outstretched, as though he had been only waiting for that question.

"Why am I to be pitied, you say? Yes! there's nothing to pity me for! I ought to be crucified, crucified on a cross, not pitied! Crucify me, oh judge, crucify me but pity me! And then I will go of myself to be crucified, for it's not merry-making I seek but tears and tribulation! . . . Do you suppose, you that sell, that this point of yours has been sweet to me? It was tribulation I sought at the bottom of it, tears and tribulation, and have found it, and I have tasted it; but He will pity us Who has had pity on all men, Who has understood all men and all things, He is the One, He too is the judge. He will come in that day and He will ask: 'Where is the daughter who gave herself for her cross, consumptive step-mother and for the little children of another? Where is the daughter who had pity upon the filthy drunkard, her earthly father, undismayed by his beastliness?' And He will say, 'Come to me! I have already forgiven thee once. . . . I have forgiven thee once. . . . Thy sins which are many are forgiven thee for thou hast loved much. . . .' And he will forgive my Sonia, He will forgive, I know it . . . I felt it in my heart when I was with her just now! And He will judge and will forgive all, the good and the evil, the wise and the meek. . . . And when He has done with all of them, then He will summon us. 'You too come forth,' He will say, 'Come forth ye drunkards, come forth, ye weak ones, come forth, ye children of shame!' And we shall all come forth, without shame and shall stand before him. And He will say unto us, 'Ye are swine, made in the Image of the Beast and with his mark; but come ye also!' And the wise ones and those of understanding will say, 'Oh Lord, why dost Thou receive these men?' And He will say, 'This is why I receive them, oh ye wise, this is why I receive them, oh ye of understanding, that not one of them believed himself to be worthy of this.' And He will hold out His hands to us and we shall fall down before him . . . and we shall weep . . . and we shall understand all things! Then we shall understand all! . . . and all will understand, Katerina Ivanovna even . . . she will understand. . . . Lord, Thy kingdom come!" And he sank down on the bench exhausted, and helpless, looking at no one, apparently oblivious of his surroundings and plunged in deep thought. His words had created a certain impression; there was a moment of silence; but soon laughter and oaths were heard again.

"That's his notion!"

"Talked himself silly!"

"A fine clerk he is!"

And so on, and so on.

"Let us go, sir," said Marmeladov all at once, raising his head and addressing Raskolnikov—"come along with me . . . Kozel's house, looking into the yard. I'm going to Katerina Ivanovna—time I did."

Raskolnikov had for some time been wanting to go and he had meant to help him. Marmeladov was much unsteadier on his legs than in his speech and leaned heavily on the young man. They had two or three hundred paces to go. The drunken man was more and more overcome by dismay and confusion as they drew nearer the house.

"It's not Katerina Ivanovna I am afraid of now," he muttered in agitation—"and that she will begin pulling my hair. What does my hair matter! Bother my hair! That's what I say! Indeed it will be better if she does begin pulling it, that's not what I am afraid of . . . it's her eyes I am afraid of . . . yes, her eyes . . . the red on her cheeks, too, frightens me . . . and her breathing too. . . . Have you noticed how people in that disease breathe . . . when they are excited? I am frightened of the children's crying, too. . . . For if Sonia has not taken them food . . . I don't know what's happened! I don't know! But blows I am not afraid of. . . . Know, sir, that such blows are not a pain to me, but even an enjoyment. In fact I can't get on without it. . . . It's better so. Let her strike me, it relieves her heart . . . it's better so . . . There is the house. The house of Kozel, the cabinet maker . . . a German, well-to-do. Lead the way!"

They went in from the yard and up to the fourth storey. The staircase got darker and darker as they went up. It was nearly eleven o'clock and although in summer in Petersburg there is no real night, yet it was quite dark at the top of the stairs.

A grimy little door at the very top of the stairs stood ajar. A very poor-looking room about ten paces long was lighted up by a candle-end; the whole of it was visible from the entrance. It was all in disorder, littered up with rags of all sorts, especially children's garments. Across the furthest corner was stretched a ragged sheet. Behind it probably was the bed. There was nothing in the room except two chairs and a sofa covered with American leather, full of holes, before which stood an old deal kitchen-table, unpainted and uncovered. At the edge of the table stood a smouldering tallow-candle in an iron candlestick. It appeared that the family had a room to themselves, not part of a room, but their room was practically a passage. The door leading to the

other rooms, or rather cupboards, into which Amalia Lippevechsel's flat was divided stood half open, and there was shouting,
uproar and laughter within. People seemed to be playing cards
and drinking tea there. Words of the most unceremonious kind
flew out from time to time.

Raskolnikov recognised Katerina Ivanovna at once. She was
a rather tall, slim and graceful woman, terribly emaciated, with
magnificent dark brown hair and with a hectic flush in her cheeks.
She was pacing up and down in her little room, pressing her hands
against her chest; her lips were parched and her breathing came
in nervous broken gasps. Her eyes glittered as in fever and
looked about with a harsh immovable stare. And that consumptive and excited face with the last flickering light of the candle-end
playing upon it made a sickening impression. She seemed to
Raskolnikov about thirty years old and was certainly a strange
wife for Marmeladov. . . . She had not heard them and did not
notice them coming in. She seemed to be lost in thought, hearing
and seeing nothing. The room was close, but she had not opened
the window; a stench rose from the staircase, but the door on to
the stairs was not closed. From the inner rooms clouds of tobacco
smoke floated in, she kept coughing, but did not close the door.
The youngest child, a girl of six, was asleep, sitting curled up on
the floor with her head on the sofa. A boy a year older stood
crying and shaking in the corner, probably he had just had a
beating. Beside him stood a girl of nine years old, tall and thin,
wearing a thin and ragged chemise with an ancient cashmere
pelisse flung over her bare shoulders, long outgrown and barely
reaching her knees. Her arm, as thin as a stick, was round her
brother's neck. She was trying to comfort him, whispering something to him, and doing all she could to keep him from whimpering again. At the same time her large dark eyes, which looked
larger still from the thinness of her frightened face, were watching her mother with alarm. Marmeladov did not enter the door,
but dropped on his knees in the very doorway, pushing Raskolnikov in front of him. The woman seeing a stranger stopped
indifferently facing him, coming to herself for a moment and
apparently wondering what he had come for. But evidently she

decided that he was going into the next room, as he had to pass through hers to get there. Taking no further notice of him, she walked towards the outer door to close it and uttered a sudden scream on seeing her husband on his knees in the doorway.

"Ah!" she cried out in a frenzy, "he has come back! The criminal! the monster! . . . And where is the money? What's in your pocket, show me! And your clothes are all different! Where are your clothes? Where is the money! speak!"

And she fell to searching him. Marmeladov submissively and obediently held up both arms to facilitate the search. Not a farthing was there.

"Where is the money?" she cried—"Mercy on us, can he have drunk it all? There were twelve silver roubles left in the chest!" and in a fury she seized him by the hair and dragged him into the room. Marmeladov seconded her efforts by meekly crawling along on his knees.

"And this is a consolation to me! This does not hurt me, but is a positive con-so-la-tion, ho-nou-red sir," he called out, shaken to and fro by his hair and even once striking the ground with his forehead. The child asleep on the floor woke up, and began to cry. The boy in the corner losing all control began trembling and screaming and rushed to his sister in violent terror, almost in a fit. The eldest girl was shaking like a leaf.

"He's drunk it! he's drunk it all," the poor woman screamed in despair—"and his clothes are gone! And they are hungry, hungry!"—and wringing her hands she pointed to the children. "Oh, accursed life! And you, are you not ashamed?"—she pounced all at once upon Raskolnikov—"from the tavern! Have you been drinking with him? You have been drinking with him, too! Go away!"

The young man was hastening away without uttering a word. The inner door was thrown wide open and inquisitive faces were peering in at it. Coarse laughing faces with pipes and cigarettes and heads wearing caps thrust themselves in at the doorway. Further in could be seen figures in dressing gowns flung open, in costumes of unseemly scantiness, some of them with cards in their hands. They were particularly diverted, when Marmeladov,

dragged about by his hair, shouted that it was a consolation to
him. They even began to come into the room; at last a sinister
shrill outcry was heard: this came from Amalia Lippevechsel herself pushing her way amongst them and trying to restore order
after her own fashion and for the hundredth time to frighten the
poor woman by ordering her with coarse abuse to clear out of the
room next day. As he went out, Raskolnikov had time to put his
hand into his pocket, to snatch up the coppers he had received in
exchange for his rouble in the tavern and to lay them unnoticed
on the window. Afterwards on the stairs, he changed his mind and
would have gone back.

"What a stupid thing I've done," he thought to himself,
"they have Sonia and I want it myself." But reflecting that it
would be impossible to take it back now and that in any case he
would not have taken it, he dismissed it with a wave of his hand
and went back to his lodging. "Sonia wants pomatum too," he
said as he walked along the street, and he laughed malignantly—
"such smartness costs money. . . . Hm! And maybe Sonia herself
will be bankrupt to-day, for there is always a risk, hunting big
game . . . digging for gold . . . then they would all be without
a crust to-morrow except for my money. Hurrah for Sonia! What
a mine they've dug there! And they're making the most of it! Yes,
they are making the most of it! They've wept over it and grown
used to it. Man grows used to everything, the scoundrel!"

He sank into thought.

"And what if I am wrong," he cried suddenly after a moment's thought. "What if man is not really a scoundrel, man in
general, I mean, the whole race of mankind—then all the rest is
prejudice, simply artificial terrors and there are no barriers and
it's all as it should be."

3

He waked up late next day after a broken sleep. But his sleep
had not refreshed him; he waked up bilious, irritable, ill-tem-
pered, and looked with hatred at his room. It was a tiny cupboard

of a room about six paces in length. It had a poverty-stricken appearance with its dusty yellow paper peeling off the walls, and it was so low-pitched that a man of more than average height was ill at ease in it and felt every moment that he would knock his head against the ceiling. The furniture was in keeping with the room: there were three old chairs, rather rickety; a painted table in the corner on which lay a few manuscripts and books; the dust that lay thick upon them showed that they had been long untouched. A big clumsy sofa occupied almost the whole of one wall and half the floor space of the room; it was once covered with chintz, but was now in rags and served Raskolnikov as a bed. Often he went to sleep on it, as he was, without undressing, without sheets, wrapped in his old student's overcoat, with his head on one little pillow, under which he heaped up all the linen he had, clean and dirty, by way of a bolster. A little table stood in front of the sofa.

It would have been difficult to sink to a lower ebb of disorder, but to Raskolnikov in his present state of mind this was positively agreeable. He had got completely away from every one, like a tortoise in its shell, and even the sight of the servant girl who had to wait upon him and looked sometimes into his room made him writhe with nervous irritation. He was in the condition that overtakes some monomaniacs entirely concentrated upon one thing. His landlady had for the last fortnight given up sending him in meals, and he had not yet thought of expostulating with her, though he went without his dinner. Nastasya, the cook and only servant, was rather pleased at the lodger's mood and had entirely given up sweeping and doing his room, only once a week or so she would stray into his room with a broom. She waked him up that day.

"Get up, why are you asleep!" she called to him. "It's past nine, I have brought you some tea; will you have a cup? I should think you're fairly starving?"

Raskolnikov opened his eyes, started and recognised Nastasya.

"From the landlady, eh?" he asked, slowly and with a sickly face sitting up on the sofa.

"From the landlady, indeed!"

She set before him her own cracked teapot full of weak and stale tea and laid two yellow lumps of sugar by the side of it.

"Here, Nastasya, take it please," he said, fumbling in his pocket (for he had slept in his clothes) and taking out a handful of coppers—"run and buy me a loaf. And get me a little sausage, the cheapest, at the pork-butcher's."

"The loaf I'll fetch you this very minute, but wouldn't you rather have some cabbage soup instead of sausage? It's capital soup, yesterday's. I saved it for you yesterday, but you came in late. It's fine soup."

When the soup had been brought, and he had begun upon it, Nastasya sat down beside him on the sofa and began chatting. She was a country peasant-woman, and a very talkative one.

"Praskovya Pavlovna means to complain to the police about you," she said.

He scowled.

"To the police? What does she want?"

"You don't pay her money and you won't turn out of the room. That's what she wants, to be sure."

"The devil, that's the last straw," he muttered, grinding his teeth, "no, that would not suit me . . . just now. She is a fool," he added aloud. "I'll go and talk to her to-day."

"Fool she is and no mistake, just as I am. But why, if you are so clever, do you lie here like a sack and have nothing to show for it? One time you used to go out, you say, to teach children. But why is it you do nothing now?"

"I am doing . . ." Raskolnikov began sullenly and reluctantly.

"What are you doing?"

"Work . . ."

"What sort of work?"

"I am thinking," he answered seriously after a pause.

Nastasya was overcome with a fit of laughter. She was given to laughter and when anything amused her, she laughed inaudibly, quivering and shaking all over till she felt ill.

"And have you made much money by your thinking?" she managed to articulate at last.

"One can't go out to give lessons without boots. And I'm sick of it."

"Don't quarrel with your bread and butter."

"They pay so little for lessons. What's the use of a few coppers?" he answered, reluctantly, as though replying to his own thought.

"And you want to get a fortune all at once?"

He looked at her strangely.

"Yes, I want a fortune," he answered firmly, after a brief pause.

"Don't be in such a hurry, you quite frighten me! Shall I get you the loaf or not?"

"As you please."

"Ah, I forgot! A letter came for you yesterday when you were out."

"A letter? for me! from whom?"

"I can't say. I gave three copecks of my own to the postman for it. Will you pay me back?"

"Then bring it to me, for God's sake, bring it," cried Raskolnikov greatly excited—"good God!"

A minute later the letter was brought him. That was it: from his mother, from the province of R——. He turned pale when he took it. It was a long while since he had received a letter, but another feeling also suddenly stabbed his heart.

"Nastasya, leave me alone, for goodness' sake; here are your three copecks, but for goodness' sake, make haste and go!"

The letter was quivering in his hand; he did not want to open it in her presence; he wanted to be left *alone* with this letter. When Nastasya had gone out, he lifted it quickly to his lips and kissed it; then he gazed intently at the address, the small, sloping handwriting, so dear and familiar, of the mother who had once taught him to read and write. He delayed; he seemed almost afraid of something. At last he opened it; it was a thick heavy letter, weighing over two ounces, two large sheets of note paper were covered with very small handwriting.

"My dear Rodya," wrote his mother—"it's two months since I last had a talk with you by letter which has distressed me and even kept me awake at night, thinking. But I am sure you will not blame me for my inevitable silence. You know how I love you; you are all we have to look to, Dounia and I, you are our all, our one hope, our one stay. What a grief it was to me when I heard that you had given up the university some months ago, for want of means to keep yourself and that you had lost your lessons and your other work! How could I help you out of my hundred and twenty roubles a year pension? The fifteen roubles I sent you four months ago I borrowed, as you know, on security of my pension, from Vassily Ivanovitch Vahrushin a merchant of this town. He is a kind-hearted man and was a friend of your father's too. But having given him the right to receive the pension, I had to wait till the debt was paid off and that is only just done, so that I've been unable to send you anything all this time. But now, thank God, I believe I shall be able to send you something more and in fact we may congratulate ourselves on our good fortune now, of which I hasten to inform you. In the first place, would you have guessed, dear Rodya, that your sister has been living with me for the last six weeks and we shall not be separated in the future. Thank God, her sufferings are over, but I will tell you everything in order, so that you may know just how everything has happened and all that we have hitherto concealed from you. When you wrote to me two months ago that you had heard that Dounia had a great deal to put up with in the Svidrigaïlovs' house, when you wrote that and asked me to tell you all about it—what could I write in answer to you? If I had written the whole truth to you, I dare say you would have thrown up everything and have come to us, even if you had to walk all the way, for I know your character and your feelings, and you would not let your sister be insulted. I was in despair myself, but what could I do? And, besides, I did not know the whole truth myself then. What made it all so difficult was that Dounia received a hundred roubles in advance when she took the place as governess in their family, on condition of part of her salary being deducted every month, and so it was impossible to throw up the situation without repaying the debt. This sum (now I can explain it all to you, my precious Rodya) she took chiefly in order to send you sixty roubles, which you needed so terribly then and which you received from us last year. We deceived you then, writing that this money came from Dounia's savings, but that was not so, and now I tell you all about it, because, thank God, things have suddenly changed for the better, and that you may know how Dounia loves you and what a heart she has. At first indeed Mr. Svidrigaïlov treated her very rudely and used to make disrespectful and jeering remarks at table. . . . But I don't want to go into all those painful details, so as not to worry you for nothing when it is now all over. In short, in spite of the kind and generous behaviour of Marfa Petrovna, Mr. Svidrigaïlov's wife, and all the rest of the household, Dounia had a very hard time, especially when Mr. Svidrigaïlov, relapsing into his old regimental habits, was under the influence of Bacchus. And how do you think it was all explained later on? Would you believe that the crazy fellow had conceived a passion for Dounia from the beginning, but had concealed it under a show of rudeness and contempt. Possibly he was ashamed and horrified himself at his own flighty hopes, considering his years and his being the father of a family; and that made him angry with Dounia. And possibly, too, he hoped by his rude and sneering behaviour to hide the truth from others. But at last he lost all control and had the face to make Dounia an open and shameful proposal, promising her all sorts of inducements and offering, besides, to throw up everything and take her to another estate of his, or even abroad. You can imagine all she went through! To leave her situation at once was impossible not only on account of the money debt, but also to spare the feelings of Marfa Petrovna, whose suspicions would have been aroused; and then Dounia would have been the cause of a rupture in the family. And it would have meant a terrible scandal for Dounia too; that would have been inevitable. There were various other reasons owing to which Dounia could not hope to escape from that awful house for another six weeks. You know Dounia, of course; you know how clever she is and what a strong will she has. Dounia can endure a great deal and even in the most difficult cases she has the fortitude to

maintain her firmness. She did not even write to me about everything for fear of upsetting me, although we were constantly in
communication. It all ended very unexpectedly. Marfa Petrovna
accidentally overheard her husband imploring Dounia in the garden, and, putting quite a wrong interpretation on the position,
threw the blame upon her, believing her to be the cause of it all.
An awful scene took place between them on the spot in the
garden; Marfa Petrovna went so far as to strike Dounia, refused
to hear anything and was shouting at her for a whole hour and
then gave orders that Dounia should be packed off at once to me
in a plain peasant's cart, into which they flung all her things, her
linen and her clothes, all pell-mell, without folding it up and
packing it. And a heavy shower of rain came on, too, and Dounia,
insulted and put to shame, had to drive with a peasant in an open
cart all the seventeen versts into town. Only think now what
answer could I have sent to the letter I received from you two
months ago and what could I have written? I was in despair; I
dared not write to you the truth because you would have been
very unhappy, mortified and indignant, and yet what could you
do? You could only perhaps ruin yourself, and, besides, Dounia
would not allow it; and fill up my letter with trifles when my heart
was so full of sorrow, I could not. For a whole month the town
was full of gossip about this scandal, and it came to such a pass
that Dounia and I dared not even go to church on account of the
contemptuous looks, whispers, and even remarks made aloud
about us. All our acquaintances avoided us, nobody even bowed
to us in the street, and I learnt that some shopmen and clerks were
intending to insult us in a shameful way, smearing the gates of our
house with pitch, so that the landlord began to tell us we must
leave. All this was set going by Marfa Petrovna, who managed to
slander Dounia and throw dirt at her in every family. She knows
every one in the neighbourhood, and that month she was continually coming into the town, and as she is rather talkative and fond
of gossiping about her family affairs and particularly of complaining to all and each of her husband—which is not at all right—so
in a short time she had spread her story not only in the town, but
over the whole surrounding district. It made me ill, but Dounia

bore it better than I did, and if only you could have seen how she
endured it all and tried to comfort me and cheer me up! She is
an angel! But by God's mercy, our sufferings were cut short: Mr.
Svidrigaïlov returned to his senses and repented and, probably
feeling sorry for Dounia, he laid before Marfa Petrovna a complete and unmistakable proof of Dounia's innocence, in the form
of a letter Dounia had been forced to write and give to him,
before Marfa Petrovna came upon them in the garden. This letter, which remained in Mr. Svidrigaïlov's hands after her departure, she had written to refuse personal explanations and secret
interviews, for which he was entreating her. In that letter she
reproached him with great heat and indignation for the baseness
of his behaviour in regard to Marfa Petrovna, reminding him that
he was the father and head of a family and telling him how
infamous it was of him to torment and make unhappy a defenceless girl, unhappy enough already. Indeed, dear Rodya, the letter
was so nobly and touchingly written that I sobbed when I read
it and to this day I cannot read it without tears. Moreover, the
evidence of the servants, too, cleared Dounia's reputation; they
had seen and known a great deal more than Mr. Svidrigaïlov had
himself supposed—as indeed is always the case with servants.
Marfa Petrovna was completely taken aback, and 'again crushed'
as she said herself to us, but she was completely convinced of
Dounia's innocence. The very next day, being Sunday, she went
straight to the Cathedral, knelt down and prayed with tears to Our
Lady to give her strength to bear this new trial and to do her duty.
Then she came straight from the Cathedral to us, told us the
whole story, wept bitterly and, fully penitent, she embraced
Dounia and besought her to forgive her. The same morning,
without any delay, she went round to all the houses in the town
and everywhere, shedding tears, she asserted in the most flattering terms Dounia's innocence and the nobility of her feelings and
her behaviour. What was more, she showed and read to every one
the letter in Dounia's own handwriting to Mr. Svidrigaïlov and
even allowed them to take copies of it—which I must say I think
was superfluous. In this way she was busy for several days in
driving about the whole town, because some people had taken

offence through precedence having been given to others. And therefore they had to take turns, so that in every house she was expected before she arrived, and every one knew that on such and such a day Marfa Petrovna would be reading the letter in such and such a place and people assembled for every reading of it, even many who had heard it several times already both in their own houses and in other people's. In my opinion a great deal, a very great deal of all this was unnecessary; but that's Marfa Petrovna's character. Anyway she succeeded in completely re-establishing Dounia's reputation and the whole ignominy of this affair rested as an indelible disgrace upon her husband, as the only person to blame, so that I really began to feel sorry for him; it was really treating the crazy fellow too harshly. Dounia was at once asked to give lessons in several families, but she refused. All of a sudden every one began to treat her with marked respect and all this did much to bring about the event by which, one may say, our whole fortunes are now transformed. You must know, dear Rodya, that Dounia has a suitor and that she has already consented to marry him. I hasten to tell you all about the matter, and though it has been arranged without asking your consent, I think you will not be aggrieved with me or with your sister on that account, for you will see that we could not wait and put off our decision till we heard from you. And you could not have judged all the facts without being on the spot. This was how it happened. He is already of the rank of a counsellor, Pyotr Petrovitch Luzhin, and is distantly related to Marfa Petrovna, who has been very active in bringing the match about. It began with his expressing through her his desire to make our acquaintance. He was properly received, drank coffee with us and the very next day he sent us a letter in which he very courteously made an offer and begged for a speedy and decided answer. He is a very busy man and is in a great hurry to get to Petersburg, so that every moment is precious to him. At first, of course, we were greatly surprised, as it had all happened so quickly and unexpectedly. We thought and talked it over the whole day. He is a well-to-do man, to be depended upon, he has two posts in the government and has already made his fortune. It is true that he is forty-five years old, but he is of a fairly prepossessing appearance, and might still be thought attractive by women, and he is altogether a very respectable and presentable man, only he seems a little morose and somewhat conceited. But possibly that may only be the impression he makes at first sight. And beware, dear Rodya, when he comes to Petersburg, as he shortly will do, beware of judging him too hastily and severely, as your way is, if there is anything you do not like in him at first sight. I give you this warning, although I feel sure that he will make a favourable impression upon you. Moreover, in order to understand any man one must be deliberate and careful to avoid forming prejudices and mistaken ideas, which are very difficult to correct and get over afterwards. And Pyotr Petrovitch, judging by many indications, is a thoroughly estimable man. At his first visit, indeed, he told us that he was a practical man, but still he shares, as he expressed it, many of the convictions 'of our most rising generation' and he is an opponent of all prejudices. He said a good deal more, for he seems a little conceited and likes to be listened to, but this is scarcely a vice. I, of course, understood very little of it, but Dounia explained to me that, though he is not a man of great education, he is clever and seems to be good-natured. You know your sister's character, Rodya. She is a resolute, sensible, patient and generous girl, but she has a passionate heart, as I know very well. Of course, there is no great love either on his side, or on hers, but Dounia is a clever girl and has the heart of an angel, and will make it her duty to make her husband happy who on his side will make her happiness his care. Of that we have no good reason to doubt, though it must be admitted the matter has been arranged in great haste. Besides he is a man of great prudence and he will see, to be sure, of himself, that his own happiness will be the more secure, the happier Dounia is with him. And as for some defects of character, for some habits and even certain differences of opinion—which indeed are inevitable even in the happiest marriages—Dounia has said that, as regards all that, she relies on herself, that there is nothing to be uneasy about, and that she is ready to put up with a great deal, if only their future relationship can be an honourable and straightforward one. He struck me, for instance, at first, as rather abrupt, but that may well come from his being an outspoken man, and that is no doubt how it is. For instance, at his second visit, after he had received Dounia's consent, in the course of conversation, he declared that before making Dounia's acquaintance, he had made up his mind to marry a girl of good reputation, without dowry and, above all, one who had experienced poverty, because, as he explained, a man ought not to be indebted to his wife, but that it is better for a wife to look upon her husband as her benefactor. I must add that he expressed it more nicely and politely than I have done, for I have forgotten his actual phrases and only remember the meaning. And, besides, it was obviously not said of design, but slipped out in the heat of conversation, so that he tried afterwards to correct himself and smooth it over, but all the same it did strike me as somewhat rude, and I said so afterwards to Dounia. But Dounia was vexed, and answered that 'words are not deeds,' and that, of course, is perfectly true. Dounia did not sleep all night before she made up her mind, and, thinking that I was asleep, she got out of bed and was walking up and down the room all night; at last she knelt down before the ikon and prayed long and fervently and in the morning she told me that she had decided.

"I have mentioned already that Pyotr Petrovitch is just setting off for Petersburg, where he has a great deal of business, and he wants to open a legal bureau. He has been occupied for many years in conducting civil and commercial litigation, and only the other day he won an important case. He has to be in Petersburg because he has an important case before the Senate. So, Rodya dear, he may be of the greatest use to you, in every way indeed, and Dounia and I have agreed that from this very day you could definitely enter upon your career and might consider that your future is marked out and assured for you. Oh, if only this comes to pass! This would be such a benefit that we could only look upon it as a providential blessing. Dounia is dreaming of nothing else. We have even ventured already to drop a few words on the subject to Pyotr Petrovitch. He was cautious in his answer, and said that, of course, as he could not get on without a secretary, it would be better to be paying a salary to a relation than to a stranger, if only the former were fitted for the duties (as though there could be doubt of your being fitted!) but then he expressed doubts whether your studies at the university would leave you time for work at his office. The matter dropped for the time, but Dounia is thinking of nothing else now. She has been in a sort of fever for the last few days, and has already made a regular plan for your becoming in the end an associate and even a partner in Pyotr Petrovitch's business, which might well be, seeing that you are a student of law. I am in complete agreement with her, Rodya, and share all her plans and hopes, and think there is every probability of realising them. And in spite of Pyotr Petrovitch's evasiveness, very natural at present (since he does not know you), Dounia is firmly persuaded that she will gain everything by her good influence over her future husband; this she is reckoning upon. Of course we are careful not to talk of any of these more remote plans to Pyotr Petrovitch, especially of your becoming his partner. He is a practical man and might take this very coldly, it might all seem to him simply a day-dream. Nor has either Dounia or I breathed a word to him of the great hopes we have of his helping us to pay for your university studies; we have not spoken of it in the first place, because it will come to pass of itself, later on, and he will no doubt without wasting words offer to do it of himself, (as though he could refuse Dounia that) the more readily since you may by your own efforts become his right hand in the office, and receive this assistance not as a charity, but as a salary earned by your own work. Dounia wants to arrange it all like this and I quite agree with her. And we have not spoken of our plans for another reason, that is, because I particularly wanted you to feel on an equal footing when you first meet him. When Dounia spoke to him with enthusiasm about you, he answered that one could never judge of a man without seeing him close, for oneself, and that he looked forward to forming his own opinion when he makes your acquaintance. Do you know, my precious Rodya, I think that perhaps for some reasons (nothing to do with Pyotr Petrovitch though, simply for my own personal, perhaps old-womanish, fancies) I should do better to go on living by myself, apart, than with them, after the wedding. I am convinced that he will be generous and delicate enough to invite me and to urge me to remain with my daughter for the future, and if he has said nothing about it hitherto, it is simply because it has been taken for granted; but I shall refuse. I have noticed more than once in my life that husbands don't quite get on with their mothers-in-law, and I don't want to be the least bit in any one's way, and for my own sake, too, would rather be quite independent, so long as I have a crust of bread of my own, and such children as you and Dounia. If possible, I would settle somewhere near you, for the most joyful piece of news, dear Rodya, I have kept for the end of my letter: know then, my dear boy, that we may, perhaps, be all together in a very short time and may embrace one another again after a separation of almost three years! It is settled *for certain* that Dounia and I are to set off for Petersburg, exactly when I don't know, but very, very soon, possibly in a week. It all depends on Pyotr Petrovitch who will let us know when he has had time to look round him in Petersburg. To suit his own arrangements he is anxious to have the ceremony as soon as possible, even before the fast of Our Lady, if it could be managed, or if that is too soon to be ready, immediately after. Oh, with what happiness I shall press you to my heart! Dounia is all excitement at the joyful thought of seeing you, she said one day in joke that she would be ready to marry Pyotr Petrovitch for that alone. She is an angel! She is not writing anything to you now, and has only told me to write that she has so much, so much to tell you that she is not going to take up her pen now, for a few lines would tell you nothing, and it would only mean upsetting herself; she bids me send you her love and innumerable kisses. But although we shall be meeting so soon, perhaps I shall send you as much money as I can in a day or two. Now that every one has heard that Dounia is to marry Pyotr Petrovitch, my credit has suddenly improved and I know that Afanasy Ivanovitch will trust me now even to seventy-five roubles on the security of my pension, so that perhaps I shall be able to send you twenty-five or even thirty roubles. I would send you more, but I am uneasy about our travelling expenses; for though Pyotr Petrovitch has been so kind as to undertake part of the expenses of the journey, that is to say, he has taken upon himself the conveyance of our bags and big trunk (which will be conveyed through some acquaintances of his), we must reckon upon some expenses on our arrival in Petersburg, where we can't be left without a half-penny, at least for the first few days. But we have calculated it all, Dounia and I, to the last penny, and we see that the journey will not cost very much. It is only ninety versts from us to the railway and we have come to an agreement with a driver we know, so as to be in readiness; and from there Dounia and I can travel quite comfortably third class. So that I may very likely be able to send to you not twenty-five, but thirty roubles. But enough; I have covered two sheets already and there is no space left for more; our whole history, but so many events have happened! And now, my precious Rodya, I embrace you and send you a mother's blessing till we meet. Love Dounia your sister, Rodya; love her as she loves you and understand that she loves you beyond everything, more than herself. She is an angel and you, Rodya, you are everything to us—our one hope, our one consolation. If only you are happy, we shall be happy. Do you still say your prayers, Rodya, and believe in the mercy of our Creator and our Redeemer? I am afraid in my heart that you may have been visited by the new spirit of infidelity that is abroad to-day! If it is so, I pray for you. Remember, dear boy, how in your childhood, when your father was living, you used to lisp your prayers at my knee, and how happy we all were in those days. Good-bye, till we meet then—I embrace you warmly, warmly, with many kisses.

"Yours till death
"PULCHERIA RASKOLNIKOV."

Almost from the first, while he read the letter, Raskolnikov's face was wet with tears; but when he finished it, his face was pale and distorted and a bitter, wrathful and malignant smile was on his lips. He laid his head down on his threadbare dirty pillow and pondered, pondered a long time. His heart was beating violently, and his brain was in a turmoil. At last he felt cramped and stifled in the little yellow room that was like a cupboard or a box. His eyes and his mind craved for space. He took up his hat and went out, this time without dread of meeting any one; he had forgotten his dread. He turned in the direction of the Vassilyevsky Ostrov, walking along Vassilyevsky Prospect, as though hastening on some business, but he walked, as his habit was, without noticing his way, muttering and even speaking aloud to himself, to the astonishment of the passersby. Many of them took him to be drunk.

4

His mother's letter had been a torture to him, but as regards the chief fact in it, he had felt not one moment's hesitation, even whilst he was reading the letter. The essential question was settled, and irrevocably settled, in his mind: "Never such a marriage while I am alive and Mr. Luzhin be damned!" "The thing is perfectly clear," he muttered to himself, with a malignant smile anticipating the triumph of his decision. "No, mother, no, Dounia, you won't deceive me! and then they apologise for not asking my advice and for taking the decision without me! I dare say! They imagine it is arranged now and can't be broken off; but we will see whether it can or not! A magnificent excuse: 'Pyotr Petrovitch is such a busy man that even his wedding has to be in post-haste, almost by express.' No, Dounia, I see it all and I know what you want to say to me; and I know too what you were thinking about, when you walked up and down all night, and what your prayers were like before the Holy Mother of Kazan who stands in mother's bedroom. Bitter is the ascent to Golgotha. . . . Hm . . . so it is finally settled; you have determined to marry a sensible business man, Avdotya Romanovna, one who has a fortune (has *already* made his fortune, that is so much more solid and impressive) a man who holds two government posts and who shares the ideas of our most rising generation, as mother writes, and who *seems* to be kind, as Dounia herself observes. That *seems* beats everything! And that very Dounia for that very *'seems'* is marrying him! Splendid! splendid!

". . . But I should like to know why mother has written to

me about 'our most rising generation'? Simply as a descriptive touch, or with the idea of prepossessing me in favour of Mr. Luzhin? Oh, the cunning of them! I should like to know one thing more: how far they were open with one another that day and night and all this time since? Was it all put into *words,* or did both understand that they had the same thing at heart and in their minds, so that there was no need to speak of it aloud, and better not to speak of it. Most likely it was partly like that, from mother's letter it's evident: he struck her as rude *a little,* and mother in her simplicity took her observations to Dounia. And she was sure to be vexed and 'answered her angrily.' I should think so! Who would not be angered when it was quite clear without any naive questions and when it was understood that it was useless to discuss it. And why does she write to me, 'love Dounia, Rodya, and she loves you more than herself'? Has she a secret conscience-prick at sacrificing her daughter to her son? 'You are our one comfort, you are everything to us.' Oh, mother!''

His bitterness grew more and more intense, and if he had happened to meet Mr. Luzhin at the moment, he might have murdered him.

"Hm . . . yes, that's true," he continued, pursuing the whirling ideas that chased each other in his brain, "it is true that 'it needs time and care to get to know a man,' but there is no mistake about Mr. Luzhin. The chief thing is he is 'a man of business and *seems* kind,' that was something, wasn't it, to send the bags and big box for them! A kind man, no doubt after that! But his *bride* and her mother are to drive in a peasant's cart covered with sacking (I know. I have been driven in it). No matter! It is only ninety versts and then they can 'travel very comfortably, third class,' for a thousand versts! Quite right, too. One must cut one's coat according to one's cloth, but what about you, Mr. Luzhin? She is your bride. . . . And you must be aware that her mother has to raise money on her pension for the journey. To be sure it's a matter of business, a partnership for mutual benefit, with equal shares and expenses;—food and drink provided, but pay for your tobacco. The business man has got the better of them, too. The luggage will cost less than their fares and very likely go for nothing. How is it that they don't both see all that, or is it that they don't want to see? And they are pleased, pleased! And to think that this is only the first blossoming, and that the real fruits are to come! But what really matters is not the stinginess, is not the meanness, but the *tone* of the whole thing. For that will be the tone after marriage, it's a foretaste of it. And mother too, why should she be so lavish? What will she have by the time she gets to Petersburg? Three silver roubles or two 'paper ones' as *she* says. . . . that old woman . . . hm. What does she expect to live upon in Petersburg afterwards? She has her reasons already for guessing that she *could not* live with Dounia after the marriage, even for the first few months. The good man has no doubt let slip something on that subject also, though mother would deny it: 'I shall refuse,' says she. On whom is she reckoning then? Is she counting on what is left of her hundred and twenty roubles of pension when Afanasy Ivanovitch's debt is paid? She knits woollen shawls and embroiders cuffs, ruining her old eyes. And all her shawls don't add more than twenty roubles a year to her hundred and twenty, I know that. So she is building all her hopes all the time on Mr. Luzhin's generosity; 'he will offer it of himself, he will press it on me.' You may wait a long time for that! That's how it always is with these Schilleresque noble hearts; till the last moment every goose is a swan with them, till the last moment, they hope for the best and will see nothing wrong, and although they have an inkling of the other side of the picture, yet they won't face the truth till they are forced to; the very thought of it makes them shiver; they thrust the truth away with both hands, until the man they deck out in false colours puts a fool's cap on them with his own hands. I should like to know whether Mr. Luzhin has any orders of merit; I bet he has the Anna in his buttonhole and that he puts it on when he goes to dine with contractors or merchants. He will be sure to have it for his wedding, too! Enough of him, confound him!

"Well, . . . mother I don't wonder at, it's like her, God bless her, but how could Dounia? Dounia, darling, as though I did not know you! You were nearly twenty when I saw you last: I understood you then. Mother writes that 'Dounia can put up with a great deal.' I know that very well. I knew that two years and a half ago, and for the last two and a half years I have been thinking about it, thinking of just that, that 'Dounia can put up with a great deal.' If she could put up with Mr. Svidrigaïlov and all the rest of it, she certainly can put up with a great deal. And now mother and she have taken it into their heads that she can put up with Mr. Luzhin, who propounds the theory of the superiority of wives raised from destitution and owing everything to their husbands' bounty—who propounds it, too, almost at the first interview. Granted that he 'let it slip,' though he is a sensible man, (yet maybe it was not a slip at all, but he meant to make himself clear as soon as possible) but Dounia, Dounia? She understands the man, of course, but she will have to live with the man. Why! she'd live on black bread and water, she would not sell her soul, she would not barter her moral freedom for comfort; she would not barter it for all Schleswig-Holstein, much less Mr. Luzhin's money. No, Dounia was not that sort when I knew her and . . . she is still the same, of course! Yes, there's no denying, the Svidrigaïlovs are a bitter pill! It's a bitter thing to spend one's life a governess in the provinces for two hundred roubles, but I know she would rather be a nigger on a plantation or a Lett with a German master, than degrade her soul, and her moral dignity, by binding herself for ever to a man whom she does not respect and with whom she has nothing in common—for her own advantage. And if Mr. Luzhin had been of unalloyed gold, or one huge diamond, she would never have consented to become his legal concubine. Why is she consenting then? What's the point of it? What's the answer? It's clear enough: for herself, for her comfort, to save her life she would not sell herself, but for some one else she is doing it! For one she loves, for one she adores, she will sell herself! That's what it all amounts to; for her brother, for her mother, she will sell herself! She will sell everything! In such cases, we 'overcome our moral feeling if necessary,' freedom, peace, conscience even, all, all are brought into the market. Let my life go, if only my dear ones may be happy! More than that, we become casuists, we learn to be Jesuitical and for a time maybe we can soothe ourselves, we can persuade ourselves that it is one's duty for a good object. That's just like us, it's as clear as daylight. It's clear that Rodion Romanovitch Raskolnikov is the central figure in the business, and no one else. Oh, yes, she can ensure his happiness, keep him in the university, make him a partner in the office, make his whole future secure; perhaps he may even be a rich man later on, prosperous, respected, and may even end his life a famous man! But my mother? It's all Rodya, precious Rodya, her firstborn! For such a son who would not sacrifice such a daughter! Oh, loving, over-partial hearts! Why, for his sake we would not shrink even from Sonia's fate. Sonia, Sonia Marmeladov, the eternal victim so long as the world lasts. Have you taken the measure of your sacrifice, both of you? Is it right? Can you bear it? Is it any use? Is there sense in it? And let me tell you, Dounia, Sonia's life is no worse than life with Mr. Luzhin. 'There can be no question of love' mother writes. And what if there can be no respect either, if on the contrary there is aversion, contempt, repulsion, what then? So you will have to 'keep up your appearance,' too. Is not that so? Do you understand what that smartness means? Do you understand that the Luzhin smartness is just the same thing as Sonia's and may be worse, viler, baser, because in your case, Dounia, it's a bargain for luxuries, after all, but with Sonia it's simply a question of starvation. It has to be paid for, it has to be paid for, Dounia, this smartness. And what if it's more than you can bear afterwards, if you regret it? The bitterness, the misery, the curses, the tears hidden from all the world, for you are not a Marfa Petrovna. And how will your mother feel then? Even now she is uneasy, she is worried, but then, when she sees it all clearly? And I? Yes, indeed, what have you taken me for? I won't have your sacrifice, Dounia, I won't have it, mother! It shall not be, so long as I am alive, it shall not, it shall not! I won't accept it!"

He suddenly paused in his reflections and stood still.

"It shall not be? But what are you going to do to prevent it? You'll forbid it? And what right have you? What can you promise them on your side to give you such a right? Your whole life, your whole future, you will devote to them *when you have finished your studies and obtained a post?* Yes, we have heard all that before, and that's all *words,* but now? Now something must be done, now, do you understand that? And what are you doing now? You are living upon them. They borrow on their hundred roubles pension. They borrow from the Svidrigaïlovs. How are you going to save them from Svidrigaïlovs, from Afanasy Ivanovitch Vahrushin, oh, future millionaire Zeus who would arrange their lives for them? In another ten years? In another ten years, mother will be blind with knitting shawls, maybe with weeping too. She will be worn to a shadow with fasting; and my sister? Imagine for a moment what may have become of your sister in ten years? What may happen to her during those ten years? Can you fancy?"

So he tortured himself, fretting himself with such questions, and finding a kind of enjoyment in it. And yet all these questions were not new ones suddenly confronting him, they were old familiar aches. It was long since they had first begun to grip and rend his heart. Long, long ago his present anguish had its first beginnings; it had waxed and gathered strength, it had matured and concentrated, until it had taken the form of a fearful, frenzied and fantastic question, which tortured his heart and mind, clamouring insistently for an answer. Now his mother's letter had burst on him like a thunderclap. It was clear that he must not now suffer passively, worrying himself over unsolved questions, but that he must do something, do it at once, and do it quickly. Anyway he must decide on something, or else . . .

"Or throw up life altogether!" he cried suddenly, in a frenzy —"accept one's lot humbly as it is, once for all and stifle everything in oneself, giving up all claim to activity, life and love!"

"Do you understand, sir, do you understand what it means when you have absolutely nowhere to turn?" Marmeladov's question came suddenly into his mind "for every man must have somewhere to turn. . . ."

He gave a sudden start; another thought, that he had had yesterday, slipped back into his mind. But he did not start at the thought recurring to him, for he knew, he had *felt beforehand,* that it must come back, he was expecting it; besides it was not only yesterday's thought. The difference was that a month ago, yesterday even, the thought was a mere dream: but now . . . now it appeared not a dream at all, it had taken a new menacing and quite unfamiliar shape, and he suddenly became aware of this himself. . . . He felt a hammering in his head, and there was a darkness before his eyes.

He looked round hurriedly, he was searching for something. He wanted to sit down and was looking for a seat; he was walking along the K—— Boulevard. There was a seat about a hundred paces in front of him. He walked towards it as fast as he could; but on the way he met with a little adventure which absorbed all his attention. Looking for the seat, he had noticed a woman walking some twenty paces in front of him, but at first he took no more notice of her than of other objects that crossed his path. It had happened to him many times going home not to notice the road by which he was going, and he was accustomed to walk like that. But there was at first sight something so strange about the woman in front of him, that gradually his attention was riveted upon her, at first reluctantly and, as it were, resentfully, and then more and more intently. He felt a sudden desire to find out what it was that was so strange about the woman. In the first place, she appeared to be a girl quite young, and she was walking in the great heat bareheaded and with no parasol or gloves, waving her arms about in an absurd way. She had on a dress of some light silky material, but put on strangely awry, not properly hooked up, and torn open at the top of the skirt, close to the waist: a great piece was rent and hanging loose. A little kerchief was flung about her bare throat, but lay slanting on one side. The girl was walking unsteadily, too, stumbling and staggering from side to side. She drew Raskolnikov's whole attention at last. He overtook the girl at the seat, but, on reaching it, she dropped down on it, in the corner; she let her head sink on the back of the seat and closed her eyes, apparently in extreme exhaustion. Looking at her close-ly, he saw at once that she was completely drunk. It was a strange and shocking sight. He could hardly believe that he was not mistaken. He saw before him the face of a quite young, fair-haired girl—sixteen, perhaps not more than fifteen years old, a pretty little face, but flushed and heavy looking and, as it were, swollen.

The girl seemed hardly to know what she was doing; she crossed one leg over the other, lifting it indecorously, and showed every sign of being unconscious that she was in the street.

Raskolnikov did not sit down, but he felt unwilling to leave her, and stood facing her in perplexity. This boulevard was never much frequented; and now, at two o'clock, in the stifling heat, it was quite deserted. And yet on the further side of the boulevard, about fifteen paces away, a gentleman was standing on the edge of the pavement, he, too, would apparently have liked to approach the girl with some object of his own. He, too, had probably seen her in the distance and had followed her, but found Raskolnikov in his way. He looked angrily at him, though he tried to escape his notice, and stood impatiently biding his time, till the unwelcome man in rags should have moved away. His intentions were unmistakable. The gentleman was a plump, thickly-set man, about thirty, fashionably dressed, with a high colour, red lips and moustaches. Raskolnikov felt furious; he had a sudden longing to insult this fat dandy in some way. He left the girl for a moment and walked towards the gentleman.

"Hey! You Svidrigaïlov! What do you want here?" he shouted, clenching his fists and laughing, spluttering with rage.

"What do you mean?" the gentleman asked sternly, scowling in haughty astonishment.

"Get away, that's what I mean."

"How dare you, you low fellow!"

He raised his cane. Raskolnikov rushed at him with his fists, without reflecting that the stout gentleman was a match for two men like himself. But at that instant some one seized him from behind, and a police constable stood between them.

"That's enough, gentlemen, no fighting, please, in a public place. What do you want? Who are you?" he asked Raskolnikov sternly, noticing his rags.

Raskolnikov looked at him intently. He had a straight-forward, sensible, soldierly face, with grey moustaches and whiskers.

"You are just the man I want," Raskolnikov cried, catching at his arm. "I am a student, Raskolnikov. . . . You may as well know that too," he added, addressing the gentleman, "come along, I have something to show you."

And taking the policeman by the hand he drew him towards the seat.

"Look here, hopelessly drunk, and she has just come down the boulevard. There is no telling who and what she is, she does not look like a professional. It's more likely she has been given drink and deceived somewhere . . . for the first time . . . you understand? and they've put her out into the street like that. Look at the way her dress is torn, and the way it has been put on: she has been dressed by somebody, she has not dressed herself, and dressed by unpractised hands, by a man's hands; that's evident. And now look there: I don't know that dandy with whom I was going to fight, I see him for the first time, but, he, too has seen her on the road, just now, drunk, not knowing what she is doing, and now he is very eager to get hold of her, to get her away somewhere while she is in this state . . . that's certain, believe me, I am not wrong. I saw him myself watching her and following her, but I prevented him, and he is just waiting for me to go away. Now he has walked away a little, and is standing still, pretending to make a cigarette. . . . Think how can we keep her out of his hands, and how are we to get her home?"

The policeman saw it all in a flash. The stout gentleman was easy to understand, he turned to consider the girl. The policeman bent over to examine her more closely, and his face worked with genuine compassion.

"Ah, what a pity!" he said, shaking his head—"why, she is quite a child! She has been deceived, you can see that at once. Listen, lady," he began addressing her, "where do you live?" The girl opened her weary and sleepy-looking eyes, gazed blankly at the speaker and waved her hand.

"Here," said Raskolnikov feeling in his pocket and finding twenty copecks, "here, call a cab and tell him to drive her to her address. The only thing is to find out her address!"

"Missy, missy!" the policeman began again, taking the money. "I'll fetch you a cab and take you home myself. Where shall I take you, eh? Where do you live?"

"Go away! They won't let me alone," the girl muttered, and once more waved her hand.

"Ach, ach, how shocking! It's shameful, missy, it's a shame!" He shook his head again, shocked, sympathetic and indignant.

"It's a difficult job," the policeman said to Raskolnikov, and as he did so, he looked him up and down in a rapid glance. He, too, must have seemed a strange figure to him: dressed in rags and handing him money!

"Did you meet her far from here?" he asked him.

"I tell you she was walking in front of me, staggering, just here, in the boulevard. She only just reached the seat and sank down on it."

"Ah, the shameful things that are done in the world nowadays, God have mercy on us! An innocent creature like that, drunk already! She has been deceived, that's a sure thing. See how her dress has been torn too. . . . Ah, the vice one sees nowadays! And as likely as not she belongs to gentlefolk too, poor ones maybe. . . . There are many like that nowadays. She looks refined, too, as though she were a lady," and he bent over her once more.

Perhaps he had daughters growing up like that, "looking like ladies and refined" with pretensions to gentility and smartness. . . .

"The chief thing is," Raskolnikov persisted, "to keep her out of this scoundrel's hands! Why should he outrage her! It's as clear as day what he is after; ah, the brute, he is not moving off!"

Raskolnikov spoke aloud and pointed to him. The gentleman heard him, and seemed about to fly into a rage again, but thought better of it, and confined himself to a contemptuous look. He then walked slowly another ten paces away and again halted.

"Keep her out of his hands we can," said the constable thoughtfully, "if only she'd tell us where to take her, but as it is. . . . Missy, hey, missy!" he bent over her once more.

She opened her eyes fully all of a sudden, looked at him intently, as though realising something, got up from the seat and walked away in the direction from which she had come. "Oh shameful wretches, they won't let me alone!" she said, waving her hand again. She walked quickly, though staggering as before. The dandy followed her, but along another avenue, keeping his eye on her.

"Don't be anxious, I won't let him have her," the policeman said resolutely, and he set off after them.

"Ah, the vice one sees nowadays!" he repeated aloud, sighing.

At that moment something seemed to sting Raskolnikov; in an instant a complete revulsion of feeling came over him.

"Hey, here!" he shouted after the policeman.

The latter turned round.

"Let them be! What is it to do with you? Let her go! Let him amuse himself." He pointed at the dandy, "What is it to do with you?"

The policeman was bewildered, and stared at him open-eyed. Raskolnikov laughed.

"Well!" ejaculated the policeman, with a gesture of contempt, and he walked after the dandy and the girl, probably taking Raskolnikov for a madman or something even worse.

"He has carried off my twenty copecks," Raskolnikov murmured angrily when he was left alone. "Well, let him take as much from the other fellow to allow him to have the girl and so let it end. And why did I want to interfere? Is it for me to help? Have I any right to help? Let them devour each other alive—what is it to me? How did I dare to give him twenty copecks? Were they mine?"

In spite of those strange words he felt very wretched. He sat down on the deserted seat. His thought strayed aimlessly. . . . He found it hard to fix his mind on anything at that moment. He longed to forget himself altogether, to forget everything, and then to wake up and begin life anew. . . .

"Poor girl!" he said, looking at the empty corner where she had sat—"She will come to herself and weep, and then her mother will find out. . . . She will give her a beating, a horrible, shameful beating and then maybe, turn her out of doors. . . . And even if she does not, the Darya Frantsovnas will get wind of it, and the girl will soon be slipping out on the sly here and there. Then there will be the hospital directly (that's always the luck of those girls with respectable mothers, who go wrong on the sly) and then . . . again the hospital . . . drink . . . the taverns . . . and more hospital, in two or three years—a wreck, and her life over at eighteen or nineteen. . . . Have not I seen cases like that? And how have they been brought to it? Why, they've all come to it like that. Ugh! But what does it matter? That's as it should be, they tell us. A certain percentage, they tell us, must every year go . . . that way . . . to the devil, I suppose, so that the rest may remain chaste, and not be interfered with. A percentage! What splendid words they have; they are so scientific, so consolatory. . . . Once you've said 'percentage,' there's nothing more to worry about. If we had any other word . . . maybe we might feel more uneasy. . . . But what if Dounia were one of the percentage! Of another one if not that one?

"But where am I going?" he thought suddenly. "Strange, I came out for something. As soon as I had read the letter I came out. . . . I was going to Vassilyevsky Ostrov, to Razumihin. That's what it was . . . now I remember. What for, though? And what put the idea of going to Razumihin into my head just now? That's curious."

He wondered at himself. Razumihin was one of his old comrades at the university. It was remarkable that Raskolnikov had hardly any friends at the university; he kept aloof from every one, went to see no one, and did not welcome any one who came to see him, and indeed every one soon gave him up. He took no part in the students' gatherings, amusements or conversations. He worked with great intensity without sparing himself, and he was respected for this, but no one liked him. He was very poor, and there was a sort of haughty pride and reserve about him, as though he were keeping something to himself. He seemed to some of his comrades to look down upon them all as children, as though he were superior in development, knowledge and convictions, as though their beliefs and interests were beneath him.

With Razumihin he had got on, or, at least, he was more unreserved and communicative with him. Indeed it was impossible to be on any other terms with Razumihin. He was an exceptionally good-humoured and candid youth, good-natured to the point of simplicity, though both depth and dignity lay concealed under that simplicity. The better of his comrades understood this, and all were fond of him. He was extremely intelligent, though he was certainly rather a simpleton at times. He was of striking appearance—tall, thin, blackhaired and always badly shaved. He was sometimes uproarious and was reputed to be of great physical strength. One night, when out in a festive company, he had with one blow laid a gigantic policeman on his back. There was no limit to his drinking powers, but he could abstain from drink altogether; he sometimes went too far in his pranks; but he could do without pranks altogether. Another thing striking about Razumihin, no failure distressed him, and it seemed as though no unfavourable circumstances could crush him. He could lodge anywhere, and bear the extremes of cold and hunger. He was very poor, and kept himself entirely on what he could earn by work of one sort or another. He knew of no end of resources by which to earn money. He spent one whole winter without lighting his stove, and used to declare that he liked it better, because one slept more soundly in the cold. For the present he, too, had been obliged to give up the university, but it was only for a time, and he was working with all his might to save enough to return to his studies again. Raskolnikov had not been to see him for the last four months, and Razumihin did not even know his address. About two months before, they had met in the street, but Raskolnikov had turned away and even crossed to the other side that he might not be observed. And though Razumihin noticed him, he passed him by, as he did not want to annoy him.

5

"Of course, I've been meaning lately to go to Razumihin's to ask for work, to ask him to get me lessons or something . . ." Raskolnikov thought, "but what help can he be to me now? Suppose he gets me lessons, suppose he shares his last farthing with me, if he has any farthings, so that I could get some boots and make myself tidy enough to give lessons . . . hm . . . Well and what then? What shall I do with the few coppers I earn? That's not what I want now. It's really absurd for me to go to Razumihin. . . ."

The question why he was now going to Razumihin agitated him even more than he was himself aware; he kept uneasily seeking for some sinister significance in this apparently ordinary action.

"Could I have expected to set it all straight and to find a way out by means of Razumihin alone?" he asked himself in perplexity.

He pondered and rubbed his forehead, and, strange to say, after long musing, suddenly, as if it were spontaneously and by chance, a fantastic thought came into his head.

"Hm . . . to Razumihin's," he said all at once, calmly, as though he had reached a final determination. "I shall go to Razumihin's of course, but . . . not now. I shall go to him . . . on the next day after It, when It will be over and everything will begin afresh. . . ."

And suddenly he realised what he was thinking.

"After It," he shouted, jumping up from the seat, "but is It really going to happen? Is it possible it really will happen?" He left the seat, and went off almost at a run; he meant to turn back, homewards, but the thought of going home suddenly filled him with intense loathing; in that hole, in that awful little cupboard of his, all *this* had for a month past been growing up in him; and he walked on at random.

His nervous shudder had passed into a fever that made him feel shivering; in spite of the heat he felt cold. With a kind of effort he began almost unconsciously, from some inner craving, to stare at all the objects before him, as though looking for something to distract his attention; but he did not succeed, and kept dropping every moment into brooding. When with a start he lifted his head again and looked around, he forgot at once what he had just been thinking about and even where he was going. In this way he walked right across Vassilyevsky Ostrov, came out on to the Lesser Neva, crossed the bridge and turned towards the islands. The greenness and freshness were at first restful to his weary eyes after the dust of the town and the huge houses that hemmed him in and weighed upon him. Here there were no taverns, no stifling closeness, no stench. But soon these new pleasant sensations passed into morbid irritability. Sometimes he stood still before a brightly painted summer villa standing among green foliage, he gazed through the fence, he saw in the distance smartly dressed women on the verandahs and balconies, and children running in the gardens. The flowers especially caught his attention; he gazed at them longer than at anything. He was met, too, by luxurious carriages and by men and women on horseback; he watched them with curious eyes and forgot about them before they had vanished from his sight. Once he stood still and counted his money; he found he had thirty copecks. "Twenty to the policeman, three to Nastasya for the letter, so I must have given forty-seven or fifty to the Marmeladovs yesterday," he thought, reckoning it up for some unknown reason, but he soon forgot with what object he had taken the money out of his pocket. He recalled it on passing an eating-house or tavern, and felt that he was hungry. . . . Going into the tavern he drank a glass of vodka and ate a pie of some sort. He finished eating it as he walked away. It was a long while since he had taken vodka and it had an effect upon him at once, though he only drank a wine-glassful. His legs felt suddenly heavy and a great drowsiness came upon him. He turned homewards, but reaching Petrovsky Ostrov he stopped completely exhausted, turned off the road into the bushes, sank down upon the grass and instantly fell asleep.

In a morbid condition of the brain, dreams often have a singular actuality, vividness, and extraordinary semblance of reality. At times monstrous images are created, but the setting and the whole picture are so truthlike and filled with details so delicate, so unexpectedly, but so artistically consistent, that the dreamer, were he an artist like Pushkin or Turgenev even, could never have invented them in the waking state. Such sick dreams always remain long in the memory and make a powerful impression on the overwrought and deranged nervous system.

Raskolnikov had a fearful dream. He dreamt he was back in

his childhood in the little town of his birth. He was a child about seven years old, walking into the country with his father on the evening of a holiday. It was a grey and heavy day, the country was exactly as he remembered it; indeed he recalled it far more vividly in his dream than he had done in memory. The little town stood on a level flat as bare as the hand, not even a willow near it; only in the far distance, a copse lay, a dark blur on the very edge of the horizon. A few paces beyond the last market garden stood a tavern, a big tavern, which had always aroused in him a feeling of aversion, even of fear, when he walked by it with his father. There was always a crowd there, always shouting, laughter and abuse, hideous hoarse singing and often fighting. Drunken and horrible-looking figures were hanging about the tavern. He used to cling close to his father, trembling all over when he met them. Near the tavern the road became a dusty track, the dust of which was always black. It was a winding road, and about a hundred paces further on, it turned to the right to the graveyard. In the middle of the graveyard stood a stone church with a green cupola where he used to go to mass two or three times a year with his father and mother, when a service was held in memory of his grandmother, who had long been dead, and whom he had never seen. On these occasions they used to take on a white dish tied up in a table napkin a special sort of rice pudding with raisins stuck in it in the shape of a cross. He loved that church, the old-fashioned, unadorned ikons and the old priest with the shaking head. Near his grandmother's grave, which was marked by a stone, was the little grave of his younger brother who had died at six months old. He did not remember him at all, but he had been told about his little brother, and whenever he visited the graveyard he used religiously and reverently to cross himself and to bow down and kiss the little grave. And now he dreamt that he was walking with his father past the tavern on the way to the graveyard; he was holding his father's hand and looking with dread at the tavern. A peculiar circumstance attracted his attention: there seemed to be some kind of festivity going on, there were crowds of gaily dressed townspeople, peasant women, their husbands, and riff-raff of all sorts, all singing and all more or less drunk. Near the entrance of the tavern stood a cart, but a strange cart. It was one of those big carts usually drawn by heavy cart-horses and laden with casks of wine or other heavy goods. He always liked looking at those great cart-horses, with their long manes, thick legs, and slow even pace, drawing along a perfect mountain with no appearance of effort, as though it were easier going with a load than without it. But now, strange to say, in the shafts of such a cart he saw a thin little sorrel beast, one of those peasants' nags which he had often seen straining their utmost under a heavy load of wood or hay, especially when the wheels were stuck in the mud or in a rut. And the peasants would be at them so cruelly, sometimes even about the nose and eyes and he felt so sorry, so sorry for them that he almost cried, and his mother always used to take him away from the window. All of a sudden there was a great uproar of shouting, singing and the balalaïka, and from the tavern a number of big and very drunken peasants came out, wearing red and blue shirts and coats thrown over their shoulders.

"Get in, get in!" shouted one of them, a young thick-necked peasant with a fleshy face red as a carrot. "I'll take you all, get in!"

But at once there was an outbreak of laughter and exclamations in the crowd.

"Take us all with a beast like that!"

"Why, Mikolka, are you crazy to put a nag like that in such a cart?"

"And this mare is twenty if she is a day, mates!"

"Get in, I'll take you all," Mikolka shouted again, leaping first into the cart, seizing the reins and standing straight up in front. "The bay has gone with Marvey," he shouted from the cart—"and this brute, mates, is just breaking my heart, I feel as if I could kill her. She's just eating her head off. Get in, I tell you! I'll make her gallop! She'll gallop!" and he picked up the whip, preparing himself with relish to flog the little mare.

"Get in! Come along!" The crowd laughed. "D'you hear, she'll gallop!"

"Gallop indeed! She has not had a gallop in her for the last ten years!"

"She'll jog along!"

"Don't you mind her, mates, bring a whip each of you, get ready!"

"All right! Give it to her!"

They all clambered into Mikolka's cart, laughing and making jokes. Six men got in and there was still room for more. They hauled in a fat, rosy-cheeked woman. She was dressed in red cotton, in a pointed, beaded headdress and thick leather shoes; she was cracking nuts and laughing. The crowd round them was laughing too and indeed, how could they help laughing? That wretched nag was to drag all the cartload of them at a gallop! Two young fellows in the cart were just getting whips ready to help Mikolka. With the cry of "now," the mare tugged with all her might, but far from galloping, could scarcely move forward; she struggled with her legs, gasping and shrinking from the blows of the three whips which were showered upon her like hail. The laughter in the cart and in the crowd was redoubled, but Mikolka flew into a rage and furiously thrashed the mare, as though he supposed she really could gallop.

"Let me get in, too, mates," shouted a young man in the crowd whose appetite was aroused.

"Get in, all get in," cried Mikolka, "she will draw you all. I'll beat her to death!" And he thrashed and thrashed at the mare, beside himself with fury.

"Father, father," he cried, "father, what are they doing? Father, they are beating the poor horse!"

"Come along, come along!" said his father. "They are drunken and foolish, they are in fun; come away, don't look!" and he tried to draw him away, but he tore himself away from his hand, and, beside himself with horror, ran to the horse. The poor beast was in a bad way. She was gasping, standing still, then tugging again and almost falling.

"Beat her to death," cried Mikolka, "it's come to that. I'll do for her!"

"What are you about, are you a Christian, you devil?" shouted an old man in the crowd.

"Did any one ever see the like? A wretched nag like that pulling such a cartload," said another.

"You'll kill her," shouted the third.

"Don't meddle! It's my property. I'll do what I choose. Get in, more of you! Get in, all of you! I will have her go at a gallop! . . ."

All at once laughter broke into a roar and covered everything: the mare, roused by the shower of blows, began feebly kicking. Even the old man could not help smiling. To think of a wretched little beast like that trying to kick!

Two lads in the crowd snatched up whips and ran to the mare to beat her about the ribs. One ran each side.

"Hit her in the face, in the eyes, in the eyes," cried Mikolka.

"Give us a song, mates," shouted some one in the cart and every one in the cart joined in a riotous song, jingling a tambourine and whistling. The woman went on cracking nuts and laughing.

. . . He ran beside the mare, ran in front of her, saw her being whipped across the eyes, right in the eyes! He was crying, he felt choking, his tears were streaming. One of the men gave him a cut with the whip across the face, he did not feel it. Wringing his hands and screaming, he rushed up to the grey-headed old man with the grey beard, who was shaking his head in disapproval. One woman seized him by the hand and would have taken him away, but he tore himself from her and ran back to the mare. She was almost at the last gasp, but began kicking once more.

"I'll teach you to kick," Mikolka shouted ferociously. He threw down the whip, bent forward and picked up from the bottom of the cart a long, thick shaft, he took hold of one end with both hands and with an effort brandished it over the mare.

"He'll crush her," was shouted round him. "He'll kill her!"

"It's my property," shouted Mikolka and brought the shaft down with a swinging blow. There was a sound of a heavy thud.

"Thrash her, thrash her! Why have you stopped?" shouted voices in the crowd.

And Mikolka swung the shaft a second time and it fell a second time on the spine of the luckless mare. She sank back on her haunches, but lurched forward and tugged forward with all her force, tugged first on one side and then on the other, trying to move the cart. But the six whips were attacking her in all directions, and the shaft was raised again and fell upon her a third time, then a fourth, with heavy measured blows. Mikolka was in a fury that he could not kill her at one blow.

"She's a tough one," was shouted in the crowd.

"She'll fall in a minute, mates, there will soon be an end of her," said an admiring spectator in the crowd.

"Fetch an axe to her! Finish her off," shouted a third.

"I'll show you! Stand off," Mikolka screamed frantically; he threw down the shaft, stooped down in the cart and picked up an iron crowbar. "Look out," he shouted, and with all his might he dealt a stunning blow at the poor mare. The blow fell; the mare staggered, sank back, tried to pull, but the bar fell again with a swinging blow on her back and she fell on the ground like a log.

"Finish her off," shouted Mikolka and he leapt, beside himself, out of the cart. Several young men, also flushed with drink, seized anything they could come across—whips, sticks, poles, and ran to the dying mare. Mikolka stood on one side and began dealing random blows with the crowbar. The mare stretched out her head, drew a long breath and died.

"You butchered her," some one shouted in the crowd.

"Why wouldn't she gallop then?"

"My property!" shouted Mikolka, with bloodshot eyes, brandishing the bar in his hands. He stood as though regretting that he had nothing more to beat.

"No mistake about it, you are not a Christian," many voices were shouting in the crowd.

But the poor boy, beside himself, made his way screaming through the crowd to the sorrel nag, put his arms round her bleeding dead head and kissed it, kissed the eyes and kissed the lips. . . . Then he jumped up and flew in a frenzy with his little fists out at Mikolka. At that instant his father who had been running after him, snatched him up and carried him out of the crowd.

"Come along, come! Let us go home," he said to him.

"Father! Why did they . . . kill . . . the poor horse!" he sobbed, but his voice broke and the words came in shrieks from his panting chest.

"They are drunk. . . . They are brutal . . . it's not our business!" said his father. He put his arms round his father but he felt choked, choked. He tried to draw a breath, to cry out—and woke up.

He waked up, gasping for breath, his hair soaked with perspiration, and stood up in terror.

"Thank God, that was only a dream," he said, sitting down under a tree and drawing deep breaths. "But what is it? Is it some fever coming on? Such a hideous dream!"

He felt utterly broken; darkness and confusion were in his soul. He rested his elbows on his knees and leaned his head on his hands.

"Good God!" he cried, "can it be, can it be, that I shall really take an axe, that I shall strike her on the head, split her skull open . . . that I shall tread in the sticky warm blood, break the lock, steal and tremble; hide, all spattered in the blood . . . with the axe. . . . Good God, can it be?"

He was shaking like a leaf as he said this.

"But why am I going on like this?" he continued, sitting up again, as it were in profound amazement. "I knew that I could never bring myself to it, so what have I been torturing myself for till now? Yesterday, yesterday, when I went to make that . . . *experiment*, yesterday I realised completely that I could never bear to do it. . . . Why am I going over it again, then? Why am I hesitating? As I came down the stairs yesterday, I said myself that it was base, loathsome, vile, vile . . . the very thought of it made me feel sick and filled me with horror.

"No, I couldn't do it, I couldn't do it! Granted, granted that there is no flaw in all that reasoning, that all that I have concluded this last month is clear as day, true as arithmetic. . . . My God! Anyway I couldn't bring myself to it! I couldn't do it, I couldn't do it! Why, why then am I still . . . ?"

He rose to his feet, looked round in wonder as though surprised at finding himself in this place, and went towards the bridge. He was pale, his eyes glowed, he was exhausted in every limb, but he seemed suddenly to breathe more easily. He felt he had cast off that fearful burden that had so long been weighing upon him, and all at once there was a sense of relief and peace in his soul. "Lord," he prayed, "show me my path—I renounce that accursed . . . dream of mine."

Crossing the bridge, he gazed quietly and calmly at the Neva, at the glowing red sun setting in the glowing sky. In spite of his weakness he was not conscious of fatigue. It was as though an abscess that had been forming for a month past in his heart had suddenly broken. Freedom, freedom! He was free from that spell, that sorcery, that obsession!

Later on, when he recalled that time and all that happened to him during those days, minute by minute, point by point, he was superstitiously impressed by one circumstance, which though in itself not very exceptional, always seemed to him afterwards the predestined turning-point of his fate. He could never understand and explain to himself why, when he was tired and worn out, when it would have been more convenient for him to go home by the shortest and most direct way, he had returned by the Hay Market where he had no need to go. It was obviously and quite unnecessarily out of his way, though not much so. It is true that it happened to him dozens of times to return home without noticing what streets he passed through. But why, he was always asking himself, why had such an important, such a decisive and at the same time such an absolutely chance meeting happened in the Hay Market (where he had moreover no reason to go) at the very hour, the very minute of his life when he was just in the very mood and in the very circumstances in which that meeting was able to exert the gravest and most decisive influence on his whole destiny? As though it had been lying in wait for him on purpose!

It was about nine o'clock when he crossed the Hay Market. At the tables and the barrows, at the booths and the shops, all the market people were closing their establishments or clearing away and packing up their wares and, like their customers, were going home. Rag pickers and costermongers of all kinds were crowding round the taverns in the dirty and stinking courtyards of the Hay

Market. Raskolnikov particularly liked this place and the neighbouring alleys, when he wandered aimlessly in the streets. Here
his rags did not attract contemptuous attention, and one could
walk about in any attire without scandalising people. At the
corner of an alley a huckster and his wife had two tables set out
with tapes, thread, cotton handkerchiefs, &c. They, too, had got
up to go home, but were lingering in conversation with a friend,
who had just come up to them. This friend was Lizaveta Ivanovna,
or, as every one called her, Lizaveta, the younger sister of the old
pawnbroker, Alyona Ivanovna, whom Raskolnikov had visited
the previous day to pawn his watch and make his *experiment*.
. . . He already knew all about Lizaveta and she knew him a little
too. She was a single woman of about thirty-five, tall, clumsy,
timid, submissive and almost idiotic. She was a complete slave and
went in fear and trembling of her sister, who made her work day
and night, and even beat her. She was standing with a bundle
before the huckster and his wife, listening earnestly and doubtful-
ly. They were talking of something with special warmth. The
moment Raskolnikov caught sight of her, he was overcome by a
strange sensation as it were of intense astonishment, though there
was nothing astonishing about this meeting.

"You could make up your mind for yourself, Lizaveta Ivanovna," the huckster was saying aloud. "Come round tomorrow
about seven. They will be here too."

"To-morrow?" said Lizaveta slowly and thoughtfully, as
though unable to make up her mind.

"Upon my word, what a fright you are in of Alyona Ivanovna," gabbled the huckster's wife, a lively little woman. "I look at
you, you are like some little babe. And she is not your own sister
either—nothing but a stepsister and what a hand she keeps over
you!"

"But this time don't say a word to Alyona Ivanovna," her
husband interrupted; "that's my advice, but come round to us
without asking. It will be worth your while. Later on your sister
herself may have a notion."

"Am I to come?"

"About seven o'clock to-morrow. And they will be here. You will be able to decide for yourself."

"And we'll have a cup of tea," added his wife.

"All right, I'll come," said Lizaveta, still pondering, and she began slowly moving away.

Raskolnikov had just passed and heard no more. He passed softly, unnoticed, trying not to miss a word. His first amazement was followed by a thrill of horror, like a shiver running down his spine. He had learnt, he had suddenly quite unexpectedly learnt, that the next day at seven o'clock Lizaveta, the old woman's sister and only companion, would be away from home and that therefore at seven o'clock precisely the old woman *would be left alone.*

He was only a few steps from his lodging. He went in like a man condemned to death. He thought of nothing and was incapable of thinking; but he felt suddenly in his whole being that he had no more freedom of thought, no will, and that everything was suddenly and irrevocably decided.

Certainly, if he had to wait whole years for a suitable opportunity, he could not reckon on a more certain step towards the success of the plan than that which had just presented itself. In any case, it would have been difficult to find out beforehand and with certainty, with greater exactness and less risk, and without dangerous inquiries and investigations, that next day at a certain time an old woman, on whose life an attempt was contemplated, would be at home and entirely alone.

6

Later on Raskolnikov happened to find out why the huckster and his wife had invited Lizaveta. It was a very ordinary matter and there was nothing exceptional about it. A family who had come to the town and been reduced to poverty were selling their household goods and clothes, all women's things. As the things would have fetched little in the market, they were looking for a dealer. This was Lizaveta's business. She undertook such jobs and was frequently employed, as she was very honest and always fixed a fair price and stuck to it. She spoke as a rule little and, as we have said already, she was very submissive and timid.

But Raskolnikov had become superstitious of late. The traces of superstition remained in him long after, and were almost ineradicable. And in all this he was always afterwards disposed to see something strange and mysterious, as it were the presence of some peculiar influences and coincidences. In the previous winter a student he knew called Pokorev, who had left for Harkov, had chanced in conversation to give him the address of Alyona Ivanovna, the old pawnbroker, in case he might want to pawn anything. For a long while he did not go to her, for he had lessons and managed to get along somehow. Six weeks ago he had remembered the address; he had two articles that could be pawned: his father's old silver watch and a little gold ring with three red stones, a present from his sister at parting. He decided to take the ring. When he found the old woman he had felt an insurmountable repulsion for her at the first glance, though he knew nothing special about her. He got two roubles from her and went into a miserable little tavern on his way home. He asked for tea, sat down and sank into deep thought. A strange idea was pecking at his brain like a chicken in the egg, and very, very much absorbed him.

Almost beside him at the next table there was sitting a student, whom he did not know and had never seen, and with him a young officer. They had played a game of billiards and began drinking tea. All at once he heard the student mention to the officer the pawnbroker Alyona Ivanovna and give him her address. This of itself seemed strange to Raskolnikov; he had just come from her and here at once he heard her name. Of course it was a chance, but he could not shake off a very extraordinary impression, and here some one seemed to be speaking expressly for him; the student began telling his friend various details about Alyona Ivanovna.

"She is first rate," he said. "You can always get money from her. She is as rich as a Jew, she can give you five thousand roubles at a time and she is not above taking a pledge for a rouble. Lots of our fellows have had dealings with her. But she is an awful old harpy. . . ."

And he began describing how spiteful and uncertain she was, how if you were only a day late with your interest the pledge was lost; how she gave a quarter of the value of an article and took five and even seven percent. a month on it and so on. The student chattered on, saying that she had a sister Lizaveta, whom the wretched little creature was continually beating, and kept in complete bondage like a small child, though Lizaveta was at least six feet high.

"There's a phenomenon for you," cried the student and he laughed.

They began talking about Lizaveta. The student spoke about her with a peculiar relish and was continually laughing and the officer listened with great interest and asked him to send Lizaveta to do some mending for him. Raskolnikov did not miss a word and learned everything about her. Lizaveta was younger than the old woman and was her half-sister, being the child of a different mother. She was thirty-five. She worked day and night for her sister, and besides doing the cooking and the washing, she did sewing and worked as a charwoman and gave her sister all she earned. She did not dare to accept an order or job of any kind without her sister's permission. The old woman had already made her will, and Lizaveta knew of it, and by this will she would not get a farthing; nothing but the movables, chairs and so on; all the money was left to a monastery in the province of N——, that prayers might be said for her in perpetuity. Lizaveta was of lower rank than her sister, unmarried and awfully uncouth in appearance, remarkably tall with long feet that looked as if they were bent outwards. She always wore battered goatskin shoes, and was clean in her person. What the student expressed most surprise and amusement about was the fact that Lizaveta was continually with child.

"But you say she is hideous?" observed the officer.

"Yes, she is so dark-skinned and looks like a soldier dressed up, but you know she is not at all hideous. She has such a good-natured face and eyes. Strikingly so. And the proof of it is that lots of people are attracted by her. She is such a soft, gentle creature, ready to put up with anything, always willing, willing to do anything. And her smile is really very sweet."

"You seem to find her attractive yourself," laughed the officer.

"From her queerness. No, I'll tell you what. I could kill that damned old woman and make off with her money, I assure you, without the faintest conscience-prick," the student added with warmth. The officer laughed again while Raskolnikov shuddered. How strange it was!

"Listen, I want to ask you a serious question," the student said hotly. "I was joking of course, but look here; on one side we have a stupid, senseless, worthless, spiteful, ailing, horrid old woman, not simply useless but doing actual mischief, who has not an idea what she is living for herself, and who will die in a day or two in any case. You understand? You understand?"

"Yes, yes, I understand," answered the officer, watching his excited companion attentively.

"Well, listen then. On the other side, fresh young lives thrown away for want of help and by thousands, on every side! A hundred thousand good deeds could be done and helped, on that old woman's money which will be buried in a monastery! Hundreds, thousands perhaps, might be set on the right path; dozens of families saved from destitution, from ruin, from vice, from the Lock hospitals—and all with her money. Kill her, take her money and with the help of it devote oneself to the service of humanity and the good of all. What do you think, would not one tiny crime be wiped out by thousands of good deeds? For one life thousands would be saved from corruption and decay. One death, and a hundred lives in exchange—it's simple arithmetic! Besides, what value has the life of that sickly, stupid, ill-natured old woman in the balance of existence! No more than the life of a louse, of a black beetle, less in fact because the old woman is doing harm. She is wearing out the lives of others; the other day she bit Lizaveta's finger out of spite; it almost had to be amputated."

"Of course she does not deserve to live," remarked the officer, "but there it is, it's nature."

"Oh, well, brother, but we have to correct and direct nature, and, but for that, we should drown in an ocean of prejudice. But for that, there would never have been a single great man. They talk of duty, conscience—I don't want to say anything against duty and conscience;—but the point is what do we mean by them. Stay, I have another question to ask you. Listen!"

"No, you stay, I'll ask you a question. Listen!"

"Well?"

"You are talking and speechifying away, but tell me, would you kill the old woman *yourself?*"

"Of course not! I was only arguing the justice of it. . . . It's nothing to do with me. . . ."

"But I think, if you would not do it yourself, there's no justice about it. . . . Let us have another game."

Raskolnikov was violently agitated. Of course, it was all ordinary youthful talk and thought, such as he had often heard before in different forms and on different themes. But why had he happened to hear such a discussion and such ideas at the very moment when his own brain was just conceiving . . . *the very same ideas?* And why, just at the moment when he had brought away the embryo of his idea from the old woman had he dropped at once upon a conversation about her? This coincidence always seemed strange to him. This trivial talk in a tavern had an immense influence on him in his later action; as though there had really been in it something preordained, some guiding hint. . . .

On returning from the Hay Market he flung himself on the sofa and sat for a whole hour without stirring. Meanwhile it got dark; he had no candle and, indeed, it did not occur to him to light up. He could never recollect whether he had been thinking about anything at that time. At last he was conscious of his former fever and shivering, and he realised with relief that he could lie down on the sofa. Soon heavy, leaden sleep came over him, as it were crushing him.

He slept an extraordinarily long time and without dreaming. Nastasya, coming into his room at ten o'clock the next morning, had difficulty in rousing him. She brought him in tea and bread. The tea was again the second brew and again in her own teapot.

"My goodness, how he sleeps!" she cried indignantly. "And he is always asleep."

He got up with an effort. His head ached, he stood up, took a turn in his garret and sank back on the sofa again.

"Going to sleep again," cried Nastasya. "Are you ill, eh?"

He made no reply.

"Do you want some tea?"

"Afterwards," he said with an effort, closing his eyes again and turning to the wall.

Nastasya stood over him.

"Perhaps he really is ill," she said, turned and went out. She came in again at two o'clock with soup. He was lying as before. The tea stood untouched. Nastasya felt positively offended and began wrathfully rousing him.

"Why are you lying like a log?" she shouted, looking at him with repulsion.

He got up, and sat down again, but said nothing and stared at the floor.

"Are you ill or not?" asked Nastasya and again received no answer. "You'd better go out and get a breath of air," she said after a pause. "Will you eat it or not?"

"Afterwards," he said weakly. "You can go."

And he motioned her out.

She remained a little longer, looked at him with compassion and went out.

A few minutes afterwards, he raised his eyes and looked for a long while at the tea and the soup. Then he took the bread, took up a spoon and began to eat.

He ate a little, three or four spoonfuls, without appetite as it were mechanically. His head ached less. After his meal he stretched himself on the sofa again, but now he could not sleep; he lay without stirring, with his face in the pillow. He was haunted by daydreams and such strange daydreams; in one, that kept recurring, he fancied that he was in Africa, in Egypt, in some sort of oasis. The caravan was resting, the camels were peacefully lying down; the palms stood all round in a complete circle; all the party were at dinner. But he was drinking water from a spring which flowed gurgling close by. And it was so cool, it was wonderful, wonderful, blue, cold water running among the parti-coloured stones and over the clean sand which glistened here and there like gold. . . . Suddenly he heard a clock strike. He started, roused himself, raised his head, looked out of the window, and seeing how late it was, suddenly jumped up wide awake as though some one had pulled him off the sofa. He crept on tiptoe to the door, stealthily opened it and began listening on the staircase. His heart beat terribly. But all was quiet on the stairs as if every one was asleep. . . . It seemed to him strange and monstrous that he could have slept in such forgetfulness from the previous day and had done nothing, had prepared nothing yet. . . . And meanwhile perhaps it had struck six. And his drowsiness and stupefaction were followed by an extraordinary, feverish, as it were, distract-ed, haste. But the preparations to be made were few. He concen-trated all his energies on thinking of everything and forgetting nothing; and his heart kept beating and thumping so that he could hardly breathe. First he had to make a noose and sew it into his overcoat—a work of a moment. He rummaged under his pillow and picked out amongst the linen stuffed away under it, a worn out, old unwashed shirt. From its rags he tore a long strip, a couple of inches wide and about sixteen inches long. He folded this strip in two, took off his wide, strong summer overcoat of some stout cotton material (his only outer garment) and began sewing the two ends of the rag on the inside, under the left armhole. His hands shook as he sewed, but he did it successfully so that nothing showed outside when he put the coat on again. The needle and thread he had got ready long before and they lay on his table in a piece of paper. As for the noose, it was a very ingenious device of his own; the noose was intended for the axe. It was impossible for him to carry the axe through the street in his hands. And if hidden under his coat he would still have had to support it with his hand, which would have been noticeable.

Now he had only to put the head of the axe in the noose, and it would hang quietly under his arm on the inside. Putting his hand in his coat pocket, he could hold the end of the handle all the way, so that it did not swing; and as the coat was very full, a regular sack in fact, it could not be seen from outside that he was holding something with the hand that was in the pocket. This noose, too, he had designed a fortnight before.

When he had finished with this, he thrust his hand into a little opening between his sofa and the floor, fumbled in the left corner and drew out the *pledge,* which he had got ready long before and hidden there. This pledge was, however, only a smoothly planed piece of wood the size and thickness of a silver cigarette case. He picked up this piece of wood in one of his wanderings in a court-yard where there was some sort of a workshop. Afterwards he had added to the wood a thin smooth piece of iron, which he had also picked up at the same time in the street. Putting the iron which was a little the smaller on the piece of wood, he fastened them very firmly, crossing and recrossing the thread round them; then wrapped them carefully and daintily in clean white paper and tied up the parcel so that it would be very difficult to untie it. This was in order to divert the attention of the old woman for a time, while she was trying to undo the knot, and so to gain a moment. The iron strip was added to give weight, so that the woman might not guess the first minute that the "thing" was made of wood. All this had been stored by him beforehand under the sofa. He had only just got the pledge out when he heard some one suddenly about in the yard.

"It struck six long ago."

"Long ago! My God!"

He rushed to the door, listened, caught up his hat and began to descend his thirteen steps cautiously, noiselessly, like a cat. He had still the most important thing to do—to steal the axe from the kitchen. That the deed must be done with an axe he had decided long ago. He had also a pocket pruning-knife, but he could not rely on the knife and still less on his own strength, and so resolved finally on the axe. We may note in passing, one peculiarity in regard to all the final resolutions taken by him in the matter; they had one strange characteristic; the more final they were, the more hideous and the more absurd they at once became in his eyes. In spite of all his agonising inward struggle, he never for a single instant all that time could believe in the carrying out of his plans.

And, indeed, if it had ever happened that everything to the least point could have been considered and finally settled, and no uncertainty of any kind had remained, he would, it seems, have renounced it all as something absurd, monstrous and impossible. But a whole mass of unsettled points and uncertainties remained. As for getting the axe, that trifling business cost him no anxiety, for nothing could be easier. Nastasya was continually out of the house, especially in the evenings; she would run in to the neighbours or to a shop, and always left the door ajar. It was the one thing the landlady was always scolding her about. And so when the time came, he would only have to go quietly into the kitchen and to take the axe, and an hour later (when everything was over) go in and put it back again. But these were doubtful points. Supposing he returned an hour later to put it back, and Nastasya had come back and was on the spot. He would of course have to go by and wait till she went out again. But supposing she were in the meantime to miss the axe, look for it, make an outcry—that would mean suspicion or at least grounds for suspicion.

But those were all trifles which he had not even begun to consider, and indeed he had no time. He was thinking of the chief point, and put off trifling details, until he *could believe in it all.* But that seemed utterly unattainable. So it seemed to himself at least. He could not imagine, for instance, that he would sometime leave off thinking, get up and simply go there. . . . Even his late experiment (*i.e.* his visit with the object of a final survey of the place) was simply an attempt at an experiment, far from being the real thing, as though one should say "come, let us go and try it—why dream about it!"—and at once he had broken down and had run away cursing, in a frenzy with himself. Meanwhile it would seem, as regards the moral question, that his analysis was complete; his casuistry had become keen as a razor, and he could not find rational objections in himself. But in the last resort he simply ceased to believe in himself, and doggedly, slavishly sought arguments in all directions, fumbling for them, as though some one were forcing and drawing him to it.

At first—long before indeed—he had been much occupied with one question; why almost all crimes are so badly concealed and so easily detected, and why almost all criminals leave such obvious traces? He had come gradually to many different and curious conclusions, and in his opinion the chief reason lay not so much in the material impossibility of concealing the crime, as in the criminal himself. Almost every criminal is subject to a failure of will and reasoning power by a childish and phenomenal heedlessness, at the very instant when prudence and caution are most essential. It was his conviction that this eclipse of reason and failure of will power attacked a man like a disease, developed gradually and reached its highest point just before the perpetration of the crime, continued with equal violence at the moment of the crime and for longer or shorter time after, according to the individual case, and then passed off like any other disease. The question whether the disease gives rise to the crime, or whether the crime from its own peculiar nature is always accompanied by something of the nature of disease, he did not yet feel able to decide.

When he reached these conclusions, he decided that in his own case there could not be such a morbid reaction, that his reason and will would remain unimpaired at the time of carrying out his design, for the simple reason that his design was "not a crime. . . ." We will omit all the process by means of which he arrived at this last conclusion; we have run too far ahead already. . . . We may add only that the practical, purely material difficulties of the affair occupied a secondary position in his mind. "One has but to keep all one's will power and reason to deal with them, and they will all be overcome at the time when once one has familiarised oneself with the minutest details of the business. . . ." But this preparation had never been begun. His final decisions were what he came to trust least, and when the hour struck, it all came to pass quite differently, as it were accidentally and unexpectedly.

One trifling circumstance upset his calculations, before he had even left the staircase. When he reached the landlady's kitchen, the door of which was open as usual, he glanced cautiously in to see whether, in Nastasya's absence, the landlady herself was there, or if not, whether the door to her own room was closed, so that she might not peep out when he went in for the axe. But what was his amazement when he suddenly saw that Nastasya was not only at home in the kitchen, but was occupied there, taking linen out of a basket and hanging it on a line. Seeing him, she left off hanging the clothes, turned to him and stared at him all the time he was passing. He turned away his eyes, and walked past as though he noticed nothing. But it was the end of everything; he had not the axe! He was overwhelmed.

"What made me think," he reflected, as he went under the gateway, "what made me think that she would be sure not to be at home at that moment! Why, why, why did I assume this so certainly?"

He was crushed and even humiliated. He could have laughed at himself in his anger. . . . A dull animal rage boiled within him.

He stood hesitating in the gateway. To go into the street, to go for a walk for appearance' sake was revolting; to go back to his room, even more revolting. "And what a chance I have lost for ever!" he muttered, standing aimlessly in the gateway, just opposite the porter's little dark room, which was also open. Suddenly he started. From the porter's room, two paces away from him, something shining under the bench to the right caught his eye. . . . He looked about him—nobody. He approached the room on tiptoe, went down two steps into it and in a faint voice called the porter. "Yes, not at home! Somewhere near though, in the yard, for the door is wide open." He dashed to the axe (it was an axe) and pulled it out from under the bench, where it lay between two chunks of wood; at once before going out, he made it fast in the noose, he thrust both hands into his pockets and went out of the room; no one had noticed him! "When reason fails, the devil helps!" he thought with a strange grin. This chance raised his spirits extraordinarily.

He walked along quietly and sedately, without hurry, to avoid awakening suspicion. He scarcely looked at the passers-by, tried to escape looking at their faces at all, and to be as little noticeable as possible. Suddenly he thought of his hat. "Good heavens! I had the money the day before yesterday and did not get a cap to wear instead!" A curse rose from the bottom of his soul.

Glancing out of the corner of his eye into a shop, he saw by a clock on the wall that it was ten minutes past seven. He had to make haste and at the same time to go someway round, so as to approach the house from the other side. . . .

When he had happened to imagine all this beforehand, he had sometimes thought that he would be very much afraid. But he was not very much afraid now, was not afraid at all, indeed. His mind was even occupied by irrelevant matters, but by nothing for long. As he passed the Yusupov garden, he was deeply absorbed in considering the building of great fountains, and of their refreshing effect on the atmosphere in all the squares. By degrees he passed to the conviction that if the summer garden were extended to the field of Mars, and perhaps joined to the garden of the Mihailovsky Palace, it would be a splendid thing and a great benefit to the town. Then he was interested by the question why in all great towns men are not simply driven by necessity, but in some peculiar way inclined to live in those parts of the town where there are no gardens nor fountains; where there is most dirt and smell and all sorts of nastiness. Then his own walks through the Hay Market came back to his mind, and for a moment he waked up to reality. "What nonsense!" he thought, "better think of nothing at all!"

"So probably men led to execution clutch mentally at every object that meets them on the way," flashed through his mind, but simply flashed, like lightning; he made haste to dismiss this thought. . . . And by now he was near; here was the house, here was the gate. Suddenly a clock somewhere struck once. "What! can it be half-past seven? Impossible, it must be fast!"

Luckily for him, everything went well again at the gates. At that very moment, as though expressly for his benefit, a huge waggon of hay had just driven in at the gate, completely screening him as he passed under the gateway, and the waggon had scarcely had time to drive through into the yard, before he had slipped in a flash to the right. On the other side of the waggon he could hear shouting and quarrelling; but no one noticed him and no one met him. Many windows looking into that huge quadrangular yard were open at that moment, but he did not raise his head—he had not the strength to. The staircase leading to the old woman's room was close by, just on the right of the gateway. He was already on the stairs. . . .

Drawing a breath, pressing his hand against his throbbing heart, and once more feeling for the axe and setting it straight, he began softly and cautiously ascending the stairs, listening every minute. But the stairs, too, were quite deserted; all the doors were shut; he met no one. One flat indeed on the first floor was wide open and painters were at work in it, but they did not glance at him. He stood still, thought a minute and went on. "Of course it would be better if they had not been here, but . . . it's two storeys above them."

And here was the fourth storey, here was the door, here was the flat opposite, the empty one. The flat underneath the old woman's was apparently empty also; the visiting card nailed on the door had been torn off—they had gone away! . . . He was out of breath. For one instant the thought floated through his mind "Shall I go back?" But he made no answer and began listening at the old woman's door, a dead silence. Then he listened again on the staircase, listened long and intently . . . then looked about him for the last time, pulled himself together, drew himself up, and once more tried the axe in the noose. "Am I very pale?" he wondered. "Am I not evidently agitated? She is mistrustful. . . . Had I better wait a little longer . . . till my heart leaves off thumping?"

But his heart did not leave off. On the contrary, as though to spite him, it throbbed more and more violently. He could stand it no longer, he slowly put out his hand to the bell and rang. Half a minute later he rang again, more loudly.

No answer. To go on ringing was useless and out of place. The old woman was, of course, at home, but she was suspicious and alone. He had some knowledge of her habits . . . and once more he put his ear to the door. Either his senses were peculiarly keen (which it is difficult to suppose), or the sound was really very distinct. Anyway, he suddenly heard something like the cautious touch of a hand on the lock and the rustle of a skirt at the very door. Some one was standing stealthily close to the lock and just as he was doing on the outside was secretly listening within, and seemed to have her ear to the door. . . . He moved a little on purpose and muttered something aloud that he might not have the appearance of hiding, then rang a third time, but quietly, soberly and without impatience. Recalling it afterwards, that moment stood out in his mind vividly, distinctly, for ever; he could not make out how he had had such cunning, for his mind was as it were clouded at moments and he was almost unconscious of his body. . . . An instant later he heard the latch unfastened.

7

The door was as before opened a tiny crack, and again two sharp and suspicious eyes stared at him out of the darkness. Then Raskolnikov lost his head and nearly made a great mistake.

Fearing the old woman would be frightened by their being alone, and not hoping that the sight of him would disarm her suspicions, he took hold of the door and drew it towards him to prevent the old woman from attempting to shut it again. Seeing this she did not pull the door back, but she did not let go the handle so that he almost dragged her out with it on to the stairs. Seeing that she was standing in the doorway not allowing him to pass, he advanced straight upon her. She stepped back in alarm, tried to say something, but seemed unable to speak and stared with open eyes at him.

"Good evening, Alyona Ivanovna," he began, trying to speak easily, but his voice would not obey him, it broke and shook. "I have come . . . I have brought something . . . but we'd better come in . . . to the light. . . ."

And leaving her, he passed straight into the room uninvited. The old woman ran after him; her tongue was unloosed.

"Good heavens! What is it? Who is it? What do you want?"

"Why, Alyona Ivanovna, you know me . . . Raskolnikov
. . . here, I brought you the pledge I promised the other day
. . ." and he held out the pledge.

The old woman glanced for a moment at the pledge, but at
once stared in the eyes of her uninvited visitor. She looked intently, maliciously and mistrustfully. A minute passed; he even fancied something like a sneer in her eyes, as though she had already
guessed everything. He felt that he was losing his head, that he
was almost frightened, so frightened that if she were to look like
that and not say a word for another half minute, he thought he
would have run away from her.

"Why do you look at me as though you did not know me?"
he said suddenly, also with malice. "Take it if you like, if not I'll
go elsewhere, I am in a hurry."

He had not even thought of saying this, but it was suddenly
said of itself. The old woman recovered herself, and her visitor's
resolute tone evidently restored her confidence.

"But why, my good sir, all of a minute. . . . What is it?" she
asked, looking at the pledge.

"The silver cigarette case; I spoke of it last time, you know."

She held out her hand.

"But how pale you are, to be sure . . . and your hands are
trembling too? Have you been bathing, or what?"

"Fever," he answered abruptly. "You can't help getting pale
. . . if you've nothing to eat," he added, with difficulty articulating
the words.

His strength was failing him again. But his answer sounded
like the truth; the old woman took the pledge.

"What is it?" she asked once more, scanning Raskolnikov
intently and weighing the pledge in her hand.

"A thing . . . cigarette case. . . . Silver. . . . Look at it."

"It does not seem somehow like silver. . . . How he has
wrapped it up!"

Trying to untie the string and turning to the window, to the
light (all her windows were shut, in spite of the stifling heat), she
left him altogether for some seconds and stood with her back to

him. He unbuttoned his coat and freed the axe from the noose, but did not yet take it out altogether, simply holding it in his right hand under the coat. His hands were fearfully weak, he felt them every moment growing more numb and more wooden. He was afraid he would let the axe slip and fall. . . . A sudden giddiness came over him.

"But what has he tied it up like this for?" the old woman cried with vexation and moved towards him.

He had not a minute more to lose. He pulled the axe quite out, swung it with both arms, scarcely conscious of himself, and almost without effort, almost mechanically, brought the blunt side down on her head. He seemed not to use his own strength in this. But as soon as he had once brought the axe down, his strength returned to him.

The old woman was as always bareheaded. Her thin, light hair, streaked with grey, thickly smeared with grease, was plaited in a rat's tail and fastened by a broken horn comb which stood out on the nape of her neck. As she was so short, the blow fell on the very top of her skull. She cried out, but very faintly, and suddenly sank all of a heap on the floor, raising her hands to her head. In one hand she still held "the pledge." Then he dealt her another and another blow with the blunt side and on the same spot. The blood gushed as from an overturned glass, the body fell back. He stepped back, let it fall, and at once bent over her face; she was dead. Her eyes seemed to be starting out of their sockets, the brow and the whole face were drawn and contorted convulsively.

He laid the axe on the ground near the dead body and felt at once in her pocket (trying to avoid the streaming body)—the same right hand pocket from which she had taken the key on his last visit. He was in full possession of his faculties, free from confusion or giddiness, but his hands were still trembling. He remembered afterwards that he had been particularly collected and careful, trying all the time not to get smeared with blood. . . . He pulled out the keys at once, they were all, as before, in one bunch on a steel ring. He ran at once into the bedroom with them. It was a very small room with a whole shrine of holy images. Against the other wall stood a big bed, very clean and covered with a silk patchwork wadded quilt. Against a third wall was a chest of drawers. Strange to say, so soon as he began to fit the keys into the chest, so soon as he heard their jingling, a convulsive shudder passed over him. He suddenly felt tempted again to give it all up and go away. But that was only for an instant; it was too late to go back. He positively smiled at himself, when suddenly another terrifying idea occurred to his mind. He suddenly fancied that the old woman might be still alive and might recover her senses. Leaving the keys in the chest, he ran back to the body, snatched up the axe and lifted it once more over the old woman, but did not bring it down. There was no doubt that she was dead. Bending down and examining her again more closely, he saw clearly that the skull was broken and even battered in on one side. He was about to feel it with his finger, but drew back his hand and indeed it was evident without that. Meanwhile there was a perfect pool of blood. All at once he noticed a string on her neck; he tugged at it, but the string was strong and did not snap and besides, it was soaked with blood. He tried to pull it out from the front of the dress, but something held it and prevented its coming. In his impatience he raised the axe again to cut the string from above on the body, but did not dare, and with difficulty, smearing his hand and the axe in the blood, after two minutes' hurried effort, he cut the string and took it off without touching the body with the axe; he was not mistaken—it was a purse. On the string were two crosses, one of Cyprus wood and one of copper, and an image in silver filigree, and with them a small greasy chamois leather purse with a steel rim and ring. The purse was stuffed very full; Raskolnikov thrust it in his pocket without looking at it, flung the crosses on the old woman's body and rushed back into the bedroom, this time taking the axe with him.

He was in terrible haste, he snatched the keys, and began trying them again. But he was unsuccessful. They would not fit in the locks. It was not so much that his hands were shaking, but that he kept making mistakes; though he saw for instance that a key was not the right one and would not fit, still he tried to put it in. Suddenly he remembered and realised that the big key with the deep notches, which was hanging there with the small keys could not possibly belong to the chest of drawers (on his last visit this had struck him), but to some strong box, and that everything perhaps was hidden in that box. He left the chest of drawers, and at once felt under the bedstead, knowing that old women usually keep boxes under their beds. And so it was; there was a good-sized box under the bed, at least a yard in length, with an arched lid covered with red leather and studded with steel nails. The notched key fitted at once and unlocked it. At the top, under a white sheet, was a coat of red brocade lined with hareskin; under it was a silk dress, then a shawl and it seemed as though there was nothing below but clothes. The first thing he did was to wipe his blood-stained hands on the red brocade. "It's red, and on red blood will be less noticeable," the thought passed through his mind; then he suddenly came to himself. "Good God, am I going out of my senses?" he thought with terror.

But no sooner did he touch the clothes than a gold watch slipped from under the fur coat. He made haste to turn them all over. There turned out to be various articles made of gold among the clothes—probably all pledges, unredeemed or waiting to be redeemed—bracelets, chains, ear-rings, pins and such things. Some were in cases, others simply wrapped in newspaper, carefully and exactly folded, and tied round with tape. Without any delay, he began filling up the pockets of his trousers and overcoat without examining or undoing the parcels and cases; but he had not time to take many. . . .

He suddenly heard steps in the room where the old woman lay. He stopped short and was still as death. But all was quiet, so it must have been his fancy. All at once he heard distinctly a faint cry, as though some one had uttered a low broken moan. Then again dead silence for a minute or two. He sat squatting on his heels by the box and waited holding his breath. Suddenly he jumped up, seized the axe and ran out of the bedroom.

In the middle of the room stood Lizaveta with a big bundle in her arms. She was gazing in stupefaction at her murdered sister, white as a sheet and seeming not to have the strength to cry out. Seeing him run out of the bedroom, she began faintly quivering all over, like a leaf, a shudder ran down her face; she lifted her hand, opened her mouth, but still did not scream. She began slowly backing away from him into the corner, staring intently, persistently at him, but still uttered no sound, as though she could not get breath to scream. He rushed at her with the axe; her mouth twitched piteously, as one sees babies' mouths, when they begin to be frightened, stare intently at what frightens them and are on the point of screaming. And this hapless Lizaveta was so simple and had been so thoroughly crushed and scared that she did not even raise a hand to guard her face, though that was the most necessary and natural action at the moment, for the axe was raised over her face. She only put up her empty left hand, but not to her face, slowly holding it out before her as though motioning him away. The axe fell with the sharp edge just on the skull and split at one blow all the top of the head. She fell heavily at once. Raskolnikov completely lost his head, snatched up her bundle, dropped it again and ran into the entry.

Fear gained more and more mastery over him, especially after this second, quite unexpected murder. He longed to run away from the place as fast as possible. And if at that moment he had been capable of seeing and reasoning more correctly, if he had been able to realise all the difficulties of his position, the hopelessness, the hideousness and the absurdity of it, if he could have understood how many obstacles and, perhaps, crimes he had still to overcome or to commit, to get out of that place and to make his way home, it is very possible that he would have flung up everything, and would have gone to give himself up, and not from fear, but from simple horror and loathing of what he had done. The feeling of loathing especially surged up within him and grew stronger every minute. He would not now have gone to the box or even into the room for anything in the world.

But a sort of blankness, even dreaminess had begun by degrees to take possession of him; at moments he forgot himself, or rather forgot what was of importance, and caught at trifles. Glancing, however, into the kitchen and seeing a bucket half full of water on a bench, he bethought him of washing his hands and the axe. His hands were sticky with blood. He dropped the axe with the blade in the water, snatched a piece of soap that lay in a broken saucer on the window, and began washing his hands in the bucket. When they were clean, he took out the axe, washed the blade and spent a long time, about three minutes, washing the wood where there were spots of blood rubbing them with soap. Then he wiped it all with some linen that was hanging to dry on a line in the kitchen and then he was a long while attentively examining the axe at the window. There was no trace left on it, only the wood was still damp. He carefully hung the axe in the noose under his coat. Then as far as was possible, in the dim light in the kitchen, he looked over his overcoat, his trousers and his boots. At the first glance there seemed to be nothing but stains on the boots. He wetted the rag and rubbed the boots. But he knew he was not looking thoroughly, that there might be something quite noticeable that he was overlooking. He stood in the middle of the room, lost in thought. Dark agonising ideas rose in his mind—the idea that he was mad and that at that moment he was incapable of reasoning, of protecting himself, that he ought perhaps to be doing something utterly different from what he was now doing. "Good God!" he muttered "I must fly, fly," and he rushed into the entry. But here a shock of terror awaited him such as he had never known before.

He stood and gazed and could not believe his eyes: the door, the outer door from the stairs, at which he had not long before waited and rung, was standing unfastened and at least six inches open. No lock, no bolt, all the time, all that time! The old woman had not shut it after him perhaps as a precaution. But, good God! Why, he had seen Lizaveta afterwards! And how could he, how could he have failed to reflect that she must have come in somehow! She could not have come through the wall!

He dashed to the door and fastened the latch.

"But no, the wrong thing again. I must get away, get away. . . ."

He unfastened the latch, opened the door and began listening on the staircase.

He listened a long time. Somewhere far away, it might be in the gateway, two voices were loudly and shrilly shouting, quar-

relling and scolding. "What are they about?" He waited patient-
ly. At last all was still, as though suddenly cut off; they had
separated. He was meaning to go out, but suddenly, on the floor
below, a door was noisily opened and some one began going
downstairs humming a tune. "How is it they all make such a
noise!" flashed through his mind. Once more he closed the door
and waited. At last all was still, not a soul stirring. He was just
taking a step towards the stairs when he heard fresh footsteps.

The steps sounded very far off, at the very bottom of the
stairs, but he remembered quite clearly and distinctly that from
the first sound he began for some reason to suspect that this was
some one coming *there,* to the fourth floor, to the old woman.
Why? Were the sounds somehow peculiar, significant? The steps
were heavy, even and unhurried. Now *he* had passed the first
floor, now he was mounting higher, it was growing more and
more distinct! He could hear his heavy breathing. And now the
third storey had been reached. Coming here! And it seemed to
him all at once that he was turned to stone, that it was like a dream
in which one is being pursued, nearly caught and will be killed,
and is rooted to the spot and cannot even move one's arms.

At last when the unknown was mounting to the fourth floor,
he suddenly started, and succeeded in slipping neatly and quickly
back into the flat and closing the door behind him. Then he took
the hook and softly, noiselessly, fixed it in the catch. Instinct
helped him. When he had done this, he crouched holding his
breath, by the door. The unknown visitor was by now also at the
door. They were now standing opposite one another, as he had
just before been standing with the old woman, when the door
divided them and he was listening.

The visitor panted several times. "He must be a big, fat
man," thought Raskolnikov, squeezing the axe in his hand. It
seemed like a dream indeed. The visitor took hold of the bell and
rang loudly.

As soon as the tin bell tinkled, Raskolnikov seemed to be
aware of something moving in the room. For some seconds he
listened quite seriously. The unknown rang again, waited and
suddenly tugged violently and impatiently at the handle of the

door. Raskolnikov gazed in horror at the hook shaking in its fastening, and in blank terror expected every minute that the fastening would be pulled out. It certainly did seem possible, so violently was he shaking it. He was tempted to hold the fastening, but *he* might be aware of it. A giddiness came over him again. "I shall fall down!" flashed through his mind, but the unknown began to speak and he recovered himself at once.

"What's up? Are they asleep or murdered? D-damn them!" he bawled in a thick voice, "Hey, Alyona Ivanovna, old witch! Lizaveta Ivanovna, hey, my beauty! open the door! Oh, damn them! Are they asleep or what?"

And again, enraged, he tugged with all his might a dozen times at the bell. He must certainly be a man of authority and an intimate acquaintance.

At this moment light hurried steps were heard not far off, on the stairs. Some one else was approaching. Raskolnikov had not heard them at first.

"You don't say there's no one at home," the new-comer cried in a cheerful, ringing voice, addressing the first visitor, who still went on pulling the bell. "Good evening, Koch."

"From his voice he must be quite young," thought Raskolnikov.

"Who the devil can tell? I've almost broken the lock," answered Koch. "But how do you come to know me?"

"Why! The day before yesterday I beat you three times running at billiards at Gambrinus'."

"Oh!"

"So they are not at home? That's queer? It's awfully stupid though. Where could the old woman have gone? I've come on business."

"Yes; and I have business with her, too."

"Well, what can we do? Go back, I suppose. Aie—aie! And I was hoping to get some money!" cried the young man.

"We must give it up, of course, but what did she fix this time for? The old witch fixed the time for me to come herself. It's out of my way. And where the devil she can have got to, I can't make out. She sits here from year's end to year's end, the old hag; her legs are bad and yet here all of a sudden she is out for a walk!"

"Hadn't we better ask the porter?"

"What?"

"Where she's gone and when she'll be back."

"Hm. . . . Damn it all! . . . We might ask. . . . But you know she never does go anywhere."

And he once more tugged at the door-handle.

"Damn it all. There's nothing to be done, we must go!"

"Stay!" cried the young man suddenly. "Do you see how the door shakes if you pull it?"

"Well?"

"That shows it's not locked, but fastened with the hook! Do you hear how the hook clanks?"

"Well?"

"Why, don't you see? That proves that one of them is at home. If they were all out, they would have locked the door from outside with the key and not with the hook from inside. There, do you hear how the hook is clanking? To fasten the hook on the inside they must be at home, don't you see. So there they are sitting inside and don't open the door!"

"Well! And so they must be!" cried Koch, astonished. "What are they about in there!" And he began furiously shaking the door.

"Stay!" cried the young man again. "Don't pull at it! There must be something wrong. . . . Here, you've been ringing and pulling at the door and still they don't open! So either they've both fainted or . . ."

"What?"

"I tell you what. Let's go and fetch the porter, let him wake them up."

"All right."

Both were going down.

"Stay. You stop here while I run down for the porter."

"What for?"

"Well, you'd better."

"All right."

"I'm studying the law you see! It's evident, e-vi-dent there's something wrong here!" the young man cried hotly, and he ran downstairs.

Koch remained. Once more he softly touched the bell which gave one tinkle, then gently, as though reflecting and looking about him, began touching the door-handle, pulling it and letting it go to make sure once more that it was only fastened by the hook. Then puffing and panting he bent down and began looking at the keyhole; but the key was in the lock on the inside and so nothing could be seen.

Raskolnikov stood keeping tight hold of the axe. He was in a sort of delirium. He was even making ready to fight when they should come in. While they were knocking and talking together, the idea several times occurred to him to end it all at once and shout to them through the door. Now and then he was tempted to swear at them, to jeer at them, while they could not open the door! "Only make haste!" was the thought that flashed through his mind.

"But what the devil is he about? . . ." Time was passing, one minute, and another—no one came. Koch began to be restless.

"What the devil?" he cried suddenly and in impatience deserting his sentry duty, he, too, went down, hurrying and thumping with his heavy boots on the stairs. The steps died away.

"Good heavens! What am I to do?"

Raskolnikov unfastened the hook, opened the door—there was no sound. Abruptly, without any thought at all, he went out, closing the door as thoroughly as he could, and went downstairs.

He had gone down three flights when he suddenly heard a loud noise below—where could he go! There was nowhere to hide. He was just going back to the flat.

"Hey there! Catch the brute!"

Somebody dashed out of a flat below, shouting, and rather fell than ran down the stairs, bawling at the top of his voice.

"Mitka! Mitka! Mitka! Mitka! Mitka! Blast him!"

The shout ended in a shriek; the last sounds came from the yard; all was still. But at the same instant several men talking loud and fast began noisily mounting the stairs. There were three or four of them. He distinguished the ringing voice of the young man. "They!"

Filled with despair he went straight to meet them, feeling "come what must!" If they stopped him—all was lost; if they let him pass—all was lost too; they would remember him. They were approaching; they were only a flight from him—and suddenly deliverance! A few steps from him on the right, there was an empty flat with the door wide open, the flat on the second floor where the painters had been at work, and which, as though for his benefit, they had just left. It was they, no doubt, who had just run down, shouting. The floor had only just been painted, in the middle of the room stood a pail and a broken pot with paint and brushes. In one instant he had whisked in at the open door and hidden behind the wall and only in the nick of time; they had already reached the landing. Then they turned and went on up to the fourth floor, talking loudly. He waited, went out on tiptoe and ran down the stairs.

No one was on the stairs, nor in the gateway. He passed quickly through the gateway and turned to the left in the street.

He knew, he knew perfectly well that at that moment they were at the flat, that they were greatly astonished at finding it unlocked, as the door had just been fastened, that by now they were looking at the bodies, that before another minute had passed they would guess and completely realise that the murderer had just been there, and had succeeded in hiding somewhere, slipping by them and escaping. They would guess most likely that he had been in the empty flat, while they were going upstairs. And meanwhile he dared not quicken his pace much, though the next turning was still nearly a hundred yards away. "Should he slip through some gateway and wait somewhere in an unknown street? No, hopeless! Should he fling away the axe? Should he take a cab? Hopeless, hopeless!"

At last he reached the turning. He turned down it more dead than alive. Here he was half way to safety, and here understood it; it was less risky because there was a great crowd of people, and he was lost in it like a grain of sand. But all he had suffered had so weakened him that he could scarcely move. Perspiration ran down him in drops, his neck was all wet. "My word, he has been going it!" some one shouted at him when he came out on the canal bank.

He was only dimly conscious of himself now, and the farther he went the worse it was. He remembered however, that on coming out on to the canal bank, he was alarmed at finding few people there and so being more conspicuous, and he had thought of turning back. Though he was almost falling from fatigue, he went a long way round so as to get home from quite a different direction.

He was not fully conscious when he passed through the gateway of his house! he was already on the staircase before he recollected the axe. And yet he had a very grave problem before him, to put it back and to escape observation as far as possible in doing so. He was of course incapable of reflecting that it might perhaps be far better not to restore the axe at all, but to drop it later on in somebody's yard. But it all happened fortunately, the door of the porter's room was closed but not locked, so that it seemed most likely that the porter was at home. But he had so completely lost all power of reflection that he walked straight to the door and opened it. If the porter had asked him "What do you want?" he would perhaps have simply handed him the axe. But again the porter was not at home, and he succeeded in putting the axe back under the bench and even covering it with the chunk of wood as before. He met no one, not a soul, afterwards on the way to his room; the landlady's door was shut. When he was in his room, he flung himself on the sofa just as he was—he did not sleep, but sank into blank forgetfulness. If any one had come into his room then, he would have jumped up at once and screamed. Scraps and shreds of thoughts were simply swarming in his brain, but he could not catch at one, he could not rest on one, in spite of all his efforts. . . .

PART TWO—

1

So he lay a very long while. Now and then he seemed to wake up, and at such moments he noticed that it was far into the night, but it did not occur to him to get up. At last he noticed that it was beginning to get light. He was lying on his back, still dazed from his recent oblivion. Fearful, despairing cries rose shrilly from the street, sounds which he heard every night, indeed, under his window after two o'clock. They woke him up now.

"Ah! the drunken men are coming out of the taverns," he thought, "it's past two o'clock," and at once he leaped up, as though some one had pulled him from the sofa.

"What! Past two o'clock!"

He sat down on the sofa—and instantly recollected everything! All at once, in one flash, he recollected everything.

For the first moment he thought he was going mad. A dreadful chill came over him; but the chill was from the fever that had begun long before in his sleep. Now he was suddenly taken with violent shivering, so that his teeth chattered and all his limbs were shaking. He opened the door and began listening; everything in the house was asleep. With amazement he gazed at himself and everything in the room around him, wondering how he could have come in the night before without fastening the door, and have flung himself on the sofa without undressing, without even taking his hat off. It had fallen off and was lying on the floor near his pillow.

"If any one had come in, what would he have thought? That I'm drunk but . . ."

He rushed to the window. There was light enough, and he began hurriedly looking himself all over from head to foot, all his clothes; were there no traces? But there was no doing it like that; shivering with cold, he began taking off everything and looking over again. He turned everything over to the last threads and rags, and mistrusting himself, went through his search three times.

But there seemed to be nothing, no trace, except in one place, where some thick drops of congealed blood were clinging to the frayed edge of his trousers. He picked up a big claspknife and cut off the frayed threads. There seemed to be nothing more.

Suddenly he remembered that the purse and the things he had taken out of the old woman's box were still in his pockets! He had not thought till then of taking them out and hiding them! He had not even thought of them while he was examining his clothes! What next? Instantly he rushed to take them out, and fling them on the table. When he had pulled out everything, and turned the pocket inside out to be sure there was nothing left, he carried the whole heap to the corner. The paper had come off the bottom of the wall and hung there in tatters. He began stuffing all the things into the hole under the paper: "They're in! All out of sight, and the purse too!" he thought gleefully, getting up and gazing blankly at the hole which bulged out more than ever. Suddenly he shuddered all over with horror; "My God!" he whispered in despair: "what's the matter with me? Is that hidden? Is that the way to hide things?"

He had not reckoned on having trinkets to hide. He had only thought of money, and so had not prepared a hiding-place.

"But now, now, what am I glad of?" he thought. "Is that hiding things? My reason's deserting me—simply!"

He sat down on the sofa in exhaustion and was at once shaken by another unbearable fit of shivering. Mechanically he drew from a chair beside him his old student's winter coat, which was still warm though almost in rags, covered himself up with it and once more sank into drowsiness and delirium. He lost consciousness.

Not more than five minutes had passed when he jumped up a second time, and at once pounced in a frenzy on his clothes again.

"How could I go to sleep again with nothing done? Yes, yes; I have not taken the loop off the armhole! I forgot it, forgot a thing like that! Such a piece of evidence!"

He pulled off the noose, hurriedly cut it to pieces and threw the bits among his linen under the pillow.

"Pieces of torn linen couldn't rouse suspicion, whatever happened; I think not, I think not, any way!" he repeated, standing in the middle of the room, and with painful concentration he fell to gazing about him again, at the floor and everywhere, trying to make sure he had not forgotten anything. The conviction, that all his faculties, even memory, and the simplest power of reflection were failing him, began to be an insufferable torture.

"Surely it isn't beginning already! Surely it isn't my punishment coming upon me? It is!"

The frayed rags he had cut off his trousers were actually lying on the floor in the middle of the room, where any one coming in would see them!

"What is the matter with me!" he cried again, like one distraught.

Then a strange idea entered his head; that, perhaps, all his clothes were covered with blood, that, perhaps, there were a great many stains, but that he did not see them, did not notice them because his perceptions were failing, were going to pieces . . . his reason was clouded. . . . Suddenly he remembered that there had been blood on the purse too. "Ah! Then there must be blood on the pocket too, for I put the wet purse in my pocket!"

In a flash he had turned the pocket inside out and, yes!— there were traces, stains on the lining of the pocket!

"So my reason has not quite deserted me, so I still have some sense and memory, since I guessed it of myself," he thought triumphantly, with a deep sigh of relief: "It's simply the weakness of fever, a moment's delirium," and he tore the whole lining out of the left pocket of his trousers. At that instant the sunlight fell on his left boot; on the sock which poked out from the boot, he fancied there were traces! He flung off his boots: "traces indeed! The tip of the sock was soaked with blood"; he must have unwarily stepped into that pool. . . . "But what am I to do with this now? Where am I to put the sock and rags and pocket?"

He gathered them all up in his hands and stood in the middle of the room.

"In the stove? But they would ransack the stove first of all. Burn them? But what can I burn them with? There are no matches even. No, better go out and throw it all away somewhere. Yes, better throw it away," he repeated, sitting down on the sofa again, "and at once, this minute, without lingering . . ."

But his head sank on the pillow instead. Again the unbearable icy shivering came over him; again he drew his coat over him.

And for a long while, for some hours, he was haunted by the impulse to "go off somewhere at once, this moment, and fling it all away, so that it may be out of sight and done with, at once, at once!" Several times he tried to rise from the sofa but could not.

He was thoroughly waked up at last by a violent knocking at his door.

"Open, do, are you dead or alive? He keeps sleeping here!" shouted Nastasya, banging with her fist on the door. "For whole days together he's snoring here like a dog! A dog he is too. Open I tell you. It's past ten."

"Maybe he's not at home," said a man's voice.

"Ha! that's the porter's voice. . . . What does he want?"

He jumped up and sat on the sofa. The beating of his heart was a positive pain.

"Then who can have latched the door?" retorted Nastasya.

"He's taken to bolting himself in! As if he were worth stealing! Open, you stupid, wake up!"

"What do they want? Why the porter? All's discovered. Resist or open? Come what may! . . ."

He half rose, stooped forward and unlatched the door.

His room was so small that he could undo the latch without leaving the bed. Yes; the porter and Nastasya were standing there.

Nastasya stared at him in a strange way. He glanced with a defiant and desperate air at the porter, who without a word held out a grey folded paper sealed with bottle-wax.

"A notice from the office," he announced, as he gave him the paper.

"From what office?"

"A summons to the police office, of course. You know which office."

"To the police? . . . What for? . . ."

"How can I tell? You're sent for, so you go."

The man looked at him attentively, looked round the room and turned to go away.

"He's downright ill!" observed Nastasya, not taking her eyes off him. The porter turned his head for a moment. "He's been in a fever since yesterday," she added.

Raskolnikov made no response and held the paper in his hands, without opening it. "Don't you get up then," Nastasya went on compassionately, seeing that he was letting his feet down from the sofa. "You're ill, and so don't go; there's no such hurry. What have you got there?"

He looked; in his right hand he held the shreds he had cut from his trousers, the sock, and the rags of the pocket. So he had been asleep with them in his hand. Afterwards reflecting upon it, he remembered that half waking up in his fever, he had grasped all this tightly in his hand and so fallen asleep again.

"Look at the rags he's collected and sleeps with them, as though he has got hold of a treasure . . ."

And Nastasya went off into her hysterical giggle.

Instantly he thrust them all under his great coat and fixed his eyes intently upon her. Far as he was from being capable of rational reflection at that moment, he felt that no one would behave like that with a person who was going to be arrested. "But . . . the police?"

"You'd better have some tea! Yes? I'll bring it, there's some left."

"No . . . I'm going; I'll go at once," he muttered, getting on to his feet.

"Why, you'll never get downstairs!"

"Yes, I'll go."

"As you please."

She followed the porter out.

At once he rushed to the light to examine the sock and the rags.

"There are stains, but not very noticeable; all covered with dirt, and rubbed and already discoloured. No one who had no suspicion could distinguish anything. Nastasya from a distance could not have noticed, thank God!" Then with a tremor he broke the seal of the notice and began reading; he was a long while reading, before he understood. It was an ordinary summons from the district police station to appear that day at half past nine at the office of the district superintendent.

"But when has such a thing happened? I never have anything to do with the police! And why just to-day?" he thought in agonising bewilderment. "Good God, only get it over soon!"

He was flinging himself on his knees to pray, but broke into laughter—not at the idea of prayer, but at himself.

He began, hurriedly dressing, "if I'm lost, I am lost, I don't care! Shall I put the sock on?" he suddenly wondered, "it will get dustier still and the traces will be gone."

But no sooner had he put it on than he pulled it off again in loathing and horror. He pulled it off, but reflecting that he had no other socks, he picked it up and put it on again—and again he laughed.

"That's all conventional, that's all relative, merely a way of looking at it," he thought in a flash, but only on the top surface of his mind, while he was shuddering all over, "there I've got it on! I have finished by getting it on!"

But his laughter was quickly followed by despair.

"No, it's too much for me . . ." he thought. His legs shook. "From fear," he muttered. His head swam and ached with fever. "It's a trick! They want to decoy me there and confound me over everything," he mused, as he went out on to the stairs—"the worst of it is I'm almost light-headed. . . . I may blurt out something stupid . . ."

On the stairs he remembered that he was leaving all the things just as they were in the hole in the wall, "and very likely, it's on purpose to search when I'm out," he thought, and stopped short. But he was possessed by such despair, such cynicism of misery, if one may so call it, that with a wave of his hand he went on. "Only to get it over!"

In the street the heat was insufferable again; not a drop of rain had fallen all those days. Again dust, bricks, and mortar, again the stench from the shops and pot-houses, again the drunken men, the Finnish pedlars and half-broken-down cabs. The sun shone straight in his eyes, so that it hurt him to look out of them, and he felt his head going round—as a man in a fever is apt to feel when he comes out into the street on a bright sunny day.

When he reached the turning into *the* street, in an agony of trepidation he looked down it . . . at *the* house . . . and at once averted his eyes.

"If they question me, perhaps I'll simply tell," he thought, as he drew near the police station.

The police station was about a quarter of a mile off. It had lately been moved to new rooms on the fourth floor of a new house. He had been once for a moment in the old office but long ago. Turning in at the gateway, he saw on the right a flight of stairs which a peasant was mounting with a book in his hand. "A house-porter, no doubt; so then, the office is here," and he began ascending the stairs on the chance. He did not want to ask questions of any one.

"I'll go in, fall on my knees, and confess everything . . ." he thought, as he reached the fourth floor.

The staircase was steep, narrow and all sloppy with dirty water. The kitchens of the flats opened on to the stairs and stood open almost the whole day. So there was a fearful smell and heat. The staircase was crowded with porters going up and down with their books under their arms, policemen, and persons of all sorts and both sexes. The door of the office, too, stood wide open. Peasants stood waiting within. There, too, the heat was stifling and there was a sickening smell of fresh paint and stale oil from the newly decorated rooms.

After waiting a little, he decided to move forward into the next room. All the rooms were small and low-pitched. A fearful impatience drew him on and on. No one paid attention to him. In the second room some clerks sat writing, dressed hardly better than he was, and rather a queer-looking set. He went up to one of them.

"What is it?"

He showed the notice he had received.

"You are a student?" the man asked, glancing at the notice.

"Yes, formerly a student."

The clerk looked at him, but without the slightest interest. He was a particularly unkempt person with the look of a fixed idea in his eye.

"There would be no getting anything out of him, because he has no interest in anything," thought Raskolnikov.

"Go in there to the head clerk," said the clerk, pointing towards the furthest room.

He went into that room—the fourth in order; it was a small room and packed full of people, rather better dressed than in the outer rooms. Among them were two ladies. One, poorly dressed in mourning, sat at the table opposite the chief clerk, writing something at his dictation. The other, a very stout, buxom woman with a purplish-red, blotchy face, excessively smartly dressed with a brooch on her bosom as big as a saucer, was standing on one side, apparently waiting for something. Raskolnikov thrust his notice upon the head clerk. The latter glanced at it, said: "Wait a minute," and went on attending to the lady in mourning.

He breathed more freely. "It can't be that!"

By degrees he began to regain confidence, he kept urging himself to have courage and be calm.

"Some foolishness, some trifling carelessness, and I may betray myself! Hm! . . . it's a pity there's no air here," he added, "it's stifling. . . . It makes one's head dizzier than ever . . . and one's mind too . . ."

He was conscious of a terrible inner turmoil. He was afraid of losing his self-control; he tried to catch at something and fix his mind on it, something quite irrelevant, but he could not succeed in this at all. Yet the head clerk greatly interested him, he kept hoping to see through him and guess something from his face.

He was a very young man, about two and twenty, with a dark mobile face that looked older than his years. He was fashionably dressed and foppish, with his hair parted in the middle, well combed and pomaded, and wore a number of rings on his well-scrubbed fingers and a gold chain on his waistcoat. He said a couple of words in French to a foreigner who was in the room, and said them fairly correctly.

"Luise Ivanovna, you can sit down," he said casually to the gaily-dressed, purple-faced lady, who was still standing as though not venturing to sit down, though there was a chair beside her.

"Ich danke," said the latter, and softly, with a rustle of silk she sank into the chair. Her light blue dress trimmed with white lace floated about the table like an air-balloon and filled almost half the room. She smelt of scent. But she was obviously embarrassed at filling half the room and smelling so strongly of scent; and though her smile was impudent as well as cringing, it betrayed evident uneasiness.

The lady in mourning had done at last, and got up. All at once, with some noise, an officer walked in very jauntily, with a peculiar swing of his shoulders at each step. He tossed his cockaded cap on the table and sat down in an easy-chair. The smart lady positively skipped from her seat on seeing him, and fell to curtsying in a sort of ecstasy; but the officer took not the smallest notice of her, and she did not venture to sit down again in his presence. He was the assistant superintendent. He had a reddish moustache that stood out horizontally on each side of his face, and extremely small features, expressive of nothing much except a certain insolence. He looked askance and rather indignantly at Raskolnikov; he was so very badly dressed, and in spite of his humiliating position, his bearing was by no means in keeping with his clothes. Raskolnikov had unwarily fixed a very long and direct look on him, so that he felt positively affronted.

"What do you want?" he shouted, apparently astonished that such a ragged fellow was not annihilated by the majesty of his glance.

"I was summoned . . . by a notice . . ." Raskolnikov faltered.

"For the recovery of money due, from *the student,*" the head clerk interfered hurriedly, tearing himself from his papers. "Here!" and he flung Raskolnikov a document and pointed out the place. "Read that!"

"Money? What money?" thought Raskolnikov, "but . . . then . . . it's certainly not *that.*"

And he trembled with joy. He felt sudden intense indescribable relief. A load was lifted from his back.

"And pray, what time were you directed to appear, sir?" shouted the assistant superintendent, seeming for some unknown reason more and more aggrieved. "You are told to come at nine, and now it's twelve!"

"The notice was only brought me a quarter of an hour ago," Raskolnikov answered loudly over his shoulder. To his own surprise he, too, grew suddenly angry and found a certain pleasure in it. "And it's enough that I have come here ill with fever."

"Kindly refrain from shouting!"

"I'm not shouting, I'm speaking very quietly, it's you who are shouting at me. I'm a student, and allow no one to shout at me."

The assistant superintendent was so furious that for the first minute he could only splutter inarticulately. He leaped up from his seat.

"Be silent! You are in a government office. Don't be impudent, sir!"

"You're in a government office, too," cried Raskolnikov, "and you're smoking a cigarette as well as shouting, so you are showing disrespect to all of us."

He felt an indescribable satisfaction at having said this.

The head clerk looked at him with a smile. The angry assistant superintendent was obviously disconcerted.

"That's not your business!" he shouted at last with unnatural loudness. "Kindly make the declaration demanded of you. Show him, Alexandr Grigorievitch. There is a complaint against you! You don't pay your debts! You're a fine bird!"

But Raskolnikov was not listening now; he had eagerly clutched at the paper, in haste to find an explanation. He read it once, and a second time, and still did not understand.

"What is this?" he asked the head clerk.

"It is for the recovery of money on an I.O.U., a writ. You must either pay it, with all expenses, costs and so on, or give a written declaration when you can pay it, and at the same time an undertaking not to leave the capital without payment, and not to sell or conceal your property. The creditor is at liberty to sell your property, and proceed against you according to the law."

"But I . . . am not in debt to any one!"

"That's not our business. Here, an I.O.U. for a hundred and fifteen roubles, legally attested, and due for payment, has been brought us for recovery, given by you to the widow of the assessor Zarnitsyn, nine months ago, and paid over by the widow Zarnitsyn to one Mr. Tchebarov. We therefore summon you hereupon."

"But she is my landlady!"

"And what if she is your landlady?"

The head clerk looked at him with a condescending smile of compassion, and at the same time with a certain triumph, as at a novice under fire for the first time—as though he would say: "Well, how do you feel now?" But what did he care now for an I.O.U., for a writ of recovery! Was that worth worrying about now, was it worth attention even! He stood, he read, he listened, he answered, he even asked questions himself, but all mechanically. The triumphant sense of security, of deliverance from overwhelming danger, that was what filled his whole soul that moment without thought for the future, without analysis, without suppositions or surmises, without doubts and without questioning. It was an instant of full, direct, purely instinctive joy. But at that very moment something like a thunderstorm took place in the office. The assistant superintendent, still shaken by Raskolnikov's disrespect, still fuming and obviously anxious to keep up his wounded dignity, pounced on the unfortunate smart lady, who had been gazing at him ever since he came in with an exceedingly silly smile.

"You shameful hussy!" he shouted suddenly at the top of his voice. (The lady in mourning had left the office.) "What was going on at your house last night? Eh! A disgrace again, you're a scandal to the whole street. Fighting and drinking again. Do you want the house of correction? Why, I have warned you ten times over that I would not let you off the eleventh! And here you are again, again, you . . . you . . . !"

The paper fell out of Raskolnikov's hands, and he looked

wildly at the smart lady who was so unceremoniously treated. But he soon saw what it meant, and at once began to find positive amusement in the scandal. He listened with pleasure, so that he longed to laugh and laugh . . . all his nerves were on edge.

"Ilya Petrovitch!" the head clerk was beginning anxiously, but stopped short, for he knew from experience that the enraged assistant could not be stopped except by force.

As for the smart lady, at first she positively trembled before the storm. But strange to say, the more numerous and violent the terms of abuse became, the more amiable she looked, and the more seductive the smiles she lavished on the terrible assistant. She moved uneasily, and curtsied incessantly, waiting impatiently for a chance of putting in her word; and at last she found it.

"There was no sort of noise or fighting in my house, Mr. Captain," she pattered all at once, like peas dropping, speaking Russian confidently, though with a strong German accent, "and no sort of scandal, and his honour came drunk, and it's the whole truth I am telling, Mr. Captain, and I am not to blame . . . Mine is an honourable house, Mr. Captain, and honourable behaviour, Mr. Captain, and I always, always dislike any scandal myself. But he came quite tipsy, and asked for three bottles again, and then he lifted up one leg, and began playing the piano-forte with one foot, and that is not at all right in an honourable house, and he *ganz* broke the piano, and it was very bad manners indeed and I said so. And he took up a bottle and began hitting every one with it. And then I called the porter, and Karl came, and he took Karl and hit him in the eye; and he hit Henriette in the eye, too, and gave me five slaps on the cheek. And it was so ungentlemanly in an honourable house, Mr. Captain, and I screamed. And he opened the window over the canal, and stood in the window, squealing like a little pig; it was a disgrace. The idea of squealing like a little pig at the window into the street! Fie upon him! And Karl pulled him away from the window by his coat, and it is true, Mr. Captain, he tore *sein Rock*. And then he shouted that *man muss* pay him fifteen roubles damages. And I did pay him, Mr. Captain, five roubles for *sein Rock*. And he is an ungentlemanly visitor and caused all the scandal. 'I will show you up,' he said, 'for I can write to all the papers about you.' "

"Then he was an author?"

"Yes, Mr. Captain, and what an ungentlemanly visitor in an honourable house. . . ."

"Now then! Enough! I have told you already . . ."

"Ilya Petrovitch!" the head clerk repeated significantly.

The assistant glanced rapidly at him; the head clerk slightly shook his head.

". . . So I tell you this, most respectable Luise Ivanovna, and I tell it you for the last time," the assistant went on. "If there is a scandal in your honourable house once again, I will put you yourself in the lock-up, as it is called in polite society. Do you hear? So a literary man, an author took five roubles for his coattail in an 'honourable house'? A nice set, these authors!"

And he cast a contemptuous glance at Raskolnikov. "There was a scandal the other day in a restaurant, too. An author had eaten his dinner and would not pay; 'I'll write a satire on you,' says he. And there was another of them on a steamer last week used the most disgraceful language to the respectable family of a civil councillor, his wife and daughter. And there was one of them turned out of a confectioner's shop the other day. They are like that, authors, literary men, students, town-criers . . . Pfoo! You get along! I shall look in upon you myself one day. Then you had better be careful! Do you hear?"

With hurried deference, Luise Ivanovna fell to curtsying in all directions, and so curtsied herself to the door. But at the door, she stumbled backwards against a good-looking officer with a fresh, open face and splendid thick fair whiskers. This was the superintendent of the district himself, Nikodim Fomitch. Luise Ivanovna made haste to curtsy almost to the ground, and with mincing little steps, she fluttered out of the office.

"Again thunder and lightning—a hurricane!" said Nikodim Fomitch to Ilya Petrovitch in a civil and friendly tone. "You are aroused again, you are fuming again! I heard it on the stairs!"

"Well, what then!" Ilya Petrovitch drawled; with gentlemanly nonchalance; and he walked with some papers to another table, with a jaunty swing of his shoulders at each step. "Here, if you will kindly look: an author, or a student, has been one at least, does not pay his debts, has given an I.O.U. won't clear out of his room, and complaints are constantly being lodged against him, and here he has been pleased to make a protest against my smoking in his presence! He behaves like a cad himself, and just look at him, please. Here's the gentleman, and very attractive he is!"

"Poverty is not a vice, my friend, but we know you go off like powder, you can't bear a slight, I daresay you took offence at something and went too far yourself," continued Nikodim Fomitch, turning affably to Raskolnikov. "But you were wrong there; he is a capital fellow, I assure you, but explosive, explosive! He gets hot, fires up, boils over, and no stopping him! And then it's all over! And at the bottom he's a heart of gold! His nickname in the regiment was the Explosive Lieutenant . . ."

"And what a regiment it was, too," cried Ilya Petrovitch, much gratified at this agreeable banter, though still sulky.

Raskolnikov had a sudden desire to say something exceptionally pleasant to them all. "Excuse me, Captain," he began easily, suddenly addressing Nikodim Fomitch, "will you enter into my position. . . . I am ready to ask pardon, if I have been ill-mannered. I am a poor student, sick and shattered (shattered was the word he used) by poverty. I am not studying, because I cannot keep myself now, but I shall get money. . . . I have a mother and sister in the province of X. They will send it to me, and I will pay. My landlady is a good-hearted woman, but she is so exasperated at my having lost my lessons, and not paying her for the last four months, that she does not even send up my dinner . . . and I don't understand this I.O.U. at all. She is asking me to pay her on this I.O.U. How am I to pay her? Judge for yourselves! . . ."

"But that is not our business, you know," the head clerk was observing.

"Yes, yes. I perfectly agree with you. But allow me to explain . . ." Raskolnikov put in again, still addressing Nikodim Fomitch, but trying his best to address Ilya Petrovitch also, though the latter persistently appeared to be rummaging among his papers and to be contemptuously oblivious of him. "Allow me to explain that I have been living with her for nearly three years and at first . . . at first . . . for why should I not confess it, at the very beginning I promised to marry her daughter, it was a verbal promise, freely given . . . she was a girl . . . indeed, I liked her, though I was not in love with her . . . a youthful affair in fact . . . that is, I mean to say, that my landlady gave me credit freely in those days, and I led a life of . . . I was very heedless . . ."

"Nobody asks you for these personal details, sir, we've no time to waste," Ilya Petrovitch interposed roughly and with a note of triumph; but Raskolnikov stopped him hotly, though he suddenly found it exceedingly difficult to speak.

"But excuse me, excuse me. It is for me to explain . . . how it all happened . . . In my turn . . . though I agree with you . . . it is unnecessary. But a year ago, the girl died of typhus. I remained lodging there as before, and when my landlady moved into her present quarters, she said to me . . . and in a friendly way . . . that she had complete trust in me, but still, would I not give her an I.O.U. for one hundred and fifteen roubles, all the debt I owed her. She said if only I gave her that, she would trust me again, as much as I liked, and that she would never, never—those were her own words—make use of that I.O.U. till I could pay of myself . . . and now, when I have lost my lessons and have nothing to eat, she takes action against me. What am I to say to that?"

"All these affecting details are no business of ours," Ilya Petrovitch interrupted rudely. "You must give a written under-taking, but as for your love affairs and all these tragic events, we have nothing to do with that."

"Come now . . . you are harsh," muttered Nikodim Fomitch, sitting down at the table and also beginning to write. He looked a little ashamed.

"Write!" said the head clerk to Raskolnikov.

"Write what?" the latter asked, gruffly.

"I will dictate to you."

Raskolnikov fancied that the head clerk treated him more casually and contemptuously after his speech, but strange to say he suddenly felt completely indifferent to any one's opinion, and this revulsion took place in a flash, in one instant. If he had cared to think a little, he would have been amazed indeed that he could have talked to them like that a minute before, forcing his feelings upon them. And where had those feelings come from? Now if the whole room had been filled, not with police officers, but with those nearest and dearest to him, he would not have found one human word for them, so empty was his heart. A gloomy sensation of agonising, everlasting solitude and remoteness, took conscious form in his soul. It was not the meanness of his sentimental effusions before Ilya Petrovitch, nor the meanness of the latter's triumph over him that had caused this sudden revulsion in his heart. Oh, what had he to do now with his own baseness, with all these petty vanities, officers, German women, debts, police offices? If he had been sentenced to be burnt at that moment, he would not have stirred, would hardly have heard the sentence to the end. Something was happening to him entirely new, sudden and unknown. It was not that he understood, but he felt clearly with all the intensity of sensation that he could never more appeal to these people in the police office with sentimental effusions like his recent outburst, or with anything whatever; and that if they had been his own brothers and sisters and not police officers, it would have been utterly out of the question to appeal to them in any circumstance of life. He had never experienced such a strange and awful sensation. And what was most agonising—it was more a sensation than a conception or idea, a direct sensation, the most agonising of all the sensations he had known in his life.

The head clerk began dictating to him the usual form of declaration, that he could not pay, that he undertook to do so at a future date, that he would not leave the town, nor sell his property, and so on.

"But you can't write, you can hardly hold the pen," observed the head clerk, looking with curiosity at Raskolnikov. "Are you ill?"

"Yes, I am giddy. Go on!"

"That's all. Sign it."

The head clerk took the paper, and turned to attend to others.

Raskolnikov gave back the pen; but instead of getting up and going away, he put his elbows on the table and pressed his head in his hands. He felt as if a nail were being driven into his skull. A strange idea suddenly occurred to him, to get up at once, to go up to Nikodim Fomitch, and tell him everything that had happened yesterday, and then to go with him to his lodgings and to show him the things in the hole in the corner. The impulse was so strong that he got up from his seat to carry it out. "Hadn't I better think a minute?" flashed through his mind. "No, better cast off the burden without thinking." But all at once he stood still, rooted to the spot. Nikodim Fomitch was talking eagerly with Ilya Petrovitch, and the words reached him:

"It's impossible, they'll both be released. To begin with, the whole story contradicts itself. Why should they have called the porter, if it had been their doing? To inform against themselves? Or as a blind? No, that would be too cunning! Besides, Pestryakov, the student, was seen at the gate by both the porters and a woman as he went in. He was walking with three friends, who left him only at the gate, and he asked the porters to direct him, in the presence of the friends. Now, would he have asked his way if he had been going with such an object? As for Koch, he spent half an hour at the silversmith's below, before he went up to the old woman and he left him at exactly a quarter to eight. Now just consider . . ."

"But excuse me, how do you explain this contradiction? They state themselves that they knocked and the door was locked; yet three minutes later when they went up with the porter, it turned out the door was unfastened."

"That's just it; the murderer must have been there and bolted himself in; and they'd have caught him for a certainty if Koch had not been an ass and gone to look for the porter too. *He* must have seized the interval to get downstairs and slip by them somehow. Koch keeps crossing himself and saying: 'If I had been there, he would have jumped out and killed me with his axe.' He is going to have a thanksgiving service—ha, ha!"

"And no one saw the murderer?"

"They might well not see him; the house is a regular Noah's Ark," said the head clerk, who was listening.

"It's clear, quite clear," Nikodim Fomitch repeated warmly.

"No, it is anything but clear," Ilya Petrovitch maintained.

Raskolnikov picked up his hat and walked towards the door, but he did not reach it. . . .

When he recovered consciousness, he found himself sitting in a chair, supported by some one on the right side, while some one else was standing on the left, holding a yellowish glass filled with yellow water, and Nikodim Fomitch standing before him, looking intently at him. He got up from the chair.

"What's this? Are you ill?" Nikodim Fomitch asked, rather sharply.

"He could hardly hold his pen when he was signing," said the head clerk, settling back in his place, and taking up his work again.

"Have you been ill long?" cried Ilya Petrovitch from his place, where he, too, was looking through papers. He had, of course, come to look at the sick man when he fainted, but retired at once when he recovered.

"Since yesterday," muttered Raskolnikov in reply.

"Did you go out yesterday?"

"Yes."

"Though you were ill?"

"Yes."

"At what time?"

"About seven."

"And where did you go, may I ask?"

"Along the street."

"Short and clear."

Raskolnikov, white as a handkerchief, had answered sharply, jerkily, without dropping his black feverish eyes before Ilya Petrovitch's stare.

"He can scarcely stand upright. And you . . ." Nikodim Fomitch was beginning.

"No matter," Ilya Petrovitch pronounced rather peculiarly.

Nikodim Fomitch would have made some further protest,

but glancing at the head clerk who was looking very hard at him, he did not speak. There was a sudden silence. It was strange.

"Very well, then," concluded Ilya Petrovitch, "we will not detain you."

Raskolnikov went out. He caught the sound of eager conversation on his departure; and above the rest rose the questioning voice of Nikodim Fomitch. In the street, his faintness passed off completely.

"A search—there will be a search at once," he repeated to himself, hurrying home. "The brutes! they suspect."

His former terror mastered him completely again.

2

"And what if there has been a search already? What if I find them in my room?"

But here was his room. Nothing and no one in it. No one had peeped in. Even Nastasya had not touched it. But heavens! how could he have left all those things in the hole?

He rushed to the corner, slipped his hand under the paper, pulled the things out and filled his pockets with them. There were eight articles in all: two little boxes with ear-rings or something of the sort, he hardly looked to see; then four small leather cases. There was a chain, too, merely wrapped in newspaper and something else in newspaper, that looked like a decoration. . . . He put them all in the different pockets of his overcoat, and the remaining pocket of his trousers, trying to conceal them as much as possible. He took the purse, too. Then he went out of his room, leaving the door open. He walked quickly and resolutely, and though he felt shattered, he had his senses about him. He was afraid of pursuit, he was afraid that in another half-hour, another quarter of an hour perhaps, instructions would be issued for his pursuit, and so at all costs, he must hide all traces before then. He must clear everything up while he still had some strength, some reasoning power left him. . . . Where was he to go?

That had long been settled: "Fling them into the canal, and

all traces hidden in the water, the thing would be at an end." So he had decided in the night of his delirium when several times he had had the impulse to get up and go away, to make haste, and get rid of it all. But to get rid of it, turned out to be a very difficult task. He wandered along the bank of the Ekaterininsky Canal for half an hour or more and looked several times at the steps running down to the water, but he could not think of carrying out his plan; either rafts stood at the steps' edge, and women were washing clothes on them, or boats were moored there, and people were swarming everywhere. Moreover he could be seen and noticed from the banks on all sides; it would look suspicious for a man to go down on purpose, stop, and throw something into the water. And what if the boxes were to float instead of sinking? And of course they would. Even as it was, every one he met seemed to stare and look round, as if they had nothing to do but to watch him. "Why is it, or can it be my fancy?" he thought.

At last the thought struck him that it might be better to go to the Neva. There were not so many people there, he would be less observed, and it would be more convenient in every way, above all it was further off. He wondered how he could have been wandering for a good half-hour, worried and anxious in this dangerous part without thinking of it before. And that half-hour he had lost over an irrational plan, simply because he had thought of it in delirium! He had become extremely absent and forgetful and he was aware of it. He certainly must make haste.

He walked towards the Neva along V—— Prospect, but on the way another idea struck him. "Why to the Neva? Would it not be better to go somewhere far off, to the Islands again, and there hide the things in some solitary place, in a wood or under a bush, and mark the spot perhaps?" And though he felt incapable of clear judgment, the idea seemed to him a sound one. But he was not destined to go there. For coming out of V—— Prospect towards the square, he saw on the left a passage leading between two blank walls to a courtyard. On the right hand, the blank unwhitewashed wall of a four-storied house stretched far into the court; on the left, a wooden hoarding ran parallel with it for twenty paces into the court, and then turned sharply to the left.

Here was a deserted fenced-off place where rubbish of different sorts was lying. At the end of the court, the corner of a low, smutty, stone shed, apparently part of some workshop, peeped from behind the hoarding. It was probably a carriage builder's or carpenter's shed; the whole place from the entrance was black with coal dust. Here would be the place to throw it, he thought. Not seeing any one in the yard, he slipped in, and at once saw near the gate a sink, such as is often put in yards where there are many workmen or cab-drivers; and on the hoarding above had been scribbled in chalk the time-honoured witticism, "Standing here strictly forbidden." This was all the better, for there would be nothing suspicious about his going in. "Here I could throw it all in a heap and get away!"

Looking round once more, with his hand already in his pocket, he noticed against the outer wall, between the entrance and the sink, a big unhewn stone, weighing perhaps sixty pounds. The other side of the wall was a street. He could hear passers-by, always numerous in that part, but he could not be seen from the entrance, unless some one came in from the street, which might well happen indeed, so there was need of haste.

He bent down over the stone, seized the top of it firmly in both hands, and using all his strength turned it over. Under the stone was a small hollow in the ground, and he immediately emptied his pocket into it. The purse lay at the top, and yet the hollow was not filled up. Then he seized the stone again and with one twist turned it back, so that it was in the same position again, though it stood a very little higher. But he scraped the earth about it and pressed it at the edges with his foot. Nothing could be noticed.

Then he went out, and turned into the square. Again an intense, almost unbearable joy overwhelmed him for an instant, as it had in the police office. "I have buried my tracks! And who, who can think of looking under that stone? It has been lying there most likely ever since the house was built, and will lie as many years more. And if it were found, who would think of me? It is all over! No clue!" And he laughed. Yes, he remembered that he began laughing a thin, nervous noiseless laugh, and went on laughing all the time he was crossing the square. But when he reached the K—— Boulevard where two days before he had come upon that girl, his laughter suddenly ceased. Other ideas crept into his mind. He felt all at once that it would be loathsome to pass that seat on which after the girl was gone, he had sat and pondered, and that it would be hateful, too, to meet that whiskered policeman to whom he had given the twenty copecks: "Damn him!"

He walked, looking about him angrily and distractedly. All his ideas now seemed to be circling round some single point, and he felt that there really was such a point, and that now, now, he was left facing that point—and for the first time, indeed, during the last two months.

"Damn it all!" he thought suddenly, in a fit of ungovernable fury. "If it has begun, then it has begun. Hang the new life! Good Lord, how stupid it is! . . . And what lies I told to-day! How despicably I fawned upon that wretched Ilya Petrovitch! But that is all folly! What do I care for them all, and my fawning upon them! It is not that at all! It is not that at all!"

Suddenly he stopped; a new utterly unexpected and exceedingly simple question perplexed and bitterly confounded him.

"If it all has really been done deliberately and not idiotically, if I really had a certain and definite object, how is it I did not even glance into the purse and don't know what I had there, for which I have undergone these agonies, and have deliberately undertaken this base, filthy degrading business? And here I wanted at once to throw into the water the purse together with all the things which I had not seen either . . . how's that?"

Yes, that was so, that was all so. Yet he had known it all before, and it was not a new question for him, even when it was decided in the night without hesitation and consideration, as though so it must be, as though it could not possibly be otherwise. . . . Yes, he had known it all, and understood it all; it surely had all been settled even yesterday at the moment when he was bending over the box and pulling the jewel-cases out of it. . . . Yes, so it was.

"It is because I am very ill," he decided grimly at last, "I have been worrying and fretting myself, and I don't know what I am doing. . . . Yesterday and the day before yesterday and all this time I have been worrying myself. . . . I shall get well and I shall not worry. . . . But what if I don't get well at all? Good God, how sick I am of it all!"

He walked on without resting. He had a terrible longing for some distraction, but he did not know what to do, what to attempt. A new overwhelming sensation was gaining more and more mastery over him every moment; this was an immeasurable, almost physical, repulsion for everything surrounding him, an obstinate, malignant feeling of hatred. All who met him were loathsome to him—he loathed their faces, their movements, their gestures. If any one had addressed him, he felt that he might have spat at him or bitten him. . . .

He stopped suddenly, on coming out on the bank of the Little Neva, near the bridge to Vassilyevsky Ostrov. "Why, he lives here, in that house," he thought, "why, I have not come to Razumihin of my own accord! Here it's the same thing over again. . . . Very interesting to know, though; have I come on purpose or have I simply walked here by chance? Never mind, I said the day before yesterday that I would go and see him the day *after;* well, and so I will! Besides I really cannot go further now."

He went up to Razumihin's room on the fifth floor.

The latter was at home in his garret, busily writing at the moment, and he opened the door himself. It was four months since they had seen each other. Razumihin was sitting in a ragged dressing-gown, with slippers on his bare feet, unkempt, unshaven and unwashed. His face showed surprise.

"Is it you?" he cried. He looked his comrade up and down; then after a brief pause, he whistled. "As hard up as all that! Why, brother, you've cut me out!" he added, looking at Raskolnikov's rags. "Come sit down, you are tired, I'll be bound."

And when he had sunk down on the American leather sofa, which was in even worse condition than his own, Razumihin saw at once that his visitor was ill.

"Why, you are seriously ill, do you know that?" He began feeling his pulse. Raskolnikov pulled away his hand.

"Never mind," he said, "I have come for this; I have no lessons. . . . I wanted . . . but I don't want lessons. . . ."

"But I say! You are delirious, you know!" Razumihin observed, watching him carefully.

"No, I am not."

Raskolnikov got up from the sofa. As he had mounted the stairs to Razumihin's, he had not realised that he would be meeting his friend face to face. Now, in a flash, he knew, that what he was least of all disposed for at that moment was to be face to face with any one in the wide world. His spleen rose within him. He almost choked with rage at himself as soon as he crossed Razumihin's threshold.

"Good-bye," he said abruptly, and walked to the door.

"Stop, stop! You queer fish."

"I don't want to," said the other, again pulling away his hand.

"Then, why the devil have you come? Are you mad, or what? Why, this is . . . almost insulting! I won't let you go like that."

"Well, then, I came to you because I know no one but you who could help . . . to begin . . . because you are kinder than any one—cleverer, I mean, and can judge . . . and now I see that I want nothing. Do you hear? Nothing at all . . . no one's services . . . no one's sympathy. I am by myself . . . alone. Come, that's enough. Leave me alone."

"Stay a minute, you sweep! You are a perfect madman. As you like for all I care. I have no lessons, do you see, and I don't care about that, but there's a bookseller, Heruvimov—and he takes the place of a lesson. I would not exchange him for five lessons. He's doing publishing of a kind, and issuing natural science manuals and what a circulation they have! The very titles are worth the money! You always maintained that I was a fool, but by Jove, my boy, there are greater fools than I am! Now he is setting up for being advanced, not that he has an inkling of anything, but, of course, I encourage him. Here are two signatures of the German text—in my opinion, the crudest charlatanism; it discusses the question, 'Is woman a human being?' And, of course, triumphantly proves that she is. Heruvimov is going to bring out this work as a contribution to the woman question; I am translating it; he will expand these two and a half signatures into six, we shall make up a gorgeous title half a page long and bring it out at half a rouble. It will do! He pays me six roubles the signature, it works out to fifteen roubles for the job, and I've had six already in advance. When we have finished this, we are going to begin a translation about whales, and then some of the dullest scandals out of the second part of *Les Confessions* we have marked for translation; somebody has told Heruvimov, that Rousseau was a kind of Radishchev. You may be sure I don't contradict him, hang him! Well, would you like to do the second signature of *'Is woman a human being?'* If you would, take the German and pens and paper—all those are provided, and take three roubles; for as I have had six roubles in advance on the whole thing, three roubles come to you for your share. And when you have finished the signature there will be another three roubles for you. And please don't think I am doing you a service; quite the contrary, as soon as you came in, I saw how you could help me; to begin with, I am weak in spelling, and secondly, I am sometimes utterly adrift in German, so that I make it up as I go along for the most part. The only comfort is, that it's bound to be a change for the better. Though who can tell, maybe it's sometimes for the worse. Will you take it?"

Raskolnikov took the German sheets in silence, took the three roubles and without a word went out. Razumihin gazed after him in astonishment. But when Raskolnikov was in the next street, he turned back, mounted the stairs to Razumihin's again and laying on the table the German article and the three roubles, went out again, still without uttering a word.

"Are you raving, or what?" Razumihin shouted, roused to fury at last. "What farce is this? You'll drive me crazy too . . . what did you come to see me for, damn you?"

"I don't want . . . translation," muttered Raskolnikov from the stairs.

"Then what the devil do you want?" shouted Razumihin from above. Raskolnikov continued descending the staircase in silence.

"Hey, there! Where are you living?"

No answer.

"Well, confound you then!"

But Raskolnikov was already stepping into the street. On the Nikolaevsky Bridge he was roused to full consciousness again by an unpleasant incident. A coachman, after shouting at him two or three times, gave him a violent lash on the back with his whip, for having almost fallen under his horses' hoofs. The lash so infuriated him that he dashed away to the railing (for some unknown reason he had been walking in the very middle of the bridge in the traffic). He angrily clenched and ground his teeth. He heard laughter, of course.

"Serves him right!"

"A pickpocket I dare say."

"Pretending to be drunk, for sure, and getting under the wheels on purpose; and you have to answer for him."

"It's a regular profession, that's what it is."

But while he stood at the railing, still looking angry and bewildered after the retreating carriage, and rubbing his back, he suddenly felt some one thrust money into his hand. He looked. It was an elderly woman in a kerchief and goatskin shoes, with a girl, probably her daughter, wearing a hat, and carrying a green parasol.

"Take it, my good man, in Christ's name."

He took it and they passed on. It was a piece of twenty copecks. From his dress and appearance they might well have taken him for a beggar asking alms in the streets, and the gift of the twenty copecks he doubtless owed to the blow, which made them feel sorry for him.

He closed his hand on the twenty copecks, walked on for ten paces, and turned facing the Neva, looking towards the palace. The sky was without a cloud and the water was almost bright blue, which is so rare in the Neva. The cupola of the cathedral, which is seen at its best from the bridge about twenty paces from the

chapel, glittered in the sunlight, and in the pure air every orna-
ment on it could be clearly distinguished. The pain from the lash
went off, and Raskolnikov forgot about it; one uneasy and not
quite definite idea occupied him now completely. He stood still,
and gazed long and intently into the distance; this spot was especially familiar to him. When he was attending the university, he
had hundreds of times—generally on his way home—stood still
on this spot, gazed at this truly magnificent spectacle and almost
always marvelled at a vague and mysterious emotion it roused in
him. It left him strangely cold; this gorgeous picture was for him
blank and lifeless. He wondered every time at his sombre and
enigmatic impression and, mistrusting himself, put off finding the
explanation of it. He vividly recalled those old doubts and perplexities, and it seemed to him that it was no mere chance that he
recalled them now. It struck him as strange and grotesque, that
he should have stopped at the same spot as before, as though he
actually imagined he could think the same thoughts, be interested
in the same theories and pictures that had interested him
. . . so short a time ago. He felt it almost amusing, and yet it wrung
his heart. Deep down, hidden far away out of sight all that seemed
to him now—all his old past, his old thoughts, his old problems
and theories, hid old impressions and that picture and himself and
all, all. . . . He felt as though he were flying upwards, and everything were vanishing from his sight. Making an unconscious
movement with his hand, he suddenly became aware of the piece
of money in his fist. He opened his hand, stared at the coin, and
with a sweep of his arm flung it into the water; then he turned
and went home. It seemed to him, he had cut himself off from
every one and from everything at that moment.

Evening was coming on when he reached home, so that he
must have been walking about six hours. How and where he came
back he did not remember. Undressing, and quivering like an
over-driven horse, he lay down on the sofa, drew his greatcoat
over him, and at once sank into oblivion. . . .

It was dusk when he was waked up by a fearful scream. Good
God, what a scream! Such unnatural sounds, such howling, wailing, grinding, tears, blows and curses he had never heard.

He could never have imagined such brutality, such frenzy. In terror he sat up in bed, almost swooning with agony. But the fighting, wailing and cursing grew louder and louder. And then to his intense amazement, he caught the voice of his landlady. She was howling, shrieking and wailing, rapidly, hurriedly, incoherently, so that he could not make out what she was talking about; she was beseeching, no doubt, not to be beaten, for she was being mercilessly beaten on the stairs. The voice of her assailant was so horrible from spite and rage that it was almost a croak; but he, too, was saying something, and just as quickly and indistinctly, hurrying and spluttering. All at once Raskolnikov trembled; he recognized the voice—it was the voice of Ilya Petrovitch. Ilya Petrovitch here and beating the landlady! He is kicking her, banging her head against the steps—that's clear, that can be told from the sounds, from the cries and the thuds. How is it, is the world topsy-turvy? He could hear people running in crowds from all the storeys and all the staircases; he heard voices, exclamations, knocking, doors banging. "But why, why, and how could it be?" he repeated, thinking seriously that he had gone mad. But no, he heard too distinctly! And they would come to him then next, "for no doubt . . . it's all about that . . . about yesterday. . . . Good God!" He would have fastened his door with the latch, but he could not lift his hand . . . besides, it would be useless. Terror gripped his heart like ice, tortured him and numbed him. . . . But at last all this uproar, after continuing about ten minutes, began gradually to subside. The landlady was moaning and groaning; Ilya Petrovitch was still uttering threats and curses. . . . But at last he, too, seemed to be silent, and now he could not be heard. "Can he have gone away? Good Lord!" Yes, and now the landlady is going too, still weeping and moaning . . . and then her door slammed. . . . Now the crowd was going from the stairs to their rooms, exclaiming, disputing, calling to one another, raising their voices to a shout, dropping them to a whisper. There must have been numbers of them—almost all the inmates of the block. "But, good God, how could it be! And why, why had he come here!"

Raskolnikov sank worn out on the sofa, but could not close

his eyes. He lay for half an hour in such anguish, such an intolerable sensation of infinite terror as he had never experienced before. Suddenly a bright light flashed into his room. Nastasya came in with a candle and a plate of soup. Looking at him carefully and ascertaining that he was not asleep, she set the candle on the table and began to lay out what she had brought—bread, salt, a plate, a spoon.

"You've eaten nothing since yesterday, I warrant. You've been trudging about all day, and you're shaking with fever."

"Nastasya . . . what were they beating the landlady for?"

She looked intently at him.

"Who beat the landlady?"

"Just now . . . half an hour ago, Ilya Petrovitch, the assistant-superintendent, on the stairs. . . . Why was he ill-treating her like that, and . . . why was he here?"

Nastasya scrutinised him, silent and frowning, and her scrutiny lasted a long time. He felt uneasy, even frightened at her searching eyes.

"Nastasya, why don't you speak?" he said timidly at last in a weak voice.

"It's the blood," she answered at last softly, as though speaking to herself.

"Blood? What blood?" he muttered, growing white and turning towards the wall.

Nastasya still looked at him without speaking.

"Nobody has been beating the landlady," she declared at last in a firm, resolute voice.

He gazed at her, hardly able to breathe.

"I heard it myself. . . . I was not asleep . . . I was sitting up," he said still more timidly. "I listened a long while. The assistant-superintendent came. . . . Every one ran out on to the stairs from all the flats."

"No one has been here. That's the blood crying in your ears. When there's no outlet for it and it gets clotted, you begin fancying things. . . . Will you eat something?"

He made no answer. Nastasya still stood over him, watching him.

"Give me something to drink . . . Nastasya."

She went downstairs and returned with a white earthenware jug of water. He remembered only swallowing one sip of the cold water and spilling some on his neck. Then followed forgetfulness.

3

He was not completely unconscious, however, all the time he was ill; he was in a feverish state, sometimes delirious, sometimes half conscious. He remembered a great deal afterwards. Sometimes it seemed as though there were a number of people round him; they wanted to take him away somewhere, there was a great deal of squabbling and discussing about him. Then he would be alone in the room; they had all gone away afraid of him, and only now and then opened the door a crack to look at him; they threatened him, plotted something together, laughed, and mocked at him. He remembered Nastasya often at his bedside; he distinguished another person, too, whom he seemed to know very well, though he could not remember who he was, and this fretted him, even made him cry. Sometimes he fancied he had been lying there a month; at other times it all seemed part of the same day. But of *that*—of *that* he had no recollection, and yet every minute he felt that he had forgotten something he ought to remember. He worried and tormented himself trying to remember, moaned, flew into a rage, or sank into awful, intolerable terror. Then he struggled to get up, would have run away, but some one always prevented him by force, and he sank back into impotence and forgetfulness. At last he returned to complete consciousness.

It happened at ten o'clock in the morning. On fine days the sun shone into the room at that hour, throwing a streak of light on the right wall and the corner near the door. Nastasya was standing beside him with another person, a complete stranger, who was looking at him very inquisitively. He was a young man with a beard, wearing a full, short-waisted coat, and looked like a messenger. The landlady was peeping in at the half-opened door. Raskolnikov sat up.

"Who is this, Nastasya?" he asked, pointing to the young man.

"I say, he's himself again!" she said.

"He is himself," echoed the man.

Concluding that he had returned to his senses, the landlady closed the door and disappeared. She was always shy and dreaded conversations or discussions. She was a woman of forty, not at all bad-looking, fat and buxom, with black eyes and eyebrows, good-natured from fatness and laziness, and absurdly bashful.

"Who . . . are you?" he went on, addressing the man. But at that moment the door was flung open, and, stooping a little, as he was so tall, Razumihin came in.

"What a cabin it is!" he cried. "I am always knocking my head. You call this a lodging! So you are conscious, brother? I've just heard the news from Pashenka."

"He has just come to," said Nastasya.

"Just come to," echoed the man again, with a smile.

"And who are you?" Razumihin asked, suddenly addressing him. "My name is Vrazumihin, at your service; not Razumihin, as I am always called, but Vrazumihin, a student and gentleman; and he is my friend. And who are you?"

"I am the messenger from our office, from the merchant Shelopaev, and I've come on business."

"Please sit down." Razumihin seated himself on the other side of the table. "It's a good thing you've come to, brother," he went on to Raskolnikov. "For the last four days you have scarcely eaten or drunk anything. We had to give you tea in spoonfuls. I brought Zossimov to see you twice. You remember Zossimov? He examined you carefully and said at once it was nothing serious —something seemed to have gone to your head. Some nervous nonsense, the result of bad feeding, he says you have not had enough beer and radish, but it's nothing much, it will pass and you will be all right. Zossimov is a first-rate fellow! He is making quite a name. Come, I won't keep you," he said, addressing the man again. "Will you explain what you want? You must know,

Rodya, this is the second time they have sent from the office; but it was another man last time, and I talked to him. Who was it came before?"

"That was the day before yesterday, I venture to say, if you please, sir. That was Alexey Semyonovitch; he is in our office, too."

"He was more intelligent than you, don't you think so?"

"Yes, indeed, sir, he is of more weight than I am."

"Quite so; go on."

"At your mamma's request, through Afanasy Ivanovitch Vahrushin, of whom I presume you have heard more than once, a remittance is sent to you from our office," the man began, addressing Raskolnikov. "If you are in an intelligible condition, I've thirty-five roubles to remit to you, as Semyon Semyonovitch has received from Afanasy Ivanovitch at your mamma's request instructions to that effect, as on previous occasions. Do you know him, sir?"

"Yes, I remember . . . Vahrushin," Raskolnikov said dreamily.

"You hear, he knows Vahrushin," cried Razumihin. "He is in 'an intelligible condition'! And I see you are an intelligent man too. Well, it's always pleasant to hear words of wisdom."

"That's the gentleman, Vahrushin, Afanasy Ivanovitch. And at the request of your mamma, who has sent you a remittance once before in the same manner through him, he did not refuse this time also, and sent instructions to Semyon Semyonovitch some days since to hand you thirty-five roubles in the hope of better to come."

"That 'hoping for better to come' is the best thing you've said, though 'your mamma' is not bad either. Come then, what do you say? Is he fully conscious, eh?"

"That's all right. If only he can sign this little paper."

"He can scrawl his name. Have you got the book?"

"Yes, here's the book."

"Give it to me. Here, Rodya, sit up. I'll hold you. Take the pen and scribble 'Raskolnikov' for him. For just now, brother, money is sweeter to us than treacle."

"I don't want it," said Raskolnikov, pushing away the pen.

"Not want it?"

"I won't sign it."

"How the devil can you do without signing it?"

"I don't want . . . the money."

"Don't want the money! Come, brother, that's nonsense, I bear witness. Don't trouble, please, it's only that he is on his travels again. But that's pretty common with him at all times though. . . . You are a man of judgment and we will take him in hand, that is, more simply, take his hand and he will sign it. Here."

"But I can come another time."

"No, no. Why should we trouble you? You are a man of judgment. . . . Now, Rodya, don't keep your visitor, you see he is waiting," and he made ready to hold Raskolnikov's hand in earnest.

"Stop, I'll do it alone," said the latter, taking the pen and signing his name.

The messenger took out the money and went away.

"Bravo! And now, brother, are you hungry?"

"Yes," answered Raskolnikov.

"Is there any soup?"

"Some of yesterday's," answered Nastasya, who was still standing there.

"With potatoes and rice in it?"

"Yes."

"I know it by heart. Bring soup and give us some tea."

"Very well."

Raskolnikov looked at all this with profound astonishment and a dull, unreasoning terror. He made up his mind to keep quiet and see what would happen. "I believe I am not wandering. I believe it's reality," he thought.

In a couple of minutes Nastasya returned with the soup, and announced that the tea would be ready directly. With the soup she brought two spoons, two plates, salt, pepper, mustard for the beef, and so on. The table was set as it had not been for a long time. The cloth was clean.

"It would not be amiss, Nastasya, if Praskovya Pavlovna were to send us up a couple of bottles of beer. We could empty them."

"Well, you are a cool hand," muttered Nastasya, and she departed to carry out his orders.

Raskolnikov still gazed wildly with strained attention. Meanwhile Razumihin sat down on the sofa beside him, as clumsily as a bear put his left arm round Raskolnikov's head, although he was able to sit up, and with his right hand gave him a spoonful of soup, blowing on it that it might not burn him. But the soup was only just warm. Raskolnikov swallowed one spoonful greedily, then a second, then a third. But after giving him a few more spoonfuls of soup, Razumihin suddenly stopped, and said that he must ask Zossimov whether he ought to have more.

Nastasya came in with two bottles of beer.

"And will you have tea?"

"Yes."

"Cut along, Nastasya, and bring some tea, for tea we may venture on without the faculty. But here is the beer!" He moved back to his chair, pulled the soup and meat in front of him, and began eating as though he had not touched food for three days.

"I must tell you, Rodya, I dine like this here every day now," he mumbled with his mouth full of beef, "and it's all Pashenka, your dear little landlady, who sees to that; she loves to do anything for me. I don't ask for it, but, of course, I don't object. And here's Nastasya with the tea. She is a quick girl. Nastasya, my dear, won't you have some beer?"

"Get along with your nonsense!"

"A cup of tea, then?"

"A cup of tea, maybe."

"Pour it out. Stay, I'll pour it out myself. Sit down."

He poured out two cups, left his dinner, and sat on the sofa again. As before, he put his left arm round the sick man's head, raised him up and gave him tea in spoonfuls, again blowing each spoonful steadily and earnestly, as though this process was the principal and most effective means towards his friend's recovery. Raskolnikov said nothing and made no resistance, though he felt quite strong enough to sit up on the sofa without support and could not merely have held a cup or a spoon, but even perhaps could have walked about. But from some queer, almost animal, cunning he conceived the idea of hiding his strength and lying low for a time, pretending if necessary not to be yet in full possession of his faculties, and meanwhile listening to find out what was going on. Yet he could not overcome his sense of repugnance. After sipping a dozen spoonfuls of tea, he suddenly released his head, pushed the spoon away capriciously, and sank back on the pillow. There were actually real pillows under his head now, down pillows in clean cases, he observed that, too, and took note of it.

"Pashenka must give us some raspberry jam to-day to make him some raspberry tea," said Razumihin, going back to his chair and attacking his soup and beer again.

"And where is she to get raspberries for you?" asked Nastasya, balancing a saucer on her five outspread fingers and sipping tea through a lump of sugar.

"She'll get it at the shop, my dear. You see, Rodya, all sorts of things have been happening while you have been laid up. When you decamped in that rascally way without leaving your address, I felt so angry that I resolved to find you out and punish you. I set to work that very day. How I ran about making inquiries for you! This lodging of yours I had forgotten, though I never remembered it, indeed, because I did not know it; and as for your old lodgings, I could only remember it was at the Five Corners, Harlamov's house. I kept trying to find that Harlamov's house, and afterwards it turned out that it was not Harlamov's, but Buch's. How one muddles up sound sometimes! So I lost my temper, and I went on the chance to the address bureau next day, and only fancy, in two minutes they looked you up! Your name is down there."

"My name!"

"I should think so; and yet a General Kobelev they could not find while I was there. Well, it's a long story. But as soon as I did land on this place, I soon got to know all your affairs—all, all, brother, I know everything; Nastasya here will tell you. I made the acquaintance of Nikodim Fomitch and Ilya Petrovitch, and the house-porter and Mr. Zametov, Alexandr Grigorievitch, the head clerk in the police office, and, last, but not least, of Pashenka; Nastasya here knows. . . ."

"He's got round her," Nastasya murmured, smiling slyly.

"Why don't you put the sugar in your tea, Nastasya Nikifo-rovna?"

"You are a one!" Nastasya cried suddenly, going off into a giggle. "I am not Nikiforovna, but Petrovna," she added suddenly, recovering from her mirth.

"I'll make a note of it. Well, brother, to make a long story short, I was going in for a regular explosion here to uproot all malignant influences in the locality, but Pashenka won the day. I had not expected, brother, to find her so . . . prepossessing. Eh, what do you think?"

Raskolnikov did not speak, but he still kept his eyes fixed upon him, full of alarm.

"And all that could be wished, indeed, in every respect," Razumihin went on, not at all embarrassed by his silence.

"Ah, the sly dog!" Nastasya shrieked again. This conversation afforded her unspeakable delight.

"It's a pity, brother, that you did not set to work in the right way at first. You ought to have approached her differently. She is, so to speak, a most unaccountable character. But we will talk about her character later. . . . How could you let things come to such a pass that she gave up sending you your dinner? And that I.O.U.? You must have been mad to sign an I.O.U. And that promise of marriage when her daughter, Natalya Yegorovna, was alive? . . . I know all about it! But I see that's a delicate matter and I am an ass; forgive me. But, talking of foolishness, do you know Praskovya Pavlovna is not nearly so foolish as you would think at first sight?"

"No," mumbled Raskolnikov, looking away, but feeling that it was better to keep up the conversation.

"She isn't, is she?" cried Razumihin, delighted to get an answer out of him. "But she is not very clever either, eh? She is essentially, essentially an unaccountable character! I am sometimes quite at a loss, I assure you. . . . She must be forty; she says she is thirty-six, and of course she has every right to say so. But I swear I judge her intellectually, simply from the metaphysical point of view; there is a sort of symbolism sprung up between us, a sort of algebra or what not! I don't understand it! Well, that's all nonsense. Only, seeing that you are not a student now and have lost your lessons and your clothes, and that through the young lady's death she has no need to treat you as a relation, she suddenly took fright; and as you hid in your den and dropped all your old relations with her, she planned to get rid of you. And she's been cherishing that design a long time, but was sorry to lose the I.O.U., for you assured her yourself that your mother would pay."

"It was base of me to say that. . . . My mother herself is almost a beggar . . . and I told a lie to keep my lodging . . . and be fed," Raskolnikov said loudly and distinctly.

"Yes, you did very sensibly. But the worst of it is that at that point Mr. Tchebarov turns up, a business man. Pashenka would never have thought of doing anything on her own account, she is too retiring; but the business man is by no means retiring, and first thing he puts the question, 'Is there any hope of realising the I.O.U.?' Answer: there is, because he has a mother who would save her Rodya with her hundred and twenty-five roubles pension, if she has to starve herself; and a sister, too, who would go into bondage for his sake. That's what he was building upon. . . . Why do you start? I know all the ins and outs of your affairs now, my dear boy—it's not for nothing that you were so open with Paskenka when you were her prospective son-in-law, and I say all this as a friend. . . . But I tell you what it is; an honest and sensitive man is open; and a business man 'listens and goes on eating' you up. Well, then she gave the I.O.U. by way of payment to this Tchebarov, and without hesitation he made a formal demand for payment. When I heard of all this I wanted to blow him up, too, to clear my conscience, but by that time harmony reigned between me and Pashenka, and I insisted on stopping the whole affair, engaging that you would pay. I went security for you, brother. Do you understand? We called Tchebarov, flung him ten

roubles and got the I.O.U. back from him, and here I have the
honour of presenting it to you. She trusts your word now. Here,
take it, you see I have torn it."

Razumihin put the note on the table. Raskolnikov looked at
him and turned to the wall without uttering a word. Even Razumihin felt a twinge.

"I see, brother," he said a moment later, "that I have been
playing the fool again. I thought I should amuse you with my
chatter, and I believe I have only made you cross."

"Was it you I did not recognise when I was delirious?"
Raskolnikov asked, after a moment's pause without turning his
head.

"Yes, and you flew into a rage about it, especially when I
brought Zametov one day."

"Zametov? The head clerk? What for?" Raskolnikov turned
round quickly and fixed his eyes on Razumihin.

"What's the matter with you? . . . What are you upset about?
He wanted to make your acquaintance because I talked to him a
lot about you. . . . How could I have found out so much except
from him? He is a capital fellow, brother, first-rate . . . in his own
way, of course. Now we are friends—see each other almost every
day. I have moved into this part, you know. I have only just
moved. I've been with him to Luise Ivanovna once or twice. . .
. Do you remember Luise, Luise Ivanovna?"

"Did I say anything in delirium?"

"I should think so! You were beside yourself."

"What did I rave about?"

"What next? What did you rave about? What people do rave
about. . . . Well, brother, now I must not lose time. To work."
He got up from the table and took up his cap.

"What did I rave about?"

"How he keeps on! Are you afraid of having let out some
secret? Don't worry yourself; you said nothing about a countess.
But you said a lot about a bulldog, and about ear-rings and chains,
and about Krestovsky Island, and some porter, and Nikodim
Fomitch and Ilya Petrovitch, the assistant superintendent. And
another thing that was of special interest to you was your own

sock. You whined, 'Give me my sock.' Zametov hunted all about your room for your socks, and with his own scented, ring-be-decked fingers he gave you the rag. And only then were you comforted, and for the next twenty-four hours you held the wretched thing in your hand; we could not get it from you. It is most likely somewhere under your quilt at this moment. And then you asked so piteously for fringe for your trousers. We tried to find out what sort of fringe, but we could not make it out. Now to business! Here are thirty-five roubles; I take ten of them, and shall give you an account of them in an hour or two. I will let Zossimov know at the same time, though he ought to have been here long ago, for it is nearly twelve. And you, Nastasya, look in pretty often while I am away, to see whether he wants a drink or anything else. And I will tell Pashenka what is wanted myself. Good-bye!"

"He calls her Pashenka! Ah, he's a deep one!" said Nastasya as he went out; then she opened the door and stood listening, but could not resist running downstairs after him. She was very eager to hear what he would say to the landlady. She was evidently quite fascinated by Razumihin.

No sooner had she left the room than the sick man flung off the bedclothes and leapt out of bed like a madman. With burning, switching impatience he had waited for them to be gone so that he might set to work. But to what work? Now, as though to spite him, it eluded him.

"Good God, only tell me one thing: do they know of it yet or not? What if they know it and are only pretending, mocking me while I am laid up, and then they will come in and tell me that it's been discovered long ago and that they have only . . . What am I to do now? That's what I've forgotten, as though on purpose; forgotten it all at once, I remembered a minute ago."

He stood in the middle of the room and gazed in miserable bewilderment about him; he walked to the door, opened it, lis-tened; but that was not what he wanted. Suddenly, as though recalling something, he rushed to the corner where there was a hole under the paper, began examining it, put his hand into the hole, fumbled—but that was not it. He went to the stove, opened it and began rummaging in the ashes; the frayed edges of his trousers and the rags cut off his pocket were lying there just as he had thrown them. No one had looked, then! Then he remembered, the sock about which Razumihin had just been telling him. Yes, there it lay on the sofa under the quilt, but it was so covered with dust and grime that Zametov could not have seen anything on it.

"Bah, Zametov! The police office! And why am I sent for to the police office? Where's the notice? Bah! I am mixing it up; that was then. I looked at my sock then, too, but now . . . now I have been ill. But what did Zametov come for? Why did Razumihin bring him?" he muttered, helplessly sitting on the sofa again. "What does it mean? Am I still in delirium, or is it real? I believe it is real. . . . Ah, I remember, I must escape! Make haste to escape. Yes, I must, I must escape! Yes . . . but where? And where are my clothes? I've no boots. They've taken them away! They've hidden them! I understand! Ah, here is my coat—they passed that over! And here is money on the table, thank God! And here's the I.O.U. . . . I'll take the money and go and take another lodging. They won't find me! . . . Yes, but the address bureau? They'll find me, Razumihin will find me. Better escape altogether . . . far away . . . to America, and let them do their worst! And take the I.O.U. . . . it would be of use there. . . . What else shall I take? They think I am ill! They don't know that I can walk, ha-ha-ha! I could see by their eyes that they know all about it! If only I could get downstairs! And what if they have set a watch there—policemen! What's this tea? Ah, and here is beer left, half a bottle, cold!"

He snatched up the bottle, which still contained a glassful of beer, and gulped it down with relish, as though quenching a flame in his breast. But in another minute the beer had gone to his head, and a faint and even pleasant shiver ran down his spine. He lay down and pulled the quilt over him. His sick and incoherent thoughts grew more and more disconnected, and soon a light, pleasant drowsiness came upon him. With a sense of comfort he nestled his head in the pillow, wrapped more closely about him the soft, wadded quilt which had replaced the old, ragged greatcoat, sighed softly and sank into a deep, sound, refreshing sleep.

He woke up, hearing some one come in. He opened his eyes and saw Razumihin standing in the doorway, uncertain whether to come in or not. Raskolnikov sat up quickly on the sofa and gazed at him, as though trying to recall something.

"Ah, you are not asleep! Here I am! Nastasya, bring in the parcel!" Razumihin shouted down the stairs. "You shall have the account directly."

"What time is it?" asked Raskolnikov, looking round uneasily.

"Yes, you had a fine sleep, brother, it's almost evening, it will be six o'clock directly. You have slept more than six hours."

"Good heaven! Have I?"

"And why not? It will do you good. What's the hurry? A tryst, is it? We've all time before us. I've been waiting for the last three hours for you; I've been up twice and found you asleep. I've called on Zossimov twice; not at home, only fancy! But no matter, he will turn up. And I've been out on my own business, too. You know I've been moving to-day, moving with my uncle. I have an uncle living with me now. But that's no matter, to business. Give me the parcel, Nastasya. We will open it directly. And how do you feel now, brother?"

"I am quite well, I am not ill. Razumihin, have you been here long?"

"I tell you I've been waiting for the last three hours."

"No, before."

"How do you mean?"

"How long have you been coming here?"

"Why I told you all about it this morning. Don't you remember?"

Raskolnikov pondered. The morning seemed like a dream to him. He could not remember alone, and looked inquiringly at Razumihin.

"Hm!" said the latter, "he has forgotten. I fancied then that you were not quite yourself. Now you are better for your sleep. . . . You really look much better. First rate! Well, to business. Look here, my dear boy."

He began untying the bundle, which evidently interested him.

"Believe me, brother, this is something specially near my heart. For we must make a man of you. Let's begin from the top. Do you see this cap?" he said, taking out of the bundle a fairly good, though cheap, and ordinary cap. "Let me try it on."

"Presently, afterwards," said Raskolnikov, waving it off pettishly.

"Come, Rodya, my boy, don't oppose it, afterwards will be too late; and I shan't sleep all night, but I bought it by guess, without measure. Just right!" he cried triumphantly, fitting it on, "just your size! A proper head-covering is the first thing in dress and a recommendation in its own way. Tolstyakov, a friend of mine, is always obliged to take off his pudding basin when he goes into any public place where other people wear their hats or caps. People think he does it from slavish politeness, but it's simply because he is ashamed of his bird's nest; he is such a bashful fellow! Look, Nastasya, here are two specimens of headgear: this Palmerston"—he took from the corner Raskolnikov's old, battered hat, which for some unknown reason he called a Palmerston —"or this jewel! Guess the price, Rodya, what do you suppose I paid for it, Nastasya!" he said, turning to her, seeing that Raskolnikov did not speak.

"Twenty copecks, no more, I dare say," answered Nastasya.

"Twenty copecks, silly!" he cried, offended. "Why, nowadays you would cost more than that—eighty copecks! And that only because it has been worn. And it's bought on condition that when's it's worn out, they will give you another next year. Yes, on my word! Well, now let us pass to the United States of America, as they called them at school. I assure you I am proud of these breeches," and he exhibited to Raskolnikov a pair of light, summer trousers of grey woollen material. "No holes, no spots, and quite respectable, although a little worn; and a waistcoat to match, quite in the fashion. And its being worn really is an improvement, it's softer, smoother. . . . You see, Rodya, to my thinking, the great thing for getting on in the world is always to keep to the seasons; if you don't insist on having asparagus in January, you

keep your money in your purse! and it's the same with this pur-
chase. It's summer now, so I've been buying summer things—
warmer materials will be wanted for autumn, so you will have to
throw these away in any case . . . especially as they will be done
for by then from their own lack of coherence if not your higher
standard of luxury. Come, price them! What do you say? Two
roubles twenty-five copecks! And remember the condition: if you
wear these out, you will have another suit for nothing! They only
do business on that system at Fedyaev's; if you've bought a thing
once, you are satisfied for life, for you will never go there again
of your own free will. Now for the boots. What do you say? You
see that they are a bit worn, but they'll last a couple of months,
for it's foreign work and foreign leather; the secretary of the
English Embassy sold them last week—he had only worn them six
days, but he was very short of cash. Price—a rouble and a half.
A bargain?"

"But perhaps they won't fit," observed Nastasya.

"Not fit? Just look!" and he pulled out of his pocket Raskolnikov's old, broken boot, stiffly coated with dry mud. "I did not
go empty-handed—they took the size from this monster. We all
did our best. And as to your linen, your landlady has seen to that.
Here, to begin with are three shirts, hempen but with a fashionable front. . . . Well now then, eighty copecks the cap, two roubles
twenty-five copecks the suit—together three roubles five copecks
—a rouble and a half for the boots—for, you see, they are very
good—and that makes four roubles fifty-five copecks; five roubles
for the underclothes—they were bought in the lot—which makes
exactly nine roubles fifty-five copecks. Forty-five copecks change
in coppers. Will you take it? And so, Rodya, you are set up with
a complete new rig-out, for your overcoat will serve, and even has
a style of its own. That comes from getting one's clothes from
Sharmer's! As for your socks and other things, I leave them to
you; we've twenty-five roubles left. And as for Pashenka and
paying for your lodging, don't you worry. I tell you she'll trust
you for anything. And now, brother, let me change your linen,
for I daresay you will throw off your illness with your shirt."

"Let me be! I don't want to!" Raskolnikov waved him off.

He had listened with disgust to Razumihin's efforts to be playful about his purchases.

"Come, brother, don't tell me I've been trudging around for nothing," Razumihin insisted. "Nastasya, don't be bashful, but help me—that's it," and in spite of Raskolnikov's resistance he changed his linen. The latter sank back on the pillows and for a minute or two said nothing.

"It will be long before I get rid of them," he thought. "What money was all that bought with?" he asked at last, gazing at the wall.

"Money? Why, your own, what the messenger brought from Vahrushin, your mother sent it. Have you forgotten that, too?"

"I remember now," said Raskolnikov after a long, sullen silence. Razumihin looked at him, frowning and uneasy.

The door opened and a tall, stout man whose appearance seemed familiar to Raskolnikov came in.

"Zossimov! At last!" cried Razumihin, delighted.

4

Zossimov was a tall, fat man with a puffy, colourless, clean-shaven face and straight flaxen hair. He wore spectacles, and a big gold ring on his fat finger. He was twenty-seven. He had on a light grey fashionable loose coat, light summer trousers, and everything about him loose, fashionable and spick and span; his linen was irreproachable, his watch-chain was massive. In manner he was slow and, as it were, nonchalant, and at the same time studiously free and easy; he made efforts to conceal his self-importance, but it was apparent at every instant. All his acquaintances found him tedious, but said he was clever at his work.

"I've been to you twice to-day, brother. You see, he's come to himself," cried Razumihin.

"I see, I see; and how do we feel now, eh?" said Zossimov to Raskolnikov, watching him carefully and, sitting down at the foot of the sofa, he settled himself as comfortably as he could.

"He is still depressed," Razumihin went on. "We've just changed his linen and he almost cried."

"That's very natural; you might have put it off if he did not wish it. . . . His pulse is first-rate. Is your head still aching, eh?"

"I am well, I am perfectly well!" Raskolnikov declared positively and irritably. He raised himself on the sofa and looked at them with glittering eyes, but sank back on to the pillow at once and turned to the wall. Zossimov watched him intently.

"Very good. . . . Going on all right," he said lazily. "Has he eaten anything?"

They told him, and asked what he might have.

"He may have anything . . . soup, tea . . . mushrooms and cucumbers, of course, you must not give him; he'd better not have meat either, and . . . but no need to tell you that!" Razumihin and he looked at each other. "No more medicine or anything. I'll look at him again to-morrow. Perhaps, to-day even . . . but never mind . . ."

"To-morrow evening I shall take him for a walk," said Razumihin. "We are going to the Yusupov garden and then to the Palais de Crystal."

"I would not disturb him to-morrow at all, but I don't know . . . a little, maybe . . . but we'll see."

"Ach, what a nuisance! I've got a house-warming party to-night; it's only a step from here. Couldn't he come? He could lie on the sofa. You are coming?" Razumihin said to Zossimov. "Don't forget, you promised."

"All right, only rather later. What are you going to do?"

"Oh, nothing—tea, vodka, herrings. There will be a pie . . . just our friends."

"And who?"

"All neighbours here, almost all new friends, except my old uncle, and he is new too—he only arrived in Petersburg yesterday to see to some business of his. We meet once in five years."

"What is he?"

"He's been stagnating all his life as a district postmaster; gets a little pension. He is sixty-five—not worth talking about. . . . But

I am fond of him. Porfiry Petrovitch, the head of the Investigation Department here . . . But you know him."

"Is he a relation of yours, too?"

"A very distant one. But why are you scowling? Because you quarrelled once, won't you come then?"

"I don't care a damn for him."

"So much the better. Well, there will be some students, a teacher, a government clerk, a musician, an officer and Zametov."

"Do tell me, please, what you or he"—Zossimov nodded at Raskolnikov—"can have in common with this Zametov?"

"Oh, you particular gentleman! Principles! You are worked by principles, as it were by springs; you won't venture to turn round on your own account. If a man is a nice fellow, that's the only principle I go upon. Zametov is a delightful person."

"Though he does take bribes."

"Well, he does! and what of it? I don't care if he does take bribes," Razumihin cried with unnatural irritability. "I don't praise him for taking bribes. I only say he is a nice man in his own way! But if one looks at men in all ways—are there many good ones left? Why, I am sure I shouldn't be worth a baked onion myself . . . perhaps with you thrown in."

"That's too little; I'd give two for you."

"And I wouldn't give more than one for you. No more of your jokes! Zametov is no more than a boy. I can pull his hair and one must draw him not repel him. You'll never improve a man by repelling him, especially a boy. One has to be twice as careful with a boy. Oh, you progressive dullards! You don't understand. You harm yourselves running another man down. . . . But if you want to know, we really have something in common."

"I should like to know what."

"Why, it's all about a house-painter. . . . We are getting him out of a mess! Though indeed there's nothing to fear now. The matter is absolutely self-evident. We only put on steam."

"A painter?"

"Why, haven't I told you about it? I only told you the beginning then about the murder of the old pawnbroker-woman. Well, the painter is mixed up in it . . ."

"Oh, I heard about that murder before and was rather interested in it . . . partly . . . for one reason. . . . I read about it in the papers, too. . . ."

"Lizaveta was murdered, too," Nastasya blurted out, suddenly addressing Raskolnikov. She remained in the room all the time, standing by the door listening.

"Lizaveta," murmured Raskolnikov hardly audibly.

"Lizaveta, who sold old clothes. Didn't you know her? She used to come here. She mended a shirt for you, too."

Raskolnikov turned to the wall where in the dirty, yellow paper he picked out one clumsy, white flower with brown lines on it and began examining how many petals there were in it, how many scallops in the petals and how many lines on them. He felt his arms and legs as lifeless as though they had been cut off. He did not attempt to move, but stared obstinately at the flower.

"But what about the painter?" Zossimov interrupted Nastasya's chatter with marked displeasure. She sighed and was silent.

"Why, he was accused of the murder," Razumihin went on hotly.

"Was there evidence against him then?"

"Evidence, indeed! Evidence that was no evidence, and that's what we have to prove. It was just as they pitched on those fellows, Koch and Pestryakov, at first. Foo! how stupidly it's all done, it makes one sick, though it's not one's business! Pestryakov may be coming to-night. . . . By the way, Rodya, you've heard about the business already; it happened before you were ill, the day before you fainted at the police office while they were talking about it."

Zossimov looked curiously at Raskolnikov. He did not stir.

"But I say, Razumihin, I wonder at you. What a busybody you are!" Zossimov observed.

"Maybe I am, but we will get him off anyway," shouted Razumihin, bringing his fist down on the table. "What's the most offensive is not their lying—one can always forgive lying—lying is a delightful thing, for it leads to truth—what is offensive is that they lie and worship their own lying. . . . I respect Porfiry, but . . . What threw them out at first? The door was locked, and when they came back with the porter it was open. So it followed that Koch and Pestryakov were the murderers—that was their logic!"

"But don't excite yourself; they simply detained them, they could not help that. . . . And, by the way, I've met that man Koch. He used to buy unredeemed pledges from the old woman? Eh?"

"Yes, he is a swindler. He buys up bad debts, too. He makes a profession of it. But enough of him! Do you know what makes me angry? It's their sickening rotten, petrified routine. . . . And this case might be the means of introducing a new method. One can show from the psychological data alone how to get on the track of the real man. 'We have facts,' they say. But facts are not everything—at least half the business lies in how you interpret them!"

"Can you interpret them, then?"

"Anyway, one can't hold one's tongue when one has a feeling, a tangible feeling, that one might be a help if only. . . . Eh! Do you know the details of the case?"

"I am waiting to hear about the painter."

"Oh, yes! Well, here's the story. Early on the third day after the murder, when they were still dandling Koch and Pestryakov —though they accounted for every step they took and it was as plain as a pikestaff—an unexpected fact turned up. A peasant called Dushkin, who keeps a dram-shop facing the house, brought to the police office a jeweller's case containing some gold ear-rings, and told a long rigmarole. 'The day before yesterday, just after eight o'clock'—mark the day and the hour!—'a journeyman house-painter, Nikolay, who had been in to see me already that day, brought me this box of gold ear-rings and stones, and asked me to give him two roubles for them. When I asked him where he got them, he said that he picked them up in the street. I did not ask him anything more.' I am telling you Dushkin's story. 'I gave him a note'—a rouble that is—'for I thought if he did not pawn it with me he would with another. It would all come to the same thing—he'd spend it on drink, so the thing had better be with me. The further you hide it the quicker you will find it, and if anything turns up, if I hear any rumours, I'll take it to the police.' Of course, that's all taradiddle; he lies like a horse, for I know this Dushkin, he is a pawnbroker and a receiver of stolen goods, and he did not cheat Nikolay out of a thirty-rouble trinket in order to give it to the police. He was simply afraid. But no matter, to return to Dushkin's story. 'I've known this peasant, Nikolay Dementyev, from a child; he comes from the same province and district of Zaraïsk, we are both Ryazan men. And though Nikolay is not a drunkard, he drinks, and I knew he had a job in that house, painting work with Dmitri, who comes from the same village, too. As soon as he got the rouble he changed it, had a couple of glasses, took his change and went out. But I did not see Dmitri with him then. And the next day I heard that some one had murdered Alyona Ivanovna and her sister, Lizaveta Ivanovna, with an axe. I knew them, and I felt suspicious about the ear-rings at once, for I knew the murdered woman lent money on pledges. I went to the house, and began to make careful inquiries without saying a word to any one. First of all I asked, "Is Nikolay here?" Dmitri told me that Nikolay had gone off on the spree; he had come home at daybreak drunk, stayed in the house about ten minutes, and went out again. Dmitri didn't see him again and is finishing the job alone. And their job is on the same staircase as the murder, on the second floor. When I heard all that I did not say a word to any one'—that's Dushkin's tale—'but I found out what I could about the murder, and went home feeling as suspicious as ever. And at eight o'clock this morning'—that was the third day, you understand—'I saw Nikolay coming in, not sober, though not so very drunk—he could understand what was said to him. He sat down on the bench and did not speak. There was only one stranger in the bar and a man I knew asleep on a bench and our two boys. "Have you seen Dmitri?" said I. "No, I haven't," said he. "And you've not been here either?" "Not since the day before yesterday," said he. "And where did you sleep last night?" "In Peski, with the Kolomensky men." "And where did you get those ear-rings?" I asked. "I found them in the street," and the way he said it was a bit queer; he did not look at me. "Did you hear what happened that very evening, at that very hour, on that same staircase?" said I. "No," said he, "I had not heard," and all the while he was listening, his eyes were staring out of his head and he turned as white as chalk. I told him all about it and he took his hat and began getting up. I wanted to keep him. "Wait a bit, Nikolay," said I, "won't you have a drink?" And I signed to the boy to hold the door, and I came out from behind the bar; but he darted out and down the street to the turning at a run. I have not seen him since. Then my doubts were at an end—it was his doing, as clear as could be. . . ."

"I should think so," said Zossimov.

"Wait! Hear the end. Of course they sought high and low for Nikolay; they detained Dushkin and searched his house; Dmitri, too, was arrested; the Kolomensky men also were turned inside out. And the day before yesterday they arrested Nikolay in a tavern at the end of the town. He had gone there, taken the silver cross off his neck and asked for a dram for it. They gave it to him. A few minutes afterwards the woman went to the cowshed, and through a crack in the wall she saw in the stable adjoining he had made a noose of his sash from the beam, stood on a block of wood, and was trying to put his neck in the noose. The woman screeched her hardest; people ran in. 'So that's what you are up to!' 'Take me,' he says, 'to such-and-such a police officer; I'll confess everything.' Well, they took him to that police station—that is here—with a suitable escort. So they asked him this and that, how old he is, 'twenty-two,' and so on. At the question, 'When you were working with Dmitri, didn't you see any one on the staircase at such-and-such a time?'—answer: 'To be sure folks may have gone up and down, but I did not notice them.' 'And didn't you hear anything, any noise, and so on?' 'We heard nothing special.' 'And did you hear, Nikolay, that on the same day Widow So-and-so and her sister were murdered and robbed?' 'I never knew a thing about it. The first I heard of it was from Afanasy Pavlovitch the day before yesterday.' 'And where did you find the ear-rings?' 'I found them on the pavement.' 'Why didn't you go to work with Dmitri the other day?' 'Because I was drinking.' 'And where were you drinking?' 'Oh, in such and such a place.' 'Why did you run away from Dushkin's?' 'Because I was awfully frightened.' 'What were you frightened of?' 'That I should be accused.' 'How could you be frightened, if you felt free from guilt?' Now, Zossimov, you may not believe me, that question was put literally in those words. I know it for a fact, it was repeated to me exactly! What do you say to that?"

"Well, anyway, there's the evidence."

"I am not talking of the evidence now, I am talking about that question, of their own idea of themselves. Well, so they squeezed and squeezed him and he confessed: 'I did not find it in the street, but in the flat where I was painting with Dmitri.' 'And how was that?' 'Why, Dmitri and I were painting there all day, and we were just getting ready to go, and Dmitri took a brush and painted my face, and he ran off and I after him. I ran after him, shouting my hardest, and at the bottom of the stairs I ran right against the porter and some gentlemen—and how many gentlemen were there I don't remember. And the porter swore at me, and the other porter swore, too, and the porter's wife came out, and swore at us, too; and a gentleman came into the entry with a lady, and he swore at us, too, for Dmitri and I lay right across the way. I got hold of Dmitri's hair and knocked him down and began beating him. And Dmitri, too, caught me by the hair and began beating me. But we did it all not for temper, but in a friendly way, for sport. And then Dmitri escaped and ran into the street, and I ran after him; but I did not catch him, and went back to the flat alone; I had to clear up my things. I began putting them together, expecting Dmitri to come, and there in the passage, in the corner by the door, I stepped on the box. I saw it lying there wrapped up in paper. I took off the paper, saw some little hooks, undid them, and in the box were the ear-rings. . . .' "

"Behind the door? Lying behind the door? Behind the door?" Raskolnikov cried suddenly, staring with a blank look of terror at Razumihin, and he slowly sat up on the sofa, leaning on his hand.

"Yes . . . why? What's the matter? What's wrong?" Razumihin, too, got up from his seat.

"Nothing," Raskolnikov answered faintly, turning to the wall. All were silent for a while.

"He must have waked from a dream," Razumihin said at last,

looking inquiringly at Zossimov. The latter slightly shook his head.

"Well, go on," said Zossimov. "What next?"

"What next? As soon as he saw the ear-rings, forgetting Dmitri and everything, he took up his cap and ran to Dushkin and, as we know, got a rouble from him. He told a lie saying he found them in the street, and went off drinking. He keeps repeating his old story about the murder: 'I knew nothing of it, never heard of it till the day before yesterday.' 'And why didn't you come to the police till now?' 'I was frightened.' 'And why did you try to hang yourself?' 'From anxiety.' 'What anxiety?' 'That I should be accused of it.' Well, that's the whole story. And now what do you suppose they deduced from that?"

"Why, there's no supposing. There's a clue, such as it is, a fact. You wouldn't have your painter set free?"

"Now they've simply taken him for the murderer. They haven't a shadow of doubt."

"That's nonsense. You are excited. But what about the ear-rings? You must admit that, if on the very same day and hour ear-rings from the old woman's box have come into Nikilay's hands, they must have come there somehow. That's a good deal in such a case."

"How did they get there? How did they get there?" cried Razumihin. "How can you, a doctor, whose duty it is to study man and who has more opportunity than any one else for studying human nature—how can you fail to see the character of the man in the whole story? Don't you see at once that the answers he has given in the examination are the holy truth? They came into his hand precisely as he has told us—he stepped on the box and picked it up."

"The holy truth! But didn't he own himself that he told a lie at first?"

"Listen to me, listen attentively. The porter and Koch and Pestryakov and the other porter and the wife of the first porter and the woman who was sitting in the porter's lodge and the man Kryukov, who had just got out of a cab at that minute and went in at the entry with a lady on his arm, that is eight or ten witnesses, agree that Nikolay had Dmitri on the ground, was lying on him beating him, while Dmitri hung on to his hair, beating him, too. They lay right across the way, blocking the thoroughfare. They were sworn at on all sides while they 'like children' (the very words of the witnesses) were falling over one another, squealing, fighting and laughing with the funniest faces, and, chasing one another like children, they ran into the street. Now take careful note. The bodies upstairs were warm, you understand, warm when they found them! If they, or Nikolay alone, had murdered them and broken open the boxes, or simply taken part in the robbery, allow me to ask you one question: do their state of mind, their squeals and giggles and childish scuffling at the gate fit in with axes, bloodshed, fiendish cunning, robbery? They'd just killed them, not five or ten minutes before, for the bodies were still warm, and at once, leaving the flat open, knowing that people would go there at once, flinging away their booty, they rolled about like children, laughing and attracting general attention. And there are a dozen witnesses to swear to that!''

"Of course it is strange! It's impossible, indeed, but . . .''

"No, brother, no *buts.* And if the ear-rings' being found in Nikolay's hands at the very day and hour of the murder constitutes an important piece of circumstantial evidence against him—although the explanation given by him accounts for it, and therefore it does not tell seriously against him—one must take into consideration the facts which prove him innocent, especially as they are facts that *cannot be denied.* And do you suppose, from the character of our legal system, that they will accept, or that they are in a position to accept, this fact—resting simply on a psychological impossibility—as irrefutable and conclusively breaking down the circumstantial evidence for the prosecution? No, they won't accept it, they certainly won't, because they found the jewel-case and the man tried to hang himself, 'which he could not have done if he hadn't felt guilty.' That's the point, that's what excites me, you must understand!''

"Oh, I see you are excited! Wait a bit. I forgot to ask you; what proof is there that the box came from the old woman?''

"That's been proved,'' said Razumihin with apparent reluctance, frowning. "Koch recognised the jewel-case and gave the name of the owner, who proved conclusively that it was his."

"That's bad. Now another point. Did any one see Nikolay at the time that Koch and Pestryakov were going upstairs at first, and is there no evidence about that?"

"Nobody did see him," Razumihin answered with vexation. "That's the worst of it. Even Koch and Pestryakov did not notice them on their way upstairs, though, indeed, their evidence could not have been worth much. They said they saw the flat was open, and that there must be work going on in it, but they took no special notice and could not remember whether there actually were men at work in it."

"Hm! . . . So the only evidence for the defence is that they were beating one another and laughing. That constitutes a strong presumption, but . . . How do you explain the facts yourself?"

"How do I explain them? What is there to explain? It's clear. At any rate, the direction in which explanation is to be sought is clear, and the jewel-case points to it. The real murderer dropped those ear-rings. The murderer was upstairs, locked in, when Koch and Pestryakov knocked at the door. Koch, like an ass, did not stay at the door; so the murderer popped out and ran down, too, for he had no other way of escape. He hid from Koch, Pestryakov and the porter in the flat when Nikolay and Dmitri had just run out of it. He stopped there while the porter and others were going upstairs, waited till they were out of hearing, and then went calmly downstairs at the very minute when Dmitri and Nikolay ran out into the street and there was no one in the entry; possibly he was seen, but not noticed. There are lots of people going in and out. He must have dropped the ear-rings out of his pocket when he stood behind the door, and did not notice he dropped them, because he had other things to think of. The jewel-case is a conclusive proof that he did stand there. . . . That's how I explain it."

"Too clever! No, my boy, you're too clever. That beats everything."

"But, why, why?"

"Why, because everything fits too well . . . it's too melo-dramatic."

"A-ach!" Razumihin was exclaiming, but at that moment the door opened and a personage came in who was a stranger to all present.

5

This was a gentleman no longer young, of a stiff and portly appearance, and a cautious and sour countenance. He began by stopping short in the doorway, staring about him with offensive and undisguised astonishment, as though asking himself what sort of place he had come to. Mistrustfully and with an affectation of being alarmed and almost affronted, he scanned Raskolnikov's low and narrow "cabin." With the same amazement he stared at Raskolnikov, who lay undressed, dishevelled, unwashed, on his miserable dirty sofa, looking fixedly at him. Then with the same deliberation he scrutinised the uncouth, unkempt figure and un-shaven face of Razumihin, who looked him boldly and inquiring-ly in the face without rising from his seat. A constrained silence lasted for a couple of minutes, and then, as might be expected, some scene-shifting took place. Reflecting, probably from certain fairly unmistakable signs, that he would get nothing in this "cab-in" by attempting to over-awe them, the gentleman softened somewhat, and civilly, though with some severity, emphasising every syllable of his question, addressed Zossimov:

"Rodion Romanovitch Raskolnikov, a student, or formerly a student?"

Zossimov made a slight movement, and would have an-swered, had not Razumihin anticipated him.

"Here he is lying on the sofa! What do you want?"

This familiar "what do you want" seemed to cut the ground from the feet of the pompous gentleman. He was turning to Razumihin, but checked himself in time and turned to Zossimov again.

"This is Raskolnikov," mumbled Zossimov, nodding towards him. Then he gave a prolonged yawn, opening his mouth as wide as possible. Then he lazily put his hand into his waistcoat-pocket, pulled out a huge gold watch in a round hunter's case, opened it, looked at it and as slowly and lazily proceeded to put it back.

Raskolnikov himself lay without speaking, on his back, gazing persistently, though without understanding, at the stranger. Now that his face was turned away from the strange flower on the paper, it was extremely pale and wore a look of anguish, as though he had just undergone an agonising operation or just been taken from the rack. But the new-comer gradually began to arouse his attention, then his wonder, then suspicion and even alarm. When Zossimov said "This is Raskolnikov" he jumped up quickly, sat on the sofa and with an almost defiant, but weak and breaking, voice articulated:

"Yes, I am Raskolnikov! What do you want?"

The visitor scrutinised him and pronounced impressively:

"Pyotr Petrovitch Luzhin. I believe I have reason to hope that my name is not wholly unknown to you?"

But Raskolnikov, who had expected something quite different, gazed blankly and dreamily at him, making no reply, as though he heard the name of Pyotr Petrovitch for the first time.

"Is it possible that you can up to the present have received no information?" asked Pyotr Petrovitch, somewhat disconcerted.

In reply Raskolnikov sank languidly back on the pillow, put his hands behind his head and gazed at the ceiling. A look of dismay came into Luzhin's face. Zossimov and Razumihin stared at him more inquisitively than ever, and at last he showed unmistakable signs of embarrassment.

"I had presumed and calculated," he faltered, "that a letter posted more than ten days, if not a fortnight ago . . ."

"I say, why are you standing in the doorway?" Razumihin interrupted suddenly. "If you've something to say, sit down. Nastasya and you are so crowded. Nastasya, make room. Here's a chair, thread your way in!"

He moved his chair back from the table, made a little space

between the table and his knees, and waited in a rather cramped position for the visitor to "thread his way in." The minute was so chosen that it was impossible to refuse, and the visitor squeezed his way through, hurrying and stumbling. Reaching the chair, he sat down, looking suspiciously at Razumihin.

"No need to be nervous," the latter blurted out. "Rodya has been ill for the last five days and delirious for three, but now he is recovering and has got an appetite. This is his doctor, who has just had a look at him. I am a comrade of Rodya's, like him, formerly a student, and now I am nursing him; so don't you take any notice of us, but go on with your business."

"Thank you. But shall I not disturb the invalid by my presence and conversation?" Pyotr Petrovitch asked of Zossimov.

"N-no," mumbled Zossimov; "you may amuse him." He yawned again.

"He has been conscious a long time, since the morning," went on Razumihin, whose familiarity seemed so much like unaffected good-nature that Pyotr Petrovitch began to be more cheerful, partly, perhaps, because this shabby and impudent person had introduced himself as a student.

"Your mamma," began Luzhin.

"Hm!" Razumihin cleared his throat loudly. Luzhin looked at him inquiringly.

"That's all right, go on."

Luzhin shrugged his shoulders.

"Your mamma had commenced a letter to you while I was sojourning in her neighbourhood. On my arrival here I purposely allowed a few days to elapse before coming to see you, in order that I might be fully assured that you were in full possession of the tidings; but now, to my astonishment . . ."

"I know, I know!" Raskolnikov cried suddenly with impatient vexation. "So you are the *fiancé?* I know, and that's enough!"

There was no doubt about Pyotr Petrovitch's being offended this time, but he said nothing. He made a violent effort to understand what it all meant. There was a moment's silence.

Meanwhile Raskolnikov, who had turned a little towards him

when he answered, began suddenly staring at him again with marked curiosity, as though he had not had a good look at him yet, or as though something new had struck him; he rose from his pillow on purpose to stare at him. There certainly was something peculiar in Pyotr Petrovitch's whole appearance, something which seemed to justify the title of "fiancé" so unceremoniously applied to him. In the first place, it was evident, far too much so indeed, that Pyotr Petrovitch had made eager use of his few days in the capital to get himself up and rig himself out in expectation of his betrothed—a perfectly innocent and permissible proceeding, indeed. Even his own, perhaps too complacent, consciousness of the agreeable improvement in his appearance might have been forgiven in such circumstances, seeing that Pyotr Petrovitch had taken up the rôle of fiancé. All his clothes were fresh from the tailor's and were all right, except for being too new and too distinctly appropriate. Even the stylish new round hat had the same significance. Pyotr Petrovitch treated it too respectfully and held it too carefully in his hands. The exquisite pair of lavender gloves, real Louvain, told the same tale, if only from the fact of his not wearing them, but carrying them in his hand for show. Light and youthful colours predominated in Pyotr Petrovitch's attire. He wore a charming summer jacket of a fawn shade, light thin trousers, a waistcoat of the same, new and fine linen, a cravat of the lightest cambric with pink stripes on it, and the best of it was, this all suited Pyotr Petrovitch. His very fresh and even handsome face looked younger than his forty-five years at all times. His dark, mutton-chop whiskers made an agreeable setting on both sides, growing thickly about his shining, clean-shaven chin. Even his hair, touched here and there with grey, though it had been combed and curled at a hairdresser's, did not give him a stupid appearance, as curled hair usually does, by inevitably suggesting a German on his wedding-day. If there really was something unpleasing and repulsive in his rather good-looking and imposing countenance, it was due to quite other causes. After scanning Mr. Luzhin unceremoniously, Raskolnikov smiled malignantly, sank back on the pillow and stared at the ceiling as before.

But Mr. Luzhin hardened his heart and seemed to determine to take no notice of their oddities.

"I feel the greatest regret at finding you in this situation," he began, again breaking the silence with an effort. "If I had been aware of your illness I should have come earlier. But you know what business is. I have, too, a very important legal affair in the Senate, not to mention other preoccupations which you may well conjecture. I am expecting your mamma and sister any minute."

Raskolnikov made a movement and seemed about to speak; his face showed some excitement. Pyotr Petrovitch paused, waited, but as nothing followed, he went on:

". . . Any minute. I have found a lodging for them on their arrival."

"Where?" asked Raskolnikov weakly.

"Very near here, in Bakaleyev's house."

"That's in Voskresensky," put in Razumihin. "There are two storeys of rooms, let by a merchant called Yushin; I've been there."

"Yes, rooms . . ."

"A disgusting place—filthy, stinking and, what's more, of doubtful character. Things have happened there, and there are all sorts of queer people living there. And I went there about a scandalous business. It's cheap, though . . ."

"I could not, of course, find out so much about it, for I am a stranger in Petersburg myself," Pyotr Petrovitch replied huffily. "However, the two rooms are exceedingly clean, and as it is for so short a time . . . I have already taken a permanent, that is, our future flat," he said, addressing Raskolnikov, "and I am having it done up. And meanwhile I am myself cramped for room in a lodging with my friend Andrey Semyonovitch Lebeziatnikov, in the flat of Madame Lippevechsel; it was he who told me of Bakaleyev's house, too . . ."

"Lebeziatnikov?" said Raskolnikov slowly, as if recalling something.

"Yes, Andrey Semyonovitch Lebeziatnikov, a clerk in the Ministry. Do you know him?"

"Yes . . . no," Raskolnikov answered.

"Excuse me, I fancied so from your inquiry. I was once his guardian. . . . A very nice young man and advanced. I like to meet young people: one learns new things from them." Luzhin looked round hopefully at them all.

"How do you mean?" asked Razumihin.

"In the most serious and essential matters," Pyotr Petrovitch replied, as though delighted at the question. "You see, it's ten years since I visited Petersburg. All the novelties, reforms, ideas have reached us in the provinces, but to see it all more clearly one must be in Petersburg. And it's my notion that you observe and learn most by watching the younger generation. And I confess I am delighted . . ."

"At what?"

"Your question is a wide one. I may be mistaken, but I fancy I find clearer views, more, so to say, criticism, more practicality . . ."

"That's true," Zossimov let drop.

"Nonsense! There's no practicality." Razumihin flew at him. "Practicality is a difficult thing to find; it does not drop down from heaven. And for the last two hundred years we have been divorced from all practical life. Ideas, if you like, are fermenting," he said to Pyotr Petrovitch, "and desire for good exists, though it's in a childish form, and honesty you may find, although there are crowds of brigands. Anyway, there's no practicality. Practicality goes well shod."

"I don't agree with you," Pyotr Petrovitch replied, with evident enjoyment. "Of course, people do get carried away and make mistakes, but one must have indulgence; those mistakes are merely evidence of enthusiasm for the cause and of abnormal external environment. If little has been done, the time has been but short; of means I will not speak. It's my personal view, if you care to know, that something has been accomplished already. New valuable ideas, new valuable works are circulating in the place of our old dreamy and romantic authors. Literature is taking a maturer form, many injurious prejudices have been rooted up and turned into ridicule. . . . In a word, we have cut ourselves off

irrevocably from the past, and that, to my thinking, is a great thing
. . ."

"He's learnt it by heart to show off!" Raskolnikov pronounced suddenly.

"What?" asked Pyotr Petrovitch, not catching his words; but
he received no reply.

"That's all true," Zossimov hastened to interpose.

"Isn't it so?" Pyotr Petrovitch went on, glancing affably at
Zossimov. "You must admit," he went on, addressing Razumihin
with a shade of triumph and superciliousness—he almost added
"young man"—"that there is an advance, or, as they say now,
progress in the name of science and economic truth . . ."

"A commonplace."

"No, not a commonplace! Hitherto, for instance, if I were
told, 'love thy neighbour,' what came of it?" Pyotr Petrovitch
went on, perhaps with excessive haste. "It came to my tearing my
coat in half to share with my neighbour and we both were left half
naked. As a Russian proverb has it, 'catch several hares and you
won't catch one.' Science now tells us, love yourself before all
men, for everything in the world rests on self-interest. You love
yourself and manage your own affairs properly and your coat
remains whole. Economic truth adds that the better private affairs
are organised in society—the more whole coats, so to say—the
firmer are its foundations and the better is the common welfare
organised too. Therefore, in acquiring wealth solely and exclusively for myself, I am acquiring so to speak, for all, and helping
to bring to pass my neighbour's getting a little more than a torn
coat; and that not from private, personal liberality, but as a consequence of the general advance. The idea is simple, but unhappily
it has been a long time reaching us, being hindered by idealism
and sentimentality. And yet it would seem to want very little wit
to perceive it . . ."

"Excuse me, I've very little wit myself," Razumihin cut in
sharply, "and so let us drop it. I began this discussion with an
object, but I've grown so sick during the last three years of this
chattering to amuse oneself, of this incessant flow of common-
places, always the same, that, by Jove, I blush even when other

people talk like that. You are in a hurry, no doubt, to exhibit your acquirements; and I don't blame you, that's quite pardonable. I only wanted to find out what sort of man you are, for so many unscrupulous people have got hold of the progressive cause of late and have so distorted in their own interests everything they touched, that the whole cause has been dragged in the mire. That's enough!"

"Excuse me, sir," said Luzhin, affronted, and speaking with excessive dignity. "Do you mean to suggest so unceremoniously that I too . . ."

"Oh, my dear sir . . . how could I? . . . Come, that's enough," Razumihin concluded, and he turned abruptly to Zossimov to continue their previous conversation.

Pyotr Petrovitch had the good sense to accept the disavowal. He made up his mind to take leave in another minute or two.

"I trust our acquaintance," he said, addressing Raskolnikov, "may, upon your recovery and in view of the circumstances of which you are aware, become closer. . . . Above all, I hope for your return to health . . ."

Raskolnikov did not even turn his head. Pyotr Petrovitch began getting up from his chair.

"One of her customers must have killed her," Zossimov declared positively.

"Not a doubt of it," replied Razumihin. "Porfiry doesn't give his opinion, but is examining all who have left pledges with her there."

"Examining them?" Raskolnikov asked aloud.

"Yes. What then?"

"Nothing."

"How does he get hold of them?" asked Zossimov.

"Koch has given the names of some of them, other names are on the wrappers of the pledges and some have come forward of themselves."

"It must have been a cunning and practised ruffian! The boldness of it! The coolness!"

"That's just what it wasn't!" interposed Razumihin. "That's what throws you all off the scent. But I maintain that he is not

cunning, nor practised, and probably this was his first crime! The
supposition that it was a calculated crime and a cunning criminal
doesn't work. Suppose him to have been inexperienced, and it's
clear that it was only a chance that saved him—and chance may
do anything. Why, he did not foresee obstacles, perhaps! And
how did he set to work? He took jewels worth ten or twenty
roubles, stuffing his pockets with them, ransacked the old woman's trunk, her rags—and they found fifteen hundred roubles,
besides notes, in a box in the top drawer of the chest! He did not
know how to rob; he could only murder. It was his first crime,
I assure you, his first crime; he lost his head. And he got off more
by luck than good counsel!"

"You are talking of the murder of the old pawnbroker, I
believe?" Pyotr Petrovitch put in, addressing Zossimov. He was
standing, hat and gloves in hand, but before departing he felt
disposed to throw off a few more intellectual phrases. He was
evidently anxious to make a favourable impression and his vanity
overcame his prudence.

"Yes. You've heard of it?"

"Oh, yes, being in the neighbourhood."

"Do you know the details?"

"I can't say that; but another circumstance interests me in the
case—the whole question, so to say. Not to speak of the fact that
crime has been greatly on the increase among the lower classes
during the last five years, not to speak of the cases of robbery and
arson everywhere, what strikes me as the strangest thing is that
in the higher classes, too, crime is increasing proportionately. In
one place one hears of a student's robbing the mail on the high
road; in another place people of good social position forge false
banknotes; in Moscow of late a whole gang has been captured
who used to forge lottery tickets, and one of the ringleaders was
a lecturer in universal history; then our secretary abroad was
murdered from some obscure motive of gain. . . . And if this old
woman, the pawnbroker, has been murdered by some one of a
higher class in society—for peasants don't pawn gold trinkets—
how are we to explain this demoralisation of the civilised part of
our society?"

"There are many economic changes," put in Zossimov.

"How are we to explain it?" Razumihin caught him up. "It might be explained by our inveterate impracticality."

"How do you mean?"

"What answer had your lecturer in Moscow to make to the question why he was forging notes? 'Everybody is getting rich one way or another, so I want to make haste to get rich too.' I don't remember the exact words, but the upshot was that he wants money for nothing, without waiting or working! We've grown used to having everything ready-made, to walking on crutches, to having our food chewed for us. Then the great hour struck,* and every man showed himself in his true colours."

"But morality? And so to speak, principles . . ."

"But why do you worry about it?" Raskolnikov interposed suddenly. "It's in accordance with your theory!"

"In accordance with my theory?"

"Why, carry out logically the theory you were advocating just now, and it follows that people may be killed . . ."

"Upon my word!" cried Luzhin.

"No, that's not so," put in Zossimov.

Raskolnikov lay with a white face and twitching upper lip, breathing painfully.

"There's a measure in all things," Luzhin went on superciliously. "Economic ideas are not an incitement to murder, and one has but to suppose . . ."

"And is it true," Raskolnikov interposed once more suddenly, again in a voice quivering with fury and delight in insulting him, "is it true that you told your *fiancée* . . . within an hour of her acceptance, that what pleased you most . . . was that she was a beggar . . . because it was better to raise a wife from poverty, so that you may have complete control over her, and reproach her with your being her benefactor?"

"Upon my word," Luzhin cried wrathfully and irritably, crimson with confusion, "to distort my words in this way! Excuse me, allow me to assure you that the report which has reached you,

---

* The emancipation of the serfs in 1861 is meant.—TRANSLATOR'S NOTE.

or rather let me say, has been conveyed to you, has no foundation in truth, and I . . . suspect who . . . in a word . . . this arrow . . . in a word, your mamma . . . She seemed to me in other things, with all her excellent qualities, of a somewhat highflown and romantic way of thinking. . . . But I was a thousand miles from supposing that she would misunderstand and misrepresent things in so fanciful a way. . . . And indeed . . . indeed . . ."

"I tell you what," cried Raskolnikov, raising himself on his pillow and fixing his piercing, glittering eyes upon him, "I tell you what."

"What?" Luzhin stood still, waiting with a defiant and offended face. Silence lasted for some seconds.

"Why, if ever again . . . you dare to mention a single word . . . about my mother . . . I shall send you flying downstairs!"

"What's the matter with you?" cried Razumihin.

"So that's how it is?" Luzhin turned pale and bit his lip. "Let me tell you, sir," he began deliberately, doing his utmost to restrain himself but breathing hard, "at the first moment I saw you you were ill-disposed to me, but I remained here on purpose to find out more. I could forgive a great deal in a sick man and a connection, but you . . . never after this . . ."

"I am not ill," cried Raskolnikov.

"So much the worse . . ."

"Go to hell!"

But Luzhin was already leaving without finishing his speech, squeezing between the table and the chair; Razumihin got up this time to let him pass. Without glancing at any one, and not even nodding to Zossimov, who had for some time been making signs to him to let the sick man alone, he went out, lifting his hat to the level of his shoulder to avoid crushing it as he stooped to go out of the door. And even the curve of his spine was expressive of the horrible insult he had received.

"How could you—how could you!" Razumihin said, shaking his head in perplexity.

"Let me alone—let me alone all of you!" Raskolnikov cried in a frenzy. "Will you ever leave off tormenting me? I am not afraid of you! I am not afraid of any one, any one now! Get away from me! I want to be alone, alone, alone!"

"Come along," said Zossimov, nodding to Razumihin.

"But we can't leave him like this!"

"Come along," Zossimov repeated insistently, and he went out. Razumihin thought a minute and ran to overtake him.

"It might be worse not to obey him," said Zossimov on the stairs. "He mustn't be irritated."

"What's the matter with him?"

"If only he could get some favourable shock, that's what would do it! At first he was better. . . . You know he has got something on his mind! Some fixed idea weighing on him. . . . I am very much afraid so; he must have!"

"Perhaps it's that gentleman, Pyotr Petrovitch. From his conversation I gather he is going to marry his sister, and that he had received a letter about it just before his illness. . . ."

"Yes, confound the man! he may have upset the case altogether. But have you noticed, he takes no interest in anything, he does not respond to anything except one point on which he seems excited—that's the murder?"

"Yes, yes," Razumihin agreed, "I noticed that, too. He is interested, frightened. It gave him a shock on the day he was ill in the police office; he fainted."

"Tell me more about that this evening and I'll tell you something afterwards. He interests me very much! In half an hour I'll go and see him again. . . . There'll be no inflammation though."

"Thanks! And I'll wait with Pashenka meantime and will keep watch on him through Nastasya. . . ."

Raskolnikov, left alone, looked with impatience and misery at Nastasya, but she still lingered.

"Won't you have some tea now?" she asked.

"Later! I am sleepy! Leave me."

He turned abruptly to the wall; Nastasya went out.

6

But as soon as she went out, he got up, latched the door, undid the parcel which Razumihin had brought in that evening and had tied up again, and began dressing. Strange to say, he seemed immediately to have become perfectly calm; not a trace of his recent delirium nor of the panic fear that had haunted him of late. It was the first moment of a strange sudden calm. His movements were precise and definite; a firm purpose was evident in them. "To-day, to-day," he muttered to himself. He understood that he was still weak, but his intense spiritual concentration gave him strength and self-confidence. He hoped, moreover, that he would not fall down in the street. When he had dressed in entirely new clothes, he looked at the money lying on the table, and after a moment's thought put it in his pocket. It was twenty-five roubles. He took also all the copper change from the ten roubles spent by Razumihin on the clothes. Then he softly unlatched the door, went out, slipped downstairs and glanced in at the open kitchen door. Nastasya was standing with her back to him, blowing up the landlady's samovar. She heard nothing. Who would have dreamed of his going out, indeed? A minute later he was in the street.

It was nearly eight o'clock, the sun was setting. It was as stifling as before, but he eagerly drank in the stinking, dusty town air. His head felt rather dizzy; a sort of savage energy gleamed suddenly in his feverish eyes and his wasted, pale and yellow face. He did not know and did not think where he was going, he had one thought only "that all *this* must be ended to-day, once for all, immediately; that he would not return home without it, because he *would not go on living like that*." How, with what to make an end? He had not an idea about it, he did not even want to think of it. He drove away thought; thought tortured him. All he knew, all he felt was that everything must be changed "one way or another," he repeated with desperate and immovable self-confidence and determination.

From old habit he took his usual walk in the direction of the Hay Market. A dark-haired young man with a barrel organ was standing in the road in front of a little general shop and was grinding out a very sentimental song. He was accompanying a girl of fifteen, who stood on the pavement in front of him. She was dressed up in a crinoline, a mantle and a straw hat with a flame-coloured feather in it, all very old and shabby. In a strong and rather agreeable voice, cracked and coarsened by street singing, she sang in hope of getting a copper from the shop. Raskolnikov joined two or three listeners, took out a five copeck piece and put it in the girl's hand. She broke off abruptly on a sentimental high note, shouted sharply to the organ grinder "Come on," and both moved on to the next shop.

"Do you like street music?" said Raskolnikov, addressing a middle-aged man standing idly by him. The man looked at him, startled and wondering.

"I love to hear singing to a street organ," said Raskolnikov, and his manner seemed strangely out of keeping with the subject —"I like it on cold, dark, damp autumn evenings—they must be damp—when all the passers-by have pale green, sickly faces, or better still when wet snow is falling straight down, when there's no wind—you know what I mean? and the street lamps shine through it. . . ."

"I don't know. . . . Excuse me . . ." muttered the stranger, frightened by the question and Raskolnikov's strange manner, and he crossed over to the other side of the street.

Raskolnikov walked straight on and came out at the corner of the Hay Market, where the huckster and his wife had talked with Lizaveta; but they were not there now. Recognising the place, he stopped, looked round and addressed a young fellow in a red shirt who stood gaping before a corn chandler's shop.

"Isn't there a man who keeps a booth with his wife at this corner?"

"All sorts of people keep booths here," answered the young man, glancing superciliously at Raskolnikov.

"What's his name?"

"What he was christened."

"Aren't you a Zaraïsky man, too? Which province?"

The young man looked at Raskolnikov again.

"It's not a province, your excellency, but a district. Graciously forgive me, your excellency!"

"Is that a tavern at the top there?"

"Yes, it's an eating-house and there's a billiard-room and you'll find princesses there too. . . . La-la!"

Raskolnikov crossed the square. In that corner there was a dense crowd of peasants. He pushed his way into the thickest part of it, looking at the faces. He felt an unaccountable inclination to enter into conversation with people. But the peasants took no notice of him; they were all shouting in groups together. He stood and thought a little and took a turning to the right in the direction of V.

He had often crossed that little street which turns at an angle, leading from the market-place to Sadovy Street. Of late he had often felt drawn to wander about this district, when he felt depressed, that he might feel more so.

Now he walked along, thinking of nothing. At that point there is a great block of buildings, entirely let out in dram shops and eating-houses; women were continually running in and out, bare-headed and in their indoor clothes. Here and there they gathered in groups, on the pavement, especially about the entrances to various festive establishments in the lower storeys. From one of these a loud din, sounds of singing, the tinkling of a guitar and shouts of merriment, floated into the street. A crowd of women were thronging round the door; some were sitting on the steps, others on the pavement, others were standing talking. A drunken soldier, smoking a cigarette, was walking near them in the road, swearing; he seemed to be trying to find his way somewhere, but had forgotten where. One beggar was quarrelling with another, and a man dead drunk was lying right across the road. Raskolnikov joined the throng of women, who were talking in husky voices. They were bare-headed and wore cotton dresses and goatskin shoes. There were women of forty and some not more than seventeen; almost all had blackened eyes.

He felt strangely attracted by the singing and all the noise and uproar in the saloon below. . . . Some one could be heard within dancing frantically, marking time with his heels to the sounds of the guitar and of a thin falsetto voice singing a jaunty air. He listened intently, gloomily and dreamily, bending down at the entrance and peeping inquisitively in from the pavement.

> *"Oh, my handsome soldier*
> *Don't beat me for nothing,"*

trilled the thin voice of the singer. Raskolnikov felt a great desire to make out what he was singing, as though everything depended on that.

"Shall I go in?" he thought. "They are laughing. From drink. Shall I get drunk?"

"Won't you come in?" one of the women asked him. Her voice was still musical and less thick than the others, she was young and not repulsive—the only one of the group.

"Why, she's pretty," he said, drawing himself up and looking at her.

She smiled, much pleased at the compliment.

"You're very nice looking yourself," she said.

"Isn't he thin though!" observed another woman in a deep bass. "Have you just come out of a hospital?"

"They're all generals' daughters it seems, but they have all snub noses," interposed a tipsy peasant with a sly smile on his face, wearing a loose coat. "See how jolly they are."

"Go along with you!"

"I'll go, sweetie!"

And he darted down into the saloon below. Raskolnikov moved on.

"I say, sir," the girl shouted after him.

"What is it?"

She hesitated.

"I'll always be pleased to spend an hour with you, kind gentleman, but now I feel shy. Give me six copecks for a drink, there's a nice young man!"

Raskolnikov gave her what came first—fifteen copecks.

"Ah, what a good-natured gentleman!"

"What's your name?"

"Ask for Duclida."

"Well, that's too much," one of the women observed, shaking her head at Duclida. "I don't know how you can ask like that. I believe I should drop with shame. . . ."

Raskolnikov looked curiously at the speaker. She was a pock-marked wench of thirty, covered with bruises, with her upper lip swollen. She made her criticism quietly and earnestly. "Where is it," thought Raskolnikov. "Where is it I've read that some one condemned to death says or thinks, an hour before his death, that if he had to live on some high rock, on such a narrow ledge that he'd only room to stand, and the ocean, everlasting darkness, everlasting solitude, everlasting tempest around him, if he had to remain standing on a square yard of space all his life, a thousand years, eternity, it were better to live so than to die at once! Only to live, to live and live! Life, whatever it may be! . . . How true it is! Good God, how true! Man is a vile creature! . . . And vile is he who calls him vile for that," he added a moment later.

He went into another street. "Bah, the Palais de Crystal! Razumihin was just talking of the Palais de Crystal. But what on earth was it I wanted? Yes, the newspapers. . . . Zossimov said he'd read it in the papers. Have you the papers?" he asked, going into a very spacious and positively clean restaurant, consisting of several rooms, which were however rather empty. Two or three people were drinking tea, and in a room further away were sitting four men drinking champagne. Raskolnikov fancied that Zametov was one of them, but he could not be sure at that distance. "What if it is!" he thought.

"Will you have vodka?" asked the waiter.

"Give me some tea and bring me the papers, the old ones for the last five days and I'll give you something."

"Yes, sir, here's to-day's. No vodka?"

The old newspapers and the tea were brought. Raskolnikov sat down and began to look through them.

"Oh, damn . . . these are the items of intelligence. An accident on a staircase, spontaneous combustion of a shopkeeper from alcohol, a fire in Peski . . . a fire in the Petersburg quarter . . . another fire in the Petersburg quarter. . . . Ah, here it is!" He found at last what he was seeking and began to read it. The lines danced before his eyes, but he read it all and began eagerly seeking later additions in the following numbers. His hands shook with nervous impatience as he turned the sheets. Suddenly some one sat down beside him at his table. He looked up, it was the head clerk Zametov, looking just the same, with the rings on his fingers and the watch-chain, with the curly, black hair, parted and pomaded, with the smart waistcoat, rather shabby coat and doubtful linen. He was in a good humour, at least he was smiling very gaily and good-humouredly. His dark face was rather flushed from the champagne he had drunk.

"What, you here?" he began in surprise, speaking as though he'd known him all his life. "Why, Razumihin told me only yesterday you were unconscious. How strange! And do you know I've been to see you?"

Raskolnikov knew he would come up to him. He laid aside the papers and turned to Zametov. There was a smile on his lips, and a new shade of irritable impatience was apparent in that smile.

"I know you have," he answered. "I've heard it. You looked for my sock. . . . And you know Razumihin has lost his heart to you? He says you've been with him to Luise Ivanovna's, you know the woman you tried to befriend, for whom you winked to the Explosive Lieutenant and he would not understand. Do you remember? How could he fail to understand—it was quite clear, wasn't it?"

"What a hot head he is!"

"The explosive one?"

"No, your friend Razumihin."

"You must have a jolly life, Mr. Zametov; entrance free to the most agreeable places. Who's been pouring champagne into you just now?"

"We've just been . . . having a drink together. . . . You talk about pouring it into me!"

"By way of a fee! You profit by everything!" Raskolnikov laughed, "it's all right, my dear boy," he added, slapping Zametov on the shoulder. "I am not speaking from temper, but in a friendly way, for sport, as that workman of yours said when he was scuffling with Dmitri, in the case of the old woman. . . ."

"How do you know about it?"

"Perhaps I know more about it than you do."

"How strange you are.... I am sure you are still very unwell. You oughtn't to have come out."

"Oh, do I seem strange to you?"

"Yes. What are you doing, reading the papers?"

"Yes."

"There's a lot about the fires."

"No, I am not reading about the fires." Here he looked mysteriously at Zametov; his lips were twisted again in a mocking smile. "No, I am not reading about the fires," he went on, winking at Zametov. "But confess now, my dear fellow, you're awfully anxious to know what I am reading about?"

"I am not in the least. Mayn't I ask a question? Why do you keep on . . . ?"

"Listen, you are a man of culture and education?"

"I was in the sixth class at the gymnasium," said Zametov with some dignity.

"Sixth class! Ah, my cocksparrow! With your parting and your rings—you are a gentleman of fortune. Foo, what a charming boy!" Here Raskolnikov broke into a nervous laugh right in Zametov's face. The latter drew back, more amazed than offended.

"Foo, how strange you are!" Zametov repeated very seriously. "I can't help thinking you are still delirious."

"I am delirious? You are fibbing, my cocksparrow! So I am strange? You find me curious, do you?"

"Yes, curious."

"Shall I tell you what I was reading about, what I was looking for? See what a lot of papers I've made them bring me. Suspicious, eh?"

"Well, what is it?"

"You prick up your ears?"

"How do you mean—prick up my ears?"

"I'll explain that afterwards, but now, my boy, I declare to you . . . no, better 'I confess' . . . No, that's not right either; 'I make a deposition and you take it.' I depose that I was reading, that I was looking and searching. . . ." he screwed up his eyes and paused. "I was searching—and came here on purpose to do it—for news of the murder of the old pawnbroker woman," he articulated at last, almost in a whisper, bringing his face exceedingly close to the face of Zametov. Zametov looked at him steadily, without moving or drawing his face away. What struck Zametov afterwards as the strangest part of it all was that silence followed for exactly a minute, and that they gazed at one another all the while.

"What if you have been reading about it?" he cried at last, perplexed and impatient. "That's no business of mine! What of it?"

"The same old woman," Raskolnikov went on in the same whisper, not heeding Zametov's explanation, "about whom you were talking in the police office, you remember, when I fainted. Well, do you understand now?"

"What do you mean? Understand . . . what?" Zametov brought out, almost alarmed.

Raskolnikov's set and earnest face was suddenly transformed, and he suddenly went off into the same nervous laugh as before, as though utterly unable to restrain himself. And in one flash he recalled with extraordinary vividness of sensation a moment in the recent past, that moment when he stood with the axe behind the door, while the latch trembled and the men outside swore and shook it, and he had a sudden desire to shout at them, to swear at them, to put out his tongue at them, to mock them, to laugh, and laugh, and laugh!

"You are either mad, or . . ." began Zametov, and he broke off, as though stunned by the idea that had suddenly flashed into his mind.

"Or? Or what? What? Come, tell me!"

"Nothing," said Zametov, getting angry, "it's all nonsense!"

Both were silent. After his sudden fit of laughter Raskolnikov became suddenly thoughtful and melancholy. He put his elbow on the table and leaned his head on his hand. He seemed to have completely forgotten Zametov. The silence lasted for some time.

"Why don't you drink your tea? It's getting cold," said Zametov.

"What! Tea? Oh, yes. . . ." Raskolnikov sipped the glass, put a morsel of bread in his mouth and, suddenly looking at Zametov, seemed to remember everything and pulled himself together. At the same moment his face resumed its original mocking expression. He went on drinking tea.

"There have been a great many of these crimes lately," said Zametov. "Only the other day I read in the *Moscow News* that a whole gang of false coiners had been caught in Moscow. It was a regular society. They used to forge tickets!"

"Oh, but it was a long time ago! I read about it a month ago," Raskolnikov answered calmly. "So you consider them criminals?" he added smiling.

"Of course they are criminals."

"They? They are children, simpletons, not criminals! Why, half a hundred people meeting for such an object—what an idea! Three would be too many, and then they want to have more faith in one other than in themselves! One has only to blab in his cups and it all collapses. Simpletons! They engaged untrustworthy people to change the notes—what a thing to trust to a casual stranger! Well, let us suppose that these simpletons succeed and each makes a million, and what follows for the rest of their lives? Each is dependent on the others for the rest of his life! Better hang oneself at once! And they did not know how to change the notes either; the man who changed the notes took five thousand roubles, and his hands trembled. He counted the first four thousand, but did not count the fifth thousand—he was in such a hurry to get the money into his pocket and run away. Of course he roused suspicion. And the whole thing came to a crash through one fool! Is it possible?"

"That his hands trembled?" observed Zametov, "yes, that's quite possible. That I feel quite sure is possible. Sometimes one can't stand things."

"Can't stand that?"

"Why, could you stand it then? No, I couldn't. For the sake of a hundred roubles to face such a terrible experience! To go with false notes into a bank where it's their business to spot that sort of thing! No, I should not have the face to do it. Would you?"

Raskolnikov had an intense desire again "to put his tongue out." Shivers kept running down his spine.

"I should do it quite differently," Raskolnikov began. "This is how I would change the notes: I'd count the first thousand three or four times backwards and forwards, look at every note and then I'd set to the second thousand; I'd count that half way through and then hold some fifty rouble note to the light, then turn it, then hold it to the light again—to see whether it was a good one? 'I am afraid,' I would say. 'A relation of mine lost twenty-five roubles the other day through a false note,' and then I'd tell them the whole story. And after I began counting the third, 'no, excuse me,' I would say, 'I fancy I made a mistake in the seventh hundred in that second thousand, I am not sure.' And so I would give up the third thousand and go back to the second and so on to the end. And when I had finished, I'd pick out one from the fifth and one from the second thousand and take them again to the light and ask again 'change them, please,' and put the clerk into such a stew that he would not know how to get rid of me. When I'd finished and had gone out, I'd come back, 'No, excuse me,' and ask for some explanation. That's how I'd do it."

"Foo, what terrible things you say!" said Zametov, laughing. "But all that is only talk. I dare say when it came to deeds you'd make a slip. I believe that even a practised, desperate man cannot always reckon on himself, much less you and I. To take an example near home—that old woman murdered in our district. The murderer seems to have been a desperate fellow, he risked everything in open daylight, was saved by a miracle—but his hands shook, too. He did not succeed in robbing the place, he couldn't stand it. That was clear from the . . ."

Raskolnikov seemed offended.

"Clear? Why don't you catch him then?" he cried, maliciously gibing at Zametov.

"Well, they will catch him."

"Who? You? Do you suppose you could catch him? You've a tough job! A great point for you is whether a man is spending money or not. If he had no money and suddenly begins spending, he must be the man. So that any child can mislead you."

"The fact is they always do that, though," answered Zametov. "A man will commit a clever murder at the risk of his life and then at once he goes drinking in a tavern. They are caught spending money, they are not all as cunning as you are. You wouldn't go to a tavern, of course?"

Raskolnikov frowned and looked steadily at Zametov.

"You seem to enjoy the subject and would like to know how I should behave in that case, too?" he asked with displeasure.

"I should like to," Zametov answered firmly and seriously. Somewhat too much earnestness began to appear in his words and looks.

"Very much?"

"Very much!"

"All right then. This is how I should behave," Raskolnikov began, again bringing his face close to Zametov's, again staring at him and speaking in a whisper, so that the latter positively shuddered. "This is what I should have done. I should have taken the money and jewels, I should have walked out of there and have gone straight to some deserted place with fences round it and scarcely any one to be seen, some kitchen garden or place of that sort. I should have looked out beforehand some stone weighing a hundredweight or more which had been lying in the corner from the time the house was built. I would lift that stone—there would be sure to be a hollow under it, and I would put the jewels and money in that hole. Then I'd roll the stone back so that it would look as before, would press it down with my foot and walk away. And for a year or two, three maybe, I would not touch it. And, well, they could search! There'd be no trace."

"You are a madman," said Zametov, and for some reason he too spoke in a whisper, and moved away from Raskolnikov, whose eyes were glittering. He had turned fearfully pale and his upper lip was twitching and quivering. He bent down as close as possible to Zametov, and his lips began to move without uttering a word. This lasted for half a minute; he knew what he was doing, but could not restrain himself. The terrible word trembled on his lips, like the latch on that door; in another moment it will break out, in another moment he will let it go, he will speak out.

"And what if it was I who murdered the old woman and Lizaveta?" he said suddenly and—realised what he had done.

Zametov looked wildly at him and turned white as the table-cloth. His face wore a contorted smile.

"But is it possible?" he brought out faintly. Raskolnikov looked wrathfully at him.

"Own up that you believed it, yes, you did?"

"Not a bit of it, I believe it less than ever now," Zametov cried hastily.

"I've caught my cocksparrow! So you did believe it before, if now you believe it less than ever?"

"Not at all," cried Zametov, obviously embarrassed. "Have you been frightening me so as to lead up to this?"

"You don't believe it then? What were you talking about behind my back when I went out of the police office? And why did the explosive lieutenant question me after I fainted? Hey, there," he shouted to the waiter, getting up and taking his cap, "how much?"

"Thirty copecks," the latter replied, running up.

"And here is twenty copecks for vodka. See what a lot of money!" he held out his shaking hand to Zametov with notes in it. "Red notes and blue, twenty-five roubles. Where did I get them? And where did my new clothes come from? You know I had not a copeck. You've cross-examined my landlady, I'll be bound. . . . Well, that's enough! *Assez causé!* Till we meet again!"

He went out, trembling all over from a sort of wild hysterical sensation, in which there was an element of insufferable rapture. Yet he was gloomy and terribly tired. His face was twisted as after a fit. His fatigue increased rapidly. Any shock, any irritating sensation stimulated and revived his energies at once, but his strength failed as quickly when the stimulus was removed.

Zametov, left alone, sat for a long time in the same place, plunged in thought. Raskolnikov had unwittingly worked a revolution in his brain on a certain point and had made up his mind for him conclusively.

"Ilya Petrovitch is a blockhead," he decided.

Raskolnikov had hardly opened the door of the restaurant when he stumbled against Razumihin on the steps. They did not see each other till they almost knocked against each other. For a moment they stood looking each other up and down. Razumihin was greatly astounded, then anger, real anger gleamed fiercely in his eyes.

"So here you are!" he shouted at the top of his voice—"you ran away from your bed! And here I've been looking for you under the sofa! We went up to the garret. I almost beat Nastasya on your account. And here he is after all. Rodya! What is the meaning of it? Tell me the whole truth! Confess! Do you hear?"

"It means that I'm sick to death of you all and I want to be alone," Raskolnikov answered calmly.

"Alone? When you are not able to walk, when your face is as white as a sheet and you are gasping for breath! Idiot! . . . What have you been doing in the Palais de Crystal? Own up at once!"

"Let me go!" said Raskolnikov and tried to pass him. This was too much for Razumihin; he gripped him firmly by the shoulder.

"Let you go? You dare tell me to let you go? Do you know what I'll do with you directly? I'll pick you up, tie you up in a bundle, carry you home under my arm and lock you up!"

"Listen, Razumihin," Raskolnikov began quietly, apparently calm—"can't you see that I don't want your benevolence? A strange desire you have to shower benefits on a man who . . . curses them, who feels them a burden in fact! Why did you seek me out at the beginning of my illness? Maybe I was very glad to die. Didn't I tell you plainly enough to-day that you were torturing me, that I was . . . sick of you! You seem to want to torture people! I assure you that all that is seriously hindering my recovery, because it's continually irritating me. You saw Zossimov went away just now to avoid irritating me. You leave me alone too, for goodness' sake! What right have you, indeed, to keep me by force? Don't you see that I am in possession of all my faculties now? How, how can I persuade you not to persecute me with your kindness? I may be ungrateful, I may be mean, only let me be, for God's sake, let me be! Let me be, let me be!"

He began calmly, gloating beforehand over the venomous phrases he was about to utter, but finished, panting for breath, in a frenzy, as he had been with Luzhin.

Razumihin stood a moment, thought and let his hand drop.

"Well, go to hell then," he said gently and thoughtfully. "Stay," he roared, as Raskolnikov was about to move. "Listen to me. Let me tell you, that you are all a set of babbling, posing idiots! If you've any little trouble you brood over it like a hen over an egg. And you are plagiarists even in that! There isn't a sign of independent life in you! You are made of spermaceti ointment and you've lymph in your veins instead of blood. I don't believe in any one of you! In any circumstances the first thing for all of you is to be unlike a human being! Stop!" he cried with redoubled fury, noticing that Raskolnikov was again making a movement—"hear me out! You know I'm having a house-warming this evening, I dare say they've arrived by now, but I left my uncle there—I just ran in—to receive the guests. And if you weren't a fool, a common fool, a perfect fool, if you were an original instead of a translation . . . you see, Rodya, I recognise you're a clever fellow, but you're a fool!—and if you weren't a fool you'd come round to me this evening instead of wearing out your boots in the street! Since you have gone out, there's no help for it! I'd give you a snug easy chair, my land lady has one . . . a cup of tea, company. . . . Or you could lie on the sofa—any way you would be with us. . . . Zossimov will be there too. Will you come?"

"No."

"R-rubbish!" Razumihin shouted, out of patience. "How do you know? You can't answer for yourself! You don't know anything about it. . . . Thousands of times I've fought tooth and nail with people and run back to them afterwards. . . . One feels ashamed and goes back to a man! So remember, Potchinkov's house on the third storey. . . ."

"Why, Mr. Razumihin, I do believe you'd let anybody beat you from sheer benevolence."

"Beat? Whom? Me? I'd twist his nose off at the mere idea! Potchinkov's house, 47, Babushkin's flat. . . ."

"I shall not come, Razumihin." Raskolnikov turned and walked away.

"I bet you will," Razumihin shouted after him. "I refuse to know you if you don't! Stay, hey, is Zametov in there?"

"Yes."

"Did you see him?"

"Yes."

"Talked to him?"

"Yes."

"What about? Confound you, don't tell me then. Potchinkov's house, 47, Babushkin's flat, remember!"

Raskolnikov walked on and turned the corner into Sadovy Street. Razumihin looked after him thoughtfully. Then with a wave of his hand he went into the house but stopped short of the stairs.

"Confound it," he went on almost aloud. "He talked sensibly but yet . . . I am a fool! As if madmen didn't talk sensibly! And this was just what Zossimov seemed afraid of." He struck his finger on his forehead. "What if . . . how could I let him go off alone? He may drown himself. . . . Ach, what a blunder! I can't." And he ran back to overtake Raskolnikov, but there was no trace of him. With a curse he returned with rapid steps to the Palais de Crystal to question Zametov.

Raskolnikov walked straight to X—— Bridge, stood in the middle, and leaning both elbows on the rail stared into the distance. On parting with Razumihin, he felt so much weaker that he could scarcely reach this place. He longed to sit or lie down somewhere in the street. Bending over the water, he gazed mechanically at the last pink flush of the sunset, at the row of houses growing dark in the gathering twilight, at one distant attic window on the left bank, flashing as though on fire in the last rays of the setting sun, at the darkening water of the canal, and the water seemed to catch his attention. At last red circles flashed before his eyes, the houses seemed moving, the passersby, the canal banks, the carriages, all danced before his eyes. Suddenly he started, saved again perhaps from swooning by an uncanny and hideous sight. He became aware of some one standing on the right side of him; he looked and saw a tall woman with a kerchief on her head, with a long, yellow, wasted face and red sunken eyes. She was looking straight at him, but obviously she saw nothing and recognised no one. Suddenly she leaned her right hand on the parapet, lifted her right leg over the railing, then her left and threw herself into the canal. The filthy water parted and swallowed up its victim for a moment, but an instant later the drowning woman floated to the surface, moving slowly with the current, her head and legs in the water, her skirt inflated like a balloon over her back.

"A woman drowning! A woman drowning!" shouted dozens of voices; people ran up, both banks were thronged with spectators, on the bridge people crowded about Raskolnikov, pressing up behind him.

"Mercy on it! it's our Afrosinya!" a woman cried tearfully close by. "Mercy! save her! kind people, pull her out!"

"A boat, a boat" was shouted in the crowd. But there was no need of a boat; a policeman ran down the steps to the canal, threw off his great coat and his boots and rushed into the water. It was easy to reach her: she floated within a couple of yards from the steps, he caught hold of her clothes with his right hand and with his left seized a pole which a comrade held out to him; the drowning woman was pulled out at once. They laid her on the granite pavement of the embankment. She soon recovered consciousness, raised her head, sat up and began sneezing and coughing, stupidly wiping her wet dress with her hands. She said nothing.

"She's drunk herself out of her senses," the same woman's voice wailed at her side. "Out of her senses. The other day she tried to hang herself, we cut her down. I ran out to the shop just now, left my little girl to look after her—and here she's in trouble again! A neighbour, gentleman, a neighbour, we live close by, the second house from the end, see yonder. . . ."

The crowd broke up. The police still remained round the woman, some one mentioned the police station. . . . Raskolnikov looked on with a strange sensation of indifference and apathy. He felt disgusted. "No, that's loathsome . . . water . . . it's not good enough," he muttered to himself. "Nothing will come of it," he added, "no use to wait. What about the police office . . . ? And why isn't Zametov at the police office? The police office is open till ten o'clock. . . ." He turned his back to the railing and looked about him.

"Very well then!" he said resolutely; he moved from the bridge and walked in the direction of the police office. His heart felt hollow and empty. He did not want to think. Even his depression had passed, there was not a trace now of the energy with which he had set out "to make an end of it all." Complete apathy had succeeded to it.

"Well, it's a way out of it," he thought, walking slowly and listlessly along the canal bank. "Anyway I'll make an end, for I want to. . . . But is it a way out? What does it matter! There'll be the square yard of space—ha! But what an end! Is it really the end? Shall I tell them or not? Ah . . . damn! How tired I am! If I could find somewhere to sit or lie down soon! What I am most ashamed of is its being so stupid. But I don't care about that either! What idiotic ideas come into one's head."

To reach the police office he had to go straight forward and take the second turning to the left. It was only a few paces away. But at the first turning he stopped and, after a minute's thought, turned into a side street and went two streets out of his way, possibly without any object, or possibly to delay a minute and gain time. He walked, looking at the ground; suddenly some one seemed to whisper in his ear; he lifted his head and saw that he was standing at the very gate of *the* house. He had not passed it, he had not been near it since *that* evening. An overwhelming, unaccountable prompting drew him on. He went into the house, passed through the gateway, then into the first entrance on the right, and began mounting the familiar staircase to the fourth storey. The narrow, steep staircase was very dark. He stopped at each landing and looked round him with curiosity; on the first landing the framework of the window had been taken out. "That wasn't so then," he thought. Here was the flat on the second

storey where Nikolay and Dmitri had been working. "It's shut up
and the door newly painted. So it's to let." Then the third storey
and the fourth. "Here!" He was perplexed to find the door of the
flat wide open. There were men there, he could hear voices; he
had not expected that. After brief hesitation he mounted the last
stairs and went into the flat. It, too, was being done up; there were
workmen in it. This seemed to amaze him; he somehow fancied
that he would find everything as he left it, even perhaps the
corpses in the same places on the floor. And now, bare walls, no
furniture; it seemed strange. He walked to the window and sat
down on the window sill. There were two workmen, both young
fellows, but one much younger than the other. They were paper-
ing the walls with a new white paper covered with lilac flowers,
instead of the old, dirty, yellow one. Raskolnikov for some reason
felt horribly annoyed by this. He looked at the new paper with
dislike, as though he felt sorry to have it all so changed. The
workmen had obviously stayed beyond their time and now they
were hurriedly rolling up their paper and getting ready to go
home. They took no notice of Raskolnikov's coming in; they were
talking. Raskolnikov folded his arms and listened.

"She comes to me in the morning," said the elder to the
younger, "very early, all dressed up. 'Why are you preening and
prinking?' says I. 'I am ready to do anything to please you, Tit
Vassilitch!' That's a way of going on! And she dressed up like a
regular fashion book!"

"And what is a fashion book?" the younger one asked. He
obviously regarded the other as an authority.

"A fashion book is a lot of pictures, coloured, and they come
to the tailors here every Saturday, by post from abroad, to show
folks how to dress, the male sex as well as the female. They're
pictures. The gentlemen are generally wearing fur coats and as for
the ladies' fluffles, they're beyond anything you can fancy."

"There's nothing you can't find in Petersburg," the younger
cried enthusiastically, "except father and mother, there's everything!"

"Except them, there's everything to be found, my boy," the
elder declared sententiously.

Raskolnikov got up and walked into the other room where the strong box, the bed, and the chest of drawers had been; the room seemed to him very tiny without furniture in it. The paper was the same; the paper in the corner showed where the case of ikons had stood. He looked at it and went to the window. The elder workman looked at him askance.

"What do you want?" he asked suddenly.

Instead of answering Raskolnikov went into the passage and pulled the bell. The same bell, the same cracked note. He rang it a second and a third time; he listened and remembered. The hideous and agonisingly fearful sensation he had felt then began to come back more and more vividly. He shuddered at every ring and it gave him more and more satisfaction.

"Well, what do you want? Who are you?" the workman shouted, going out to him. Raskolnikov went inside again.

"I want to take a flat," he said. "I am looking round."

"It's not the time to look at rooms at night; and you ought to come up with the porter."

"The floors have been washed, will they be painted?" Raskolnikov went on. "Is there no blood?"

"What blood?"

"Why, the old woman and her sister were murdered here. There was a perfect pool there."

"But who are you?" the workman cried, uneasy.

"Who am I?"

"Yes."

"You want to know? Come to the police station, I'll tell you."

The workmen looked at him in amazement.

"It's time for us to go, we are late. Come along, Alyoshka. We must lock up," said the elder workman.

"Very well, come along," said Raskolnikov indifferently, and going out first, he went slowly downstairs. "Hey, porter," he cried in the gateway.

At the entrance several people were standing, staring at the passers-by; the two porters, a peasant woman, a man in a long coat and a few others. Raskolnikov went straight up to them.

"What do you want?" asked one of the porters.

"Have you been to the police office?"

"I've just been there. What do you want?"

"Is it open?"

"Of course."

"Is the assistant there?"

"He was there for a time. What do you want?"

Raskolnikov made no reply, but stood beside them lost in thought.

"He's been to look at the flat," said the elder workman, coming forward.

"Which flat?"

"Where we are at work. 'Why have you washed away the blood?' says he. 'There has been a murder here,' says he and I've come to take it.' And he began ringing at the bell, all but broke it. 'Come to the police station,' says he. 'I'll tell you everything there.' He wouldn't leave us."

The porter looked at Raskolnikov, frowning and perplexed.

"Who are you?" he shouted as impressively as he could.

"I am Rodion Romanovitch Raskolnikov, formerly a student, I live in Shil's house, not far from here, flat Number 14, ask the porter, he knows me." Raskolnikov said all this in a lazy, dreamy voice, not turning round, but looking intently into the darkening street.

"Why have you been to the flat?"

"To look at it."

"What is there to look at?"

"Take him straight to the police station," the man in the long coat jerked in abruptly.

Raskolnikov looked intently at him over his shoulder and said in the same slow, lazy tone:

"Come along."

"Yes, take him," the man went on more confidently. "Why was he going into *that*, what's in his mind, eh?"

"He's not drunk, but God knows what's the matter with him," muttered the workman.

"But what do you want?" the porter shouted again, beginning to get angry in earnest—"Why are you hanging about?"

"You funk the police station then?" said Raskolnikov jeeringly.

"How funk it? Why are you hanging about?"

"He's a rogue!" shouted the peasant woman.

"Why waste time talking to him?" cried the other porter, a huge peasant in a full open coat and with keys on his belt. "Get along! He is a rogue and no mistake. Get along!"

And seizing Raskolnikov by the shoulder he flung him into the street. He lurched forward, but recovered his footing, looked at the spectators in silence and walked away.

"Strange man!" observed the workman.

"There are strange folks about nowadays," said the woman.

"You should have taken him to the police station all the same," said the man in the long coat.

"Better have nothing to do with him," decided the big porter. "A regular rogue! Just what he wants, you may be sure, but once take him up, you won't get rid of him. . . . We know the sort!"

"Shall I go there or not?" thought Raskolnikov, standing in the middle of the thoroughfare at the cross roads, and he looked about him, as though expecting from some one a decisive word. But no sound came, all was dead and silent like the stones on which he walked, dead to him, to him alone. . . . All at once at the end of the street, two hundred yards away, in the gathering dusk he saw a crowd and heard talk and shouts. In the middle of the crowd stood a carriage. . . . A light gleamed in the middle of the street. "What is it?" Raskolnikov turned to the right and went up to the crowd. He seemed to clutch at everything and smiled coldly when he recognised it, for he had fully made up his mind to go to the police station and knew that it would all soon be over.

7

An elegant carriage stood in the middle of the road with a pair of spirited grey horses; there was no one in it, and the coachman had got off his box and stood by; the horses were being held by the bridle . . . A mass of people had gathered round, the police standing in front. One of them held a lighted lantern which he was turning on something lying close to the wheels. Every one was talking, shouting, exclaiming; the coachman seemed at a loss and kept repeating:

"What a misfortune! Good Lord, what a misfortune!"

Raskolnikov pushed his way in as far as he could, and succeeded at last in seeing the object of the commotion and interest. On the ground a man who had been run over lay apparently unconscious, and covered with blood; he was very badly dressed, but not like a workman. Blood was flowing from his head and face; his face was crushed, mutilated and disfigured. He was evidently badly injured.

"Merciful heaven!" wailed the coachman, "what more could I do? If I'd been driving fast or had not shouted to him, but I was going quietly, not in a hurry. Every one could see I was going along just like everybody else. A drunken man can't walk straight, we all know. . . . I saw him crossing the street, staggering and almost falling. I shouted again and a second and a third time, then I held the horses in, but he fell straight under their feet! Either he did it on purpose or he was very tipsy. . . . The horses are young and ready to take fright . . . they started, he screamed . . . that made them worse. That's how it happened!"

"That's just how it was," a voice in the crowd confirmed.

"He shouted, that's true, he shouted three times," another voice declared.

"Three times it was, we all heard it," shouted a third.

But the coachman was not very much distressed and frightened. It was evident that the carriage belonged to a rich and important person who was awaiting it somewhere; the police, of course, were in no little anxiety to avoid upsetting his arrangements. All they had to do was to take the injured man to the police station and the hospital. No one knew his name.

Meanwhile Raskolnikov had squeezed in and stooped closer over him. The lantern suddenly lighted up the unfortunate man's face. He recognised him.

"I know him! I know him!" he shouted, pushing to the front. "It's a government clerk retired from the service, Marmeladov. He lives close by in Kozel's house. . . . Make haste for a doctor! I will pay, see." He pulled money out of his pocket and showed it to the policeman. He was in violent agitation.

The police were glad that they had found out who the man was. Raskolnikov gave his own name and address, and, as earnestly as if it had been his father, he besought the police to carry the unconscious Marmeladov to his lodging at once.

"Just here, three houses away," he said eagerly, "the house belongs to Kozel, a rich German. He was going home, no doubt drunk. I know him, he is a drunkard. He has a family there, a wife, children, he has one daughter. . . . It will take time to take him to the hospital, and there is sure to be a doctor in the house. I'll pay, I'll pay! At least he will be looked after at home . . . they will help him at once. But he'll die before you get him to the hospital." He managed to slip something unseen into the policeman's hand. But the thing was straightforward and legitimate, and in any case help was closer here. They raised the injured man; people volunteered to help.

Kozel's house was thirty yards away. Raskolnikov walked behind, carefully holding Marmeladov's head and showing the way.

"This way, this way! We must take him upstairs head foremost. Turn round! I'll pay, I'll make it worth your while," he muttered.

Katerina Ivanovna had just begun, as she always did at every free moment, walking to and fro in her little room from window to stove and back again, with her arms folded across her chest, talking to herself and coughing. Of late she had begun to talk more than ever to her eldest girl, Polenka, a child of ten, who, though there was much she did not understand, understood very well that her mother needed her, and so always watched her with her big clever eyes and strove her utmost to appear to understand. This time Polenka was undressing her little brother, who had been unwell all day and was going to bed. The boy was waiting for her to take off his shirt, which had to be washed at night. He was sitting straight and motionless on a chair, with a silent, serious face, with his legs stretched out straight before him—heels together and toes turned out.

He was listening to what his mother was saying to his sister, sitting perfectly still with pouting lips and wide-open eyes, just as all good little boys have to sit when they are undressed to go to bed. A little girl, still younger, dressed literally in rags, stood at the screen, waiting for her turn. The door on to the stairs was open to relieve them a little from the clouds of tobacco smoke which floated in from the other rooms and brought on long terrible fits of coughing in the poor, consumptive woman. Katerina Ivanovna seemed to have grown even thinner during that week and the hectic flush on her face was brighter than ever.

"You wouldn't believe, you can't imagine, Polenka," she said, walking about the room, "what a happy luxurious life we had in my papa's house and how this drunkard has brought me, and will bring you all, to ruin! Papa was a civil colonel and only a step from being a governor; so that every one who came to see him said, 'We look upon you, Ivan Mihailovitch, as our governor!' When I . . . when . . ." she coughed violently, "oh, cursed life," she cried, clearing her throat and pressing her hands to her breast, "when I . . . when at the last ball . . . at the marshal's . . . Princess Bezzemelny saw me—who gave me the blessing when your father and I were married Polenka—she asked at once 'Isn't that the pretty girl who danced the shawl dance at the breaking up?' (You must mend that tear, you must take your needle and darn it as I showed you, or to-morrow—cough, cough, cough—he will make the hole bigger," she articulated with effort.) "Prince Schegolskoy, a kammerjunker, had just come from Petersburg then . . . he danced the mazurka with me and wanted to make me an offer next day; but I thanked him in flattering expressions and told him that my heart had long been another's. That other was your father, Polya; papa was fearfully angry. . . . Is the water ready? Give me the shirt, and the stockings! Lida," said she to the youngest one, "you must manage without your chemise to-night . . . and lay your stockings out with it . . . I'll wash them together. . . . How is it that drunken vagabond doesn't come in? He has worn his shirt till it looks like a dishclout, he has torn it to rags! I'd do it all together, so as not to have to work two nights running! Oh, dear! (Cough, cough, cough, cough!) Again! What's this?" she cried, noticing a crowd in the passage and the men who were pushing into her room, carrying a burden. "What is it? What are they bringing? Mercy on us!"

"Where are we to put him?" asked the policeman, looking round when Marmeladov, unconscious and covered with blood, had been carried in.

"On the sofa! Put him straight on the sofa, with his head this way," Raskolnikov showed him.

"Run over in the road! Drunk!" some one shouted in the passage.

Katerina Ivanovna stood, turning white and gasping for breath. The children were terrified. Little Lida screamed, rushed to Polenka and clutched at her, trembling all over.

Having laid Marmeladov down, Raskolnikov flew to Katerina Ivanovna.

"For God's sake be calm, don't be frightened!" he said, speaking quickly, "he was crossing the road and was run over by a carriage, don't be frightened, he will come to, I told them to bring him here . . . I've been here already, you remember? He will come to; I'll pay!"

"He's done it this time!" Katerina Ivanovna cried despairingly and she rushed to her husband.

Raskolnikov noticed at once that she was not one of those women who swoon easily. She instantly placed under the luckless man's head a pillow, which no one had thought of and began undressing and examining him. She kept her head, forgetting herself, biting her trembling lips and stifling the screams which were ready to break from her.

Raskolnikov meanwhile induced some one to run for a doctor. There was a doctor, it appeared, next door but one.

"I've sent for a doctor," he kept assuring Katerina Ivanovna, "don't be uneasy, I'll pay. Haven't you water? . . . and give me a napkin or a towel, anything, as quick as you can. . . . He is injured, but not killed, believe me. . . . We shall see what the doctor says!"

Katerina Ivanovna ran to the window; there, on a broken chair in the corner, a large earthenware basin full of water had been stood, in readiness for washing her children's and husband's linen that night. This washing was done by Katerina Ivanovna at night at least twice a week, if not oftener. For the family had come to such a pass that they were practically without change of linen, and Katerina Ivanovna could not endure uncleanliness and, rather than see dirt in the house, she preferred to wear herself out at night, working beyond her strength when the rest were asleep, so as to get the wet linen hung on a line and dry by the morning. She took up the basin of water at Raskolnikov's request, but almost fell down with her burden. But the latter had already succeeded in finding a towel, wetted it and begun washing the blood off Marmeladov's face.

Katerina Ivanovna stood by, breathing painfully and pressing her hands to her breast. She was in need of attention herself. Raskolnikov began to realise that he might have made a mistake in having the injured man brought here. The policeman, too, stood in hesitation.

"Polenka," cried Katerina Ivanovna, "run to Sonia, make haste. If you don't find her at home, leave word that her father has been run over and that she is to come here at once . . . when she comes in. Run, Polenka! there, put on the shawl."

"Run your fastest!" cried the little boy on the chair suddenly, after which he relapsed into the same dumb rigidity, with round eyes, his heels thrust forward and his toes spread out.

Meanwhile the room had become so full of people that you couldn't have dropped a pin. The policemen left, all except one, who remained for a time, trying to drive out the people who came in from the stairs. Almost all Madame Lippevechsel's lodgers had streamed in from the inner rooms of the flat; at first they were squeezed together in the doorway, but afterwards they overflowed into the room. Katerina Ivanovna flew into a fury.

"You might let him die in peace, at least," she shouted at the crowd, "is it a spectacle for you to gape at? With cigarettes! (Cough, cough, cough!) You might as well keep your hats on. . . . And there is one in his hat! . . . Get away! You should respect the dead, at least!"

Her cough choked her—but her reproaches were not without result. They evidently stood in some awe of Katerina Ivanovna. The lodgers, one after another, squeezed back into the doorway with that strange inner feeling of satisfaction which may be observed in the presence of a sudden accident, even in those nearest and dearest to the victim, from which no living man is exempt, even in spite of the sincerest sympathy and compassion.

Voices outside were heard, however, speaking of the hospital and saying that they'd no business to make a disturbance here.

"No business to die!" cried Katerina Ivanovna, and she was rushing to the door to vent her wrath upon them, but in the doorway came face to face with Madame Lippevechsel who had only just heard of the accident and ran in to restore order. She was a particularly quarrelsome and irresponsible German.

"Ah, my God!" she cried, clasping her hands, "your husband drunken horses have trampled! To the hospital with him! I am the landlady!"

"Amalia Ludwigovna, I beg you to recollect what you are saying," Katerina Ivanovna began haughtily (she always took a haughty tone with the landlady that she might "remember her place" and even now could not deny herself this satisfaction). "Amalia Ludwigovna . . ."

"I have you once before told that you that you to call me Amalia Ludwigovna may not dare; I am Amalia Ivanovna."

"You are not Amalia Ivanovna, but Amalia Ludwigovna, and as I am not one of your despicable flatterers like Mr. Lebeziatnikov, who's laughing behind the door at this moment (a laugh and a cry of 'they are at it again' was in fact audible at the door) so I shall always call you Amalia Ludwigovna, though I fail to understand why you dislike that name. You can see for yourself what has happened to Semyon Zaharovitch; he is dying. I beg you to close that door at once and to admit no one. Let him at least die in peace! Or I warn you the Governor-General, himself, shall be informed of your conduct to-morrow. The prince knew me as a girl; he remembers Semyon Zaharovitch well and has often been a benefactor to him. Every one knows that Semyon Zaharovitch had many friends and protectors, whom he abandoned himself from an honourable pride, knowing his unhappy weakness, but now (she pointed to Raskolnikov) a generous young man has come to our assistance, who has wealth and connections and whom Semyon Zaharovitch has known from a child. You may rest assured, Amalia Ludwigovna . . ."

All this was uttered with extreme rapidity, getting quicker and quicker, but a cough suddenly cut short Katerina Ivanovna's eloquence. At that instant the dying man recovered consciousness and uttered a groan; she ran to him. The injured man opened his eyes and without recognition or understanding gazed at Raskolnikov who was bending over him. He drew deep, slow, painful breaths; blood oozed at the corners of his mouth and drops of perspiration came out on his forehead. Not recognising Raskolnikov, he began looking round uneasily. Katerina Ivanovna looked at him with a sad but stern face, and tears trickled from her eyes.

"My God! His whole chest is crushed! How he is bleeding," she said in despair. "We must take off his clothes. Turn a little, Semyon Zaharovitch, if you can," she cried to him.

Marmeladov recognised her.

"A priest," he articulated huskily.

Katerina Ivanovna walked to the window, laid her head against the window frame and exclaimed in despair:

"Oh, cursed life!"

"A priest," the dying man said again after a moment's silence.

"They've gone for him," Katerina Ivanovna shouted to him; he obeyed her shout and was silent. With sad and timid eyes he looked for her; she returned and stood by his pillow. He seemed a little easier but not for long.

Soon his eyes rested on little Lida, his favourite, who was shaking in the corner, as though she were in a fit, and staring at him with her wondering childish eyes.

"A—ah," he signed towards her uneasily. He wanted to say something.

"What now?" cried Katerina Ivanovna.

"Barefoot, barefoot!" he muttered, indicating with frenzied eyes the child's bare feet.

"Be silent," Katerina Ivanovna cried irritably, "you know why she is barefooted."

"Thank God, the doctor," exclaimed Raskolnikov, relieved.

The doctor came in, a precise little old man, a German, looking about him mistrustfully; he went up to the sick man, took his pulse, carefully felt his head and with the help of Katerina Ivanovna he unbuttoned the blood-stained shirt, and bared the injured man's chest. It was gashed, crushed and fractured, several ribs on the right side were broken. On the left side, just over the heart, was a large, sinister-looking yellowish-black bruise—a cruel kick from the horse's hoof. The doctor frowned. The policeman told him that he was caught in the wheel and turned round with it for thirty yards on the road.

"It's wonderful that he has recovered consciousness," the doctor whispered softly to Raskolnikov.

"What do you think of him?" he asked.

"He will die immediately."

"Is there really no hope?"

"Not the faintest! He is at the last gasp. . . . His head is badly injured, too . . . Him . . . I could bleed him if you like, but . . . it would be useless. He is bound to die within the next five or ten minutes."

"Better bleed him then."

"If you like. . . . But I warn you it will be perfectly useless."

At that moment other steps were heard; the crowd in the passage parted, and the priest, a little, grey old man, appeared in the doorway bearing the sacrament. A policeman had gone for him at the time of the accident. The doctor changed places with him, exchanging glances with him. Raskolnikov begged the doctor to remain a little while. He shrugged his shoulders and remained.

All stepped back. The confession was soon over. The dying man probably understood little; he could only utter indistinct broken sounds. Katerina Ivanovna took little Lida, lifted the boy from the chair, knelt down in the corner by the stove and made the children kneel in front of her. The little girl was still trembling; but the boy, kneeling on his little bare knees, lifted his hand rhythmically, crossing himself with precision and bowed down, touching the floor with his forehead, which seemed to afford him especial satisfaction. Katerina Ivanovna bit her lips and held back her tears; she prayed, too, now and then pulling straight the boy's shirt, and managed to cover the girl's bare shoulders with a kerchief, which she took from the chest without rising from her knees or ceasing to pray. Meanwhile the door from the inner rooms was opened inquisitively again. In the passage the crowd of spectators from all the flats on the staircase grew denser and denser, but they did not venture beyond the threshold. A single candle-end lighted up the scene.

At that moment Polenka forced her way through the crowd at the door. She came in panting from running so fast, took off her kerchief, looked for her mother, went up to her and said, "She's coming, I met her in the street." Her mother made her kneel beside her.

Timidly and noiselessly a young girl made her way through the crowd, and strange was her appearance in that room, in the midst of want, rags, death and despair. She, too, was in rags, her attire was all of the cheapest, but decked out in gutter finery of a special stamp, unmistakably betraying its shameful purpose. Sonia stopped short in the doorway and looked about her bewildered, unconscious of everything. She forgot her fourth-hand, gaudy silk dress, so unseemly here with its ridiculous long train, and her immense crinoline that filled up the whole doorway, and her light-coloured shoes, and the parasol she brought with her, though it was no use at night, and the absurd round straw hat with its flaring flame-coloured feather. Under this rakishly-tilted hat was a pale, frightened little face with lips parted and eyes staring in terror. Sonia was a small thin girl of eighteen with fair hair, rather pretty, with wonderful blue eyes. She looked intently at the bed and the priest; she too was out of breath with running. At last whispers, some words in the crowd probably, reached her. She looked down and took a step forward into the room, still keeping close to the door.

The service was over. Katerina Ivanovna went up to her husband again. The priest stepped back and turned to say a few words of admonition and consolation to Katerina Ivanovna on leaving.

"What am I to do with these?" she interrupted sharply and irritably, pointing to the little ones.

"God is merciful; look to the Most High for succour," the priest began.

"Ach! He is merciful, but not to us."

"That's a sin, a sin, madam," observed the priest, shaking his head.

"And isn't that a sin?" cried Katerina Ivanovna, pointing to the dying man.

"Perhaps those who have involuntarily caused the accident will agree to compensate you, at least for the loss of his earnings."

"You don't understand!" cried Katerina Ivanovna angrily waving her hand. "And why should they compensate me? Why, he was drunk and threw himself under the horses! What earnings? He brought us in nothing but misery. He drank everything away, the drunkard! He robbed us to get drink, he wasted their lives and mine for drink! And thank God he's dying! One less to keep!"

"You must forgive in the hour of death, that's a sin, madam, such feelings are a great sin."

Katerina Ivanovna was busy with the dying man; she was giving him water, wiping the blood and sweat from his head, setting his pillow straight, and had only turned now and then for a moment to address the priest. Now she flew at him almost in a frenzy.

"Ah, father! That's words and only words! Forgive! If he'd not been run over, he'd have come home to-day drunk and his only shirt dirty and in rags and he'd have fallen asleep like a log, and I should have been sousing and rinsing till daybreak, washing his rags and the children's and then drying them by the window and as soon as it was daylight I should have been darning them. That's how I spend my nights! . . . What's the use of talking of forgiveness! I have forgiven as it is!"

A terrible hollow cough interrupted her words. She put her handkerchief to her lips and showed it to the priest, pressing her other hand to her aching chest. The handkerchief was covered with blood. The priest bowed his head and said nothing.

Marmeladov was in the last agony; he did not take his eyes off the face of Katerina Ivanovna, who was bending over him again. He kept trying to say something to her; he began moving his tongue with difficulty and articulating indistinctly, but Katerina Ivanovna, understanding that he wanted to ask her forgiveness, called peremptorily to him:

"Be silent! No need! I know what you want to say!" And the sick man was silent, but at the same instant his wandering eyes strayed to the doorway and he saw Sonia.

Till then he had not noticed her: she was standing in the shadow in a corner.

"Who's that? Who's that?" he said suddenly in a thick gasping voice, in agitation, turning his eyes in horror towards the door where his daughter was standing, and trying to sit up.

"Lie down! Lie do-own!" cried Katerina Ivanovna.

With unnatural strength he had succeeded in propping himself on his elbow. He looked wildly and fixedly for some time on his daughter, as though not recognising her. He had never seen her before in such attire. Suddenly he recognised her, crushed and ashamed in her humiliation and gaudy finery, meekly awaiting her turn to say good-bye to her dying father. His face showed intense suffering.

"Sonia! Daughter! Forgive!" he cried, and he tried to hold out his hand to her, but losing his balance, he fell off the sofa, face downwards on the floor. They rushed to pick him up, they put him on the sofa; but he was dying. Sonia with a faint cry ran up, embraced him and remained so without moving. He died in her arms.

"He's got what he wanted," Katerina Ivanovna cried, seeing her husband's dead body. "Well, what's to be done now? How am I to bury him! What can I give them to-morrow to eat?"

Raskolnikov went up to Katerina Ivanovna.

"Katerina Ivanovna," he began, "last week your husband told me all his life and circumstances. . . . Believe me, he spoke of you with passionate reverence. From that evening, when I learnt how devoted he was to you all and how he loved and respected you especially, Katerina Ivanovna, in spite of his unfortunate weakness, from that evening we became friends. . . . Allow me now . . . to do something . . . to repay my debt to my dead friend. Here are twenty roubles I think—and if that can be of any assistance to you, then . . . I . . . in short, I will come again, I will be sure to come again . . . I shall, perhaps, come again to-morrow. . . . Good-bye!"

And he went quickly out of the room, squeezing his way through the crowd to the stairs. But in the crowd he suddenly jostled against Nikodim Fomitch, who had heard of the accident and had come to give instructions in person. They had not met since the scene at the police station, but Nikodim Fomitch knew him instantly.

"Ah, is that you?" he asked him.

"He's dead," answered Raskolnikov. "The doctor and the priest have been, all as it should have been. Don't worry the poor woman too much, she is in consumption as it is. Try and cheer her up, if possible . . . you are a kind-hearted man, I know . . ." he added with a smile, looking straight in his face.

"But you are spattered with blood," observed Nikodim Fomitch, noticing in the lamplight some fresh stains on Raskolnikov's waistcoat.

"Yes . . . I'm covered with blood," Raskolnikov said with a peculiar air; then he smiled, nodded and went downstairs.

He walked down slowly and deliberately, feverish but not conscious of it, entirely absorbed in a new overwhelming sensation of life and strength that surged up suddenly within him. This sensation might be compared to that of a man condemned to death who has suddenly been pardoned. Halfway down the staircase he was overtaken by the priest on his way home; Raskolnikov let him pass, exchanging a silent greeting with him. He was just descending the last steps when he heard rapid footsteps behind him. Some one overtook him; it was Polenka. She was running after him, calling "Wait! wait!"

He turned round. She was at the bottom of the staircase and stopped short a step above him. A dim light came in from the yard. Raskolnikov could distinguish the child's thin but pretty little face, looking at him with a bright childish smile. She had run after him with a message which she was evidently glad to give.

"Tell me, what is your name? . . . and where do you live?" she said hurriedly in a breathless voice.

He laid both hands on her shoulders and looked at her with a sort of rapture. It was such a joy to him to look at her, he could not have said why.

"Who sent you?"

"Sister Sonia sent me," answered the girl, smiling still more brightly.

"I knew it was sister Sonia sent you."

"Mamma sent me, too . . . when sister Sonia was sending me, mamma came up, too, and said 'Run fast, Polenka.' "

"Do you love sister Sonia?"

"I love her more than any one," Polenka answered with a peculiar earnestness, and her smile became graver.

"And will you love me?"

By way of answer he saw the little girl's face approaching him, her full lips naïvely held out to kiss him. Suddenly her arms as thin as sticks held him tightly, her head rested on his shoulder and the little girl wept softly, pressing her face against him.

"I am sorry for father," she said a moment later, raising her tear-stained face and brushing away the tears with her hands. "It's nothing but misfortunes now," she added suddenly with that peculiarly sedate air which children try hard to assume when they want to speak like grown-up people.

"Did your father love you?"

"He loved Lida most," she went on very seriously without a smile, exactly like grown-up people, "he loved her because she is little and because she is ill, too. And he always used to bring her presents. But he taught us to read and me grammar and scripture, too," she added with dignity. "And mother never used to say anything, but we knew that she liked it and father knew it, too. And mother wants to teach me French, for it's time my education began."

"And do you know your prayers?"

"Of course, we do! We knew them long ago. I say my prayers to myself as I am a big girl now, but Kolya and Lida say them aloud with mother. First they repeat the 'Ave Maria' and then another prayer: 'Lord, forgive and bless sister Sonia,' and then another, 'Lord, forgive and bless our second father.' For our elder father is dead and this is another one, but we do pray for the other as well."

"Polenka, my name is Rodion. Pray sometimes for me, too. 'And Thy servant Rodion,' nothing more."

"I'll pray for you all the rest of my life," the little girl declared hotly, and suddenly smiling again she rushed at him and hugged him warmly once more.

Raskolnikov told her his name and address and promised to be sure to come next day. The child went away quite enchanted with him. It was past ten when he came out into the street. In five minutes he was standing on the bridge at the spot where the woman had jumped in.

"Enough," he pronounced resolutely and triumphantly. "I've done with fancies, imaginary terrors and phantoms! Life is Real! haven't I lived just now? My life has not yet died with that old woman! The Kingdom of Heaven to her—and now enough, madam, leave me in peace! Now for the reign of reason and light . . . and of will, and of strength . . . and now we will see! We will try our strength!" he added defiantly, as though challenging some power of darkness. "And I was ready to consent to live in a square of space!

"I am very weak at this moment, but . . . I believe my illness is all over. I knew it would be over when I went out. By the way, Potchinkov's house is only a few steps away. I certainly must go to Razumihin even if it were not close by . . . let him win his bet! Let us give him some satisfaction, too—no matter! Strength, strength is what one wants, you can get nothing without it, and strength must be won by strength—that's what they don't know," he added proudly and self-confidently and he walked with flagging footsteps from the bridge. Pride and self-confidence grew continually stronger in him; he was becoming a different man every moment. What was it had happened to work this revolution in him? He did not know himself; like a man catching at a straw, he suddenly felt that he, too, 'could live, that there was still life for him, that his life had not died with the old woman.' Perhaps he was in too great a hurry with his conclusion, but he did not think of that.

"But I did ask her to remember 'Thy servant Rodion' in her prayers," the idea struck him. "Well, that was . . . in case of emergency," he added and laughed himself at his boyish sally. He was in the best of spirits.

He easily found Razumihin; the new lodger was already known at Potchinkov's and the porter at once showed him the way. Half-way upstairs he could hear the noise and animated conversation of a big gathering of people. The door was wide open on the stairs; he could hear exclamations and discussion. Razumihin's room was fairly large; the company consisted of fifteen people. Raskolnikov stopped in the entry, where two of the landlady's servants were busy behind a screen with two samovars, bottles, plates and dishes of pie and savouries, brought up from the landlady's kitchen. Raskolnikov sent in for Razumihin. He ran out delighted. At the first glance it was apparent that he had had a great deal to drink and, though no amount of liquor made Razumihin quite drunk, this time he was perceptibly affected by it.

"Listen," Raskolnikov hastened to say, "I've only just come to tell you you've won your bet and that no one really knows what may not happen to him. I can't come in; I am so weak that I shall fall down directly. And so good evening and good-bye! Come and see me to-morrow."

"Do you know what? I'll see you home. If you say you're weak yourself, you must . . ."

"And your visitors? Who is the curly-headed one who has just peeped out?"

"He? Goodness only knows! Some friend of uncle's I expect, or perhaps he has come without being invited . . . I'll leave uncle with them, he is an invaluable person, pity I can't introduce you to him now. But confound them all now! They won't notice me, and I need a little fresh air, for you've come just in the nick of time—another two minutes and I should have come to blows! They are talking such a lot of wild stuff . . . you simply can't imagine what men will say! Though why shouldn't you imagine? Don't we talk nonsense ourselves? And let them . . . that's the way to learn not to! . . . Wait a minute, I'll fetch Zossimov."

Zossimov pounced upon Raskolnikov almost greedily; he showed a special interest in him; soon his face brightened.

"You must go to bed at once," he pronounced, examining the patient as far as he could, "and take something for the night. Will you take it? I got it ready some time ago . . . a powder."

"Two, if you like," answered Raskolnikov. The powder was taken at once.

"It's a good thing you are taking him home," observed Zossimov to Razumihin—"we shall see how he is to-morrow, to-day he's not at all amiss: a considerable change since the afternoon. Live and learn . . ."

"Do you know what Zossimov whispered to me when we were coming out?" Razumihin blurted out, as soon as they were in the street. "I won't tell you everything, brother, because they are such fools. Zossimov told me to talk freely to you on the way and get you to talk freely to me, and afterwards I am to tell him about it, for he's got a notion in his head that you are . . . mad or close on it. Only fancy! In the first place, you've three times the brains he has; in the second, if you are not mad, you needn't care a hang that he has got such a wild idea; and thirdly, that piece of beef whose specialty is surgery has gone mad on mental diseases, and what's brought him to this conclusion about you was your conversation to-day with Zametov."

"Zametov told you all about it?"

"Yes, and he did well. Now I understand what it all means and so does Zametov. . . . Well, the fact is, Rodya . . . the point is . . . I am a little drunk now. . . . But that's . . . no matter . . . the point is that this idea . . . you understand? was just being hatched in their brains . . . you understand? That is, no one ventured to say it aloud, because the idea is too absurd and especially since the arrest of that painter, that bubble's burst and gone for ever. But why are they such fools? I gave Zametov a bit of a thrashing at the time—that's between ourselves, brother; please don't let out a hint that you know of it; I've noticed he is a ticklish subject; it was at Luise Ivanovna's. But to-day, to-day it's all cleared up. That Ilya Petrovitch is at the bottom of it! He took advantage of your fainting at the police station, but he is ashamed of it himself now; I know that . . ."

Raskolnikov listened greedily. Razumihin was drunk enough to talk too freely.

"I fainted then because it was so close and the smell of paint," said Raskolnikov.

"No need to explain that! And it wasn't the paint only: the fever had been coming on for a month; Zossimov testifies to that! But how crushed that boy is now, you wouldn't believe! 'I am not worth his little finger,' he says. Yours, he means. He has good feelings at times, brother. But the lesson, the lesson you gave him to-day in the Palais de Crystal, that was too good for anything! You frightened him at first, you know, he nearly went into convulsions! You almost convinced him again of the truth of all that hideous nonsense, and then you suddenly—put out your tongue at him: 'There now, what do you make of it?' It was perfect! He is crushed, annihilated now! It was masterly, by Jove, it's what they deserve! Ah, that I wasn't there! He was hoping to see you awfully. Porfiry, too, wants to make your acquaintance . . ."

"Ah! . . . he too . . . but why did they put me down as mad?"

"Oh, not mad. I must have said too much, brother. . . . What struck him, you see, was that only that subject seemed to interest you; now it's clear why it did interest you; knowing all the circumstances . . . and how that irritated you and worked in with your illness . . . I am a little drunk, brother, only, confound him, he has some idea of his own . . . I tell you, he's mad on mental diseases. But don't you mind him . . ."

For half a minute both were silent.

"Listen, Razumihin," began Raskolnikov, "I want to tell you plainly: I've just been at a death-bed, a clerk who died . . . I gave them all my money . . . and besides I've just been kissed by some one who, if I had killed any one, would just the same . . . in fact I saw some one else there . . . with a flame-coloured feather . . . but I am talking nonsense; I am very weak, support me . . . we shall be at the stairs directly . . ."

"What's the matter? What's the matter with you?" Razumihin asked anxiously.

"I am a little giddy, but that's not the point, I am so sad, so sad . . . like a woman. Look, what's that? Look, look!"

"What is it?"

"Don't you see? A light in my room, you see? Through the crack . . ."

They were already at the foot of the last flight of stairs, at the level of the landlady's door, and they could, as a fact, see from below that there was a light in Raskolnikov's garret.

"Queer! Nastasya, perhaps," observed Razumihin.

"She is never in my room at this time and she must be in bed long ago, but . . . I don't care! Good-bye!"

"What do you mean? I am coming with you, we'll come in together!"

"I know we are going in together, but I want to shake hands here and say good-bye to you here. So give me your hand, good-bye!"

"What's the matter with you, Rodya?"

"Nothing . . . come along . . . you shall be witness."

They began mounting the stairs, and the idea struck Razumihin that perhaps Zossimov might be right after all. "Ah, I've upset him with my chatter!" he muttered to himself.

When they reached the door they heard voices in the room.

"What is it?" cried Razumihin.

Raskolnikov was the first to open the door; he flung it wide and stood still in the doorway, dumbfounded.

His mother and sister were sitting on his sofa and had been waiting an hour and a half for him. Why had he never expected, never thought of them, though the news that they had started, were on their way and would arrive immediately, had been repeated to him only that day? They had spent that hour and a half plying Nastasya with questions. She was still standing before them and had told them everything by now. They were beside themselves with alarm when they heard of his "running away" to-day, ill and, as they understood from her story, delirious! "Good Heavens, what had become of him?" Both had been weeping, both had been in anguish for that hour and a half.

A cry of joy, of ecstasy, greeted Raskolnikov's entrance. Both rushed to him. But he stood like one dead; a sudden intolerable sensation struck him like a thunderbolt. He did not lift his arms to embrace them, he could not. His mother and sister clasped him in their arms, kissed him, laughed and cried. He took a step, tottered and fell to the ground, fainting.

Anxiety, cries of horror, moans . . . Razumihin who was standing in the doorway flew into the room, seized the sick man in his strong arms and in a moment had him on the sofa.

"It's nothing, nothing!" he cried to the mother and sister—"it's only a faint, a mere trifle! Only just now the doctor said he was much better, that he is perfectly well! Water! See, he is coming to himself, he is all right again!"

And seizing Dounia by the arm so that he almost dislocated it, he made her bend down to see that "he is all right again." The mother and sister looked on him with emotion and gratitude, as their Providence. They had heard already from Nastasya all that had been done for their Rodya during his illness, by this "very competent young man," as Pulcheria Alexandrovna Raskolnikov called him that evening in conversation with Dounia.

PART THREE—

1

Raskolnikov got up, and sat down on the sofa. He waved his hand weakly to Razumihin to cut short the flow of warm and incoherent consolations he was addressing to his mother and sister, took them both by the hand and for a minute or two gazed from one to the other without speaking. His mother was alarmed by his expression. It revealed an emotion agonisingly poignant, and at the same time something immovable, almost insane. Pulcheria Alexandrovna began to cry.

Avdotya Romanovna was pale; her hand trembled in her brother's.

"Go home . . . with him," he said in a broken voice, pointing to Razumihin, "good-bye till to-morrow; to-morrow everything . . . Is it long since you arrived?"

"This evening, Rodya," answered Pulcheria Alexandrovna, "the train was awfully late. But, Rodya, nothing would induce me to leave you now! I will spend the night here, near you . . ."

"Don't torture me!" he said with a gesture of irritation.

"I will stay with him," cried Razumihin, "I won't leave him for a moment. Bother all my visitors! Let them rage to their hearts' content! My uncle is presiding there."

"How, how can I thank you!" Pulcheria Alexandrovna was beginning, once more pressing Razumihin's hands, but Raskolnikov interrupted her again.

"I can't have it! I can't have it!" he repeated irritably, "don't worry me! Enough, go away . . . I can't stand it!"

"Come, mamma, come out of the room at least for a minute," Dounia whispered in dismay; "we are distressing him, that's evident."

"Mayn't I look at him after three years?" wept Pulcheria Alexandrovna.

"Stay," he stopped them again, "you keep interrupting me, and my ideas get muddled. . . . Have you seen Luzhin?"

"No, Rodya, but he knows already of our arrival. We have

heard, Rodya, that Pyotr Petrovitch was so kind as to visit you to-day," Pulcheria Alexandrovna added somewhat timidly.

"Yes . . . he was so kind . . . Dounia, I promised Luzhin I'd throw him downstairs and told him to go to hell. . . ."

"Rodya, what are you saying! Surely, you don't mean to tell us . . ." Pulcheria Alexandrovna began in alarm, but she stopped, looking at Dounia.

Avdotya Romanovna was looking attentively at her brother, waiting for what would come next. Both of them had heard of the quarrel from Nastasya, so far as she had succeeded in understanding and reporting it, and were in painful perplexity and suspense.

"Dounia," Raskolnikov continued with an effort, "I don't want that marriage, so at the first opportunity to-morrow you must refuse Luzhin, so that we may never hear his name again."

"Good Heavens!" cried Pulcheria Alexandrovna.

"Brother, think what you are saying!" Avdotya Romanovna began impetuously, but immediately checked herself. "You are not fit to talk now, perhaps; you are tired," she added gently.

"You think I am delirious? No . . . You are marrying Luzhin for *my* sake. But I won't accept the sacrifice. And so write a letter before to-morrow, to refuse him . . . Let me read it in the morning and that will be the end of it!"

"That I can't do!" the girl cried, offended, "what right have you . . ."

"Dounia, you are hasty, too, be quiet, to-morrow . . . Don't you see . . ." the mother interposed in dismay. "Better come away!"

"He is raving," Razumihin cried tipsily, "or how would he dare! To-morrow all this nonsense will be over . . . to-day he certainly did drive him away. That was so. And Luzhin got angry, too . . . He made speeches here, wanted to show off his learning and he went out crest-fallen. . . ."

"Then it's true?" cried Pulcheria Alexandrovna.

"Good-bye till to-morrow, brother," said Dounia compassionately—"let us go, mother . . . Good-bye, Rodya."

"Do you hear, sister," he repeated after them, making a last effort, "I am not delirious; this marriage is—an infamy. Let me act like a scoundrel, but you mustn't . . . one is enough . . . and though I am a scoundrel, I wouldn't own such a sister. It's me or Luzhin! Go now. . . ."

"But you're out of your mind! Despot!" roared Razumihin; but Raskolnikov did not and perhaps could not answer. He lay down on the sofa, and turned to the wall, utterly exhausted. Avdotya Romanovna looked with interest at Razumihin; her black eyes flashed; Razumihin positively started at her glance.

Pulcheria Alexandrovna stood overwhelmed.

"Nothing would induce me to go," she whispered in despair to Razumihin. "I will stay somewhere here . . . escort Dounia home."

"You'll spoil everything," Razumihin answered in the same whisper, losing patience—"come out on to the stairs, anyway. Nastasya, show a light! I assure you," he went on in a half whisper on the stairs—"that he was almost beating the doctor and me this afternoon! Do you understand? The doctor himself! Even he gave way and left him, so as not to irritate him. I remained downstairs on guard, but he dressed at once and slipped off. And he will slip off again if you irritate him, at this time of night, and will do himself some mischief. . . ."

"What are you saying?"

"And Avdotya Romanovna can't possibly be left in those lodgings without you. Just think where you are staying! That blackguard Pyotr Petrovitch couldn't find you better lodgings . . . But you know I've had a little to drink, and that's what makes me . . . swear; don't mind it. . . ."

"But I'll go to the landlady here," Pulcheria Alexandrovna insisted, "I'll beseech her to find some corner for Dounia and me for the night. I can't leave him like that, I cannot!"

This conversation took place on the landing just before the landlady's door. Nastasya lighted them from a step below. Razumihin was in extraordinary excitement. Half an hour earlier, while he was bringing Raskolnikov home, he had indeed talked too freely, but he was aware of it himself, and his head was clear in spite of the vast quantities he had imbibed. Now he was in a state bordering on ecstasy, and all that he had drunk seemed to fly to his head with redoubled effect. He stood with the two ladies, seizing both by their hands, persuading them, and giving them reasons with astonishing plainness of speech, and at almost every word he uttered, probably to emphasize his arguments, he squeezed their hands painfully as in a vice. He stared at Avdotya Romanovna without the least regard for good manners. They sometimes pulled their hands out of his huge bony paws, but far from noticing what was the matter, he drew them all the closer to him. If they'd told him to jump head foremost from the staircase, he would have done it without thought or hesitation in their service. Though Pulcheria Alexandrovna felt that the young man was really too eccentric and pinched her hand too much, in her anxiety over her Rodya she looked on his presence as providential, and was unwilling to notice all his peculiarities. But though Avdotya Romanovna shared her anxiety, and was not of timorous disposition, she could not see the glowing light in his eyes without wonder and almost alarm. It was only the unbounded confidence inspired by Nastasya's account of her brother's queer friend, which prevented her from trying to run away from him, and to persuade her mother to do the same. She realised, too, that even running away was perhaps impossible now. Ten minutes later, however, she was considerably reassured; it was characteristic of Razumihin that he showed his true nature at once, whatever mood he might be in, so that people quickly saw the sort of man they had to deal with.

"You can't go to the landlady, that's perfect nonsense!" he cried. "If you stay, though you are his mother, you'll drive him to a frenzy, and then goodness knows what will happen! Listen, I'll tell you what I'll do: Nastasya will stay with him now, and I'll conduct you both home, you can't be in the streets alone; Petersburg is an awful place in that way . . . But no matter! Then I'll run straight back here and a quarter of an hour later, on my word of honour, I'll bring you news how he is, whether he is asleep, and all that. Then, listen! Then I'll run home in a twinkling—I've a lot of friends there, all drunk—I'll fetch Zossimov—that's the doctor who is looking after him, he is there, too, but he is not drunk; he is not drunk, he is never drunk! I'll drag him to Rodya, and then to you, so that you'll get two reports in the hour—from the doctor, you understand, from the doctor himself, that's a very different thing from my account of him! If there's anything wrong, I swear I'll bring you here myself, but, if it's all right, you go to bed. And I'll spend the night here, in the passage, he won't hear me, and I'll tell Zossimov to sleep at the landlady's, to be at hand. Which is better for him: you or the doctor? So come home then! But the landlady is out of the question; it's all right for me, but it's out of the question for you: she wouldn't take you, for she's . . . for she's a fool . . . She'd be jealous on my account of Avdotya Romanovna and of you, too, if you want to know . . . of Avdotya Romanovna certainly. She is an absolutely, absolutely unaccountable character! But I am a fool, too! . . . No matter! Come along! Do you trust me? Come, do you trust me or not?"

"Let us go, mother," said Avdotya Romanovna, "he will certainly do what he has promised. He has saved Rodya already, and if the doctor really will consent to spend the night here, what could be better?"

"You see, you . . . you . . . understand me, because you are an angel!" Razumihin cried in ecstasy, "let us go! Nastasya! Fly upstairs and sit with him with a light; I'll come in a quarter of an hour."

Though Pulcheria Alexandrovna was not perfectly convinced, she made no further resistance. Razumihin gave an arm to each and drew them down the stairs. He still made her uneasy, as though he was competent and good-natured, was he capable of carrying out his promise? He seemed in such a condition. . . .

"Ah, I see you think I am in such a condition!" Razumihin broke in upon her thoughts, guessing them, as he strolled along the pavement with huge steps, so that the two ladies could hardly keep up with him, a fact he did not observe, however. "Nonsense! That is . . . I am drunk like a fool, but that's not it; I am not drunk from wine. It's seeing you has turned my head . . . But don't mind me! Don't take any notice: I am talking nonsense, I am not worthy of you . . . I am utterly unworthy of you! The minute I've taken you home, I'll pour a couple of pailfuls of water

over my head in the gutter here, and then I shall be all right
. . . If only you knew how I love you both! Don't laugh, and don't
be angry! You may be angry with any one, but not with me! I am
his friend, and therefore I am your friend, too, I want to be
. . . I had a presentiment . . . Last year there was a moment
. . . though it wasn't a presentiment really, for you seem to have
fallen from heaven. And I expect I shan't sleep all night . . .
Zossimov was afraid a little time ago that he would go mad
. . . that's why he mustn't be irritated."

"What do you say?" cried the mother.

"Did the doctor really say that?" asked Avdotya Romanovna, alarmed.

"Yes, but it's not so, not a bit of it. He gave him some
medicine, a powder, I saw it, and then your coming here.
. . . Ah! It would have been better if you had come to-morrow.
It's a good thing we went away. And in an hour Zossimov himself
will report to you about everything. He is not drunk! And I shan't
be drunk . . . And what made me get so tight? Because they got
me into an argument, damn them! I've sworn never to argue!
They talk such trash! I almost came to blows! I've left my uncle
to preside. Would you believe, they insist on complete absence
of individualism and that's just what they relish! Not to be themselves, to be as unlike themselves as they can. That's what they
regard as the highest point of progress. If only their nonsense
were their own, but as it is . . ."

"Listen!" Pulcheria Alexandrovna interrupted timidly, but it
only added fuel to the flames.

"What do you think?" shouted Razumihin, louder than ever,
"you think I am attacking them for talking nonsense? Not a bit!
I like them to talk nonsense. That's man's one privilege over all
creation. Through error you come to the truth! I am a man
because I err! You never reach any truth without making fourteen
mistakes and very likely a hundred and fourteen. And a fine thing,
too, in its way; but we can't even make mistakes on our own
account! Talk nonsense, but talk your own nonsense, and I'll kiss
you for it. To go wrong in one's own way is better than to go right
in some one else's. In the first case you are a man, in the second

you're no better than a bird. Truth won't escape you, but life can be cramped. There have been examples. And what are we doing now? In science, development, thought, invention, ideals, aims, liberalism, judgment, experience and everything, everything, everything, we are still in the preparatory class at school. We prefer to live on other people's ideas, it's what we are used to! Am I right, am I right?" cried Razumihin, pressing and shaking the two ladies' hands.

"Oh, mercy, I do not know," cried poor Pulcheria Alexandrovna.

"Yes, yes . . . though I don't agree with you in everything," added Avdotya Romanovna earnestly and at once uttered a cry, for he squeezed her hand so painfully.

"Yes, you say yes . . . well after that you . . . you . . ." he cried in a transport, "you are a fount of goodness, purity, sense . . . and perfection. Give me your hand . . . you give me yours, too! I want to kiss your hands here at once, on my knees . . ." and he fell on his knees on the pavement, fortunately at that time deserted.

"Leave off, I entreat you, what are you doing?" Pulcheria Alexandrovna cried, greatly distressed.

"Get up, get up!" said Dounia laughing, though she, too, was upset.

"Not for anything till you let me kiss your hands! That's it! Enough! I get up and we'll go on! I am a luckless fool, I am unworthy of you and drunk . . . and I am ashamed. . . . I am not worthy to love you, but to do homage to you is the duty of every man who is not a perfect beast! And I've done homage. . . . Here are your lodgings, and for that alone Rodya was right in driving your Pyotr Petrovitch away. . . . How dare he! how dare he put you in such lodgings! It's a scandal! Do you know the sort of people they take in here? And you his betrothed! You are his betrothed? Yes. Well, then, I'll tell you, your *fiancé* is a scoundrel."

"Excuse me, Mr. Razumihin, you are forgetting . . ." Pulcheria Alexandrovna was beginning.

"Yes, yes, you are right, I did forget myself, I am ashamed

of it," Razumihin made haste to apologise. "But . . . but you can't be angry with me for speaking so! For I speak sincerely and not because . . . hm, hm! That would be disgraceful; in fact not because I'm in . . . hm! Well, anyway I won't say why, I daren't. . . . But we all saw to-day when he came in that that man is not of our sort. Not because he had his hair curled at the barber's, not because he was in such a hurry to show his wit, but because he is a spy, a speculator, because he is a skinflint and a buffoon. That's evident. Do you think him clever? No, he is a fool, a fool. And is he a match for you? Good heavens! Do you see, ladies?" he stopped suddenly on the way upstairs to their rooms, "though all my friends there are drunk, yet they are all honest, and though we do talk a lot of trash, and I do, too, yet we shall talk our way to the truth at last, for we are on the right path, while Pyotr Petrovitch . . . is not on the right path. Though I've been calling them all sorts of names just now, I do respect them all . . . though I don't respect Zametov, I like him, for he is a puppy, and that bullock Zossimov, because he is an honest man and knows his work. But enough, it's all said and forgiven. Is it forgiven? Well, then, let's go on. I know this corridor, I've been here, there was a scandal here at Number 3. . . . Where are you here? Which number? eight? Well, lock yourselves in for the night, then. Don't let anybody in. In a quarter of an hour I'll come back with news, and half an hour later I'll bring Zossimov, you'll see! Good-bye, I'll run."

"Good heavens, Dounia, what is going to happen?" said Pulcheria Alexandrovna, addressing her daughter with anxiety and dismay.

"Don't worry yourself, mother," said Dounia, taking off her hat and cape. "God has sent this gentleman to our aid, though he has come from a drinking party. We can depend on him, I assure you. And all that he has done for Rodya. . . ."

"Ah. Dounia, goodness knows whether he will come! How could I bring myself to leave Rodya? . . . And how different, how different I had fancied our meeting! How sullen he was, as though not pleased to see us. . . ."

Tears came into her eyes.

"No, it's not that, mother. You didn't see, you were crying all the time. He is quite unhinged by serious illness—that's the reason."

"Ah, that illness! What will happen, what will happen? And how he talked to you, Dounia!" said the mother, looking timidly at her daughter, trying to read her thoughts and already half consoled by Dounia's standing up for her brother, which meant that she had already forgiven him. "I am sure he will think better of it to-morrow," she added, probing her further.

"And I am sure that he will say the same to-morrow . . . about that," Avdotya Romanovna said finally. And, of course, there was no going beyond that, for this was a point which Pulcheria Alexandrovna was afraid to discuss. Dounia went up and kissed her mother. The latter warmly embraced her without speaking. Then she sat down to wait anxiously for Razumihin's return, timidly watching her daughter who walked up and down the room with her arms folded, lost in thought. This walking up and down when she was thinking was a habit of Avdotya Romanovna's and the mother was always afraid to break in on her daughter's mood at such moments.

Razumihin, of course, was ridiculous in his sudden drunken infatuation for Avdotya Romanovna. Yet apart from his eccentric condition, many people would have thought it justified if they had seen Avdotya Romanovna, especially at that moment when she walking to and fro with folded arms, pensive and melancholy. Avdotya Romanovna was remarkably good looking; she was tall, strikingly well-proportioned, strong and self-reliant—the latter quality was apparent in every gesture, though it did not in the least detract from the grace and softness of her movements. In face she resembled her brother, but she might be described as really beautiful. Her hair was dark brown, a little lighter than her brother's; there was a proud light in her almost black eyes and yet at times a look of extraordinary kindness. She was pale, but it was a healthy pallor; her face was radiant with freshness and vigour. Her mouth was rather small; the full red lower lip projected a little as did her chin; it was the only irregularity in her beautiful face, but it gave it a peculiarly individual and almost haughty expression. Her face was always more serious and thoughtful than gay; but how well smiles, how well youthful, lighthearted, irresponsible, laughter suited her face! It was natural enough that a warm, open, simple-hearted, honest giant like Razumihin, who had never seen any one like her and was not quite sober at the time, should lose his head immediately. Besides, as chance would have it, he saw Dounia for the first time transfigured by her love for her brother and her joy at meeting him. Afterwards he saw her lower lip quiver with indignation at her brother's insolent, cruel and ungrateful words—and his fate was sealed.

He had spoken the truth, moreover, when he blurted out in his drunken talk on the stairs that Praskovya Pavlovna, Raskolnikov's eccentric landlady, would be jealous of Pulcheria Alexandrovna as well as of Avdotya Romanovna on his account. Although Pulcheria Alexandrovna was forty-three, her face still retained traces of her former beauty; she looked much younger than her age, indeed, which is almost always the case with women who retain serenity of spirit, sensitiveness and pure sincere warmth of heart to old age. We may add in parenthesis that to preserve all this is the only means of retaining beauty to old age. Her hair had begun to grow grey and thin, there had long been little crow's foot wrinkles round her eyes, her cheeks were hollow and sunken from anxiety and grief, and yet it was a handsome face. She was Dounia over again, twenty years older, but without the projecting underlip. Pulcheria Alexandrovna was emotional, but not sentimental, timid and yielding, but only to a certain point. She could give way and accept a great deal even of what was contrary to her convictions, but there was a certain barrier fixed by honesty, principle and the deepest convictions which nothing would induce her to cross.

Exactly twenty minutes after Razumihin's departure, there came two subdued but hurried knocks at the door: he had come back.

"I won't come in, I haven't time," he hastened to say when the door was opened. "He sleeps like a top, soundly, quietly, and God grant he may sleep ten hours. Nastasya's with him; I told her not to leave till I came. Now I am fetching Zossimov, he will report to you and then you'd better turn in; I can see you are too tired to do anything. . . ."

And he ran off down the corridor.

"What a very competent and . . . devoted young man!" cried Pulcheria Alexandrovna exceedingly delighted.

"He seems a splendid person!" Avdotya Romanovna replied with some warmth, resuming her walk up and down the room.

It was nearly an hour later when they heard footsteps in the corridor and another knock at the door. Both women waited this time completely relying on Razumihin's promise; he actually had succeeded in bringing Zossimov. Zossimov had agreed at once to desert the drinking party to go to Raskolnikov's, but he came reluctantly and with the greatest suspicion to see the ladies, mistrusting Razumihin in his exhilarated condition. But his vanity was at once reassured and flattered; he saw that they were really expecting him as an oracle. He stayed just ten minutes and succeeded in completely convincing and comforting Pulcheria Alexandrovna. He spoke with marked sympathy, but with the reserve and extreme seriousness of a young doctor at an important consultation. He did not utter a word on any other subject and did not display the slightest desire to enter into more personal relations with the two ladies. Remarking at his first entrance the dazzling beauty of Avdotya Romanovna, he endeavoured not to notice her at all during his visit and addressed himself solely to Pulcheria Alexandrovna. All this gave him extraordinary inward satisfaction. He declared that he thought the invalid at this moment going on very satisfactorily. According to his observations the patient's illness was due partly to his unfortunate material surroundings during the last few months, but it had partly also a moral origin, "was so to speak the product of several material and moral influences, anxieties, apprehensions, troubles, certain ideas . . . and so on." Noticing stealthily that Avdotya Romanovna was following his words with close attention, Zossimov allowed himself to enlarge on this theme. On Pulcheria Alexandrovna's anxiously and timidly inquiring as to "some suspicion of insanity," he replied with a composed and candid smile that his words had been exaggerated; that certainly the patient had some fixed idea, something approaching a monomania—he, Zossimov, was now particularly studying this interesting branch of medicine—but that it must be recollected that until to-day the patient had been in delirium and . . . and that no doubt the presence of his family would have a favourable effect on his recovery and distract his mind, "if only all fresh shocks can be avoided," he added significantly. Then he got up, took leave with an impressive and affable bow, while blessings, warm gratitude, and entreaties were showered upon him, and Avdotya Romanovna spontaneously offered her hand to him. He went out exceedingly pleased with his visit and still more so with himself.

"We'll talk to-morrow; go to bed at once!" Razumihin said in conclusion, following Zossimov out. "I'll be with you to-morrow morning as early as possible with my report."

"That's a fetching little girl, Avdotya Romanovna," remarked Zossimov, almost licking his lips as they both came out into the street.

"Fetching? You said fetching?" roared Razumihin and he flew at Zossimov and seized him by the throat. "If you ever dare . . . Do you understand? Do you understand?" he shouted, shaking him by the collar and squeezing him against the wall. "Do you hear?"

"Let me go, you drunken devil," said Zossimov, struggling and when he had let him go, he stared at him and went off into a sudden guffaw. Razumihin stood facing him in gloomy and earnest reflection.

"Of course, I am an ass," he observed, sombre as a storm cloud, "but still . . . you are another."

"No, brother, not at all such another. I am not dreaming of any folly."

They walked along in silence and only when they were close to Raskolnikov's lodgings, Razumihin broke the silence in considerable anxiety.

"Listen," he said, "you're a first-rate fellow, but among your other failings, you're a loose fish, that, I know, and a dirty one, too. You are a feeble, nervous wretch, and a mass of whims, you're getting fat and lazy and can't deny yourself anything—and

I call that dirty because it leads on straight into the dirt. You've let yourself get so slack that I don't know how it is you are still a good, even a devoted doctor. You—a doctor—sleep on a feather bed and get up at night to your patients! In another three or four years you won't get up for your patients. . . . But hang it all, that's not the point! . . . You are going to spend to-night in the landlady's flat here. (Hard work I've had to persuade her!) And I'll be in the kitchen. So here's a chance for you to get to know her better. . . . It's not as you think! There's not a trace of anything of the sort, brother . . . !"

"But I don't think!"

"Here you have modesty, brother, silence, bashfulness, a savage virtue . . . and yet she's sighing and melting like wax, simply melting! Save me from her, by all that's unholy! She's most prepossessing. . . . I'll repay you, I'll do anything. . . ."

Zossimov laughed more violently than ever.

"Well, you are smitten! But what am I to do with her?"

"It won't be much trouble, I assure you. Talk any rot you like to her, as long as you sit by her and talk. You're a doctor, too; try curing her of something. I swear you won't regret it. She has a piano, and you know, I strum a little. I have a song there, a genuine Russian one: 'I shed hot tears.' She likes the genuine article—and well, it all began with that song; Now you're a regular performer, a maître, a Rubinstein. . . . I assure you, you won't regret it!"

"But have you made her some promise? Something signed? A promise of marriage, perhaps?"

"Nothing, nothing, absolutely nothing of the kind! Besides she is not that sort at all. . . . Tchebarov tried that. . . ."

"Well, then, drop her!"

"But I can't drop her like that!"

"Why can't you?"

"Well, I can't, that's all about it! There's an element of attraction here, brother."

"Then why have you fascinated her?"

"I haven't fascinated her; perhaps, I was fascinated myself in my folly. But she won't care a straw whether it's you or I, so long

as somebody sits beside her, sighing. . . . I can't explain the
position, brother . . . look here, you are good at mathematics, and
working at it now . . . begin teaching her the integral calculus;
upon my soul, I'm not joking. I'm in earnest, it'll be just the same
to her. She will gaze at you and sigh for a whole year together.
I talked to her once for two days at a time about the Prussian
House of Lords (for one must talk of something)—she just sighed
and perspired! And you mustn't talk of love—she's bashful to
hysterics—but just let her see you can't tear yourself away—that's
enough. It's fearfully comfortable; you're quite at home, you can
read, sit, lie about, write. You may even venture on a kiss, if
you're careful."

"But what do I want with her?"

"Ach, I can't make you understand! You see, you are made
for each other! I have often been reminded of you! . . . You'll
come to it in the end! So does it matter whether it's sooner or
later? There's the featherbed element here, brother,—ach! and
not only that! There's an attraction here—here you have the end
of the world, an anchorage, a quiet haven, the navel of the earth,
the three fishes that are the foundation of the world, the essence
of pancakes, of savoury fish-pies, of the evening samovar, of soft
sighs and warm shawls, and hot stoves to sleep on—as snug as
though you were dead, and yet you're alive—the advantages of
both at once! Well, hang it, brother, what stuff I'm talking, it's
bedtime! Listen. I sometimes wake up at night; so I'll go in and
look at him. But there's no need, it's all right. Don't you worry
yourself, yet if you like, you might just look in once, too. But if
you notice anything, delirium or fever—wake me at once. But
there can't be. . . ."

2

Razumihin waked up next morning at eight o'clock, troubled
and serious. He found himself confronted with many new and
unlooked-for perplexities. He had never expected that he would
ever wake up feeling like that. He remembered every detail of

the previous day and he knew that a perfectly novel experience had befallen him, that he had received an impression unlike anything he had known before. At the same time he recognised clearly that the dream which had fired his imagination was hopelessly unattainable—so unattainable that he felt positively ashamed of it, and he hastened to pass to the other more practical cares and difficulties bequeathed him by that "thrice accursed yesterday."

The most awful recollection of the previous day was the way he had shown himself "base and mean," not only because he had been drunk, but because he had taken advantage of the young girl's position to abuse her *fiancé* in his stupid jealousy, knowing nothing of their mutual relations and obligations and next to nothing of the man himself. And what right had he to criticise him in that hasty and unguarded manner? Who had asked for his opinion! Was it thinkable that such a creature as Avdotya Romanovna would be marrying an unworthy man for money? So there must be something in him. The lodgings? But after all how could he know the character of the lodgings? He was furnishing a flat . . . Foo, how despicable it all was! And what justification was it that he was drunk? Such a stupid excuse was even more degrading! In wine is truth, and the truth had all come out, "that is, all the uncleanness of his coarse and envious heart!" And would such a dream ever be permissible to him, Razumihin? What was he beside such a girl—he, the drunken noisy braggart of last night? "Was it possible to imagine so absurd and cynical a juxtaposition?" Razumihin blushed desperately at the very idea and suddenly the recollection forced itself vividly upon him of how he had said last night on the stairs that the landlady would be jealous of Avdotya Romanovna . . . that was simply intolerable. He brought his fist down heavily on the kitchen stove, hurt his hand and sent one of the bricks flying.

"Of course," he muttered to himself a minute later with a feeling of self-abasement, "of course, all these infamies can never be wiped out or smoothed over . . . and so it's useless even to think of it, and I must go to them in silence and do my duty

. . . in silence, too. . . . and not ask forgiveness, and say nothing . . . for all is lost now!"

And yet as he dressed he examined his attire more carefully than usual. He hadn't another suit—if he had had, perhaps he wouldn't have put it on. "I would have made a point of not putting it on." But in any case he could not remain a cynic and a dirty sloven; he had no right to offend the feelings of others, especially when they were in need of his assistance and asking him to see them. He brushed his clothes carefully. His linen was always decent; in that respect he was especially clean.

He washed that morning scrupulously—he got some soap from Nastasya—he washed his hair, his neck and especially his hands. When it came to the question whether to shave his stubbly chin or not (Praskovya Pavlovna had capital razors that had been left by her late husband), the question was angrily answered in the negative. "Let it stay as it is! What if they think that I shaved on purpose to . . . ? They certainly would think so! Not on any account!"

"And . . . the worst of it was he was so coarse, so dirty, he had the manners of a pothouse; and . . . and even admitting that he knew he had some of the essentials of a gentleman . . . what was there in that to be proud of? Every one ought to be a gentleman and more than that . . . and all the same (he remembered) he, too, had done little things . . . not exactly dishonest, and yet. . . . and what thoughts he sometimes had; hm . . . and to set all that beside Avdotya Romanovna! Confound it! So be it! Well, he'd make a point then of being dirty, greasy, pothouse in his manners and he wouldn't care! He'd be worse!"

He was engaged in such monologues when Zossimov, who had spent the night in Praskovya Pavlovna's parlour, came in.

He was going home and was in a hurry to look at the invalid first. Razumihin informed him that Raskolnikov was sleeping like a dormouse. Zossimov gave orders that they shouldn't wake him and promised to see him again about eleven.

"If he is still at home," he added. "Damn it all! If one can't control one's patients, how is one to cure them! Do you know whether *he* will go to them, or whether *they* are coming here?"

"They are coming, I think," said Razumihin, understanding the object of the question, "and they will discuss their family affairs, no doubt. I'll be off. You, as the doctor, have more right to be here than I."

"But I am not a father confessor; I shall come and go away; I've plenty to do besides looking after them."

"One thing worries me," interposed Razumihin, frowning. "On the way home I talked a lot of drunken nonsense to him . . . all sort of things . . . and amongst them that you were afraid that he . . . might become insane."

"You told the ladies so, too."

"I know it was stupid! You may beat me if you like! Did you think so seriously?"

"That's nonsense, I tell you, how could I think it seriously! You, yourself, described him as a monomaniac when you fetched me to him . . . and we added fuel to the fire yesterday, you did, that is, with your story about the painter; it was a nice conversation, when he was, perhaps, mad on that very point! If only I'd known what happened then at the police station and that some wretch . . . had insulted him with this suspicion! Hm . . . I would not have allowed that conversation yesterday. These monomaniacs will make a mountain out of a molehill . . . and see their fancies as solid realities. . . . As far as I remember, it was Zametov's story that cleared up half the mystery to my mind. Why, I know one case in which a hypochondriac, a man of forty, cut the throat of a little boy of eight, because he couldn't endure the jokes he made every day at table! And in this case his rags, the insolent police officer, the fever and this suspicion! All that working upon a man half frantic with hypochondria, and with his morbid exceptional vanity! That may well have been the starting-point of illness. Well, bother it all! . . . And, by the way, that Zametov certainly is a nice fellow, but hm . . . he shouldn't have told all that last night. He is an awful chatterbox!"

"But whom did he tell it to? You and me?"

"And Porfiry."

"What does that matter?"

"And by the way, have you any influence on them, his

mother and sister? Tell them to be more careful with him to-day.
. . ."

"They'll get on all right!" Razumihin answered reluctantly.

"Why is he so set against this Luzhin? A man with money and
she doesn't seem to dislike him . . . and they haven't a farthing
I suppose? eh?"

"But what business is it of yours?" Razumihin cried with
annoyance. "How can I tell whether they've a farthing? Ask them
yourself and perhaps you'll find out. . . ."

"Foo, what an ass you are sometimes! Last night's wine has
not gone off yet. . . . Good-bye; thank your Praskovya Pavlovna
from me for my night's lodging. She locked herself in, made no
reply to my *bonjour* through the door; she was up at seven
o'clock, the samovar was taken in to her from the kitchen. I was
not vouchsafed a personal interview. . . ."

At nine o'clock precisely Razumihin reached the lodgings at
Bakaleyev's house. Both ladies were waiting for him with nervous
impatience. They had risen at seven o'clock or earlier. He entered
looking as black as night, bowed awkwardly and was at once
furious with himself for it. He had reckoned without his host:
Pulcheria Alexandrovna fairly rushed at him, seized him by both
hands and was almost kissing them. He glanced timidly at Avdotya Romanovna, but her proud countenance wore at that moment an expression of such gratitude and friendliness, such
complete and unlooked-for respect (in place of the sneering looks
and ill-disguised contempt he had expected), that it threw him
into greater confusion than if he had been met with abuse. Fortunately there was a subject for conversation, and he made haste to
snatch at it.

Hearing that everything was going well and that Rodya had
not yet waked, Pulcheria Alexandrovna declared that she was
glad to hear it, because "she had something which it was very,
very necessary to talk over beforehand." Then followed an inquiry about breakfast and an invitation to have it with them; they
had waited to have it with him. Avdotya Romanovna rang the
bell: it was answered by a ragged dirty waiter, and they asked him
to bring tea which was served at last, but in such a dirty and

disorderly way, that the ladies were ashamed. Razumihin vigorously attacked the lodgings, but, remembering Luzhin, stopped in embarrassment and was greatly relieved by Pulcheria Alexandrovna's questions, which showered in a continual stream upon him.

He talked for three quarters of an hour, being constantly interrupted by their questions, and succeeded in describing to them all the most important facts he knew of the last year of Raskolnikov's life, concluding with a circumstantial account of his illness. He omitted, however, many things, which were better omitted, including the scene at the police station with all its consequences. They listened eagerly to his story, and, when he thought he had finished and satisfied his listeners, he found that they considered he had hardly begun.

"Tell me, tell me! What do you think . . . ?" Excuse me, I still don't know your name!" Pulcheria Alexandrovna put in hastily.

"Dmitri Prokofitch."

"I should like very, very much to know, Dmitri Prokofitch . . . how he looks . . . on things in general now, that is, how can I explain, what are his likes and dislikes? Is he always so irritable? Tell me, if you can, what are his hopes and so to say his dreams? Under what influences is he now? In a word, I should like . . ."

"Ah, mother, how can he answer all that at once?" observed Dounia.

"Good heavens, I had not expected to find him in the least like this, Dmitri Prokofitch!"

"Naturally," answered Razumihin. "I have no mother, but my uncle comes every year and almost every time he can scarcely recognise me, even in appearance, though he is a clever man; and your three years' separation means a great deal. What am I to tell you? I have known Rodion for a year and a half; he is morose, gloomy, proud and haughty, and of late—and perhaps for a long time before—he has been suspicious and fanciful. He has a noble nature and a kind heart. He does not like showing his feelings and would rather do a cruel thing than open his heart freely. Sometimes, though, he is not at all morbid, but simply cold and inhumanly callous; it's as though he were alternating between two characters. Sometimes he is fearfully reserved! He says he is so busy that everything is a hindrance, and yet he lies in bed doing nothing. He doesn't jeer at things, not because he hasn't the wit, but as though he hadn't time to waste on such trifles. He never listens to what is said to him. He is never interested in what interests other people at any given moment. He thinks very highly of himself and perhaps he is right. Well, what more? I think your arrival will have a most beneficial influence upon him."

"God grant it may," cried Pulcheria Alexandrovna, distressed by Razumihin's account of her Rodya.

And Razumihin ventured to look more boldly at Avdotya Romanovna at last. He glanced at her often while he was talking, but only for a moment and looked away again at once. Avdotya Romanovna sat at the table, listening attentively, then got up again and began walking to and fro with her arms folded and her lips compressed, occasionally putting in a question, without stopping her walk. She had the same habit of not listening to what was said. She was wearing a dress of thin dark stuff and she had a white transparent scarf round her neck. Razumihin soon detected signs of extreme poverty in their belongings. Had Avdotya Romanovna been dressed like a queen, he felt that he would not be afraid of her, but perhaps just because she was poorly dressed and that he noticed all the misery of her surroundings, his heart was filled with dread and he began to be afraid of every word he uttered, every gesture he made, which was very trying for a man who already felt diffident.

"You've told us a great deal that is interesting about my brother's character . . . and have told it impartially. I am glad. I thought that you were too uncritically devoted to him," observed Avdotya Romanovna with a smile. "I think you are right that he needs a woman's care," she added thoughtfully.

"I didn't say so; but I daresay you are right, only . . ."

"What?"

"He loves no one and perhaps he never will," Razumihin declared decisively.

"You mean he is not capable of love?"

"Do you know, Avdotya Romanovna, you are awfully like your brother, in everything, indeed!" he blurted out suddenly to his own surprise, but remembering at once what he had just before said of her brother, he turned as red as a crab and was overcome with confusion. Avdotya Romanovna couldn't help laughing when she looked at him.

"You may both be mistaken about Rodya," Pulcheria Alexandrovna remarked, slightly piqued. "I am not talking of our present difficulty, Dounia. What Pyotr Petrovitch writes in this letter and what you and I have supposed may be mistaken, but you can't imagine, Dmitri Prokofitch, how moody and, so to say, capricious he is. I never could depend on what he would do when he was only fifteen. And I am sure that he might do something now that nobody else would think of doing . . . Well, for instance, do you know how a year and a half ago he astounded me and gave me a shock that nearly killed me, when he had the idea of marrying that girl—what was her name—his landlady's daughter?"

"Did you hear about that affair?" asked Avdotya Romanovna.

"Do you suppose—" Pulcheria Alexandrovna continued warmly. "Do you suppose that my tears, my entreaties, my illness, my possible death from grief, our poverty would have made him pause? No, he would calmly have disregarded all obstacles. And yet it isn't that he doesn't love us!"

"He has never spoken a word of that affair to me," Razumihin answered cautiously. "But I did hear something from Praskovya Pavlovna herself, though she is by no means a gossip. And what I heard certainly was rather strange."

"And what did you hear?" both the ladies asked at once.

"Well, nothing very special. I only learned that the marriage, which only failed to take place through the girl's death, was not at all to Praskovya Pavlovna's liking. They say, too, the girl was not at all pretty, in fact I am told positively ugly . . . and such an invalid . . . and queer. But she seems to have had some good qualities. She must have had some good qualities or it's quite inexplicable. . . . She had no money either and he wouldn't have considered her money. . . . But it's always difficult to judge in such matters."

"I am sure she was a good girl," Avdotya Romanovna observed briefly.

"God forgive me, I simply rejoiced at her death. Though I don't know which of them would have caused most misery to the other—he to her or she to him," Pulcheria Alexandrovna concluded. Then she began tentatively questioning him about the scene on the previous day with Luzhin, hesitating and continually glancing at Dounia, obviously to the latter's annoyance. This incident more than all the rest evidently caused her uneasiness, even consternation. Razumihin described it in detail again, but this time he added his own conclusions: he openly blamed Raskolnikov for intentionally insulting Pyotr Petrovitch, not seeking to excuse him on the score of his illness.

"He had planned it before his illness," he added.

"I think so, too," Pulcheria Alexandrovna agreed with a dejected air. But she was very much surprised at hearing Razumihin express himself so carefully and even with a certain respect about Pyotr Petrovitch. Avdotya Romanovna, too, was struck by it.

"So this is your opinion of Pyotr Petrovitch?" Pulcheria Alexandrovna could not resist asking.

"I can have no other opinion of your daughter's future husband," Razumihin answered firmly and with warmth, "and I don't say it simply from vulgar politeness, but because . . . simply because Avdotya Romanovna has of her own free will deigned to accept this man. If I spoke so rudely of him last night, it was because I was disgustingly drunk and . . . mad besides; yes, mad, crazy, I lost my head completely . . . and this morning I am ashamed of it."

He crimsoned and ceased speaking. Avdotya Romanovna flushed, but did not break the silence. She had not uttered a word from the moment they began to speak of Luzhin.

Without her support Pulcheria Alexandrovna obviously did not know what to do. At last, faltering and continually glancing at her daughter, she confessed that she was exceedingly worried by one circumstance.

"You see, Dmitri Prokofitch," she began. "I'll be perfectly open with Dmitri Prokofitch, Dounia?"

"Of course, mother," said Avdotya Romanovna emphatically.

"This is what it is," she began in haste, as though the permission to speak of her trouble lifted a weight off her mind. "Very early this morning we got a note from Pyotr Petrovitch in reply to our letter announcing our arrival. He promised to meet us at the station, you know; instead of that he sent a servant to bring us the address of these lodgings and to show us the way; and he sent a message that he would be here himself this morning. But this morning this note came from him. You'd better read it yourself; there is one point in it which worries me very much . . . you will soon see what that is, and . . . tell me your candid opinion, Dmitri Prokofitch! You know Rodya's character better than any one and no one can advise us better than you can. Dounia, I must tell you, made her decision at once, but I still don't feel sure how to act and I . . . I've been waiting for your opinion."

Razumihin opened the note which was dated the previous evening and read as follows:

"DEAR MADAM, Pulcheria Alexandrovna, I have the honour to inform you that owing to unforeseen obstacles I was rendered unable to meet you at the railway station; I sent a very competent person with the same object in view. I likewise shall be deprived of the honour of an interview with you to-morrow morning by business in the Senate that does not admit of delay, and also that I may not intrude on your family circle while you are meeting your son, and Avdotya Romanovna her brother. I shall have the honour of visiting you and paying you my respects at your lodgings not later than to-morrow evening at eight o'clock precisely, and herewith I venture to present my earnest and, I may add, imperative request that Rodion Romanovitch may not be present at our interview—as he offered me a gross and unprecedented affront on the occasion of my visit to him in his illness yesterday, and, moreover, since I desire from you personally an indispensable and circumstantial explanation upon a certain point, in regard to which I wish to learn your own interpretation. I have the honour to inform you, in anticipation, that if, in spite of my request, I meet Rodion Romanovitch, I shall be compelled to withdraw immediately and then you have only yourself to blame. I write on the assumption that Rodion Romanovitch who appeared so ill at my visit, suddenly recovered two hours later and so, being able to leave the house, may visit you also. I was confirmed in that belief by the testimony of my own eyes in the lodging of a drunken man who was run over and has since died, to whose daughter, a young woman of notorious behaviour, he gave twenty-five roubles on the pretext of the funeral, which gravely surprised me knowing what pains you were at to raise that sum. Herewith expressing my special respect to your estimable daughter, Avdotya Romanovna, I beg you to accept the respectful homage of

> "Your humble servant,
> "P. LUZHIN."

"What am I to do now, Dmitri Prokofitch?" began Pulcheria Alexandrovna, almost weeping. "How can I ask Rodya not to come? Yesterday he insisted so earnestly on our refusing Pyotr Petrovitch and now we are ordered not to receive Rodya! He will come on purpose if he knows, and . . . what will happen then?"

"Act on Avdotya Romanovna's decision," Razumihin answered calmly at once.

"Oh, dear me! She says . . . goodness knows what she says, she doesn't explain her object! She says that it would be best, at least, not that it would be best, but that it's absolutely necessary that Rodya should make a point of being here at eight o'clock and that they must meet. . . . I didn't want even to show him the letter, but to prevent him from coming by some stratagem with your help . . . because he is so irritable. . . . Besides I don't understand about that drunkard who died and that daughter, and how he could have given the daughter all the money . . . which . . ."

"Which cost you such sacrifice, mother," put in Avdotya Romanovna.

"He was not himself yesterday," Razumihin said thoughtfully, "if you only knew what he was up to in a restaurant yesterday, though there was sense in it too. . . . Hm! He did say something, as we were going home yesterday evening, about a dead man and a girl, but I didn't understand a word. . . . But last night, I myself . . ."

"The best thing, mother, will be for us to go to him ourselves and there I assure you we shall see at once what's to be done. Besides, it's getting late—good heavens, it's past ten," she cried looking at a splendid gold enamelled watch which hung round her neck on a thin Venetian chain, and looked entirely out of keeping with the rest of her dress. "A present from her fiancé," thought Razumihin.

"We must start, Dounia, we must start," her mother cried in a flutter. "He will be thinking we are still angry after yesterday, from our coming so late. Merciful heavens!"

While she said this she was hurriedly putting on her hat and mantle; Dounia, too, put on her things. Her gloves, as Razumihin noticed, were not merely shabby but had holes in them, and yet this evident poverty gave the two ladies an air of special dignity, which is always found in people who know how to wear poor clothes. Razumihin looked reverently at Dounia and felt proud of escorting her. "The queen who mended her stockings in prison," he thought, "must have looked then every inch a queen and even more a queen than at sumptuous banquets and levées."

"My God," exclaimed Pulcheria Alexandrovna, "little did I think that I should ever fear seeing my son, my darling, darling Rodya! I am afraid, Dmitri Prokofitch," she added, glancing at him timidly.

"Don't be afraid, mother," said Dounia, kissing her, "better have faith in him."

"Oh, dear, I have faith in him, but I haven't slept all night," exclaimed the poor woman.

They came out into the street.

"Do you know, Dounia, when I dozed a little this morning

I dreamed of Marfa Petrovna . . . she was all in white . . . she came up to me, took my hand, and shook her head at me, but so sternly as though she were blaming me. . . . Is that a good omen? Oh, dear me! You don't know, Dmitri Prokofitch, that Marfa Petrovna's dead!"

"No, I didn't know; who is Marfa Petrovna?"

"She died suddenly; and only fancy . . ."

"Afterwards, mamma," put in Dounia. "He doesn't know who Marfa Petrovna is."

"Ah, you don't know? And I was thinking that you knew all about us. Forgive me, Dmitri Prokofitch, I don't know what I am thinking about these last few days. I look upon you really as a providence for us, and so I took it for granted that you knew all about us. I look on you as a relation. . . . Don't be angry with me for saying so. Dear me, what's the matter with your right hand? Have you knocked it?"

"Yes, I bruised it," muttered Razumihin overjoyed.

"I sometimes speak too much from the heart, so that Dounia finds fault with me. . . . But, dear me, what a cupboard he lives in! I wonder whether he is awake? Does this woman, his landlady, consider it a room? Listen, you say he does not like to show his feelings, so perhaps I shall annoy him with my . . . weaknesses? Do advise me, Dmitri Prokofitch, how am I to treat him? I feel quite distracted, you know."

"Don't question him too much about anything if you see him frown! don't ask him too much about his health; he doesn't like that."

"Ah, Dmitri Prokofitch, how hard it is to be a mother! But here are the stairs. . . . What an awful staircase!"

"Mother, you are quite pale, don't distress yourself, darling," said Dounia caressing her, then with flashing eyes she added: "He ought to be happy at seeing you, and you are tormenting yourself so."

"Wait, I'll peep in and see whether he has waked up."

The ladies slowly followed Razumihin, who went on before, and when they reached the landlady's door on the fourth storey, they noticed that her door was a tiny crack open and that two keen black eyes were watching them from the darkness within. When their eyes met, the door was suddenly shut with such a slam that Pulcheria Alexandrovna almost cried out.

3

"He is well, quite well!" Zossimov cried cheerfully as they entered.

He had come in ten minutes earlier and was sitting in the same place as before, on the sofa. Raskolnikov was sitting in the opposite corner, fully dressed and carefully washed and combed, as he had not been for some time past. The room was immediately crowded, yet Nastasya managed to follow the visitors in and stayed to listen.

Raskolnikov really was almost well, as compared with his condition the day before, but he was still pale, listless, and sombre. He looked like a wounded man or one who has undergone some terrible physical suffering. His brows were knitted, his lips compressed, his eyes feverish. He spoke little and reluctantly, as though performing a duty, and there was a restlessness in his movements.

He only wanted a sling on his arm or a bandage on his finger to complete the impression of a man with a painful abscess or a broken arm. The pale, sombre face lighted up for a moment when his mother and sister entered, but this only gave it a look of more intense suffering, in place of its listless dejection. The light soon died away, but the look of suffering remained, and Zossimov, watching and studying his patient with all the zest of a young doctor beginning to practise, noticed in him no joy at the arrival of his mother and sister, but a sort of bitter, hidden determination to bear another hour or two of inevitable torture. He saw later that almost every word of the following conversation seemed to touch on some sore place and irritate it. But at the same time he marvelled at the power of controlling himself and hiding his feelings in a patient who the previous day had, like a monomaniac, fallen into a frenzy at the slightest word.

"Yes, I see myself now that I am almost well," said Raskolnikov, giving his mother and sister a kiss of welcome which made Pulcheria Alexandrovna radiant at once. "And I don't say this *as I did yesterday,*" he said addressing Razumihin, with a friendly pressure of his hand.

"Yes, indeed, I am quite surprised at him to-day," began Zossimov, much delighted at the ladies' entrance, for he had not succeeded in keeping up a conversation with his patient for ten minutes. "In another three or four days, if he goes on like this, he will be just as before, that is, as he was a month ago, or two . . . or perhaps even three. This has been coming on for a long while. . . . eh? Confess, now, that it has been perhaps your own fault?" he added, with a tentative smile, as though still afraid of irritating him.

"It is very possible," answered Raskolnikov coldly.

"I should say, too," continued Zossimov with zest, "that your complete recovery depends solely on yourself. Now that one can talk to you, I should like to impress upon you that it is essential to avoid the elementary, so to speak, fundamental causes tending to produce your morbid condition: in that case you will be cured, if not, it will go from bad to worse. These fundamental causes I don't know, but they must be known to you. You are an intelligent man, and must have observed yourself, of course. I fancy the first stage of your derangement coincides with your leaving the university. You must not be left without occupation, and so, work and a definite aim set before you might, I fancy, be very beneficial."

"Yes, yes; you are perfectly right. . . . I will make haste and return to the university: and then everything will go smoothly. . . ."

Zossimov, who had begun his sage advice partly to make an effect before the ladies, was certainly somewhat mystified, when, glancing at his patient, he observed unmistakable mockery on his face. This lasted an instant, however. Pulcheria Alexandrovna began at once thanking Zossimov, especially for his visit to their lodging the previous night.

"What! he saw you last night?" Raskolnikov asked, as

though startled. "Then you have not slept either after your journey."

"Ach, Rodya, that was only till two o'clock. Dounia and I never go to bed before two at home."

"I don't know how to thank him either," Raskolnikov went on suddenly frowning and looking down. "Setting aside the question of payment—forgive me for referring to it (he turned to Zossimov)—I really don't know what I have done to deserve such special attention from you! I simply don't understand it . . . and . . . and . . . it weighs upon me, indeed, because I don't understand it. I tell you so candidly."

"Don't be irritated." Zossimov forced himself to laugh. "Assume that you are my first patient—well—we fellows just beginning to practise love our first patients as if they were our children, and some almost fall in love with them. And, of course, I am not rich in patients."

"I say nothing about him," added Raskolnikov, pointing to Razumihin, "though he has had nothing from me either but insult and trouble."

"What nonsense he is talking! Why, you are in a sentimental mood to-day, are you?" shouted Razumihin.

If he had had more penetration he would have seen that there was no trace of sentimentality in him, but something indeed quite the opposite. But Avdotya Romanovna noticed it. She was intently and uneasily watching her brother.

"As for you, mother, I don't dare to speak," he went on, as though repeating a lesson learned by heart. "It is only to-day that I have been able to realise a little how distressed you must have been here yesterday, waiting for me to come back."

When he had said this, he suddenly held out his hand to his sister, smiling without a word. But in this smile there was a flash of real unfeigned feeling. Dounia caught it at once, and warmly pressed his hand, overjoyed and thankful. It was the first time he had addressed her since their dispute the previous day. The mother's face lighted up with ecstatic happiness at the sight of this conclusive unspoken reconciliation. "Yes, that is what I love him for," Razumihin, exaggerating it all, muttered to himself, with a vigorous turn in his chair. "He has these movements."

"And how well he does it all," the mother was thinking to herself. "What generous impulses he has, and how simply, how delicately he put an end to all the misunderstanding with his sister—simply by holding out his hand at the right minute and looking at her like that. . . . And what fine eyes he has, and how fine his whole face is! . . . He is even better looking than Dounia. . . . But, good heavens, what a suit—how terribly he's dressed! . . . Vasya, the messenger boy in Afanasy Ivanitch's shop, is better dressed! I could rush at him and hug him . . . weep over him—but I am afraid. . . . Oh, dear, he's so strange! He's talking kindly, but I'm afraid! Why, what am I afraid of? . . . ."

"Oh, Rodya, you wouldn't believe," she began suddenly, in haste to answer his words to her, "how unhappy Dounia and I were yesterday! Now that it's all over and done with and we are quite happy again—I can tell you. Fancy, we ran here almost straight from the train to embrace you and that woman—ah, here she is! Good morning, Nastasya! . . . She told us at once that you were lying in a high fever and had just run away from the doctor in delirium, and they were looking for you in the streets. You can't imagine how we felt! I couldn't help thinking of the tragic end of Lieutenant Potanchikov, a friend of your father's—you can't remember him, Rodya—who ran out in the same way in a high fever and fell into the well in the courtyard and they couldn't pull him out till next day. Of course, we exaggerated things. We were on the point of rushing to find Pyotr Petrovitch to ask him to help. . . . Because we were alone, utterly alone," she said plaintively and stopped short, suddenly, recollecting it was still somewhat dangerous to speak of Pyotr Petrovitch, although "we are quite happy again."

"Yes, yes. . . . Of course it's very annoying. . . ." Raskolnikov muttered in reply, but with such a preoccupied and inattentive air that Dounia gazed at him in perplexity.

"What else was it I wanted to say," he went on trying to recollect. "Oh, yes; mother, and you too, Dounia, please don't think that I didn't mean to come and see you to-day and was waiting for you to come first."

"What are you saying, Rodya?" cried Pulcheria Alexandrovna. She, too, was surprised.

"Is he answering us as a duty?" Dounia wondered. "Is he being reconciled and asking forgiveness as though he were performing a rite or repeating a lesson?"

"I've only just waked up, and wanted to go to you, but was delayed owing to my clothes; I forgot yesterday to ask her . . . Nastasya . . . to wash out the blood . . . I've only just got dressed."

"Blood! What blood?" Pulcheria Alexandrovna asked in alarm.

"Oh, nothing—don't be uneasy. It was when I was wandering about yesterday, rather delirious, I chanced upon a man who had been run over . . . a clerk . . ."

"Delirious? But you remember everything!" Razumihin interrupted.

"That's true," Raskolnikov answered with special carefulness. "I remember everything even to the slightest detail, and yet—why I did that and went there and said that, I can't clearly explain now."

"A familiar phenomenon," interposed Zossimov, "actions are sometimes performed in a masterly and most cunning way, while the direction of the actions is deranged and dependent on various morbid impressions—it's like a dream."

"Perhaps it's a good thing really that he should think me almost a madman," thought Raskolnikov.

"Why, people in perfect health act in the same way too," observed Dounia, looking uneasily at Zossimov.

"There is some truth in your observation," the latter replied. "In that sense we are certainly all not infrequently like madmen, but with the slight difference that the deranged are somewhat madder, for we must draw a line. A normal man, it is true, hardly exists. Among dozens—perhaps hundreds of thousands—hardly one is to be met with."

At the word "madman," carelessly dropped by Zossimov in his chatter on his favourite subject, every one frowned.

Raskolnikov sat seeming not to pay attention, plunged in thought with a strange smile on his pale lips. He was still meditating on something.

"Well, what about the man who was run over? I interrupted you!" Razumihin cried hastily.

"What?" Raskolnikov seemed to wake up. "Oh . . . I got spattered with blood helping to carry him to his lodging. By the way, mamma, I did an unpardonable thing yesterday. I was literally out of my mind. I gave away all the money you sent me . . . to his wife for the funeral. She's a widow now, in consumption, a poor creature . . . three little children, starving . . . nothing in the house . . . there's a daughter, too . . . perhaps you'd have given it yourself if you'd seen them. But I had no right to do it I admit, especially as I knew how you needed the money yourself. To help others one must have the right to do it, or else *Crevez, chiens, si vous n'êtes pas contents.*" He laughed, "That's right, isn't it, Dounia?"

"No, it's not," answered Dounia firmly.

"Bah! you, too, have ideals," he muttered, looking at her almost with hatred, and smiling sarcastically. "I ought to have considered that. . . . Well, that's praiseworthy, and it's better for you . . . and if you reach a line you won't overstep, you will be unhappy . . . and if you overstep it, maybe you will be still unhappier. . . . But all that's nonsense," he added irritably, vexed at being carried away. "I only meant to say that I beg your forgiveness, mother," he concluded, shortly and abruptly.

"That's enough, Rodya, I am sure that everything you do is very good," said his mother, delighted.

"Don't be too sure," he answered, twisting his mouth into a smile.

A silence followed. There was a certain constraint in all this conversation, and in the silence, and in the reconciliation, and in the forgiveness, and all were feeling it.

"It is as though they were afraid of me," Raskolnikov was thinking to himself, looking askance at his mother and sister.

Pulcheria Alexandrovna was indeed growing more timid the longer she kept silent.

"Yet in their absence I seemed to love them so much," flashed through his mind.

"Do you know, Rodya, Marfa Petrovna is dead," Pulcheria Alexandrovna suddenly blurted out.

"What Marfa Petrovna?"

"Oh, mercy on us—Marfa Petrovna Svidrigaïlov. I wrote you so much about her."

"A-a-h! Yes, I remember. . . . So she's dead! Oh, really?" he roused himself suddenly, as if waking up. "What did she die of?"

"Only imagine, quite suddenly," Pulcheria Alexandrovna answered hurriedly, encouraged by his curiosity. "On the very day I was sending you that letter! Would you believe it, that awful man seems to have been the cause of her death. They say he beat her dreadfully."

"Why, were they on such bad terms?" he asked, addressing his sister.

"Not at all. Quite the contrary indeed. With her, he was always very patient, considerate even. In fact, all those seven years of their married life he gave way to her, too much so indeed, in many cases. All of a sudden he seems to have lost patience."

"Then he could not have been so awful if he controlled himself for seven years? You seem to be defending him, Dounia?"

"No, no, he's an awful man! I can imagine nothing more awful!" Dounia answered, almost with a shudder, knitting her brows, and sinking into thought.

"That had happened in the morning," Pulcheria Alexandrovna went on hurriedly. "And directly afterwards she ordered the horses to be harnessed to drive to the town immediately after dinner. She always used to drive to the town in such cases. She ate a very good dinner, I am told. . . ."

"After the beating?"

"That was always her . . . habit; and immediately after dinner, so as not to be late in starting, she went to the bath-house. . . . You see, she was undergoing some treatment with baths. They have a cold spring there, and she used to bathe in it regularly every day, and no sooner had she got into the water when she suddenly had a stroke!"

"I should think so," said Zossimov.

"And did he beat her badly?"

"What does that matter!" put in Dounia.

"H'm! But I don't know why you want to tell us such gossip, mother," said Raskolnikov irritably, as it were in spite of himself.

"Ah, my dear, I don't know what to talk about," broke from Pulcheria Alexandrovna.

"Why, are you all afraid of me?" he asked, with a constrained smile.

"That's certainly true," said Dounia, looking directly and sternly at her brother. "Mother was crossing herself with terror as she came up the stairs."

His face worked, as though in convulsion.

"Ach, what are you saying, Dounia! Don't be angry, please, Rodya. . . . Why did you say that, Dounia?" Pulcheria Alexandrovna began, overwhelmed—"You see, coming here, I was dreaming all the way, in the train, how we should meet, how we should talk over everything together. . . . And I was so happy, I did not notice the journey! But what am I saying? I am happy now. . . . You should not, Dounia. . . . I am happy now—simply in seeing you, Rodya. . . ."

"Hush, mother," he muttered in confusion, not looking at her, but pressing her hand. "We shall have time to speak freely of everything!"

As he said this, he was suddenly overwhelmed with confusion and turned pale. Again that awful sensation he had known of late passed with deadly chill over his soul. Again it became suddenly plain and perceptible to him that he had just told a fearful lie—that he would never now be able to speak freely of everything—that he would never again be able to *speak* of anything to any one. The anguish of this thought was such that for a moment he almost forgot himself. He got up from his seat, and not looking at any one walked towards the door.

"What are you about?" cried Razumihin, clutching him by the arm.

He sat down again, and began looking about him, in silence. They were all looking at him in perplexity.

"But what are you all so dull for?" he shouted, suddenly and quite unexpectedly. "Do say something! What's the use of sitting like this? Come, do speak. Let us talk. . . . We meet together and sit in silence. . . . Come, anything!"

"Thank God; I was afraid the same thing as yesterday was beginning again," said Pulcheria Alexandrovna, crossing herself.

"What is the matter, Rodya?" asked Avdotya Romanovna, distrustfully.

"Oh, nothing! I remembered something," he answered, and suddenly laughed.

"Well, if you remembered something; that's all right! . . . I was beginning to think . . ." muttered Zossimov, getting up from the sofa. "It is time for me to be off. I will look in again perhaps . . . if I can . . ." He made his bows, and went out.

"What an excellent man!" observed Pulcheria Alexandrovna.

"Yes, excellent, splendid, well-educated, intelligent," Raskolnikov began, suddenly speaking with surprising rapidity, and a liveliness he had not shown till then. "I can't remember where I met him before my illness. . . . I believe I have met him somewhere—— . . . And this is a good man, too," he nodded at Razumihin. "Do you like him, Dounia?" he asked her; and suddenly, for some unknown reason, laughed.

"Very much," answered Dounia.

"Foo—what a pig you are," Razumihin protested, blushing in terrible confusion, and he got up from his chair. Pulcheria Alexandrovna smiled faintly, but Raskolnikov laughed aloud.

"Where are you off to?"

"I must go."

"You need not at all. Stay. Zossimov has gone, so you must. Don't go. What's the time? Is it twelve o'clock? What a pretty watch you have got, Dounia. But why are you all silent again? I do all the talking."

"It was a present from Marfa Petrovna," answered Dounia.

"And a very expensive one!" added Pulcheria Alexandrovna.

"A-ah! What a big one! Hardly like a lady's."

"I like that sort," said Dounia.

"So it is not a present from her fiancé," thought Razumihin, and was unreasonably delighted.

"I thought it was Luzhin's present," observed Raskolnikov.

"No, he has not made Dounia any presents yet."

"A-ah! And do you remember, mother, I was in love and wanted to get married?" he said suddenly, looking at his mother, who was disconcerted by the sudden change of subject and the way he spoke of it.

"Oh, yes, my dear."

Pulcheria Alexandrovna exchanged glances with Dounia and Razumihin.

"H'm, yes. What shall I tell you? I don't remember much indeed. She was such a sickly girl," he went on, growing dreamy and looking down again. "Quite an invalid. She was fond of giving alms to the poor, and was always dreaming of a nunnery, and once she burst into tears when she began talking to me about it. Yes, yes, I remember. I remember very well. She was an ugly little thing. I really don't know what drew me to her then—I think it was because she was always ill. If she had been lame or hunchback, I believe I should have liked her better still," he smiled dreamily. "Yes, it was a sort of spring delirium."

"No, it was not only spring delirium," said Dounia, with warm feeling.

He fixed a strained intent look on his sister, but did not hear or did not understand her words. Then, completely lost in thought, he got up, went up to his mother, kissed her, went back to his place and sat down.

"You love her even now?" said Pulcheria Alexandrovna, touched.

"Her? Now? Oh, yes. . . . You ask about her? No . . . that's all now as it were, in another world . . . and so long ago. And indeed everything happening here seems somehow far away."

He looked attentively at them. "You now . . . I seem to be looking at you from a thousand miles away . . . but, goodness knows why we are talking of that! And what's the use of asking about it," he added with annoyance, and biting his nails, he fell into dreamy silence again.

"What a wretched lodging you have, Rodya! It's like a tomb," said Pulcheria Alexandrovna, suddenly breaking the oppressive silence. "I am sure it's quite half through your lodging you have become so melancholy."

"My lodging," he answered, listlessly. "Yes, the lodging had a great deal to do with it. . . . I thought that, too. . . . If only you knew, though, what a strange thing you said just now, mother," he said, laughing strangely.

A little more, and their companionship, this mother and this sister, with him after three years' absence, this intimate tone of conversation, in face of the utter impossibility of really speaking about anything, would have been beyond his power of endurance. But there was one urgent matter which must be settled one way or the other that day—so he had decided when he woke. Now he was glad to remember it, as a means of escape.

"Listen, Dounia," he began, gravely and drily, "of course I beg your pardon for yesterday, but I consider it my duty to tell you again that I do not withdraw from my chief point. It is me or Luzhin. If I am a scoundrel, you must not be. One is enough. If you marry Luzhin, I cease at once to look on you as a sister."

"Rodya, Rodya! It is the same as yesterday again," Pulcheria Alexandrovna cried, mournfully. "And why do you call yourself a scoundrel? I can't bear it. You said the same yesterday."

"Brother," Dounia answered firmly and with the same dryness. "In all this there is a mistake on your part. I thought it over at night, and found out the mistake. It is all because you seem to fancy I am sacrificing myself to some one and for some one. That is not the case at all. I am simply marrying for my own sake, because things are hard for me. Though, of course, I shall be glad if I succeed in being useful to my family. But that is not the chief motive for my decision. . . ."

"She is lying," he thought to himself, biting his nails vindictively. "Proud creature! She won't admit she wants to do it out of charity! Too haughty! Oh, base characters! They even love as though they hate. . . . Oh, how I . . . hate them all!"

"In fact," continued Dounia, "I am marrying Pyotr Petrovitch because of two evils I choose the less. I intend to do honestly all he expects of me, so I am not deceiving him. . . . Why did you smile just now?" She, too, flushed, and there was a gleam of anger in her eyes.

"All?" he asked, with a malignant grin.

"Within certain limits. Both the manner and form of Pyotr Petrovitch's courtship showed me at once what he wanted. He may, of course, think too well of himself, but I hope he esteems me, too. . . . Why are you laughing again?"

"And why are you blushing again? You are lying, sister. You are intentionally lying, simply from feminine obstinacy, simply to hold your own against me. . . . You cannot respect Luzhin. I have seen him and talked with him. So you are selling yourself for money, and so in any case you are acting basely, and I am glad at least that you can blush for it."

"It is not true. I am not lying," cried Dounia, losing her composure. "I would not marry him if I were not convinced that he esteems me and thinks highly of me. I would not marry him if I were not firmly convinced that I can respect him. Fortunately, I can have convincing proof of it this very day . . . and such a marriage is not a vileness, as you say! And even if you were right, if I really had determined on a vile action, is it not merciless on your part to speak to me like that? Why do you demand of me a heroism that perhaps you have not either? It is despotism; it is tyranny. If I ruin any one, it is only myself. . . . I am not committing a murder. Why do you look at me like that? Why are you so pale? Rodya, darling, what's the matter?"

"Good heavens! You have made him faint," cried Pulcheria Alexandrovna.

"No, no, nonsense! It's nothing. A little giddiness—not fainting. You have fainting on the brain. H'm, yes, what was I saying? Oh, yes. In what way will you get convincing proof to-day that you can respect him, and that he . . . esteems you, as you said. I think you said to-day?"

"Mother, show Rodya Pyotr Petrovitch's letter," said Dounia.

With trembling hands, Pulcheria Alexandrovna gave him the letter. He took it with great interest, but, before opening it, he suddenly looked with a sort of wonder at Dounia.

"It is strange," he said, slowly, as though struck by a new idea. "What am I making such a fuss for? What is it all about? Marry whom you like!"

He said this as though to himself, but said it aloud, and looked for some time at his sister, as though puzzled. He opened the letter at last, still with the same look of strange wonder on his face. Then, slowly and attentively, he began reading, and read it through twice. Pulcheria Alexandrovna showed marked anxiety, and all indeed expected something particular.

"What surprises me," he began, after a short pause, handing the letter to his mother, but not addressing any one in particular, "is that he is a business man, a lawyer, and his conversation is pretentious indeed, and yet he writes such an uneducated letter."

They all started. They had expected something quite different.

"But they all write like that, you know," Razumihin observed, abruptly.

"Have you read it?"

"Yes."

"We showed him, Rodya. We . . . consulted him just now," Pulcheria Alexandrovna began, embarrassed.

"That's just the jargon of the courts," Razumihin put in. "Legal documents are written like that to this day."

"Legal? Yes, it's just legal—business language—not so very uneducated, and not quite educated—business language!"

"Pyotr Petrovitch makes no secret of the fact that he had a cheap education, he is proud indeed of having made his own way," Avdotya Romanovna observed, somewhat offended by her brother's tone.

"Well, if he's proud of it, he has reason, I don't deny it. You seem to be offended, sister, at my making only such a frivolous criticism on the letter, and to think that I speak of such trifling matters on purpose to annoy you. It is quite the contrary, an observation apropos of the style occurred to me that is by no means irrelevant as things stand. There is one expression, 'blame yourselves' put in very significantly and plainly, and there is besides a threat that he will go away at once if I am present. That threat to go away is equivalent to a threat to abandon you both if you are disobedient, and to abandon you now after summoning you to Petersburg. Well, what do you think? Can one resent such an expression from Luzhin, as we should if he (he pointed to Razumihin) had written it, or Zossimov, or one of us?"

"N-no," answered Dounia, with more animation. "I saw clearly that it was too naïvely expressed, and that perhaps he simply has no skill in writing . . . that is a true criticism, brother. I did not expect, indeed . . ."

"It is expressed in legal style, and sounds coarser than perhaps he intended. But I must disillusion you a little. There is one expression in the letter, one slander about me, and rather a contemptible one. I gave the money last night to the widow, a woman in consumption, crushed with trouble, and not 'on the pretext of the funeral,' but simply to pay for the funeral, and not to the daughter—a young woman, as he writes, of notorious behaviour (whom I saw last night for the first time in my life)—but to the widow. In all this I see a too hasty desire to slander me and to raise dissension between us. It is expressed again in legal jargon, that is to say, with a too obvious display of the aim, and with a very naïve eagerness. He is a man of intelligence, but to act sensibly, intelligence is not enough. It all shows the man and . . . I don't think he has a great esteem for you. I tell you this simply to warn you, because I sincerely wish for your good . . ."

Dounia did not reply. Her resolution had been taken. She was only awaiting the evening.

"Then what is your decision, Rodya?" asked Pulcheria Alexandrovna, who was more uneasy than ever at the sudden, new businesslike tone of his talk.

"What decision?"

"You see Pyotr Petrovitch writes that you are not to be with us this evening, and that he will go away if you come. So will you . . . come?"

"That, of course, is not for me to decide, but for you first, if you are not offended by such a request; and secondly, by Dounia, if she, too, is not offended. I will do what you think best," he added drily.

"Dounia has already decided, and I fully agree with her," Pulcheria Alexandrovna hastened to declare.

"I decided to ask you, Rodya, to urge you not to fail to be with us at this interview," said Dounia. "Will you come?"

"Yes."

"I will ask you, too, to be with us at eight o'clock," she said, addressing Razumihin. "Mother, I am inviting him, too."

"Quite right, Dounia. Well, since you have decided," added Pulcheria Alexandrovna, "so be it. I shall feel easier myself. I do not like concealment and deception. Better let us have the whole truth. . . . Pyotr Petrovitch may be angry or not, now!"

4

At that moment the door was softly opened, and a young girl walked into the room, looking timidly about her. Every one turned towards her with surprise and curiosity. At first sight, Raskolnikov did not recognise her. It was Sofya Semyonovna Marmeladov. He had seen her yesterday for the first time, but at such a moment, in such surroundings and in such a dress, that his memory retained a very different image of her. Now she was a modestly and poorly-dressed young girl, very young, indeed almost like a child, with a modest and refined manner, with a candid but somewhat frightened-looking face. She was wearing a very plain indoor dress, and had on a shabby old-fashioned hat, but she still carried a parasol. Unexpectedly finding the room full of people, she was not so much embarrassed as completely over-whelmed with shyness, like a little child. She was even about to retreat. "Oh . . . it's you!" saidRaskolnikov, extremely astonished, and he, too, was confused. He at once recollected that his mother and sister knew through Luzhin's letter of "some young woman of notorious behaviour." He had only just been protesting against Luzhin's calumny and declaring that he had seen the girl last night for the first time, and suddenly she had walked in. He remembered, too, that he had not protested against the expression "of notorious behaviour." All this passed vaguely and fleetingly through his brain, but looking at her more intently, he saw that the humiliated creature was so humiliated that he felt suddenly sorry for her. When she made a movement to retreat in terror, it sent a pang to his heart.

"I did not expect you," he said, hurriedly, with a look that made her stop. "Please sit down. You come, no doubt, from Katerina Ivanovna. Allow me—not there. Sit here. . . ."

At Sonia's entrance, Razumihin, who had been sitting on one of Raskolnikov's three chairs, close to the door, got up to allow her to enter. Raskolnikov had at first shown her the place on the sofa where Zossimov had been sitting, but feeling that the sofa which served him as a bed, was too *familiar* a place, he hurriedly motioned her to Razumihin's chair.

"You sit here," he said to Razumihin, putting him on the sofa.

Sonia sat down, almost shaking with terror, and looked timidly at the two ladies. It was evidently almost inconceivable to herself that she could sit down beside them. At the thought of it, she was so frightened that she hurriedly got up again, and in utter confusion addressed Raskolnikov.

"I . . . I . . . have come for one minute. Forgive me for disturbing you," she began falteringly. "I come from Katerina Ivanovna, and she had no one to send. Katerina Ivanovna told me to beg you . . . to be at the service . . . in the morning . . . at the Mitrofanievsky . . . and then . . . to us . . . to her . . . to do her the honour . . . she told me to beg you . . ." Sonia stammered and ceased speaking.

"I will try, certainly, most certainly," answered Raskolnikov. He, too, stood up, and he, too, faltered and could not finish his sentence. "Please sit down," he said, suddenly. "I want to talk to you. You are perhaps in a hurry, but please, be so kind, spare me two minutes,'' and he drew up a chair for her.

Sonia sat down again, and again timidly she took a hurried, frightened look at the two ladies, and dropped her eyes. Raskolnikov's pale face flushed, a shudder passed over him, his eyes glowed.

"Mother," he said, firmly and insistently, "this is Sofya Semyonovna Marmeladov, the daughter of that unfortunate Mr. Marmeladov, who was run over yesterday before my eyes, and of whom I was just telling you."

Pulcheria Alexandrovna glanced at Sonia, and slightly screwed up her eyes. In spite of her embarrassment before Rodya's urgent and challenging look, she could not deny herself that satisfaction. Dounia gazed gravely and intently into the poor girl's face, and scrutinised her with perplexity. Sonia, hearing herself introduced, tried to raise her eyes again, but was more embarrassed than ever.

"I wanted to ask you," said Raskolnikov, hastily, "how things were arranged yesterday. You were not worried by the police, for instance?"

"No, that was all right . . . it was too evident, the cause of death . . . they did not worry us . . . only the lodgers are angry."

"Why?"

"At the body's remaining so long. You see it is hot now. So that, to-day, they will carry it to the cemetery, into the chapel, until to-morrow. At first Katerina Ivanovna was unwilling, but now she sees herself that it's necessary . . ."

"To-day, then?"

"She begs you to do us the honour to be in the church to-morrow for the service, and then to be present at the funeral lunch."

"She is giving a funeral lunch?"

"Yes . . . just a little. . . . She told me to thank you very much for helping us yesterday. But for you, we should have had nothing for the funeral."

All at once her lips and chin began trembling, but, with an effort, she controlled herself, looking down again.

During the conversation, Raskolnikov watched her carefully. She had a thin, very thin, pale little face, rather irregular and
angular, with a sharp little nose and chin. She could not have been
called pretty, but her blue eyes were so clear, and when they
lighted up, there was such a kindliness and simplicity in her
expression that one could not help being attracted. Her face, and
her whole figure indeed, had another peculiar characteristic. In
spite of her eighteen years, she looked almost a little girl—almost
a child. And in some of her gestures, this childishness seemed
almost absurd.

"But has Katerina Ivanovna been able to manage with such
small means? Does she even mean to have a funeral lunch?"
Raskolnikov asked, persistently keeping up the conversation.

"The coffin will be plain, of course . . . and everything will
be plain, so it won't cost much. Katerina Ivanovna and I have
reckoned it all out, so that there will be enough left . . . and
Katerina Ivanovna was very anxious it should be so. You know
one can't . . . it's a comfort to her . . . she is like that, you know.
. . ."

"I understand, I understand . . . of course . . . why do you
look at my room like that? My mother has just said it is like a
tomb."

"You gave us everything yesterday," Sonia said suddenly, in
reply, in a loud rapid whisper; and again she looked down in
confusion. Her lips and chin were trembling once more. She had
been struck at once by Raskolnikov's poor surroundings, and now
these words broke out spontaneously. A silence followed. There
was a light in Dounia's eyes, and even Pulcheria Alexandrovna
looked kindly at Sonia.

"Rodya," she said, getting up, "we shall have dinner together, of course. Come, Dounia. . . . And you, Rodya, had better
go for a little walk, and then rest and lie down before you come
to see us. . . . I am afraid we have exhausted you. . . ."

"Yes, yes, I'll come," he answered, getting up fussily. "But
I have something to see to."

"But surely you will have dinner together?" cried Razumihin, looking in surprise at Raskolnikov. "What do you mean?"

"Yes, yes, I am coming . . . of course, of course! And you stay a minute. You do not want him just now, do you, mother? Or perhaps I am taking him from you?"

"Oh, no, no. And will you, Dmitri Prokofitch, do us the favour of dining with us?"

"Please do," added Dounia.

Razumihin bowed, positively radiant. For one moment, they were all strangely embarrassed.

"Good-bye, Rodya, that is till we meet. I do not like saying good-bye. Good-bye, Nastasya. Ah, I have said good-bye again."

Pulcheria Alexandrovna meant to greet Sonia, too; but it somehow failed to come off, and she went in a flutter out of the room.

But Avdotya Romanovna seemed to await her turn, and following her mother out, gave Sonia an attentive, courteous bow. Sonia, in confusion, gave a hurried, frightened curtsy. There was a look of poignant discomfort in her face, as though Avdotya Romanovna's courtesy and attention were oppressive and painful to her.

"Dounia, good-bye," called Raskolnikov, in the passage. "Give me your hand."

"Why, I did give it you. Have you forgotten?" said Dounia, turning warmly and awkwardly to him.

"Never mind, give it to me again." And he squeezed her fingers warmly.

Dounia smiled, flushed, pulled her hand away, and went off quite happy.

"Come, that's capital," he said to Sonia, going back and looking brightly at her. "God give peace to the dead, the living have still to live. That is right, isn't it?"

Sonia looked surprised at the sudden brightness of his face. He looked at her for some moments in silence. The whole history of the dead father floated before his memory in those moments. . . .

"Heavens, Dounia," Pulcheria Alexandrovna began, as soon as they were in the street, "I really feel relieved myself at coming

away—more at ease. How little did I think yesterday in the train
that I could ever be glad of that."

"I tell you again, mother, he is still very ill. Don't you see
it? Perhaps worrying about us upset him. We must be patient, and
much, much can be forgiven."

"Well, you were not very patient!" Pulcheria Alexandrovna
caught her up, hotly and jealously. "Do you know, Dounia, I was
looking at you two. You are the very portrait of him, and not so
much in face as in soul. You are both melancholy, both morose
and hot tempered, both haughty and both generous. . . . Surely
he can't be an egoist, Dounia. Eh? When I think of what is in store
for us this evening, my heart sinks!"

"Don't be uneasy, mother. What must be, will be."

"Dounia, only think what a position we are in! What if Pyotr
Petrovitch breaks it off?" poor Pulcheria Alexandrovna blurted
out, incautiously.

"He won't be worth much if he does," answered Dounia,
sharply and contemptuously.

"We did well to come away," Pulcheria Alexandrovna hurriedly broke in. "He was in a hurry about some business or other.
If he gets out and has a breath of air . . . it is fearfully close in
his room. . . . But where is one to get a breath of air here. The
very streets here feel like shut-up rooms. Good heavens! what a
town! . . . stay . . . this side . . . they will crush you—carrying
something. Why, it is a piano they have got, I declare . . . how
they push . . . I am very much afraid of that young woman, too."

"What young woman, mother?"

"Why, that Sofya Semyonovna, who was there just now."

"Why?"

"I have a presentiment, Dounia. Well, you may believe it or
not, but as soon as she came in, that very minute, I felt that she
was the chief cause of the trouble. . . ."

"Nothing of the sort!" cried Dounia, in vexation. "What
nonsense, with your presentiments, mother! He only made her
acquaintance the evening before, and he did not know her when
she came in."

"Well, you will see. . . . She worries me; but you will see, you will see! I was so frightened. She was gazing at me with those eyes. I could scarcely sit still in my chair when he began introducing her, do you remember? It seems so strange, but Pyotr Petrovitch writes like that about her, and he introduces her to us—to you! So he must think a great deal of her."

"People will write anything. We were talked about and written about, too. Have you forgotten? I am sure that she is a good girl, and that it is all nonsense."

"God grant it may be!"

"And Pyotr Petrovitch is a contemptible slanderer," Dounia snapped out, suddenly.

Pulcheria Alexandrovna was crushed; the conversation was not resumed.

"I will tell you what I want with you," said Raskolnikov, drawing Razumihin to the window.

"Then I will tell Katerina Ivanovna that you are coming," Sonia said hurriedly, preparing to depart.

"One minute, Sofya Semyonovna. We have no secrets. You are not in our way. I want to have another word or two with you. Listen!" he turned suddenly to Razumihin again. "You know that . . . what's his name . . . Porfiry Petrovitch?"

"I should think so! He is a relation. Why?" added the latter, with interest.

"Is not he managing that case . . . you know about that murder? . . . You were speaking about it yesterday."

"Yes . . . well?" Razumihin's eyes opened wide.

"He was inquiring for people who had pawned things, and I have some pledges there, too—trifles—a ring my sister gave me as a keepsake when I left home, and my father's silver watch—they are only worth five or six roubles altogether . . . but I value them. So what am I to do now? I do not want to lose the things, especially the watch. I was quaking just now, for fear mother would ask to look at it, when we spoke of Dounia's watch. It is the only thing of father's left us. She would be ill if it were lost. You know what women are. So tell me what to do. I know I ought to have given notice at the police station, but would it not be better to go straight to Porfiry? Eh? What do you think? The matter might be settled more quickly. You see mother may ask for it before dinner."

"Certainly not to the police station. Certainly to Porfiry," Razumihin shouted in extraordinary excitement. "Well, how glad I am. Let us go at once. It is a couple of steps. We shall be sure to find him."

"Very well, let us go."

"And he will be very, very glad to make your acquaintance. I have often talked to him of you at different times. I was speaking of you yesterday. Let us go. So you knew the old woman? So that's it! It is all turning out splendidly. . . . Oh, yes, Sofya Ivanovna . . ."

"Sofya Semyonovna," corrected Raskolnikov. "Sofya Semyonovna, this is my friend Razumihin, and he is a good man."

"If you have to go now," Sonia was beginning, not looking at Razumihin at all, and still more embarrassed.

"Let us go," decided Raskolnikov. "I will come to you today, Sofya Semyonovna. Only tell me where you live."

He was not exactly ill at ease, but seemed hurried, and avoided her eyes. Sonia gave her address, and flushed as she did so. They all went out together.

"Don't you lock up?" asked Razumihin, following him on to the stairs.

"Never," answered Raskolnikov. "I have been meaning to buy a lock for these two years. People are happy who have no need of locks," he said, laughing, to Sonia. They stood still in the gateway.

"Do you go to the right, Sofya Semyonovna? How did you find me, by the way?" he added, as though he wanted to say something quite different. He wanted to look at her soft clear eyes, but this was not easy.

"Why, you gave your address to Polenka yesterday."

"Polenka? Oh, yes; Polenka, that is the little girl. She is your sister? Did I give her the address?"

"Why, had you forgotten?"

"No, I remember."

"I had heard my father speak of you . . . only I did not know your name, and he did not know it. And now I came . . . and as I had learnt your name, I asked to-day, 'Where does Mr. Raskolnikov live?' I did not know you had only a room too. . . . Good-bye, I will tell Katerina Ivanovna."

She was extremely glad to escape at last; she went away looking down, hurrying to get out of sight as soon as possible, to walk the twenty steps to the turning on the right and to be at last alone, and then moving rapidly along, looking at no one, noticing nothing, to think, to remember, to meditate on every word, every detail. Never, never had she felt anything like this. Dimly and unconsciously a whole new world was opening before her. She remembered suddenly that Raskolnikov meant to come to her that day, perhaps that morning, perhaps at once!

"Only not to-day, please, not to-day!" she kept muttering with a sinking heart, as though entreating some one, like a frightened child. "Mercy! to me . . . to that room . . . he will see . . . oh, dear!"

She was not capable at that instant of noticing an unknown gentleman who was watching her and following at her heels. He had accompanied her from the gateway. At the moment when Razumihin, Raskolnikov, and she stood still at parting on the pavement, this gentleman, who was just passing, started on hearing Sonia's words: "and I asked where Mr. Raskolnikov lived?" He turned a rapid but attentive look upon all three, especially upon Raskolnikov, to whom Sonia was speaking; then looked back and noted the house. All this was done in an instant as he passed, and trying not to betray his interest, he walked on more slowly as though waiting for something. He was waiting for Sonia; he saw that they were parting, and that Sonia was going home.

"Home? Where? I've seen that face somewhere," he thought. "I must find out."

At the turning he crossed over, looked round, and saw Sonia coming the same way, noticing nothing. She turned the corner. He followed her on the other side. After about fifty paces he crossed over again, overtook her and kept two or three yards behind her.

He was a man about fifty, rather tall and thickly set, with broad high shoulders which made him look as though he stooped a little. He wore good and fashionable clothes, and looked like a gentleman of position. He carried a handsome cane, which he tapped on the pavement at each step; his gloves were spotless. He had a broad, rather pleasant face with high cheek-bones and a fresh colour, not often seen in Petersburg. His flaxen hair was still abundant, and only touched here and there with grey, and his thick square beard was even lighter than his hair. His eyes were blue and had a cold and thoughtful look; his lips were crimson. He was a remarkedly well-preserved man and looked much younger than his years.

When Sonia came out on the canal bank, they were the only two persons on the pavement. He observed her dreaminess and preoccupation. On reaching the house where she lodged, Sonia turned in at the gate; he followed her, seeming rather surprised. In the courtyard she turned to the right corner. "Bah!" muttered the unknown gentleman, and mounted the stairs behind her. Only then Sonia noticed him. She reached the third storey, turned down the passage, and rang at No. 9. On the door was inscribed in chalk, "Kapernaumov, Tailor." "Bah!" the stranger repeated again, wondering at the strange coincidence, and he rang next door, at No. 8. The doors were two or three yards apart.

"You lodge at Kapernaumov's," he said, looking at Sonia and laughing. "He altered a waistcoat for me yesterday. I am staying close here at Madame Resslich's. How odd!" Sonia looked at him attentively.

"We are neighbours," he went on gaily. "I only came to town the day before yesterday. Good-bye for the present."

Sonia made no reply; the door opened and she slipped in. She felt for some reason ashamed and uneasy.

On the way to Porfiry's, Razumihin was obviously excited.

"That's capital, brother," he repeated several times, "and I am glad! I am glad!"

"What are you glad about?" Raskolnikov thought to himself.

"I didn't know that you pledged things at that old woman's,

too. And . . . was it long ago? I mean, was it long since you were there?"

"What a simple-hearted fool he is!"

"When was it?" Raskolnikov stopped still to recollect. "Two or three days before her death it must have been. But I am not going to redeem the things now," he put in with a sort of hurried and conspicuous solicitude about the things. "I've not more than a silver rouble left . . . after last night's accursed delirium!"

He laid special emphasis on the delirium.

"Yes, yes," Razumihin hastened to agree—with what was not clear. "Then that's why you . . . were struck . . . partly . . . you know in your delirium you were continually mentioning some rings or chains! Yes, yes . . . that's clear, it's all clear now."

"Hullo! How that idea must have got about among them. Here this man will go to the stake for me, and I find him delighted at having it *cleared up* why I spoke of rings in my delirium! What a hold the idea must have on all of them!"

"Shall we find him?" he asked suddenly.

"Oh, yes," Razumihin answered quickly. "He is a nice fellow, you will see, brother. Rather clumsy, that is to say, he is a man of polished manners, but I mean clumsy in a different sense. He is an intelligent fellow, very much so indeed, but he has his own range of ideas. . . . He is incredulous, sceptical, cynical . . . he likes to impose on people, or rather to make fun of them. His is the old, circumstantial method. . . . But he understands his work . . . thoroughly. . . . Last year he cleared up a case of murder in which the police had hardly a clue. He is very, very anxious to make your acquaintance."

"On what grounds is he so anxious?"

"Oh, it's not exactly . . . you see, since you've been ill I happen to have mentioned you several times. . . . So, when he heard about you . . . about your being a law student and not able to finish your studies, he said, 'What a pity!' And so I concluded . . . from everything together, not only that; yesterday, Zametov . . . you know, Rodya, I talked some nonsense on the way home to you yesterday, when I was drunk . . . I am afraid, brother, of your exaggerating it, you see."

"What? That they think I am a madman? Maybe they are right," he said with a constrained smile.

"Yes, yes. . . . That is, pooh, no! . . . But all that I said (and there was something else too) it was all nonsense, drunken nonsense."

"But why are you apologizing? I am so sick of it all!" Raskolnikov cried with exaggerated irritability. It was partly assumed, however.

"I know, I know, I understand. Believe me, I understand. One's ashamed to speak of it."

"If you are ashamed, then don't speak of it."

Both were silent. Razumihin was more than ecstatic and Raskolnikov perceived it with repulsion. He was alarmed, too, by what Razumihin had just said about Porfiry.

"I shall have to pull a long face with him too," he thought, with a beating heart, and he turned white, "and do it naturally, too. But the most natural thing would be to do nothing at all. Carefully do nothing at all! No, *carefully* would not be natural again. . . . Oh, well, we shall see how it turns out. . . . We shall see . . . directly. Is it a good thing to go or not? The butterfly flies to the light. My heart is beating, that's what's bad!"

"In this grey house," said Razumihin.

"The most important thing, does Porfiry know that I was at the old hag's flat yesterday . . . and asked about the blood? I must find that out instantly, as soon as I go in, find out from his face; otherwise . . . I'll find out, if it's my ruin."

"I say, brother," he said suddenly, addressing Razumihin, with a sly smile, "I have been noticing all day that you seem to be curiously excited. Isn't it so?"

"Excited? Not a bit of it," said Razumihin, stung to the quick.

"Yes, brother, I assure you it's noticeable. Why, you sat on your chair in a way you never do sit, on the edge somehow, and you seemed to be writhing all the time. You kept jumping up for nothing. One moment you were angry, and the next your face looked like a sweetmeat. You even blushed; especially when you were invited to dinner, you blushed awfully."

"Nothing of the sort, nonsense! What do you mean?"

"But why are you wriggling out of it, like a schoolboy? By Jove, there he's blushing again."

"What a pig you are!"

"But why are you so shamefaced about it? Romeo! Stay, I'll tell of you to-day. Ha-ha-ha! I'll make mother laugh, and some one else, too . . ."

"Listen, listen, listen, this is serious. . . . What next, you fiend!" Razumihin was utterly overwhelmed, turning cold with horror. "What will you tell them? Come, brother . . . foo, what a pig you are!"

"You are like a summer rose. And if only you knew how it suits you; a Romeo over six foot high! And how you've washed to-day—you cleaned your nails, I declare. Eh? That's something unheard of! Why, I do believe you've got pomatum on your hair! Bend down."

"Pig!"

Raskolnikov laughed as though he could not restrain himself. So laughing, they entered Porfiry Petrovitch's flat. This is what Raskolnikov wanted: from within they could be heard laughing as they came in, still guffawing in the passage.

"Not a word here or I'll . . . brain you!" Razumihin whispered furiously, seizing Raskolnikov by the shoulder.

5

Raskolnikov was already entering the room. He came in looking as though he had the utmost difficulty not to burst out laughing again. Behind him Razumihin strode in gawky and awkward, shamefaced and red as a peony, with an utterly crest-fallen and ferocious expression. His face and whole figure really were ridiculous at that moment and amply justified Raskolnikov's laughter. Raskolnikov, not waiting for an introduction, bowed to Porfiry Petrovitch, who stood in the middle of the room looking inquiringly at them. He held out his hand and shook hands, still apparently making desperate efforts to subdue his mirth and utter a few words to introduce himself. But he had no sooner succeeded in assuming a serious air and muttering something when he suddenly glanced again as though accidentally at Razumihin, and could no longer control himself: his stifled laughter broke out the more irresistibly the more he tried to restrain it. The extraordinary ferocity with which Razumihin received this "spontaneous" mirth gave the whole scene the appearance of most genuine fun and naturalness. Razumihin strengthened this impression as though on purpose.

"Fool! You fiend," he roared, waving his arm which at once struck a little round table with an empty tea-glass on it. Everything was sent flying and crashing.

"But why break chairs, gentlemen? You know it's a loss to the Crown," Porfiry Petrovitch quoted gaily.

Raskolnikov was still laughing, with his hand in Porfiry Petrovitch's, but anxious not to overdo it, awaited the right moment to put a natural end to it. Razumihin, completely put to confusion by upsetting the table and smashing the glass, gazed gloomily at the fragments, cursed and turned sharply to the window where he stood looking out with his back to the company with a fiercely scowling countenance, seeing nothing. Porfiry Petrovitch laughed and was ready to go on laughing, but obviously looked for explanations. Zametov had been sitting in the corner, but he rose at the visitors' entrance and was standing in expectation with a smile on his lips, though he looked with surprise and even it seemed incredulity at the whole scene and at Raskolnikov with a certain embarrassment. Zametov's unexpected presence struck Raskolnikov unpleasantly.

"I've got to think of that," he thought. "Excuse me, please," he began, affecting extreme embarrassment. "Raskolnikov."

"Not at all, very pleasant to see you . . . and how pleasantly you've come in. . . . Why, won't he even say good-morning?" Porfiry Petrovitch nodded at Razumihin.

"Upon my honour I don't know why he is in such a rage with me. I only told him as we came along that he was like Romeo . . . and proved it. And that was all, I think!"

"Pig!" ejaculated Razumihin, without turning round.

"There must have been very grave grounds for it, if he is so furious at the word," Porfiry laughed.

"Oh, you sharp lawyer! ... Damn you all!" snapped Razumihin, and suddenly bursting out laughing himself, he went up to Porfiry with a more cheerful face as though nothing had happened. "That'll do! We are all fools. To come to business. This is my friend Rodion Romanovitch Raskolnikov; in the first place he has heard of you and wants to make your acquaintance, and secondly, he has a little matter of business with you. Bah! Zametov, what brought you here? Have you met before? Have you known each other long?"

"What does this mean?" thought Raskolnikov uneasily.

Zametov seemed taken aback, but not very much so.

"Why, it was at your rooms we met yesterday," he said easily.

"Then I have been spared the trouble. All last week he was begging me to introduce him to you. Porfiry and you have sniffed each other out without me. Where is your tobacco?"

Porfiry Petrovitch was wearing a dressing-gown, very clean linen, and trodden-down slippers. He was a man of about five and thirty, short, stout even to corpulence, and clean shaven. He wore his hair cut short and had a large round head, particularly prominent at the back. His soft, round, rather snub-nosed face was of a sickly yellowish colour, but had a vigorous and rather ironical expression. It would have been good-natured, except for a look in the eyes, which shone with a watery, mawkish light under almost white, blinking eyelashes. The expression of those eyes was strangely out of keeping with his somewhat womanish figure, and gave it something far more serious than could be guessed at first sight.

As soon as Porfiry Petrovitch heard that his visitor had a little matter of business with him, he begged him to sit down on the sofa and sat down himself on the other end, waiting for him to explain his business, with that careful and over-serious attention which is at once oppressive and embarrassing, especially to a stranger, and especially if what you are discussing is in your own opinion of far too little importance for such exceptional solemnity. But in brief and coherent phrases Raskolnikov explained his business clearly and exactly, and was so well satisfied with himself that he even succeeded in taking a good look at Porfiry. Porfiry Petrovitch did not once take his eyes off him. Razumihin, sitting opposite at the same table, listened warmly and impatiently, looking from one to the other every moment with rather excessive interest.

"Fool," Raskolnikov swore to himself.

"You have to give information to the police," Porfiry replied, with a most businesslike air, "that having learnt of this incident, that is of the murder, you beg to inform the lawyer in charge of the case that such and such things belong to you, and that you desire to redeem them . . . or . . . but they will write to you."

"That's just the point, that at the present moment," Raskolnikov tried his utmost to feign embarrassment, "I am not quite in funds . . . and even this trifling sum is beyond me . . . I only wanted, you see, for the present to declare that the things are mine, and that when I have money. . . ."

"That's no matter," answered Porfiry Petrovitch, receiving his explanation of his pecuniary position coldly, "but you can, if you prefer, write straight to me, to say, that having been informed of the matter, and claiming such and such as your property, you beg . . ."

"On an ordinary sheet of paper?" Raskolnikov interrupted eagerly, again interested in the financial side of the question.

"Oh, the most ordinary," and suddenly Porfiry Petrovitch looked with obvious irony at him, screwing up his eyes and as it were winking at him. But perhaps it was Raskolnikov's fancy, for it all lasted but a moment. There was certainly something of the sort, Raskolnikov could have sworn he winked at him, goodness knows why.

"He knows," flashed through his mind like lightning.

"Forgive my troubling you about such trifles," he went on, a little disconcerted, "the things are only worth five roubles, but I prize them particularly for the sake of those from whom they

came to me, and I must confess that I was alarmed when I heard
. . ."

"That's why you were so much struck when I mentioned to
Zossimov that Porfiry was inquiring for every one who had
pledges!" Razumihin put in with obvious intention.

This was really unbearable. Raskolnikov could not help
glancing at him with a flash of vindictive anger in his black eyes,
but immediately recollected himself.

"You seem to be jeering at me, brother?" he said to him,
with a well-feigned irritability. "I dare say I do seem to you
absurdly anxious about such trash; but you mustn't think me
selfish or grasping for that, and these two things may be anything
but trash in my eyes. I told you just now that the silver watch,
though it's not worth a cent, is the only thing left us of my father's.
You may laugh at me, but my mother is here," he turned suddenly to Porfiry, "and if she knew," he turned again hurriedly to
Razumihin, carefully making his voice tremble, "that the watch
was lost, she would be in despair! You know what women are!"

"Not a bit of it! I didn't mean that at all! Quite the contrary!"
shouted Razumihin distressed.

"Was it right? Was it natural? Did I overdo it?" Raskolnikov
asked himself in a tremor. "Why did I say that about women?"

"Oh, your mother is with you?" Porfiry Petrovitch inquired.

"Yes."

"When did she come?"

"Last night."

Porfiry paused as though reflecting.

"Your things would not in any case be lost," he went on
calmly and coldly. "I have been expecting you here for some
time."

And as though that was a matter of no importance, he carefully offered the ash-tray to Razumihin, who was ruthlessly scattering
cigarette ash over the carpet. Raskolnikov shuddered, but Porfiry
did not seem to be looking at him, and was still concerned with
Razumihin's cigarette.

"What? Expecting him? Why, did you know that he had
pledges *there?*" cried Razumihin.

Porfiry Petrovitch addressed himself to Raskolnikov.

"Your things, the ring and the watch, were wrapped up together, and on the paper your name was legibly written in pencil, together with the date on which you left them with her . . ."

"How observant you are!" Raskolnikov smiled awkwardly, doing his very utmost to look him straight in the face, but he failed, and suddenly added:

"I say that because I suppose there were a great many pledges . . . so that it must be difficult to remember them all. . . . But you remember them all so clearly, and . . . and . . ."

"Stupid! Feeble!" he thought. "Why did I add that?"

"But we know all who had pledges, and you are the only one who hasn't come forward," Porfiry answered with hardly perceptible irony.

"I haven't been quite well."

"I heard that too. I heard, indeed, that you were in great distress about something. You look pale still."

"I am not pale at all. . . . No, I am quite well," Raskolnikov snapped out rudely and angrily, completely changing his tone. His anger was mounting, he could not repress it. "And in my anger I shall betray myself," flashed through his mind again. "Why are they torturing me?"

"Not quite well!" Razumihin caught him up. "What next! He was unconscious and delirious till yesterday. Would you believe, Porfiry, as soon as our backs were turned, he dressed, though he could hardly stand, and gave us the slip and went off on a spree somewhere till midnight, delirious all the time! Would you believe it! Extraordinary!"

"Really delirious? You don't say so!" Porfiry shook his head in a womanish way.

"Nonsense! Don't you believe it! But you don't believe it anyway," Raskolnikov let slip in his anger. But Porfiry Petrovitch did not seem to catch those strange words.

"But how could you have gone out if you hadn't been delirious?" Razumihin got hot suddenly. "What did you go out for? What was the object of it? And why on the sly? Were you in your senses when you did it? Now that all danger is over I can speak plainly."

"I was awfully sick of them yesterday." Raskolnikov addressed Porfiry suddenly with a smile of insolent defiance, "I ran away from them to take lodgings where they wouldn't find me, and took a lot of money with me. Mr. Zametov there saw it. I say, Mr. Zametov, was I sensible or delirious yesterday; settle our dispute."

He could have strangled Zametov at that moment, so hateful were his expression and his silence to him.

"In my opinion you talked sensibly and even artfully, but you were extremely irritable," Zametov pronounced drily.

"And Nikodim Fomitch was telling me to-day," put in Porfiry Petrovitch, "that he met you very late last night in the lodging of a man who had been run over."

"And there," said Razumihin, "weren't you mad then? You gave your last penny to the widow for the funeral. If you wanted to help, give fifteen or twenty even, but keep three roubles for yourself at least, but he flung away all the twenty-five at once!"

"Maybe I found a treasure somewhere and you know nothing of it? So that's why I was liberal yesterday. . . . Mr. Zametov knows I've found a treasure! Excuse us, please, for disturbing you for half an hour with such trivialities," he said turning to Porfiry Petrovitch, with trembling lips. "We are boring you, aren't we?"

"Oh no, quite the contrary, quite the contrary! If only you knew how you interest me! It's interesting to look on and listen . . . and I am really glad you have come forward at last."

"But you might give us some tea! My throat's dry," cried Razumihin.

"Capital idea! Perhaps we will all keep you company. Wouldn't you like . . . something more essential before tea?"

"Get along with you!"

Porfiry Petrovitch went out to order tea.

Raskolnikov's thoughts were in a whirl. He was in terrible exasperation.

"The worst of it is they don't disguise it; they don't care to stand on ceremony! And how if you didn't know me at all, did you come to talk to Nikodim Fomitch about me? So they didn't care to hide that they are tracking me like a pack of dogs. They simply spit in my face." He was shaking with rage. "Come, strike me openly, don't play with me like a cat with a mouse. It's hardly civil, Porfiry Petrovitch, but perhaps I won't allow it! I shall get up and throw the whole truth in your ugly faces, and you'll see how I despise you." He could hardly breathe. "And what if it's only my fancy? What if I am mistaken, and through inexperience I get angry and don't keep up my nasty part? Perhaps it's all unintentional. All their phrases are the usual ones, but there is something about them. . . . It all might be said, but there is something. Why did he say bluntly, 'With her'? Why did Zametov add that I spoke artfully? Why do they speak in that tone? Yes, the tone. . . . Razumihin is sitting here, why does he see nothing? That innocent blockhead never does see anything! Feverish again! Did Porfiry wink at me just now? Of course it's nonsense! What could he wink for? Are they trying to upset my nerves or are they teasing me? Either it's all fancy or they know! Even Zametov is rude. . . . Is Zametov rude? Zametov has changed his mind. I foresaw he would change his mind! He is at home here, while it's my first visit. Porfiry does not consider him a visitor; sits with his back to him. They're as thick as thieves, no doubt, over me! Not a doubt they were talking about me before we came. Do they know about the flat? If only they'd make haste! When I said that I ran away to take a flat he let it pass. . . . I put that in cleverly about a flat, it may be of use afterwards. . . . Delirious, indeed . . . ha-ha-ha! He knows all about last night! He didn't know of my mother's arrival! The hag had written the date on in pencil! You are wrong, you won't catch me! There are no facts . . . it's all supposition! You produce facts! The flat even isn't a fact but delirium. I know what to say to them. . . . Do they know about the flat? I won't go without finding out. What did I come for? But my being angry now, maybe is a fact! Fool, how irritable I am! Perhaps that's right; to play the invalid. . . . He is feeling me. He will try to catch me. Why did I come?"

All this flashed like lightning through his mind.

Porfiry Petrovitch returned quickly. He became suddenly more jovial.

"Your party yesterday, brother, has left my head rather. ... And I am out of sorts altogether," he began in quite a different tone, laughing to Razumihin.

"Was it interesting? I left you yesterday at the most interesting point. Who got the best of it?"

"Oh, no one, of course. They got on to everlasting questions, floated off into space."

"Only fancy, Rodya, what we got on to yesterday. Whether there is such a thing as crime. I told you that we talked our heads off."

"What is there strange? It's an everyday social question," Raskolnikov answered casually.

"The question wasn't put quite like that," observed Porfiry.

"Not quite, that's true," Razumihin agreed at once, getting warm and hurried as usual. "Listen, Rodion, and tell us your opinion, I want to hear it. I was fighting tooth and nail with them and wanted you to help me. I told them you were coming. ... It began with the socialist doctrine. You know their doctrine; crime is a protest against the abnormality of the social organization and nothing more, and nothing more; no other causes admitted! ..."

"You are wrong there," cried Porfiry Petrovitch; he was noticeably animated and kept laughing as he looked at Razumihin which made him more excited than ever.

"Nothing is admitted," Razumihin interrupted with heat.

"I am not wrong. I'll show you their pamphlets. Everything with them is 'the influence of environment,' and nothing else. Their favourite phrase! From which it follows that, if society is normally organized, all crime will cease at once, since there will be nothing to protest against and all men will become righteous in one instant. Human nature is not taken into account, it is excluded, it's not supposed to exist! They don't recognise that humanity, developing by a historical living process, will become at last a normal society, but they believe that a social system that has come out of some mathematical brain is going to organise all humanity at once and make it just and sinless in an instant, quicker than any living process! That's why they instinctively dislike history, 'nothing but ugliness and stupidity in it,' and they explain it all as stupidity! That's why they dislike the *living* process of life; they don't want a *living soul!* The living soul demands life, the soul won't obey the rules of mechanics, the soul is an object of suspicion, the soul is retrograde! But what they want though it smells of death and can be made of india-rubber, at least is not alive, has no will, is servile and won't revolt! And it comes in the end to their reducing everything to the building of walls and the planning of rooms and passages in a phalanstery! The phalanstery is ready, indeed, but your human nature is not ready for the phalanstery—it wants life, it hasn't completed its vital process, it's too soon for the graveyard! You can't skip over nature by logic. Logic presupposes three possibilities, but there are millions! Cut away a million, and reduce it all to the question of comfort! That's the easiest solution of the problem! It's seductively clear and you mustn't think about it. That's the great thing, you mustn't think! The whole secret of life in two pages of print!"

"Now he is off, beating the drum! Catch hold of him, do!" laughed Porfiry. "Can you imagine," he turned to Raskolnikov, "six people holding forth like that last night, in one room, with punch as a preliminary! No, brother, you are wrong, environment accounts for a great deal in crime; I can assure you of that."

"Oh, I know it does, but just tell me: a man of forty violates a child of ten; was it environment drove him to it?"

"Well, strictly speaking, it did," Porfiry observed with noteworthy gravity; "a crime of that nature may be very well ascribed to the influence of environment."

Razumihin was almost in a frenzy. "Oh, if you like," he roared. "I'll prove to you that your white eyelashes may very well be ascribed to the Church of Ivan the Great's being two hundred and fifty feet high, and I will prove it clearly, exactly, progressively, and even with a Liberal tendency! I undertake to! Will you bet on it?"

"Done! Let's hear, please, how he will prove it!"

"He is always humbugging, confound him," cried Razumihin, jumping up and gesticulating. "What's the use of talking to you! He does all that on purpose; you don't know him, Rodion! He took their side yesterday, simply to make fools of them. And the things he said yesterday! And they were delighted! He can keep it up for a fortnight together. Last year he persuaded us that he was going into a monastery: he stuck to it for two months. Not long ago he took it into his head to declare he was going to get married, that he had everything ready for the wedding. He ordered new clothes indeed. We all began to congratulate him. There was no bride, nothing, all pure fantasy!"

"Ah, you are wrong! I got the clothes before. It was the new clothes in fact that made me think of taking you in."

"Are you such a good dissembler?" Raskolnikov asked carelessly.

"You wouldn't have supposed it, eh? Wait a bit, I shall take you in, too. Ha-ha-ha! No, I'll tell you the truth. All these questions about crime, environment, children, recall to my mind an article of yours which interested me at the time. 'On Crime' . . . or something of the sort, I forget the title, I read it with pleasure two months ago in the *Periodical Review.*"

"My article? In the *Periodical Review?*" Raskolnikov asked in astonishment. "I certainly did write an article upon a book six months ago when I left the university, but I sent it to the *Weekly Review.*"

"But it came out in the *Periodical.*"

"And the *Weekly Review* ceased to exist, so that's why it wasn't printed at the time."

"That's true; but when it ceased to exist, the *Weekly Review* was amalgamated with the *Periodical,* and so your article appeared two months ago in the latter. Didn't you know?"

Raskolnikov had not known.

"Why, you might get some money out of them for the article! What a strange person you are! You lead such a solitary life that you know nothing of matters that concern you directly. It's a fact, I assure you."

"Bravo, Rodya! I knew nothing about it either!" cried Razumihin. "I'll run to-day to the reading-room and ask for the

number. Two months ago? What was the date? It doesn't matter
though, I will find it. Think of not telling us!"

"How did you find out that the article was mine? It's only
signed with an initial."

"I only learnt it by chance, the other day. Through the
editor; I know him. . . . I was very much interested."

"It analysed, if I remember, the psychology of a criminal
before and after the crime."

"Yes, and you maintained that the perpetration of a crime is
always accompanied by illness. Very, very original, but . . . it was
not that part of your article that interested me so much, but an
idea at the end of the article which I regret to say you merely
suggested without working it out clearly. There is, if you recollect, a suggestion that there are certain persons who can . . . that
is, not precisely are able to, but have a perfect right to commit
breaches of morality and crimes, and that the law is not for them."

Raskolnikov smiled at the exaggerated and intentional dis-
tortion of his idea.

"What? What do you mean? A right to crime? But not because of the influence of environment?" Razumihin inquired with
some alarm even.

"Not, not exactly because of it," answered Porfiry. "In his
article all men are divided into 'ordinary' and 'extraordinary.'
Ordinary men have to live in submission, have no right to transgress the law, because, don't you see, they are ordinary. But
extraordinary men have a right to commit any crime and to transgress the law in any way, just because they are extraordinary. That
was your idea, if I am not mistaken?"

"What do you mean? That can't be right?" Razumihin muttered in bewilderment.

Raskolnikov smiled again. He saw the point at once, and
knew where they wanted to drive him. He decided to take up the
challenge.

"That wasn't quite my contention," he began simply and
modestly. "Yet I admit that you have stated it almost correctly;
perhaps, if you like, perfectly so." (It almost gave him pleasure
to admit this.) "The only difference is that I don't contend that

extraordinary people are always bound to commit breaches of morals, as you call it. In fact, I doubt whether such an argument could be published. I simply hinted that an 'extraordinary' man has the right . . . that is not an official right, but an inner right to decide in his own conscience to overstep . . . certain obstacles, and only in case it is essential for the practical fulfilment of his idea (sometimes, perhaps, of benefit to the whole of humanity). You say that my article isn't definite; I am ready to make it as clear as I can. Perhaps I am right in thinking you want me to; very well. I maintain that if the discoveries of Kepler and Newton could not have been made known except by sacrificing the lives of one, a dozen, a hundred, or more men, Newton would have had the right, would indeed have been in duty bound . . . to *eliminate* the dozen or the hundred men for the sake of making his discoveries known to the whole of humanity. But it does not follow from that that Newton had a right to murder people right and left and to steal every day in the market. Then, I remember, I maintain in my article that all . . . well, legislators and leaders of men, such as Lycurgus, Solon, Mahomet, Napoleon, and so on, were all without exception criminals, from the very fact that, making a new law, they transgressed the ancient one, handed down from their ancestors and held sacred by the people, and they did not stop short at bloodshed either, if that bloodshed—often of inno-cent persons fighting bravely in defence of ancient law—were of use to their cause. It's remarkable, in fact, that the majority, indeed, of these benefactors and leaders of humanity were guilty of terrible carnage. In short, I maintain that all great men or even men a little out of the common, that is to say capable of giving some new word, must from their very nature be criminals—more or less, of course. Otherwise it's hard for them to get out of the common rut; and to remain in the common rut is what they can't submit to, from their very nature again, and to my mind they ought not, indeed, to submit to it. You see that there is nothing particularly new in all that. The same thing has been printed and read a thousand times before. As for my division of people into ordinary and extraordinary, I acknowledge that it's somewhat arbitrary, but I don't insist upon exact numbers. I only believe in my leading idea that men are *in general* divided by a law of nature into two categories, inferior (ordinary), that is, so to say, material that serves only to reproduce its kind, and men who have the gift or the talent to utter *a new word*. There are, of course, innumerable sub-divisions, but the distinguishing features of both categories are fairly well marked. The first category, generally speaking, are men conservative in temperament and law-abiding; they live under control and love to be controlled. To my thinking it is their duty to be controlled, because that's their vocation, and there is nothing humiliating in it for them. The second category all transgress the law; they are destroyers or disposed to destruction according to their capacities. The crimes of these men are of course relative and varied; for the most part they seek in very varied ways the destruction of the present for the sake of the better. But if such a one is forced for the sake of his idea to step over a corpse or wade through blood, he can, I maintain, find within himself, in his conscience, a sanction for wading through blood—that depends on the idea and its dimensions, note that. It's only in that sense I speak of their right to crime in my article (you remember it began with the legal question). There's no need for such anxiety, however; the masses will scarcely ever admit this right, they punish them or hang them (more or less), and in doing so fulfil quite justly their conservative vocation. But the same masses set these criminals on a pedestal in the next generation and worship them (more or less). The first category is always the man of the present, the second the man of the future. The first preserve the world and people it, the second move the world and lead it to its goal. Each class has an equal right to exist. In fact, all have equal rights with me—and *vive la guerre éternelle*—till the New Jerusalem, of course!"

"Then you believe in the New Jerusalem, do you?"

"I do," Raskolnikov answered firmly; as he said these words and during the whole preceding tirade he kept his eyes on one spot on the carpet.

"And . . . and do you believe in God? Excuse my curiosity."

"I do," repeated Raskolnikov, raising his eyes to Porfiry.

"And . . . do you believe in Lazarus' rising from the dead?"

"I . . . I do. Why do you ask all this?"

"You believe it literally?"

"Literally."

"You don't say so. . . . I asked from curiosity. Excuse me. But let us go back to the question; they are not always executed. Some, on the contrary . . ."

"Triumph in their lifetime? Oh, yes, some attain their ends in this life, and then . . ."

"They begin executing other people?"

"If it's necessary; indeed, for the most part they do. Your remark is very witty."

"Thank you. But tell me this: how do you distinguish those extraordinary people from the ordinary ones? Are there signs at their birth? I feel there ought to be more exactitude, more external definition. Excuse the natural anxiety of a practical law-abiding citizen, but couldn't they adopt a special uniform, for instance, couldn't they wear something, be branded in some way? For you know if confusion arises and a member of one category imagines that he belongs to the other, begins to 'eliminate obstacles,' as you so happily expressed it, then . . ."

"Oh, that very often happens! That remark is wittier than the other."

"Thank you."

"No reason to; but take note that the mistake can only arise in the first category, that is among the ordinary people (as I perhaps unfortunately called them). In spite of their predisposition to obedience very many of them, through a playfulness of nature, sometimes vouchsafed even to the cow, like to imagine themselves advanced people, 'destroyers,' and to push themselves into the 'new movement,' and this quite sincerely. Meanwhile the really *new* people are very often unobserved by them, or even despised as reactionaries of grovelling tendencies. But I don't think there is any considerable danger here, and you really need not be uneasy for they never go very far. Of course, they might have a thrashing sometimes for letting their fancy run away with them and to teach them their place, but no more; in fact, even this isn't necessary as they castigate themselves, for they are very conscientious: some perform this service for one another and others chastise themselves with their own hands. . . . They will impose various public acts of penitence upon themselves with a beautiful and edifying effect; in fact you've nothing to be uneasy about. . . . It's a law of nature."

"Well, you have certainly set my mind more at rest on that score; but there's another thing worries me. Tell me, please, are there many people who have the right to kill others, these extraordinary people? I am ready to bow down to them, of course, but you must admit it's alarming if there are a great many of them, eh?"

"Oh, you needn't worry about that either," Raskolnikov went on in the same tone. "People with new ideas, people with the faintest capacity for saying something *new,* are extremely few in number, extraordinarily so in fact. One thing only is clear, that the appearance of all these grades and sub-divisions of men must follow with unfailing regularity some law of nature. That law, of course, is unknown at present, but I am convinced that it exists, and one day may become known. The vast mass of mankind is mere material, and only exists in order by some great effort, by some mysterious process, by means of some crossing of races and stocks, to bring into the world at last perhaps one man out of a thousand with a spark of independence. One in ten thousand perhaps—I speak roughly, approximately—is born with some independence, and with still greater independence one in a hundred thousand. The man of genius is one of millions, and the great geniuses, the crown of humanity, appear on earth perhaps one in many thousand millions. In fact I have not peeped into the retort in which all this takes place. But there certainly is and must be a definite law, it cannot be a matter of chance."

"Why, are you both joking?" Razumihin cried at last. "There you sit, making fun of one another. Are you serious, Rodya?"

Raskolnikov raised his pale and almost mournful face and made no reply. And the unconcealed, persistent, nervous, and *discourteous* sarcasm of Porfiry seemed strange to Razumihin beside that quiet and mournful face.

"Well, brother, if you are really serious . . . You are right, of course, in saying that it's not new, that it's like what we've read and heard a thousand times already; but what is really *original* in all this, and is exclusively your own, to my horror, is that you sanction bloodshed *in the name* of *conscience,* and, excuse my saying so, with such fanaticism. . . . That, I take it, is the point of your article. But that sanction of bloodshed *by conscience* is to my mind . . . more terrible than the official, legal sanction of bloodshed. . . ."

"You are quite right, it is more terrible," Porfiry agreed.

"Yes, you must have exaggerated! There is some mistake, I shall read it. You can't think that! I shall read it."

"All that is not in the article, there's only a hint of it," said Raskolnikov.

"Yes, yes." Porfiry couldn't sit still. "Your attitude to crime is pretty clear to me now, but . . . excuse me for my impertinence (I am really ashamed to be worrying you like this), you see, you've removed my anxiety as to the two grades' getting mixed, but . . . there are various practical possibilities that make me uneasy! What if some man or youth imagines that he is a Lycurgus or Mahomet—a future one of course—and suppose he begins to remove all obstacles. . . . He has some great enterprise before him and needs money for it . . . and tries to get it . . . do you see?"

Zametov gave a sudden guffaw in his corner. Raskolnikov did not even raise his eyes to him.

"I must admit," he went on calmly, "that such cases certainly must arise. The vain and foolish are particularly apt to fall into that snare; young people especially."

"Yes, you see. Well then?"

"What then?" Raskolnikov smiled in reply; "that's not my fault. So it is and so it always will be. He said just now (he nodded at Razumihin) that I sanction bloodshed. Society is too well protected by prisons, banishment, criminal investigators, penal servitude. There's no need to be uneasy. You have but to catch the thief."

"And what if we do catch him?"

"Then he gets what he deserves."

"You are certainly logical. But what of his conscience?"

"Why do you care about that?"

"Simply from humanity."

"If he has a conscience he will suffer for his mistake. That will be his punishment—as well as the prison."

"But the real geniuses," asked Razumihin frowning, "those who have the right to murder? Oughtn't they to suffer at all even for the blood they've shed?"

"Why the word *ought?* It's not a matter of permission or prohibition. He will suffer if he is sorry for his victim. Pain and suffering are always inevitable for a large intelligence and a deep heart. The really great men must, I think, have great sadness on earth," he added dreamily, not in the tone of the conversation.

He raised his eyes, looked earnestly at them all, smiled, and took his cap. He was too quiet by comparison with his manner at his entrance, and he felt this. Every one got up.

"Well, you may abuse me, be angry with me if you like," Porfiry Petrovitch began again, "but I can't resist. Allow me one little question (I know I am troubling you). There is just one little notion I want to express, simply that I may not forget it."

"Very good, tell me your little notion," Raskolnikov stood waiting, pale and grave before him.

"Well, you see . . . I really don't know how to express it properly. . . . It's a playful, psychological idea. . . . When you were writing your article, surely you couldn't have helped, he-he, fancying yourself . . . just a little, an 'extraordinary' man, uttering a *new word* in your sense. . . . That's so, isn't it?"

"Quite possibly," Raskolnikov answered contemptuously. Razumihin made a movement.

"And, if so, could you bring yourself in case of worldly difficulties and hardship or for some service to humanity—to overstep obstacles? . . . For instance, to rob and murder?"

And again he winked with his left eye, and laughed noiselessly just as before.

"If I did I certainly should not tell you," Raskolnikov answered with defiant and haughty contempt.

"No, I was only interested on account of your article, from a literary point of view . . ."

"Foo, how obvious and insolent that is," Raskolnikov thought with repulsion.

"Allow me to observe," he answered drily, "that I don't consider myself a Mahomet or a Napoleon, nor any personage of that kind, and not being one of them I cannot tell you how I should act."

"Oh, come, don't we all think ourselves Napoleons now in Russia?" Porfiry Petrovitch said with alarming familiarity.

Something peculiar betrayed itself in the very intonation of his voice.

"Perhaps it was one of these future Napoleons who did for Alyona Ivanovna last week?" Zametov blurted out from the corner.

Raskolnikov did not speak, but looked firmly and intently at Porfiry. Razumihin was scowling gloomily. He seemed before this to be noticing something. He looked angrily around. There was a minute of gloomy silence. Raskolnikov turned to go.

"Are you going already?" Porfiry said amiably, holding out his hand with excessive politeness. "Very, very glad of your acquaintance. As for your request, have no uneasiness, write just as I told you, or, better still, come to me there yourself in a day or two . . . to-morrow, indeed. I shall be there at eleven o'clock for certain. We'll arrange it all; we'll have a talk. As one of the last to be *there,* you might perhaps be able to tell us something," he added with a most good-natured expression.

"You want to cross-examine me officially in due form?" Raskolnikov asked sharply.

"Oh, why? That's not necessary for the present. You misunderstand me. I lose no opportunity, you see, and . . . I've talked with all who had pledges. . . . I obtained evidence from some of them, and you are the last. . . . Yes, by the way," he cried, seemingly suddenly delighted, "I just remember, what was I thinking of?" he turned to Razumihin, "you were talking my ears off about that Nikolay . . . of course, I know, I know very well," he turned to Raskolnikov, "that the fellow is innocent, but what

is one to do? We had to trouble Dmitri too. . . . This is the point,
this is all: when you went up the stairs it was past seven, wasn't
it?"

"Yes," answered Raskolnikov, with an unpleasant sensation
at the very moment he spoke that he need not have said it.

"Then when you went upstairs between seven and eight,
didn't you see in a flat that stood open on a second storey, do you
remember, two workmen or at least one of them? They were
painting there, didn't you notice them? It's very, very important
for them."

"Painters? No, I didn't see them," Raskolnikov answered
slowly, as though ransacking his memory, while at the same instant he was racking every nerve, almost swooning with anxiety
to conjecture as quickly as possible where the trap lay and not to
overlook anything. "No, I didn't see them, and I don't think I
noticed a flat like that open. . . . But on the fourth storey" (he
had mastered the trap now and was triumphant) "I remember
now that some one was moving out of the flat opposite Alyona
Ivanovna's. . . . I remember . . . I remember it clearly. Some
porters were carrying out a sofa and they squeezed me against the
wall. But painters . . . no, I don't remember that there were any
painters, and I don't think that there was a flat open anywhere,
no, there wasn't."

"What do you mean?" Razumihin shouted suddenly, as
though he had reflected and realised. "Why, it was on the day of
the murder the painters were at work, and he was there three days
before? What are you asking?"

"Foo! I have muddled it!" Porfiry slapped himself on the
forehead. "Deuce take it! This business is turning my brain!" he
addressed Raskolnikov somewhat apologetically. "It would be
such a great thing for us to find out whether any one had seen
them between seven and eight at the flat, so I fancied you could
perhaps have told us something. . . . I quite muddled it."

"Then you should be more careful," Razumihin observed
grimly.

The last words were uttered in the passage. Porfiry Petrovitch saw them to the door with excessive politeness.

They went out into the street gloomy and sullen, and for some steps they did not say a word. Raskolnikov drew a deep breath.

6

"I don't believe it, I can't believe it!" repeated Razumihin, trying in perplexity to refute Raskolnikov's arguments. They were by now approaching Bakaleyev's lodgings, where Pulcheria Alexandrovna and Dounia had been expecting them a long while. Razumihin kept stopping on the way in the heat of discussion, confused and excited by the very fact that they were for the first time speaking openly about *it*.

"Don't believe it, then!" answered Raskolnikov, with a cold, careless smile. "You were noticing nothing as usual, but I was weighing every word."

"You are suspicious. That is why you weighed their words . . . h'm . . . certainly, I agree, Porfiry's tone was rather strange, and still more that wretch Zametov! . . . You are right, there was something about him—but why? Why?"

"He has changed his mind since last night."

"Quite the contrary! If they had that brainless idea, they would do their utmost to hide it, and conceal their cards, so as to catch you afterwards. . . . But it was all impudent and careless."

"If they had had facts—I mean, real facts—or at least grounds for suspicion, then they would certainly have tried to hide their game, in the hope of getting more (they would have made a search long ago besides). But they have no facts, not one. It is all mirage—all ambiguous. Simply a floating idea. So they try to throw me out by impudence. And perhaps, he was irritated at having no facts, and blurted it out in his vexation—or perhaps he has some plan . . . he seems an intelligent man. Perhaps he wanted to frighten me by pretending to know. They have a psychology of their own, brother. But it is loathsome explaining it all. Stop!"

"And it's insulting, insulting! I understand you. But . . . since we have spoken openly now (and it is an excellent thing that we

have at last—I am glad) I will own now frankly that I noticed it
in them long ago, this idea. Of course the merest hint only—an
insinuation—but why an insinuation even? How dare they? What
foundation have they? If only you knew how furious I have been.
Think only! Simply because a poor student, unhinged by poverty
and hypochondria, on the eve of a severe delirious illness (note
that), suspicious, vain, proud, who has not seen a soul to speak
to for six months, in rags and in boots without soles, has to face
some wretched policemen and put up with their insolence; and
the unexpected debt thrust under his nose, the I.O.U. presented by
Tchebarov, the new paint, thirty degrees Reaumur and a stifling
atmosphere, a crowd of people, the talk about the murder of a
person where he had been just before, and all that on an empty
stomach—he might well have a fainting fit! And that, that is what
they found it all on! Damn them! I understand how annoying it
is, but in your place, Rodya, I would laugh at them, or better still,
spit in their ugly faces, and spit a dozen times in all directions. I'd
hit out in all directions, neatly too, and so I'd put an end to it.
Damn them! Don't be downhearted. It's a shame!"

"He really has put it well, though," Raskolnikov thought.

"Damn them? But the cross-examination again, to-morrow?" he said with bitterness. "Must I really enter into explanations with them? I feel vexed as it is that I condescended to speak
to Zametov yesterday in the restaurant. . . ."

"Damn it! I will go myself to Porfiry. I will squeeze it out
of him, as one of the family: he must let me know the ins and outs
of it all! And as for Zametov . . ."

"At last he sees through him!" thought Raskolnikov.

"Stay!" cried Razumihin, seizing him by the shoulder again.
"Stay! you were wrong. I have thought it out. You are wrong!
How was that a trap? You say that the question about the workmen was a trap. But if you had done *that,* could you have said you
had seen them painting the flat . . . and the workmen? On the
contrary, you would have seen nothing, even if you had seen it.
Who would own it against himself?"

"If I had done *that thing,* I should certainly have said that I had seen the workmen and the flat," Raskolnikov answered, with reluctance and obvious disgust.

"But why speak against yourself?"

"Because only peasants, or the most inexperienced novices deny everything flatly at examinations. If a man is ever so little developed and experienced, he will certainly try to admit all the external facts that can't be avoided, but will seek other explanations of them, will introduce some special, unexpected turn, that will give them another significance and put them in another light. Porfiry might well reckon that I should be sure to answer so, and say I had seen them to give an air of truth, and then make some explanation."

"But he would have told you at once, that the workmen could not have been there two days before, and that therefore you must have been there on the day of the murder at eight o'clock. And so he would have caught you over a detail."

"Yes, that is what he was reckoning on, that I should not have time to reflect, and should be in a hurry to make the most likely answer, and so would forget that the workmen could not have been there two days before."

"But how could you forget it?"

"Nothing easier. It is in just such stupid things clever people are most easily caught. The more cunning a man is, the less he suspects that he will be caught in a simple thing. The more cunning a man is, the simpler the trap he must be caught in. Porfiry is not such a fool as you think. . . ."

"He is a knave then, if that is so!"

Raskolnikov could not help laughing. But at the very moment, he was struck by the strangeness of his own frankness, and the eagerness with which he had made this explanation, though he had kept up all the preceding conversation with gloomy repulsion, obviously with a motive, from necessity.

"I am getting a relish for certain aspects!" he thought to himself. But almost at the same instant, he became suddenly uneasy, as though an unexpected and alarming idea had occurred to him. His uneasiness kept on increasing. They had just reached the entrance to Bakaleyev's.

"Go in alone!" said Raskolnikov suddenly. "I will be back directly."

"Where are you going? Why, we are just here."

"I can't help it. . . . I will come in half an hour. Tell them."

"Say what you like, I will come with you."

"You, too, want to torture me!" he screamed, with such bitter irritation, such despair in his eyes that Razumihin's hands dropped. He stood for some time on the steps, looking gloomily at Raskolnikov striding rapidly away in the direction of his lodging. At last, gritting his teeth and clenching his fist, he swore he would squeeze Porfiry like a lemon that very day, and went up the stairs to reassure Pulcheria Alexandrovna, who was by now alarmed at their long absence.

When Raskolnikov got home, his hair was soaked with sweat and he was breathing heavily. He went rapidly up the stairs, walked into his unlocked room and at once fastened the latch. Then in senseless terror he rushed to the corner, to that hole under the paper where he had put the thing; put his hand in, and for some minutes felt carefully in the hole, in every crack and fold of the paper. Finding nothing, he got up and drew a deep breath. As he was reaching the steps of Bakaleyev's, he suddenly fancied that something, a chain, a stud or even a bit of paper in which they had been wrapped with the old woman's handwriting on it, might somehow have slipped out and been lost in some crack, and then might suddenly turn up as unexpected, conclusive evidence against him.

He stood as though lost in thought, and a strange, humiliated, half senseless smile strayed on his lips. He took his cap at last and went quietly out of the room. His ideas were all tangled. He went dreamily through the gateway.

"Here he is himself," shouted a loud voice.

He raised his head.

The porter was standing at the door of his little room and was pointing him out to a short man who looked like an artisan, wearing a long coat and a waistcoat, and looking at a distance remarkably like a woman. He stooped, and his head in a greasy cap hung forward. From his wrinkled flabby face he looked over fifty; his little eyes were lost in fat and they looked out grimly, sternly and discontentedly.

"What is it?" Raskolnikov asked, going up to the porter.

The man stole a look at him from under his brows and he looked at him attentively, deliberately; then he turned slowly and went out of the gate into the street without saying a word.

"What is it?" cried Raskolnikov.

"Why, he there was asking whether a student lived here, mentioned your name and whom you lodged with. I saw you coming and pointed you out and he went away. It's funny."

The porter too seemed rather puzzled, but not much so, and after wondering for a moment he turned and went back to his room.

Raskolnikov ran after the stranger, and at once caught sight of him walking along the other side of the street with the same even, deliberate step with his eyes fixed on the ground, as though in meditation. He soon overtook him, but for some time walked behind him. At last, moving on to a level with him, he looked at his face. The man noticed him at once, looked at him quickly, but dropped his eyes again; and so they walked for a minute side by side without uttering a word.

"You were inquiring for me . . . of the porter?" Raskolnikov said at last, but in a curiously quiet voice.

The man made no answer; he didn't even look at him. Again they were both silent.

"Why do you . . . come and ask for me . . . and say nothing. . . . What's the meaning of it?"

Raskolnikov's voice broke and he seemed unable to articulate the words clearly.

The man raised his eyes this time and turned a gloomy sinister look at Raskolnikov.

"Murderer!" he said suddenly in a quiet but clear and distinct voice.

Raskolnikov went on walking beside him. His legs felt suddenly weak, a cold shiver ran down his spine, and his heart seemed to stand still for a moment, then suddenly began throbbing as though it were set free. So they walked for about a hundred paces, side by side in silence.

The man did not look at him.

"What do you mean . . . what is. . . . Who is a murderer?" muttered Raskolnikov hardly audibly.

"*You* are a murderer," the man answered still more articulately and emphatically, with a smile of triumphant hatred, and again he looked straight into Raskolnikov's pale face and stricken eyes.

They had just reached the cross roads. The man turned to the left without looking behind him. Raskolnikov remained standing, gazing after him. He saw him turn round fifty paces away and look back at him still standing there. Raskolnikov could not see clearly, but he fancied that he was again smiling the same smile of cold hatred and triumph.

With slow faltering steps, with shaking knees, Raskolnikov made his way back to his little garret, feeling chilled all over. He took off his cap and put it on the table, and for ten minutes he stood without moving. Then he sank exhausted on the sofa and with a weak moan of pain he stretched himself on it. So he lay for half an hour.

He thought of nothing. Some thoughts or fragments of thoughts, some images without order or coherence floated before his mind—faces of people he had seen in his childhood or met somewhere once, whom he would never have recalled, the belfry of the church at V., the billiard table in a restaurant and some officers playing billiards, the smell of cigars in some underground tobacco shop, a tavern room, a back staircase quite dark, all sloppy with dirty water and strewn with egg shells, and the Sunday bells floating in from somewhere. . . . The images followed one another, whirling like a hurricane. Some of them he liked and tried to clutch at, but they faded and all the while there was an oppression within him, but it was not overwhelming, sometimes it was even pleasant. . . . The slight shivering still persisted, but that too was an almost pleasant sensation.

He heard the hurried footsteps of Razumihin; he closed his eyes and pretended to be asleep. Razumihin opened the door and stood for some time in the doorway as though hesitating, then he stepped softly into the room and went cautiously to the sofa. Raskolnikov heard Nastasya's whisper:

"Don't disturb him! Let him sleep. He can have his dinner later."

"Quite so," answered Razumihin. Both withdrew carefully and closed the door. Another half-hour passed. Raskolnikov opened his eyes, turned on his back again, clasping his hands behind his head.

"Who is he? Who is that man who sprang out of the earth? Where was he, what did he see? He has seen it all, that's clear. Where was he then? And from where did he see? Why has he only now sprung out of the earth? And how could he see? Is it possible? Hm . . ." continued Raskolnikov, turning cold and shivering, "and the jewel case Nikolay found behind the door—was that possible? A clue? You miss an infinitesimal line and you can build it into a pyramid of evidence! A fly flew by and saw it! Is it possible?" He felt with sudden loathing how weak, how physically weak he had become. "I ought to have known it," he thought with a bitter smile. "And how dared I, knowing myself, knowing how I should be, take up an axe and shed blood! I ought to have known beforehand. . . . Ah, but I did know!" he whispered in despair. At times he came to a standstill at some thought.

"No, those men are not made so. The real *Master* to whom all is permitted storms Toulon, makes a massacre in Paris, *forgets* an army in Egypt, *wastes* half a million men in the Moscow expedition and gets off with a jest at Vilna. And altars are set up to him after his death, and so *all* is permitted. No, such people it seems are not of flesh but of bronze!"

One sudden irrelevant idea almost made him laugh. Napoleon, the pyramids, Waterloo, and a wretched skinny old woman, a pawnbroker with a red trunk under her bed—it's a nice hash for Porfiry Petrovitch to digest! How can they digest it! It's too inartistic. "A Napoleon creep under an old woman's bed! Ugh, how loathsome!"

At moments he felt he was raving. He sank into a state of feverish excitement. "The old woman is of no consequence," he thought, hotly and incoherently. "The old woman was a mistake perhaps, but she is not what matters! The old woman was only an illness. . . . I was in a hurry to overstep. . . . I didn't kill a human being, but a principle! I killed the principle, but I didn't overstep, I stopped on this side. . . . I was only capable of killing. And it seems I wasn't even capable of that . . . Principle? Why was that fool Razumihin abusing the socialists? They are industrious, commercial people; 'the happiness of all' is their case. No, life is only given to me once and I shall never have it again; I don't want to wait for 'the happiness of all.' I want to live myself, or else better not live at all. I simply couldn't pass by my mother starving, keeping my trouble in my pocket while I waited for the 'happiness of all.' I am putting my little brick into the happiness of all and so my heart is at peace. Ha-ha! Why have you let me slip? I only live once, I too want. . . . Ech, I am an aesthetic louse and nothing more." he added suddenly, laughing like a madman. "Yes, I am certainly a louse," he went on, clutching at the idea, gloating over it and playing with it with vindictive pleasure. "In the first place, because I can reason that I am one, and secondly, because for a month past I have been troubling benevolent Providence, calling it to witness that not for my own fleshly lusts did I undertake it, but with a grand and noble object—ha-ha! Thirdly, because I aimed at carrying it out as justly as possible, weighing, measuring and calculating. Of all the lice I picked out the most useless one and proposed to take from her only as much as I needed for the first step, no more nor less (so the rest would have gone to a monastery, according to her will, ha-ha!). And what shows that I am utterly a louse," he added, grinding his teeth, "is that I am perhaps viler and more loathsome than the louse I killed, and *I felt beforehand* that I should tell myself so *after* killing her. Can anything be compared with the horror of that! The vulgarity! The abjectness! I understand the 'prophet' with his sabre, on his steed: Allah commands and 'trembling' creation, and not *to have desires,* for that's not for you! . . . I shall never, never forgive the old woman!"

His hair was soaked with sweat, his quivering lips were parched, his eyes were fixed on the ceiling.

"Mother, sister—how I loved them! Why do I hate them now? Yes, I hate them, I feel a physical hatred for them, I can't bear them near me. . . . I went up to my mother and kissed her, I remember. . . . To embrace her and think if she only knew . . . shall I tell her then? That's just what I might do. . . . H'm. *She* must be the same as I am," he added, straining himself to think, as it were struggling with delirium. "Ah, how I hate the old woman now! I feel I should kill her again if she came to life! Poor Lizaveta! Why did she come in? . . . It's strange though, why is it I scarcely ever think of her, as though I hadn't killed her! Lizaveta! Sonia! Poor gentle things, with gentle eyes. . . . Dear women! Why don't they weep? Why don't they moan? They give up everything . . . their eyes are soft and gentle. . . . Sonia, Sonia! Gentle Sonia!"

He lost consciousness; it seemed strange to him that he didn't remember how he got into the street. It was late evening. The twilight had fallen and the full moon was shining more and more brightly; but there was a peculiar breathlessness in the air. There were crowds of people in the street; workmen and business people were making their way home; other people had come out for a walk; there was a smell of mortar, dust and stagnant water. Raskolnikov walked along, mournful and anxious; he was distinctly aware of having come out with a purpose, of having to do something in a hurry, but what it was he had forgotten. Suddenly he stood still and saw a man standing on the other side of the street, beckoning to him. He crossed over to him, but at once the man turned and walked away with his head hanging, as though he had made no sign to him. "Stay, did he really beckon?" Raskolnikov wondered, but he tried to overtake him. When he was within ten paces he recognised him and was frightened; it was the same man with stooping shoulders in the long coat. Raskolnikov followed him at a distance; his heart was beating; they went down a turning; the man still did not look round. "Does he know I am following him?" thought Raskolnikov. The man went into the gateway of a big house. Raskolnikov hastened to the gate and looked in to see whether he would look round and sign to him. In the courtyard the man did turn round and again seemed to beckon him. Raskolnikov at once followed him into the yard, but the man was gone. He must have gone up the first staircase. Raskolnikov rushed after him. He heard slow measured steps two flights above. The staircase seemed strangely familiar. He reached the window on the first floor; the moon shone through the panes with a melancholy and mysterious light; then he reached the second floor. Bah! this is the flat where the painters were at work . . . but how was it he did not recognise it at once? The steps of the man above had died away. "So he must have stopped or hidden somewhere." He reached the third storey, should he go on? There was a stillness that was dreadful. . . . But he went on. The sound of his own footsteps scared and frightened him. How dark it was! The man must be hiding in some corner here. Ah! the flat was standing wide open, he hesitated and went in. It was very dark and empty in the passage, as though everything had been removed; he crept on tiptoe into the parlour which was flooded with moonlight. Everything there was as before, the chairs, the looking-glass, the yellow sofa and the pictures in the frames. A huge, round, copper-red moon looked in at the windows. "It's the moon that makes it so still, weaving some mystery," thought Raskolnikov. He stood and waited, waited a long while, and the more silent the moonlight, the more violently his heart beat, till it was painful. And still the same hush. Suddenly he heard a momentary sharp crack like the snapping of a splinter and all was still again. A fly flew up suddenly and struck the window pane with a plaintive buzz. At that moment he noticed in the corner between the window and the little cupboard something like a cloak hanging on the wall. "Why is that cloak here?" he thought, "it wasn't there before. . . ." He went up to it quietly and felt that there was some one hiding behind it. He cautiously moved the cloak and saw, sitting on a chair in the corner, the old woman bent double so that he couldn't see her face; but it was she. He stood over her. "She is afraid," he thought. He stealthily took the axe from the noose and struck her one blow, then another on the skull. But strange to say she did not stir, as though she were made of wood. He was frightened, bent down nearer and tried to look at her; but she, too, bent her head lower. He bent right down to the ground and peeped up into her face from below, he peeped and turned cold with horror: the old woman was sitting and laughing, shaking with noiseless laughter, doing her utmost that he should not hear it. Suddenly he fancied that the door from the bedroom was opened a little and that there was laughter and whispering within. He was overcome with frenzy and he began hitting the old woman on the head with all his force, but at every blow of the axe the laughter and whispering from the bedroom grew louder and the old woman was simply shaking with mirth. He was rushing away, but the passage was full of people, the doors of the flats stood open and on the landing, on the stairs and everywhere below there were people, rows of heads, all looking, but huddled together in silence and expectation. Something gripped his heart, his legs were rooted to the spot, they would not move. . . . He tried to scream and woke up.

He drew a deep breath—but his dream seemed strangely to persist: his door was flung open and a man whom he had never seen stood in the doorway watching him intently.

Raskolnikov had hardly opened his eyes and he instantly closed them again. He lay on his back without stirring.

"Is it still a dream?" he wondered and again raised his eyelids hardly perceptibly; the stranger was standing in the same place, still watching him.

He stepped cautiously into the room, carefully closing the door after him, went up to the table, paused a moment, still keeping his eyes on Raskolnikov and noiselessly seated himself on the chair by the sofa; he put his hat on the floor beside him and leaned his hands on his cane and his chin on his hands. It was evident that he was prepared to wait indefinitely. As far as Raskolnikov could make out from his stolen glances, he was a man no longer young, stout, with a full, fair, almost whitish beard.

Ten minutes passed. It was still light, but beginning to get dusk. There was complete stillness in the room. Not a sound came from the stairs. Only a big fly buzzed and fluttered against the window pane. It was unbearable at last. Raskolnikov suddenly got up and sat on the sofa.

"Come, tell me what you want."

"I knew you were not asleep, but only pretending," the stranger answered oddly, laughing calmly. "Arkady Ivanovitch Svidrigaïlov, allow me to introduce myself. . . ."

PART FOUR—

1

"Can this be still a dream?" Raskolnikov thought once more. He looked carefully and suspiciously at the unexpected visitor.

"Svidrigaïlov! What nonsense! It can't be!" he said at last aloud in bewilderment.

His visitor did not seem at all surprised at this exclamation.

"I've come to you for two reasons. In the first place, I wanted to make your personal acquaintance, as I have already heard a great deal about you that is interesting and flattering; secondly, I cherish the hope that you may not refuse to assist me in a matter directly concerning the welfare of your sister, Avdotya Romanovna. For without your support she might not let me come near her now, for she is prejudiced against me, but with your assistance I reckon on . . ."

"You reckon wrongly," interrupted Raskolnikov.

"They only arrived yesterday, may I ask you?"

Raskolnikov made no reply.

"It was yesterday, I know. I only arrived myself the day before. Well, let me tell you this, Rodion Romanovitch, I don't consider it necessary to justify myself, but kindly tell me what was there particularly criminal on my part in all this business, speaking without prejudice, with common sense?"

Raskolnikov continued to look at him in silence.

"That in my own house I persecuted a defenceless girl and 'insulted her with my infamous proposals'—is that it? (I am anticipating you.) But you've only to assume that I, too, am a man *et nihil humanum* . . . in a word, that I am capable of being attracted and falling in love (which does not depend on our will), then everything can be explained in the most natural manner. The question is, am I a monster, or am I myself a victim? And what if I am a victim? In proposing to the object of my passion to elope with me to America or Switzerland, I may have cherished the deepest respect for her, and may have thought that I was promoting our mutual happiness! Reason is the slave of passion, you know; why, probably, I was doing more harm to myself than any one!"

"But that's not the point," Raskolnikov interrupted with disgust. "It's simply that whether you are right or wrong, we dislike you. We don't want to have anything to do with you. We show you the door. Go out!"

Svidrigaïlov broke into a sudden laugh.

"But you're . . . but there's no getting round you," he said, laughing in the frankest way. "I hoped to get round you, but you took up the right line at once!"

"But you are trying to get round me still!"

"What of it? What of it?" cried Svidrigaïlov, laughing openly. "But this is what the French call *bonne guerre,* and the most innocent form of deception! . . . But still you have interrupted me; one way or another, I repeat again: there would never have been any unpleasantness except for what happened in the garden. Marfa Petrovna . . ."

"You have got rid of Marfa Petrovna, too, so they say?" Raskolnikov interrupted rudely.

"Oh, you've heard that, too, then? You'd be sure to, though. . . . But as for your question, I really don't know what to say, though my own conscience is quite at rest on that score. Don't suppose that I am in any apprehension about it. All was regular and in order; the medical inquiry diagnosed apoplexy due to bathing immediately after a heavy dinner and a bottle of wine, and indeed it could have proved nothing else. But I'll tell you what I have been thinking to myself of late, on my way here in the train, especially: didn't I contribute to all that . . . calamity, morally, in a way, by irritation or something of the sort. But I came to the conclusion that that, too, was quite out of the question."

Raskolnikov laughed.

"I wonder you trouble yourself about it!"

"But what are you laughing at? Only consider, I struck her just twice with a switch—there were no marks even . . . don't regard me as a cynic, please; I am perfectly aware how atrocious it was of me and all that; but I know for certain, too, that Marfa Petrovna was very likely pleased at my, so to say, warmth. The story of your sister had been wrung out to the last drop; for the last three days Marfa Petrovna had been forced to sit at home; she had nothing to show herself with in the town. Besides, she had bored them so with that letter (you heard about her reading the letter). And all of a sudden those two switches fell from heaven! Her first act was to order the carriage to be got out. . . . Not to speak of the fact that there are cases when women are very, very glad to be insulted in spite of all their show of indignation. There are instances of it with every one; human beings in general, indeed, greatly love to be insulted, have you noticed that? But it's particularly so with women. One might even say it's their only amusement."

At one time Raskolnikov thought of getting up and walking out and so finishing the interview. But some curiosity and even a sort of prudence made him linger for a moment.

"You are fond of fighting?" he asked carelessly.

"No, not very," Svidrigaïlov answered, calmly. "And Marfa Petrovna and I scarcely ever fought. We lived very harmoniously, and she was always pleased with me. I only used the whip twice in all our seven years (not counting a third occasion of a very ambiguous character). The first time, two months after our marriage, immediately after we arrived in the country, and the last time was that of which we are speaking. Did you suppose I was such a monster, such a reactionary, such a slave driver? Ha, ha! By the way, do you remember, Rodion Romanovitch, how a few years ago, in those days of beneficent publicity, a nobleman, I've forgotten his name, was put to shame everywhere, in all the papers, for having thrashed a German woman in the railway train.

You remember? It was in those days, that very year I believe, the 'disgraceful action of the *Age*' took place (you know, 'The Egyptian Nights,' that public reading, you remember? The dark eyes, you know! Ah, the golden days of our youth, where are they?). Well, as for the gentleman who thrashed the German, I feel no sympathy with him, because after all what need is there for sympathy? But I must say that there are sometimes such provoking 'Germans' that I don't believe there is a progressive who could quite answer for himself. No one looked at the subject from that point of view then, but that's the truly humane point of view, I assure you."

After saying this, Svidrigaïlov broke into a sudden laugh again. Raskolnikov saw clearly that this was a man with a firm purpose in his mind and able to keep it to himself.

"I expect you've not talked to any one for some days?" he asked.

"Scarcely any one. I suppose you are wondering at my being such an adaptable man?"

"No, I am only wondering at your being too adaptable a man."

"Because I am not offended at the rudeness of your questions? Is that it? But why take offence? As you asked, so I answered," he replied, with a surprising expression of simplicity. "You know, there's hardly anything I take interest in," he went on, as it were dreamily, "especially now, I've nothing to do. . . . You are quite at liberty to imagine though that I am making up to you with a motive, particularly as I told you I want to see your sister about something. But I'll confess frankly, I am very much bored. The last three days especially, so I am delighted to see you. . . . Don't be angry, Rodion Romanovitch, but you seem to be somehow awfully strange yourself. Say what you like, there's something wrong with you, and now, too . . . not this very minute, I mean, but now, generally. . . . Well, well, I won't, I won't, don't scowl! I am not such a bear, you know, as you think."

Raskolnikov looked gloomily at him.

"You are not a bear, perhaps, at all," he said. "I fancy indeed that you are a man of very good breeding, or at least know how on occasion to behave like one."

"I am not particularly interested in any one's opinion," Svidragaïlov answered, dryly and even with a shade of haughtiness, "and therefore why not be vulgar at times when vulgarity is such a convenient cloak for our climate . . . and especially if one has a natural propensity that way," he added, laughing again.

"But I've heard you have many friends here. You are, as they say, 'not without connections.' What can you want with me, then, unless you've some special object?"

"That's true that I have friends here," Svidrigaïlov admitted, not replying to the chief point. "I've met some already. I've been lounging about for the last three days, and I've seen them, or they've seen me. That's a matter of course. I am well dressed and reckoned not a poor man; the emancipation of the serfs hasn't affected me; my property consists chiefly of forests and water meadows. The revenue has not fallen off; but . . . I am not going to see them, I was sick of them long ago. I've been here three days and have called on no one. . . . What a town it is! How has it come into existence among us, tell me that? A town of officials and students of all sorts. Yes, there's a great deal I didn't notice when I was here eight years ago, kicking up my heels. . . . My only hope now is in anatomy, by Jove, it is!"

"Anatomy?"

"But as for these clubs, Dussauts, parades, or progress, indeed, may be—well, all that can go on without me," he went on, again without noticing the question. "Besides, who wants to be a card-sharper?"

"Why, have you been a card-sharper then?"

"How could I help being? There was a regular set of us, men of the best society, eight years ago; we had a fine time. And all men of breeding, you know, poets, men of property. And indeed as a rule in our Russian society, the best manners are found among those who've been thrashed, have you noticed that? I've deteriorated in the country. But I did get into prison for debt, through a low Greek who came from Nezhin. Then Marfa Petrovna turned up; she bargained with him and bought me off for thirty

thousand silver pieces (I owed seventy thousand). We were united in lawful wedlock and she bore me off into the country like
a treasure. You know she was five years older than I. She was very
fond of me. For seven years I never left the country. And, take
note, that all my life she held a document over me, the I.O.U. for
thirty thousand roubles, so if I were to elect to be restive about
anything I should be trapped at once! And she would have done
it! Women find nothing incompatible in that."

"If it hadn't been for that, would you have given her the
slip?"

"I don't know what to say. It was scarcely the document
restrained me. I didn't want to go anywhere else. Marfa Petrovna
herself invited me to go abroad, seeing I was bored, but I've been
abroad before, and always felt sick there. For no reason, but the
sunrise, the bay of Naples, the sea—you look at them and it makes
you sad. What's most revolting is that one is really sad! No, it's
better at home. Here at least one blames others for everything
and excuses oneself. I should have gone perhaps on an expedition
to the North Pole, because *j'ai le vin mauvais* and hate drinking,
and there's nothing left but wine. I have tried it. But, I say, I've
been told Berg is going up in a great balloon next Sunday from
the Yusupov Garden and will take up passengers at a fee. Is it
true?"

"Why, would you go up?"

"I . . . No, oh, no," muttered Svidrigaïlov really seeming to
be deep in thought.

"What does he mean? Is he in earnest?" Raskolnikov wondered.

"No, the document didn't restrain me," Svidrigaïlov went
on, meditatively. "It was my own doing, not leaving the country,
and nearly a year ago Marfa Petrovna gave me back the document
on my name day and made me a present of a considerable sum
of money, too. She had a fortune, you know. 'You see how I trust
you, Arkady Ivanovitch'—that was actually her expression. You
don't believe she used it? But do you know I managed the estate
quite decently, they know me in the neighbourhood. I ordered

books, too. Marfa Petrovna at first approved, but afterwards she was afraid of my over-studying."

"You seem to be missing Marfa Petrovna very much?"

"Missing her? Perhaps. Really, perhaps I am. And, by the way, do you believe in ghosts?"

"What ghosts?"

"Why, ordinary ghosts."

"Do you believe in them?"

"Perhaps not, *pour vous plaire*. . . . I wouldn't say no exactly."

"Do you see them, then?"

Svidrigaïlov looked at him rather oddly.

"Marfa Petrovna is pleased to visit me," he said, twisting his mouth into a strange smile.

"How do you mean 'she is pleased to visit you'?"

"She has been three times. I saw her first on the very day of the funeral, an hour after she was buried. It was the day before I left to come here. The second time was the day before yesterday, at daybreak, on the journey at the station of Malaya Vishera, and the third time was two hours ago in the room where I am staying. I was alone."

"Were you awake?"

"Quite awake. I was wide awake every time. She comes, speaks to me for a minute and goes out at the door—always at the door. I can almost hear her."

"What made me think that something of the sort must be happening to you?" Raskolnikov said suddenly.

At the same moment he was surprised at having said it. He was much excited.

"What! Did you think so?" Svidrigaïlov asked in astonishment. "Did you really? Didn't I say that there was something in common between us, eh?"

"You never said so!" Raskolnikov cried sharply and with heat.

"Didn't I?"

"No!"

"I thought I did. When I came in and saw you lying with

your eyes shut, pretending, I said to myself at once 'here's the man.' "

"What do you mean by 'the man'? What are you talking about?" cried Raskolnikov.

"What do I mean? I really don't know. . . ." Svidrigaïlov muttered ingenuously, as though he, too, were puzzled.

For a minute they were silent. They stared in each other's faces.

"That's all nonsense!" Raskolnikov shouted with vexation. "What does she say when she comes to you?"

"She! Would you believe it, she talks of the silliest trifles and—man is a strange creature—it makes me angry. The first time she came in (I was tired you know: the funeral service, the funeral ceremony, the lunch afterwards. At last I was left alone in my study. I lighted a cigar and began to think), she came in at the door. 'You've been so busy to-day, Arkady Ivanovitch, you have forgotten to wind the dining room clock,' she said. All those seven years I've wound that clock every week, and if I forgot it she would always remind me. The next day I set off on my way here. I got out at the station at daybreak; I'd been asleep, tired out, with my eyes half open, I was drinking some coffee. I looked up and there was suddenly Marfa Petrovna sitting beside me with a pack of cards in her hands. 'Shall I tell your fortune for the journey, Arkady Ivanovitch?' She was a great hand at telling fortunes. I shall never forgive myself for not asking her to. I ran away in a fright, and, besides, the bell rang. I was sitting to-day, feeling very heavy after a miserable dinner from a cookshop; I was sitting smoking, all of a sudden Marfa Petrovna again. She came in very smart in a new green silk dress with a long train. 'Good day, Arkady Ivanovitch! How do you like my dress? Aniska can't make like this.' (Aniska was a dressmaker in the country, one of our former serf girls who had been trained in Moscow, a pretty wench.) She stood turning round before me. I looked at the dress, and then I looked carefully, very carefully, at her face. 'I wonder you trouble to come to me about such trifles, Marfa Petrovna.' 'Good gracious, you won't let one disturb you about anything!' To tease her I said, 'I want to get married, Marfa

Petrovna.' 'That's just like you, Arkady Ivanovitch; it does you
very little credit to come looking for a bride when you've hardly
buried your wife. And if you could make a good choice, at least,
but I know it won't be for your happiness or hers, you will only
be a laughing-stock to all good people.' Then she went out and
her train seemed to rustle. Isn't it nonsense, eh?''

"But perhaps you are telling lies?" Raskolnikov put in.

"I rarely lie," answered Svidrigaïlov thoughtfully, apparently not noticing the rudeness of the question.

"And in the past, have you ever seen ghosts before?"

"Y-yes, I have seen them, but only once in my life, six years
ago. I had a serf, Filka; just after his burial I called out forgetting
'Filka, my pipe!' He came in and went to the cupboard where my
pipes were. I sat still and thought 'he is doing it out of revenge,'
because we had a violent quarrel just before his death. 'How dare
you come in with a hole in your elbow,' I said. 'Go away, you
scamp!' He turned and went out, and never came again. I didn't
tell Marfa Petrovna at the time. I wanted to have a service sung
for him, but I was ashamed.''

"You should go to a doctor."

"I know I am not well, without your telling me, though I
don't know what's wrong; I believe I am five times as strong as
you are. I didn't ask you whether you believe that ghosts are seen,
but whether you believe that they exist.''

"No, I won't believe it!" Raskolnikov cried, with positive
anger.

"What do people generally say?" muttered Svidrigaïlov, as
though speaking to himself, looking aside and bowing his head:
"They say, 'You are ill, so what appears to you is only unreal
fantasy.' But that's not strictly logical. I agree that ghosts only
appear to the sick, but that only proves that they are unable to
appear except to the sick, not that they don't exist.''

"Nothing of the sort," Raskolnikov insisted irritably.

"No? You don't think so?" Svidrigaïlov went on, looking at
him deliberately. "But what do you say to this argument (help me
with it): ghosts are as it were shreds and fragments of other
worlds, the beginning of them. A man in health has, of course,

no reason to see them, because he is above all a man of this earth and is bound for the sake of completeness and order to live only in this life. But as soon as one is ill, as soon as the normal earthly order of the organism is broken, one begins to realise the possibility of another world; and the more seriously ill one is, the closer becomes one's contact with that other world, so that as soon as the man dies he steps straight into that world. I thought of that long ago. If you believe in a future life, you could believe in that, too."

"I don't believe in a future life," said Raskolnikov.

Svidrigaïlov sat lost in thought.

"And what if there are only spiders there, or something of that sort," he said suddenly.

"He is a madman," thought Raskolnikov.

"We always imagine eternity as something beyond our conception, something vast, vast! But why must it be vast? Instead of all that, what if it's one little room, like a bath-house in the country, black and grimy and spiders in every corner, and that's all eternity is? I sometimes fancy it like that."

"Can it be you can imagine nothing juster and more comforting than that?" Raskolnikov cried, with a feeling of anguish.

"Juster? And how can we tell, perhaps that is just, and do you know it's what I would certainly have made it," answered Svidrigaïlov, with a vague smile.

This horrible answer sent a cold chill through Raskolnikov. Svidrigaïlov raised his head, looked at him, and suddenly began laughing.

"Only think," he cried, "half an hour ago we had never seen each other, we regarded each other as enemies; there is a matter unsettled between us; we've thrown it aside, and away we've gone into the abstract! Wasn't I right in saying that we were birds of a feather?"

"Kindly allow me," Raskolnikov went on irritably, "to ask you to explain why you have honoured me with your visit . . . and . . . and I am in a hurry, I have no time to waste. I want to go out."

"By all means, by all means. Your sister, Avdotya Romanovna, is going to be married to Mr. Luzhin, Pyotr Petrovitch?"

"Can you refrain from any question about my sister and from mentioning her name? I can't understand how you dare utter her name in my presence, if you really are Svidrigaïlov."

"Why, but I've come here to speak about her; how can I avoid mentioning her?"

"Very good, speak, but make haste."

"I am sure that you must have formed your own opinion of this Mr. Luzhin, who is a connection of mine through my wife, if you have only seen him for half an hour, or heard any facts about him. He is no match for Avdotya Romanovna. I believe Avdotya Romanovna is sacrificing herself generously and imprudently for the sake of . . . for the sake of her family. I fancied from all I had heard of you that you would be very glad if the match could be broken off without the sacrifice of worldly advantages. Now I know you personally, I am convinced of it."

"All this is very naïve . . . excuse me, I should have said impudent on your part," said Raskolnikov.

"You mean to say that I am seeking my own ends. Don't be uneasy, Rodion Romanovitch, if I were working for my own advantage, I would not have spoken out so directly. I am not quite a fool. I will confess something psychologically curious about that: just now, defending my love for Avdotya Romanovna, I said I was myself the victim. Well, let me tell you that I've no feeling of love now, not the slightest, so that I wonder myself indeed, for I really did feel something . . ."

"Through idleness and depravity," Raskolnikov put in.

"I certainly am idle and depraved, but your sister has such qualities that even I could not help being impressed by them. But that's all nonsense, as I see myself now."

"Have you seen that long?"

"I began to be aware of it before, but was only perfectly sure of it the day before yesterday, almost at the moment I arrived in Petersburg. I still fancied in Moscow, though, that I was coming to try to get Avdotya Romanovna's hand and to cut out Mr. Luzhin."

"Excuse me for interrupting you; kindly be brief, and come to the object of your visit. I am in a hurry, I want to go out. . . ."

"With the greatest pleasure. On arriving here and determining on a certain . . . journey, I should like to make some necessary preliminary arrangements. I left my children with an aunt; they are well provided for; and they have no need of me personally. And a nice father I should make, too! I have taken nothing but what Marfa Petrovna gave me a year ago. That's enough for me. Excuse me, I am just coming to the point. Before the journey which may come off, I want to settle Mr. Luzhin, too. It's not that I detest him so much, but it was through him I quarrelled with Marfa Petrovna when I learned that she had dished up this marriage. I want now to see Avdotya Romanovna through your mediation, and if you like in your presence, to explain to her that in the first place she will never gain anything but harm from Mr. Luzhin. Then begging her pardon for all past unpleasantness, to make her a present of ten thousand roubles and so assist the rupture with Mr. Luzhin, a rupture to which I believe she is herself not disinclined, if she could see the way to it."

"You are certainly mad," cried Raskolnikov not so much angered as astonished. "How dare you talk like that!"

"I knew you would scream at me; but in the first place, though I am not rich, this ten thousand roubles is perfectly free; I have absolutely no need for it. If Avdotya Romanovna does not accept it, I shall waste it in some more foolish way. That's the first thing. Secondly, my conscience is perfectly easy; I make the offer with no ulterior motive. You may not believe it, but in the end Avdotya Romanovna and you will know. The point is, that I did actually cause your sister, whom I greatly respect, some trouble and unpleasantness, and so, sincerely regretting it, I want—not to compensate, not to repay her for the unpleasantness, but simply to do something to her advantage, to show that I am not, after all, privileged to do nothing but harm. If there were a millionth fraction of self interest in my offer, I should not have made it so openly; and I should not have offered her ten thousand only, when five weeks ago I offered her more. Besides, I may, perhaps, very soon marry a young lady, and that alone ought to prevent suspicion of any design on Avdotya Romanovna. In conclusion, let me say that in marrying Mr. Luzhin, she is taking money just the same, only from another man. Don't be angry, Rodion Romanovitch, think it over coolly and quietly."

Svidrigaïlov himself was exceedingly cool and quiet as he was saying this.

"I beg you to say no more," said Raskolnikov. "In any case this is unpardonable impertinence."

"Not in the least. Then a man may do nothing but harm to his neighbour in this world, and is prevented from doing the tiniest bit of good by trivial conventional formalities. That's absurd. If I died, for instance, and left that sum to your sister in my will, surely she wouldn't refuse it?"

"Very likely she would."

"Oh, no, indeed. However, if you refuse it, so be it, though ten thousand roubles is a capital thing to have on occasion. In any case I beg you to repeat what I have said to Avdotya Romanovna."

"No, I won't."

"In that case, Rodion Romanovitch, I shall be obliged to try and see her myself and worry her by doing so."

"And if I do tell her, will you not try to see her?"

"I don't know really what to say. I should like very much to see her once more."

"Don't hope for it."

"I'm sorry. But you don't know me. Perhaps we may become better friends."

"You think we may become friends?"

"And why not?" Svidrigaïlov said, smiling. He stood up and took his hat. "I didn't quite intend to disturb you and I came here without reckoning on it . . . though I was very much struck by your face this morning."

"Where did you see me this morning?" Raskolnikov asked uneasily.

"I saw you by chance. . . . I kept fancying there is something about you like me. . . . But don't be uneasy. I am not intrusive;

I used to get on all right with card-sharpers, and I never bored Prince Svirbey, a great personage who is a distant relation of mine, and I could write about Raphael's *Madonna* in Madam Prilukov's album, and I never left Marfa Petrovna's side for seven years, and I used to stay the night at Viazemsky's house in the Hay Market in the old days, and I may go up in a balloon with Berg, perhaps."

"Oh, all right. Are you starting soon on your travels, may I ask?"

"What travels?"

"Why, on that 'journey'; you spoke of it yourself."

"A journey? Oh, yes. I did speak of a journey. Well, that's a wide subject. . . . If only you knew what you are asking," he added, and gave a sudden, loud, short laugh. "Perhaps I'll get married instead of the journey. They're making a match for me."

"Here?"

"Yes."

"How have you had time for that?"

"But I am very anxious to see Avdotya Romanovna once. I earnestly beg it. Well, good-bye for the present. Oh, yes, I have forgotten something. Tell your sister, Rodion Romanovitch, that Marfa Petrovna remembered her in her will and left her three thousand roubles. That's absolutely certain. Marfa Petrovna arranged it a week before her death, and it was done in my presence. Avdotya Romanovna will be able to receive the money in two or three weeks."

"Are you telling the truth?"

"Yes, tell her. Well, your servant. I am staying very near you."

As he went out, Svidrigaïlov ran up against Razumihin in the doorway.

2

It was nearly eight o'clock. The two young men hurried to Bakaleyev's, to arrive before Luzhin.

"Why, who was that?" asked Razumihin, as soon as they were in the street.

"It was Svidrigaïlov, that landowner in whose house my sister was insulted when she was their governess. Through his persecuting her with his attentions, she was turned out by his wife, Marfa Petrovna. This Marfa Petrovna begged Dounia's forgiveness afterwards, and she's just died suddenly. It was of her we were talking this morning. I don't know why I'm afraid of that man. He came here at once after his wife's funeral. He is very strange, and is determined on doing something. . . . We must guard Dounia from him . . . that's what I wanted to tell you, do you hear?"

"Guard her! What can he do to harm Avdotya Romanovna? Thank you, Rodya, for speaking to me like that. . . . We will, we will guard her. Where does he live?"

"I don't know."

"Why didn't you ask? What a pity! I'll find out, though."

"Did you see him?" asked Raskolnikov after a pause.

"Yes, I noticed him, I noticed him well."

"You did really see him? You saw him clearly?" Raskolnikov insisted.

"Yes, I remember him perfectly, I should know him in a thousand; I have a good memory for faces."

They were silent again.

"Hm! . . . that's all right," muttered Raskolnikov. "Do you know, I fancied . . . I keep thinking that it may have been an hallucination."

"What do you mean? I don't understand you."

"Well, you all say," Raskolnikov went on, twisting his mouth into a smile, "that I am mad. I thought just now that perhaps I really am mad, and have only seen a phantom."

"What do you mean?"

"Why, who can tell? Perhaps I am really mad, and perhaps everything that happened all these days may be only imagination."

"Ach, Rodya, you have been upset again! . . . But what did he say, what did he come for?"

Raskolnikov did not answer. Razumihin thought a minute.

"Now let me tell you my story," he began, "I came to you, you were asleep. Then we had dinner and then I went to Porfiry's, Zametov was still with him. I tried to begin, but it was no use. I couldn't speak in the right way. They don't seem to understand and can't understand, but are not a bit ashamed. I drew Porfiry to the window, and began talking to him, but it was still no use. He looked away and I looked away. At last I shook my fist in his ugly face, and told him as a cousin I'd brain him. He merely looked at me, I cursed and came away. That was all. It was very stupid. To Zametov I didn't say a word. But, you see, I thought I'd made a mess of it, but as I went downstairs a brilliant idea struck me; why should we trouble? Of course if you were in any danger or anything, but why need you care? You needn't care a hang for them. We shall have a laugh at them afterwards, and if I were in your place I'd mystify them more than ever. How ashamed they'll be afterwards! Hang them! We can thrash them afterwards, but let's laugh at them now!"

"To be sure," answered Raskolnikov. "But what will you say to-morrow?" he thought to himself. Strange to say, till that moment it had never occurred to him to wonder what Razumihin would think when he knew. As he thought it, Raskolnikov looked at him. Razumihin's account of his visit to Porfiry had very little interest for him, so much had come and gone since then.

In the corridor they came upon Luzhin; he had arrived punctually at eight, and was looking for the number, so that all three went in together without greeting or looking at one another. The young men walked in first, while Pyotr Petrovitch, for good manners, lingered a little in the passage, taking off his coat. Pulcheria Alexandrovna came forward at once to greet him in the doorway, Dounia was welcoming her brother. Pyotr Petrovitch walked in and quite amiably, though with redoubled dignity, bowed to the ladies. He looked, however, as though he were a little put out and could not yet recover himself. Pulcheria Alexandrovna, who seemed also a little embarrassed, hastened to make them all sit down at the round table where a samovar was boiling. Dounia and Luzhin were facing one another on opposite sides of the table. Razumihin and Raskolnikov were facing Pulcheria Alexandrovna, Razumihin was next to Luzhin and Raskolnikov was beside his sister.

A moment's silence followed. Pyotr Petrovitch deliberately drew out a cambric handkerchief reeking of scent and blew his nose with an air of a benevolent man who felt himself slighted, and was firmly resolved to insist on an explanation. In the passage the idea had occurred to him to keep on his overcoat and walk away, and so give the two ladies a sharp and emphatic lesson and make them feel the gravity of the position. But he could not bring himself to do this. Besides, he could not endure uncertainty and he wanted an explanation: if his request had been so openly disobeyed, there was something behind it, and in that case it was better to find it out beforehand; it rested with him to punish them and there would always be time for that.

"I trust you had a favourable journey," he inquired officially of Pulcheria Alexandrovna.

"Oh, very, Pyotr Petrovitch."

"I am gratified to hear it. And Avdotya Romanovna is not over fatigued either?"

"I am young and strong, I don't get tired, but it was a great strain for mother," answered Dounia.

"That's unavoidable; our national railways are of terrible length. 'Mother Russia,' as they say, is a vast country. . . . In spite of all my desire to do so, I was unable to meet you yesterday. But I trust all passed off without inconvenience?"

"Oh, no, Pyotr Petrovitch, it was all terribly disheartening," Pulcheria Alexandrovna hastened to declare with peculiar intonation, "and if Dmitri Prokofitch had not been sent us, I really believe by God Himself, we should have been utterly lost. Here, he is! Dmitri Prokofitch Razumihin," she added, introducing him to Luzhin.

"I had the pleasure . . . yesterday," muttered Pyotr Petrovitch with a hostile glance sidelong at Razumihin; then he scowled and was silent.

Pyotr Petrovitch belonged to that class of persons, on the surface very polite in society, who make a great point of punctiliousness, but who, directly they are crossed in anything, are completely disconcerted, and become more like sacks of flour than elegant and lively men of society. Again all was silent; Raskolnikov was obstinately mute, Avdotya Romanovna was unwilling to open the conversation too soon. Razumihin had nothing to say, so Pulcheria Alexandrovna was anxious again.

"Marfa Petrovna is dead, have you heard?" she began having recourse to her leading item of conversation.

"To be sure, I heard so. I was immediately informed, and I have come to make you acquainted with the fact that Arkady Ivanovitch Svidrigaïlov set off in haste for Petersburg immediately after his wife's funeral. So at least I have excellent authority for believing."

"To Petersburg? here?" Dounia asked in alarm and looked at her mother.

"Yes, indeed, and doubtless not without some design, having in view the rapidity of his departure, and all the circumstances preceding it."

"Good heavens! won't he leave Dounia in peace even here?" cried Pulcheria Alexandrovna.

"I imagine that neither you nor Avdotya Romanovna have any grounds for uneasiness, unless, of course, you are yourselves desirous of getting into communication with him. For my part I am on my guard, and am now discovering where he is lodging."

"Oh, Pyotr Petrovitch, you would not believe what a fright you have given me," Pulcheria Alexandrovna went on. "I've only seen him twice, but I thought him terrible, terrible! I am convinced that he was the cause of Marfa Petrovna's death."

"It's impossible to be certain about that. I have precise information. I do not dispute that he may have contributed to accelerate the course of events by the moral influence, so to say, of the affront; but as to the general conduct and moral characteristics of that personage, I am in agreement with you. I do not know whether he is well off now, and precisely what Marfa Petrovna left him; this will be known to me within a very short period; but no doubt here in Petersburg, if he has any pecuniary resources, he will relapse at once into his old ways. He is the most depraved, and abjectly vicious specimen of that class of men. I have considerable reason to believe that Marfa Petrovna, who was so unfortunate as to fall in love with him and to pay his debts eight years ago, was of service to him also in another way. Solely by her exertions and sacrifices, a criminal charge, involving an element of fantastic and homicidal brutality for which he might well have been sentenced to Siberia, was hushed up. That's the sort of man he is, if you care to know."

"Good heavens!" cried Pulcheria Alexandrovna. Raskolnikov listened attentively.

"Are you speaking the truth when you say that you have good evidence of this?" Dounia asked sternly and emphatically.

"I only repeat what I was told in secret by Marfa Petrovna. I must observe that from the legal point of view the case was far from clear. There was, and I believe still is, living here a woman called Resslich, a foreigner, who lent small sums of money at interest, and did other commissions, and with this woman Svidrigaïlov had for a long while close and mysterious relations. She had a relation, a niece I believe, living with her, a deaf and dumb girl of fifteen, or perhaps not more than fourteen. Resslich hated this girl, and grudged her every crust; she used to beat her mercilessly. One day the girl was found hanging in the garret. At the inquest the verdict was suicide. After the usual proceedings the matter ended, but, later on, information was given that the child had been . . . cruelly outraged by Svidrigaïlov. It is true, this was not clearly established, the information was given by another German woman of loose character whose word could not be trusted; no statement was actually made to the police, thanks to Marfa Petrovna's money and exertions; it did not get beyond gossip. And yet the story is a very significant one. You heard, no doubt, Avdotya Romanovna, when you were with them the story of the servant Philip who died of ill treatment he received six years ago, before the abolition of serfdom."

"I heard on the contrary that this Philip hanged himself."

"Quite so, but what drove him, or rather perhaps disposed him, to suicide, was the systematic persecution and severity of Mr. Svidrigaïlov."

"I don't know that," answered Dounia, drily. "I only heard a queer story that Philip was a sort of hypochondriac, a sort of domestic philosopher, the servants used to say, 'he read himself silly,' and that he hanged himself partly on account of Mr. Svidrigaïlov's mockery of him and not his blows. When I was there he behaved well to the servants, and they were actually fond of him, though they certainly did blame him for Philip's death."

"I perceive, Avdotya Romanovna, that you seem disposed to undertake his defence all of a sudden," Luzhin observed, twisting his lips into an ambiguous smile, "there's no doubt that he is an astute man, and insinuating where ladies are concerned, of which Marfa Petrovna, who has died so strangely, is a terrible instance. My only desire has been to be of service to you and your mother with my advice, in view of the renewed efforts which may certainly be anticipated from him. For my part it's my firm conviction, that he will end in a debtor's prison again. Marfa Petrovna had not the slightest intention of settling anything substantial on him, having regard for his children's interests, and, if she left him anything, it would only be the merest sufficiency, something insignificant and ephemeral, which would not last a year for a man of his habits."

"Pyotr Petrovitch, I beg you," said Dounia, "say no more of Mr. Svidrigaïlov. It makes me miserable."

"He has just been to see me," said Raskolnikov, breaking his silence for the first time.

There were exclamations from all, and they all turned to him. Even Pyotr Petrovitch was roused.

"An hour and a half ago, he came in when I was asleep, waked me, and introduced himself." Raskolnikov continued. "He was fairly cheerful and at ease, and quite hopes that we shall become friends. He is particularly anxious by the way, Dounia, for an interview with you, at which he asked me to assist. He has a proposition to make to you, and he told me about it. He told me, too, that a week before her death Marfa Petrovna left you three thousand roubles in her will, Dounia, and that you can receive the money very shortly."

"Thank God!" cried Pulcheria Alexandrovna, crossing herself. "Pray for her soul, Dounia!"

"It's a fact!" broke from Luzhin.

"Tell us, what more?" Dounia urged Raskolnikov.

"Then he said that he wasn't rich and all the estate was left to his children who are now with an aunt, then that he was staying somewhere not far from me, but where, I don't know, I didn't ask. . . ."

"But what, what does he want to propose to Dounia?" cried Pulcheria Alexandrovna in a fright. "Did he tell you?"

"Yes."

"What was it?"

"I'll tell you afterwards."

Raskolnikov ceased speaking and turned his attention to his tea.

Pyotr Petrovitch looked at his watch.

"I am compelled to keep a business engagement, and so I shall not be in your way," he added with an air of some pique and he began getting up.

"Don't go, Pyotr Petrovitch," said Dounia, "you intended to spend the evening. Besides, you wrote yourself that you wanted to have an explanation with mother."

"Precisely so, Avdotya Romanovna," Pyotr Petrovitch answered impressively, sitting down again, but still holding his hat. "I certainly desired an explanation with you and your honoured mother upon a very important point indeed. But as your brother cannot speak openly in my presence to some proposals of Mr. Svidrigaïlov, I, too, do not desire and am not able to speak openly . . . in the presence of others . . . of certain matters of the greatest gravity. Moreover, my most weighty and urgent request has been disregarded. . . ."

Assuming an aggrieved air, Luzhin relapsed into dignified silence.

"Your request that my brother should not be present at our meeting was disregarded solely at my instance," said Dounia. "You wrote that you had been insulted by my brother; I think that this must be explained at once, and you must be reconciled. And if Rodya really has insulted you, then he *should* and *will* apologize."

Pyotr Petrovitch took a stronger line.

"There are insults, Avdotya Romanovna, which no goodwill can make us forget. There is a line in everything which it is dangerous to overstep; and when it has been overstepped, there is no return."

"That wasn't what I was speaking of exactly, Pyotr Petrovitch," Dounia interrupted with some impatience. "Please understand that our whole future depends now on whether all this is explained and set right as soon as possible. I tell you frankly at the start that I cannot look at it in any other light, and if you have the least regard for me, all this business must be ended to-day, however hard that may be. I repeat that if my brother is to blame he will ask your forgiveness."

"I am surprised at your putting the question like that," said Luzhin, getting more and more irritated. "Esteeming, and so to say, adoring you, I may at the same time, very well indeed, be able to dislike some member of your family. Though I lay claim to the happiness of your hand, I cannot accept duties incompatible with . . ."

"Ah, don't be so ready to take offence, Pyotr Petrovitch," Dounia interrupted with feeling, "and be the sensible and generous man I have always considered, and wish to consider, you to be. I've given you a great promise, I am your betrothed. Trust me in this matter and, believe me, I shall be capable of judging impartially. My assuming the part of judge is as much a surprise for my brother as for you. When I insisted on his coming to our interview to-day after your letter, I told him nothing of what I meant to do. Understand that, if you are not reconciled, I must choose between you—it must be either you or he. That is how the question rests on your side and on his. I don't want to be mistaken in my choice, and I must not be. For your sake I must break off with my brother, for my brother's sake I must break off with you. I can find out for certain now whether he is a brother to me, and I want to know it; and of you, whether I am dear to you, whether you esteem me, whether you are the husband for me."

"Avdotya Romanovna," Luzhin declared huffily, "your words are of too much consequence to me; I will say more, they are offensive in view of the position I have the honour to occupy in relation to you. To say nothing of your strange and offensive setting me on a level with an impertinent boy, you admit the possibility of breaking your promise to me. You say 'you or he,' showing thereby of how little consequence I am in your eyes . . . I cannot let this pass considering the relationship and . . . the obligations existing between us."

"What!" cried Dounia, flushing. "I set your interest beside all that has hitherto been most precious in my life, what has made up the *whole* of my life, and here you are offended at my making too *little* account of you."

Raskolnikov smiled sarcastically, Razumihin fidgeted, but Pyotr Petrovitch did not accept the reproof; on the contrary, at every word he became more persistent and irritable, as though he relished it.

"Love for the future partner of your life, for your husband, ought to outweigh your love for your brother," he pronounced sententiously, "and in any case I cannot be put on the same level. . . . Although I said so emphatically that I would not speak openly in your brother's presence, nevertheless, I intend now to ask your honoured mother for a necessary explanation on a point of great importance closely affecting my dignity. Your son," he turned to Pulcheria Alexandrovna, "yesterday in the presence of Mr. Razsudkin (or . . . I think that's it? excuse me I have forgotten your surname," he bowed politely to Razumihin) "insulted me by misrepresenting the idea I expressed to you in a private conversation, drinking coffee, that is, that marriage with a poor girl who has had experience of trouble is more advantageous from the conjugal point of view than with one who has lived in luxury, since it is more profitable for the moral character. Your son intentionally exaggerated the significance of my words and made them ridiculous, accusing me of malicious intentions, and, as far as I could see, relied upon your correspondence with him. I shall consider myself happy, Pulcheria Alexandrovna, if it is possible for you to convince me of an opposite conclusion, and thereby considerately reassure me. Kindly let me know in what terms precisely you repeated my words in your letter to Rodion Romanovitch."

"I don't remember," faltered Pulcheria Alexandrovna. "I repeated them as I understood them. I don't know how Rodya repeated them to you, perhaps he exaggerated."

"He could not have exaggerated them, except at your instigation."

"Pyotr Petrovitch," Pulcheria Alexandrovna declared with dignity, "the proof that Dounia and I did not take your words in a very bad sense is the fact that we are here."

"Good, mother," said Dounia approvingly.

"Then this is my fault again," said Luzhin, aggrieved.

"Well, Pyotr Petrovitch, you keep blaming Rodion, but you yourself have just written what was false about him," Pulcheria Alexandrovna added, gaining courage.

"I don't remember writing anything false."

"You wrote," Raskolnikov said sharply, not turning to Luzhin, "that I gave money yesterday not to the widow of the man who was killed, as was the fact, but to his daughter (whom I had never seen till yesterday). You wrote this to make dissension between me and my family, and for that object added coarse expressions about the conduct of a girl whom you don't know. All that is mean slander."

"Excuse me, sir," said Luzhin, quivering with fury. "I enlarged upon your qualities and conduct in my letter solely in response to your sister's and mother's inquiries how I found you and what impression you made on me. As for what you've alluded to in my letter, be so good as to point out one word of falsehood, show, that is, that you didn't throw away your money, and that there are not worthless persons in that family, however unfortunate."

"To my thinking, you with all your virtues are not worth the little finger of that unfortunate girl at whom you throw stones."

"Would you go so far then as to let her associate with your mother and sister?"

"I have done so already, if you care to know. I made her sit down to-day with mother and Dounia."

"Rodya!" cried Pulcheria Alexandrovna. Dounia crimsoned, Razumihin knitted his brows. Luzhin smiled with lofty sarcasm.

"You may see for yourself, Avdotya Romanovna," he said, "whether it is possible for us to agree. I hope now that this question is at an end, once and for all. I will withdraw, that I may not hinder the pleasures of family intimacy, and the discussion of secrets." He got up from his chair and took his hat. "But in withdrawing, I venture to request that for the future I may be spared similar meetings, and, so to say, compromises. I appeal particularly to you, honoured Pulcheria Alexandrovna, on this subject, the more as my letter was addressed to you and to no one else."

Pulcheria Alexandrovna was a little offended.

"You seem to think we are completely under your authority, Pyotr Petrovich. Dounia has told you the reason your desire was disregarded, she had the best intentions. And indeed you write as though you were laying commands upon me. Are we to consider every desire of yours as a command? Let me tell you on the contrary that you ought to show particular delicacy and consideration for us now, because we have thrown up everything, and have come here relying on you, and so we are in any case in a sense in your hands."

"That is not quite true, Pulcheria Alexandrovna, especially at the present moment, when the news has come of Marfa Petrovna's legacy, which seems indeed very apropos, judging from the new tone you take to me," he added sarcastically.

"Judging from that remark, we may certainly presume that you were reckoning on our helplessness," Dounia observed irritably.

"But now in any case I cannot reckon on it, and I particularly desire not to hinder your discussion of the secret proposals of Arkady Ivanovitch Svidrigaïlov, which he has entrusted to your brother and which have, I perceive, a great and possibly a very agreeable interest for you."

"Good heavens!" cried Pulcheria Alexandrovna.

Razumihin could not sit still on his chair.

"Aren't you ashamed now, sister?" asked Raskolnikov.

"I am ashamed, Rodya," said Dounia. "Pyotr Petrovitch, go away," she turned to him, white with anger.

Pyotr Petrovitch had apparently not at all expected such a conclusion. He had too much confidence in himself, in his power and in the helplessness of his victims. He could not believe it even now. He turned pale, and his lips quivered.

"Avdotya Romanovna, if I go out of this door now, after such a dismissal, then, you may reckon on it, I will never come back. Consider what you are doing. My word is not to be shaken."

"What insolence!" cried Dounia, springing up from her seat. "I don't want you to come back again."

"What! So that's how it stands!" cried Luzhin, utterly unable to the last moment to believe in the rupture and so completely thrown out of his reckoning now. "So that's how it stands! But do you know, Avdotya Romanovna, that I might protest?"

"What right have you to speak to her like that?" Pulcheria Alexandrovna intervened hotly. "And what can you protest about? What rights have you? Am I to give my Dounia to a man like you? Go away, leave us altogether! We are to blame for having agreed to a wrong action, and I above all. . . ."

"But you have bound me, Pulcheria Alexandrovna," Luzhin stormed in a frenzy, "by your promise, and now you deny it and . . . besides . . . I have been led on account of that into expenses. . . ."

This last complaint was so characteristic of Pyotr Petrovitch, that Raskolnikov, pale with anger and with the effort of restraining it, could not help breaking into laughter. But Pulcheria Alexandrovna was furious.

"Expenses? What expenses? Are you speaking of our trunk? But the conductor brought it for nothing for you. Mercy on us, we have bound you! What are you thinking about, Pyotr Petrovitch, it was you bound us, hand and foot, not we!"

"Enough, mother, no more please," Avdotya Romanovna implored. "Pyotr Petrovitch, do be kind and go!"

"I am going, but one last word," he said, quite unable to control himself. "Your mamma seems to have entirely forgotten that I made up my mind to take you, so to speak, after the gossip of the town had spread all over the district in regard to your reputation. Disregarding public opinion for your sake and reinstating your reputation, I certainly might very well reckon on a fitting return, and might indeed look for gratitude on your part. And my eyes have only now been opened! I see myself that I may have acted very, very recklessly in disregarding the universal verdict. . . ."

"Does the fellow want his head smashed?" cried Razumihin, jumping up.

"You are a mean and spiteful man!" cried Dounia.

"Not a word! Not a movement!" cried Raskolnikov, holding Razumihin back; then going close up to Luzhin, "Kindly leave the room!" he said quietly and distinctly, "and not a word more or . . ."

Pyotr Petrovitch gazed at him for some seconds with a pale face that worked with anger, then he turned, went out, and rarely has any man carried away in his heart such vindictive hatred as he felt against Raskolnikov. Him, and him alone, he blamed for everything. It is noteworthy that as he went downstairs he still imagined that his case was perhaps not utterly lost, and that, so far as the ladies were concerned, all might "very well indeed" be set right again.

3

The fact was that up to the last moment he had never expected such an ending; he had been overbearing to the last degree, never dreaming that two destitute and defenceless women could escape from his control. This conviction was strengthened by his vanity and conceit, a conceit to the point of fatuity. Pyotr Petrovitch, who had made his way up from insignificance, was morbidly given to self-admiration, had the highest opinion of his intelligence and capacities, and sometimes even gloated in solitude over his image in the glass. But what he loved and valued above all was the money he had amassed by his labour, and by all sorts of devices: that money made him the equal of all who had been his superiors.

When he had bitterly reminded Dounia that he had decided to take her in spite of evil report, Pyotr Petrovitch had spoken with perfect sincerity and had, indeed, felt genuinely indignant at such "black ingratitude." And yet, when he made Dounia his offer, he was fully aware of the groundlessness of all the gossip. The story had been everywhere contradicted by Marfa Petrovna, and was by then disbelieved by all the townspeople, who were warm in Dounia's defence. And he would not have denied that he knew all that at the time. Yet he still thought highly of his own resolution in lifting Dounia to his level and regarded it as something heroic. In speaking of it to Dounia, he had let out the secret feeling he cherished and admired, and he could not understand that others should fail to admire it too. He had called on Raskolnikov with the feelings of a benefactor who is about to reap the fruits of his good deeds and to hear agreeable flattery. And as he went downstairs now, he considered himself most undeservedly injured and unrecognised.

Dounia was simply essential to him; to do without her was unthinkable. For many years he had voluptuous dreams of marriage, but he had gone on waiting and amassing money. He brooded with relish, in profound secret, over the image of a girl—virtuous, poor (she must be poor), very young, very pretty, of good birth and education, very timid, one who had suffered much, and was completely humbled before him, one who would all her life look on him as her saviour, worship him, admire him and only him. How many scenes, how many amorous episodes he had imagined on this seductive and playful theme, when his work was over! And, behold, the dream of so many years was all but realised; the beauty and education of Avdotya Romanovna had impressed him; her helpless position had been a great allurement; in her he had found even more than he dreamed of. Here was a girl of pride, character, virtue, of education and breeding superior to his own (he felt that), and this creature would be slavishly grateful all her life for his heroic condescension, and would humble herself in the dust before him, and he would have absolute, unbounded power over her! . . . Not long before, he had, too, after long reflection and hesitation, made an important change in his career and was now entering on a wider circle of business. With this change his cherished dreams of rising into a higher class of society seemed likely to be realised. . . . He was, in fact, determined to try his fortune in Petersburg. He knew that women could do a very great deal. The fascination of a charming, virtuous, highly educated woman might make his way easier, might do wonders in attracting people to him, throwing an aureole round him, and now everything was in ruins! This sudden horrible rupture affected him like a clap of thunder; it was like a hideous joke, an absurdity. He had only been a tiny bit masterful, had not even time to speak out, had simply made a joke, been carried away—and it had ended so seriously. And, of course, too, he did love Dounia in his own way; he already possessed her in his dreams—and all at once! No! The next day, the very next day, it must all be set right, smoothed over, settled. Above all he must crush that conceited milksop who was the cause of it all. With a sick feeling he could not help recalling Razumihin too, but, he soon reassured himself on that score; as though a fellow like that could be put on a level with him! The man he really dreaded in earnest was Svidrigaïlov. . . . He had, in short, a great deal to attend to. . . .

"No, I, I am more to blame than any one!" said Dounia, kissing and embracing her mother. "I was tempted by his money, but on my honour, brother, I had no idea he was such a base man. If I had seen through him before, nothing would have tempted me! Don't blame me, brother!"

"God has delivered us! God has delivered us!" Pulcheria Alexandrovna muttered, but half consciously, as though scarcely able to realise what had happened.

They were all relieved, and in five minutes they were laughing. Only now and then Dounia turned white and frowned, remembering what had passed. Pulcheria Alexandrovna was surprised to find that she, too, was glad: she had only that morning thought rupture with Luzhin a terrible misfortune. Razumihin was delighted. He did not yet dare to express his joy fully, but he was in a fever of excitement as though a ton-weight had fallen off his heart. Now he had the right to devote his life to them, to serve them. . . . Anything might happen now! But he felt afraid to think of further possibilities and dared not let his imagination range. But Raskolnikov sat still in the same place, almost sullen and indifferent. Though he had been the most insistent on getting rid of Luzhin, he seemed now the least concerned at what had happened. Dounia could not help thinking that he was still angry with her, and Pulcheria Alexandrovna watched him timidly.

"What did Svidrigaïlov say to you?" said Dounia, approaching him.

"Yes, yes!" cried Pulcheria Alexandrovna.

Raskolnikov raised his head.

"He wants to make you a present of ten thousand roubles and he desires to see you once in my presence."

"See her! On no account!" cried Pulcheria Alexandrovna. "And how dare he offer her money!"

Then Raskolnikov repeated (rather drily) his conversation with Svidrigaïlov, omitting his account of the ghostly visitations of Marfa Petrovna, wishing to avoid all unnecessary talk.

"What answer did you give him?" asked Dounia.

"At first I said I would not take any message to you. Then he said that he would do his utmost to obtain an interview with you without my help. He assured me that his passion for you was a passing infatuation, now he has no feeling for you. He doesn't want you to marry Luzhin. . . . His talk was altogether rather muddled."

"How do you explain him to yourself, Rodya? How did he strike you?"

"I must confess I don't quite understand him. He offers you ten thousand, and yet says he is not well off. He says he is going away, and in ten minutes he forgets he has said it. Then he says he is going to be married and has already fixed on the girl. . . . No doubt he has a motive, and probably a bad one. But it's odd that he should be so clumsy about it if he had any designs against you. . . . Of course, I refused this money on your account, once for all. Altogether, I thought him very strange. . . . One might almost think he was mad. But I may be mistaken; that may only be the part he assumes. The death of Marfa Petrovna seems to have made a great impression on him."

"God rest her soul," exclaimed Pulcheria Alexandrovna. "I shall always, always pray for her! Where should we be now, Dounia, without this three thousand! It's as though it had fallen from heaven! Why, Rodya, this morning we had only three roubles in our pocket and Dounia and I were just planning to pawn her watch, so as to avoid borrowing from that man until he offered help."

Dounia seemed strangely impressed by Svidrigaïlov's offer. She still stood meditating.

"He has got some terrible plan," she said in a half whisper to herself, almost shuddering.

Raskolnikov noticed this disproportionate terror.

"I fancy I shall have to see him more than once again," he said to Dounia.

"We will watch him! I will track him out!" cried Razumihin, vigorously. "I won't lose sight of him. Rodya has given me leave. He said to me himself just now. 'Take care of my sister.' Will you give me leave, too, Avdotya Romanovna?"

Dounia smiled and held out her hand, but the look of anxiety did not leave her face. Pulcheria Alexandrovna gazed at her timidly, but the three thousand roubles had obviously a soothing effect on her.

A quarter of an hour later, they were all engaged in a lively conversation. Even Raskolnikov listened attentively for some time, though he did not talk. Razumihin was the speaker.

"And why, why should you go away?" he flowed on ecstatically. "And what are you to do in a little town? The great thing is, you are all here together and you need one another—you do need one another, believe me. For a time, anyway. . . . Take me into partnership and I assure you we'll plan a capital enterprise. Listen! I'll explain it all in detail to you, the whole project! It all flashed into my head this morning, before anything had happened. . . . I tell you what; I have an uncle, I must introduce him to you (a most accommodating and respectable old man). This uncle has got a capital of a thousand roubles, and he lives on his pension and has no need of that money. For the last two years he has been bothering me to borrow it from him and pay him six per cent. interest. I know what that means; he simply wants to help me. Last year I had no need of it, but this year I resolved to borrow it as soon as he arrived. Then you lend me another thousand of your three and we have enough for a start, so we'll go into partnership, and what are we going to do?"

Then Razumihin began to unfold his project, and he explained at length that almost all our publishers and booksellers know nothing at all of what they are selling, and for that reason they are usually bad publishers, and that any decent publications pay as a rule and give a profit, sometimes a considerable one. Razumihin had, indeed, been dreaming of setting up as a publisher. For the last two years he had been working in publishers' offices, and knew three European languages well, though he had told Raskolnikov six days before that he was "schwach" in German with an object of persuading him to take half his translation and half the payment for it. He had told a lie, then, and Raskolnikov knew he was lying.

"Why, why should we let our chance slip when we have one of the chief means of success—money of our own!" cried Razumihin warmly. "Of course there will be a lot of work, but we will work, you, Avdotya Romanovna, I, Rodion. . . . You get a splendid profit on some books nowadays! And the great point of the business is that we shall know just what wants translating, and we shall be translating, publishing, learning all at once. I can be of use because I have experience. For nearly two years I've been scuttling about among the publishers, and now I know every detail of their business. You need not be a saint to make pots, believe me! And why, why should we let our chance slip! Why, I know—and I kept the secret—two or three books which one might get a hundred roubles simply for thinking of translating and publishing. Indeed, and I would not take five hundred for the very idea of one of them. And what do you think? If I were to tell a publisher, I dare say he'd hesitate—they are such blockheads! And as for the business side, printing, paper, selling, you trust to me, I know my way about. We'll begin in a small way and go on to a large. In any case it will get us our living and we shall get back our capital."

Dounia's eyes shone.

"I like what you are saying, Dmitri Prokofitch!" she said.

"I know nothing about it, of course," put in Pulcheria Alexandrovna, "it may be a good idea, but again God knows. It's new and untried. Of course, we must remain here at least for a time." She looked at Rodya.

"What do you think, brother?" said Dounia.

"I think he's got a very good idea," he answered. "Of course, it's too soon to dream of a publishing firm, but we certainly might bring out five or six books and be sure of success. I know of one book myself which would be sure to go well. And as for his being able to manage it, there's no doubt about that either. He knows the business. . . . But we can talk it over later. . . ."

"Hurrah!" cried Razumihin. "Now, stay, there's a flat here in this house, belonging to the same owner. It's a special flat apart, not communicating with these lodgings. It's furnished, rent moderate, three rooms. Suppose you take them to begin with. I'll pawn your watch to-morrow and bring you the money, and everything can be arranged then. You can all three live together, and Rodya will be with you. But where are you off to, Rodya?"

"What, Rodya, you are going already?" Pulcheria Alexandrovna asked in dismay.

"At such a minute?" cried Razumihin.

Dounia looked at her brother with incredulous wonder. He held his cap in his hand, he was preparing to leave them.

"One would think you were burying me or saying good-bye for ever," he said somewhat oddly. He attempted to smile, but it did not turn out a smile. "But who knows, perhaps it is the last time we shall see each other . . ." he let slip accidentally. It was what he was thinking, and it somehow was uttered aloud.

"What is the matter with you?" cried his mother.

"Where are you going, Rodya?" asked Dounia rather strangely.

"Oh, I'm quite obliged to . . ." he answered vaguely, as though hesitating what he would say. But there was a look of sharp determination in his white face.

"I meant to say . . . as I was coming here . . . I meant to tell you, mother, and you, Dounia, that it would be better for us to part for a time. I feel ill, I am not at peace. . . . I will come afterwards, I will come of myself . . . when it's possible, I remember you and love you. . . . Leave me, leave me alone. I decided this even before . . . I'm absolutely resolved on it. Whatever may come to me, whether I come to ruin or not, I want to be alone. Forget me altogether, it's better. Don't inquire about me. When I can, I'll come of myself or . . . I'll send for you. Perhaps it will all come back, but now if you love me, give me up . . . else I shall begin to hate you, I feel it. . . . Good-bye!"

"Good God!" cried Pulcheria Alexandrovna. Both his mother and his sister were terribly alarmed. Razumihin was also.

"Rodya, Rodya, be reconciled with us! Let us be as before!" cried his poor mother.

He turned slowly to the door and slowly went out of the room. Dounia overtook him.

"Brother, what are you doing to mother?" she whispered, her eyes flashing with indignation.

He looked dully at her.

"No matter, I shall come. . . . I'm coming," he muttered in an undertone, as though not fully conscious of what he was saying, and he went out of the room.

"Wicked, heartless egoist!" cried Dounia.

"He is insane, but not heartless. He is mad! Don't you see it? You're heartless after that!" Razumihin whispered in her ear, squeezing her hand tightly. "I shall be back directly," he shouted to the horror-stricken mother, and he ran out of the room.

Raskolnikov was waiting for him at the end of the passage.

"I knew you would run after me," he said. "Go back to

them—be with them . . . be with them to-morrow and always.
. . . I . . . perhaps I shall come . . . if I can. Good-bye."

And without holding out his hand he walked away.

"But where are you going? What are you doing? What's the
matter with you? How can you go on like this?" Razumihin
muttered, at his wits' end.

Raskolnikov stopped once more.

"Once for all, never ask me about anything. I have nothing
to tell you. Don't come to see me. Maybe I'll come here.
. . . Leave me, but *don't leave* them. Do you understand me?"

It was dark in the corridor, they were standing near the lamp.
For a minute they were looking at one another in silence. Razumihin remembered that minute all his life. Raskolnikov's burning
and intent eyes grew more penetrating every moment, piercing
into his soul, into his consciousness. Suddenly Razumihin started.
Something strange, as it were, passed between them. . . . Some
idea, some hint as it were, slipped, something awful, hideous, and
suddenly understood on both sides. . . . Razumihin turned pale.

"Do you understand now?" said Raskolnikov, his face
twitching nervously. "Go back, go to them," he said suddenly,
and turning quickly, he went out of the house.

I will not attempt to describe how Razumihin went back to
the ladies, how he soothed them, how he protested that Rodya
needed rest in his illness, protested that Rodya was sure to come,
that he would come every day, that he was very, very much upset,
that he must not be irritated, that he, Razumihin, would watch
over him, would get him a doctor, the best doctor, a consultation.
. . . In fact from that evening Razumihin took his place with them
as a son and a brother.

4

Raskolnikov went straight to the house on the canal bank
where Sonia lived. It was an old green house of three storeys. He
found the porter and obtained from him vague directions as to the
whereabouts of Kapernaumov, the tailor. Having found in the

corner of the courtyard the entrance to the dark and narrow staircase, he mounted to the second floor and came out into a gallery that ran round the whole second storey over the yard. While he was wandering in the darkness, uncertain where to turn for Kapernaumov's door, a door opened three paces from him; he mechanically took hold of it.

"Who is there?" a woman's voice asked uneasily.

"It's I . . . come to see you," answered Raskolnikov and he walked into the tiny entry.

On a broken chair stood a candle in a battered copper candlestick.

"It's you! Good heavens!" cried Sonia weakly and she stood rooted to the spot.

"Which is your room? This way?" and Raskolnikov, trying not to look at her, hastened in.

A minute later Sonia, too, came in with the candle, set down the candlestick and, completely disconcerted, stood before him inexpressibly agitated and apparently frightened by his unexpected visit. The colour rushed suddenly to her pale face and tears came into her eyes. . . . She felt sick and ashamed and happy, too. . . . Raskolnikov turned away quickly and sat on a chair by the table. He scanned the room in a rapid glance.

It was a large but exceeding low-pitched room, the only one let by the Kapernaumovs, to whose rooms a closed door led in the wall on the left. In the opposite side on the right hand wall was another door, always kept locked. That led to the next flat, which formed a separate lodging. Sonia's room looked like a barn; it was a very irregular quadrangle and this gave it a grotesque appearance. A wall with three windows looking out on to the canal ran aslant so that one corner formed a very acute angle, and it was difficult to see in it without very strong light. The other corner was disporportionately obtuse. There was scarcely any furniture in the big room: in the corner on the right was a bedstead, beside it, nearest the door, a chair. A plain, deal table covered by a blue cloth stood against the same wall, close to the door into the other flat. Two rush-bottom chairs stood by the table. On the opposite wall near the acute angle stood a small plain wooden chest of drawers looking, as it were, lost in a desert. That was all there was in the room. The yellow, scratched and shabby wall-paper was black in the corners. It must have been damp and full of fumes in the winter. There was every sign of poverty; even the bedstead had no curtain.

Sonia looked in silence at her visitor, who was so attentively and unceremoniously scrutinising her room, and even began at last to tremble with terror, as though she was standing before her judge and the arbiter of her destinies.

"I am late. . . . It's eleven, isn't it?" he asked, still not lifting his eyes.

"Yes," muttered Sonia, "oh, yes, it is," she added, hastily, as though in that lay her means of escape. "My landlady's clock has just struck. . . . I heard it myself. . . ."

"I've come to you for the last time," Raskolnikov went on gloomily, although this was the first time. "I may perhaps not see you again . . ."

"Are you . . . going away?"

"I don't know . . . to-morrow. . . ."

"Then you are not coming to Katerina Ivanovna to-morrow?" Sonia's voice shook.

"I don't know. I shall know to-morrow morning. . . . Never mind that: I've come to say one word. . . ."

He raised his brooding eyes to her and suddenly noticed that he was sitting down while she was all the while standing before him.

"Why are you standing? Sit down," he said in a changed voice, gentle and friendly.

She sat down. He looked kindly and almost compassionately at her.

"How thin you are! What a hand! Quite transparent, like a dead hand."

He took her hand. Sonia smiled faintly.

"I have always been like that," she said.

"Even when you lived at home?"

"Yes."

"Of course, you were," he added abruptly and the expression of his face and the sound of his voice changed again sudden-ly.

He looked round him once more.

"You rent this room from the Kapernaumovs?"

"Yes. . . ."

"They live there, through that door?"

"Yes. . . . They have another room like this."

"All in one room?"

"Yes."

"I should be afraid in your room at night," he observed gloomily.

"They are very good people, very kind," answered Sonia, who still seemed bewildered, "and all the furniture, everything . . . everything is theirs. And they are very kind and the children, too, often come to see me."

"They all stammer, don't they?"

"Yes. . . . He stammers and he's lame. And his wife, too. . . . It's not exactly that she stammers, but she can't speak plainly. She is a very kind woman. And he used to be a house serf. And there are seven children . . . and it's only the eldest one that stammers and the others are simply ill . . . but they don't stammer. . . . But where did you hear about them?" she added with some surprise.

"Your father told me, then. He told me all about you. . . . And how you went out at six o'clock and came back at nine and how Katerina Ivanovna knelt down by your bed."

Sonia was confused.

"I fancied I saw him to-day," she whispered hesitatingly.

"Whom?"

"Father. I was walking in the street, out there at the corner, about ten o'clock and he seemed to be walking in front. It looked just like him. I wanted to go to Katerina Ivanovna. . . ."

"You were walking in the streets?"

"Yes," Sonia whispered abruptly, again overcome with con-fusion and looking down.

"Katerina Ivanovna used to beat you, I daresay?"

"Oh no, what are you saying? No!" Sonia looked at him almost with dismay.

"You love her, then?"

"Love her? Of course!" said Sonia with plaintive emphasis, and she clasped her hands in distress. "Ah, you don't. . . . If you only knew! You see, she is quite like a child. . . . Her mind is quite unhinged, you see . . . from sorrow. And how clever she used to be . . . how generous . . . how kind! Ah, you don't understand, you don't understand!"

Sonia said this as though in despair, wringing her hands in excitement and distress. Her pale cheeks flushed, there was a look of anguish in her eyes. It was clear that she was stirred to the very depths, that she was longing to speak, to champion, to express something. A sort of *insatiable* compassion, if one may so express it, was reflected in every feature of her face.

"Beat me! how can you? Good heavens, beat me! And if she did beat me, what then? What of it? You know nothing, nothing about it. . . . She is so unhappy . . . ah, how unhappy! And ill. . . . She is seeking righteousness, she is pure. She has such faith that there must be righteousness everywhere and she expects it. . . . And if you were to torture her, she wouldn't do wrong. She doesn't see that it's impossible for people to be righteous and she is angry at it. Like a child, like a child. She is good!"

"And what will happen to you?"

Sonia looked at him inquiringly.

"They are left on your hands, you see. They were all on your hands before, though. . . . And your father came to you to beg for drink. Well, how will it be now?"

"I don't know," Sonia articulated mournfully.

"Will they stay there?"

"I don't know. . . . They are in debt for the lodging, but the landlady, I hear, said to-day that she wanted to get rid of them, and Katerina Ivanovna says that she won't stay another minute."

"How is it she is so bold? She relies upon you?"

"Oh, no, don't talk like that. . . . We are one, we live like one." Sonia was agitated again and even angry, as though a canary or some other little bird were to be angry. "And what could she do? What, what could she do?" she persisted, getting hot and excited. "And how she cried to-day! Her mind is unhinged, haven't you noticed it? At one minute she is worrying like a child that everything should be right to-morrow, the lunch and all that. . . . Then she is wringing her hands, spitting blood, weeping, and all at once she will begin knocking her head against the wall, in despair. Then she will be comforted again. She builds all her hopes on you; she says that you will help her now and that she will borrow a little money somewhere and go to her native town with me and set up a boarding school for the daughters of gentlemen and take me to superintend it, and we will begin a new splendid life. And she kisses and hugs me, comforts me, and you know she has such faith, such faith in her fancies! One can't contradict her. And all the day long she has been washing, cleaning, mending. She dragged the wash tub into the room with her feeble hands and sank on the bed, gasping for breath. We went this morning to the shops to buy shoes for Polenka and Lida for theirs are quite worn out. Only the money we'd reckoned wasn't enough, not nearly enough. And she picked out such dear little boots, for she has taste, you don't know. And there in the shop she burst out crying before the shopmen because she hadn't enough. . . . Ah, it was sad to see her. . . ."

"Well, after that I can understand your living like this," Raskolnikov said with a bitter smile.

"And aren't you sorry for them? Aren't you sorry?" Sonia flew at him again. "Why, I know, you gave your last penny yourself, though you'd seen nothing of it, and if you'd seen everything, oh dear! And how often, how often I've brought her to tears! Only last week! Yes, I! Only a week before his death. I was cruel! And how often I've done it! Ah, I've been wretched at the thought of it all day!"

Sonia wrung her hands as she spoke at the pain of remembering it.

"You were cruel?"

"Yes, I—I. I went to see them," she went on, weeping, "and father said, 'read me something, Sonia, my head aches, read to me, here's a book.' He had a book he had got from Andrey

Semyonovitch Lebeziatnikov, he lives there, he always used to get hold of such funny books. And I said, 'I can't stay,' as I didn't want to read, and I'd gone in chiefly to show Katerina Ivanovna some collars. Lizaveta, the pedlar, sold me some collars and cuffs cheap, pretty, new, embroidered ones. Katerina Ivanovna liked them very much; she put them on and looked at herself in the glass and was delighted with them. 'Make me a present of them, Sonia,' she said, 'please do.' *'Please do,'* she said, she wanted them so much. And when could she wear them? They just reminded her of her old happy days. She looked at herself in the glass, admired herself, and she has no clothes at all, no things of her own, hasn't had all these years! And she never asks any one for anything; she is proud, she'd sooner give away everything. And these she asked for, she liked them so much. And I was sorry to give them. 'What use are they to you, Katerina Ivanovna?' I said. I spoke like that to her, I ought not to have said that! She gave me such a look. And she was so grieved, so grieved at my refusing her. And it was so sad to see. . . . And she was not grieved for the collars, but for my refusing, I saw that. Ah, if only I could bring it all back, change it, take back those words! Ah, if I . . . but it's nothing to you!"

"Did you know Lizaveta, the pedlar?"

"Yes. . . . Did you know her?" Sonia asked with some surprise.

"Katerina Ivanovna is in consumption, rapid consumption; she will soon die," said Raskolnikov after a pause, without answering her question.

"Oh, no, no, no!"

And Sonia unconsciously clutched both his hands, as though imploring that she should not.

"But it will be better if she does die."

"No, not better, not at all better!" Sonia unconsciously repeated in dismay.

"And the children? What can you do except take them to live with you?"

"Oh, I don't know," cried Sonia, almost in despair, and she put her hands to her head.

It was evident that that idea had very often occurred to her before and he had only roused it again.

"And, what, if even now, while Katerina Ivanovna is alive, you get ill and are taken to the hospital, what will happen then?" he persisted pitilessly.

"How can you? That cannot be!"

And Sonia's face worked with awful terror.

"Cannot be?" Raskolnikov went on with a harsh smile. "You are not insured against it, are you? What will happen to them then? They will be in the street, all of them, she will cough and beg and knock her head against some wall, as she did to-day, and the children will cry. . . . Then she will fall down, be taken to the police station and to the hospital, she will die, and the children . . ."

"Oh, no. . . . God will not let it be!" broke at last from Sonia's overburdened bosom.

She listened, looking imploringly at him, clasping her hands in dumb entreaty, as though it all depended upon him.

Raskolnikov got up and began to walk about the room. A minute passed. Sonia was standing with her hands and her head hanging in terrible dejection.

"And can't you save? Put by for a rainy day?" he asked, stopping suddenly before her.

"No," whispered Sonia.

"Of course not. Have you tried?" he added almost ironically.

"Yes."

"And it didn't come off! Of course not! No need to ask."

And again he paced the room. Another minute passed.

"You don't get money every day?"

Sonia was more confused than ever and colour rushed into her face again.

"No," she whispered with a painful effort.

"It will be the same with Polenka, no doubt," he said suddenly.

"No, no! It can't be, no!" Sonia cried aloud in desperation, as though she had been stabbed. "God would not allow anything so awful!"

"He lets others come to it."

"No, no! God will protect her, God!" she repeated beside herself.

"But, perhaps, there is no God at all," Raskolnikov answered with a sort of malignance, laughed and looked at her.

Sonia's face suddenly changed; a tremor passed over it. She looked at him with unutterable reproach, tried to say something, but could not speak and broke into bitter, bitter sobs, hiding her face in her hands.

"You say Katerina Ivanovna's mind is unhinged; your own mind is unhinged," he said after a brief silence.

Five minutes passed. He still paced up and down the room in silence, not looking at her. At last he went up to her; his eyes glittered. He put his two hands on her shoulders and looked straight into her tearful face. His eyes were hard, feverish and piercing, his lips were twitching. All at once he bent down quickly and dropping to the ground, kissed her foot. Sonia drew back from him as from a madman. And certainly he looked like a madman.

"What are you doing to me?" she muttered, turning pale, and a sudden anguish clutched at her heart.

He stood up at once.

"I did not bow down to you, I bowed down to all the suffering of humanity," he said wildly and walked away to the window. "Listen," he added, turning to her a minute later. "I said just now to an insolent man that he was not worth your little finger . . . and that I did my sister honour making her sit beside you."

"Ach, you said that to them! And in her presence?" cried Sonia, frightened. "Sit down with me! An honour! Why, I'm . . . dishonourable. . . . Ah, why did you say that?"

"It was not because of your dishonour and your sin I said that of you, but because of your great suffering. But you are a great sinner, that's true," he added almost solemnly, "and your worst sin is that you have destroyed and betrayed yourself *for nothing.* Isn't that fearful? Isn't it fearful that you are living in this filth which you loathe so, and at the same time you know yourself (you've only to open your eyes) that you are not helping any one by it, not saving any one from anything! Tell me," he went on almost in a frenzy, "how this shame and degradation can exist in you side by side with other, opposite, holy feelings? It would be better, a thousand times better and wiser to leap into the water and end it all!"

"But what would become of them?" Sonia asked faintly, gazing at him with eyes of anguish, but not seeming surprised at his suggestion.

Raskolnikov looked strangely at her. He read it all in her face; so she must have had that thought already, perhaps many times, and earnestly she had thought out in her despair how to end it and so earnestly, that now she scarcely wondered at his suggestion. She had not even noticed the cruelty of his words. (The significance of his reproaches and his peculiar attitude to her shame she had, of course, not noticed either, and that, too, was clear to him.) But he saw how monstrously the thought of her disgraceful, shameful position was torturing her and had long tortured her. "What, what," he thought, "could hitherto have hindered her from putting an end to it?" Only then he realised what those poor little orphan children and that pitiful half-crazy Katerina Ivanovna, knocking her head against the wall in her consumption, meant for Sonia.

But, nevertheless, it was clear to him again that with her character and the amount of education she had after all received, she could not in any case remain so. He was still confronted by the question how could she have remained so long in that position without going out of her mind, since she could not bring herself to jump into the water? Of course he knew that Sonia's position was an exceptional case, though unhappily not unique and not infrequent, indeed; but that very exceptionalness, her tinge of education, her previous life might, one would have thought, have killed her at the first step on that revolting path. What held her up—surely not depravity? All that infamy had obviously only touched her mechanically, not one drop of real depravity had penetrated to her heart; he saw that. He saw through her as she stood before him. . . .

"There are three ways before her," he thought, "the canal, the madhouse, or . . . at last to sink into depravity which obscures the mind and turns the heart to stone."

The last idea was the most revolting, but he was a sceptic, he was young, abstract, and therefore cruel, and so he could not help believing that the last end was the most likely.

"But can that be true?" he cried to himself. "Can that creature who has still preserved the purity of her spirit be consciously drawn at last into that sink of filth and iniquity? Can the process already have begun? Can it be that she has only been able to bear it till now, because vice has begun to be less loathsome to her? No, no, that cannot be!" he cried, as Sonia had just before. "No, what has kept her from the canal till now is the idea of sin and they, the children. . . . And if she has not gone out of her mind . . . but who says she has not gone out of her mind? Is she in her senses? Can one talk, can one reason as she does? How can she sit on the edge of the abyss of loathsomeness into which she is slipping and refuse to listen when she is told of danger? Does she expect a miracle? No doubt she does. Doesn't that all mean madness?"

He stayed obstinately at that thought. He liked that explanation indeed better than any other. He began looking more intently at her.

"So you pray to God a great deal, Sonia?" he asked her.

Sonia did not speak; he stood beside her waiting for an answer.

"What should I be without God?" she whispered rapidly, forcibly, glancing at him with suddenly flashing eyes, and squeezing his hand.

"Ah, so that is it!" he thought.

"And what does God do for you?" he asked, probing her further.

Sonia was silent a long while, as though she could not answer. Her weak chest kept heaving with emotion.

"Be silent! Don't ask! You don't deserve!" she cried suddenly, looking sternly and wrathfully at him.

"That's it, that's it," he repeated to himself.

"He does everything," she whispered quickly, looking down again.

"That's the way out! That's the explanation," he decided, scrutinising her with eager curiosity, with a new, strange, almost morbid feeling. He gazed at that pale, thin, irregular, angular little face, those soft blue eyes, which could flash with such fire, such stern energy, that little body still shaking with indignation and anger—and it all seemed to him more and more strange, almost impossible. "She is a religious maniac!" he repeated to himself.

There was a book lying on the chest of drawers. He had noticed it every time he paced up and down the room. Now he took it up and looked at it. It was the New Testament in the Russian translation. It was bound in leather, old and worn.

"Where did you get that?" he called to her across the room.

She was still standing in the same place, three steps from the table.

"It was brought me," she answered, as it were unwillingly, not looking at him.

"Who brought it?"

"Lizaveta, I asked her for it."

"Lizaveta! strange!" he thought.

Everything about Sonia seemed to him stranger and more wonderful every moment. He carried the book to the candle and began to turn over the pages.

"Where is the story of Lazarus?" he asked suddenly.

Sonia looked obstinately at the ground and would not answer. She was standing sideways to the table.

"Where is the raising of Lazarus? Find it for me, Sonia."

She stole a glance at him.

"You are not looking in the right place. . . . It's in the fourth gospel," she whispered sternly, without looking at him.

"Find it and read it to me," he said. He sat down with his

elbow on the table, leaned his head on his hand and looked away sullenly, prepared to listen.

"In three weeks' time they'll welcome me in the madhouse! I shall be there if I am not in a worse place," he muttered to himself.

Sonia heard Raskolnikov's request distrustfully and moved hesitatingly to the table. She took the book however.

"Haven't you read it?" she asked, looking up at him across the table.

Her voice became sterner and sterner.

"Long ago. . . . When I was at school. Read!"

"And haven't you heard it in church?"

"I . . . haven't been. Do you often go?"

"N-no," whispered Sonia.

Raskolnikov smiled.

"I understand. . . . And you won't go to your father's funeral to-morrow?"

"Yes, I shall. I was at church last week, too. . . . I had a requiem service."

"For whom?"

"For Lizaveta. She was killed with an axe."

His nerves were more and more strained. His head began to go round.

"Were you friends with Lizaveta?"

"Yes. . . . She was good . . . she used to come . . . not often . . . she couldn't. . . . We used to read together and . . . talk. She will see God."

The last phrase sounded strange in his ears. And here was something new again: the mysterious meetings with Lizaveta and both of them—religious maniacs.

"I shall be a religious maniac myself soon! It's infectious!"

"Read!" he cried irritably and insistently.

Sonia still hesitated. Her heart was throbbing. She hardly dared to read to him. He looked almost with exasperation at the "unhappy lunatic."

"What for? You don't believe? . . ." she whispered softly and as it were breathlessly.

"Read! I want you to," he persisted. "You used to read to Lizaveta."

Sonia opened the book and found the place. Her hands were shaking, her voice failed her. Twice she tried to begin and could not bring out the first syllable.

"Now a certain man was sick named Lazarus of Bethany. . . ." she forced herself at last to read, but at the third word her voice broke like an overstrained string. There was a catch in her breath.

Raskolnikov saw in part why Sonia could not bring herself to read to him and the more he saw this, the more roughly and irritably he insisted on her doing so. He understood only too well how painful it was for her to betray and unveil all that was her *own*. He understood that these feelings really were her *secret treasure*, which she had kept perhaps for years, perhaps from childhood, while she lived with an unhappy father and a distracted stepmother crazed by grief, in the midst of starving children and unseemly abuse and reproaches. But at the same time he knew now and knew for certain that, although it filled her with dread and suffering, yet she had a tormenting desire to read and to read to *him* that he might hear it, and to read *now* whatever might come of it! . . . He read this in her eyes, he could see it in her intense emotion. She mastered herself, controlled the spasm in her throat and went on reading the eleventh chapter of St. John. She went on to the nineteenth verse:

"And many of the Jews came to Martha and Mary to comfort them concerning their brother.

Then Martha as soon as she heard that Jesus was coming went and met Him: but Mary sat still in the house.

Then said Martha unto Jesus, Lord, if Thou hadst been here, my brother had not died.

But I know that even now whatsoever Thou wilt ask of God, God will give it Thee. . . ."

Then she stopped again with a shamefaced feeling that her voice would quiver and break again.

"Jesus said unto her, thy brother shall rise again.

Martha saith unto Him, I know that he shall rise again in the resurrection, at the last day.

Jesus said unto her, I am the resurrection and the life: he that believeth in Me though he were dead, yet shall he live.

And whosoever liveth and believeth in Me shall never die. Believest thou this?

She saith unto Him,"

(And drawing a painful breath, Sonia read distinctly and forcibly as though she were making a public confession of faith.)

"Yea, Lord: I believe that Thou art the Christ, the Son of God Which should come into the world."

She stopped and looked up quickly at him, but controlling herself went on reading. Raskolnikov sat without moving, his elbows on the table and his eyes turned away. She read to the thirty-second verse.

"Then when Mary was come where Jesus was and saw Him, she fell down at His feet, saying unto Him, Lord if Thou hadst been here, my brother had not died.

When Jesus therefore saw her weeping, and the Jews also weeping which came with her, He groaned in the spirit and was troubled,

And said, Where have ye laid him? They said unto Him, Lord, come and see.

Jesus wept.

Then said the Jews, behold how He loved him!

And some of them said, could not this Man which opened the eyes of the blind, have caused that even this man should not have died?"

Raskolnikov turned and looked at her with emotion. Yes, he had known it! She was trembling in a real physical fever. He had expected it. She was getting near the story of the greatest miracle and a feeling of immense triumph came over her. Her voice rang out like a bell; triumph and joy gave it power. The lines danced before her eyes, but she knew what she was reading by heart. At the last verse "Could not this Man which opened the eyes of the blind . . ." dropping her voice she passionately reproduced the doubt, the reproach and censure of the blind disbelieving Jews, who in another moment would fall at His feet as though struck by thunder, sobbing and believing. . . . "And *he, he*—too, is blinded and unbelieving, he, too, will hear, he, too, will believe, yes, yes! At once, now," was what she was dreaming, and she was quivering with happy anticipation.

"Jesus therefore again groaning in Himself cometh to the grave. It was a cave, and a stone lay upon it.

Jesus said, Take ye away the stone. Martha, the sister of him that was dead, saith unto Him, Lord by this time he stinketh: for he hath been dead four days."

She laid emphasis on the word *four.*

"Jesus saith unto her, Said I not unto thee that if thou would-est believe, thou shouldest see the glory of God?

Then they took away the stone from the place where the dead was laid. And Jesus lifted up His eyes and said, Father, I thank Thee that Thou hast heard Me.

And I knew that Thou hearest Me always; but because of the people which stand by I said it, that they may believe that Thou hast sent Me.

And when He thus had spoken, He cried with a loud voice, Lazarus, come forth.

And he that was dead came forth."

(She read loudly, cold and trembling with ecstasy, as though she were seeing it before her eyes.)

"Bound hand and foot with graveclothes; and his face was bound about with a napkin. Jesus saith unto them, Loose him and let him go.

Then many of the Jews which came to Mary and had seen the things which Jesus did believed on Him."

She could read no more, closed the book and got up from her chair quickly.

"That is all about the raising of Lazarus," she whispered severely and abruptly, and turning away she stood motionless, not daring to raise her eyes to him. She still trembled feverishly. The candle-end was flickering out in the battered candlestick, dimly lighting up in the poverty-stricken room the murderer and the harlot who had so strangely been reading together the eternal book. Five minutes or more passed.

"I came to speak of something," Raskolnikov said aloud, frowning. He got up and went to Sonia. She lifted her eyes to him in silence. His face was particularly stern and there was a sort of savage determination in it.

"I have abandoned my family to-day," he said, "my mother and sister. I am not going to see them. I've broken with them completely."

"What for?" asked Sonia amazed. Her recent meeting with his mother and sister had left a great impression which she could not analyse. She heard his news almost with horror.

"I have only you now," he added. "Let us go together. . . . I've come to you, we are both accursed, let us go our way together!"

His eyes glittered "as though he were mad," Sonia thought, in her turn.

"Go where?" she asked in alarm and she involuntarily stepped back.

"How do I know? I only know it's the same road, I know that and nothing more. It's the same goal!"

She looked at him and understood nothing. She knew only that he was terribly, infinitely unhappy.

"No one of them will understand, if you tell them, but I have understood. I need you, that is why I have come to you."

"I don't understand," whispered Sonia.

"You'll understand later. Haven't you done the same? You, too, have transgressed . . . have had the strength to transgress. You have laid hands on yourself, you have destroyed a life . . . *your own* (it's all the same!). You might have lived in spirit and understanding, but you'll end in the Hay Market. . . . But you won't be able to stand it, and if you remain alone you'll go out of your mind like me. You are like a mad creature already. So we must go together on the same road! Let us go!"

"What for? What's all this for?" said Sonia, strangely and violently agitated by his words.

"What for? Because you can't remain like this, that's why!

You must look things straight in the face at last, and not weep like a child and cry that God won't allow it. What will happen, if you should really be taken to the hospital to-morrow? She is mad and in consumption, she'll soon die, and the children? Do you mean to tell me Polenka won't come to grief? Haven't you seen children here at the street corners sent out by their mothers to beg? I've found out where those mothers live and in what surroundings. Children can't remain children there! At seven the child is vicious and a thief. Yet children, you know, are the image of Christ: 'theirs is the kingdom of Heaven.' He bade us honour and love them, they are the humanity of the future. . . ."

"What's to be done, what's to be done?" repeated Sonia, weeping hysterically and wringing her hands.

"What's to be done? Break what must be broken, once for all, that's all, and take the suffering on oneself. What, you don't understand? You'll understand later. . . . Freedom and power, and above all, power! Over all trembling creation and all the antheap! . . . That's the goal, remember that! That's my farewell message. Perhaps it's the last time I shall speak to you. If I don't come to-morrow, you'll hear of it all, and then remember these words. And some day later on, in years to come, you'll understand perhaps what they meant. If I come to-morrow, I'll tell you who killed Lizaveta. . . . Good-bye."

Sonia started with terror.

"Why, do you know who killed her?" she asked, chilled with horror, looking wildly at him.

"I know and will tell . . . you, only you. I have chosen you out. I'm not coming to you to ask forgiveness, but simply to tell you. I chose you out long ago to hear this, when your father talked of you and when Lizaveta was alive, I thought of it. Good-bye, don't shake hands. To-morrow!"

He went out. Sonia gazed at him as at a madman. But she herself was like one insane and felt it. Her head was going round.

"Good heavens, how does he know who killed Lizaveta? What did those words mean? It's awful!" But at the same time *the idea* did not enter her head, not for a moment! "Oh, he must be terribly unhappy! . . . He has abandoned his mother and sister.

. . . What for? What has happened? And what had he in his mind? What did he say to her? He had kissed her foot and said . . . said (yes, he had said it clearly) that he could not live without her. . . . Oh, merciful heavens!"

Sonia spent the whole night feverish and delirious. She jumped up from time to time, wept and wrung her hands, then sank again into feverish sleep and dreamt of Polenka, Katerina Ivanovna and Lizaveta, of reading the gospel and him . . . him with pale face, with burning eyes . . . kissing her feet, weeping.

On the other side of the door on the right, which divided Sonia's room from Madame Resslich's flat, was a room which had long stood empty. A card was fixed on the gate and a notice stuck in the windows over the canal advertising it to let. Sonia had long been accustomed to the room's being uninhabited. But all that time Mr. Svidrigaïlov had been standing, listening at the door of the empty room. When Raskolnikov went out he stood still, thought a moment, went on tiptoe to his own room which adjoined the empty one, brought a chair and noiselessly carried it to the door that led to Sonia's room. The conversation had struck him as interesting and remarkable, and he had greatly enjoyed it—so much so that he brought a chair that he might not in the future, to-morrow, for instance, have to endure the inconvenience of standing a whole hour, but might listen in comfort.

5

When next morning at eleven o'clock punctually Raskolnikov went into the department of the investigation of criminal causes and sent his name in to Porfiry Petrovitch, he was surprised at being kept waiting so long: it was at least ten minutes before he was summoned. He had expected that they would pounce upon him. But he stood in the waiting-room, and people, who apparently had nothing to do with him, were continually passing to and fro before him. In the next room which looked like an office, several clerks were sitting writing and obviously they had no notion who or what Raskolnikov might be. He looked uneasily and suspiciously about him to see whether there was not some guard, some mysterious watch being kept on him to prevent his escape. But there was nothing of the sort: he saw only the faces of clerks absorbed in petty details, then other people, no one seemed to have any concern with him. He might go where he liked for them. The conviction grew stronger in him that if that enigmatic man of yesterday, that phantom sprung out of the earth, had seen everything, they would not have let him stand and wait like that. And would they have waited till he elected to appear at eleven? Either the man had not yet given information, or ... or simply he knew nothing, had seen nothing (and how could he have seen anything?) and so all that had happened to him the day before was again a phantom exaggerated by his sick and overstrained imagination. This conjecture had begun to grow strong the day before, in the midst of all his alarm and despair. Thinking it all over now and preparing for a fresh conflict, he was suddenly aware that he was trembling—and he felt a rush of indignation at the thought that he was trembling with fear at facing that hateful Porfiry Petrovitch. What he dreaded above all was meeting that man again; he hated him with an intense, unmitigated hatred and was afraid his hatred might betray him. His indignation was such that he ceased trembling at once; he made ready to go in with a cold and arrogant bearing and vowed to himself to keep as silent as possible, to watch and listen and for once at least to control his overstrained nerves. At that moment he was summoned to Porfiry Petrovitch.

He found Porfiry Petrovitch alone in his study. His study was a room neither large nor small, furnished with a large writing-table, that stood before a sofa, upholstered in checked material, a bureau, a bookcase in the corner and several chairs—all government furniture, of polished yellow wood. In the further wall there was a closed door, beyond it there were, no doubt, other rooms. On Raskolnikov's entrance Porfiry Petrovitch had at once closed the door by which he had come in and they remained alone. He met his visitor with an apparently genial and good-tempered air, and it was only after a few minutes that Raskolnikov saw signs of a certain awkwardness in him, as though he had been thrown out of his reckoning or caught in something very secret.

"Ah, my dear fellow! Here you are . . . in our domain" . . . began Porfiry, holding out both hands to him. "Come, sit down, old man . . . or perhaps you don't like to be called 'my dear fellow' and 'old man'—*tout court?* Please don't think it too familiar. . . . Here, on the sofa."

Raskolnikov sat down, keeping his eyes fixed on him. "In our domain," the apologies for familiarity, the French phrase *tout court,* were all characteristic signs.

"He held out both hands to me, but he did not give me one—he drew it back in time," struck him suspiciously. Both were watching each other, but when their eyes met, quick as lightning they looked away.

"I brought you this paper . . . about the watch. Here it is. Is it all right or shall I copy it again?"

"What? A paper? Yes, yes, don't be uneasy, it's all right," Porfiry Petrovitch said as though in haste, and after he had said it he took the paper and looked at it. "Yes, it's all right. Nothing more is needed," he declared with the same rapidity and he laid the paper on the table.

A minute later when he was talking of something else he took it from the table and put it on his bureau.

"I believe you said yesterday you would like to question me . . . formally . . . about my acquaintance with the murdered woman?" Raskolnikov was beginning again. "Why did I put in 'I believe' " passed through his mind in a flash. "Why am I so uneasy at having put in that *'I believe'?"* came in a second flash. And he suddenly felt that his uneasiness at the mere contact with Porfiry, at the first words, at the first looks, had grown in an instant to monstrous proportions, and that this was fearfully dangerous. His nerves were quivering, his emotion was increasing. "It's bad, it's bad! I shall say too much again."

"Yes, yes, yes! There's no hurry, there's no hurry," muttered Porfiry Petrovitch, moving to and fro about the table without any apparent aim, as it were making dashes towards the window, the bureau and the table, at one moment avoiding Raskolnikov's suspicious glance, then again standing still and looking him straight in the face.

His fat round little figure looked very strange, like a ball rolling from one side to the other and rebounding back.

"We've plenty of time. Do you smoke? have you your own? Here, a cigarette!" he went on, offering his visitor a cigarette. "You know I am receiving you here, but my own quarters are through there, you know, my government quarters. But I am living outside for the time, I had to have some repairs done here. It's almost finished now. . . . Government quarters, you know, are a capital thing. Eh, what do you think?"

"Yes, a capital thing," answered Raskolnikov, looking at him almost ironically.

"A capital thing, a capital thing," repeated Porfiry Petrovitch, as though he had just thought of something quite different. "Yes, a capital thing," he almost shouted at last, suddenly staring at Raskolnikov and stopping short two steps from him.

This stupid repetition was too incongruous in its ineptitude with the serious, brooding and enigmatic glance he turned upon his visitor.

But this stirred Raskolnikov's spleen more than ever and he could not resist an ironical and rather incautious challenge.

"Tell me, please," he asked suddenly, looking almost insolently at him and taking a kind of pleasure in his own insolence. "I believe it's a sort of legal rule, a sort of legal tradition—for all investigating lawyers—to begin their attack from afar, with a trivial, or at least an irrelevant subject, so as to encourage, or rather, to divert the man they are cross-examining, to disarm his caution and then all at once to give him an unexpected knock-down blow with some fatal question. Isn't that so? It's a sacred tradition, mentioned, I fancy, in all the manuals of the art?"

"Yes, yes. . . . Why, do you imagine that was why I spoke about government quarters . . . eh?"

And as he said this Porfiry Petrovitch screwed up his eyes and winked; a good-humoured, crafty look passed over his face. The wrinkles on his forehead were smoothed out, his eyes contracted, his features broadened and he suddenly went off into a

nervous prolonged laugh, shaking all over and looking Raskolnikov straight in the face. The latter forced himself to laugh, too,
but when Porfiry, seeing that he was laughing, broke into such
a guffaw that he turned almost crimson, Raskolnikov's repulsion
overcame all precaution; he left off laughing, scowled and stared
with hatred at Porfiry, keeping his eyes fixed on him while his
intentionally prolonged laughter lasted. There was lack of precaution on both sides, however, for Porfiry Petrovitch seemed to be
laughing in his visitor's face and to be very little disturbed at the
annoyance with which the visitor received it. The latter fact was
very significant in Raskolnikov's eyes: he saw that Porfiry Petrovitch had not been embarrassed just before either, but that he,
Raskolnikov, had perhaps fallen into a trap; that there must be
something, some motive here unknown to him; that, perhaps,
everything was in readiness and in another moment would break
upon him . . .

He went straight to the point at once, rose from his seat and
took his cap.

"Porfiry Petrovitch," he began resolutely, though with considerable irritation, "yesterday you expressed a desire that I
should come to you for some inquiries (he laid special stress on
the word 'inquiries'). I have come and, if you have anything to
ask me, ask it, and if not, allow me to withdraw. I have no time
to spare. . . . I have to be at the funeral of that man who was run
over, of whom you . . . know also," he added, feeling angry at
once at having made this addition and more irritated at his anger,
"I am sick of it all, do you hear, and have long been. It's partly
what made me ill. In short," he shouted, feeling that the phrase
about his illness was still more out of place, "in short, kindly
examine me or let me go, at once. And if you must examine me,
do so in the proper form! I will not allow you to do so otherwise,
and so meanwhile, good-bye, as we have evidently nothing to
keep us now."

"Good heavens! What do you mean? What shall I question
you about?" cackled Porfiry Petrovitch with a change of tone,
instantly leaving off laughing. "Please don't disturb yourself," he
began fidgeting from place to place and fussily making Raskol-

nikov sit down. "There's no hurry, there's no hurry, it's all non-sense. Oh, no, I'm very glad you've come to see me at last . . . I look upon you simply as a visitor. And as for my confounded laughter, please excuse it, Rodion Romanovitch. Rodion Romanovitch? That is your name? . . . It's my nerves, you tickled me so with your witty observation; I assure you, sometimes I shake with laughter like an india-rubber ball for half an hour at a time. . . . I'm often afraid of an attack of paralysis. Do sit down. Please do, or I shall think you are angry . . ."

Raskolnikov did not speak; he listened, watching him, still frowning angrily. He did sit down, but still held his cap.

"I must tell you one thing about myself, my dear Rodion Romanovitch," Porfiry Petrovitch continued, moving about the room and again avoiding his visitor's eyes. "You see, I'm a bache-lor, a man of no consequence and not used to society; besides, I have nothing before me, I'm set, I'm running to seed and . . . and have you noticed, Rodion Romanovitch, that in our Petersburg circles, if two clever men meet who are not intimate, but respect each other, like you and me, it takes them half an hour before they can find a subject for conversation—they are dumb, they sit opposite each other and feel awkward. Every one has subjects of conversation, ladies for instance . . . people in high society always have their subjects of conversation, *c'est de ri-gueur*, but people of the middle sort like us, thinking people that is, are always tongue-tied and awkward. What is the reason of it? Whether it is the lack of public interest, or whether it is we are so honest we don't want to deceive one another, I don't know. What do you think? Do put down your cap, it looks as if you were just going, it makes me uncomfortable . . . I am so delighted . . ."

Raskolnikov put down his cap and continued listening in silence with a serious frowning face to the vague and empty chatter of Porfiry Petrovitch. "Does he really want to distract my attention with his silly babble?"

"I can't offer you coffee here; but why not spend five minutes with a friend," Porfiry pattered on, "and you know all these official duties . . . please don't mind my running up and down, excuse it, my dear fellow, I am very much afraid of offending you, but exercise is absolutely indispensable for me. I'm always sitting and so glad to be moving about for five minutes . . . I suffer from my sedentary life . . . I always intend to join a gymnasium; they say that officials of all ranks, even Privy Councillors may be seen skipping gaily there; there you have it, modern science . . . yes, yes. . . . But as for my duties here, inquiries and all such formalities . . . you mentioned inquiries yourself just now . . . I assure you these interrogations are sometimes more embarrassing for the interrogator than for the interrogated. . . . You made the observation yourself just now very aptly and wittily. (Raskolnikov had made no observation of the kind.) One gets into a muddle! A regular muddle! One keeps harping on the same note, like a drum! There is to be a reform and we shall be called by a different name, at least, he-he-he! And as for our legal tradition, as you so wittily called it, I thoroughly agree with you. Every prisoner on trial, even the rudest peasant knows, that they begin by disarming him with irrelevant questions (as you so happily put it) and then deal him a knock-down blow, he-he-he!—your felicitous comparison, he-he! So you really imagined that I meant by government quarters . . . he-he! You are an ironical person. Come, I won't go on! Ah, by the way, yes! One word leads to another. You spoke of formality just now, apropos of the inquiry, you know. But what's the use of formality? In many cases it's nonsense. Sometimes one has a friendly chat and gets a good deal more out of it. One can always fall back on formality, allow me to assure you. And after all, what does it amount to? An examining lawyer cannot be bounded by formality at every step. The work of investigation is, so to speak, a free art in its own way, he-he-he!"

Porfiry Petrovitch took breath a moment. He had simply babbled on uttering empty phrases, letting slip a few enigmatic words and again reverting to incoherence. He was almost running about the room, moving his fat little legs quicker and quicker, looking at the ground, with his right hand behind his back, while with his left making gesticulations that were extraordinarily incongruous with his words. Raskolnikov suddenly noticed that as he ran about the room he seemed twice to stop for a moment near the door, as though he were listening.

"Is he expecting anything?"

"You are certainly quite right about it," Porfiry began gaily, looking with extraordinary simplicity at Raskolnikov (which startled him and instantly put him on his guard), "certainly quite right in laughing so wittily at our legal forms, he-he! Some of these elaborate psychological methods are exceedingly ridiculous and perhaps useless, if one adheres too closely to the forms. Yes . . . I am talking of forms again. Well, if I recognise, or more strictly speaking, if I suspect some one or other to be a criminal in any case entrusted to me . . . you're reading for the law, of course, Rodion Romanovitch?"

"Yes, I was . . ."

"Well, then it is a precedent for you for the future—though don't suppose I should venture to instruct you after the articles you publish about crime! No, I simply make bold to state it by way of fact, if I took this man or that for a criminal, why, I ask, should I worry him prematurely, even though I had evidence against him? In one case I may be bound, for instance, to arrest a man at once, but another may be in quite a different position, you know, so why shouldn't I let him walk about the town a bit, he-he-he! But I see you don't quite understand, so I'll give you a clearer example. If I put him in prison too soon, I may very likely give him, so to speak, moral support, he-he! You're laughing?"

Raskolnikov had no idea of laughing. He was sitting with compressed lips, his feverish eyes fixed on Porfiry Petrovitch's.

"Yet that is the case, with some types especially, for men are so different. You say evidence. Well, there may be evidence. But evidence, you know, can generally be taken two ways. I am an examining lawyer and a weak man, I confess it. I should like to make a proof, so to say, mathematically clear, I should like to make a chain of evidence such as twice two are four, it ought to be a direct, irrefutable proof! And if I shut him up too soon—even though I might be convinced *he* was the man, I should very likely be depriving myself of the means of getting further evidence against him. And how? By giving him, so to speak, a definite position, I shall put him out of suspense and set his mind at rest, so that he will retreat into his shell. They say that at Sevastopol, soon after Alma, the clever people were in a terrible fright that the enemy would attack openly and take Sevastopol at once. But when they saw that the enemy preferred a regular siege, they were delighted, I am told and reassured, for the thing would drag on for two months at least. You're laughing, you don't believe me again? Of course, you're right, too. You're right, you're right. These are all special cases, I admit. But you must observe this, my dear Rodion Romanovitch, the general case, the case for which all legal forms and rules are intended, for which they are calculated and laid down in books, does not exist at all, for the reason that every case, every crime for instance, so soon as it actually occurs, at once becomes a thoroughly special case and sometimes a case unlike any that's gone before. Very comic cases of that sort sometimes occur. If I leave one man quite alone, if I don't touch him and don't worry him, but let him know or at least suspect every moment that I know all about it and am watching him day and night, and if he is in continual suspicion and terror, he'll be bound to lose his head. He'll come of himself, or maybe do something which will make it as plain as twice two are four—it's delightful. It may be so with a simple peasant, but with one of our sort, an intelligent man cultivated on a certain side, it's a dead certainty. For, my dear fellow, it's a very important matter to know on what side a man is cultivated. And then there are nerves, there are nerves, you have overlooked them! Why, they are all sick, nervous and irritable! . . . And then how they all suffer from spleen! That I assure you is a regular gold mine for us. And it's no anxiety to me, his running about the town free! Let him, let him walk about for a bit! I know well enough that I've caught him and that he won't escape me. Where could he escape to, he-he? Abroad, perhaps? A Pole will escape abroad, but not here, especially as I am watching and have taken measures. Will he escape into the depths of the country perhaps? But you know, peasants live there, real rude Russian peasants. A modern cultivated man would prefer prison to living with such strangers as our peasants.

He-he! But that's all nonsense, and on the surface. It's not merely that he has nowhere to run to, he is *psychologically* unable to escape me, he-he! What an expression! Through a law of nature he can't escape me if he had anywhere to go. Have you seen a butterfly round a candle? That's how he will keep circling and circling round me. Freedom will lose its attractions. He'll begin to brood, he'll weave a tangle round himself, he'll worry himself to death! What's more he will provide me with a mathematical proof—if I only give him long enough interval. . . . And he'll keep circling round me, getting nearer and nearer and then—flop! He'll fly straight into my mouth and I'll swallow him, and that will be very amusing, he-he-he! You don't believe me?"

Raskolnikov made no reply; he sat pale and motionless, still gazing with the same intensity into Porfiry's face.

"It's a lesson," he thought, turning cold. "This is beyond the cat playing with a mouse, like yesterday. He can't be showing off his power with no motive . . . prompting me; he is far too clever for that . . . he must have another object. What is it? It's all nonsense, my friend, you are pretending, to scare me! You've no proofs and the man I saw had no real existence. You simply want to make me lose my head, to work me up beforehand and so to crush me. But you are wrong, you won't do it even though you have some trap for me . . . let us see what you have in store for me."

And he braced himself to face a terrible and unknown ordeal. At times he longed to fall on Porfiry and strangle him. This anger was what he dreaded from the beginning. He felt that his parched lips were flecked with foam, his heart was throbbing. But he was still determined not to speak till the right moment. He realised that this was the best policy in his position, because instead of saying too much he would be irritating his enemy by his silence and provoking him into speaking too freely. Anyhow, this was what he hoped for.

"No, I see you don't believe me, you think I am playing a harmless joke on you," Porfiry began again, getting more and more lively, chuckling at every instant and again pacing round the room. "And, to be sure, you're right: God has given me a figure that can awaken none but comic ideas in other people; a buffoon; but let me tell you and I repeat it, excuse an old man, my dear Rodion Romanovitch, you are a man still young, so to say, in your first youth and so you put intellect above everything, like all young people. Playful wit and abstract arguments fascinate you and that's for all the world like the old Austrian Hofkriegsrath, as far as I can judge of military matters that is: on paper they'd beaten Napoleon and taken him prisoner, and there in their study they worked it all out in the cleverest fashion, but look you, General Mack surrendered with all his army, he-he-he! I see, I see, Rodion Romanovitch, you are laughing at a civilian like me, taking examples out of military history! But I can't help it, it's my weakness. I am fond of military science. And I'm ever so fond of reading all military histories. I've certainly missed my proper career. I ought to have been in the army, upon my word I ought. I shouldn't have been a Napoleon, but I might have been a major, he-he-he! Well, I'll tell you the whole truth, my dear fellow, about this *special case,* I mean: actual fact and a man's temperament, my dear sire, are weighty matters and it's astonishing how they sometimes deceive the sharpest calculation! I—I listen to an old man— am speaking seriously, Rodion Romanovitch (as he said this Porfiry Petrovitch who was scarcely five and thirty actually seemed to have grown old; even his voice changed and he seemed to shrink together) moreover, I'm a candid man . . . am I a candid man or not? What do you say? I fancy I really am: I tell you these things for nothing and don't even expect a reward for it, he-he! Well, to proceed, wit in my opinion is a splendid thing, it is, so to say, an adornment of nature and a consolation of life, and what tricks it can play! So that it sometimes is hard for a poor examining lawyer to know where he is, especially when he's liable to be carried away by his own fancy, too, for you know he is a man after all. But the poor fellow is saved by the criminal's temperament, worse luck for him! But young people carried away by their own wit don't think of that 'when they overstep all obstacles' as you wittily and cleverly expressed it yesterday. He will lie—that is, the man who is a *special case,* the incognito, and he will lie well, in the cleverest fashion; you might think he would triumph and enjoy the fruits of his wit, but at the most interesting, the most flagrant moment he will faint. Of course there may be illness and a stuffy room as well, but anyway! Anyway he's given us the idea! He lied incomparably, but he didn't reckon on his temperament. That's what betrays him! Another time he will be carried away by his playful wit into making fun of the man who suspects him, he will turn pale as it were on purpose to mislead, but his paleness will be *too natural,* too much like the real thing, again he has given us an idea! Though his questioner may be deceived at first, he will think differently next day if he is not a fool, and, of course, it is like that at every step! He puts himself forward where he is not wanted, speaks continually when he ought to keep silent, brings in all sorts of allegorical allusions, he-he! Comes and asks why didn't you take me long ago, he-he-he! And that can happen, you know, with the cleverest man, the psychologist, the literary man. The temperament reflects everything like a mirror! Gaze into it and admire what you see! But why are you so pale, Rodion Romanovitch? Is the room stuffy? Shall I open the window?"

"Oh, don't trouble, please," cried Raskolnikov and he suddenly broke into a laugh. "Please don't trouble."

Porfiry stood facing him, paused a moment and suddenly he too laughed. Raskolnikov got up from the sofa, abruptly checking his hysterical laughter.

"Porfiry Petrovitch," he began, speaking loudly and distinctly, though his legs trembled and he could scarcely stand. "I see clearly at last that you actually suspect me of murdering that old woman and her sister Lizaveta. Let me tell you for my part that I am sick of this. If you find that you have a right to prosecute me legally, to arrest me, then prosecute me, arrest me. But I will not let myself be jeered at to my face and worried . . ."

His lips trembled, his eyes glowed with fury and he could not restrain his voice.

"I won't allow it!" he shouted, bringing his fist down on the table. "Do you hear that, Porfiry Petrovitch? I won't allow it."

"Good heavens! What does it mean?" cried Porfiry Petrovitch, apparently quite frightened. "Rodion Romanovitch, my dear fellow, what is the matter with you?"

"I won't allow it," Raskolnikov shouted again.

"Hush, my dear man! They'll hear and come in. Just think, what could we say to them?" Porfiry Petrovitch whispered in horror, bringing his face close to Raskolnikov's.

"I won't allow it, I won't allow it," Raskolnikov repeated mechanically, but he too spoke in a sudden whisper.

Porfiry turned quickly and ran to open the window.

"Some fresh air! And you must have some water, my dear fellow. You're ill!" and he was running to the door to call for some when he found a decanter of water in the corner. "Come, drink a little," he whispered, rushing up to him with the decanter. "It will be sure to do you good."

Porfiry Petrovitch's alarm and sympathy were so natural that Raskolnikov was silent and began looking at him with wild curiosity. He did not take the water, however.

"Rodion Romanovitch, my dear fellow, you'll drive yourself out of your mind, I assure you, ach, ach! Have some water, do drink a little."

He forced him to take the glass. Raskolnikov raised it mechanically to his lips, but set it on the table again with disgust.

"Yes, you've had a little attack! You'll bring back your illness again, my dear fellow," Porfiry Petrovitch cackled with friendly sympathy, though he still looked rather disconcerted. "Good heavens, you must take more care of yourself! Dmitri Prokofitch was here, came to see me yesterday—I know, I know, I've a nasty, ironical temper, but what they made of it! . . . Good heavens, he came yesterday after you'd been. We dined and he talked and talked away, and I could only throw up my hands in despair! Did he come from you? But do sit down, for mercy's sake, sit down!"

"No, not from me, but I knew he went to you and why he went," Raskolnikov answered sharply.

"You knew?"

"I knew. What of it?"

"Why this, Rodion Romanovitch, that I know more than that about you; I know about everything. I know how you went *to take a flat* at night when it was dark and how you rang the bell and asked about the blood, so that the workmen and the porter did not know what to make of it. Yes, I understand your state of mind at that time . . . but you'll drive yourself mad like that, upon my word! You'll lose your head! You're full of generous indignation at the wrongs you've received, first from destiny, and then from the police officers, and so you rush from one thing to another to force them to speak out and make an end of it all, because you are sick of all this suspicion and foolishness. That's so, isn't it? I have guessed how you feel, haven't I? Only in that way you'll lose your head and Razumihin's, too; he's too *good* a man for such a position, you must know that. You are ill and he is good and your illness is infectious for him . . . I'll tell you about it when you are more yourself. . . . But do sit down, for goodness' sake. Please rest, you look shocking, do sit down."

Raskolnikov sat down; he no longer shivered, he was hot all over. In amazement he listened with strained attention to Porfiry Petrovitch who still seemed frightened as he looked after him with friendly solicitude. But he did not believe a word he said, though he felt a strange inclination to believe. Porfiry's unexpected words about the flat had utterly overwhelmed him. "How can it be, he knows about the flat then," he thought suddenly, "and he tells it me himself!"

"Yes, in our legal practice there was a case almost exactly similar, a case of morbid psychology," Porfiry went on quickly. "A man confessed to murder and how he kept it up! It was a regular hallucination; he brought forward facts, he imposed upon every one and why? He had been partly, but only partly, unintentionally the cause of a murder and when he knew that he had given the murderers the opportunity, he sank into dejection, it got on his mind and turned his brain, he began imagining things and he persuaded himself that he was the murderer. But at last the High Court of Appeals went into it and the poor fellow was acquitted and put under proper care. Thanks to the Court of Appeals! Tut-tut-tut! Why, my dear fellow, you may drive yourself into delirium if you have the impulse to work upon your nerves, to go ringing bells at night and asking about blood! I've studied all this morbid psychology in my practice. A man is sometimes tempted to jump out of a window or from a belfry. Just the same with bell-ringing. . . . It's all illness, Rodion Romanovitch! You have begun to neglect your illness. You should consult an experienced doctor, what's the good of that fat fellow? You are lightheaded! You were delirious when you did all this!"

For a moment Raskolnikov felt everything going round.

"Is it possible, is it possible," flashed through his mind, "that he is still lying? He can't be, he can't be." He rejected that idea, feeling to what a degree of fury it might drive him, feeling that that fury might drive him mad.

"I was not delirious. I knew what I was doing," he cried, straining every faculty to penetrate Porfiry's game, "I was quite myself, do you hear?"

"Yes, I hear and understand. You said yesterday you were not delirious, you were particularly emphatic about it! I understand all you can tell me! A-ach! . . . Listen, Rodion Romanovitch, my dear fellow. If you were actually a criminal, or were somehow mixed up in this damnable business, would you insist that you were not delirious but in full possession of your faculties? And so emphatically and persistently? Would it be possible? Quite impossible, to my thinking. If you had anything on your conscience, you certainly ought to insist that you were delirious. That's so, isn't it?"

There was a note of slyness in this inquiry. Raskolnikov drew back on the sofa as Porfiry bent over him and stared in silent perplexity at him.

"Another thing about Razumihin—you certainly ought to have said that he came of his own accord, to have concealed your part in it! But you don't conceal it! You lay stress on his coming at your instigation."

Raskolnikov had not done so. A chill went down his back.

"You keep telling lies," he said slowly and weakly, twisting his lips into a sickly smile, "you are trying again to show that you know all my game, that you know all I shall say beforehand," he said, conscious himself that he was not weighing his words as he ought. "You want to frighten me . . . or you are simply laughing at me. . . ."

He still stared at him as he said this and again there was a light of intense hatred in his eyes.

"You keep lying," he said. "You know perfectly well that the best policy for the criminal is to tell the truth as nearly as possible . . . to conceal as little as possible. I don't believe you!"

"What a wily person you are!" Porfiry tittered, "there's no catching you; you've a perfect monomania. So you don't believe me? But still you do believe me, you believe a quarter; I'll soon make you believe the whole, because I have a sincere liking for you and genuinely wish you good."

Raskolnikov's lips trembled.

"Yes, I do," went on Porfiry, touching Raskolnikov's arm genially, "you must take care of your illness. Besides, your mother and sister are here now; you must think of them. You must soothe and comfort them and you do nothing but frighten them . . ."

"What has that to do with you? How do you know it? What concern is it of yours? You are keeping watch on me and want to let me know it?"

"Good heavens! Why, I learnt it all from you yourself! You don't notice that in your excitement you tell me and others everything. From Razumihin, too, I learnt a number of interesting details yesterday. No, you interrupted me, but I must tell you that, for all your wit, your suspiciousness makes you lose the common-sense view of things. To return to bell-ringing, for instance. I, an examining lawyer, have betrayed a precious thing like that, a real fact (for it is a fact worth having), and you see nothing in it! Why, if I had the slightest suspicion of you, should I have acted like that? No, I should first have disarmed your suspicions and not let you see I knew of that fact, should have diverted your attention and suddenly have dealt you a knockdown blow (your expression) saying: 'And what were you doing, sir, pray, at ten or nearly eleven at the murdered woman's flat and why did you ring the bell and why did you ask about blood? And why did you invite the porters to go with you to the police station, to the lieutenant? That's how I ought to have acted if I had a grain of suspicion of you. I ought to have taken your evidence in due

form, searched your lodging and perhaps have arrested you, too
. . . so I have no suspicion of you, since I have not done that! But
you can't look at it normally and you see nothing, I say again."

Raskolnikov started so that Porfiry Petrovitch could not fail
to perceive it.

"You are lying all the while," he cried, "I don't know your
object, but you are lying. You did not speak like that just now and
I cannot be mistaken!"

"I am lying?" Porfiry repeated, apparently incensed, but
preserving a good-humoured and ironical face, as though he were
not in the least concerned at Raskolnikov's opinion of him. "I am
lying . . . but how did I treat you just now, I, the examining
lawyer? Prompting you and giving you every means for your
defence; illness, I said, delirium, injury, melancholy and the police officers and all the rest of it? Ah! He-he-he! Though, indeed,
all those psychological means of defence are not very reliable and
cut both ways: illness, delirium, I don't remember—that's all
right, but why, my good sir, in your illness and in your delirium
were you haunted by just those delusions and not by any others?
There may have been others, eh? He-he-he!"

Raskolnikov looked haughtily and contemptuously at him.

"Briefly," he said loudly and imperiously, rising to his feet
and in so doing pushing Porfiry back a little, "briefly, I want to
know, do you acknowledge me perfectly free from suspicion or
not? Tell me, Porfiry Petrovitch, tell me once for all and make
haste!"

"What a business I'm having with you!" cried Porfiry with
a perfectly good-humoured, sly and composed face. "And why do
you want to know, why do you want to know so much, since they
haven't begun to worry you? Why, you are like a child asking for
matches! And why are you so uneasy? Why do you force yourself
upon us, eh? He-he-he!"

"I repeat," Raskolnikov cried furiously. "that I can't put up
with it!"

"With what? Uncertainty?" interrupted Porfiry.

"Don't jeer at me! I won't have it! I tell you I won't have

it. I can't and I won't, do you hear, do you hear?" he shouted, bringing his fist down on the table again.

"Hush! Hush! They'll overhear! I warn you seriously, take care of yourself. I am not joking," Porfiry whispered, but this time there was not the look of old womanish good-nature and alarm in his face. Now he was peremptory, stern, frowning and for once laying aside all mystification.

But this was only for an instant. Raskolnikov, bewildered, suddenly fell into actual frenzy, but, strange to say, he again obeyed the command to speak quietly, though he was in a perfect paroxysm of fury.

"I will not allow myself to be tortured," he whispered, instantly recognising with hatred that he could not help obeying the command and driven to even greater fury by the thought. "Arrest me, search me, but kindly act in due form and don't play with me! Don't dare!"

"Don't worry about the form," Porfiry interrupted with the same sly smile, as it were, gloating with enjoyment over Raskolnikov. "I invited you to see me quite in a friendly way."

"I don't want your friendship and I spit on it! Do you hear? And, here, I take my cap and go. What will you say now if you mean to arrest me?"

He took up his cap and went to the door.

"And won't you see my little surprise?" chuckled Porfiry, again taking him by the arm and stopping him at the door.

He seemed to become more playful and good-humoured which maddened Raskolnikov.

"What surprise?" he asked, standing still and looking at Porfiry in alarm.

"My little surprise, it's sitting there behind the door, he-he-he! (he pointed to the locked door.) I locked him in that he should not escape."

"What is it? Where? What? . . ."

Raskolnikov walked to the door and would have opened it, but it was locked.

"It's locked, here is the key!"

And he brought a key out of his pocket.

"You are lying," roared Raskolnikov without restraint, "you lie, you damned punchinello!" and he rushed at Porfiry who retreated to the other door, not at all alarmed.

"I understand it all! You are lying and mocking so that I may betray myself to you . . ."

"Why, you could not betray yourself any further, my dear Rodion Romanovitch. You are in a passion. Don't shout, I shall call the clerks."

"You are lying! Call the clerks! You knew I was ill and tried to work me into a frenzy to make me betray myself, that was your object! Produce your facts! I understand it all. You've no evidence, you have only wretched rubbishly suspicions like Zametov's! You knew my character, you wanted to drive me to fury and then to knock me down with priests and deputies. . . . Are you waiting for them? eh! What are you waiting for? Where are they? Produce them?"

"Why deputies, my good man? What things people will imagine! And to do so would not be acting in form as you say, you don't know the business, my dear fellow. . . . And there's no escaping form, as you see," Porfiry muttered, listening at the door through which a noise could be heard.

"Ah, they're coming," cried Raskolnikov. "You've sent for them! You expected them! Well, produce them all: your deputies, your witnesses, what you like! . . . I am ready!"

But at this moment a strange incident occurred, something so unexpected that neither Raskolnikov nor Porfiry Petrovitch could have looked for such a conclusion to their interview.

6

When he remembered the scene afterwards, this is how Raskolnikov saw it.

The noise behind the door increased, and suddenly the door was opened a little.

"What is it?" cried Porfiry Petrovitch, annoyed. "Why, I gave orders . . ."

For an instant there was no answer, but it was evident that there were several persons at the door, and that they were apparently pushing somebody back.

"What is it?" Porfiry Petrovitch repeated, uneasily.

"The prisoner Nikolay has been brought," some one answered.

"He is not wanted! Take him away! Let him wait! What's he doing here? How irregular!" cried Porfiry, rushing to the door.

"But he . . ." began the same voice, and suddenly ceased.

Two seconds, not more, were spent in actual struggle, then some one gave a violent shove, and then a man, very pale, strode into the room.

This man's appearance was at first sight very strange. He stared straight before him, as though seeing nothing. There was a determined gleam in his eyes; at the same time there was a deathly pallor in his face, as though he were being led to the scaffold. His white lips were faintly twitching.

He was dressed like a workman and was of medium height, very young, slim, his hair cut in a round crop, with thin spare features. The man whom he had thrust back followed him into the room and succeeded in seizing him by the shoulder; he was a warder; but Nikolay pulled his arm away.

Several persons crowded inquisitively into the doorway. Some of them tried to get in. All this took place almost instantaneously.

"Go away, it's too soon! Wait till you are sent for! . . . Why have you brought him so soon?" Porfiry Petrovitch muttered, extremely annoyed, and as it were thrown out of his reckoning.

But Nikolay suddenly knelt down.

"What's the matter?" cried Porfiry, surprised.

"I am guilty! Mine is the sin! I am the murderer," Nikolay articulated suddenly, rather breathless, but speaking fairly loudly.

For ten seconds there was silence as though all had been struck dumb; even the warden stepped back, mechanically retreated to the door, and stood immovable.

"What is it?" cried Porfiry Petrovitch, recovering from his momentary stupefaction.

"I . . . am the murderer," repeated Nikolay, after a brief pause.

"What . . . you . . . what . . . whom did you kill?" Porfiry Petrovitch was obviously bewildered.

Nikolay again was silent for a moment.

"Alyona Ivanovna and her sister Lizaveta Ivanovna, I . . . killed . . . with an axe. Darkness came over me," he added suddenly, and was again silent.

He still remained on his knees. Porfiry Petrovitch stood for some moments as though meditating, but suddenly roused himself and waved back the uninvited spectators. They instantly vanished and closed the door. Then he looked towards Raskolnikov, who was standing in the corner, staring wildly at Nikolay, and moved towards him, but stopped short, looked from Nikolay to Raskolnikov and then again at Nikolay, and seeming unable to restrain himself darted at the latter.

"You're in too great a hurry," he shouted at him, almost angrily. "I didn't ask you what came over you. . . . Speak, did you kill them?"

"I am the murderer. . . . I want to give evidence," Nikolay pronounced.

"Ach! What did you kill them with?"

"An axe. I had it ready."

"Ach, he is in a hurry! Alone?"

Nikolay did not understand the question.

"Did you do it alone?"

"Yes, alone. And Mitka is not guilty and had no share in it."

"Don't be in a hurry about Mitka! A-ach! How was it you ran downstairs like that at the time? The porters met you both!"

"It was to put them off the scent. . . . I ran after Mitka," Nikolay replied hurriedly, as though he had prepared the answer.

"I knew it!" cried Porfiry, with vexation. "It's not his own tale he is telling," he muttered as though to himself, and suddenly his eyes rested on Raskolnikov again.

He was apparently so taken up with Nikolay that for a moment he had forgotten Raskolnikov. He was a little taken aback.

"My dear Rodion Rimanovitch, excuse me!" He flew up to

him, "this won't do; I'm afraid you must go . . . it's no good your staying . . . I will . . . you see, what a surprise! . . . Good-bye!"

And taking him by the arm, he showed him to the door.

"I suppose you didn't expect it?" said Raskolnikov who, though he had not yet fully grasped the situation, had regained his carriage.

"You did not expect it either, my friend. See how your hand is trembling! He-he!"

"You're trembling, too, Porfiry Petrovitch!"

"Yes, I am; I didn't expect it."

They were already at the door; Porfiry was impatient for Raskolnikov to be gone.

"And your little surprise, aren't you going to show it to me?" Raskolnikov said, sarcastically.

"Why, his teeth are chattering as he asks, he-he! You are an ironical person! Come, till we meet!"

"I believe we can say *good-bye!*"

"That's in God's hands," muttered Porfiry, with an unnatural smile.

As he walked through the office, Raskolnikov noticed that many people were looking at him. Among them he saw the two porters from *the* house, whom he had invited that night to the police station. They stood there waiting. But he was no sooner on the stairs than he heard the voice of Porfiry Petrovitch behind him. Turning round, he saw the latter running after him, out of breath.

"One word, Rodion Romanovitch; as to all the rest, it's in God's hands, but as a matter of form there are some questions I shall have to ask you . . . so we shall meet again, shan't we?"

And Porfiry stood still, facing him with a smile.

"Shan't we?" he added again.

He seemed to want to say something more, but could not speak out.

"You must forgive me, Porfiry Petrovitch, for what has just passed . . . I lost my temper," began Raskolnikov, who had so far regained his courage that he felt irresistibly inclined to display his coolness.

"Don't mention it, don't mention it," Porfiry replied, almost gleefully. "I myself, too . . . I have a wicked temper, I admit it! But we shall meet again. If it's God's will, we may see a great deal of one another."

"And will get to know each other through and through?" added Raskolnikov.

"Yes; know each other through and through," assented Porfiry Petrovitch, and he screwed up his eyes looking earnestly at Raskolnikov. "Now you're going to a birthday party?"

"To a funeral."

"Of course, the funeral! Take care of yourself, and get well."

"I don't know what to wish you," said Raskolnikov, who had begun to descend the stairs, but looked back again. "I should like to wish you success, but your office is such a comical one."

"Why comical?" Porfiry Petrovitch had turned to go, but he seemed to prick up his ears at this.

"Why, how you must have been torturing and harassing that poor Nikolay psychologically, after your fashion, till he confessed! You must have been at him day and night, proving to him that he was the murderer, and now that he has confessed, you'll begin vivisecting him again. 'You are lying,' you'll say. 'You are not the murderer! You can't be! It's not your own tale you are telling!' You must admit it's a comical business!"

"He-he-he! You noticed then that I said to Nikolay just now that it was not his own tale he was telling?"

"How could I help noticing it!"

"He-he! You are quick-witted. You notice everything! You've really a playful mind! And you always fasten on the comic side . . . he-he! They say that was the marked characteristic of Gogol, among the writers."

"Yes, of Gogol."

"Yes, of Gogol. . . . I shall look forward to meeting you."

"So shall I."

Raskolnikov walked straight home. He was so muddled and bewildered that on getting home he sat for a quarter of an hour on the sofa, trying to collect his thoughts. He did not attempt to think about Nikolay; he was stupefied; he felt that his confession was something inexplicable, amazing—something beyond his understanding. But Nikolay's confession was an actual fact. The consequences of this fact were clear to him at once, its falsehood could not fail to be discovered, and then they would be after him again. Till then, at least, he was free and must do something for himself, for the danger was imminent.

But how imminent? His position gradually became clear to him. Remembering, sketchily, the main outlines of his recent scene with Porfiry, he could not help shuddering again with horror. Of course, he did not yet know all Porfiry's aims, he could not see into all his calculations. But he had already partly shown his hand, and no one knew better than Raskolnikov how terrible Porfiry's "lead" had been for him. A little more and he *might* have given himself away completely, circumstantially. Knowing his nervous temperament and from the first glance seeing through him, Porfiry, though playing a bold game, was bound to win. There's no denying that Raskolnikov had compromised himself seriously, but no *facts* had come to light as yet; there was nothing positive. But was he taking a true view of the position? Wasn't he mistaken? What had Porfiry been trying to get at? Had he really some surprise prepared for him? And what was it? Had he really been expecting something or not? How would they have parted if it had not been for the unexpected appearance of Nikolay?

Porfiry had shown almost all his cards—of course, he had risked something in showing them—and if he had really had anything up his sleeve (Raskolnikov reflected), he would have shown that, too. What was that "surprise"? Was it a joke? Had it meant anything? Could it have concealed anything like a fact, a piece of positive evidence? His yesterday's visitor? What had become of him? Where was he to-day? If Porfiry really had any evidence, it must be connected with him. . . .

He sat on the sofa with his elbows on his knees and his face hidden in his hands. He was still shivering nervously. At last he got up, took his cap, thought a minute, and went to the door.

He had a sort of presentiment that for to-day, at least, he might consider himself out of danger. He had a sudden sense almost of joy; he wanted to make haste to Katerina Ivanovna's.

He would be too late for the funeral, of course, but he would be in time for the memorial dinner, and there at once he would see Sonia.

He stood still, thought a moment, and a suffering smile came for a moment on to his lips.

"To-day! To-day," he repeated to himself. "Yes, to-day! So it must be. . . ."

But as he was about to open the door, it began opening of itself. He started and moved back. The door opened gently and slowly, and there suddenly appeared a figure—yesterday's visitor *from underground.*

The man stood in the doorway, looked at Raskolnikov without speaking, and took a step forward into the room. He was exactly the same as yesterday; the same figure, the same dress, but there was a great change in his face; he looked dejected and sighed deeply. If he had only put his hand up to his cheek and leaned his head on one side he would have looked exactly like a peasant woman.

"What do you want?" asked Raskolnikov, numb with terror.

The man was still silent, but suddenly he bowed down almost to the ground, touching it with his finger.

"What is it?" cried Raskolnikov.

"I have sinned," the man articulated softly.

"How?"

"By evil thoughts."

They looked at one another.

"I was vexed. When you came, perhaps in drink, and bade the porters go to the police station and asked about the blood, I was vexed that they let you go and took you for drunken. I was so vexed that I lost my sleep. And remembering the address we came here yesterday and asked for you. . . ."

"Who came?" Raskolnikov interrupted, instantly beginning to recollect.

"I did, I've wronged you."

"Then you came from that house?"

"I was standing at the gate with them . . . don't you remember? We have carried on our trade in that house for years past.

We cure and prepare hides, we take work home . . . most of all I was vexed. . . ."

And the whole scene of the day before yesterday in the gateway came clearly before Raskolnikov's mind; he recollected that there had been several people there besides the porters, women among them. He remembered one voice had suggested taking him straight to the police station. He could not recall the face of the speaker, and even now he did not recognise it, but he remembered that he had turned round and made him some answer. . . .

So this was the solution of yesterday's horror. The most awful thought was that he had been actually almost lost, had almost done for himself on account of such a *trivial* circumstance. So this man could tell nothing except his asking about the flat and the blood stains. So Porfiry, too, had nothing but that *delirium*, no facts but this *psychology* which *cuts both ways*, nothing positive. So if no more facts come to light (and they must not, they must not!) then . . . then what can they do to him? How can they convict him, even if they arrest him? And Porfiry then had only just heard about the flat and had not known about it before.

"Was it you who told Porfiry . . . that I'd been there?" he cried, struck by a sudden idea.

"What Porfiry?"

"The head of the detective department?"

"Yes. The porters did not go there, but I went."

"To-day?"

"I got there two minutes before you. And I heard, I heard it all, how he worried you."

"Where? What? When?"

"Why, in the next room. I was sitting there all the time."

PART FIVE—

1

The morning that followed the fateful interview with Dounia and her mother brought sobering influences to bear on Pyotr Petrovitch. Intensely unpleasant as it was, he was forced little by little to accept as a fact beyond recall what had seemed to him only the day before fantastic and incredible. The black snake of wounded vanity had been gnawing at his heart all night. When he got out of bed, Pyotr Petrovitch immediately looked in the looking-glass. He was afraid that he had jaundice. However his health seemed unimpaired so far, and looking at his noble, clear-skinned countenance which had grown fattish of late, Pyotr Petrovitch for an instant was positively comforted in the conviction that he would find another bride and, perhaps, even a better one. But coming back to the sense of his present position, he turned aside and spat vigorously, which excited a sarcastic smile in Andrey Semyonovitch Lebeziatnikov, the young friend with whom he was staying. That smile Pyotr Petrovitch noticed, and at once set it down against his young friend's account. He had set down a good many points against him of late. His anger was redoubled when he reflected that he ought not to have told Andrey Semyonovitch about the result of yesterday's interview. That was the second mistake he had made in temper, through impulsiveness and irritability. . . . Moreover, all that morning one unpleasantness followed another. He even found a hitch awaiting him in his legal case in the Senate. He was particularly irritated by the owner of the flat which had been taken in view of his approaching marriage and was being redecorated at his own expense; the owner, a rich German tradesman, would not entertain the idea of breaking the contract which had just been signed and insisted on the full forfeit money, though Pyotr Petrovitch would be giving him back the flat practically redecorated. In the same way the upholsterers refused to return a single rouble of the instalment paid for the furniture purchased but not yet removed to the flat.

"Am I to get married simply for the sake of the furniture?"

Pyotr Petrovitch ground his teeth and at the same time once more he had a gleam of desperate hope. "Can all that be really so irrevocably over? Is it no use to make another effort?" The thought of Dounia sent a voluptuous pang through his heart. He endured anguish at that moment, and if it had been possible to slay Raskolnikov instantly by wishing it, Pyotr Petrovitch would promptly have uttered the wish.

"It was my mistake, too, not to have given them money," he thought, as he returned dejectedly to Lebeziatnikov's room, "and why on earth was I such a Jew? It was false economy! I meant to keep them without a penny so that they should turn to me as their providence, and look at them! Foo! If I'd spent some fifteen hundred roubles on them for the trousseau and presents, on knick-knacks, dressing-cases, jewellery, materials, and all that sort of trash from Knopp's and the English shop, my position would have been better and . . . stronger! They could not have refused me so easily! They are the sort of people that would feel bound to return money and presents if they broke it off; and they would find it hard to do it! And their consciences would prick them: how can we dismiss a man who has hitherto been so generous and delicate? . . . H'm! I've made a blunder."

And grinding his teeth again, Pyotr Petrovitch called himself a fool—but not aloud, of course.

He returned home, twice as irritated and angry as before. The preparations for the funeral dinner at Katerina Ivanovna's excited his curiosity as he passed. He had heard about it the day before; he fancied, indeed, that he had been invited, but absorbed in his own cares he had paid no attention. Inquiring of Madame Lippevechsel who was busy laying the table while Katerina Ivanovna was away at the cemetery, he heard that the entertainment was to be a great affair, that all the lodgers had been invited, among them some who had not known the dead man, that even Andrey Semyonovitch Lebeziatnikov was incited in spite of his previous quarrel with Katerina Ivanovna, that he, Pyotr Petrovitch, was not only invited, but was eagerly expected as he was the most important of the lodgers. Amalia Ivanovna herself had been invited with great ceremony in spite of the recent unpleasantness, and so she was very busy with preparations and was taking a positive pleasure in them; she was moreover dressed up to the nines, all in new black silk, and she was proud of it. All this suggested an idea to Pyotr Petrovitch and he went into his room, or rather Lebeziatnikov's, somewhat thoughtful. He had learnt that Raskolnikov was to be one of the guests.

Andrey Semyonovitch had been at home all the morning. The attitude of Pyotr Petrovitch to this gentleman was strange, though perhaps natural. Pyotr Petrovitch had despised and hated him from the day he came to stay with him and at the same time he seemed somewhat afraid of him. He had not come to stay with him on his arrival in Petersburg simply from parsimony, though that had been perhaps his chief object. He had heard of Andrey Semyonovitch, who had once been his ward, as a leading young progressive who was taking an important part in certain interesting circles, the doings of which were a legend in the provinces. It had impressed Pyotr Petrovitch. These powerful omniscient circles who despised every one and showed every one up had long inspired in him a peculiar but quite vague alarm. He had not, of course, been able to form even an approximate notion of what they meant. He, like every one, had heard that there were, especially in Petersburg, progressives of some sort, nihilists and so on, and, like many people, he exaggerated and distorted the significance of those words to an absurd degree. What for many years past he had feared more than anything was *being shown up* and this was the chief ground for his continual uneasiness at the thought of transferring his business to Petersburg. He was afraid of this as little children are sometimes panic-stricken. Some years before, when he was just entering on his own career, he had come upon two cases in which rather important personages in the province, patrons of his, had been cruelly shown up. One instance had ended in great scandal for the person attacked and the other had very nearly ended in serious trouble. For this reason Pyotr Petrovitch intended to go into the subject as soon as he reached Petersburg and, if necessary, to anticipate contingencies by seeking the favour of "our younger generation." He relied on Andrey Semyonovitch for this and before his visit to Raskolnikov he had succeeded in picking up some current phrases. He soon discovered that Andrey Semyonovitch was a commonplace simpleton, but that by no means reassured Pyotr Petrovitch. Even if he had been certain that all the progressives were fools like him, it would not have allayed his uneasiness. All the doctrines, the ideas, the systems with which Andrey Semyonovitch pestered him had no interest for him. He had his own object—he simply wanted to find out at once what was happening *here*. Had these people any power or not? Had he anything to fear from them? Would they expose any enterprise of his? And what precisely was now the object of their attacks? Could he somehow make up to them and get round them if they really were powerful? Was this the thing to do or not? Couldn't he gain something through them? In fact hundreds of questions presented themselves.

Andrey Semyonovitch was an anaemic, scrofulous little man, with strangely flaxen mutton-chop whiskers of which he was very proud. He was a clerk and had almost always something wrong with his eyes. He was rather soft-hearted, but self-confident and sometimes extremely conceited in speech which had an absurd effect, incongruous with his little figure. He was one of the lodgers most respected by Amalia Ivanovna, for he did not get drunk and paid regularly for his lodgings. Andrey Semyonovitch really was rather stupid; he attached himself to the cause of progress and "our younger generation" from enthusiasm. He was one of the numerous and varied legion of dullards, of half-animate abortions, conceited, half-educated coxcombs, who attach themselves to the idea most in fashion only to vulgarise it and who caricature every cause they serve, however sincerely.

Though Lebeziatnikov was so good-natured, he, too, was beginning to dislike Pyotr Petrovitch. This happened on both sides unconsciously. However simple Andrey Semyonovitch might be, he began to see that Pyotr Petrovitch was duping him and secretly despising him, and that "he was not the right sort of man." He had tried expounding to him the system of Fourier and the Darwinian theory, but of late Pyotr Petrovitch began to listen too sarcastically and even to be rude. The fact was he had begun instinctively to guess that Lebeziatnikov was not merely a com-

monplace simpleton, but, perhaps, a liar, too, and that he had no
connections of any consequence even in his own circle, but had
simply picked things up third-hand; and that very likely he did not
even know much about his own work of propaganda, for he was
in too great a muddle. A fine person he would be to show any
one up! It must be noted, by the way, that Pyotr Petrovitch had
during those ten days eagerly accepted the strangest praise from
Andrey Semyonovitch; he had not protested, for instance, when
Andrey Semyonovitch belauded him for being ready to contribute to the establishment of the new "commune," or to abstain
from christening his future children, or to acquiesce if Dounia
were to take a lover a month after marriage, and so on. Pyotr
Petrovitch so enjoyed hearing his own praises that he did not
disdain even such virtues when they were attributed to him.

Pyotr Petrovitch had had occasion that morning to realise
some five per cent. bonds and now he sat down to the table and
counted over bundles of notes. Andrey Semyonovitch who hardly
ever had any money walked about the room pretending to himself
to look at all those bank notes with indifference and even contempt. Nothing would have convinced Pyotr Petrovitch that Andrey Semyonovitch could really look on the money unmoved,
and the latter, on his side, kept thinking bitterly that Pyotr Petrovitch was capable of entertaining such an idea about him and
was, perhaps, glad of the opportunity of teasing his young friend
by reminding him of his inferiority and the great difference between them.

He found him incredibly inattentive and irritable, though
he, Andrey Semyonovitch, began enlarging on his favourite subject, the foundation of a new special "commune." The brief
remarks that dropped from Pyotr Petrovitch between the clicking
of the beads on the reckoning frame betrayed unmistakable and
discourteous irony. But the "humane" Andrey Semyonovitch
ascribed Pyotr Petrovitch's ill-humour to his recent breach with
Dounia and he was burning with impatience to discourse on that
theme. He had something progressive to say on the subject which
might console his worthy friend and "could not fail" to promote
his development.

"There is some sort of festivity being prepared at that
. . . at the widow's, isn't there?" Pyotr Petrovitch asked suddenly,
interrupting Andrey Semyonovitch at the most interesting Passage.

"Why, don't you know? Why, I was telling you last night
what I think about all such ceremonies. And she invited you too,
I heard. You were talking to her yesterday . . ."

"I should never have expected that beggarly fool would have
spent on this feast all the money she got from that other fool,
Raskolnikov. I was surprised just now as I came through at the
preparations there, the wines! Several people are invited. It's
beyond everything!" continued Pyotr Petrovitch, who seemed to
have some object in pursuing the conversation. "What? You say
I am asked too? When was that? I don't remember. But I shan't
go. Why should I? I only said a word to her in passing yesterday
of the possibility of her obtaining a year's salary as a destitute
widow of a government clerk. I suppose she has invited me on
that account, hasn't she? He-he-he!"

"I don't intend to go either," said Lebeziatnikov.

"I should think not, after giving her a thrashing! You might
well hesitate, he-he!"

"Who thrashed? Whom?" cried Lebeziatnikov, flustered and
blushing.

"Why, you thrashed Katerina Ivanovna a month ago. I heard
so yesterday . . . so that's what your convictions amount to
. . . and the woman question, too, wasn't quite sound, he-he-he!"
and Pyotr Petrovitch, as though comforted, went back to clicking
his beads.

"It's all slander and nonsense!" cried Lebeziatnikov, who
was always afraid of allusions to the subject. "It was not like that
at all, it was quite different. You've heard it wrong; it's a libel.
I was simply defending myself. She rushed at me first with her
nails, she pulled out all my whiskers. . . . It's permissible for any
one I should hope to defend himself and I never allow any one
to use violence to me on principle, for it's an act of despotism.
What was I to do? I simply pushed her back."

"He-he-he!" Luzhin went on laughing maliciously.

"You keep on like that because you are out of humour yourself. . . . But that's nonsense and it has nothing, nothing whatever to do with the woman question! You don't understand; I used to think, indeed, that if women are equal to men in all respects even in strength (as is maintained now) there ought to be equality in that, too. Of course, I reflected afterwards that such a question ought not really to arise, for there ought not to be fighting and in the future society, fighting is unthinkable . . . and that it would be a queer thing to seek for equality in fighting. I am not so stupid . . . though, of course, there is fighting . . . there won't be later, but at present there is . . . confound it! How muddled one gets with you! It's not on that account that I am not going. I am not going on principle, not to take part in the revolting convention of memorial dinners, that's why! Though, of course, one might go to laugh at it. . . . I am sorry there won't be any priests at it. I should certainly go if there were."

"Then you would sit down at another man's table and insult it and those who invited you. Eh?"

"Certainly not insult, but protest. I should do it with a good object. I might indirectly assist the cause of enlightenment and propaganda. It's a duty of every man to work for enlightenment and propaganda and the more harshly, perhaps, the better. I might drop a seed, an idea. . . . And something might grow up from that seed. How should I be insulting them? They might be offended at first, but afterwards they'd see I'd done them a service. You know, Terebyeva (who is in the community now) was blamed because when she left her family and . . . devoted . . . herself, she wrote to her father and mother that she wouldn't go on living conventionally and was entering on a free marriage and it was said that that was too harsh, that she might have spared them and have written more kindly. I think that's all nonsense and there's no need of softness, on the contrary, what's wanted is protest. Varents had been married seven years, she abandoned her two children, she told her husband straight out in a letter: 'I have realised that I cannot be happy with you. I can never forgive you that you have deceived me by concealing from me that there is another organisation of society by means of the communities.

I have only lately learned it from a great-hearted man to whom I have given myself and with whom I am establishing a community. I speak plainly because I consider it dishonest to deceive you. Do as you think best. Do not hope to get me back, you are too late. I hope you will be happy.' That's how letters like that ought to be written!"

"Is that Terebyeva the one you said had made a third free marriage?"

"No, it's only the second, really! But what if it were the fourth, what if it were the fifteenth, that's all nonsense! And if ever I regretted the death of my father and mother, it is now, and I sometimes think if my parents were living what a protest I would have aimed at them! I would have done something on purpose . . . I would have shown them! I would have astonished them! I am really sorry there is no one!"

"To surprise! He-he! Well, be that as you will," Pyotr Petrovitch interrupted, "but tell me this: do you know the dead man's daughter, the delicate-looking little thing? It's true what they say about her, isn't it?"

"What of it? I think, that is, it is my own personal conviction, that this is the normal condition of women. Why not? I mean, *distinguons*. In our present society, it is not altogether normal, because it is compulsory, but in the future society, it will be perfectly normal, because it will be voluntary. Even as it is, she was quite right: she was suffering and that was her asset, so to speak, her capital which she had a perfect right to dispose of. Of course, in the future society, there will be no need of assets, but her part will have another significance, rational and in harmony with her environment. As to Sofya Semyonovna personally, I regard her action as a vigorous protest against the organisation of society, and I respect her deeply for it; I rejoice indeed when I look at her!"

"I was told that you got her turned out of these lodgings." Lebeziatnikov was enraged.

"That's another slander," he yelled. "It was not so at all! That was all Katerina Ivanovna's invention, for she did not understand! And I never made love to Sofya Semyonovna! I was simply developing her, entirely disinterestedly, trying to rouse her to protest. . . . All I wanted was her protest and Sofya Semyonovna could not have remained here anyway!"

"Have you asked her to join your community?"

"You keep on laughing and very inappropriately, allow me to tell you. You don't understand! There is no such rôle in a community. The community is established that there should be no such rôles. In a community, such a rôle is essentially transformed and what is stupid here is sensible there, what, under present conditions, is unnatural becomes perfectly natural in the community. It all depends on the environment. It's all the environment and man himself is nothing. And I am on good terms with Sofya Semyonovna to this day, which is a proof that she never regarded me as having wronged her. I am trying now to attract her to the community, but on quite, quite a different footing. What are you laughing at? We are trying to establish a community of our own, a special one, on a broader basis. We have gone further in our convictions. We reject more! And meanwhile I'm still developing Sofya Semyonovna. She has a beautiful, beautiful character!"

"And you take advantage of her fine character, eh? He-he!"

"No, no! Oh, no! On the contrary."

"Oh, on the contrary! He-he-he! A queer thing to say!"

"Believe me! Why should I disguise it? In fact, I feel it strange myself how timid, chaste and modern she is with me!"

"And you, of course, are developing her . . . he-he! Trying to prove to her that all that modesty is nonsense?"

"Not at all, not at all! How coarsely, how stupidly—excuse me saying so—you misunderstand the word development! Good heavens, how . . . crude you still are! We are striving for the freedom of women and you have only one idea in your head. . . . Setting aside the general question of chastity and feminine modesty as useless in themselves and indeed prejudices, I fully accept her chastity with me, because that's for her to decide. Of course if she were to tell me herself that she wanted me, I should think myself very lucky, because I like the girl very much; but as it is, no one has ever treated her more courteously than I, with more respect for her dignity . . . I wait in hopes, that's all!"

"You had much better make her a present of something. I bet you never thought of that."

"You don't understand, as I've told you already! Of course, she is in such a position, but it's another question. Quite another question! You simply despise her. Seeing a fact which you mistakenly consider deserving of contempt, you refuse to take a humane view of a fellow creature. You don't know what a character she is! I am only sorry that of late she has quite given up reading and borrowing books. I used to lend them to her. I am sorry, too, that with all the energy and resolution in protesting—which she has already shown once—she has little self-reliance, little, so to say, independence, so as to break free from certain prejudices and certain foolish ideas. Yet she thoroughly understands some questions, for instance about kissing of hands, that is, that it's an insult to a woman for a man to kiss her hand, because it's a sign of inequality. We had a debate about it and I described it to her. She listened attentively to an account of the workmen's associations in France, too. Now I am explaining the question of coming into the room in the future society."

"And what's that, pray?"

"We had a debate lately on the question: Has a member of the community the right to enter another member's room, whether man or woman at any time . . . and we decided that he has!"

"It might be at an inconvenient moment, he-he!"

Lebeziatnikov was really angry.

"You are always thinking of something unpleasant," he cried with aversion. "Tfoo! How vexed I am that when I was expounding our system, I referred prematurely to the question of personal privacy! It's always a stumbling-block to people like you, they turn it into ridicule before they understand it. And how proud they are of it, too! Tfoo! I've often maintained that that question should not be approached by a novice till he has a firm faith in the system. And tell me, please, what do you find so shameful even in cesspools? I should be the first to be ready to clean out any cesspool you like. And it's not a question of self-sacrifice, it's simply work, honourable, useful work which is as good as any other and much better than the work of a Raphael and a Pushkin, because it is more useful.''

"And more honourable, more honourable, he-he-he!''

"What do you mean by 'more honourable'? I don't understand such expressions to describe human activity. 'More honourable,' 'nobler'—all those are old-fashioned prejudices which I reject. Everything which is *of use* to mankind is honourable. I only understand one word: *useful!* You can snigger as much as you like, but that's so!''

Pyotr Petrovitch laughed heartily. He had finished counting the money and was putting it away. But some of the notes he left on the table. The "cesspool question'' had already been a subject of dispute between them. What was absurd was that it made Lebeziatnikov really angry, while it amused Luzhin and at that moment he particularly wanted to anger his young friend.

"It's your ill-luck yesterday that makes you so ill-humoured and annoying,'' blurted out Lebeziatnikov, who in spite of his "independence'' and his "protests'' did not venture to oppose Pyotr Petrovitch and still behaved to him with some of the respect habitual in earlier years.

"You'd better tell me this,'' Pyotr Petrovitch interrupted with haughty displeasure, "can you . . . or rather are you really friendly enough with that young person to ask her to step in here for a minute? I think they've all come back from the cemetery . . . I hear the sound of steps . . . I want to see her, that young person.''

"What for?'' Lebeziatnikov asked with surprise.

"Oh, I want to. I am leaving here to-day or to-morrow and therefore I wanted to speak to her about . . . However, you may be present during the interview. It's better you should be, indeed. For there's no knowing what you might imagine.''

"I shan't imagine anything. I only asked and, if you've anything to say to her, nothing is easier than to call her in. I'll go directly and you may be sure I won't be in your way.''

Five minutes later Lebeziatnikov came in with Sonia. She came in very much surprised and overcome with shyness as usual.

She was always shy in such circumstances and was always afraid of new people, she had been as a child and was even more so now. . . . Pyotr Petrovitch met her "politely and affably," but with a certain shade of bantering familiarity which in his opinion was suitable for a man of his respectability and weight in dealing with a creature so young and so *interesting* as she. He hastened to "reassure" her and made her sit down facing him at the table. Sonia sat down, looked about her—at Lebeziatnikov, at the notes lying on the table and then again at Pyotr Petrovitch and her eyes remained riveted on him. Lebeziatnikov was moving to the door. Pyotr Petrovitch signed to Sonia to remain seated and stopped Lebeziatnikov.

"Is Raskolnikov in there? Has he come?" he asked him in a whisper.

"Raskolnikov? Yes. Why? Yes, he is there. I saw him just come in. . . . Why?"

"Well, I particularly beg you to remain here with us and not to leave me alone with this . . . young woman. I only want a few words with her, but God knows what they may make of it. I shouldn't like Raskolnikov to repeat anything. . . . You understand what I mean?"

"I understand!" Lebeziatnikov saw the point. "Yes, you are right. . . . Of course, I am convinced personally that you have no reason to be uneasy, but . . . still, you are right. Certainly I'll stay. I'll stand here at the window and not be in your way . . . I think you are right . . ."

Pyotr Petrovitch returned to the sofa, sat down opposite Sonia, looked attentively at her and assumed an extremely dignified, even severe expression, as much as to say, "don't you make any mistake, madam." Sonia was overwhelmed with embarrassment.

"In the first place, Sofya Semyonovna, will you make my excuses to your respected mamma. . . . That's right, isn't it? Katerina Ivanovna stands in the place of a mother to you?" Pyotr Petrovitch began with great dignity, though affably.

It was evident that his intentions were friendly.

"Quite so, yes; the place of a mother," Sonia answered, timidly and hurriedly.

"Then will you make my apologies to her? Through inevitable circumstances I am forced to be absent and shall not be at the dinner in spite of your mamma's kind invitation."

"Yes . . . I'll tell her . . . at once."

And Sonia hastily jumped up from her seat.

"Wait, that's not all," Pyotr Petrovitch detained her, smiling at her simplicity and ignorance of good manners, "and you know me little, my dear Sofya Semyonovna, if you suppose I would have ventured to trouble a person like you for a matter of so little consequence affecting myself only. I have another object."

Sonia sat down hurriedly. Her eyes rested again for an instant on the grey and rainbow-coloured notes that remained on the table, but she quickly looked away and fixed her eyes on Pyotr Petrovitch. She felt it horribly indecorous, especially for *her,* to look at another person's money. She stared at the gold eyeglass which Pyotr Petrovitch held in his left hand and at the massive and extremely handsome ring with a yellow stone on his middle finger. But suddenly she looked away and, not knowing where to turn, ended by staring Pyotr Petrovitch again straight in the face. After a pause of still greater dignity he continued.

"I chanced yesterday in passing to exchange a couple of words with Katerina Ivanovna, poor woman. That was sufficient to enable me to ascertain that she is in a position—preternatural, if one may so express it."

"Yes . . . preternatural . . ." Sonia hurriedly assented.

"Or it would be simpler and more comprehensible to say, ill."

"Yes, simpler and more comprehen . . . yes, ill."

"Quite so. So then from a feeling of humanity and so to speak compassion, I should be glad to be of service to her in any way, foreseeing her unfortunate position. I believe the whole of this poverty-stricken family depends now entirely on you?"

"Allow me to ask," Sonia rose to her feet, "did you say something to her yesterday of the possibility of a pension? Because she told me you had undertaken to get her one. Was that true?"

"Not in the slightest, and indeed it's an absurdity! I merely hinted at her obtaining temporary assistance as the widow of an official who had died in the service—if only she has patronage . . . but apparently your late parent had not served his full term and had not indeed been in the service at all of late. In fact, if there could be any hope, it would be very ephemeral, because there would be no claim for assistance in that case, far from it. . . . And she is dreaming of a pension already, he-he-he! . . . A go-ahead lady!"

"Yes, she is. For she is credulous and good-hearted, and she believes everything from the goodness of her heart and . . . and . . . and she is like that . . . yes . . . You must excuse her," said Sonia, and again she got up to go.

"But you haven't heard what I have to say."

"No, I haven't heard," muttered Sonia.

"Then sit down." She was terribly confused; she sat down again a third time.

"Seeing her position with her unfortunate little ones, I should be glad, as I have said before, so far as lies in my power, to be of service, that is, so far as is in my power, not more. One might for instance get up a subscription for her, or a lottery, something of the sort, such as is always arranged in such cases by friends or even outsiders desirous of assisting people. It was of that I intended to speak to you; it might be done."

"Yes, yes . . . God will repay you for it," faltered Sonia, gazing intently at Pyotr Petrovitch.

"It might be, but we will talk of it later. We might begin it to-day, we will talk it over this evening and lay the foundation so to speak. Come to me at seven o'clock. Mr. Lebeziatnikov, I hope, will assist us. But there is one circumstance of which I ought to warn you beforehand and for which I venture to trouble you, Sofya Semyonovna, to come here. In my opinion money cannot be, indeed it's unsafe to put it into Katerina Ivanovna's own hands. The dinner to-day is a proof of that. Though she has not, so to speak, a crust of bread for to-morrow and . . . well, boots or shoes, or anything; she has bought to-day Jamaica rum, and even, I believe, Madeira and . . . and coffee. I saw it as I passed through. To-morrow it will all fall upon you again, they won't have a crust of bread. It's absurd, really, and so, to my thinking, a subscription ought to be raised so that the unhappy widow should not know of the money, but only you, for instance. Am I right?"

"I don't know . . . this is only to-day, once in her life. . . . She was so anxious to do honour, to celebrate the memory. . . . And she is very sensible . . . but just as you think and I shall be very, very . . . they will all be . . . and God will reward . . . and the orphans . . ."

Sonia burst into tears.

"Very well, then, keep it in mind; and now will you accept for the benefit of your relation the small sum that I am able to spare, from me personally. I am very anxious that my name should not be mentioned in connection with it. Here . . . having so to speak anxieties of my own, I cannot do more . . ."

And Pyotr Petrovitch held out to Sonia a ten-rouble note carefully unfolded. Sonia took it, flushed crimson, jumped up, muttered something and began taking leave. Pyotr Petrovitch accompanied her ceremoniously to the door. She got out of the room at last, agitated and distressed, and returned to Katerina Ivanovna, overwhelmed with confusion.

All this time Lebeziatnikov had stood at the window or walked about the room, anxious not to interrupt the conversation; when Sonia had gone he walked up to Pyotr Petrovitch and solemnly held out his hand.

"I heard and *saw* everything," he said, laying stress on the last verb. "That is honourable, I mean to say, it's humane! You wanted to avoid gratitude, I saw! And although I cannot, I confess, in principle sympathise with private charity, for it not only fails to eradicate the evil but even promotes it, yet I must admit that I saw your action with pleasure—yes, yes, I like it."

"That's all nonsense," muttered Pyotr Petrovitch, somewhat disconcerted, looking carefully at Lebeziatnikov.

"No, it's not nonsense! A man who has suffered distress and

annoyance as you did yesterday and who yet can sympathise with the misery of others, such a man . . . even though he is making a social mistake—is still deserving of respect! I did not expect it indeed of you, Pyotr Petrovitch, especially as according to your ideas . . . oh, what a drawback your ideas are to you! How distressed you are for instance by your ill luck yesterday," cried the simple-hearted Lebeziatnikov, who felt a return of affection for Pyotr Petrovitch. "And what do you want with marriage, with *legal* marriage, my dear, noble Pyotr Petrovitch? Why do you cling to this *legality* of marriage? Well, you may beat me if you like, but I am glad, positively glad it hasn't come off, that you are free, that you are not quite lost for humanity. . . . You see, I've spoken my mind!"

"Because I don't want in your free marriage to be made a fool of and to bring up another man's children, that's why I want legal marriage," Luzhin replied in order to make some answer.

He seemed preoccupied by something.

"Children? You referred to children," Lebeziatnikov started off like a warhorse at the trumpet call. "Children are a social question and a question of first importance, I agree; but the question of children has another solution. Some refuse to have children altogether, because they suggest the institution of the family. We'll speak of children later, but now as to the question of honour, I confess that's my weak point. That horrid, military, Pushkin expression is unthinkable in the dictionary of the future. What does it mean indeed? It's nonsense, there will be no deception in a free marriage! That is only the natural consequence of a legal marriage, so to say, its corrective, a protest. So that indeed it's not humiliating . . . and if I ever, to suppose an absurdity, were to be legally married, I should be positively glad of it. I should say to my wife: 'My dear, hitherto I have loved you, now I respect you, for you've shown you can protest!' You laugh! That's because you are incapable of getting away from prejudices. Confound it all! I understand now where the unpleasantness is of being deceived in a legal marriage, but it's simply a despicable consequence of a despicable position in which both are humiliated. When the deception is open, as in a free marriage, then it does not exist, it's unthinkable. Your wife will only prove how she respects you by considering you incapable of opposing her happiness and avenging yourself on her for her new husband. Damn it all! I sometimes dream if I were to be married, foo! I mean if I were to marry, legally or not, it's just the same, I should present my wife with a lover if she had not found one for herself. 'My dear,' I should say, 'I love you, but even more than that I desire you to respect me. See!' Am I not right?"

Pyotr Petrovitch sniggered as he listened, but without much merriment. He hardly heard it indeed. He was preoccupied with something else and even Lebeziatnikov at last noticed it. Pyotr Petrovitch seemed excited and rubbed his hands. Lebeziatnikov remembered all this and reflected upon it afterwards.

2

It would be difficult to explain exactly what could have originated the idea of that senseless dinner in Katerina Ivanovna's disordered brain. Nearly ten of the twenty roubles, given by Raskolnikov for Marmeladov's funeral, were wasted upon it. Possibly Katerina Ivanovna felt obliged to honour the memory of the deceased "suitably," that all the lodgers, and still more Amalia Ivanovna, might know "that he was in no way their inferior, and perhaps very much their superior," and that no one had the right "to turn up his nose at him." Perhaps the chief element was that peculiar "poor man's pride," which compels many poor people to spend their last savings on some traditional social ceremony, simply in order to do "like other people," and not to "be looked down upon." It is very probable, too, that Katerina Ivanovna longed on this occasion, at the moment when she seemed to be abandoned by every one, to show those "wretched contemptible lodgers" that she knew "how to do things, how to entertain" and that she had been brought up "in a genteel, she might almost say aristocratic colonel's family" and had not been meant for sweeping floors and washing the children's rags at night. Even the poorest and most broken-spirited people are sometimes liable to these paroxysms of pride and vanity which take the form of an irresistible nervous craving. And Katerina Ivanovna was not broken-spirited; she might have been killed by circumstance, but her spirit could not have been broken, that is, she could not have been intimidated, her will could not be crushed. Moreover Sonia had said with good reason that her mind was unhinged. She could not be said to be insane, but for a year past she had been so harassed that her mind might well be overstrained. The later stages of consumption are apt, doctors tell us, to affect the intellect.

There was no great variety of wines, nor was there Madeira; but wine there was. There was vodka, rum and Lisbon wine, all of the poorest quality but in sufficient quantity. Besides the traditional rice and honey, there were three or four dishes, one of which consisted of pancakes, all prepared in Amalia Ivanovna's kitchen. Two samovars were boiling, that tea and punch might be offered after dinner. Katerina Ivanovna had herself seen to purchasing the provisions, with the help of one of the lodgers, an unfortunate little Pole who had somehow been stranded at Madame Lippevechsel's. He promptly put himself at Katerina Ivanovna's disposal and had been all that morning and all the day before running about as fast as his legs could carry him, and very anxious that every one should be aware of it. For every trifle he ran to Katerina Ivanovna, even hunting her out at the bazaar, at every instant called her *"Pani."* She was heartily sick of him before the end, though she had declared at first that she could not have got on without this "serviceable and magnanimous man." It was one of Katerina Ivanovna's characteristics to paint every one she met in the most glowing colours. Her praises were so exaggerated as sometimes to be embarrassing; she would invent various circumstances to the credit of her new acquaintance and quite genuinely believe in their reality. Then all of a sudden she would be disillusioned and would rudely and contemptuously repulse the person she had only a few hours before been literally adoring. She was naturally of a gay, lively and peace-loving disposition, but from continual failures and misfortunes she had come to desire so *keenly* that all should live in peace and joy and should not *dare* to break the peace, that the slightest jar, the smallest disaster reduced her almost to frenzy, and she would pass in an instant from the brightest hopes and fancies to cursing her fate and raving, and knocking her head against the wall.

Amalia Ivanovna, too, suddenly acquired extraordinary importance in Katerina Ivanovna's eyes and was treated by her with extraordinary respect, probably only because Amalia Ivanovna had thrown herself heart and soul into the preparations. She had undertaken to lay the table, to provide the linen, crockery, &c., and to cook the dishes in her kitchen, and Katerina Ivanovna had left it all in her hands and gone herself to the cemetery. Everything had been well done. Even the tablecloth was nearly clean; the crockery, knives, forks and glasses were, of course, of all shapes and patterns, lent by different lodgers, but the table was properly laid at the time fixed, and Amalia Ivanovna, feeling she had done her work well, had put on a black silk dress and a cap with new mourning ribbons and met the returning party with some pride. This pride, though justifiable, displeased Katerina Ivanovna for some reason: "as though the table could not have been laid except by Amalia Ivanovna!" She disliked the cap with new ribbons, too. "Could she be stuck up, the stupid German, because she was mistress of the house, and had consented as a favour to help her poor lodgers! As a favour! Fancy that! Katerina Ivanovna's father who had been a colonel and almost a governor had sometimes had the table set for forty persons, and then any one like Amalia Ivanovna, or rather Ludwigovna, would not have been allowed into the kitchen."

Katerina Ivanovna, however, put off expressing her feelings for the time and contented herself with treating her coldly, though she decided inwardly that she would certainly have to put Amalia Ivanovna down and set her in her proper place, for goodness only knew what she was fancying herself. Katerina Ivanovna was irritated too by the fact that hardly any of the lodgers invited had come to the funeral, except the Pole who had just managed to run into the cemetery, while to the memorial dinner the poorest and most insignificant of them had turned up, the wretched creatures, many of them not quite sober. The older and more respectable of them all, as if by common consent, stayed away. Pyotr Petrovitch Luzhin, for instance, who might be said to be the most respectable of all the lodgers, did not appear, though Katerina Ivanovna had the evening before told all the world, that is Amalia Ivanovna, Polenka, Sonia and the Pole, that he was the most generous, noble-hearted man with a large property and vast connections, who had been a friend of her first husband's, and a guest in her father's house, and that he had promised to use all his influence to secure her a considerable pension. It must be noted that when Katerina Ivanovna exalted any one's connections and fortune, it was without any ulterior motive, quite disinterestedly, for the mere pleasure of adding to the consequence of the person praised. Probably "taking his cue" from Luzhin, "that contemptible wretch Lebeziatnikov had not turned up either. What did he fancy himself? He was only asked out of kindness and because he was sharing the same room with Pyotr Petrovitch and was a friend of his, so that it would have been awkward not to invite him."

Among those who failed to appear were "the genteel lady and her old-maidish daughter," who had only been lodgers in the house for the last fortnight, but had several times complained of the noise and uproar in Katerina Ivanovna's room, especially when Marmeladov had come back drunk. Katerina Ivanovna heard this from Amalia Ivanovna who, quarrelling with Katerina Ivanovna, and threatening to turn the whole family out of doors, had shouted at her that they "were not worth the foot" of the honourable lodgers whom they were disturbing. Katerina Ivanovna determined now to invite this lady and her daughter, "whose foot she was not worth," and who had turned away haughtily when she casually met them, so that they might know that "she was more noble in her thoughts and feelings and did not harbour malice," and might see that she was not accustomed to her way of living. She had proposed to make this clear to them at dinner with allusions to her late father's governorship, and also at the same time to hint that it was exceedingly stupid of them to turn away on meeting her. The fat colonel-major (he was really a discharged officer of low rank) was also absent, but it appeared that he had been "not himself" for the last two days. The party consisted of the Pole, a wretched looking clerk with a spotty face and a greasy coat, who had not a word to say for himself, and smelt abominably, a deaf and almost blind old man who had once been in the post office and who had been from immemorial ages maintained by some one at Amalia Ivanovna's.

A retired clerk of the commissariat department came, too; he was drunk, had a loud and most unseemly laugh and only fancy— was without a waistcoat! One of the visitors sat straight down to the table without even greeting Katerina Ivanovna. Finally one person having no suit appeared in his dressing gown, but this was too much, and the efforts of Amalia Ivanovna and the Pole succeeded in removing him. The Pole brought with him, however, two other Poles who did not live at Amalia Ivanovna's and whom no one had seen here before. All this irritated Katerina Ivanovna intensely. "For whom had they made all these preparations then?" To make room for the visitors the children had not even been laid for at the table; but the two little ones were sitting on a bench in the furthest corner with their dinner laid on a box, while Polenka as a big girl had to look after them, feed them, and keep their noses wiped like well-bred children's.

Katerina Ivanovna, in fact, could hardly help meeting her guests with increased dignity, and even haughtiness. She stared at some of them with special severity, and loftily invited them to take their seats. Rushing to the conclusion that Amalia Ivanovna must be responsible for those who were absent, she began treating her with extreme nonchalance, which the latter promptly observed and resented. Such a beginning was no good omen for the end. All were seated at last.

Raskolnikov came in almost at the moment of their return from the cemetery. Katerina Ivanovna was greatly delighted to see him, in the first place, because he was the one "educated visitor, and, as every one knew, was in two years to take a professorship in the university," and secondly because he immediately and respectfully apologised for having been unable to be at the funeral. She positively pounced upon him, and made him sit on her left hand (Amalia Ivanovna was on her right). In spite of her continual anxiety that the dishes should be passed round correctly and that every one should taste them, in spite of the agonising cough which interrupted her every minute and seemed to have grown worse during the last few days she hastened to pour out in a half whisper to Raskolnikov all her suppressed feelings and her just indignation at the failure of the dinner, interspersing her remarks with lively and uncontrollable laughter at the expense of her visitors and especially of her landlady.

"It's all that cuckoo's fault! You know whom I mean? Her, her!" Katerina Ivanovna nodded towards the landlady. "Look at her, she's making round eyes, she feels that we are talking about her and can't understand. Pfoo, the owl! Ha-ha! (Cough-cough-cough.) And what does she put on that cap for? (Cough-cough-cough.) Have you noticed that she wants every one to consider that she is patronising me and doing me an honour by being here? I asked her like a sensible woman to invite people, especially those who knew my late husband, and look at the set of fools she has brought! The sweeps! Look at that one with the spotty face. And those wretched Poles, ha-ha-ha! (Cough-cough-cough.) Not one of them has ever poked his nose in here, I've never set eyes on them. What have they come here for, I ask you? There they sit in a row. Hey, *Pan!*" she cried suddenly to one of them, "have you tasted the pancakes? Take some more! Have some beer! Won't you have some vodka? Look, he's jumped up and is making his bows, they must be quite starved, poor things. Never mind, let them eat! They don't make a noise, anyway, though I'm really afraid for our landlady's silver spoons . . . Amalia Ivanovna!" she addressed her suddenly, almost aloud, "if your spoons should happen to be stolen, I won't be responsible, I warn you! Ha-ha-ha!" She laughed turning to Raskolnikov, and again nodding towards the landlady, in high glee at her sally. "She didn't understand, she didn't understand again! Look how she sits with her mouth open! An owl, a real owl! An owl in new ribbons, ha-ha-ha!"

Here her laugh turned again to an insufferable fit of coughing that lasted five minutes. Drops of perspiration stood out on her forehead and her handkerchief was stained with blood. She showed Raskolnikov the blood in silence, and as soon as she could get her breath began whispering to him again with extreme animation and a hectic flush on her cheeks.

"Do you know, I gave her the most delicate instructions, so to speak, for inviting that lady and her daughter, you understand of whom I am speaking? It needed the utmost delicacy, the greatest nicety, but she has managed things so that that fool, that conceited baggage, that provincial nonentity, simply because she is the widow of a major, and has come to try and get a pension and to fray out her skirts in the government offices, because at fifty she paints her face (everybody knows it) . . . a creature like that did not think fit to come, and has not even answered the invitation, which the most ordinary good manners required! I can't understand why Pyotr Petrovitch has not come! But where's Sonia? Where has she gone? Ah, there she is at last! what is it, Sonia, where have you been? It's odd that even at your father's funeral you should be so unpunctual. Rodion Romanovitch, make room for her beside you. That's your place, Sonia . . . take what you like. Have some of the cold entrée with jelly, that's the best. They'll bring the pancakes directly. Have they given the children some? Polenka, have you got everything? (Cough-cough-cough.) That's all right. Be a good girl, Lida, and, Kolya, don't fidget with your feet; sit like a little gentleman. What are you saying, Sonia?"

Sonia hastened to give her Pyotr Petrovitch's apologies, trying to speak loud enough for every one to hear and carefully choosing the most respectful phrases which she attributed to Pyotr Petrovitch. She added that Pyotr Petrovitch had particularly told her to say that, as soon as he possibly could, he would come immediately to discuss *business* alone with her and to consider what could be done for her, &c., &c.

Sonia knew that this would comfort Katerina Ivanovna, would flatter her and gratify her pride. She sat down beside Raskolnikov; she made him a hurried bow, glancing curiously at him. But for the rest of the time she seemed to avoid looking at him or speaking to him. She seemed absent-minded, though she kept looking at Katerina Ivanovna, trying to please her. Neither she nor Katerina Ivanovna had been able to get mourning; Sonia was wearing dark brown, and Katerina Ivanovna had on her only dress, a dark striped cotton one.

The message from Pyotr Petrovitch was very successful. Listening to Sonia with dignity, Katerina Ivanovna inquired with equal dignity how Pyotr Petrovitch was, then at once whispered almost aloud to Raskolnikov that it certainly would have been strange for a man of Pyotr Petrovitch's position and standing to find himself in such "extraordinary company," in spite of his devotion to her family and his old friendship with her father.

"That's why I am so grateful to you, Rodion Romanovitch, that you have not disdained my hospitality, even in such surroundings," she added almost aloud. "But I am sure that it was only your special affection for my poor husband that has made you keep your promise."

Then once more with pride and dignity she scanned her visitors, and suddenly inquired aloud across the table of the deaf man: "wouldn't he have some more meat, and had he been given some wine?" The old man made no answer and for a long while could not understand what he was asked, though his neighbours amused themselves by poking and shaking him. He simply gazed about him with his mouth open, which only increased the general mirth.

"What an imbecile! Look, look! Why was he brought? But as to Pyotr Petrovitch, I always had confidence in him," Katerina Ivanovna continued, "and, of course, he is not like . . ." with an extremely stern face she addressed Amalia Ivanovna so sharply and loudly that the latter was quite disconcerted, "not like your dressed up draggletails whom my father would not have taken as cooks into his kitchen, and my late husband would have done them honour if he had invited them in the goodness of his heart."

"Yes, he was fond of drink, he was fond of it, he did drink!" cried the commissariat clerk, gulping down his twelfth glass of vodka.

"My late husband certainly had that weakness, and every one knows it," Katerina Ivanovna attacked him at once, "but he was a kind and honourable man, who loved and respected his family. The worst of it was his good nature made him trust all sorts of disreputable people, and he drank with fellows who were not worth the sole of his shoe. Would you believe it, Rodion Romanovitch, they found a gingerbread cock in his pocket; he was dead drunk, but he did not forget the children!"

"A cock? Did you say a cock?" shouted the commissariat clerk.

Katerina Ivanovna did not vouchsafe a reply. She sighed, lost in thought.

"No doubt you think, like every one, that I was too severe with him," she went on, addressing Raskolnikov. "But that's not so! He respected me, he respected me very much! He was a kind-hearted man! And how sorry I was for him sometimes! He would sit in a corner and look at me, I used to feel so sorry for him, I used to want to be kind to him and then would think to myself: 'be kind to him and he will drink again,' it was only by severity that you could keep him within bounds."

"Yes, he used to get his hair pulled pretty often," roared the commissariat clerk again, swallowing another glass of vodka.

"Some fools would be the better for a good drubbing, as well as having their hair pulled. I am not talking of my late husband now!" Katerina Ivanovna snapped at him.

The flush on her cheeks grew more and more marked, her chest heaved. In another minute she would have been ready to make a scene. Many of the visitors were sniggering, evidently delighted. They began poking the commissariat clerk and whispering something to him. They were evidently trying to egg him on.

"Allow me to ask what are you alluding to," began the clerk, "that is to say, whose . . . about whom . . . did you say just now . . . But I don't care! That's nonsense! Widow! I forgive you. . . . Pass!"

And he took another drink of vodka.

Raskolnikov sat in silence, listening with disgust. He only ate from politeness, just tasting the food that Katerina Ivanovna was continually putting on his plate, to avoid hurting her feelings. He watched Sonia intently. But Sonia became more and more anxious and distressed; she, too, foresaw that the dinner would not end peaceably, and saw with terror Katerina Ivanovna's growing irritation. She knew that she, Sonia, was the chief reason for the 'genteel' ladies' contemptuous treatment of Katerina Ivanovna's invitation. She had heard from Amalia Ivanovna that the mother was positively offended at the invitation and had asked the question: "how could she let her daughter sit down beside *that young person?*" Sonia had a feeling that Katerina Ivanovna had already heard this and an insult to Sonia meant more to Katerina Ivanovna than an insult to herself, her children, or her father. Sonia knew that Katerina Ivanovna would not be satisfied now, "till she had shown those draggletails that they were both . . ." To make matters worse some one passed Sonia, from the other end of the table, a plate with two hearts pierced with an arrow, cut out of black bread. Katerina Ivanovna flushed crimson and at once said aloud across the table that the man who sent it was "a drunken ass!"

Amalia Ivanovna was foreseeing something amiss, and at the same time deeply wounded by Katerina Ivanovna's haughtiness, and to restore the good-humour of the company and raise herself in their esteem she began, apropos of nothing, telling a story about an acquaintance of hers "Karl from the chemist's," who was driving one night in a cab, and that "the cabman wanted him to kill, and Karl very much begged him not to kill, and wept and clasped hands, and frightened and from fear pierced his heart." Though Katerina Ivanovna smiled, she observed at once that Amalia Ivanovna ought not to tell anecdotes in Russian; the latter was still more offended, and she retorted that her "vater aus Berlin was a very important man, and always went with his hands in pockets." Katerina Ivanovna could not restrain herself and laughed so much that Amalia Ivanovna lost patience and could scarcely control herself.

"Listen to the owl!" Katerina Ivanovna whispered at once, her good-humour almost restored, "she meant to say he kept his hands in his pockets, but she said he put his hands in people's pockets. (Cough-cough.) And have you noticed, Rodion Romanovitch, that all these Petersburg foreigners, the Germans especially, are all stupider than we! Can you fancy any one of us

telling how 'Karl from the chemist's pierced his heart from fear'
and that the idiot instead of punishing the cabman, 'clasped his
hands and wept, and much begged.' Ah, the fool! And you know
she fancies it's very touching and does not suspect how stupid she
is! To my thinking that drunken commissariat clerk is a great deal
cleverer, anyway one can see that he has addled his brains with
drink, but you know, these foreigners are always so well behaved
and serious. . . . Look how she sits glaring! She is angry, ha-ha!
(Cough-cough-cough.)''

Regaining her good-humour, Katerina Ivanovna began at
once telling Raskolnikov that when she had obtained her pension,
she intended to open a school for the daughters of gentlemen in
her native town T——. This was the first time she had spoken to
him of the project, and she launched out into the most alluring
details. It suddenly appeared that Katerina Ivanovna had in her
hands the very certificate of honour of which Marmeladov had
spoken to Raskolnikov in the tavern, when he told him that
Katerina Ivanovna, his wife, had danced the shawl dance before
the governor and other great personages on leaving school. This
certificate of honour was obviously intended now to prove Katerina Ivanovna's right to open a boarding-school; but she had armed
herself with it chiefly with the object of overwhelming "those two
stuck-up draggletails" if they came to the dinner, and proving
incontestably that Katerina Ivanovna was of the most noble, "she
might even say aristocratic family, a colonel's daughter and was
far superior to certain adventuresses who have been so much to
the fore of late." The certificate of honour immediately passed
into the hands of the drunken guests, and Katerina Ivanovna did
not try to retain it, for it actually contained the statement *en toutes
lettres,* that her father was of the rank of a major, and also a
companion of an order, so that she really was almost the daughter
of a colonel.

Warming up, Katerina Ivanovna proceeded to enlarge on
the peaceful and happy life they would lead in T——, on the
gymnasium teachers whom she would engage to give lessons in
her boarding-school, one a most respectable old Frenchman, one
Mangot, who had taught Katerina Ivanovna herself in old days

and was still living in T——, and would no doubt teach in her school on moderate terms. Next she spoke of Sonia who would go with her to T—— and help her in all her plans. At this some one at the further end of the table gave a sudden guffaw.

Though Katerina Ivanovna tried to appear to be disdainfully unaware of it, she raised her voice and began at once speaking with conviction of Sonia's undoubted ability to assist her, of "her gentleness, patience, devotion, generosity and good education," tapping Sonia on the cheek and kissing her warmly twice. Sonia flushed crimson, and Katerina Ivanovna suddenly burst into tears, immediately observing that she was "nervous and silly, that she was too much upset, that it was time to finish, and as the dinner was over, it was time to hand round the tea."

At that moment, Amalia Ivanovna, deeply aggrieved at taking no part in the conversation, and not being listened to, made one last effort, and with secret misgivings ventured on an exceedingly deep and weighty observation, that "in the future boarding-school she would have to pay particular attention to *die Wäsche,* and that there certainly must be a good *Dame* to look after the linen, and secondly that the young ladies must not novels at night read."

Katerina Ivanovna, who certainly was upset and very tired, as well as heartily sick of the dinner, at once cut short Amalia Ivanovna, saying "she knew nothing about it and was talking nonsense, that it was the business of the laundry maid, and not of the directress of a high-class boarding-school to look after *die Wäsche,* and as for novel reading, that was simply rudeness, and she begged her to be silent." Amalia Ivanovna fired up and getting angry observed that she only "meant her good," and that "she had meant her very good," and that "it was long since she had paid her *Gold* for the lodgings."

Katerina Ivanovna at once "set her down," saying that it was a lie to say she wished her good, because only yesterday when her dead husband was lying on the table, she had worried her about the lodgings. To this Amalia Ivanovna very appropriately observed that she had invited those ladies, but "those ladies had not come, because those ladies are ladies and cannot come to a lady who is not a lady." Katerina Ivanovna at once pointed out to her, that as she was a slut she could not judge what made one really a lady. Amalia Ivanovna at once declared that her "Vater aus Berlin was a very, very important man, and both hands in pockets went, and always used to say: poof! poof!" and she leapt up from the table to represent her father, sticking her hands in her pockets, puffing her cheeks, and uttering vague sounds resembling "poof! poof!" amid loud laughter from all the lodgers, who purposely encouraged Amalia Ivanovna, hoping for a fight.

But this was too much for Katerina Ivanovna, and she at once declared, so that all could hear, that Amalia Ivanovna probably never had a father, but was simply a drunken Petersburg Finn, and had certainly once been a cook and probably something worse. Amalia Ivanovna turned as red as a lobster and squealed that perhaps Katerina Ivanovna never had a father, "but she had a vater aus Berlin and that he wore a long coat and always said poof-poof-poof!"

Katerina Ivanovna observed contemptuously that all knew what her family was and that on that very certificate of honour it was stated in print that her father was a colonel, while Amalia Ivanovna's father—if she really had one—was probably some Finnish milkman, but that probably she never had a father at all, since it was still uncertain whether her name was Amalia Ivanovna or Amalia Ludwigovna.

At this Amalia Ivanovna, lashed to fury, struck the table with her fist, and shrieked that she was Amalia Ivanovna, and not Ludwigovna, "that her *Vater* was named Johann and that he was a burgomeister, and that Katerina Ivanovan's *Vater* was quite never a burgomeister." Katerina Ivanovna rose from her chair, and with a stern and apparently calm voice (though she was pale and her chest was heaving) observed that "if she dared for one moment to set her contemptible wretch of a father on a level with her papa, she, Katerina Ivanovna, would tear her cap off her head and trample it under foot." Amalia Ivanovna ran about the room, shouting at the top of her voice, that she was mistress of the house and that Katerina Ivanovna should leave the lodgings that minute; then she rushed for some reason to collect the silver spoons from the table. There was a great outcry and uproar, the children began crying. Sonia ran to restrain Katerina Ivanovna, but when Amalia Ivanovna shouted something about "the yellow ticket," Katerina Ivanovna pushed Sonia away, and rushed at the landlady to carry out her threat.

At that minute the door opened, and Pyotr Petrovitch Luzhin appeared on the threshold. He stood scanning the party with severe and vigilant eyes. Katerina Ivanovna rushed to him.

3

"Pyotr Petrovitch," she cried, "protect me . . . you at least! Make this foolish woman understand that she can't behave like this to a lady in misfortune . . . that there is a law for such things. . . . I'll go to the governor-general himself. . . . She shall answer for it. . . . Remembering my father's hospitality protect these orphans."

"Allow me, madam. . . . Allow me." Pyotr Petrovitch waved her off. "Your papa, as you are well aware, I had not the honour of knowing" (some one laughed aloud) "and I do not intend to take part in your everlasting squabbles with Amalia Ivanovna. . . . I have come here to speak of my own affairs . . . and I want to have a word with your stepdaughter, Sofya . . . Ivanova, I think it is? Allow me to pass."

Pyotr Petrovitch, edging by her, went to the opposite corner where Sonia was.

Katerina Ivanovna remained standing where she was, as though thunderstruck. She could not understand how Pyotr Petrovitch could deny having enjoyed her father's hospitality. Though she had invented it herself, she believed in it firmly by this time. She was struck too by the businesslike, dry and even contemptuously menacing tone of Pyotr Petrovitch. All the clamour gradually died away at his entrance. Not only was this "serious business man" strikingly incongruous with the rest of the party, but it was evident, too, that he had come upon some matter of consequence, that some exceptional cause must have brought him and that therefore something was going to happen. Raskolnikov, standing beside Sonia, moved aside to let him pass; Pyotr Petrovitch did not seem to notice him. A minute later Lebeziatnikov, too, appeared in the doorway; he did not come in, but stood still, listening with marked interest, almost wonder, and seemed for a time perplexed.

"Excuse me for possibly interrupting you, but it's a matter of some importance," Pyotr Petrovitch observed, addressing the company generally. "I am glad indeed to find other persons present. Amalia Ivanovna, I humbly beg you as mistress of the house to pay careful attention to what I have to say to Sofya Ivanovna. Sofya Ivanovna," he went on, addressing Sonia, who was very much surprised and already alarmed, "immediately after your visit I found that a hundred-rouble note was missing from my table, in the room of my friend Mr. Lebeziatnikov. If in any way whatever you know and will tell us where it is now, I assure you on my word of honour and call all present to witness that the matter shall end there. In the opposite case I shall be compelled to have recourse to very serious measures and then . . . you must blame yourself."

Complete silence reigned in the room. Even the crying children were still. Sonia stood deadly pale, staring at Luzhin and unable to say a word. She seemed not to understand. Some seconds passed.

"Well, how is it to be then?" asked Luzhin, looking intently at her.

"I don't know. . . . I know nothing about it," Sonia articulated faintly at last.

"No, you know nothing?" Luzhin repeated and again he paused for some seconds. "Think a moment, mademoiselle," he began severely, but still, as it were, admonishing her. "Reflect, I am prepared to give you time for consideration. Kindly observe this: if I were not so entirely convinced I should not, you may be sure, with my experience venture to accuse you so directly. Seeing that for such direct accusation before witnesses, if false or even mistaken, I should myself in a certain sense be made responsible, I am aware of that. This morning I changed for my own purposes several five per cent. securities for the sum of approximately three thousand roubles. The account is noted down in my pocket-book. On my return home I proceeded to count the money,—as Mr. Lebeziatnikov will bear witness—and after counting two thousand three hundred roubles I put the rest in my pocket-book in my coat pocket. About five hundred roubles remained on the table and among them three notes of a hundred roubles each. At that moment you entered (at my invitation)—and all the time you were present you were exceedingly embarrassed; so that three times you jumped up in the middle of the conversation and tried to make off. Mr. Lebeziatnikov can bear witness to this. You yourself, mademoiselle, probably will not refuse to confirm my statement that I invited you through Mr. Lebeziatnikov, solely in order to discuss with you the hopeless and destitute position of your relative, Katerina Ivanovna (whose dinner I was unable to attend), and the advisability of getting up something of the nature of a subscription, lottery or the like, for her benefit. You thanked me and even shed tears. I describe all this as it took place, primarily to recall it to your mind and secondly to show you that not the slightest detail has escaped my recollection. Then I took a ten-rouble note from the table and handed it to you by way of first instalment on my part for the benefit of your relative. Mr. Lebeziatnikov saw all this. Then I accompanied you to the door,—you being still in the same state of embarrassment—after which, being left alone with Mr. Lebeziatnikov I talked to him for ten minutes,—then Mr. Lebeziatnikov went out and I returned to the table with the money lying on it, intending to count it and to put it aside, as I proposed doing before. To my surprise one hundred-rouble note had disappeared. Kindly consider the position. Mr. Lebeziatnikov I cannot suspect. I am ashamed to allude to such a supposition. I cannot have made a mistake in my reckoning, for the minute before your entrance I had finished my accounts and found the total correct. You will admit that recollecting your embarrassment, your eagerness to get away and the fact that you kept your hands for some time on the table, and taking into consideration your social position and the habits associated with it, I was, so to say, with horror

and positively against my will, *compelled* to entertain a suspicion
—a cruel, but justifiable suspicion! I will add further and repeat
that in spite of my positive conviction, I realise that I run a certain
risk in making this accusation, but as you see, I could not let it
pass. I have taken action and I will tell you why: solely, madam,
solely, owing to your black ingratitude! Why! I invite you for the
benefit of your destitute relative, I present you with my donation
of ten roubles and you, on the spot, repay me for all that with such
an action. It is too bad! You need a lesson. Reflect! Moreover, like
a true friend I beg you—and you could have no better friend at
this moment—think what you are doing, otherwise I shall be
immovable! Well, what do you say?"

"I have taken nothing," Sonia whispered in terror, "you
gave me ten roubles, here it is, take it."

Sonia pulled her handkerchief out of her pocket, untied a
corner of it, took out the ten-rouble note and gave it to Luzhin.

"And the hundred roubles you do not confess to taking?" he
insisted reproachfully, not taking the note.

Sonia looked about her. All were looking at her with such
awful, stern, ironical, hostile eyes. She looked at Raskolnikov
. . . he stood against the wall, with his arms crossed, looking at
her with glowing eyes.

"Good God!" broke from Sonia.

"Amalia Ivanovna, we shall have to send word to the police
and therefore I humbly beg you meanwhile to send for the house
porter," Luzhin said softly and even kindly.

"Gott der barmherzige! I knew she was the thief," cried
Amalia Ivanovna, throwing up her hands.

"You knew it?" Luzhin caught her up, "then I suppose you
had some reason before this for thinking so. I beg you, worthy
Amalia Ivanovna, to remember your words which have been
uttered before witnesses."

There was a buzz of loud conversation on all sides. All were
in movement.

"What!" cried Katerina Ivanovna, suddenly realising the
position, and she rushed at Luzhin. "What! You accuse her of
stealing? Sonia? Ah, the wretches, the wretches!"

And running to Sonia she flung her wasted arms round her and held her as in a vise.

"Sonia! how dared you take ten roubles from him? Foolish girl! Give it to me! Give me the ten roubles at once—here!"

And snatching the note from Sonia, Katerina Ivanovna crumpled it up and flung it straight into Luzhin's face. It hit him in the eye and fell on the ground. Amalia Ivanovna hastened to pick it up. Pyotr Petrovitch lost his temper.

"Hold that mad woman!" he shouted.

At that moment several other persons, besides Lebeziatnikov, appeared in the doorway, among them the two ladies.

"What! Mad? Am I mad? Idiot!" shrieked Katerina Ivanovna. "You are an idiot yourself, pettifogging lawyer, base man! Sonia, Sonia take his money! Sonia a thief! Why, she'd give away her last penny!" and Katerina Ivanovna broke into hysterical laughter. "Did you ever see such an idiot?" she turned from side to side. "And you too?" she suddenly saw the landlady, "and you too, sausage eater, you declare that she is a thief, you trashy Prussian hen's leg in a crinoline! She hasn't been out of this room: she came straight from you, you wretch, and sat down beside me, every one saw her. She sat here, by Rodion Romanovitch. Search her! Since she's not left the room, the money would have to be on her! Search her, search her! But if you don't find it, then excuse me, my dear fellow, you'll answer for it! I'll go to our Sovereign, to our Sovereign, to our gracious Tsar himself, and throw myself at his feet, to-day, this minute! I am alone in the world! They would let me in! Do you think they wouldn't? You're wrong, I will get in! I will get in! You reckoned on her meekness! You relied upon that! But I am not so submissive, let me tell you! You've gone too far yourself. Search her, search her!"

And Katerina Ivanovna in a frenzy shook Luzhin and dragged him towards Sonia.

"I am ready, I'll be responsible . . . but calm yourself, madam, calm yourself. I see that you are not so submissive! . . . Well, well, but as to that . . ." Luzhin muttered, "that ought to be before the police . . . though indeed there are witnesses enough as it is. . . . I am ready. . . . But in any case it's difficult for a man . . . on account of her sex. . . . But with the help of Amalia Ivanovna . . . though, of course, it's not the way to do things. . . . How is it to be done?"

"As you will! Let any one who likes search her!" cried Katerina Ivanovna. "Sonia, turn out your pockets! See. Look, monster, the pocket is empty, here was her handkerchief! Here is the other pocket, look! D'you see, d'you see?"

And Katerina Ivanovna turned—or rather snatched—both pockets inside out. But from the right pocket a piece of paper flew out and describing a parabola in the air fell at Luzhin's feet. Every one saw it, several cried out. Pyotr Petrovitch stooped down, picked up the paper in two fingers, lifted it where all could see it and opened it. It was a hundred-rouble note folded in eight. Pyotr Petrovitch held up the note showing it to every one.

"Thief! Out of my lodging. Police, police!" yelled Amalia Ivanovna. "They must to Siberia be sent! Away!"

Exclamations arose on all sides. Raskolnikov was silent, keeping his eyes fixed on Sonia, except for an occasional rapid glance at Luzhin. Sonia stood still, as though unconscious. She was hardly able to feel surprise. Suddenly the colour rushed to her cheeks; she uttered a cry and hid her face in her hands.

"No, it wasn't I! I didn't take it! I know nothing about it," she cried with a heartrending wail, and she ran to Katerina Ivanovna, who clasped her tightly in her arms, as though she would shelter her from all the world.

"Sonia! Sonia! I don't believe it! You see, I don't believe it!" she cried in the face of the obvious fact, swaying her to and fro in her arms like a baby, kissing her face continually, then snatching at her hands and kissing them, too. "You took it! How stupid these people are! Oh dear! You are fools, fools," she cried, addressing the whole room, "you don't know, you don't know what a heart she has, what a girl she is! She take it, she? She'd sell her last rag, she'd go barefoot to help you if you needed it, that's what she is! She has the yellow passport because my children were starving, she sold herself for us! Ah, husband, husband! Do you see? Do you see? What a memorial dinner for you! Merciful heavens! Defend her, why are you all standing still? Rodion Romanovitch, why don't you stand up for her? Do you believe it, too? You are not worth her little finger, all of you together! Good God! Defend her now, at least!"

The wail of the poor, consumptive, helpless woman seemed to produce a great effect on her audience. The agonised, wasted, consumptive face, the parched blood-stained lips, the hoarse voice, the tears unrestrained as a child's, the trustful, childish and yet despairing prayer for help were so piteous that every one seemed to feel for her. Pyotr Petrovitch at any rate was at once moved to *compassion*.

"Madam, madam, this incident does not reflect upon you!" he cried impressively, "no one would take upon himself to accuse you of being an instigator or even an accomplice in it, especially as you have proved her guilt by turning out her pockets, showing that you had no previous idea of it. I am most ready, most ready to show compassion, if poverty, so to speak, drove Sofya Semyonovna to it, but why did you refuse to confess, mademoiselle? Were you afraid of the disgrace? The first step? You lost your head, perhaps? One can quite understand it. . . . But how could you have lowered yourself to such an action? Gentlemen," he addressed the whole company, "gentlemen! Compassionate and so to say commiserating these people, I am ready to overlook it even now in spite of the personal insult lavished upon me! And may this disgrace be a lesson to you for the future," he said, addressing Sonia, "and I will carry the matter no further. Enough!"

Pyotr Petrovitch stole a glance at Raskolnikov. Their eyes met, and the fire in Raskolnikov's seemed ready to reduce him to ashes. Meanwhile Katerina Ivanovna apparently heard nothing. She was kissing and hugging Sonia like a madwoman. The children, too, were embracing Sonia on all sides, and Polenka,— though she did not fully understand what was wrong,—was drowned in tears and shaking with sobs, as she hid her pretty little face, swollen with weeping, on Sonia's shoulder.

"How vile!" a loud voice cried suddenly in the doorway.

Pyotr Petrovitch looked round quickly.

"What vileness!" Lebeziatnikov repeated, staring him straight in the face.

Pyotr Petrovitch gave a positive start—all noticed it and recalled it afterwards. Lebeziatnikov strode into the room.

"And you dared to call me as witness?" he said, going up to Pyotr Petrovitch.

"What do you mean? What are you talking about?" muttered Luzhin.

"I mean that you . . . are a slanderer, that's what my words mean!" Lebeziatnikov said hotly, looking sternly at him with his shortsighted eyes.

He was extremely angry. Raskolnikov gazed intently at him, as though seizing and weighing each word. Again there was a silence. Pyotr Petrovitch indeed seemed almost dumbfounded for the first moment.

"If you mean that for me, . . ." he began, stammering. "But what's the matter with you? Are you out of your mind?"

"I'm in my mind, but you are a scoundrel! Ah, how vile! I have heard everything. I kept waiting on purpose to understand it, for I must own even now it is not quite logical. . . . What you have done it all for I can't understand."

"Why, what have I done then? Give over talking in your nonsensical riddles! Or may be you are drunk!"

"You may be a drunkard, perhaps, vile man, but I am not! I never touch vodka, for it's against my convictions. Would you believe it, he, he himself, with his own hands gave Sofya Semyonovna that hundred-rouble note—I saw it, I was a witness, I'll take my oath! He did it, he!" repeated Lebeziatnikov, addressing all.

"Are you crazy, milksop?" squealed Luzhin. "She is herself before you,—she herself here declared just now before every one that I gave her only ten roubles. How could I have given it to her?"

"I saw it, I saw it," Lebeziatnikov repeated, "and although it is against my principles, I am ready this very minute to take any oath you like before the court, for I saw how you slipped it in her pocket. Only like a fool I thought you did it out of kindness! When you were saying good-bye to her at the door, while you held her hand in one hand, with the other, the left, you slipped the note into her pocket. I saw it, I saw it!"

Luzhin turned pale.

"What lies!" he cried impudently, "why, how could you, standing by the window, see the note! You fancied it with your shortsighted eyes. You are raving!"

"No, I didn't fancy it. And though I was standing some way off, I saw it all. And though it certainly would be hard to distinguish a note from the window,—that's true—I knew for certain that it was a hundred-rouble note, because, when you were going to give Sofya Semyonovna ten roubles, you took up from the table a hundred-rouble note (I saw it because I was standing near then, and an idea struck me at once, so that I did not forget you had it in your hand). You folded it and kept it in your hand all the time. I didn't think of it again until, when you were getting up, you changed it from your right hand to your left and nearly dropped it! I noticed it because the same idea struck me again, that you meant to do her a kindness without my seeing. You can fancy how I watched you and I saw how you succeeded in slipping it into her pocket. I saw it, I saw it, I'll take my oath."

Lebeziatnikov was almost breathless. Exclamations arose on all hands chiefly expressive of wonder, but some were menacing in tone. They all crowded round Pyotr Petrovitch. Katerina Ivanovna flew to Lebeziatnikov.

"I was mistaken in you! Protect her! You are the only one to take her part! She is an orphan. God has sent you!"

Katerina Ivanovna, hardly knowing what she was doing, sank on her knees before him.

"A pack of nonsense!" yelled Luzhin, roused to fury, "it's all nonsense you've been talking! 'An idea struck you, you didn't think, you noticed'—what does it amount to? So I gave it to her on the sly on purpose? What for? With what object? What have I to do with this . . . ?"

"What for? That's what I can't understand, but that what I am telling you is the fact, that's certain! So far from my being mistaken, you infamous, criminal man, I remember how, on account of it, a question occurred to me at once, just when I was thanking you and pressing your hand. What made you put it secretly in her pocket? Why you did it secretly, I mean? Could it be simply to conceal it from me, knowing that my convictions are opposed to yours and that I do not approve of private benevolence, which effects no radical cure? Well, I decided that you really were ashamed of giving such a large sum before me. Perhaps, too, I thought, he wants to give her a surprise, when she finds a whole hundred-rouble note in her pocket. (For I know some benevolent people are very fond of decking out their charitable actions in that way.) Then the idea struck me, too, that you wanted to test her, to see whether, when she found it, she would come to thank you. Then, too, that you wanted to avoid thanks and that, as the saying is, your right hand should not know . . . something of that sort, in fact. I thought of so many possibilities that I put off considering it, but still thought it indelicate to show you I knew your secret. But another idea struck me again that Sofya Semyonovna might easily lose the money before she noticed it, that was why I decided to come in here to call her out of the room and to tell her that you put a hundred roubles in her pocket. But on my way I went first to Madame Kobilatnikov's to take them the 'General Treatise on the Positive Method' and especially to recommend Piderit's article (and also Wagner's); then I come on here and what a state of things I find! Now could I, could I, have all these ideas and reflections, if I had not seen you put the hundred-rouble note in her pocket?"

When Lebeziatnikov finished his long-winded harangue with the logical deduction at the end, he was quite tired, and the perspiration streamed from his face. He could not, alas, even express himself correctly in Russian, though he knew no other language, so that he was quite exhausted, almost emaciated after this heroic exploit. But his speech produced a powerful effect. He had spoken with such vehemence, with such conviction that every one obviously believed him. Pyotr Petrovitch felt that things were going badly with him.

"What is it to do with me if silly ideas did occur to you?" he shouted, "that's no evidence. You may have dreamt it, that's all! And I tell you, you are lying, sir. You are lying and slandering from some spite against me, simply from pique, because I did not agree with your freethinking, godless, social propositions!"

But this retort did not benefit Pyotr Petrovitch. Murmurs of disapproval were heard on all sides.

"Ah, that's your line now, is it!" cried Lebeziatnikov, "that's nonsense! Call the police and I'll take my oath! There's only one thing I can't understand: what made him risk such a contemptible action. Oh, pitiful, despicable man!"

"I can explain why he risked such an action, and if necessary, I, too, will swear to it," Raskolnikov said at last in a firm voice, and he stepped forward.

He appeared to be firm and composed. Every one felt clearly, from the very look of him that he really knew about it and that the mystery would be solved.

"Now I can explain it all to myself," said Raskolnikov, addressing Lebeziatnikov. "From the very beginning of the business, I suspected that there was some scoundrelly intrigue at the bottom of it. I began to suspect it from some special circumstances known to me only, which I will explain at once to every one: they account for everything. Your valuable evidence has finally made everything clear to me. I beg all, all to listen. This gentleman (he pointed to Luzhin) was recently engaged to be married to a young lady—my sister, Avdotya Romanovna Raskolnikov. But coming to Petersburg he quarrelled with me, the day before yesterday, at our first meeting and I drove him out of my room—I have two witnesses to prove it. He is a very spiteful man. . . . The day before yesterday I did not know that he was staying here, in your room, and that consequently on the very day we quarrelled—the day before yesterday—he saw me give Katerina Ivanovna some money for the funeral, as a friend of the late Mr. Marmeladov. He at once wrote a note to my mother and informed her that I had given away all my money, not to Katerina Ivanovna, but to Sofya Semyonovna, and referred in a most contemptible way to the . . . character of Sofya Semyonovna, that is, hinted at the character of my attitude to Sofya Semyonovna. All this you understand was with the object of dividing me from my mother and sister, by insinuating that I was squandering on unworthy objects the money which they had sent me and which was all they had. Yesterday evening, before my mother and sister and in his presence, I declared that I had given the money to Katerina Ivanovna for the funeral and not to Sofya Semyonovna and that I had no acquaintance with Sofya Semyonovna and had never seen her before, indeed. At the same time I added that he, Pyotr Petrovitch Luzhin, with all his virtues was not worth Sofya Semyonovna's little finger, though he spoke so ill of her. To his question—would I let Sofya Semyonovna sit down beside my sister, I answered that I had already done so that day. Irritated that my mother and sister were unwilling to quarrel with me at his insinuations, he gradually began being unpardonably rude to them. A final rupture took place and he was turned out of the house. All this happened yesterday evening. Now I beg your special attention: consider: if he had now succeeded in proving that Sofya Semyonovna was a thief, he would have shown to my mother and sister that he was almost right in his suspicions, that he had reason to be angry at my putting my sister on a level with Sofya Semyonovna, that, in attacking me, he was protecting and preserving the honour of my sister, his betrothed. In fact he might even, through all this, have been able to estrange me from my family, and no doubt he hoped to be restored to favour with them; to say nothing of revenging himself on me personally, for he has grounds for supposing that the honour and happiness of Sofya Semyonovna are very precious to me. That was what he was working for! That's how I understand it. That's the whole reason for it and there can be no other!"

It was like this, or somewhat like this, that Raskolnikov wound up his speech which was followed very attentively, though often interrupted by exclamations from his audience. But in spite of interruptions he spoke clearly, calmly, exactly, firmly. His decisive voice, his tone of conviction and his stern face made a great impression on every one.

"Yes, yes, that's it," Lebeziatnikov assented gleefully, "that must be it, for he asked me, as soon as Sofya Semyonovna came into our room, whether you were here, whether I had seen you among Katerina Ivanovna's guests. He called me aside to the window and asked me in secret. It was essential for him that you should be here! That's it, that's it!''

Luzhin smiled contemptuously and did not speak. But he was very pale. He seemed to be deliberating on some means of escape. Perhaps he would have been glad to give up everything and get away, but at the moment this was scarcely possible. It would have implied admitting the truth of the accusations brought against him. Moreover, the company, which had already been excited by drink, was now too much stirred to allow it. The commissariat clerk, though indeed he had not grasped the whole position, was shouting louder than any one and was making some suggestions very unpleasant to Luzhin. But not all those present were drunk; lodgers came in from all the rooms. The three Poles were tremendously excited and were continually shouting at him: "The *Pan* is a *lajdak!*" and muttering threats in Polish. Sonia had been listening with strained attention, though she too seemed unable to grasp it all; she seemed as though she had just returned to consciousness. She did not take her eyes off Raskolnikov, feeling that all her safety lay in him. Katerina Ivanovna breathed hard and painfully and seemed fearfully exhausted. Amalia Ivanovna stood looking more stupid than any one, with her mouth wide open, unable to make out what had happened. She only saw that Pyotr Petrovitch had somehow come to grief.

Raskolnikov was attempting to speak again, but they did not let him. Every one was crowding round Luzhin with threats and shouts of abuse. But Pyotr Petrovitch was not intimidated. Seeing that his accusation of Sonia had completely failed, he had recourse to insolence:

"Allow me, gentlemen, allow me! Don't squeeze, let me pass!" he said, making his way through the crowd. "And no threats if you please! I assure you it will be useless, you will gain nothing by it. On the contrary, you'll have to answer, gentlemen, for violently obstructing the course of justice. The thief has been more than unmasked, and I shall prosecute. Our judges are not so blind and . . . not so drunk, and will not believe the testimony of two notorious infidels, agitators, and atheists, who accuse me from motives of personal revenge which they are foolish enough to admit. . . . Yes, allow me to pass!"

"Don't let me find a trace of you in my room! Kindly leave at once, and everything is at an end between us! When I think of the trouble I've been taking, the way I've been expounding . . . all this fortnight!"

"I told you myself to-day that I was going, when you tried to keep me; now I will simply add that you are a fool. I advise you to see a doctor for your brains and your short sight. Let me pass, gentlemen!"

He forced his way through. But the commissariat clerk was unwilling to let him off so easily: he picked up a glass from the table, brandished it in the air and flung it at Pyotr Petrovitch; but the glass flew straight at Amalia Ivanovna. She screamed, and the clerk, overbalancing, fell heavily under the table. Pyotr Petrovitch made his way to his room and half an hour later had left the house. Sonia, timid by nature, had felt before that day that she could be ill-treated more easily than any one, and that she could be wronged with impunity. Yet till that moment she had fancied that she might escape misfortune by care, gentleness and submissiveness before every one. Her disappointment was too great. She could, of course, bear with patience and almost without murmur anything, even this. But for the first minute she felt it too bitter. In spite of her triumph and her justification—when her first terror and stupefaction had passed and she could understand it all clearly —the feeling of her helplessness and of the wrong done to her made her heart throb with anguish and she was overcome with hysterical weeping. At last, unable to bear any more, she rushed out of the room and ran home, almost immediately after Luzhin's departure. When amidst loud laughter the glass flew at Amalia Ivanovna, it was more than the landlady could endure. With a shriek she rushed like a fury at Katerina Ivanovna, considering her to blame for everything.

"Out of my lodgings! At once! Quick march!"

And with these words she began snatching up everything she could lay her hands on that belonged to Katerina Ivanovna, and throwing it on the floor, Katerina Ivanovna, pale, almost fainting, and gasping for breath, jumped up from the bed where she had sunk in exhaustion and darted at Amalia Ivanovna. But the battle was too unequal: the landlady waved her away like a feather.

"What! As though that godless calumny was not enough—this vile creature attacks me! What! On the day of my husband's funeral I am turned out of my lodgings! After eating my bread and salt she turns me into the street, with my orphans! Where am I to go?" wailed the poor woman, sobbing and gasping. "Good God!" she cried with flashing eyes, "is there no justice upon earth? Whom should you protect if not us orphans? We shall see! There is law and justice on earth, there is, I will find it! Wait a bit, godless creature! Polenka, stay with the children, I'll come back. Wait for me, if you have to wait in the street. We will see whether there is justice on earth!"

And throwing over her head that green shawl which Marmeladov had mentioned to Raskolnikov, Katerina Ivanovna squeezed her way through the disorderly and drunken crowd of lodgers who still filled the room, and, wailing and tearful, she ran into the street—with a vague intention of going at once somewhere to find justice. Polenka with the two little ones in her arms crouched, terrified, on the trunk in the corner of the room, where she waited trembling for her mother to come back. Amalia Ivanovna raged about the room, shrieking, lamenting and throwing everything she came across on the floor. The lodgers talked incoherently, some commented to the best of their ability on what had happened, others quarreled and swore at one another, while others struck up a song. . . .

"Now it's time for me to go," thought Raskolnikov. "Well, Sofya Semyonovna, we shall see what you'll say now!"

And he set off in the direction of Sonia's lodgings.

4

Raskolnikov had been a vigorous and active champion of Sonia against Luzhin, although he had such a load of horror and anguish in his own heart. But having gone through so much in the morning, he found a sort of relief in a change of sensations, apart from the strong personal feeling which impelled him to defend Sonia. He was agitated too, especially at some moments by the thought of his approaching interview with Sonia: he *had* to tell her who had killed Lizaveta. He knew the terrible suffering it would be to him and, as it were, brushed away the thought of it. So when he cried as he left Katerina Ivanovna's, "Well, Sofya Semyonovna, we shall see what you'll say now!" he was still superficially excited, still vigorous and defiant from his triumph over Luzhin. But, strange to say, by the time he reached Sonia's lodging, he felt a sudden impotence and fear. He stood still in hesitation at the door, asking himself the strange question: "Must I tell her who killed Lizaveta?" It was a strange question because he felt at the very time not only that he could not help telling her, but also that he could not put off the telling. He did not yet know why it must be so, he only *felt* it, and the agonising sense of his impotence before the inevitable almost crushed him. To cut short his hesitation and suffering, he quickly opened the door and looked at Sonia from the doorway. She was sitting with her elbows on the table and her face in her hands, but seeing Raskolnikov she got up at once and came to meet him as though she were expecting him.

"What would have become of me but for you!" she said quickly, meeting him in the middle of the room.

Evidently she was in haste to say this to him. It was what she had been waiting for.

Raskolnikov went to the table and sat down on the chair from which she had only just risen. She stood facing him, two steps away, just as she had done the day before.

"Well, Sonia?" he said, and felt that his voice was trembling, "it was all due to 'your social position and the habits associated with it.' Did you understand that just now?"

Her face showed her distress.

"Only don't talk to me as you did yesterday," she interrupted him. "Please don't begin it. There is misery enough without that."

She made haste to smile, afraid that he might not like the reproach.

"I was silly to come away from there. What is happening there now? I wanted to go back directly, but I kept thinking that . . . you would come."

He told her that Amalia Ivanovna was turning them out of their lodging and that Katerina Ivanovna had run off somewhere "to seek justice."

"My God!" cried Sonia, "let's go at once. . . ."

And she snatched up her cape.

"It's everlastingly the same thing!" said Raskolnikov, irritably. "You've no thought except for them! Stay a little with me."

"But . . . Katerina Ivanovna?"

"You won't lose Katerina Ivanovna, you may be sure, she'll come to you herself since she has run out," he added peevishly. "If she doesn't find you here, you'll be blamed for it. . . ."

Sonia sat down in painful suspense. Raskolnikov was silent, gazing at the floor and deliberating.

"This time Luzhin did not want to prosecute you," he began, not looking at Sonia, "but if he had wanted to, if it had suited his plans, he would have sent you to prison if it had not been for Lebeziatnikov and me. Ah?"

"Yes," she assented in a faint voice. "Yes," she repeated, preoccupied and distressed.

"But I might easily not have been there. And it was quite an accident Lebeziatnikov's turning up."

Sonia was silent.

"And if you'd gone to prison, what then? Do you remember what I said yesterday?"

Again she did not answer. He waited.

"I thought you would cry out again 'don't speak of it, leave off.' " Raskolnikov gave a laugh, but rather a forced one. "What, silence again?" he asked a minute later. "We must talk about something, you know. It would be interesting for me to know how you would decide a certain 'problem' as Lebeziatnikov would say." (He was beginning to lose the thread.) "No, really, I am serious. Imagine, Sonia, that you had known all Luzhin's intentions beforehand. Known, that is, for a fact, that they would be the ruin of Katerina Ivanovna and the children and yourself thrown in—since you don't count yourself for anything—Polenka too . . . for she'll go the same way. Well, if suddenly it all depended on your decision whether he or they should go on living, that is whether Luzhin should go on living and doing wicked things, or Katerina Ivanovna should die? How would you decide which of them was to die? I ask you?"

Sonia looked uneasily at him. There was something peculiar in this hesitating question, which seemed approaching something in a roundabout way.

"I felt that you were going to ask some question like that," she said, looking inquisitively at him.

"I dare say you did. But how is it to be answered?"

"Why do you ask about what could not happen?" said Sonia reluctantly.

"Then it would be better for Luzhin to go on living and doing wicked things? You haven't dared to decide even that!"

"But I can't know the Divine Providence. . . . And why do you ask what can't be answered? What's the use of such foolish questions? How could it happen that it should depend on my decision—who has made me a judge to decide who is to live and who is not to live?"

"Oh, if the Divine Providence is to be mixed up in it, there is no doing anything," Raskolnikov grumbled morosely.

"You'd better say straight out what you want!" Sonia cried in distress. "You are leading up to something again. . . . Can you have come simply to torture me?"

She could not control herself and began crying bitterly. He looked at her in gloomy misery. Five minutes passed.

"Of course you're right, Sonia," he said softly at last. He was suddenly changed. His tone of assumed arrogance and helpless defiance was gone. Even his voice was suddenly weak. "I told you yesterday that I was not coming to ask forgiveness and almost the first thing I've said is to ask forgiveness. . . . I said that about Luzhin and Providence for my own sake. I was asking forgiveness, Sonia. . . ."

He tried to smile, but there was something helpless and incomplete in his pale smile. He bowed his head and hid his face in his hands.

And suddenly a strange, surprising sensation of a sort of bitter hatred for Sonia passed through his heart. As it were wondering and frightened of this sensation, he raised his head and looked intently at her; but he met her uneasy and painfully anxious eyes fixed on him; there was love in them; his hatred vanished like a phantom. It was not the real feeling; he had taken the one feeling for the other. It only meant that *that* minute had come.

He hid his face in his hands again and bowed his head. Suddenly he turned pale, got up from his chair, looked at Sonia, and without uttering a word sat down mechanically on her bed.

His sensations that moment were terribly like the moment when he had stood over the old woman with the axe in his hand and felt that "he must not lose another minute."

"What's the matter?" asked Sonia, dreadfully frightened.

He could not utter a word. This was not at all, not at all the way he had intended to "tell" and he did not understand what was happening to him now. She went up to him, softly, sat down on the bed beside him and waited, not taking her eyes off him. Her heart throbbed and sank. It was unendurable; he turned his deadly pale face to her. His lips worked, helplessly struggling to utter something. A pang of terror passed through Sonia's heart.

"What's the matter?" she repeated, drawing a little away from him.

"Nothing, Sonia, don't be frightened. . . . It's nonsense. It really is nonsense, if you think of it," he muttered, like a man in delirium. "Why have I come to torture you?" he added suddenly, looking at her. "Why, really? I keep asking myself that question, Sonia. . . ."

He had perhaps been asking himself that question a quarter of an hour before, but now he spoke helplessly, hardly knowing what he said and feeling a continual tremor all over.

"Oh, how you are suffering!" she muttered in distress, looking intently at him.

"It's all nonsense. . . . Listen, Sonia." He suddenly smiled, a pale helpless smile for two seconds. "You remember what I meant to tell you yesterday?"

Sonia waited uneasily.

"I said as I went away that perhaps I was saying good-bye for ever, but that if I came to-day I would tell you who . . . who killed Lizaveta."

She began trembling all over.

"Well, here I've come to tell you."

"Then you really meant it yesterday?" she whispered with difficulty. "How do you know?" she asked quickly, as though suddenly regaining her reason.

Sonia's face grew paler and paler, and she breathed painfully.

"I know."

She paused a minute.

"Have they found him?" she asked timidly.

"No."

"Then how do you know about *it?*" she asked again, hardly audibly and again after a minute's pause.

He turned to her and looked very intently at her.

"Guess," he said, with the same distorted helpless smile.

A shudder passed over her.

"But you . . . why do you frighten me like this?" she said, smiling like a child.

"I must be a great friend of *his* . . . since I know," Raskolnikov went on, still gazing into her face, as though he could not turn his eyes away. "He . . . did not mean to kill that Lizaveta . . . he . . . killed her accidentally. . . . He meant to kill the old woman when she was alone and he went there . . . and then Lizaveta came in . . . he killed her too."

Another awful moment passed. Both still gazed at one another.

"You can't guess, then?" he asked suddenly, feeling as though he were flinging himself down from a steeple.

"N-no . . ." whispered Sonia.

"Take a good look."

As soon as he had said this again, the same familiar sensation froze his heart. He looked at her and all at once seemed to see in her face the face of Lizaveta. He remembered clearly the expression in Lizaveta's face, when he approached her with the axe and she stepped back to the wall, putting out her hand, with childish terror in her face, looking as little children do when they begin to be frightened of something, looking intently and uneasily at what frightens them, shrinking back and holding out their little hands on the point of crying. Almost the same thing happened now to Sonia. With the same helplessness and the same terror, she looked at him for a while and, suddenly putting out her left hand, pressed her fingers faintly against his breast and slowly began to get up from the bed, moving further from him and keeping her eyes fixed even more immovably on him. Her terror infected him. The same fear showed itself on his face. In the same way he stared at her and almost with the same *childish* smile.

"Have you guessed?" he whispered at last.

"Good God!" broke in an awful wail from her bosom.

She sank helplessly on the bed with her face in the pillows, but a moment later she got up, moved quickly to him, seized both his hands and, gripping them tight in her thin fingers, began looking into his face again with the same intent stare. In this last desperate look she tried to look into him and catch some last hope. But there was no hope; there was no doubt remaining; it was all true! Later on, indeed, when she recalled that moment, she thought it strange and wondered why she had seen at once that there was no doubt. She could not have said, for instance, that she had foreseen something of the sort—and yet now, as soon as he told her, she suddenly fancied that she had really foreseen this very thing.

"Stop, Sonia, enough! don't torture me," he begged her miserably.

It was not at all, not at all like this he had thought of telling her, but this is how it happened.

She jumped up, seeming not to know what she was doing, and, wringing her hands, walked into the middle of the room; but, quickly went back and sat down again beside him, her shoulder almost touching his. All of a sudden she started as though she had been stabbed, uttered a cry and fell on her knees before him, she did not know why.

"What have you done—what have you done to yourself!" she said in despair, and, jumping up, she flung herself on his neck, threw her arms round him, and held him tight.

Raskolnikov drew back and looked at her with a mournful smile.

"You are a strange girl, Sonia—you kiss me and hug me when I tell you about that. . . . You don't think what you are doing."

"There is no one—no one in the whole world now so unhappy as you!" she cried in a frenzy, not hearing what he said, and she suddenly broke into violent hysterical weeping.

A feeling long unfamiliar to him flooded his heart and softened it at once. He did not struggle against it. Two tears started into his eyes and hung on his eyelashes.

"Then you won't leave me, Sonia?" he said, looking at her almost with hope.

"No, no, never, nowhere!" cried Sonia. "I will follow you, I will follow you everywhere. Oh, my God! Oh, how miserable I am! . . . Why, why didn't I know you before! Why didn't you come before? Oh, dear!"

"Here I have come."

"Yes, now! What's to be done now! . . . Together, together!" she repeated as it were unconsciously, and she hugged him again. "I'll follow you to Siberia!"

He recoiled at this, and the same hostile, almost haughty smile came to his lips.

"Perhaps I don't want to go to Siberia yet, Sonia," he said.

Sonia looked at him quickly.

Again after her first passionate, agonising sympathy for the unhappy man the terrible idea of the murder overwhelmed her. In his changed tone she seemed to hear the murderer speaking. She looked at him bewildered. She knew nothing as yet, why, how, with what object it had been. Now all these questions rushed at once into her mind. And again she could not believe it: "He, he is a murderer! Could it be true?"

"What's the meaning of it? Where am I?" she said in complete bewilderment, as though still unable to recover herself. "How could you, you, a man like you. . . . How could you bring yourself to it? . . . What does it mean?"

"Oh, well—to plunder. Leave off, Sonia," he answered wearily, almost with vexation.

Sonia stood as though struck dumb, but suddenly she cried: "You were hungry! It was . . . to help your mother? Yes?"

"No, Sonia, no," he muttered, turning away and hanging his head. "I was not so hungry. . . . I certainly did want to help my mother, but . . . that's not the real thing either. . . . Don't torture me, Sonia."

Sonia clasped her hands.

"Could it, could it all be true? Good God, what a truth! Who could believe it? And how could you give away your last farthing and yet rob and murder! Ah," she cried suddenly, "that money you gave Katerina Ivanovna . . . that money. . . . Can that money . . ."

"No, Sonia," he broke in hurriedly, "that money was not it. Don't worry yourself! That money my mother sent me and it came when I was ill, the day I gave it to you. . . . Razumihin saw it . . . he received it for me. . . . That money was mine—my own."

Sonia listened to him in bewilderment and did her utmost to comprehend.

"And that money. . . . I don't even know really whether there was any money," he added softly, as though reflecting. "I took a purse off her neck, made of chamois leather . . . a purse stuffed full of something . . . but I didn't look in it; I suppose I hadn't time. . . . And the things—chains and trinkets—I buried under a stone with the purse next morning in a yard off the V—— Prospect. They are all there now. . . ."

Sonia strained every nerve to listen.

"Then why . . . why, you said you did it to rob, but you took nothing?" she asked quickly, catching at a straw.

"I don't know. . . . I haven't yet decided whether to take that

money or not," he said, musing again; and, seeming to wake up
with a start, he gave a brief ironical smile. "Ach, what silly stuff
I am talking, eh?"

The thought flashed through Sonia's mind, wasn't he mad?
But she dismissed it at once. "No, it was something else." She
could make nothing of it, nothing.

"Do you know, Sonia," he said suddenly with conviction,
"let me tell you: if I'd simply killed because I was hungry," laying
stress on every word and looking enigmatically but sincerely at
her, "I should be *happy* now. You must believe that! What would
it matter to you," he cried a moment later with a sort of despair,
"what would it matter to you if I were to confess that I did wrong!
What do you gain by such a stupid triumph over me? Ah, Sonia,
was it for that I've come to you to-day?"

Again Sonia tried to say something, but did not speak.

"I asked you to go with me yesterday because you are all I
have left."

"Go where?" asked Sonia timidly.

"Not to steal and not to murder, don't be anxious," he
smiled bitterly. "We are so different. . . . And you know, Sonia,
it's only now, only this moment that I understand *where* I asked
you to go with me yesterday! Yesterday when I said it I did not
know where. I asked you for one thing, I came to you for one
thing—not to leave me. You won't leave me, Sonia?"

She squeezed his hand.

"And why, why did I tell her? Why did I let her know?" he
cried a minute later in despair, looking with infinite anguish at
her. "Here you expect an explanation from me, Sonia; you are
sitting and waiting for it, I see that. But what can I tell you? You
won't understand and will only suffer misery . . . on my account!
Well, you are crying and embracing me again. Why do you do
it? Because I couldn't bear my burden and have come to throw
it on another: you suffer too, and I shall feel better! And can you
love such a mean wretch?"

"But aren't you suffering, too?" cried Sonia.

Again a wave of the same feeling surged into his heart, and
again for an instant softened it.

"Sonia, I have a bad heart, take note of that. It may explain a great deal. I have come because I am bad. There are men who wouldn't have come. But I am a coward and . . . a mean wretch. But . . . never mind! That's not the point. I must speak now, but I don't know how to begin."

He paused and sank into thought.

"Ach, we are so different," he cried again, "we are not alike. And why, why did I come? I shall never forgive myself that."

"No, no, it was a good thing you came," cried Sonia. "It's better I should know, far better!"

He looked at her with anguish.

"What if it were really that?" he said, as though reaching a conclusion. "Yes, that's what it was! I wanted to become a Napoleon, that is why I killed her. . . . Do you understand now?"

"N-no," Sonia whispered naïvely and timidly. "Only speak, speak, I shall understand, I shall understand *in myself!*" she kept begging him.

"You'll understand? Very well, we shall see!" He paused and was for some time lost in meditation.

"It was like this: I asked myself one day this question—what if Napoleon, for instance, had happened to be in my place, and if he had not had Toulon nor Egypt nor the passage of Mont Blanc to begin his career with, but instead of all those picturesque and monumental things, there had simply been some ridiculous old hag, a pawnbroker, who had to be murdered too to get money from her trunk (for his career, you understand). Well, would he have brought himself to that, if there had been no other means? Wouldn't he have felt a pang at its being so far from monumental and . . . and sinful, too? Well, I must tell you that I worried myself fearfully over that 'question' so that I was awfully ashamed when I guessed at last (all of a sudden, somehow) that it would not have given him the least pang, that it would not even have struck him that it was not monumental . . . that he would not have seen that there was anything in it to pause over, and that, if he had had no other way, he would have strangled her in a minute without thinking about it! Well, I too . . . left off thinking about it . . . murdered her, following his example. And that's exactly how it was! Do you think it funny? Yes, Sonia, the funniest thing of all is that perhaps that's just how it was."

Sonia did not think it at all funny.

"You had better tell me straight out . . . without examples," she begged, still more timidly and scarcely audibly.

He turned to her, looked sadly at her and took her hands.

"You are right again, Sonia. Of course that's all nonsense, it's almost all talk! You see, you know of course that my mother has scarcely anything, my sister happened to have a good education and was condemned to drudge as a governess. All their hopes were centered on me. I was a student, but I couldn't keep myself at the university and was forced for a time to leave it. Even if I had lingered on like that, in ten or twelve years I might (with luck) hope to be some sort of teacher or clerk with a salary of a thousand roubles" (he repeated it as though it were a lesson) "and by that time my mother would be worn out with grief and anxiety and I could not succeed in keeping her in comfort while my sister . . . well, my sister might well have fared worse! And it's a hard thing to pass everything by all one's life, to turn one's back upon everything, to forget one's mother and decorously accept the insults inflicted on one's sister. Why should one? When one has buried them to burden oneself with others—wife and children—and to leave them again without a farthing? So I resolved to gain possession of the old woman's money and to use it for my first years without worrying my mother, to keep myself at the university and for a little while after leaving it—and to do this all on a broad, thorough scale, so as to build up a completely new career and enter upon a new life of independence. . . . Well . . . that's all. . . . Well, of course in killing the old woman I did wrong. . . . Well, that's enough."

He struggled to the end of his speech in exhaustion and let his head sink.

"Oh, that's not it, that's not it," Sonia cried in distress. "How could one . . . no, that's not right, not right."

"You see yourself that it's not right. But I've spoken truly, it's the truth."

"As though that could be the truth! Good God!"

"I've only killed a louse, Sonia, a useless, loathsome, harmful creature."

"A human being—a louse!"

"I too know it wasn't a louse," he answered, looking strangely at her. "But I am talking nonsense, Sonia," he added. "I've been talking nonsense a long time. . . . That's not it, you are right there. There were quite, quite other causes for it! I haven't talked to anyone for so long, Sonia. . . . My head aches dreadfully now."

His eyes shone with feverish brilliance. He was almost delirious; an uneasy smile strayed on his lips. His terrible exhaustion could be seen through his excitement. Sonia saw how he was suffering. She too was growing dizzy. And he talked so strangely; it seemed somehow comprehensible, but yet . . . "But how, how! Good God!" And she wrung her hands in despair.

"No, Sonia, that's not it," he began again suddenly, raising his head, as though a new and sudden train of thought had struck and as it were roused him—"that's not it! Better . . . imagine— yes, it's certainly better—imagine that I am vain, envious, malicious, base, vindictive and . . . well, perhaps with a tendency to insanity. (Let's have it all out at once! They've talked of madness already, I noticed.) I told you just now I could not keep myself at the university. But do you know that perhaps I might have done? My mother would have sent me what I needed for the fees and I could have earned enough for clothes, boots and food, no doubt. Lessons had turned up at half a rouble. Razumihin works! But I turned sulky and wouldn't. (Yes, sulkiness, that's the right word for it!) I sat in my room like a spider. You've been in my den, you've seen it. . . . And do you know, Sonia, that low ceilings and tiny rooms cramp the soul and the mind? Ah, how I hated that garret! And yet I wouldn't go out of it! I wouldn't on purpose! I didn't go out for days together, and I wouldn't work, I wouldn't even eat, I just lay there doing nothing. If Nastasya brought me anything, I ate it, if she didn't, I went all day without; I wouldn't ask, on purpose, from sulkiness! At night I had no light, I lay in the dark and I wouldn't earn money for candles. I ought to have studied, but I sold my books; and the dust lies an inch thick on the notebooks on my table. I preferred lying still and thinking.

And I kept thinking. . . . And I had dreams all the time, strange dreams of all sorts, no need to describe! Only then I began to fancy that . . . No, that's not it! Again I am telling you wrong! You see I kept asking myself then: why am I so stupid that if others are stupid—and I know they are—yet I won't be wiser? Then I saw, Sonia, that if one waits for every one to get wiser it will take too long. . . . Afterwards I understood that that would never come to pass, that men won't change and that nobody can alter it and that it's not worth wasting effort over it. Yes, that's so. That's the law of their nature, Sonia, . . . that's so! . . . And I know now, Sonia, that whoever is strong in mind and spirit will have power over them. Anyone who is greatly daring is right in their eyes. He who despises most things will be a lawgiver among them and he who dares most of all will be most in the right! So it has been till now and so it will always be. A man must be blind not to see it!"

Though Raskolnikov looked at Sonia as he said this, he no longer cared whether she understood or not. The fever had complete hold of him; he was in a sort of gloomy ecstasy (he certainly had been too long without talking to anyone). Sonia felt that his gloomy creed had become his faith and code.

"I divined then, Sonia," he went on eagerly, "that power is only vouchsafed to the man who dares to stoop and pick it up. There is only one thing, one thing needful: one has only to dare! Then for the first time in my life an idea took shape in my mind which no one had ever thought of before me, no one! I saw clear as daylight how strange it is that not a single person living in this mad world has had the daring to go straight for it all and send it flying to the devil! I . . . I wanted *to have the daring* . . . and I killed her. I only wanted to have the daring, Sonia! That was the whole cause of it!"

"Oh hush, hush," cried Sonia, clasping her hands. "You turned away from God and God has smitten you, has given you over to the devil!"

"Then, Sonia, when I used to lie there in the dark and all this became clear to me, was it a temptation of the devil, eh?"

"Hush, don't laugh, blasphemer! You don't understand, you don't understand! Oh God! He won't understand!"

"Hush, Sonia! I am not laughing. I know myself that it was the devil leading me. Hush, Sonia, hush!" he repeated with gloomy insistence. "I know it all, I have thought it all over and over and whispered it all over to myself, lying there in the dark. . . . I've argued it all over with myself, every point of it, and I know it all, all! And how sick, how sick I was then of going over it all! I have kept wanting to forget it and make a new beginning, Sonia, and leave off thinking. And you don't suppose that I went into it headlong like a fool? I went into it like a wise man, and that was just my destruction. And you mustn't suppose that I didn't know, for instance, that if I began to question myself whether I had the right to gain power—I certainly hadn't the right—or that if I asked myself whether a human being is a louse it proved that it wasn't so for me, though it might be for a man who would go straight to his goal without asking questions. . . . If I worried myself all those days, wondering whether Napoleon would have done it or not, I felt clearly of course that I wasn't Napoleon. I had to endure all the agony of that battle of ideas, Sonia, and I longed to throw it off: I wanted to murder without casuistry, to murder for my own sake, for myself alone! I didn't want to lie about it even to myself. It wasn't to help my mother I did the murder—that's nonsense—I didn't do the murder to gain wealth and power and to become a benefactor of mankind. Nonsense! I simply did it; I did the murder for myself, for myself alone, and whether I became a benefactor to others, or spent my life like a spider catching men in my web and sucking the life out of men, I couldn't have cared at that moment. . . . And it was not the money I wanted, Sonia, when I did it. It was not so much the money I wanted, but something else. . . . I know it all now. . . . Understand me! Perhaps I should never have committed a murder again. I wanted to find out something else; it was something else led me on. I wanted to find out then and quickly whether I was a louse like everybody else or a man. Whether I can step over barriers or not, whether I dare stoop to pick up or not, whether I am a trembling creature or whether I have the *right* . . ."

"To kill? Have the right to kill?" Sonia clasped her hands.

"Ach, Sonia!" he cried irritably and seemed about to make some retort, but was contemptuously silent. "Don't interrupt me, Sonia. I want to prove one thing only, that the devil led me on then and he has shown me since that I had not the right to take that path, because I am just such a louse as all the rest. He was mocking me and here I've come to you now! Welcome your guest! If I were not a louse, should I have come to you? Listen: when I went then to the old woman's I only went to *try*. . . . You may be sure of that!"

"And you murdered her!"

"But how did I murder her? Is that how men do murders? Do men go to commit a murder as I went then? I will tell you some day how I went! Did I murder the old woman? I murdered myself, not her! I crushed myself once for all, for ever. . . . But it was the devil that killed that old woman, not I. Enough, enough, Sonia, enough! Let me be!" he cried in a sudden spasm of agony, "let me be!"

He leaned his elbows on his knees and squeezed his head in his hands as in a vice.

"What suffering!" A wail of anguish broke from Sonia.

"Well, what am I to do now?" he asked, suddenly raising his head and looking at her with a face hideously distorted by despair.

"What are you to do?" she cried, jumping up, and her eyes that had been full of tears suddenly began to shine. "Stand up!" (She seized him by the shoulder, he got up, looking at her almost bewildered.) "Go at once, this very minute, stand at the cross-roads, bow down, first kiss the earth which you have defiled and then bow down to all the world and say to all men aloud, 'I am a murderer!' Then God will send you life again. Will you go, will you go?" she asked him, trembling all over, snatching his two hands, squeezing them tight in hers and gazing at him with eyes full of fire.

He was amazed at her sudden ecstasy.

"You mean Siberia, Sonia? I must give myself up?" he asked gloomily.

"Suffer and expiate your sin by it, that's what you must do."

"No! I am not going to them, Sonia!"

"But how will you go on living? What will you live for?" cried Sonia, "how is it possible now? Why, how can you talk to your mother? (Oh, what will become of them now!) But what am I saying? You have abandoned your mother and your sister already. He has abandoned them already! Oh God!" she cried, "why, he knows it all himself. How, how can he live by himself! What will become of you now?"

"Don't be a child, Sonia," he said softly. "What wrong have I done them? Why should I go to them? What should I say to them? That's only a phantom. . . . They destroy men by millions themselves and look on it as a virtue. They are knaves and scoundrels, Sonia! I am not going to them. And what should I say to them—that I murdered her, but did not dare to take the money and hid it under a stone?" he added with a bitter smile. "Why, they would laugh at me, and would call me a fool for not getting it. A coward and a fool! They wouldn't understand and they don't deserve to understand. Why should I go to them? I won't. Don't be a child, Sonia. . . ."

"It will be too much for you to bear, too much!" she repeated, holding out her hands in despairing supplication.

"Perhaps I've been unfair to myself," he observed gloomily, pondering, "perhaps after all I am a man and not a louse and I've been in too great a hurry to condemn myself. I'll make another fight for it."

A haughty smile appeared on his lips.

"What a burden to bear! And your whole life, your whole life!"

"I shall get used to it," he said grimly and thoughtfully. "Listen," he began a minute later, "stop crying, it's time to talk of the facts: I've come to tell you that the police are after me, on my track. . . ."

"Ach!" Sonia cried in terror.

"Well, why do you cry out? You want me to go to Siberia

and now you are frightened? But let me tell you: I shall not give
myself up. I shall make a struggle for it and they won't do anything to me. They've no real evidence. Yesterday I was in great
danger and believed I was lost; but to-day things are going better.
All the facts they know can be explained two ways, that's to say
I can turn their accusations to my credit, do you understand? And
I shall, for I've learnt my lesson. But they will certainly arrest me.
If it had not been for something that happened, they would have
done so to-day for certain; perhaps even now they will arrest me
to-day. . . . But that's no matter, Sonia; they'll let me out again
. . . for there isn't any real proof against me, and there won't be,
I give you my word for it. And they can't convict a man on what
they have against me. Enough. . . . I only tell you that you may
know. . . . I will try to manage somehow to put it to my mother
and sister so that they won't be frightened. . . . My sister's future
is secure, however, now, I believe . . . and my mother's must be
too. . . . Well, that's all. Be careful, though. Will you come and
see me in prison when I am there?"

"Oh, I will, I will."

They sat side by side, both mournful and dejected, as though
they had been cast up by the tempest alone on some deserted
shore. He looked at Sonia and felt how great was her love for
him, and strange to say he felt it suddenly burdensome and painful to be so loved. Yes, it was a strange and awful sensation! On
his way to see Sonia he had felt that all his hopes rested on her;
he expected to be rid of at least part of his suffering, and now,
when all her heart turned towards him, he suddenly felt that he
was immeasurably unhappier than before.

"Sonia," he said, "you'd better not come and see me when
I am in prison."

Sonia did not answer, she was crying. Several minutes
passed.

"Have you a cross on you?" she asked, as though suddenly
thinking of it.

He did not at first understand the question.

"No, of course not. Here, take this one, of cypress wood. I
have another, a copper one that belonged to Lizaveta. I changed

with Lizaveta: she gave me her cross and I gave her my little ikon. I will wear Lizaveta's now and give you this. Take it . . . it's mine! It's mine, you know," she begged him. "We will go to suffer together, and together we will bear our cross!"

"Give it me," said Raskolnikov.

He did not want to hurt her feelings. But immediately he drew back the hand he held out for the cross.

"Not now, Sonia. Better later," he added to comfort her.

"Yes, yes, better," she repeated with conviction, "when you go to meet your suffering, then put it on. You will come to me, I'll put it on you, we will pray and go together."

At that moment some one knocked three times at the door.

"Sofya Semyonovna, may I come in?" they heard in a very familiar and polite voice.

Sonia rushed to the door in a fright. The flaxen head of Mr. Lebeziatnikov appeared at the door.

5

Lebeziatnikov looked perturbed. "I've come to you, Sofya Semyonovna," he began. "Excuse me . . . I thought I should find you," he said, addressing Raskolnikov suddenly, "that is, I didn't mean anything . . . of that sort . . . But I just thought . . . Katerina Ivanovna has gone out of her mind," he blurted out suddenly, turning from Raskolnikov to Sonia.

Sonia screamed.

"At least it seems to. But . . . we don't know what to do, you see! She came back—she seems to have been turned out somewhere, perhaps beaten. . . . So it seems at least, . . . She had run to your father's former chief, she didn't find him at home: he was dining at some other general's. . . . Only fancy, she rushed off there, to the other general's, and, imagine, she was so persistent that she managed to get the chief to see her, had him fetched out from dinner, it seems. You can imagine what happened. She was turned out, of course; but, according to her own story, she abused him and threw something at him. One may well believe it.

. . . How it is she wasn't taken up, I can't understand! Now she is telling every one, including Amalia Ivanovna; but it's difficult to understand her, she is screaming and flinging herself about. . . . Oh yes, she shouts that since every one has abandoned her, she will take the children and go into the street with a barrel-organ, and the children will sing and dance, and she too, and collect money, and will go every day under the general's window . . . 'to let every one see well-born children, whose father was an official, begging in the street.' She keeps beating the children and they are all crying. She is teaching Lida to sing 'My Village,' the boy to dance, Polenka the same. She is tearing up all the clothes, and making them little caps like actors; she means to carry a tin basin and make it tinkle, instead of music. . . . She won't listen to anything. . . . Imagine the state of things! It's beyond anything!"

Lebeziatnikov would have gone on, but Sonia, who had heard him almost breathless, snatched up her cloak and hat, and ran out of the room, putting on her things as she went. Raskolnikov followed her and Lebeziatnikov came after him.

"She has certainly gone mad!" he said to Raskolnikov, as they went out into the street. "I didn't want to frighten Sofya Semyonovna, so I said 'it seemed like it,' but there isn't a doubt of it. They say that in consumption, the tubercles sometimes occur in the brain; it's a pity I know nothing of medicine. I did try to persuade her, but she wouldn't listen."

"Did you talk to her about the tubercles?"

"Not precisely of the tubercles. Besides, she wouldn't have understood! But what I say is, that if you convince a person logically that he has nothing to cry about, he'll stop crying. That's clear. Is it your conviction that he won't?"

"Life would be too easy if it were so," answered Raskolnikov.

"Excuse me, excuse me; of course it would be rather difficult for Katerina Ivanovna to understand, but do you know that in Paris they have been conducting serious experiments as to the possibility of curing the insane, simply by logical argument? One professor there, a scientific man of standing, lately dead, believed in the possibility of such treatment. His idea was that there's nothing really wrong with the physical organism of the insane, and that insanity is, so to say, a logical mistake, an error of judgment, an incorrect view of things. He gradually showed the madman his error and, would you believe it, they say he was successful? But as he made use of douches too, how far success was due to that treatment remains uncertain. . . . So it seems at least."

Raskolnikov had long ceased to listen. Reaching the house where he lived, he nodded to Lebeziatnikov and went in at the gate. Lebeziatnikov woke up with a start, looked about him and hurried on.

Raskolnikov went into his little room and stood still in the middle of it. Why had he come back here? He looked at the yellow and tattered paper, at the dust, at his sofa. . . . From the yard came a loud continuous knocking; some one seemed to be hammering . . . He went to the window, rose on tiptoe and looked out into the yard for a long time with an air of absorbed attention. But the yard was empty and he could not see who was hammering. In the house on the left he saw some open windows; on the window-sills were pots of sickly-looking geraniums. Linen was hung out of the windows . . . He knew it all by heart. He turned away and sat down on the sofa.

Never, never had he felt himself so fearfully alone!

Yes, he felt once more that he would perhaps come to hate Sonia, now that he had made her more miserable.

"Why had he gone to her to beg for her tears? What need had he to poison her life? Oh, the meanness of it!"

"I will remain alone," he said resolutely, "and she shall not come to the prison!"

Five minutes later he raised his head with a strange smile. That was a strange thought.

"Perhaps it really would be better in Siberia," he thought suddenly.

He could not have said how long he sat there with vague thoughts surging through his mind. All at once the door opened and Dounia came in. At first she stood still and looked at him from the doorway, just as he had done at Sonia; then she came in and sat down in the same place as yesterday, on the chair facing him. He looked silently and almost vacantly at her.

"Don't be angry, brother; I've only come for one minute," said Dounia.

Her face looked thoughtful but not stern. Her eyes were bright and soft. He saw that she too had come to him with love.

"Brother, now I know all, *all*. Dmitri Prokofitch has explained and told me everything. They are worrying and persecuting you through a stupid and contemptible suspicion. . . . Dmitri Prokofitch told me that there is no danger, and that you are wrong in looking upon it with such horror. I don't think so, and I fully understand how indignant you must be, and that that indignation may have a permanent effect on you. That's what I am afraid of. As for your cutting yourself off from us, I don't judge you, I don't venture to judge you, and forgive me for having blamed you for it. I feel that I too, if I had so great a trouble, should keep away from every one. I shall tell mother nothing of *this,* but I shall talk about you continually and shall tell her from you that you will come very soon. Don't worry about her; *I* will set her mind at rest; but don't you try her too much—come once at least; remember that she is your mother. And now I have come simply to say" (Dounia began to get up) "that if you should need me or should need . . . all my life or anything . . . call me, and I'll come. Good-bye!"

She turned abruptly and went towards the door.

"Dounia!" Raskolnikov stopped her and went towards her. "That Razumihin, Dmitri Prokofitch, is a very good fellow."

Dounia flushed slightly.

"Well?" she asked, waiting a moment.

"He is competent, hardworking, honest and capable of real love. . . . Good-bye, Dounia."

Dounia flushed crimson, then suddenly she took alarm.

"But what does it mean, brother? Are we really parting for ever that you . . . give me such a parting message?"

"Never mind. . . . Good-bye."

He turned away, and walked to the window. She stood a moment, looked at him uneasily, and went out troubled.

No, he was not cold to her. There was an instant (the very last one) when he had longed to take her in his arms and *say good-bye* to her, and even *to tell* her, but he had not dared even to touch her hand.

"Afterwards she may shudder when she remembers that I embraced her, and will feel that I stole her kiss."

"And would *she* stand that test?" he went on a few minutes later to himself. "No, she wouldn't; girls like that can't stand things! They never do."

And he thought of Sonia.

There was a breath of fresh air from the window. The daylight was fading. He took up his cap and went out.

He could not, of course, and would not consider how ill he was. But all this continual anxiety and agony of mind could not but affect him. And if he were not lying in high fever it was perhaps just because this continual inner strain helped to keep him on his legs and in possession of his faculties. But this artificial excitement could not last long.

He wandered aimlessly. The sun was setting. A special form of misery had begun to oppress him of late. There was nothing poignant, nothing acute about it; but there was a feeling of permanence, of eternity about it; it brought a foretaste of hopeless years of this cold leaden misery, a foretaste of an eternity "on a square yard of space." Towards evening this sensation usually began to weigh on him more heavily.

"With this idiotic, purely physical weakness, depending on the sunset or something, one can't help doing something stupid! You'll go to Dounia, as well as to Sonia," he muttered bitterly.

He heard his name called. He looked round. Lebeziatnikov rushed up to him.

"Only fancy, I've been to your room looking for you. Only fancy, she's carried out her plan, and taken away the children. Sofya Semyonovna and I have had a job to find them. She is rapping on a frying-pan and making the children dance. The children are crying. They keep stopping at the cross roads and in front of shops; there's a crowd of fools running after them. Come along!"

"And Sonia?" Raskolnikov asked anxiously, hurrying after Lebeziatnikov.

"Simply frantic. That is, it's not Sofya Semyonovna's frantic, but Katerina Ivanovna, though Sofya Semyonovna's frantic too. But Katerina Ivanovna is absolutely frantic. I tell you she is quite mad. They'll be taken to the police. You can fancy what an effect that will have. . . . They are on the canal bank, near the bridge now, not far from Sofya Semyonovna's, quite close."

On the canal bank near the bridge and not two houses away from the one where Sonia lodged, there was a crowd of people, consisting principally of gutter children. The hoarse broken voice of Katerina Ivanovna could be heard from the bridge, and it certainly was a strange spectacle likely to attract a street crowd. Katerina Ivanovna in her old dress with the green shawl, wearing a torn straw hat, crushed in a hideous way on one side, was really frantic. She was exhausted and breathless. Her wasted consumptive face looked more suffering than ever, and indeed out of doors in the sunshine a consumptive always looks worse than at home. But her excitement did not flag, and every moment her irritation grew more intense. She rushed at the children, shouted at them, coaxed them, told them before the crowd how to dance and what to sing, began explaining to them why it was necessary, and driven to desperation by their not understanding, beat them. . . . Then she would make a rush at the crowd; if she noticed any decently dressed person stopping to look, she immediately appealed to him to see what these children "from a genteel, one may say aristocratic, house" had been brought to. If she heard laughter or jeering in the crowd, she would rush at once at the scoffers and begin squabbling with them. Some people laughed, others shook their heads, but every one felt curious at the sight of the madwoman with the frightened children. The frying-pan of which Lebeziatnikov had spoken was not there, at least Raskolnikov did not see it. But instead of rapping on the pan, Katerina Ivanovna began clapping her wasted hands, when she made Lida and Kolya dance and Polenka sing. She too joined in the singing, but broke down at the second note with a fearful cough, which made her curse in despair and even shed tears. What made her most furious was the weeping and terror of Kolya and Lida. Some effort had been made to dress the children up as street singers are dressed. The boy had on a turban made of something red and white to look like a Turk. There had been no costume for Lida; she simply had a red knitted cap, or rather a night cap that had belonged to Marmeladov, decorated with a broken piece of white ostrich-feather, which had been Katerina Ivanovna's grandmother's and had been preserved as a family possession. Polenka was in her everyday dress; she looked in timid perplexity at her mother, and kept at her side, hiding her tears. She dimly realized her mother's condition, and looked uneasily about her. She was terribly fright-ened of the street and the crowd. Sonia followed Katerina Ivanov-na, weeping and beseeching her to return home, but Katerina Ivanovna was not to be persuaded.

"Lease off, Sonia, leave off," she shouted, speaking fast, panting and coughing. "You don't know what you ask; you are like a child! I've told you before that I am not coming back to that drunken German. Let every one, let all Petersburg see the chil-dren begging in the streets, though their father was an honoura-ble man who served all his life in truth and fidelity, and one may say died in the service." (Katerina Ivanovna had by now invented this fantastic story and thoroughly believed it.) "Let that wretch of a general see it! And you are silly, Sonia: what have we to eat? Tell me that. We have worried you enough, I won't go on so! Ah, Rodion Romanovitch, is that you?" she cried, seeing Raskolnikov and rushing up to him. "Explain to this silly girl, please, that nothing better could be done! Even organ-grinders earn their living, and every one will see at once that we are different, that we are an honourable and bereaved family reduced to beggary. And that general will lose his post, you'll see! We shall perform under his windows every day, and if the Tsar drives by, I'll fall on my knees, put the children before me, show them to him, and say 'Defend us, father.' He is the father of the fatherless, he is merciful, he'll protect us, you'll see, and that wretch of a general. . . . Lida, *tenez vous droite!* Kolya, you'll dance again. Why are you whimpering? Whimpering again! What are you afraid of, stupid? Goodness, what am I to do with them, Rodion Romanovitch? If you only knew how stupid they are! What's one to do with such children?"

And she, almost crying herself—which did not stop her uninterrupted, rapid flow of talk—pointed to the crying children. Raskolnikov tried to persuade her to go home, and even said, hoping to work on her vanity, that it was unseemly for her to be wandering about the streets like an organ-grinder, as she was intending to become the principal of a boarding-school.

"A boarding-school, ha-ha-ha! A castle in the air," cried Katerina Ivanovna, her laugh ending in a cough. "No, Rodion Romanovitch, that dream is over! All have forsaken us! . . . And that general. . . . You know, Rodion Romanovitch, I threw an inkpot at him—it happened to be standing in the waiting-room by the paper where you sign your name. I wrote my name, threw it at him and ran away. Oh the scoundrels, the scoundrels! But enough of them, now I'll provide for the children myself, I won't bow down to anybody! She has had to bear enough for us!" she pointed to Sonia. "Polenka, how much have you got? Show me! What, only two farthings! Oh, the mean wretches! They give us nothing, only run after us, putting their tongues out. There, what is that blockhead laughing at?" (She pointed to a man in the crowd.) "It's all because Kolya here is so stupid; I have such a bother with him. What do you want, Polenka? Tell me in French, *parlez moi français*. Why, I've taught you, you know some phrases. Else how are you to show that you are of good family, well brought-up children, and not at all like other organ-grinders? We aren't going to have a Punch and Judy show in the street, but to sing a genteel song. . . . Ah, yes. . . . What are we to sing? You keep putting me out, but we . . . you see, we are standing here, Rodion Romanovitch, to find something to sing and get money, something Kolya can dance to. . . . For, as you can fancy, our performance is all impromptu. . . . We must talk it over and rehearse it all thoroughly, and then we shall go to Nevsky, where there are far more people of good society, and we shall be noticed at once. Lida knows 'My Village' only, nothing but 'My Village,' and every one sings that. We must sing something far more genteel. . . . Well, have you thought of anything, Polenka? If only you'd help your mother! My memory's quite gone, or I should have thought of something. We really can't sing 'An Hussar.' Ah, let us sing in French, 'Cinq sous,' I have taught it you, I have taught it you. And as it is in French, people will see at once that you are children of good family, and that will be much more touching. . . . You might sing 'Marlborough s'en va-t-en guerre,' for that's quite a child's song and is sung as a lullaby in all the aristocratic houses.

> *Marlborough s'en va-t-en guerre*
> *Ne sait quand reviendra . . ."*

she began singing. "But no, better sing *'Cinq sous.'* Now, Kolya, your hands on your hips, make haste, and you, Lida, keep turning the other way, and Polenka and I will sing and clap our hands!

> *Cinq sous, cinq sous*
> *Pour monter notre ménage.*

(Cough-cough-cough!) Set your dress straight, Polenka, it's slipped down on your shoulders," she observed, panting from coughing. "Now it's particularly necessary to behave nicely and genteelly, that all may see that you are well-born children. I said at the time that the bodice should be cut longer, and made of two widths. It was your fault, Sonia, with your advice to make it shorter, and now you see the child is quite deformed by it. . . . Why, you're all crying again! What's the matter, stupids? Come, Kolya, begin. Make haste, make haste! Oh, what an unbearable child!

> *Cinq sous, cinq sous.*

A policeman again! What do you want?"

A policeman was indeed forcing his way through the crowd. But at that moment a gentleman in civilian uniform and an overcoat—a solid-looking official of about fifty with a decoration on his neck (which delighted Katerina Ivanovna and had its effect on the policeman)—approached and without a word handed her a green three-rouble note. His face wore a look of genuine sympathy. Katerina Ivanovna took it and gave him a polite, even ceremonious, bow.

"I thank you, honoured sir," she began loftily. "The causes that have induced us (take the money, Polenka: you see there are generous and honourable people who are ready to help a poor gentlewoman in distress). You see, honoured sir, these orphans of good family—I might even say of aristocratic connections—and that wretch of a general sat eating grouse . . . and stamped at my disturbing him. 'Your excellency,' I said, 'protect the orphans, for you knew my late husband, Semyon Zaharovitch, and on the very day of his death the basest of scoundrels slandered his only daughter.' . . . That policeman again! Protect me," she cried to the official. "Why is that policeman edging up to me? We have only just run away from one of them. What do you want, fool?"

"It's forbidden in the streets. You mustn't make a disturbance."

"It's you're making a disturbance. It's just the same as if I were grinding an organ. What business is it of yours?"

"You have to get a license for an organ, and you haven't got one, and in that way you collect a crowd. Where do you lodge?"

"What, a licence?" wailed Katerina Ivanovna. "I buried my husband to-day. What need of a licence?"

"Calm yourself, madam, calm yourself," began the official. "Come along; I will escort you. . . . This is no place for you in the crowd. You are ill."

"Honoured sir, honoured sir, you don't know," screamed Katerina Ivanovna. "We are going to the Nevsky. . . . Sonia, Sonia! Where is she? She is crying too! What's the matter with you all? Kolya, Lida, where are you going?" she cried suddenly in alarm. "Oh, silly children! Kolya, Lida, where are they off to? . . ."

Kolya and Lida, scared out of their wits by the crowd, and their mother's mad pranks, suddenly seized each other by the hand, and ran off at the sight of the policeman who wanted to take them away somewhere. Weeping and wailing, poor Katerina Ivanovna ran after them. She was a piteous and unseemly spectacle, as she ran, weeping and panting for breath. Sonia and Polenka rushed after them.

"Bring them back, bring them back, Sonia! Oh stupid, ungrateful children! . . . Polenka! catch them. . . . It's for your sakes I . . ."

She stumbled as she ran and fell down.

"She's cut herself, she's bleeding! Oh, dear!" cried Sonia, bending over her.

All ran up and crowded round. Raskolnikov and Lebeziatnikov were the first at her side, the official too hastened up, and behind him the policeman who muttered, "Bother!" with a gesture of impatience, feeling that the job was going to be troublesome one.

"Pass on! Pass on!" he said to the crowd that pressed forward.

"She's dying," some one shouted.

"She's gone out of her mind," said another.

"Lord have mercy upon us," said a woman, crossing herself. "Have they caught the little girl and the boy? They're being brought back, the elder one's got them. . . . Ah, the naughty imps!"

When they had examined Katerina Ivanovna carefully, they saw that she had not cut herself against a stone, as Sonia thought, but that the blood had stained the pavement red was from her chest.

"I've seen that before," muttered the official to Raskolnikov and Lebeziatnikov; "that's consumption; the blood flows and chokes the patient. I saw the same thing with a relative of my own not long ago . . . nearly a pint of blood, all in a minute. . . . What's to be done though? She is dying."

"This way, this way, to my room!" Sonia implored. "I live here! . . . See, that house, the second from here. . . . Come to me, make haste," she turned from one to the other. "Send for the doctor! Oh, dear!"

Thanks to the official's efforts, this plan was adopted, the policeman even helping to carry Katerina Ivanovna. She was carried to Sonia's room, almost unconscious, and laid on the bed.

The blood was still flowing, but she seemed to be coming to herself, Raskolnikov, Lebeziatnikov, and the official accompanied Sonia into the room and were followed by the policeman, who first drove back the crowd which followed to the very door. Polenka came in holding Kolya and Lida, who were trembling and weeping. Several persons came in too from the Kapernaumovs' room; the landlord, a lame one-eyed man of strange appearance with whiskers and hair that stood up like a brush, his wife, a woman with an everlastingly scared expression, and several open-mouthed children with wonder-struck faces. Among these, Svidrigaïlov suddenly made his appearance. Raskolnikov looked at him with surprise, not understanding where he had come from and not having noticed him in the crowd. A doctor and priest were spoken of. The official whispered to Raskolnikov that he thought it was too late now for the doctor, but he ordered him to be sent for. Kapernaumov ran himself.

Meanwhile Katerina Ivanovna had regained her breath. The bleeding ceased for a time. She looked with sick but intent and penetrating eyes at Sonia, who stood pale and trembling, wiping the sweat from her brow with a handkerchief. At last she asked to be raised. They sat her up on the bed, supporting her on both sides.

"Where are the children?" she said in a faint voice. "You've brought them, Polenka? Oh the sillies! Why did you run away. . . . Och!"

Once more her parched lips were covered with blood. She moved her eyes, looking about her.

"So that's how you live, Sonia! Never once have I been in your room."

She looked at her with a face of suffering.

"We have been your ruin, Sonia. Polenka, Lida, Kolya, come here! Well, here they are, Sonia, take them all! I hand them over to you, I've had enough! The ball is over. (Cough!) Lay me down, let me die in peace."

They laid her back on the pillow.

"What, the priest? I don't want him. You haven't got a rouble to spare. I have no sins. God must forgive me without that.

He knows how I have suffered. . . . And if He won't forgive me, I don't care!"

She sank more and more into uneasy delirium. At times she shuddered, turned her eyes from side to side, recognised every one for a minute, but at once sank into delirium again. Her breathing was hoarse and difficult, there was a sort of rattle in her throat.

"I said to him, your excellency," she ejaculated, gasping after each word. "That Amalia Ludwigovna, ah! Lida, Kolya, hands on your hips, make haste! *Glissez, glissez! pas de basque!* Tap with your heels, be a graceful child!

Du hast Diamanten und Perlen

What next? That's the thing to sing.

Du hast die schönsten Augen
Mädchen, was willst du mehr?

"What an idea! *Was willst du mehr.* What things the fool invents! Ah, yes!

In the heat of midday in the vale of Dagestan.

"Ah, how I loved it! I loved that song to distraction, Polenka! Your father, you know, used to sing it when we were engaged. . . . Oh those days! Oh that's the thing for us to sing! How does it go? I've forgotten. Remind me! How was it?"

She was violently excited and tried to sit up. At last, in a horribly hoarse, broken voice, she began, shrieking and gasping at every word, with a look of growing terror.

"In the heat of midday! . . . in the vale! . . . of Dagestan!
. . . With lead in my breast! . . ."

"Your excellency!" she wailed suddenly with a heartrending scream and a flood of tears, "protect the orphans! You have been their father's guest . . . one may say aristocratic. . . ." She started, regaining consciousness, and gazed at all with a sort of terror, but at once recognised Sonia.

"Sonia, Sonia!" she articulated softly and caressingly, as

though surprised to find her there. "Sonia darling, are you here, too?"

They lifted her up again.

"Enough! It's over! Farewell, poor thing! I am done for! I am broken!" she cried with vindictive despair, and her head fell heavily back on the pillow.

She sank into unconsciousness again, but this time it did not last long. Her pale, yellow, wasted face dropped back, her mouth fell open, her leg moved convulsively, she gave a deep, deep sigh and died.

Sonia fell upon her, flung her arms about her, and remained motionless with her head pressed to the dead woman's wasted bosom. Polenka threw herself at her mother's feet, kissing them and weeping violently. Though Kolya and Lida did not understand what had happened, they had a feeling that it was something terrible; they put their hands on each other's little shoulders, stared straight at one another and both at once opened their mouths and began screaming. They were both still in their fancy dress; one in a turban, the other in the cap with the ostrich feather.

And how did "the certificate of merit" come to be on the bed beside Katerina Ivanovna? It lay there by the pillow: Raskolnikov saw it.

He walked away to the window. Lebeziatnikov skipped up to him.

"She is dead," he said.

"Rodion Romanovitch, I must have two words with you," said Svidrigaïlov, coming up to them.

Lebeziatnikov at once made room for him and delicately withdrew. Svidrigaïlov drew Raskolnikov further away.

"I will undertake all the arrangements, the funeral and that. You know it's a question of money and, as I told you, I have plenty to spare. I will put those two little ones and Polenka into some good orphan asylum, and I will settle fifteen hundred roubles to be paid to each on coming of age, so that Sofya Semyonovna need have no anxiety about them. And I will pull her out of the mud too, for she is a good girl, isn't she? So tell Avdotya Romanovna that that is how I am spending her ten thousand."

"What is your motive for such benevolence?" asked Raskolnikov.

"Ah! you sceptical person!" laughed Svidrigaïlov. "I told you I had no need of that money. Won't you admit that it's simply done from humanity? She wasn't 'a louse,' you know" (he pointed to the corner where the dead woman lay), "was she, like some old pawnbroker woman? Come, you'll agree, is Luzhin to go on living, and doing wicked things or is she to die? And if I didn't help them, Polenka would go the same way."

He said this with an air of a sort of gay winking slyness, keeping his eyes fixed on Raskolnikov, who turned white and cold, hearing his own phrases, spoken to Sonia. He quickly stepped back and looked wildly at Svidrigaïlov.

"How do you know?" he whispered, hardly able to breathe.

"Why, I lodge here at Madame Resslich's, the other side of the wall. Here is Kapernaumov, and there lives Madame Resslich, an old and devoted friend of mine. I am a neighbour."

"You?"

"Yes," continued Svidrigaïlov, shaking with laughter. "I assure you on my honour, dear Rodion Romanovitch, that you have interested me enormously. I told you we should become friends, I foretold it. Well, here we have. And you will see what an accommodating person I am. You'll see that you can get on with me!"

PART SIX—

1

A strange period began for Raskolnikov: it was as though a fog had fallen upon him and wrapped him in a dreary solitude from which there was no escape. Recalling that period long after, he believed that his mind had been clouded at times, and that it had continued so, with intervals, till the final catastrophe. He was convinced that he had been mistaken about many things at that time, for instance as to the date of certain events. Anyway, when he tried later on to piece his recollections together, he learnt a great deal about himself from what other people told him. He had mixed up incidents and had explained events as due to circumstances which existed only in his imagination. At times he was a prey to agonies of morbid uneasiness, amounting sometimes to panic. But he remembered, too, moments, hours, perhaps whole days, of complete apathy, which came upon him as a reaction from his previous terror and might be compared with the abnormal insensibility, sometimes seen in the dying. He seemed to be trying in that latter stage to escape from a full and clear understanding of his position. Certain essential facts which required immediate consideration were particularly irksome to him. How glad he would have been to be free from some cares, the neglect of which would have threatened him with complete, inevitable ruin.

He was particularly worried about Svidrigaïlov, he might be said to be permanently thinking of Svidrigaïlov. From the time of Svidrigaïlov's too menacing and unmistakable words in Sonia's room at the moment of Katerina Ivanovna's death, the normal working of his mind seemed to break down. But although this new fact caused him extreme uneasiness, Raskolnikov was in no hurry for an explanation of it. At times, finding himself in a solitary and remote part of the town, in some wretched eating-house, sitting alone lost in thought, hardly knowing how he had come there, he suddenly thought of Svidrigaïlov. He recognised suddenly, clearly, and with dismay that he ought at once to come to an understanding with that man and to make what terms he could. Walking outside the city gates one day, he positively fancied that they had fixed a meeting there, that he was waiting for Svidrigaïlov. Another time he woke up before daybreak lying on the ground under some bushes and could not at first understand how he had come there.

But during the two or three days after Katerina Ivanovna's death, he had two or three times met Svidrigaïlov at Sonia's

lodging, where he had gone aimlessly for a moment. They exchanged a few words and made no reference to the vital subject,
as though they were tacitly agreed not to speak of it for a time.

Katerina Ivanovna's body was still lying in the coffin, Svidrigaïlov was busy making arrangements for the funeral. Sonia
too was very busy. At their last meeting Svidrigaïlov informed
Raskolnikov that he had made an arrangement, and a very satisfactory one, for Katerina Ivanovna's children; that he had,
through certain connections, succeeded in getting hold of certain
personages by whose help the three orphans could be at once
placed in very suitable institutions; that the money he had settled
on them had been of great assistance, as it is much easier to place
orphans with some property than destitute ones. He said something too about Sonia and promised to come himself in a day or
two to see Raskolnikov, mentioning that "he would like to consult with him, that there were things they must talk over.
. . ."

This conversation took place in the passage on the stairs.
Svidrigaïlov looked intently at Raskolnikov and suddenly, after a
brief pause, dropping his voice, asked: "But how is it, Rodion
Romanovitch; you don't seem yourself? You look and you listen,
but you don't seem to understand. Cheer up! We'll talk things
over; I am only sorry, I've so much to do of my own business and
other people's. Ah, Rodion Romanovitch," he added suddenly,
"what all men need is fresh air, fresh air . . . more than anything!"

He moved to one side to make way for the priest and server,
who were coming up the stairs. They had come for the requiem
service. By Svidrigaïlov's orders it was sung twice a day punctually. Svidrigaïlov went his way. Raskolnikov stood still a moment,
thought, and followed the priest into Sonia's room. He stood at
the door. They began quietly, slowly and mournfully singing the
service. From his childhood the thought of death and the presence of death had something oppressive and mysteriously awful;
and it was long since he had heard the requiem service. And there
was something else here as well, too awful and disturbing. He
looked at the children: they were all kneeling by the coffin; Polen-

ka was weeping. Behind them Sonia prayed, softly, and, as it were, timidly weeping.

"These last two days she hasn't said a word to me, she hasn't glanced at me," Raskolnikov thought suddenly. The sunlight was bright in the room; the incense rose in clouds; the priest read, "Give rest, oh Lord. . . ." Raskolnikov stayed all through the service. As he blessed them and took his leave, the priest looked round strangely. After the service, Raskolnikov went up to Sonia. She took both his hands and let her head sink on his shoulder. This slight friendly gesture bewildered Raskolnikov. It seemed strange to him that there was no trace of repugnance, no trace of disgust, no tremor in her hand. It was the furthest limit of self-abnegation, at least so he interpreted it.

Sonia said nothing. Raskolnikov pressed her hand and went out. He felt very miserable. If it had been possible to escape to some solitude, he would have thought himself lucky, even if he had to spend his whole life there. But although he had almost always been by himself of late, he had never been able to feel alone. Sometimes he walked out of the town on to the high road, once he had even reached a little wood, but the lonelier the place was, the more he seemed to be aware of an uneasy presence near him. It did not frighten him, but greatly annoyed him, so that he made haste to return to the town, to mingle with the crowd, to enter restaurants and taverns, to walk in busy thoroughfares. There he felt easier and even more solitary. One day at dusk he sat for an hour listening to songs in a tavern and he remembered that he positively enjoyed it. But at last he had suddenly felt the same uneasiness again, as though his conscience smote him. "Here I sit listening to singing, is that what I ought to be doing?" he thought. Yet he felt at once that that was not the only cause of his uneasiness; there was something requiring immediate decision, but it was something he could not clearly understand or put into words. It was a hopeless tangle. "No, better the struggle again! Better Porfiry again . . . or Svidrigaïlov. . . . Better some challenge again . . . some attack. Yes, yes!" he thought. He went out of the tavern and rushed away almost at a run. The thought of Dounia and his mother suddenly reduced him almost to a panic. That night he woke up before morning among some bushes in Krestovsky Island, trembling all over with fever; he walked home, and it was early morning when he arrived. After some hours' sleep the fever left him, but he woke up late, two o'clock in the afternoon.

He remembered that Katerina Ivanovna's funeral had been fixed for that day, and was glad that he was not present at it. Nastasya brought him some food; he ate and drank with appetite, almost with greediness. His head was fresher and he was calmer than he had been for the last three days. He even felt a passing wonder at his previous attacks of panic.

The door opened and Razumihin came in.

"Ah, he's eating, then he's not ill," said Razumihin. He took a chair and sat down at the table opposite Raskolnikov.

He was troubled and did not attempt to conceal it. He spoke with evident annoyance, but without hurry or raising his voice. He looked as though he had some special fixed determination.

"Listen," he began resolutely. "As far as I am concerned, you may all go to hell, but from what I see, it's clear to me that I can't make head or tail of it; please don't think I've come to ask you questions. I don't want to know, hang it! If you begin telling me your secrets, I dare say I shouldn't stay to listen, I should go away cursing. I have only come to find out once for all whether it's a fact that you are mad? There is a conviction in the air that you are mad or very nearly so. I admit I've been disposed to that opinion myself, judging from your stupid, repulsive and quite inexplicable actions, and from your recent behaviour to your mother and sister. Only a monster or a madman could treat them as you have; so you must be mad."

"When did you see them last?"

"Just now. Haven't you seen them since then? What have you been doing with yourself? Tell me, please. I've been to you three times already. Your mother has been seriously ill since yesterday. She had made up her mind to come to you; Avdotya Romanovna tried to prevent her; she wouldn't hear a word. 'If he is ill, if his mind is giving way, who can look after him like his mother?' she said. We all came here together, we couldn't let her

come alone all the way. We kept begging her to be calm. We
came in, you weren't here; she sat down, and stayed ten minutes,
while we stood waiting in silence. She got up and said: 'If he's
gone out, that is, if he is well, and has forgotten his mother, it's
humiliating and unseemly for his mother to stand at his door
begging for kindness.' She returned home and took to her bed;
now she is in a fever. 'I see,' she said, 'that he has time for *his girl.'*
She means by *your girl* Sofya Semyonovna, your betrothed or
your mistress, I don't know. I went at once to Sofya Semyonovna's, for I wanted to know what was going on. I looked round,
I saw the coffin, the children crying, and Sofya Semyonovna trying them on mourning dresses. No sign of you. I apologised,
came away, and reported to Avdotya Romanovna. So that's all
nonsense and you haven't got a girl; the most likely thing is that
you are mad. But here you sit, guzzling boiled beef as though
you'd not had a bite for three days. Though as far as that goes,
madmen eat too, but though you have not said a word to me yet
. . . you are not mad! That I'd swear! Above all, you are not mad.
So you may go to hell, all of you, for there's some mystery, some
secret about it, and I don't intend to worry my brains over your
secrets. So I've simply come to swear at you," he finished, getting
up, "to relieve my mind. And I know what to do now."

"What do you mean to do now?"

"What business is it of yours what I mean to do?"

"You are going in for a drinking bout."

"How . . . how did you know?"

"Why, it's pretty plain."

Razumihin paused for a minute.

"You always have been a very rational person and you've
never been mad, never," he observed suddenly with warmth.
"You're right: I shall drink. Good-bye!"

And he moved to go out.

"I was talking with my sister—the day before yesterday I
think it was—about you, Razumihin."

"About me! But . . . where can you have seen her the day
before yesterday?" Razumihin stopped short and even turned a
little pale.

One could see that his heart was throbbing slowly and violently.

"She came here by herself, sat there and talked to me."

"She did!"

"Yes."

"What did you say to her . . . I mean, about me?"

"I told her you were a very good, honest, and industrious man. I didn't tell her you love her, because she knows that herself."

"She knows that herself?"

"Well, it's pretty plain. Wherever I might go, whatever happened to me, you would remain to look after them. I, so to speak, give them into your keeping, Razumihin. I say this because I know quite well how you love her, and am convinced of the purity of your heart. I know that she too may love you and perhaps does love you already. Now decide for yourself, as you know best, whether you need go in for a drinking bout or not."

"Rodya! You see . . . well. . . . Ach, damn it! But where do you mean to go? Of course, if it's all a secret, never mind. . . . But I . . . I shall find out the secret . . . and I am sure that it must be some ridiculous nonsense and that you've made it all up. Anyway you are a capital fellow, a capital fellow!" . . .

"That was just what I wanted to add, only you interrupted, that that was a very good decision of yours not to find out these secrets. Leave it to time, don't worry about it. You'll know it all in time when it must be. Yesterday a man said to me that what a man needs is fresh air, fresh air, fresh air. I mean to go to him directly to find out what he meant by that."

Razumihin stood lost in thought and excitement, making a silent conclusion.

"He's a political conspirator! He must be. And he's on the eve of some desperate step, that's certain. It can only be that! And . . . and Dounia knows," he thought suddenly.

"So Avdotya Romanovna comes to see you," he said, weighing each syllable, "and you're going to see a man who says we need more air, and so of course that letter . . . that too must have something to do with it," he concluded to himself.

"What letter?"

"She got a letter to-day. It upset her very much—very much indeed. Too much so. I began speaking of you, she begged me not to. Then . . . then she said that perhaps we should very soon have to part . . . then she began warmly thanking me for something; then she went to her room and locked herself in."

"She got a letter?" Raskolnikov asked thoughtfully.

"Yes, and you didn't know? hm . . ."

They were both silent.

"Good-bye, Rodion. There was a time, brother, when I . . . Never mind, good-bye. You see, there was a time. . . . Well, good-bye! I must be off too. I am not going to drink. There's no need now. . . . That's all stuff!"

He hurried out; but when he had almost closed the door behind him, he suddenly opened it again, and said, looking away:

"Oh, by the way, do you remember that murder, you know Porfiry's, that old woman? Do you know the murderer has been found, he has confessed and given the proofs. It's one of those very workmen, the painter, only fancy! Do you remember I defended them here? Would you believe it, all that scene of fighting and laughing with his companion on the stairs while the porter and the two witnesses were going up, he got up on purpose to disarm suspicion. The cunning, the presence of mind of the young dog! One can hardly credit it; but it's his own explanation, he has confessed it all. And what a fool I was about it! Well, he's simply a genius of hypocrisy and resourcefulness in disarming the suspicions of the lawyers—so there's nothing much to wonder at, I suppose! Of course people like that are always possible. And the fact that he couldn't keep up the character, but confessed, makes him easier to believe in. But what a fool I was! I was frantic on their side!"

"Tell me please from whom did you hear that, and why does it interest you so?" Raskolnikov asked with unmistakable agitation.

"What next? You ask me why it interests me! . . . Well, I heard it from Porfiry, among others . . . It was from him I heard almost all about it."

"From Porfiry?"

"From Porfiry."

"What . . . what did he say?" Raskolnikov asked in dismay.

"He gave me a capital explanation of it. Psychologically, after his fashion."

"He explained it? Explained it himself?"

"Yes, yes; good-bye. I'll tell you all about it another time, but now I'm busy. There was a time when I fancied . . . But no matter, another time! . . . What need is there for me to drink now? You have made me drunk without wine. I am drunk, Rodya! Good-bye, I'm going. I'll come again very soon."

He went out.

"He's a political conspirator, there's not a doubt about it," Razumihin decided, as he slowly descended the stairs. "And he's drawn his sister in; that's quite, quite in keeping with Avdotya Romanovna's character. There are interviews between them! . . . She hinted at it too . . . So many of her words . . . and hints . . . bear that meaning! And how else can all this tangle be explained? Hm! And I was almost thinking . . . Good heavens, what I thought! Yes, I took leave of my senses and I wronged him! It was his doing, under the lamp in the corridor that day. Pfoo! What a crude, nasty, vile idea on my part! Nikolay is a brick, for confessing. . . . And how clear it all is now! His illness then, all his strange actions . . . before this, in the university, how morose he used to be, how gloomy. . . . But what's the meaning now of that letter? There's something in that, too, perhaps. Whom was it from? I suspect . . . ! No, I must find out!"

He thought of Dounia, realising all he had heard and his heart throbbed, and he suddenly broke into a run.

As soon as Razumihin went out, Raskolnikov got up, turned to the window, walked into one corner and then into another, as though forgetting the smallness of his room, and sat down again on the sofa. He felt, so to speak, renewed; again the struggle, so a means of escape had come.

"Yes, a means of escape had come! It had been too stifling, too cramping, the burden had been too agonising. A lethargy had come upon him at times. From the moment of the scene with

Nikolay at Porfiry's he had been suffocating, penned in without hope of escape. After Nikolay's confession, on that very day had come the scene with Sonia; his behaviour and his last words had been utterly unlike anything he could have imagined beforehand; he had grown feebler, instantly and fundamentally! And he had agreed at the time with Sonia, he had agreed in his heart he could not go on living alone with such a thing on his mind!

"And Svidrigaïlov was a riddle . . . He worried him, that was true, but somehow not on the same point. He might still have a struggle to come with Svidrigaïlov. Svidrigaïlov, too, might be a means of escape; but Porfiry was a different matter.

"And so Porfiry himself had explained it to Razumihin, had explained it *psychologically*. He had begun bringing in his damned psychology again! Porfiry? But to think that Porfiry should for one moment believe that Nikolay was guilty, after what had passed between them before Nikolay's appearance, after that tête-à-tête interview, which could have only *one* explanation? (During those days Raskolnikov had often recalled passages in that scene with Porfiry; he could not bear to let his mind rest on it.) Such words, such gestures had passed between them, they had exchanged such glances, things had been said in such a tone and had reached such a pass, that Nikolay, whom Porfiry had seen through at the first word, at the first gesture, could not have shaken his conviction.

"And to think that even Razumihin had begun to suspect! The scene in the corridor under the lamp had produced its effect then. He had rushed to Porfiry. . . . But what had induced the latter to receive him like that? What had been his object in putting Razumihin off with Nikolay? He must have some plan; there was some design, but what was it? It was true that a long time had passed since that morning—too long a time—and no sight nor sound of Porfiry. Well, that was a bad sign. . . ."

Raskolnikov took his cap and went out of the room, still pondering. It was the first time for a long while that he had felt clear in his mind, at least. "I must settle Svidrigaïlov," he thought, "and as soon as possible; he, too, seems to be waiting for me to come to him of my own accord." And at that moment there was such a rush of hate in his weary heart that he might have killed either of those two—Porfiry or Svidrigaïlov. At least he felt that he would be capable of doing it later, if not now.

"We shall see, we shall see," he repeated to himself.

But no sooner had he opened the door than he stumbled upon Porfiry himself in the passage. He was coming in to see him. Raskolnikov was dumbfounded for a minute, but only for one minute. Strange to say, he was not very much astonished at seeing Porfiry and scarcely afraid of him. He was simply startled, but was quickly, instantly, on his guard. "Perhaps this will mean the end? But how could Porfiry have approached so quietly, like a cat, so that he had heard nothing? Could he have been listening at the door?"

"You didn't expect a visitor, Rodion Romanovitch,"Porfiry explained, laughing. "I've been meaning to look in a long time; I was passing by and thought why not go in for five minutes. Are you going out? I won't keep you long. Just let me have one cigarette."

"Sit down, Porfiry Petrovitch, sit down." Raskolnikov gave his visitor a seat with so pleased and friendly an expression that he would have marvelled at himself, if he could have seen it.

The last moment had come, the last drops had to be drained! So a man will sometimes go through half an hour of mortal terror with a brigand, yet when the knife is at his throat at last, he feels no fear.

Raskolnikov seated himself directly facing Porfiry, and looked at him without flinching. Porfiry screwed up his eyes and began lighting a cigarette.

"Speak, speak," seemed as though it would burst from Raskolnikov's heart. "Come, why don't you speak?"

2

"Ah these cigarettes!" Porfiry Petrovitch ejaculated at last, having lighted one. "They are pernicious, positively pernicious, and yet I can't give them up! I cough, I begin to have tickling in my throat and a difficulty in breathing. You know I am a coward, I went lately to Dr. B——n; he always gives at least half an hour to each patient. He positively laughed looking at me; he sounded me: 'Tobacco's bad for you,' he said, 'your lungs are affected.' But how am I to give it up? What is there to take its place? I don't drink, that's the mischief, he-he-he, that I don't. Everything is relative, Rodion Romanovitch, everything is relative!"

"Why, he's playing his professional tricks again," Raskolnikov thought with disgust. All the circumstances of their last interview suddenly came back to him, and he felt a rush of the feeling that had come upon him then.

"I came to see you the day before yesterday, in the evening; you didn't know?" Porfiry Petrovitch went on, looking round the room. "I came into this very room. I was passing by, just as I did to-day, and I thought I'd return your call. I walked in as your door was wide open, I looked round, waited and went out without leaving my name with your servant. Don't you lock your door?"

Raskolnikov's face grew more and more gloomy. Porfiry seemed to guess his state of mind.

"I've come to have it out with you, Rodion Romanovitch, my dear fellow! I owe you an explanation and must give it to you," he continued with a slight smile, just patting Raskolnikov's knee.

But almost at the same instant a serious and careworn look came into his face; to his surprise Raskolnikov saw a touch of sadness in it. He had never seen and never suspected such an expression in his face.

"A strange scene passed between us last time we met, Rodion Romanovitch. Our first interview, too, was a strange one; but then . . . and one thing after another! This is the point: I have perhaps acted unfairly to you; I feel it. Do you remember how we parted? Your nerves were unhinged and your knees were shaking and so were mine. And, you know, our behaviour was unseemly, even ungentlemanly. And yet we are gentlemen, above all, in any case, gentlemen; that must be understood. Do you remember what we came to? . . . it was quite indecorous."

"What is he up to, what does he take me for?" Raskolnikov

asked himself in amazement, raising his head and looking with open eyes on Porfiry.

"I've decided openness is better between us," Porfiry Petrovitch went on, turning his head away and dropping his eyes, as though unwilling to disconcert his former victim and as though disdaining his former wiles. "Yes, such suspicions and such scenes cannot continue for long. Nikolay put a stop to it, or I don't know what we might not have come to. That damned workman was sitting at the time in the next room—can you realise that? You know that, of course; and I am aware that he came to you afterwards. But what you supposed then was not true: I had not sent for any one, I had made no kind of arrangements. You ask why I hadn't? What shall I say to you: it had all come upon me so suddenly. I had scarcely sent for the porters (you noticed them as you went out, I dare say). An idea flashed upon me; I was firmly convinced at the time, you see, Rodion Romanovitch. Come, I thought—even if I let one thing slip for a time, I shall get hold of something else—I shan't lose what I want, anyway. You are nervously irritable, Rodion Romanovitch, by temperament; it's out of proportion with other qualities of your heart and character, which I flatter myself I have to some extent divined. Of course I did reflect even then that it does not always happen that a man gets up and blurts out his whole story. It does happen sometimes, if you make a man lose all patience, though even then it's rare. I was capable of realising that. If I only had a fact, I thought, the least little fact to go upon, something I could lay hold of, something tangible, not merely psychological. For if a man is guilty, you must be able to get something substantial out of him; one may reckon upon most surprising results indeed. I was reckoning on your temperament, Rodion Romanovitch, on your temperament above all things! I had great hopes of you at that time."

"But what are you driving at now?" Raskolnikov muttered at last, asking the question without thinking.

"What is he talking about?" he wondered distractedly, "does he really take me to be innocent?"

"What am I driving at? I've come to explain myself, I consider it my duty, so to speak. I want to make clear to you how the whole business, the whole misunderstanding arose. I've caused you a great deal of suffering, Rodion Romanovitch. I am not a monster. I understand what it must mean for a man who has been unfortunate, but who is proud, imperious and above all, impatient, to have to bear such treatment! I regard you in any case as a man of noble character and not without elements of magnanimity, though I don't agree with all your convictions. I wanted to tell you this first, frankly and quite sincerely, for above all I don't want to deceive you. When I made your acquaintance, I felt attracted by you. Perhaps you will laugh at my saying so. You have a right to. I know you disliked me from the first and indeed you've no reason to like me. You may think what you like, but I desire now to do all I can to efface that impression and to show that I am a man of heart and conscience. I speak sincerely."

Porfiry Petrovitch made a dignified pause. Raskolnikov felt a rush of renewed alarm. The thought that Porfiry believed him to be innocent began to make him uneasy.

"It's scarcely necessary to go over everything in detail," Porfiry Petrovitch went on. "Indeed I could scarcely attempt it. To begin with there were rumours. Through whom, how, and when those rumours came to me . . . and how they affected you, I need not go into. My suspicions were aroused by a complete accident, which might just as easily not have happened. What was it? Hm! I believe there is no need to go into that either. Those rumours and that accident led to one idea in my mind. I admit it openly—for one may as well make a clean breast of it—I was the first to pitch on you. The old woman's notes on the pledges and the rest of it—that all came to nothing. Yours was one of a hundred. I happened, too, to hear of the scene at the office, from a man who described it capitally, unconsciously reproducing the scene with great vividness. It was just one thing after another, Rodion Romanovitch, my dear fellow! How could I avoid being brought to certain ideas? From a hundred rabbits you can't make a horse, a hundred suspicions don't make a proof, as the English proverb says, but that's only from the rational point of view—you can't help being partial, for after all a lawyer is only human. I thought, too, of your article in that journal, do you remember, on your first visit we talked of it? I jeered at you at the time, but that was only to lead you on. I repeat, Rodion Romanovitch, you are ill and impatient. That you were bold, headstrong, in earnest and . . . had felt a great deal I recognised long before. I, too, have felt the same, so that your article seemed familiar to me. It was conceived on sleepless nights, with a throbbing heart, in ecstasy and suppressed enthusiasm. And that proud suppressed enthusiasm in young people is dangerous! I jeered at you then, but let me tell you that, as a literary amateur, I am awfully fond of such first essays, full of the heat of youth. There is a mistiness and a chord vibrating in the mist. Your article is absurd and fantastic, but there's a transparent sincerity, a youthful incorruptible pride and the daring of despair in it. It's a gloomy article, but that's what's fine in it. I read your article and put it aside, thinking as I did so 'that man won't go the common way.' Well, I ask you, after that as a preliminary, how could I help being carried away by what followed? Oh, dear, I am not saying anything, I am not making any statement now. I simply noted it at the time. What is there in it? I reflected. There's nothing in it, that is really nothing and perhaps absolutely nothing. And it's not at all the thing for the prosecutor to let himself be carried away by notions: here I have Nikolay on my hands with actual evidence against him—you may think what you like of it, but it's evidence. He brings in his psychology, too; one has to consider him, too, for it's a matter of life and death. Why am I explaining this to you? That you may understand, and not blame my malicious behaviour on that occasion. It was not malicious, I assure you, he-he! Do you suppose I didn't come to search your room at the time? I did, I did, he-he! I was here when you were lying ill in bed, not officially, not in my own person, but I was here. Your room was searched to the last thread at the first suspicion; but *umsonst!* I thought to myself, now that man will come, will come of himself and quickly, too; if he's guilty, he's sure to come. Another man wouldn't but he will. And you remember how Mr. Razumihin began discussing the subject with you? We arranged that to excite you, so we purposely spread rumours, that he might discuss the case with you, and Razumihin is not a man to restrain his indignation. Mr.

Zametov was tremendously struck by your anger and your open daring. Think of blurting out in a restaurant 'I killed her.' It was too daring, too reckless. I thought so myself, if he is guilty he will be a formidable opponent. That was what I thought at the time. I was expecting you. But you simply bowled Zametov over and . . . well, you see, it all lies in this—that this damnable psychology can be taken two ways! Well, I kept expecting you, and so it was, you came! My heart was fairly throbbing. Ach!

"Now, why need you have come? Your laughter, too, as you came in, do you remember? I saw it all plain as daylight, but if I hadn't expected you so specially, I should not have noticed anything in your laughter. You see what influence a mood has! Mr. Razumihin then—ah, that stone, that stone under which the things were hidden! I seem to see it somewhere in a kitchen garden. It was in a kitchen garden, you told Zametov and afterwards you repeated that in my office? And when we began picking your article to pieces, how you explained it! One could take every word of yours in two senses, as though there were another meaning hidden.

"So in this way, Rodion Romanovitch, I reached the furthest limit, and knocking my head against a post, I pulled myself up, asking myself what I was about. After all, I said, you can take it all in another sense if you like, and it's more natural so, indeed. I couldn't help admitting it was more natural. I was bothered! 'No, I'd better get hold of some little fact' I said. So when I heard of the bell-ringing, I held my breath and was all in a tremor. 'Here is my little fact,' thought I, and I didn't think it over, I simply wouldn't. I would have given a thousand roubles at that minute to have seen you with my own eyes, when you walked a hundred paces beside that workman, after he had called you murderer to your face, and you did not dare to ask him a question all the way. And then what about your trembling, what about your bell-ringing in your illness, in semi-delirium?

"And so, Rodion Romanovitch, can you wonder that I played such pranks on you? And what made you come at that very minute? Some one seemed to have sent you, by Jove! And if Nikolay had not parted us . . . and do you remember Nikolay at the time? Do you remember him clearly? It was a thunderbolt, a regular thunderbolt! And how I met him! I didn't believe in the thunderbolt, not for a minute. You could see it for yourself; and how could I? Even afterwards, when you had gone and he began making very, very plausible answers on certain points, so that I was surprised at him myself, even then I didn't believe his story! You see what it is to be as firm as a rock! No, thought I, *morgen früh*. What has Nikolay got to do with it!"

"Razumihin told me just now that you think Nikolay guilty and had yourself assured him of it. . . ."

His voice failed him, and he broke off. He had been listening in indescribable agitation, as this man who had seen through and through him went back upon himself. He was afraid of believing it and did not believe it. In those still ambiguous words he kept eagerly looking for something more definite and conclusive.

"Mr. Razumihin!" cried Porfiry Petrovitch, seeming glad of a question from Raskolnikov, who had till then been silent. "He-he-he! But I had to put Mr. Razumihin off; two is company, three is none. Mr. Razumihin is not the right man, besides he is an outsider. He came running to me with a pale face. . . . But never mind him, why bring him in! To return to Nikolay, would you like to know what sort of a type he is, how I understand him, that is? To begin with, he is still a child and not exactly a coward, but something by way of an artist. Really, don't laugh at my describing him so. He is innocent and responsive to influence. He has a heart, and is a fantastic fellow. He sings and dances, he tells stories, they say, so that people come from other villages to hear him. He attends school too, and laughs till he cries if you hold up a finger to him; he will drink himself senseless—not as a regular vice, but at times, when people treat him like a child. And he stole, too, then, without knowing it himself, for 'How can it be stealing, if one picks it up?' And do you know he is an Old Believer, or rather a dissenter? There have been Wanderers* in his family, and he was for two years in his village under the spiritual guidance of a certain elder. I learnt all this from Nikolay

* A religious sect.—TRANSLATOR'S NOTE.

and from his fellow villagers. And what's more, he wanted to run
into the wilderness! He was full of fervour, prayed at night, read
the old books, 'the true' ones, and read himself crazy.

"Petersburg had a great effect upon him, especially the
women and the wine. He responds to everything and he forgot
the elder and all that. I learnt that an artist here took a fancy to
him, and used to go and see him, and now this business came
upon him.

"Well, he was frightened, he tried to hang himself! He ran
away! How can one get over the idea the people have of Russian
legal proceedings! The very word 'trial' frightens some of them.
Whose fault is it? We shall see what the new juries will do. God
grant they do good! Well, in prison, it seems, he remembered the
venerable elder, the Bible, too, made its appearance again. Do
you know, Rodion Romanovitch, the force of the word 'suffering'
among some of these people! It's not a question of suffering for
some one's benefit, but simply, 'one must suffer.' If they suffer at
the hands of the authorities, so much the better. In my time there
was a very meek and mild prisoner who spent a whole year in
prison always reading his Bible on the stove at night and he read
himself crazy, and so crazy, do you know, that one day, apropos
of nothing, he seized a brick and flung it at the governor, though
he had done him no harm. And the way he threw it too: aimed
it a yard on one side on purpose, for fear of hurting him. Well,
we know what happens to a prisoner who assaults an officer with
a weapon. So 'he took his suffering.'

"So I suspect now that Nikolay wants to take his suffering or
something of the sort. I know it for certain from facts, indeed.
Only he doesn't know that I know. What, you don't admit that
there are such fantastic people among the peasants? Lots of them.
The elder now has begun influencing him, especially since he
tried to hang himself. But he'll come and tell me all himself. You
think he'll hold out? Wait a bit, he'll take his words back. I am
waiting from hour to hour for him to come and abjure his evidence. I have come to like that Nikolay and am studying him in
detail. And what do you think? He-he! He answered me very
plausibly on some points, he obviously had collected some evi-

dence and prepared himself cleverly. But on other points he is simply at sea, knows nothing and doesn't even suspect that he doesn't know!

"No, Rodion Romanovitch, Nikolay doesn't come in! This is a fantastic, gloomy business, a modern case, an incident of today when the heart of man is troubled, when the phrase is quoted that blood 'renews,' when comfort is preached as the aim of life. Here we have bookish dreams, a heart unhinged by theories. Here we see resolution in the first stage, but resolution of a special kind: he resolved to do it like jumping over a precipice or from a bell tower and his legs shook as he went to the crime. He forgot to shut the door after him, and murdered two people for a theory. He committed the murder and couldn't take the money, and what he did manage to snatch up he hid under a stone. It wasn't enough for him to suffer agony behind the door while they battered at the door and rung the bell, no, he had to go to the empty lodging, half delirious, to recall the bell-ringing, he wanted to feel the cold shiver over again. . . . Well, that we grant, was through illness, but consider this: he is a murderer, but looks upon himself as an honest man, despises others, poses as injured innocence. No, that's not the work of a Nikolay, my dear Rodion Romanovitch!"

All that had been said before had sounded so like a recantation that these words were too great a shock. Raskolnikov shuddered as though he had been stabbed.

"Then . . . who then . . . is the murderer?" he asked in a breathless voice, unable to restrain himself.

Porfiry Petrovitch sank back in his chair, as though he were amazed at the question.

"Who is the murderer?" he repeated, as though unable to believe his ears. "Why *you,* Rodion Romanovitch! You are the murderer," he added almost in a whisper, in a voice of genuine conviction.

Raskolnikov leapt from the sofa, stood up for a few seconds and sat down again without uttering a word. His face twitched convulsively.

"Your lip is twitching just as it did before," Porfiry Petrovitch observed almost sympathetically. "You've been misunderstanding me, I think, Rodion Romanovitch," he added after a brief pause, "that's why you are so surprised. I came on purpose to tell you everything and deal openly with you."

"It was not I murdered her," Raskolnikov whispered like a frightened child caught in the act.

"No, it was you, you Rodion Romanovitch, and no one else," Porfiry whispered sternly, with conviction.

They were both silent and the silence lasted strangely long, about ten minutes. Raskolnikov put his elbow on the table and passed his fingers through his hair. Porfiry Petrovitch sat quietly waiting. Suddenly Raskolnikov looked scornfully at Porfiry.

"You are at your old tricks again, Porfiry Petrovitch! Your old method again. I wonder you don't get sick of it!"

"Oh, stop that, what does that matter now? It would be a different matter if there were witnesses present, but we are whispering alone. You see yourself that I have not come to chase and capture you like a hare. Whether you confess it or not is nothing to me now; for myself, I am convinced without it."

"If so, what did you come for?" Raskolnikov asked irritably. "I ask you the same question again: if you consider me guilty, why don't you take me to prison?"

"Oh, that's your question! I will answer you, point for point. In the first place, to arrest you so directly is not to my interest."

"How so? If you are convinced you ought. . . ."

"Ach, what if I am convinced? That's only my dream for the time. Why should I put you in safety? You know that's it, since you ask me to do it. If I confront you with that workman for instance and you say to him 'were you drunk or not? Who saw me with you? I simply took you to be drunk, and you were drunk, too.' Well, what could I answer, especially as your story is a more likely one than his, for there's nothing but psychology to support his evidence—that's almost unseemly with his ugly mug, while you hit the mark exactly, for the rascal is an inveterate drunkard and notoriously so. And I have myself admitted candidly several times already that that psychology can be taken in two ways and that the second way is stronger and looks far more probable, and that apart from that I have as yet nothing against you. And though

I shall put you in prison and indeed have come—quite contrary to etiquette—to inform you of it beforehand, yet I tell you frankly, also contrary to etiquette, that it won't be to my advantage. Well, secondly, I've come to you because . . ."

"Yes, yes, secondly?" Raskolnikov was listening breathless.

"Because, as I told you just now, I consider I owe you an explanation. I don't want you to look upon me as a monster, as I have a genuine liking for you, you may believe me or not. And in the third place I've come to you with a direct and open proposition—that you should surrender and confess. It will be infinitely more to your advantage and to my advantage too, for my task will be done. Well, is this open on my part or not?"

Raskolnikov thought a minute.

"Listen, Porfiry Petrovitch. You said just now you have nothing but psychology to go on, yet now you've gone on to mathematics. Well, what if you are mistaken yourself, now?"

"No, Rodion Romanovitch, I am not mistaken. I have a little fact even then, providence sent it me."

"What little fact?"

"I won't tell you what, Rodion Romanovitch. And in any case, I haven't the right to put it off any longer, I must arrest you. So think it over: it makes no difference to me *now* and so I speak only for your sake. Believe me, it will be better, Rodion Romanovitch."

Raskolnikov smiled malignantly.

"That's not simply ridiculous, it's positively shameless. Why, even if I were guilty, which I don't admit, what reason should I have to confess, when you tell me yourself that I shall be in greater safety in prison?"

"Ah, Rodion Romanovitch, don't put too much faith in words, perhaps prison will not be altogether a restful place. That's only theory and my theory, and what authority am I for you? Perhaps, too, even now I am hiding something from you? I can't lay bare everything, he-he! And how can you ask what advantage? Don't you know how it would lessen your sentence? You would be confessing at a moment when another man has taken the crime on himself and so has muddled the whole case. Consider that! I swear before God that I will so arrange that your confession shall come as a complete surprise. We will make a clean sweep of all these psychological points, of all suspicion against you, so that your crime will appear to have been something like an aberration, for in truth it was an aberration. I am an honest man, Rodion Romanovitch, and will keep my word."

Raskolnikov maintained a mournful silence and let his head sink dejectedly. He pondered a long while and at last smiled again, but his smile was sad and gentle.

"No!" he said, apparently abandoning all attempt to keep up appearances with Porfiry, "it's not worth it, I don't care about lessening the sentence!"

"That's just what I was afraid of!" Porfiry cried warmly and, as it seemed, involuntarily. "That's just what I feared, that you wouldn't care about the mitigation of sentence."

Raskolnikov looked sadly and expressively at him.

"Ah, don't disdain life!" Porfiry went on. "You have a great deal of it still before you. How can you say you don't want a mitigation of sentence? You are an impatient fellow!"

"A great deal of what lies before me?"

"Of life. What sort of prophet are you, do you know much about it? Seek and ye shall find. This may be God's means for bringing you to Him. And it's not for ever, the bondage. . . ."

"The time will be shortened," laughed Raskolnikov.

"Why, is it the bourgeois disgrace you are afraid of? It may be that you are afraid of it without knowing it, because you are young! But anyway *you* shouldn't be afraid of giving yourself up and confessing."

"Ach, hang it!" Raskolnikov whispered with loathing and contempt, as though he did not want to speak aloud.

He got up again as though he meant to go away, but sat down again in evident despair.

"Hang it, if you like! You've lost faith and you think that I am grossly flattering you; but how long has your life been? How much do you understand? You made up a theory and then were ashamed that it broke down and turned out to be not at all original! It turned out something base, that's true, but you are not hopelessly base. By no means so base! At least you didn't deceive yourself for long, you went straight to the furthest point at one bound. How do I regard you? I regard you as one of those men who would stand and smile at their torturer while he cuts their entrails out, if only they have found faith or God. Find it and you will live. You have long needed a change of air. Suffering, too, is a good thing. Suffer! Maybe Nikolay is right in wanting to suffer. I know you don't believe in it—but don't be over-wise; fling yourself straight into life, without deliberation; don't be afraid—the flood will bear you to the bank and set you safe on your feet again. What bank? How can I tell? I only believe that you have long life before you. I know that you take all my words now for a set speech prepared beforehand, but maybe you will remember them after. They may be of use some time. That's why I speak. It's as well that you only killed the old woman. If you'd invented another theory you might perhaps have done something a thousand times more hideous. You ought to thank God, perhaps. How do you know? Perhaps God is saving you for something. But keep a good heart and have less fear! Are you afraid of the great expiation before you? No, it would be shameful to be afraid of it. Since you have taken such a step, you must harden your heart. There is justice in it. You must fulfil the demands of justice. I know that you don't believe it, but indeed, life will bring you through. You will live it down in time. What you need now is fresh air, fresh air, fresh air!"

Raskolnikov positively started.

"But who are you? what prophet are you? From the height of what majestic calm do you proclaim these words of wisdom?"

"Who am I? I am a man with nothing to hope for, that's all. A man perhaps of feeling and sympathy, maybe of some knowledge too, but my day is over. But you are a different matter, there is life waiting for you. Though who knows, maybe your life, too, will pass off in smoke and come to nothing. Come, what does it matter, that you will pass into another class of men? It's not comfort you regret, with your heart! What of it that perhaps no one will see you for so long? It's not time, but yourself that will decide that. Be the sun and all will see you. The sun has before all to be the sun. Why are you smiling again? At my being such a Schiller? I bet you're imagining that I am trying to get round you by flattery. Well, perhaps I am, he-he-he! Perhaps you'd better not believe my word, perhaps you'd better never believe it altogether,—I'm made that way, I confess it. But let me add, you can judge for yourself, I think, how far I am a base sort of man and how far I am honest."

"When do you mean to arrest me?"

"Well, I can let you walk about another day or two. Think it over, my dear fellow, and pray to God. It's more in your interest, believe me."

"And what if I run away?" asked Raskolnikov with a strange smile.

"No, you won't run away. A peasant would run away, a fashionable dissenter would run away, the flunkey of another man's thought, for you've only to show him the end of your little finger and he'll be ready to believe in anything for the rest of his life. But you've ceased to believe in your theory already, what will you run away with? And what would you do in hiding? It would be hateful and difficult for you, and what you need more than anything in life is a definite position, an atmosphere to suit you. And what sort of atmosphere would you have? If you ran away, you'd come back to yourself. *You can't get on without us.* And if I put you in prison,—say you've been there a month, or two, or three—remember my word, you'll confess of yourself and perhaps to your own surprise. You won't know an hour before-hand that you are coming with a confession. I am convinced that you will decide, 'to take your suffering.' You don't believe my words now, but you'll come to it of yourself. For suffering, Rodion Romanovitch, is a great thing. Never mind my having grown fat, I know all the same. Don't laugh at it, there's an idea in suffering, Nikolay is right. No, you won't run away, Rodion Romanovitch."

Raskolnikov got up and took his cap. Porfiry Petrovitch also rose.

"Are you going for a walk? The evening will be fine, if only we don't have a storm. Though it would be a good thing to freshen the air."

He too took his cap.

"Porfiry Petrovitch, please don't take up the notion that I have confessed to you to-day," Raskolnikov pronounced with sullen insistence. "You're a strange man and I have listened to you from simple curiosity. But I have admitted nothing, remember that!"

"Oh, I know that, I'll remember. Look at him, he's trembling! Don't be uneasy, my dear fellow, have it your own way. Walk about a bit, you won't be able to walk too far. If anything happens, I have one request to make of you," he added, dropping his voice. "It's an awkward one, but important. If anything were to happen (though indeed I don't believe in it and think you quite incapable of it), yet in case you were taken during these forty or fifty hours with the notion of putting an end to the business in some other way, in some fantastic fashion—laying hands on yourself—(it's an absurd proposition, but you must forgive me for it) do leave a brief but precise note, only two lines and mention the stone. It will be more generous. Come, till we meet! Good thoughts and sound decisions to you!"

Porfiry went out, stooping and avoiding looking at Raskolnikov. The latter went to the window and waited with irritable impatience till he calculated that Porfiry had reached the street and moved away. Then he too went hurriedly out of the room.

3

He hurried to Svidrigaïlov's. What he had to hope from that man he did not know. But that man had some hidden power over him. Having once recognised this, he could not rest, and now the time had come.

On the way, one question particularly worried him: had Svidrigaïlov been to Porfiry's?

As far as he could judge, he would swear to it, that he had

not. He pondered again and again, went over Porfiry's visit; no, he hadn't been, of course he hadn't.

But if he had not been yet, would he go? Meanwhile, for the present he fancied he couldn't. Why? He could not have explained, but if he could, he would not have wasted much thought over it at the moment. It all worried him and at the same time he could not attend to it. Strange to say, none would have believed it perhaps, but he only felt a faint vague anxiety about his immediate future. Another, much more important anxiety tormented him—it concerned himself, but in a different, more vital way. Moreover, he was conscious of immense moral fatigue, though his mind was working better that morning than it had done of late.

And was it worth while, after all that had happened, to contend with these new trivial difficulties? Was it worth while, for instance, to manoeuvre that Svidrigaïlov should not go to Porfiry's? Was it worth while to investigate, to ascertain the facts, to waste time over any one like Svidrigaïlov?

Oh how sick he was of it all!

And yet he was hastening to Svidrigaïlov; could he be expecting something *new* from him, information, or means of escape? Men will catch at straws! Was it destiny or some instinct bringing them together? Perhaps it was only fatigue, despair; perhaps it was not Svidrigaïlov but some other whom he needed, and Svidrigaïlov had simply presented himself by chance. Sonia? But what should he go to Sonia for now? To beg her tears again? He was afraid of Sonia, too. Sonia stood before him as an irrevocable sentence. He must go his own way or hers. At that moment especially he did not feel equal to seeing her. No, would it not be better to try Svidrigaïlov? And he could not help inwardly owning that he had long felt that he must see him for some reason.

But what could they have in common? Their very evil-doing could not be of the same kind. The man, moreover, was very unpleasant, evidently depraved, undoubtedly cunning and deceitful, possibly malignant. Such stories were told about him. It is true he was befriending Katerina Ivanovna's children, but who could tell with what motive and what it meant? The man always had some design, some project.

There was another thought which had been continually hovering of late about Raskolnikov's mind, and causing him great uneasiness. It was so painful that he made distinct efforts to get rid of it. He sometimes thought that Svidrigaïlov was dogging his footsteps. Svidrigaïlov had found out his secret and had had designs on Dounia. What if he had them still? Wasn't it practically certain that he had? And what if, having learnt his secret and so having gained power over him, he were to use it as a weapon against Dounia?

This idea sometimes even tormented his dreams, but it had never presented itself so vividly to him as on his way to Svidrigaïlov. The very thought moved him to gloomy rage. To begin with, this would transform everything, even his own position; he would have at once to confess his secret to Dounia. Would he have to give himself up perhaps to prevent Dounia from taking some rash step? The letter? This morning Dounia had received a letter. From whom could she get letters in Petersburg? Luzhin, perhaps? It's true Razumihin was there to protect her; but Razumihin knew nothing of the position. Perhaps it was his duty to tell Razumihin? He thought of it with repugnance.

In any case he must see Svidrigaïlov as soon as possible, he decided finally. Thank God, the details of the interview were of little consequence, if only he could get at the root of the matter; but if Svidrigaïlov were capable . . . if he were intriguing against Dounia,—then . . .

Raskolnikov was so exhausted by what he had passed through that month that he could only decide such questions in one way; "then I shall kill him," he thought in cold despair.

A sudden anguish oppressed his heart, he stood still in the middle of the street and began looking about to see where he was and which way he was going. He found himself in X. Prospect, thirty or forty paces from the Hay Market, through which he had come. The whole second storey of the house on the left was used as a tavern. All the windows were wide open; judging from the figures moving at the windows, the rooms were full to overflowing. There were sounds of singing, of clarionet and violin, and the boom of a Turkish drum. He could hear women shrieking. He was about to turn back wondering why he had come to the X. Prospect, when suddenly at one of the end windows he saw Svidrigaïlov, sitting at a tea-table right in the open window with a pipe in his mouth. Raskolnikov was dreadfully taken aback, almost terrified. Svidrigaïlov was silently watching and scrutinising him and, what struck Raskolnikov at once, seemed to be meaning to get up and slip away unobserved. Raskolnikov at once pretended not to have seen him, but to be looking absentmindedly away, while he watched him out of the corner of his eye. His heart was beating violently. Yet, it was evident that Svidrigaïlov did not want to be seen. He took the pipe out of his mouth and was on the point of concealing himself, but as he got up and moved back his chair, he seemed to have become suddenly aware that Raskolnikov had seen him, and was watching him. What had passed between them was much the same as what happened at their first meeting in Raskolnikov's room. A sly smile came into Svidrigaïlov's face and grew broader and broader. Each knew that he was seen and watched by the other. At last Svidrigaïlov broke into a loud laugh.

"Well, well, come in if you want me; I am here!" he shouted from the window.

Raskolnikov went up into the tavern. He found Svidrigaïlov in a tiny back room, adjoining the saloon in which merchants, clerks and numbers of people of all sorts were drinking tea at twenty little tables to the desperate bawling of a chorus of singers. The click of billiard balls could be heard in the distance. On the table before Svidrigaïlov stood an open bottle, and a glass half full of champagne. In the room he found also a boy with a little hand organ, a healthy-looking red-cheeked girl of eighteen, wearing a tucked-up striped skirt, and a Tyrolese hat with ribbons. In spite of the chorus in the other room, she was singing some servants' hall song in a rather husky contralto, to the accompaniment of the organ.

"Come, that's enough," Svidrigaïlov stopped her at Raskolnikov's entrance. The girl at once broke off and stood waiting respectfully. She had sung her guttural rhymes, too, with a serious and respectful expression in her face.

"Hey, Philip, a glass!" shouted Svidrigaïlov.

"I won't drink anything," said Raskolnikov.

"As you like, I didn't mean it for you. Drink, Katia! I don't want anything more to-day, you can go." He poured her out a full glass, and laid down a yellow note.

Katia drank off her glass of wine, as women do, without putting it down, in twenty gulps, took the note and kissed Svidrigaïlov's hand, which he allowed quite seriously. She went out of the room and the boy trailed after her with the organ. Both had been brought in from the street. Svidrigaïlov had not been a week in Petersburg, but everything about him was already, so to speak, on a patriarchal footing; the waiter, Philip, was by now an old friend and very obsequious.

The door leading to the saloon had a lock on it. Svidrigaïlov was at home in this room and perhaps spent whole days in it. The tavern was dirty and wretched, not even second rate.

"I was going to see you and looking for you," Raskolnikov began, "but I don't know what made me turn from the Hay Market into the X. Prospect just now. I never take this turning. I turn to the right from the Hay Market. And this isn't the way to you. I simply turned and here you are. It is strange!"

"Why don't you say at once 'it's a miracle'?"

"Because it may be only chance."

"Oh, that's the way with all you folk," laughed Svidrigaïlov. "You won't admit it, even if you do inwardly believe it a miracle! Here you say that it may be only chance. And what cowards they all are here, about having an opinion of their own, you can't fancy, Rodion Romanovitch. I don't mean you, you have an opinion of your own and are not afraid to have it. That's how it was you attracted my curiosity."

"Nothing else?"

"Well, that's enough, you know," Svidrigaïlov was obviously exhilarated, but only slightly so, he had not had more than half a glass of wine.

"I fancy you came to see me before you knew that I was capable of having what you call an opinion of my own," observed Raskolnikov.

"Oh, well, it was a different matter. Every one has his own plans. And apropos of the miracle let me tell you that I think you have been asleep for the last two or three days. I told you of this tavern myself, there is no miracle in your coming straight here. I explained the way myself, told you where it was, and the hours you could find me here. Do you remember?"

"I don't remember," answered Raskolnikov with surprise.

"I believe you. I told you twice. The address has been stamped mechanically on your memory. You turned this way mechanically and yet precisely according to the direction, though you are not aware of it. When I told you then, I hardly hoped you understood me. You give yourself away too much, Rodion Romanovitch. And another thing, I'm convinced there are lots of people in Petersburg who talk to themselves as they walk. This is a town of crazy people. If only we had scientific men, doctors, lawyers and philosophers might make most valuable investigations in Petersburg each in his own line. There are few places where there are so many gloomy, strong and queer influences on the soul of a man as in Petersburg. The mere influences of climate mean so much. And it's the administrative centre of all Russia and its character must be reflected on the whole country. But that is neither here nor there now. The point is that I have several times watched you. You walk out of your house—holding your head high—twenty paces from home you let it sink, and fold your hands behind your back. You look and evidently see nothing before nor beside you. At last you begin moving your lips and talking to yourself, and sometimes you wave one hand and declaim, and at last stand still in the middle of the road. That's not at all the thing. Some one may be watching you besides me, and it won't do you any good. It's nothing really to do with me and I can't cure you, but, of course, you understand me."

"Do you know that I am being followed?" asked Raskolnikov, looking inquisitively at him.

"No, I know nothing about it," said Svidrigaïlov, seeming surprised.

"Well, then, let us leave me alone," Raskolnikov muttered, frowning.

"Very good, let us leave you alone."

"You had better tell me, if you come here to drink, and directed me twice to come here to you, why did you hide, and try to get away just now when I looked at the window from the street? I saw it."

"He-he! And why was it you lay on your sofa with closed eyes and pretended to be asleep, though you were wide awake while I stood in your doorway? I saw it."

"I may have had . . . reasons. You know that yourself."

"And I may have had my reasons, though you don't know them."

Raskolnikov dropped his right elbow on the table, leaned his chin in the fingers of his right hand, and stared intently at Svidrigaïlov. For a full minute he scrutinised his face, which had impressed him before. It was a strange face, like a mask; white and red, with bright red lips, with a flaxen beard, and still thick flaxen hair. His eyes were somehow too blue and their expression somehow too heavy and fixed. There was something awfully unpleasant in that handsome face, which looked so wonderfully young for his age. Svidrigaïlov was smartly dressed in light summer clothes and was particularly dainty in his linen. He wore a huge ring with a precious stone in it.

"Have I got to bother myself about you too now?" said Raskolnikov suddenly, coming with nervous impatience straight to the point. "Even though perhaps you are the most dangerous man if you care to injure me, I don't want to put myself out any more. I will show you at once that I don't prize myself as you probably think I do. I've come to tell you at once that if you keep to your former intentions with regard to my sister and if you think to derive any benefit in that direction from what has been discovered of late, I will kill you before you get me locked up. You can reckon on my word. You know that I can keep it. And in the second place if you want to tell me anything—for I keep fancying all this time that you have something to tell me—make haste and tell it, for time is precious and very likely it will soon be too late."

"Why in such haste?" asked Svidrigaïlov, looking at him curiously.

"Every one has his plans," Raskolnikov answered gloomily and impatiently.

"You urged me yourself to frankness just now, and at the first question you refuse to answer," Svidrigaïlov observed with a smile. "You keep fancying that I have aims of my own and so you look at me with suspicion. Of course it's perfectly natural in your position. But though I should like to be friends with you, I shan't trouble myself to convince you of the contrary. The game isn't worth the candle and I wasn't intending to talk to you about anything special."

"What did you want me for, then? It was you who came hanging about me."

"Why, simply as an interesting subject for observation. I liked the fantastic nature of your position—that's what it was! Besides you are the brother of a person who greatly interested me, and from that person I had in the past heard a very great deal about you, from which I gathered that you had a great influence over her; isn't that enough? Ha-ha-ha! Still I must admit that your question is rather complex, and is difficult for me to answer. Here, you, for instance, have come to me not only for a definite object, but for the sake of hearing something new. Isn't that so? Isn't that so?" persisted Svidrigaïlov with a sly smile. "Well, can't you fancy then that I, too, on my way here in the train was reckoning on you, on your telling me something new, and on my making some profit out of you! You see what rich men we are!"

"What profit could you make?"

"How can I tell you? How do I know? You see in what a tavern I spend all my time and it's my enjoyment, that's to say it's no great enjoyment, but one must sit somewhere; that poor Katia now—you saw her? . . . If only I had been a glutton now, a club gourmand, but you see I can eat this."

He pointed to a little table in the corner where the remnants of a terrible looking beef-steak and potatoes lay on a tin dish.

"Have you dined, by the way? I've had something and want nothing more. I don't drink, for instance, at all. Except for champagne I never touch anything, and not more than a glass of that all the evening, and even that is enough to make my head ache.

I ordered it just now to wind myself up, for I am just going off somewhere and you see me in a peculiar state of mind. That was why I hid myself just now like a schoolboy, for I was afraid you would hinder me. But I believe," he pulled out his watch, "I can spend an hour with you. It's half-past four now. If only I'd been something, a landowner, a father, a cavalry officer, a photographer, a journalist . . . I am nothing, no specialty, and sometimes I am positively bored. I really thought you would tell me something new."

"But what are you, and why have you come here?"

"What am I? You know, a gentleman, I served for two years in the cavalry, then I knocked about here in Petersburg, then I married Marfa Petrovna and lived in the country. There you have my biography!"

"You are a gambler, I believe?"

"No, a poor sort of gambler. A card-sharper—not a gambler."

"You have been a card-sharper then?"

"Yes, I've been a card-sharper too."

"Didn't you get thrashed sometimes?"

"It did happen. Why?"

"Why, you might have challenged them . . . altogether it must have been lively."

"I won't contradict you and besides I am no hand at philosophy. I confess that I hastened here for the sake of the women."

"As soon as you buried Marfa Petrovna?"

"Quite so," Svidrigaïlov smiled with engaging candour. "What of it? You seem to find something wrong in my speaking like that about women?"

"You ask whether I find anything wrong in vice?"

"Vice! Oh, that's what you are after! But I'll answer you in order, first about women in general; you know I am fond of talking. Tell me, what should I restrain myself for? Why should I give up women, since I have a passion for them? It's an occupation, anyway."

"So you hope for nothing here but vice?"

"Oh, very well, for vice then. You insist on its being vice.

But anyway I like a direct question. In this vice at least there is
something permanent, founded indeed upon nature and not dependent on fantasy, something present in the blood like an ever-
burning ember, for ever setting one on fire and maybe, not to be
quickly extinguished, even with years. You'll agree it's an occupation of a sort."

"That's nothing to rejoice at, it's a disease and a dangerous
one."

"Oh, that's what you think, is it? I agree, that it is a disease
like everything that exceeds moderation. And, of course, in this
one must exceed moderation. But in the first place, everybody
does so in one way or another, and in the second place, of course,
one ought to be moderate and prudent, however mean it may be,
but what am I to do? If I hadn't this, I might have to shoot myself.
I am ready to admit that a decent man ought to put up with being
bored, but yet . . ."

"And could you shoot yourself?"

"Oh, come!" Svidrigaïlov parried with disgust. "Please
don't speak of it," he added hurriedly and with none of the
bragging tone he had shown in all the previous conversation. His
face quite changed. "I admit it's an unpardonable weakness, but
I can't help it: I am afraid of death and I dislike its being talked
of. Do you know that I am to a certain extent a mystic?"

"Ah, the apparitions of Marfa Petrovna! Do they still go on
visiting you?"

"Oh, don't talk of them; there have been no more in Petersburg, confound them!" he cried with an air of irritation. "Let's
rather talk of that . . . though . . . H'm! I have not much time,
and can't stay long with you, it's a pity! I should have found plenty
to tell you."

"What's your engagement, a woman?"

"Yes, a woman, a casual incident. . . . No, that's not what I
want to talk of."

"And the hideousness, the filthiness of all your surroundings,
doesn't that affect you? Have you lost the strength to stop yourself?"

"And do you pretend to strength, too? He-he-he! You surprised me just now, Rodion Romanovitch, though I knew beforehand it would be so. You preach to me about vice and aesthetics! You—a Schiller, you—an idealist! Of course that's all as it should be and it would be surprising if it were not so, yet it is strange in reality. . . . Ah, what a pity I have no time, for you're a most interesting type! And by-the-way, are you fond of Schiller? I am awfully fond of him."

"But what a braggart you are," Raskolnikov said with some disgust.

"Upon my word, I am not," answered Svidrigaïlov laughing. "However, I won't dispute it, let me be a braggart, why not brag, if it hurts no one? I spent seven years in the country with Marfa Petrovna, so now when I come across an intelligent person like you—intelligent and highly interesting—I am simply glad to talk and besides, I've drunk that half-glass of champagne and it's gone to my head a little. And besides, there's a certain fact that has wound me up tremendously, but about that I . . . will keep quiet. Where are you off to?" he asked in alarm.

Raskolnikov had begun getting up. He felt oppressed and stifled and, as it were, ill at ease at having come here. He felt convinced that Svidrigaïlov was the most worthless scoundrel on the face of the earth.

"A-ach! Sit down, stay a little!" Svidrigaïlov begged. "Let them bring you some tea, anyway. Stay a little, I won't talk nonsense, about myself, I mean. I'll tell you something. If you like I'll tell you how a woman tried 'to save' me, as you would call it? It will be an answer to your first question indeed, for the woman was your sister. May I tell you? It will help to spend the time."

"Tell me, but I trust that you . . ."

"Oh, don't be uneasy. Besides, even in a worthless low fellow like me, Avdotya Romanovna can only excite the deepest respect."

4

"You know perhaps—yes, I told you myself," began Svidrigaïlov, "that I was in the debtors' prison here, for an immense sum, and had not any expectation of being able to pay it. There's no need to go into particulars of how Marfa Petrovna bought me out; do you know to what a point of insanity a woman can sometimes love? She was an honest woman, and very sensible, although completely uneducated. Would you believe that this honest and jealous woman, after many scenes of hysterics and reproaches, condescended to enter into a kind of contract with me which she kept throughout our married life? She was considerably older than I, and besides, she always kept a clove or something in her mouth. There was so much swinishness in my soul and honesty too, of a sort, as to tell her straight out that I couldn't be absolutely faithful to her. This confession drove her to frenzy, but yet she seems in a way to have liked my brutal frankness. She thought it showed I was unwilling to deceive her if I warned her like this beforehand and for a jealous woman, you know, that's the first consideration. After many tears an unwritten contract was drawn up between us: first, that I would never leave Marfa Petrovna and would always be her husband; secondly, that I would never absent myself without her permission; thirdly, that I would never set up a permanent mistress; fourthly, in return for this, Marfa Petrovna gave me a free hand with the maid servants, but only with her secret knowledge; fifthly, God forbid my falling in love with a woman of our class; sixthly, in case I—which God forbid—should be visited by a great serious passion I was bound to reveal it to Marfa Petrovna. On this last score, however, Marfa Petrovna was fairly at ease. She was a sensible woman and so she could not help looking upon me as a dissolute profligate incapable of real love. But a sensible woman and a jealous woman are two very different things, and that's where the trouble came in. But to judge some people impartially we must renounce certain preconceived opinions and our habitual attitude to the ordinary people about us. I have reason to have faith in your judgment rather than in any one's. Perhaps you have already heard a great deal that was ridiculous and absurd about Marfa Petrovna. She certainly had some very ridiculous ways, but I tell you frankly that I feel really sorry for the innumerable woes of which I was the cause. Well, and that's enough, I think, by way of a decorous *oraison funèbre* for the most tender wife of a most tender husband. When we quarrelled, I usually held my tongue and did not irritate her and that gentlemanly conduct rarely failed to attain its object, it influenced her, it pleased her, indeed. There were times when she was positively proud of me. But your sister she couldn't put up with, anyway. And however she came to risk taking such a beautiful creature into her house as a governess! My explanation is that Marfa Petrovna was an ardent and impressionable woman and simply fell in love herself—literally fell in love—with your sister. Well, little wonder—look at Avdotya Romanovna! I saw the danger at the first glance and what do you think, I resolved not to look at her even. But Avdotya Romanovna herself made the first step, would you believe it? Would you believe it too that Marfa Petrovna was positively angry with me at first for my persistent silence about your sister, for my careless reception of her continual adoring praises of Avdotya Romanovna. I don't know what it was she wanted! Well, of course, Marfa Petrovna told Avdotya Romanovna every detail about me. She had the unfortunate habit of telling literally every one all our family secrets and continually complaining of me; how could she fail to confide in such a delightful new friend? I expect they talked of nothing else but me and no doubt Avdotya Romanovna heard all those dark mysterious rumours that were current about me. . . . I don't mind betting that you too have heard something of the sort already?"

"I have. Luzhin charged you with having caused the death of a child. Is that true?"

"Don't refer to those vulgar tales, I beg," said Svidrigaïlov with disgust and annoyance. "If you insist on wanting to know about all that idiocy, I will tell you one day, but now . . ."

"I was told too about some footman of yours in the country whom you treated badly."

"I beg you to drop the subject," Svidrigaïlov interrupted again with obvious impatience.

"Was that the footman who came to you after death to fill your pipe? . . . you told me about it yourself," Raskolnikov felt more and more irritated.

Svidrigaïlov looked at him attentively and Raskolnikov fancied he caught a flash of spiteful mockery in that look. But Svidrigaïlov restrained himself and answered very civilly.

"Yes, it was. I see that you, too, are extremely interested and shall feel it my duty to satisfy your curiosity at the first opportunity. Upon my soul! I see that I really might pass for a romantic figure with some people. Judge how grateful I must be to Marfa Petrovna for having repeated to Avdotya Romanovna such mysterious and interesting gossip about me. I dare not guess what impression it made on her, but in any case it worked in my interests. With all Avdotya Romanovna's natural aversion and in spite of my invariably gloomy and repellent aspect—she did at last feel pity for me, pity for a lost soul. And if once a girl's heart is moved to *pity*, it's more dangerous than anything. She is bound to want to 'save him,' to bring him to his senses, and lift him up and draw him to nobler aims, and restore him to new life and usefulness,—well, we all know how far such dreams can go. I saw at once that the bird was flying into the cage of herself. And I too made ready. I think you are frowning, Rodion Romanovitch? There's no need. As you know, it all ended in smoke. (Hang it all, what a lot I am drinking!) Do you know, I always, from the very beginning, regretted that it wasn't your sister's fate to be born in the second or third century A.D., as the daughter of a reigning prince or some governor or proconsul in Asia Minor. She would undoubtedly have been one of those who would endure martyrdom and would have smiled when they branded her bosom with hot pincers. And she would have gone to it of herself. And in the fourth or fifth century she would have walked away into the Egyptian desert and would have stayed there thirty years living on roots and ecstasies and visions. She is simply thirsting to face some torture for some one, and if she can't get her torture, she'll throw herself out of a window. I've heard something of a Mr. Razumihin—he's said to be a sensible fellow; his surname suggests it, indeed. He's probably a divinity student. Well, he'd better look after your sister! I believe I understand her, and I am proud of it. But at the beginning of an acquaintance, as you know, one is apt to be more heedless and stupid. One doesn't see clearly. Hang it all, why is she so handsome? It's not my fault. In fact, it began on my side with a most irrestible physical desire. Avdotya Romanovna is awfully chaste, incredibly and phenomenally so. Take note, I tell you this about your sister as a fact. She is almost morbidly chaste, in spite of her broad intelligence, and it will stand in her way. There happened to be a girl in the house then, Parasha, a black-eyed wench, whom I had never seen before—she had just come from another village—very pretty, but incredibly stupid: she burst into tears, wailed so that she could be heard all over the place and caused scandal. One day after dinner Avdotya Romanovna followed me into an avenue in the garden and with flashing eyes *insisted* on my leaving poor Parasha alone. It was almost our first conversation by ourselves. I, of course, was only too pleased to obey her wishes, tried to appear disconcerted, embarrassed, in fact played my part not badly. Then came interviews, mysterious conversations, exhortations, entreaties, supplications, even tears—would you believe it, even tears? Think what the passion for propaganda will bring some girls to! I, of course, threw it all on my destiny, posed as hungering and thirsting for light, and finally resorted to the most powerful weapon in the subjection of the female heart, a weapon which never fails one. It's the well-known resource—flattery. Nothing in the world is harder than speaking the truth and nothing easier than flattery. If there's the hundredth part of a false note in speaking the truth, it leads to a discord, and that leads to trouble. But if all, to the last note, is false in flattery, it is just as agreeable, and is heard not without satisfaction. It may be a coarse satisfaction, but still a satisfaction. And however coarse the flattery, at least half will be sure to seem true. That's so for all stages of development and classes of society. A vestal virgin might be seduced by flattery. I can never remember without laughter how I once seduced a lady who was devoted to her husband, her children, and her principles. What fun it was and how little trouble! And the lady really had principles, of her own, anyway. All my tactics lay in simply being utterly annihilated and prostrate before her purity. I flattered her shamelessly, and as soon as I succeeded in getting a pressure of the hand, even a glance from her, I would reproach myself for having snatched it by force, and would declare that she had resisted, so that I could never have gained anything but for my being so unprincipled. I maintained that she was so innocent that she could not foresee my treachery, and yielded to me unconsciously, unawares, and so on. In fact, I triumphed, while my lady remained firmly convinced that she was innocent, chaste, and faithful to all her duties and obligations and had succumbed quite by accident. And how angry she was with me when I explained to her at last that it was my sincere conviction that she was just as eager as I. Poor Marfa Petrovna was awfully weak on the side of flattery, and if I had only cared to, I might have had all her property settled on me during her lifetime. (I am drinking an awful lot of wine now and talking too much.) I hope you won't be angry if I mention now that I was beginning to produce the same effect on Avdotya Romanovna. But I was stupid and impatient and spoiled it all. Avdotya Romanovna had several times— and one time in particular—been greatly displeased by the expression of my eyes, would you believe it? There was sometimes a light in them which frightened her and grew stronger and stronger and more unguarded till it was hateful to her. No need to go into detail, but we parted. There I acted stupidly again. I fell to jeering in the coarsest way at all such propaganda and efforts to convert me; Parasha came on to the scene again, and not she alone; in fact there was a tremendous to-do. Ah, Rodion Romanovitch, if you could only see how your sister's eyes can flash sometimes! Never mind my being drunk at this moment and having had a whole glass of wine. I am speaking the truth. I assure you that this glance has haunted my dreams; the very rustle of her dress was more than I could stand at last. I really began to think that I might become epileptic. I could never have believed that I could be moved to such a frenzy. It was essential, indeed, to be reconciled, but by then it was impossible. And imagine what I did then! To what a pitch of stupidity a man can be brought by frenzy! Never undertake anything in a frenzy, Rodion Romanovitch. I reflected that Avdotya Romanovna was after all a beggar (ach, excuse me, that's not the word . . . but does it matter if it expresses the meaning?), that she lived by her work, that she had her mother and you to keep (ach, hang it, you are frowning again), and I resolved to offer her all my money—thirty thousand roubles I could have realised then—if she would run away with me here, to Petersburg. Of course I should have vowed eternal love, rapture, and so on. Do you know, I was so wild about her at that time that if she had told me to poison Marfa Petrovna or to cut her throat and to marry herself, it would have been done at once! But it ended in the catastrophe of which you know already. You can fancy how frantic I was when I heard that Marfa Petrovna had got hold of that scoundrelly attorney, Luzhin, and had almost made a match between them—which would really have been just the same thing as I was proposing. Wouldn't it? Wouldn't it? I notice that you've begun to be very attentive . . . you interesting young man. . . ."

Svidrigaïlov struck the table with his fist impatiently. He was flushed. Raskolnikov saw clearly that the glass or glass and a half of champagne that he had sipped almost unconsciously was affecting him—and he resolved to take advantage of the opportunity. He felt very suspicious of Svidrigaïlov.

"Well, after what you have said, I am fully convinced that you have come to Petersburg with designs on my sister," he said directly to Svidrigaïlov, in order to irritate him further.

"Oh, nonsense," said Svidrigaïlov, seeming to rouse himself. "Why, I told you . . . besides your sister can't endure me."

"Yes, I am certain that she can't, but that's not the point."

"Are you so sure that she can't?" Svidrigaïlov screwed up his eyes and smiled mockingly. "You are right, she doesn't love me, but you can never be sure of what has passed between husband and wife or lover and mistress. There's always a little corner which remains a secret to the world and is only known to those two. Will you answer for it that Avdotya Romanovna regarded me with aversion?"

"From some words you've dropped, I notice that you still

have designs—and of course evil ones—on Dounia and mean to carry them out promptly."

"What, have I dropped words like that?" Svidrigaïlov asked in naïve dismay, taking not the slightest notice of the epithet bestowed on his designs.

"Why, you are dropping them even now. Why are you so frightened? What are you so afraid of now?"

"Me—afraid? Afraid of you? You have rather to be afraid of me, *cher ami*. But what nonsense. . . . I've drunk too much though, I see that. I was almost saying too much again. Damn the wine! Hi! there, water!"

He snatched up the champagne bottle and flung it without ceremony out of the window. Philip brought the water.

"That's all nonsense!" said Svidrigaïlov, wetting a towel and putting it to his head. "But I can answer you in one word and annihilate all your suspicions. Do you know that I am going to get married?"

"You told me so before."

"Did I? I've forgotten. But I couldn't have told you so for certain for I had not even seen my betrothed; I only meant to. But now I really have a betrothed and it's a settled thing, and if it weren't that I have business that can't be put off, I would have taken you to see them at once, for I should like to ask your advice. Ach, hang it, only ten minutes left! See, look at the watch. But I must tell you, for it's an interesting story, my marriage, in its own way. Where are you off to? Going again?"

"No, I'm not going away now."

"Not at all? We shall see. I'll take you there, I'll show you my betrothed, only not now. For you'll soon have to be off. You have to go to the right and I to the left. Do you know that Madame Resslich, the woman I am lodging with now; eh? I know what you're thinking, that she's the woman whose girl they say drowned herself in the winter. Come, are you listening? She arranged it all for me. You're bored, she said, you want something to fill up your time. For, you know, I am a gloomy, depressed person. Do you think I'm light-hearted? No, I'm gloomy. I do no harm, but sit in a corner without speaking a word for three

days at a time. And that Resslich is a sly hussy, I tell you. I know
what she has got in her mind; she thinks I shall get sick of it,
abandon my wife and depart, and she'll get hold of her and make
a profit out of her—in our class, of course, or higher. She told me
the father was a broken-down retired official, who has been sitting
in a chair for the last three years with his legs paralysed. The
mamma, she said, was a sensible woman. There is a son serving
in the provinces, but he doesn't help; there is a daughter, who is
married, but she doesn't visit them. And they've two little neph-
ews on their hands, as though their own children were not
enough, and they've taken from school their youngest daughter,
a girl who'll be sixteen in another month, so that then she can be
married. She was for me. We went there. How funny it was! I
present myself—a landowner, a widower, of a well-known name,
with connections, with a fortune. What if I am fifty and she is not
sixteen? Who thinks of that? But it's fascinating, isn't it? It is
fascinating, ha-ha! You should have seen how I talked to the papa
and mamma. It was worth paying to have seen me at that moment.
She comes in, curtseys, you can fancy, still in a short frock—an
unopened bud! Flushing like a sunset—she had been told, no
doubt. I don't know how you feel about female faces, but to my
mind these sixteen years, these childish eyes, shyness and tears of
bashfulness are better than beauty; and she is a perfect little
picture, too. Fair hair in little curls, like a lamb's, full little rosy
lips, tiny feet, a charmer! . . . Well, we made friends. I told them
I was in a hurry owing to domestic circumstances, and the next
day, that is the day before yesterday, we were betrothed. When
I go now I take her on my knee at once and keep her there.
. . . Well, she flushes like a sunset and I kiss her every minute.
Her mamma of course impresses on her that this is her husband
and that this must be so. It's simply delicious! The present betrothed condition is perhaps better than marriage. Here you have
what is called *la nature et la vérité*, ha-ha! I've talked to her twice,
she is far from a fool. Sometimes she steals a look at me that
positively scorches me. Her face is like Raphael's Madonna. You
know, the Sistine Madonna's face has something fantastic in it, the
face of mournful religious ecstasy. Haven't you noticed it? Well,

she's something in that line. The day after we'd been betrothed, I bought her presents to the value of fifteen hundred roubles—a set of diamonds and another of pearls and a silver dressing-case as large as this, with all sorts of things in it, so that even my Madonna's face glowed. I sat her on my knee, yesterday, and I suppose rather too unceremoniously—she flushed crimson and the tears started, but she didn't want to show it. We were left alone, she suddenly flung herself on my neck (for the first time of her own accord), put her little arms round me, kissed me, and vowed that she would be an obedient, faithful, and good wife, would make me happy, would devote all her life, every minute of her life, would sacrifice everything, everything, and that all she asks in return is my *respect*, and that she wants 'nothing, nothing more from me, no presents.' You'll admit that to hear such a confession, alone, from an angel of sixteen in a muslin frock, with little curls, with a flush of maiden shyness in her cheeks and tears of enthusiasm in her eyes is rather fascinating! Isn't it fascinating? It's worth paying for, isn't it? Well . . . listen, we'll go to see my betrothed, only not just now!"

"The fact is this monstrous difference in age and development excites your sensuality! Will you really make such a marriage?"

"Why, of course. Every one thinks of himself, and he lives most gaily who knows best how to deceive himself. Ha-ha! But why are you so keen about virtue? Have mercy on me, my good friend. I am a sinful man. Ha-ha-ha!"

"But you have provided for the children of Katerina Ivanovna. Though . . . though you had your own reasons. . . . I understand it all now."

"I am always fond of children, very fond of them," laughed Svidrigaïlov. "I can tell you one curious instance of it. The first day I came here I visited various haunts, after seven years I simply rushed at them. You probably notice that I am not in a hurry to renew acquaintance with my old friends. I shall do without them as long as I can. Do you know, when I was with Marfa Petrovna in the country, I was haunted by the thought of these places where any one who knows his way about can find a great deal. Yes, upon my soul! The peasants have vodka, the educated young people, shut out from activity, waste themselves in impossible dreams and visions and are crippled by theories; Jews have sprung up and are amassing money, and all the rest give themselves up to debauchery. From the first hour the town reeked of its familiar odours. I chanced to be in a frightful den—I like my dens dirty—it was a dance, so called, and there was a *cancan* such as I never saw in my day. Yes, there you have progress. All of a sudden I saw a little girl of thirteen, nicely dressed, dancing with a specialist in that line, with another one *vis-à-vis*. Her mother was sitting on a chair by the wall. You can't fancy what a *cancan* that was! The girl was ashamed, blushed, at last felt insulted, and began to cry. Her partner seized her and began whirling her round and performing before her; every one laughed and—I like your public, even the *cancan* public—they laughed and shouted, 'Serves her right—serves her right! Shouldn't bring children!' Well, it's not my business whether that consoling reflection was logical or not. I at once fixed on my plan, sat down by the mother, and began by saying that I too was a stranger and that people here were ill-bred and that they couldn't distinguish decent folks and treat them with respect; gave her to understand that I had plenty of money, offered to take them home in my carriage. I took them home and got to know them. They were lodging in a miserable little hole and had only just arrived from the country. She told me that she and her daughter could only regard my acquaintance as an honour. I found out that they had nothing of their own and had come to town upon some legal business. I proffered my services and money. I learnt that they had gone to the dancing saloon by mistake, believing that it was a genuine dancing class. I offered to assist in the young girl's education in French and dancing. My offer was accepted with enthusiasm as an honour—and we are still friendly. . . . If you like, we'll go and see them, only not just now."

"Stop! Enough of your vile, nasty anecdotes, depraved, vile, sensual man!"

"Schiller, you are a regular Schiller! *O la vertu va-t-elle se nicher?* But you know I shall tell you these things on purpose, for the pleasure of hearing your outcries!"

"I dare say. I can see I am ridiculous myself," muttered Raskolnikov angrily.

Svidrigaïlov laughed heartily; finally he called Philip, paid his bill, and began getting up.

"I say, but I am drunk, *assez causé,*" he said. "It's been a pleasure!"

"I should rather think it must be a pleasure!" cried Raskolnikov, getting up. "No doubt it is a pleasure for a worn-out profligate to describe such adventures with a monstrous project of the same sort in his mind—especially under such circumstances and to such a man as me. . . . It's stimulating!"

"Well, if you come to that," Svidrigaïlov answered, scrutinising Raskolnikov with some surprise, "if you come to that, you are a thorough cynic yourself. You've plenty to make you so, anyway. You can understand a great deal . . . and you can do a great deal too. But enough. I sincerely regret not having had more talk with you, but I shan't lose sight of you. . . . Only wait a bit."

Svidrigaïlov walked out of the restaurant. Raskolnikov walked out after him. Svidrigaïlov was not however very drunk, the wine had affected him for a moment, but it was passing off every minute. He was preoccupied with something of importance and was frowning. He was apparently excited and uneasy in anticipation of something. His manner to Raskolnikov had changed during the last few minutes, and he was ruder and more sneering every moment. Raskolnikov noticed all this, and he too was uneasy. He became very suspicious of Svidrigaïlov and resolved to follow him.

They came out on to the pavement.

"You go to the right, and I to the left, or if you like, the other way. Only *adieu, mon plaisir,* may we meet again."

And he walked to the right towards the Hay Market.

5

Raskolnikov walked after him.

"What's this?" cried Svidrigaïlov turning round, "I thought I said . . ."

"It means that I am not going to lose sight of you now."

"What?"

Both stood still and gazed at one another, as though measuring their strength.

"From all your half tipsy stories," Raskolnikov observed harshly, "I am *positive* that you have not given up your designs on my sister, but are pursuing them more actively than ever. I have learnt that my sister received a letter this morning. You have hardly been able to sit still all this time. . . . You may have unearthed a wife on the way, but that means nothing. I should like to make certain myself."

Raskolnikov could hardly have said himself what he wanted and of what he wished to make certain.

"Upon my word! I'll call the police!"

"Call away!"

Again they stood for a minute facing each other. At last Svidrigaïlov's face changed. Having satisfied himself that Raskolnikov was not frightened at his threat, he assumed a mirthful and friendly air.

"What a fellow! I purposely refrained from referring to your affair, though I am devoured by curiosity. It's a fantastic affair. I've put it off till another time, but you're enough to rouse the dead. . . . Well, let us go, only I warn you beforehand I am only going home for a moment, to get some money; then I shall lock up the flat, take a cab and go to spend the evening at the Islands. Now, now are you going to follow me?"

"I'm coming to your lodgings, not to see you but Sofya Semyonovna, to say I'm sorry not to have been at the funeral."

"That's as you like, but Sofya Semyonovna is not at home. She has taken the three children to an old lady of high rank, the patroness of some orphan asylums, whom I used to know years ago. I charmed the old lady by depositing a sum of money with her to provide for the three children of Katerina Ivanovna and subscribing to the institution as well. I told her too the story of Sofya Semyonovna in full detail, suppressing nothing. It pro-

duced an indescribable effect on her. That's why Sofya Semyonovna has been invited to call to-day at the X. Hotel where the
lady is staying for the time."

"No matter, I'll come all the same."

"As you like, it's nothing to me, but I won't come with you;
here we are at home. By the way, I am convinced that you regard
me with suspicion just because I have shown such delicacy and
have not so far troubled you with questions . . . you understand?
It struck you as extraordinary; I don't mind betting it's that. Well,
it teaches one to show delicacy!"

"And to listen at doors!"

"Ah, that's it, is it?" laughed Svidrigaïlov. "Yes, I should
have been surprised if you had let that pass after all that has
happened. Ha-ha! Though I did understand something of the
pranks you had been up to and were telling Sofya Semyonovna
about, what was the meaning of it? Perhaps I am quite behind the
times and can't understand. For goodness' sake, explain it, my
dear boy. Expound the latest theories!"

"You couldn't have heard anything. You're making it all
up!"

"But I'm not talking about that (though I did hear something). No, I'm talking of the way you keep sighing and groaning
now. The Schiller in you is in revolt every moment, and now you
tell me not to listen at doors. If that's how you feel, go and inform
the police that you had this mischance; you made a little mistake
in your theory. But if you are convinced that one mustn't listen
at doors, but one may murder old women at one's pleasure, you'd
better be off to America and make haste. Run, young man! There
may still be time. I'm speaking sincerely. Haven't you the money?
I'll give you the fare."

"I'm not thinking of that at all," Raskolnikov interrupted
with disgust.

"I understand (but don't put yourself out, don't discuss it if
you don't want to). I understand the questions you are worrying
over—moral ones, aren't they? Duties of citizen and man? Lay
them all aside. They are nothing to you now, ha-ha! You'll say
you are still a man and a citizen. If so you ought not to have got

into this coil. It's no use taking up a job you are not fit for. Well, you'd better shoot yourself, or don't you want to?"

"You seem trying to enrage me, to make me leave you."

"What a queer fellow! But here we are. Welcome to the staircase. You see, that's the way to Sofya Semyonovna. Look, there is no one at home. Don't you believe me? Ask Kapernaumov. She leaves the key with him. Here is Madame de Kapernaumov herself. Hey, what? She is rather deaf. Has she gone out? Where? Did you hear? She is not in and won't be till late in the evening probably. Well, come to my room; you wanted to come and see me, didn't you? Here we are. Madame Resslich's not at home. She is a woman who is always busy, an excellent woman I assure you. . . . She might have been of use to you if you had been a little more sensible. Now, see! I take this five per cent. bond out of the bureau—see what a lot I've got of them still—this one will be turned into cash to-day. I mustn't waste any more time. The bureau is locked, the flat is locked, and here we are again on the stairs. Shall we take a cab? I'm going to the Islands. Would you like a lift? I'll take this carriage. Ah, you refuse? You are tired of it! Come for a drive! I believe it will come on to rain. Never mind, we'll put down the hood. . . ."

Svidrigaïlov was already in the carriage. Raskolnikov decided that his suspicions were at least for that moment unjust. Without answering a word he turned and walked back towards the Hay Market. If he had only turned round on his way he might have seen Svidrigaïlov get out not a hundred paces off, dismiss the cab and walk along the pavement. But he had turned the corner and could see nothing. Intense disgust drew him away from Svidrigaïlov.

"To think that I could for one instant have looked for help from that coarse brute, that depraved sensualist and blackguard!" he cried.

Raskolnikov's judgment was uttered too lightly and hastily: there was something about Svidrigaïlov which gave him a certain original, even a mysterious character. As concerned his sister, Raskolnikov was convinced that Svidrigaïlov would not leave her

in peace. But it was too tiresome and unbearable to go on thinking and thinking about this.

When he was alone, he had not gone twenty paces before he
sank, as usual, into deep thought. On the bridge he stood by the
railing and began gazing at the water. And his sister was standing
close by him.

He met her at the entrance to the bridge, but passed by
without seeing her. Dounia had never met him like this in the
street before and was struck with dismay. She stood still and did
not know whether to call to him or not. Suddenly she saw Svidrigaïlov coming quickly from the direction of the Hay Market.

He seemed to be approaching cautiously. He did not go on
to the bridge, but stood aside on the pavement, doing all he could
to avoid Raskolnikov's seeing him. He had observed Dounia for
some time and had been making signs to her. She fancied he was
signalling to beg her not to speak to her brother, but to come to
him.

That was what Dounia did. She stole by her brother and went
up to Svidrigaïlov.

"Let us make haste away," Svidrigaïlov whispered to her, "I
don't want Rodion Romanovitch to know of our meeting. I must
tell you I've been sitting with him in the restaurant close by,
where he looked me up and I had great difficulty in getting rid
of him. He has somehow heard of my letter to you and suspects
something. It wasn't you who told him, of course, but if not you,
who then?"

"Well, we've turned the corner now," Dounia interrupted,
"and my brother won't see us. I have to tell you that I am going
no further with you. Speak to me here. You can tell it all in the
street."

"In the first place, I can't say it in the street; secondly, you
must hear Sofya Semyonovna too; and, thirdly, I will show you
some papers. . . . Oh well, if you won't agree to come with me,
I shall refuse to give any explanation and go away at once. But
I beg you not to forget that a very curious secret of your beloved
brother's is entirely in my keeping."

Dounia stood still, hesitating, and looked at Svidrigaïlov with searching eyes.

"What are you afraid of?" he observed quietly. "The town is not the country. And even in the country you did me more harm that I did you."

"Have you prepared Sofya Semyonovna?"

"No, I have not said a word to her and am not quite certain whether she is at home now. But most likely she is. She has buried her stepmother to-day: she is not likely to go visiting on such a day. For the time I don't want to speak to any one about it and I half regret having spoken to you. The slightest indiscretion is as bad as betrayal in a thing like this. I live there in that house, we are coming to it. That's the porter of our house—he knows me very well; you see, he's bowing; he sees I'm coming with a lady and no doubt he has noticed your face already and you will be glad of that if you are afraid of me and suspicious. Excuse my putting things so coarsely. I haven't a flat to myself; Sofya Semyonovna's room is next to mine—she lodges in the next flat. The whole floor is let out in lodgings. Why are you frightened like a child? Am I really so terrible?"

Svidrigaïlov's lips were twisted in a condescending smile; but he was in no smiling mood. His heart was throbbing and he could scarcely breathe. He spoke rather loud to cover his growing excitement. But Dounia did not notice this peculiar excitement, she was so irritated by his remark that she was frightened of him like a child and that he was so terrible to her.

"Though I know that you are not a man . . . of honour, I am not in the least afraid of you. Lead the way," she said with apparent composure, but her face was very pale.

Svidrigaïlov stopped at Sonia's room.

"Allow me to inquire whether she is at home. . . . She is not. How unfortunate! But I know she may come quite soon. If she's gone out, it can only be to see a lady about the orphans. Their mother is dead. . . . I've been meddling and making arrangements for them. If Sofya Semyonovna does not come back in ten minutes, I will send her to you, to-day if you like. This is my flat. These are my two rooms. Madame Resslich, my landlady, has the next room. Now, look this way. I will show you my chief piece of evidence: this door from my bedroom leads into two perfectly empty rooms, which are to let. Here they are . . . you must look into them with some attention."

Svidrigaïlov occupied two fairly large furnished rooms. Dounia was looking about her mistrustfully, but saw nothing special in the furniture or position of the rooms. Yet there was something to observe, for instance, that Svidrigaïlov's flat was exactly between two sets of almost uninhabited apartments. His rooms were not entered directly from the passage, but through the landlady's two almost empty rooms. Unlocking a door leading out of his bedroom, Svidrigaïlov showed Dounia the two empty rooms that were to let. Dounia stopped in the doorway, not knowing what she was called to look upon, but Svidrigaïlov hastened to explain.

"Look here, at this second large room. Notice that door, it's locked. By the door stands a chair, the only one in the two rooms. I brought it from my rooms so as to listen more conveniently. Just the other side of the door is Sofya Semyonovna's table; she sat there talking to Rodion Romanovitch. And I sat here listening on two successive evenings, for two hours each time—and of course I was able to learn something, what do you think?"

"You listened?"

"Yes, I did. Now come back to my room; we can't sit down here."

He brought Avdotya Romanovna back into his sitting-room and offered her a chair. He sat down at the opposite side of the table, at least seven feet from her, but probably there was the same glow in his eyes which had once frightened Dounia so much. She shuddered and once more looked about her distrustfully. It was an involuntary gesture; she evidently did not wish to betray her uneasiness. But the secluded position of Svidrigaïlov's lodging had suddenly struck her. She wanted to ask whether his landlady at least were at home, but pride kept her from asking. Moreover, she had another trouble in her heart incomparably greater than fear for herself. She was in great distress.

"Here is your letter," she said, laying it on the table. "Can it be true what you write? You hint at a crime committed, you say, by my brother. You hint at it too clearly; you daren't deny it now. I must tell you that I'd heard of this stupid story before you wrote and don't believe a word of it. It's a disgusting and ridiculous suspicion. I know the story and why and how it was invented. You can have no proofs. You promised to prove it. Speak! But let me warn you that I don't believe you! I don't believe you!"

Dounia said this, speaking hurriedly, and for an instant the colour rushed to her face.

"If you didn't believe it, how could you risk coming alone to my rooms? Why have you come? Simply from curiosity?"

"Don't torment me. Speak, speak!"

"There's no denying that you are a brave girl. Upon my word, I thought you would have asked Mr. Razumihin to escort you here. But he was not with you nor anywhere near. I was on the look-out. It's spirited of you, it proves you wanted to spare Rodion Romanovitch. But everything is divine in you. . . . About your brother, what am I to say to you? You've just seen him yourself. What did you think of him?"

"Surely that's not the only thing you are building on?"

"No, not on that, but on his own words. He came here on two successive evenings to see Sofya Semyonovna. I've shown you where they sat. He made a full confession to her. He is a murderer. He killed an old woman, a pawnbroker, with whom he had pawned things himself. He killed her sister too, a pedlar woman called Lizaveta, who happened to come in while he was murdering her sister. He killed them with an axe he brought with him. He murdered them to rob them and he did rob them. He took money and various things. . . . He told all this, word for word, to Sofya Semyonovna, the only person who knows his secret. But she has had no share by word or deed in the murder; she was as horrified at it as you are now. Don't be anxious, she won't betray him."

"It cannot be," muttered Dounia, with white lips. She gasped for breath. "It cannot be. There was not the slightest cause, no sort of ground. . . . It's a lie, a lie!"

"He robbed her, that was the cause, he took money and

things. It's true that by his own admission he made no use of the money or things, but hid them under a stone, where they are now. But that was because he dared not make use of them."

"But how could he steal, rob? How could he dream of it?" cried Dounia, and she jumped up from the chair. "Why, you know him, and you've seen him, can he be a thief?"

She seemed to be imploring Svidrigaïlov; she had entirely forgotten her fear.

"There are thousands and millions of combinations and possibilities, Avdotya Romanovna. A thief steals and knows he is a scoundrel, but I've heard of a gentleman who broke open the mail. Who knows, very likely he thought he was doing a gentlemanly thing! Of course I should not have believed it myself if I'd been told of it as you have, but I believe my own ears. He explained all the causes of it to Sofya Semyonovna too, but she did not believe her ears at first, yet she believed her own eyes at last."

"What . . . were the causes?"

"It's a long story, Avdotya Romanovna. Here's . . . how shall I tell you?—A theory of a sort, the same one by which I for instance consider that a single misdeed is permissible if the principal aim is right, a solitary wrongdoing and hundreds of good deeds! It's galling too, of course, for a young man of gifts and overweening pride to know that if he had, for instance, a paltry three thousand, his whole career, his whole future would be differently shaped and yet not to have that three thousand. Add to that, nervous irritability from hunger, from lodging in a whole, from rags, from a vivid sense of the charm of his social position and his sister's and mother's position too. Above all, vanity, pride and vanity, though goodness knows he may have good qualities too. . . . I am not blaming him, please don't think it; besides, it's not my business. A special little theory came in too—a theory of a sort—dividing mankind, you see, into material and superior persons, that is persons to whom the law does not apply owing to their superiority, who make laws for the rest of mankind, the material, that is. It's all right as a theory, *une théorie comme une autre*. Napoleon attracted him tremendously, that is, what affected him was that a great many men of genius have not hesitated at wrongdoing, but have overstepped the law without thinking about it. He seems to have fancied that he was a genius too—that is, he was convinced of it for a time. He has suffered a great deal and is still suffering from the idea that he could make a theory, but was incapable of boldly overstepping the law, and so he is not a man of genius. And that's humiliating for a young man of any pride, in our day especially. . . ."

"But remorse? You deny him any moral feeling then? Is he like that?"

"Ah, Avdotya Romanovna, everything is in a muddle now; not that it was ever in very good order. Russians in general are broad in their ideas, Avdotya Romanovna, broad like their land and exceedingly disposed to the fantastic, the chaotic. But it's a misfortune to be broad without a special genius. Do you remember what a lot of talk we had together on this subject, sitting in the evenings on the terrace after supper? Why, you used to reproach me with breadth! Who knows, perhaps we were talking at the very time when he was lying here thinking over his plan. There are no sacred traditions amongst us, especially in the educated class, Avdotya Romanovna. At the best some one will make them up somehow for himself out of books or from some old chronicle. But those are for the most part the learned and all old fogeys, so that it would be almost ill-bred in a man of society. You know my opinions in general, though. I never blame any one. I do nothing at all, I persevere in that. But we've talked of this more than once before. I was so happy indeed as to interest you in my opinions. . . . You are very pale, Avdotya Romanovna."

"I know his theory. I read that article of his about men to whom all is permitted. Razumihin brought it to me."

"Mr. Razumihin? Your brother's article? In a magazine? Is there such an article? I didn't know. It must be interesting. But where are you going, Avdotya Romanovna?"

"I want to see Sofya Semyonovna," Dounia articulated faintly. "How do I go to her? She has come in, perhaps. I must see her at once. Perhaps she . . ."

Avdotya Romanovna could not finish. Her breath literally failed her.

"Sofya Semyonovna will not be back till night, at least I believe not. She was to have been back at once, but if not, then she will not be in till quite late."

"Ah, then you are lying! I see . . . you were lying . . . lying all the time. . . . I don't believe you! I don't believe you!" cried Dounia, completely losing her head.

Almost fainting, she sank on to a chair which Svidrigaïlov made haste to give her.

"Avdotya Romanovna, what is it? Control yourself! Here is some water. Drink a little. . . ."

He sprinkled some water over her. Dounia shuddered and came to herself.

"It has acted violently," Svidrigaïlov muttered to himself, frowning. "Avdotya Romanovna, calm yourself! Believe me, he has friends. We will save him. Would you like me to take him abroad? I have money, I can get a ticket in three days. And as for the murder, he will do all sorts of good deeds yet, to atone for it. Calm yourself. He may become a great man yet. Well, how are you? How do you feel?"

"Cruel man! To be able to jeer at it! Let me go. . . ."

"Where are you going?"

"To him. Where is he? Do you know? Why is this door locked? We came in at that door and now it is locked. When did you manage to lock it?"

"We couldn't be shouting all over the flat on such a subject. I am far from jeering; it's simply that I'm sick of talking like this. But how can you go in such a state? Do you want to betray him? You will drive him to fury, and he will give himself up. Let me tell you, he is already being watched; they are already on his track. You will simply be giving him away. Wait a little: I saw him and was talking to him just now. He can still be saved. Wait a bit, sit down; let us think it over together. I asked you to come in order to discuss it alone with you and to consider it thoroughly. But do sit down!"

"How can you save him? Can he really be saved?"

Dounia sat down. Svidrigaïlov sat down beside her.

"It all depends on you, on you, on you alone," he began with glowing eyes, almost in a whisper and hardly able to utter the words for emotion.

Dounia drew back from him in alarm. He too was trembling all over.

"You . . . one word from you, and he is saved. I . . . I'll save him. I have money and friends. I'll send him away at once. I'll get a passport, two passports, one for him and one for me. I have friends . . . capable people. . . . If you like, I'll take a passport for you . . . for your mother. . . . What do you want with Razumihin? I love you too. . . . I love you beyond everything. . . . Let me kiss the hem of your dress, let me, let me. . . . The very rustle of it is too much for me. Tell me, 'do that,' and I'll do it. I'll do everything. I will do the impossible. What you believe, I will believe. I'll do anything—anything! Don't, don't look at me like that. Do you know that you are killing me? . . ."

He was almost beginning to rave. . . . Something seemed suddenly to go to his head. Dounia jumped up and rushed to the door.

"Open it! Open it!" she called, shaking the door. "Open it! Is there no one there?"

Svidrigaïlov got up and came to himself. His still trembling lips slowly broke into an angry mocking smile.

"There is no one at home," he said quietly and emphatically. "The landlady has gone out, and it's waste of time to shout like that. You are only exciting yourself uselessly."

"Where is the key? Open the door at once, at once, base man!"

"I have lost the key and cannot find it."

"This is an outrage," cried Dounia, turning pale as death. She rushed to the furthest corner, where she made haste to barricade herself with a little table.

She did not scream, but she fixed her eyes on her tormentor and watched every movement he made.

Svidrigaïlov remained standing at the other end of the room facing her. He was positively composed, at least in appearance, but his face was pale as before. The mocking smile did not leave his face.

"You spoke of outrage just now, Avdotya Romanovna. In that case you may be sure I've taken measures. Sofya Semyonovna is not at home. The Kapernaumovs are far away—there are five locked rooms between. I am at least twice as strong as you are and I have nothing to fear, besides. For you could not complain afterwards. You surely would not be willing actually to betray your brother? Besides, no one would believe you. How should a girl have come alone to visit a solitary man in his lodgings? So that even if you do sacrifice your brother, you could prove nothing. It is very difficult to prove an assault, Avdotya Romanovna."

"Scoundrel!" whispered Dounia indignantly.

"As you like, but observe I was only speaking by way of a general proposition. It's my personal conviction that you are perfectly right—violence is hateful. I only spoke to show you that you need have no remorse even if . . . you were willing to save your brother of your own accord, as I suggest to you. You would be simply submitting to circumstances, to violence, in fact, if we must use that word. Think about it. Your brother's and your mother's fate are in your hands. I will be your slave . . . all my life. . . . I will wait here."

Svidrigaïlov sat down on the sofa about eight steps from Dounia. She had not the slightest doubt now of his unbending determination. Besides, she knew him. Suddenly she pulled out of her pocket a revolver, cocked it and laid it in her hand on the table. Svidrigaïlov jumped up.

"Aha! So that's it, is it?" he cried, surprised but smiling maliciously. "Well, that completely alters the aspect of affairs. You've made things wonderfully easier for me, Avdotya Romanovna. But where did you get the revolver? Was it Mr. Razumihin? Why, it's my revolver, an old friend! And how I've hunted for it! The shooting lessons I've given you in the country have not been thrown away."

"It's not your revolver, it belonged to Marfa Petrovna, whom you killed, wretch! There was nothing of yours in her house. I took it when I began to suspect what you were capable of. If you dare to advance one step, I swear I'll kill you." She was frantic.

"But your brother? I ask from curiosity," said Svidrigaïlov, still standing where he was.

"Inform, if you want to! Don't stir! Don't come nearer! I'll shoot! You poisoned your wife, I know; you are a murderer yourself!" She held the revolver ready.

"Are you so positive I poisoned Marfa Petrovna?"

"You did! You hinted it yourself! you talked to me of poison. . . . I know you went to get it . . . you had it in readiness. . . . It was your doing. . . . It must have been your doing. . . . Scoundrel!"

"Even if that were true, it would have been for your sake . . . you would have been the cause."

"You are lying! I hated you always, always. . . ."

"Oho, Avdotya Romanovna! You seem to have forgotten how you softened to me in the heat of propaganda. I saw it in your eyes. Do you remember that moonlight night, when the nightingale was singing?"

"That's a lie," there was a flash of fury in Dounia's eyes, "that's a lie and a libel!"

"A lie? Well, if you like, it's a lie. I made it up. Women ought not to be reminded of such things," he smiled. "I know you will shoot, you pretty wild creature. Well, shoot away!"

Dounia raised the revolver, and deadly pale, gazed at him, measuring the distance and awaiting the first movement on his part. Her lower lip was white and quivering and her big black eyes flashed like fire. He had never seen her so handsome. The fire glowing in her eyes at the moment she raised the revolver seemed to kindle him and there was a pang of anguish in his heart. He took a step forward and a shot rang out. The bullet grazed his hair and flew into the wall behind. He stood still and laughed softly.

"The wasp has stung me. She aimed straight at my head. What's this? Blood?" he pulled out his handkerchief to wipe the blood, which flowed in a thin stream down his right temple. The bullet seemed to have just grazed the skin.

Dounia lowered the revolved and looked at Svidrigaïlov not so much in terror as in a sort of wild amazement. She seemed not to understand what she was doing and what was going on.

"Well, you missed! Fire again, I'll wait," said Svidrigaïlov softly, still smiling, but gloomily. "If you go on like that, I shall have time to seize you before you cock again."

Dounia started, quickly cocked the pistol and again raised it.

"Let me be," she cried in despair. "I swear I'll shoot again. I . . . I'll kill you."

"Well . . . at three paces you can hardly help it. But if you don't . . . then." His eyes flashed and he took two steps forward. Dounia shot again: it missed fire.

"You haven't loaded it properly. Never mind, you have another charge there. Get it ready, I'll wait."

He stood facing her, two paces away, waiting and gazing at her with wild determination, with feverishly passionate, stubborn, set eyes. Dounia saw that he would sooner die than let her go. "And . . . now, of course she would kill him, at two paces!" Suddenly she flung away the revolver.

"She's dropped it!" said Svidrigaïlov with surprise, and he drew a deep breath. A weight seemed to have rolled from his heart—perhaps not only the fear of death; indeed he may scarcely have felt it at that moment. It was the deliverance from another feeling, darker and more bitter, which he could not himself have defined.

He went to Dounia and gently put his arm round her waist. She did not resist, but, trembling like a leaf, looked at him with suppliant eyes. He tried to say something, but his lips moved without being able to utter a sound.

"Let me go," Dounia implored. Svidrigaïlov shuddered. Her voice now was quite different.

"Then you don't love me?" he asked softly. Dounia shook her head.

"And . . . and you can't? Never?" he whispered in despair. "Never!"

There followed a moment of terrible, dumb struggle in the heart of Svidrigaïlov. He looked at her with an indescribable gaze. Suddenly he withdrew his arm, turned quickly to the window and stood facing it. Another moment passed.

"Here's the key."

He took it out of the left pocket of his coat and laid it on the table behind him, without turning or looking at Dounia.

"Take it! Make haste!"

He looked stubbornly out of the window. Dounia went up to the table to take the key.

"Make haste! Make haste!" repeated Svidrigaïlov, still without turning or moving. But there seemed a terrible significance in the tone of that "make haste."

Dounia understood it, snatched up the key, flew to the door, unlocked it quickly and rushed out of the room. A minute later, beside herself, she ran out on to the canal bank in the direction of X. Bridge.

Svidrigaïlov remained three minutes standing at the window. At last he slowly turned, looked about him and passed his hand over his forehead. A strange smile contorted his face, a pitiful, sad, weak smile, a smile of despair. The blood, which was already getting dry, smeared his hand. He looked angrily at it, then wetted a towel and washed his temple. The revolver which Dounia had flung away lay near the door and suddenly caught his eye. He picked it up and examined it. It was a little pocket three-barrel revolver of old-fashioned construction. There were still two charges and one capsule left in it. It could be fired again. He thought a little, put the revolver in his pocket, took his hat and went out.

6

He spent that evening till ten o'clock, going from one low haunt to another. Katia too turned up and sang another gutter song, how a certain "villain and tyrant"

"began kissing Katia."

Svidrigaïlov treated Katia and the organ-grinder and some singers and the waiters and two little clerks. He was particularly drawn to these clerks by the fact that they both had crooked noses, one bent to the left and the other to the right. They took him finally to a pleasure garden, where he paid for their entrance. There was one lanky three-year-old pine tree and three bushes in the garden, besides a "Vauxhall," which was in reality a drinking-bar where tea too was served, and there were a few green tables and chairs standing round it. A chorus of wretched singers and a drunken, but exceedingly depressed German clown from Mü-nich with a red nose entertained the public. The clerks quarrelled with some other clerks and a fight seemed imminent. Svidrigaïlov was chosen to decide the dispute. He listened to them for a quarter of an hour, but they shouted so loud that there was no possibility of understanding them. The only fact that seemed certain was that one of them had stolen something and had even succeeded in selling it on the spot to a Jew, but would not share the spoil with his companion. Finally it appeared that the stolen object was a teaspoon belonging to the Vauxhall. It was missed and the affair began to seem troublesome. Svidrigaïlov paid for the spoon, got up, and walked out of the garden. It was about six o'clock. He had not drunk a drop of wine all this time and had ordered tea more for the sake of appearances than anything.

It was a dark and stifling evening. Threatening storm-clouds came over the sky about ten o'clock. There was a clap of thunder, and the rain came down like a waterfall. The water fell not in drops, but beat on the earth in streams. There were flashes of lightning every minute and each flash lasted while one could count five.

Drenched to the skin, he went home, locked himself in, opened the bureau, took out all his money and tore up two or three papers. Then, putting the money in his pocket, he was about to change his clothes, but, looking out of window and listening to the thunder and the rain, he gave up the idea, took up his hat and went out of the room without locking the door. He went straight to Sonia. She was at home.

She was not alone: the four Kapernaumov children were with her. She was giving them tea. She received Svidrigaïlov in respectful silence, looking wonderingly at his soaking clothes. The children all ran away at once in indescribable terror.

Svidrigaïlov sat down at the table and asked Sonia to sit beside him. She timidly prepared to listen.

"I may be going to America, Sofya Semyonovna," said Svidrigaïlov, "and as I am probably seeing you for the last time, I have come to make some arrangements. Well, did you see the lady to-day? I know what she said to you, you need not tell me." (Sonia made a movement and blushed.) "Those people have their own way of doing things. As to your sisters and your brother, they are really provided for and the money assigned to them I've put into safe keeping and have received acknowledgments. You had better take charge of the receipts, in case anything happens. Here, take them! Well, now that's settled. Here are three 5 per cent. bonds to the value of three thousand roubles. Take those for yourself, entirely for yourself, and let that be strictly between ourselves, so that no one knows of it, whatever you hear. You will need the money, for to go on living in the old way, Sofya Semyonovna, is bad, and besides there is no need for it now."

"I am so much indebted to you, and so are the children and my stepmother," said Sonia hurriedly, "and if I've said so little . . . please don't consider . . ."

"That's enough! that's enough!"

"But as for the money, Arkady Ivanovitch, I am very grateful to you, but I don't need it now. I can always earn my own living. Don't think me ungrateful. If you are so charitable, that money . . ."

"It's for you, for you, Sofya Semyonovna, and please don't waste words over it. I haven't time for it. You will want it. Rodion Romanovitch has two alternatives: a bullet in the brain or Siberia." (Sonia looked wildly at him, and started.) "Don't be uneasy, I know all about it from himself and I am not a gossip; I won't tell any one. It was good advice when you told him to give himself up and confess. It would be much better for him. Well, if it turns out to be Siberia, he will go and you will follow him. That's so, isn't it? And if so, you'll need money. You'll need it for him, do you understand? Giving it to you is the same as my giving it to him. Besides, you promised Amalia Ivanovna to pay what's owing. I heard you. How can you undertake such obligations so heedlessly, Sofya Semyonovna? It was Katerina Ivanovna's debt and not yours, so you ought not to have taken any notice of the German woman. You can't get through the world like that. If you are ever questioned about me—to-morrow or the day after you will be asked—don't say anything about my coming to see you now and don't show the money to any one or say a word about it. Well, now good-bye." (He got up.) "My greetings to Rodion Romanovitch. By the way, you'd better put the money for the present in Mr. Razumihin's keeping. You know Mr. Razumihin? Of course you do. He's not a bad fellow. Take it to him to-morrow or . . . when the time comes. And till then, hide it carefully."

Sonia too jumped up from her chair and looked in dismay at Svidrigaïlov. She longed to speak, to ask a question, but for the first moments she did not dare and did not know how to begin.

"How can you . . . how can you be going now, in such rain?"

"Why, be starting for America, and be stopped by rain! Ha, ha! Good-bye, Sofya Semyonovna, my dear! Live and live long, you will be of use to others. By the way . . . tell Mr. Razumihin I send my greetings to him. Tell him Arkady Ivanovitch Svidrigaïlov sends his greetings. Be sure to."

He went out, leaving Sonia in a state of wondering anxiety and vague apprehension.

It appeared afterwards that on the same evening, at twenty past eleven, he made another very eccentric and unexpected visit. The rain still persisted. Drenched to the skin, he walked into the little flat where the parents of his betrothed lived, in Third Street in Vassilyevsky Island. He knocked some time before he was admitted, and his visit at first caused great perturbation; but Svidrigaïlov could be very fascinating when he liked, so that the first, and indeed very intelligent surmise of the sensible parents that Svidrigaïlov had probably had so much to drink that he did not know what he was doing vanished immediately. The decrepit father was wheeled in to see Svidrigaïlov by the tender and sensible mother, who as usual began the conversation with various irrelevant questions. She never asked a direct question, but began by smiling and rubbing her hands and then, if she were obliged to ascertain something—for instance, when Svidrigaïlov would like to have the wedding—she would begin by interested and almost eager questions about Paris and the court life there, and only by degrees brought the conversation round to Third Street. On other occasions this had of course been very impressive, but this time Arkady Ivanovitch seemed particularly impatient, and insisted on seeing his betrothed at once, though he had been informed to begin with that she had already gone to bed. The girl of course appeared.

Svidrigaïlov informed her at once that he was obliged by very important affairs to leave Petersburg for a time, and therefore brought her fifteen thousand roubles and begged her accept them as a present from him, as he had long been intending to make her this trifling present before their wedding. The logical connection of the present with his immediate departure and the absolute necessity of visiting them for that purpose in pouring rain at midnight was not made clear. But it all went off very well; even the inevitable ejaculations of wonder and regret, the inevitable questions were extraordinarily few and restrained. On the other hand, the gratitude expressed was most glowing and was reinforced by tears from the most sensible of mothers. Svidrigaïlov got up, laughed, kissed his betrothed, patted her cheek, declared he would soon come back, and noticing in her eyes, together with childish curiosity, a sort of earnest dumb inquiry, reflected and kissed her again, though he felt sincere anger inwardly at the thought that his present would be immediately locked up in the keeping of the most sensible of mothers. He went away, leaving them all in a state of extraordinary excitement, but the tender mamma, speaking quietly in a half whisper, settled some of the most important of their doubts, concluding that Svidrigaïlov was a great man, a man of great affairs and connections and of great wealth—there was no knowing what he had in his mind. He would start off on a journey and give away money just as the fancy took him, so that there was nothing surprising about it. Of course it was strange that he was wet through, but Englishmen, for instance, are even more eccentric, and all these people of high society didn't think of what was said of them and didn't stand on ceremony. Possibly, indeed, he came like that on purpose to show that he was not afraid of any one. Above all, not a word should be said about it, for God knows what might come of it, and the money must be locked up, and it was most fortunate that Fedosya, the cook, had not left the kitchen. And above all not a word must be said to that old cat, Madame Resslich, and so on and so on. They sat up whispering till two o'clock, but the girl went to bed much earlier, amazed and rather sorrowful.

Svidrigaïlov meanwhile, exactly at midnight, crossed the bridge on the way back to the mainland. The rain had ceased and there was a roaring wind. He began shivering, and for one moment he gazed at the black waters of the Little Neva with a look of special interest, even inquiry. But he soon felt it very cold, standing by the water; he turned and went towards Y. Prospect. He walked along that endless street for a long time, almost half an hour, more than once stumbling in the dark on the wooden pavement, but continually looking for something on the right side of the street. He had noticed passing through this street lately that there was a hotel somewhere towards the end, built of wood, but fairly large, and its name he remembered was something like Adrianople. He was not mistaken: the hotel was so conspicuous in that God-forsaken place that he could not fail to see it even in the dark. It was a long, blackened wooden building, and in spite of the late hour there were lights in the windows and signs of life within. He went in and asked a ragged fellow who met him in the corridor for a room. The latter, scanning Svidrigaïlov, pulled himself together and led him at once to a close and tiny room in the distance, at the end of the corridor, under the stairs. There was no other, all were occupied. The ragged fellow looked inquiringly.

"Is there tea?" asked Svidrigaïlov.

"Yes, sir."

"What else is there?"

"Veal, vodka, savouries."

"Bring me tea and veal."

"And you want nothing else?" he asked with apparent surprise.

"Nothing, nothing."

The ragged man went away, completely disillusioned.

"It must be a nice place," thought Svidrigaïlov. "How was it I didn't know it? I expect I look as if I came from a café chantant and have had some adventure on the way. It would be interesting to know who stayed here."

He lighted the candle and looked at the room more carefully. It was a room so low-pitched that Svidrigaïlov could only just stand up in it; it had one window; the bed, which was very dirty, and the plain stained chair and table almost filled it up. The walls looked as though they were made of planks, covered with shabby paper, so torn and dusty that the pattern was indistinguishable, though the general colour—yellow—could still be made out. One of the walls was cut short by the sloping ceiling, though the room was not an attic, but just under the stairs.

Svidrigaïlov set down the candle, sat down on the bed and sank into thought. But a strange persistent murmur which sometimes rose to a shout in the next room attracted his attention. The murmur had not ceased from the moment he entered the room. He listened: some one was upbraiding and almost tearfully scolding, but he heard only one voice.

Svidrigaïlov got up, shaded the light with his hand and at once he saw light through a crack in the wall; he went up and peeped through. The room, which was somewhat larger than his, had two occupants. One of them, a very curly-headed man with a red inflamed face, was standing in the pose of an orator, without his coat, with his legs wide apart to preserve his balance, and smiting himself on the breast. He reproached the other with being a beggar, with having no standing whatever. He declared that he had taken the other out of the gutter and he could turn him out when he liked, and that only the finger of Providence sees it all. The object of his reproaches was sitting in a chair, and had the air of a man who wants dreadfully to sneeze, but can't. He sometimes turned sheepish and befogged eyes on the speaker, but obviously had not the slightest idea what he was talking about and scarcely heard it. A candle was burning down on the table; there were wine glasses, a nearly empty bottle of vodka, bread and cucumber, and glasses with the dregs of stale tea. After gazing attentively at this, Svidrigaïlov turned away indifferently and sat down on the bed.

The ragged attendant, returning with the tea, could not resist asking him again whether he didn't want anything more, and again receiving a negative reply, finally withdrew. Svidrigaïlov made haste to drink a glass of tea to warm himself, but could not eat anything. He began to feel feverish. He took off his coat and, wrapping himself in the blanket, lay down on the bed. He was annoyed. "It would have been better to be well for the occasion," he thought with a smile. The room was close, the candle burnt dimly, the wind was roaring outside, he heard a mouse scratching in the corner and the room smelt of mice and of leather. He lay in a sort of reverie: one thought followed another. He felt a longing to fix his imagination on something. "It must be a garden under the window," he thought. "There's a sound of trees. How I dislike the sound of trees on a stormy night, in the dark! They give one a horrid feeling." He remembered how he had disliked it when he passed Petrovsky Park just now. This reminded him of the bridge over the Little Neva and he felt cold again as he had when standing there. "I never have liked water," he thought, "even in a landscape," and he suddenly smiled again at a strange idea: "Surely now all these questions of taste and comfort ought not to matter, but I've become more particular, like an animal that picks out a special place . . . for such an occasion. I ought to have gone into the Petrovsky Park! I suppose it seemed dark, cold, ha-ha! As though I were seeking pleasant sensations! . . . By the way, why haven't I put out the candle?" he blew it out. "They've gone to bed next door," he thought, not seeing the light at the crack. "Well, now, Marfa Petrovna, now is the time for you to turn up; it's dark, and the very time and place for you. But now you won't come!"

He suddenly recalled how, an hour before carrying out his design on Dounia, he had recommended Raskolnikov to trust her to Razumihin's keeping. "I suppose I really did say it, as Raskolnikov guessed, to tease myself. But what a rogue that Raskolnikov is! He's gone through a good deal. He may be a successful rogue in time when he's got over his nonsense. But now he's *too* eager for life. These young men are contemptible on that point. But, hang the fellow! Let him please himself, it's nothing to do with me."

He could not get to sleep. By degrees Dounia's image rose before him, and a shudder ran over him. "No, I must give up all that now," he thought, rousing himself. "I must think of something else. It's queer and funny. I never had a great hatred for any one, I never particularly desired to revenge myself even, and that's a bad sign, a bad sign, a bad sign. I never liked quarrelling either, and never lost my temper—that's a bad sign too. And the promises I made her just now, too—Damnation! But—who knows?—perhaps she would have made a new man of me somehow. . . ."

He ground his teeth and sank into silence again. Again Dounia's image rose before him, just as she was when, after shooting the first time, she had lowered the revolver in terror and gazed blankly at him, so that he might have seized her twice over and she would not have lifted a hand to defend herself if he had not reminded her. He recalled how at that instant he felt almost sorry for her, how he had felt a pang at his heart . . .

"Aïe! Damnation, these thoughts again! I must put it away!"

He was dozing off; the feverish shiver had ceased, when suddenly something seemed to run over his arm and leg under the bedclothes. He started. "Ugh! hang it! I believe it's a mouse," he thought, "that's the veal I left on the table." He felt fearfully disinclined to pull off the blanket, get up, get cold, but all at once something unpleasant ran over his leg again. He pulled off the blanket and lighted the candle. Shaking with feverish chill he bent down to examine the bed: there was nothing. He shook the blanket and suddenly a mouse jumped out on the sheet. He tried to catch it, but the mouse ran to and fro in zigzags without leaving the bed, slipped between his fingers, ran over his hand and suddenly darted under the pillow. He threw down the pillow, but in one instant felt something leap on his chest and dart over his body and down his back under his shirt. He trembled nervously and woke up.

The room was dark. He was lying on the bed and wrapped up in the blanket as before. The wind was howling under the window. "How disgusting," he thought with annoyance.

He got up and sat on the edge of the bedstead with his back to the window. "It's better not to sleep at all," he decided. There was a cold damp draught from the window, however; without getting up he drew the blanket over him and wrapped himself in it. He was not thinking of anything and did not want to think. But one image rose after another, incoherent scraps of thought without beginning or end passed through his mind. He sank into drowsiness. Perhaps the cold, or the dampness, or the dark, or the wind that howled under the window and tossed the trees roused a sort of persistent craving for the fantastic. He kept dwelling on images of flowers, he fancied a charming flower garden, a bright, warm, almost hot day, a holiday—Trinity day. A fine, sumptuous country cottage in the English taste overgrown with fragrant flowers, with flower beds going round the house; the porch, wreathed in climbers, was surrounded with beds of roses. A light, cool staircase, carpeted with rich rugs, was decorated with rare plants in china pots. He noticed particularly in the windows nosegays of tender, white, heavily fragrant narcissus bending over their bright, green, thick long stalks. He was reluctant to move away from them, but he went up the stairs and came into a large, high drawing-room and again everywhere—at the windows, the doors on to the balcony, and on the balcony itself—were flowers. The floors were strewn with freshly-cut fragrant hay, the windows were open, a fresh, cool, light air came into the room. The birds were chirruping under the window, and in the middle of the room, on a table covered with a white satin shroud, stood a coffin. The coffin was covered with white silk and edged with a thick white frill; wreaths of flowers surrounded it on all sides. Among the flowers lay a girl in a white muslin dress, with her arms crossed and pressed on her bosom, as though carved out of marble. But her loose fair hair was wet; there was a wreath of roses on her head. The stern and already rigid profile of her face looked as though chiselled of marble too, and the smile on her pale lips was full of an immense unchildish misery and sorrowful appeal. Svidrigaïlov knew that girl; there was no holy image, no burning candle beside the coffin; no sound of prayers: the girl had drowned herself. She was only fourteen, but her heart was broken. And she had destroyed herself, crushed by an insult that had appalled and amazed that childish soul, had smirched that angel purity with unmerited disgrace and torn from her a last scream of despair, unheeded and brutally disregarded, on a dark night in the cold and wet while the wind howled. . . .

Svidrigaïlov came to himself, got up from the bed and went to the window. He felt for the latch and opened it. The wind lashed furiously into the little room and stung his face and his chest, only covered with his shirt, as though with frost. Under the window there must have been something like a garden, and apparently a pleasure garden. There, too, probably there were tea tables and singing in the daytime. Now drops of rain flew in at the window from the trees and bushes; it was dark as in a cellar, so that he could only just make out some dark blurs of objects. Svidrigaïlov, bending down with elbows on the window-sill, gazed for five minutes into the darkness; the boom of a cannon, followed by a second one, resounded in the darkness of the night. "Ah, the signal! The river is overflowing," he thought. "By morning it will be swirling down the street in the lower parts, flooding the basements and cellars. The cellar rats will swim out, and men will curse in the rain and wind as they drag their rubbish to their upper storeys. What time is it now?" And he had hardly thought it when, somewhere near, a clock on the wall, ticking away hurriedly, struck three.

"Aha! It will be light in an hour! Why wait? I'll go out at once straight to the park. I'll choose a great bush there drenched with rain, so that as soon as one's shoulder touches it, millions of drops drip on one's head."

He moved away from the window, shut it, lighted the candle, put on his waistcoat, his overcoat and his hat and went out, carrying the candle, into the passage to look for the ragged attendant who would be asleep somewhere in the midst of candle ends and all sorts of rubbish, to pay him for the room and leave the hotel. "It's the best minute; I couldn't chose a better."

He walked for some time through a long narrow corridor without finding any one and was just going to call out, when suddenly in a dark corner between an old cupboard and the door he caught sight of a strange object which seemed to be alive. He bent down with the candle and saw a little girl, not more than five years old, shivering and crying, with her clothes as wet as a soaking house-flannel. She did not seem afraid of Svidrigaïlov, but looked at him with blank amazement out of her big black eyes. Now and then she sobbed as children do when they have been crying a long time, but are beginning to be comforted. The child's face was pale and tired, she was numb with cold. "How can she have come here? She must have hidden here and not slept all night." He began questioning her. The child suddenly becoming animated, chattered away in her baby language, something about "mammy" and that "mammy would beat her," and about some cup that she had "bwoken." The child chattered on without stopping. He could only guess from what she said that she was a neglected child, whose mother, probably a drunken cook, in the service of the hotel, whipped and frightened her; that the child had broken a cup of her mother's and was so frightened that she had run away the evening before, had hidden for a long while somewhere outside in the rain, at last had made her way in here, hidden behind the cupboard and spent the night there, crying and trembling from the damp, the darkness and the fear that she would be badly beaten for it. He took her in his arms, went back to his room, sat her on the bed, and began undressing her. The torn shoes which she had on her stockingless feet were as wet as if they had been standing in a puddle all night. When he had undressed her, he put her on the bed, covered her up and wrapped her in the blanket from her head downwards. She fell asleep at once. Then he sank into dreary musing again.

"What folly to trouble myself," he decided suddenly with an oppressive feeling of annoyance. "What idiocy!" In vexation he took up the candle to go and look for the ragged attendant again and make haste to go away. "Damn the child!" he thought as he opened the door, but he turned again to see whether the child was asleep. He raised the blanket carefully. The child was sleeping soundly, she had got warm under the blanket, and her pale cheeks were flushed. But strange to say that flush seemed brighter and coarser than the rosy cheeks of childhood. "It's a flush of fever," thought Svidrigaïlov. It was like the flush from drinking, as though she had been given a full glass to drink. Her crimson lips were hot and glowing; but what was this? He suddenly fancied that her long black eyelashes were quivering, as though the lids were opening and a sly crafty eye peeped out with an unchildlike wink, as though the little girl were not asleep, but pretending. Yes, it was so. Her lips parted in a smile. The corners of her mouth quivered, as though she were trying to control them. But now she quite gave up all effort, now it was a grin, a broad grin; there was something shameless, provocative in that quite unchildish face; it was depravity, it was the face of a harlot, the shameless face of a French harlot. Now both eyes opened wide; they turned a glowing, shameless glance upon him; they laughed, invited him. . . . There was something infinitely hideous and shocking in that laugh, in those eyes, in such nastiness in the face of a child. "What, at five years old?" Svidrigaïlov muttered in genuine horror. "What does it mean?" And now she turned to him, her little face all aglow, holding out her arms. . . . "Accursed child!" Svidrigaïlov cried, raising his hand to strike her, but at that moment he woke up.

He was in the same bed, still wrapped in the blanket. The candle had not been lighted, and daylight was streaming in at the windows.

"I've had nightmares all night!" He got up angrily, feeling utterly shattered; his bones ached. There was a thick mist outside and he could see nothing. It was nearly five. He had overslept himself! He got up, put on his still damp jacket and overcoat. Feeling the revolver in his pocket, he took it out and then he sat down, took a notebook out of his pocket and in the most conspicuous place on the title page wrote a few lines in large letters. Reading them over, he sank into thought with his elbows on the table. The revolver and the notebook lay beside him. Some flies woke up and settled on the untouched veal, which was still on the table. He stared at them and at last with his free right hand began trying to catch one. He tried till he was tired, but could not catch it. At last, realising that he was engaged in this interesting pursuit, he started, got up and walked resolutely out of the room. A minute later he was in the street.

A thick milky mist hung over the town. Svidrigaïlov walked along the slippery dirty wooden pavement towards the Little Neva. He was picturing the waters of the Little Neva swollen in the night, Petrovsky Island, the wet paths, the wet grass, the wet trees and bushes and at last the bush. . . . He began ill-humouredly staring at the houses, trying to think of something else. There was not a cabman or a passer-by in the street. The bright yellow, wooden, little houses looked dirty and dejected with their closed shutters. The cold and damp penetrated his whole body and he began to shiver. From time to time he came across shop signs and read each carefully. At last he reached the end of the wooden pavement and came to a big stone house. A dirty, shivering dog crossed his path with its tail between its legs. A man in a great coat lay face downwards; dead drunk, across the pavement. He looked at him and went on. A high tower stood up on the left. "Bah!" he shouted, "here is a place. Why should it be Petrovsky? It will be in the presence of an official witness anyway. . . ."

He almost smiled at this new thought and turned into the street where there was the big house with the tower. At the great closed gates of the house, a little man stood with his shoulder leaning against them, wrapped in a grey soldier's coat, with a copper Achilles helmet on his head. He cast a drowsy and indifferent glance at Svidrigaïlov. His face wore that perpetual look of peevish dejection, which is so sourly printed on all faces of Jewish race without exception. They both, Svidrigaïlov and Achilles, stared at each other for a few minutes without speaking. At last it struck Achilles as irregular for a man not drunk to be standing three steps from him, staring and not saying a word.

"What do you want here?" he said, without moving or changing his position.

"Nothing, brother, good morning," answered Svidrigaïlov.

"This isn't the place."

"I am going to foreign parts, brother."

"To foreign parts?"

"To America."

"America?"

Svidrigaïlov took out the revolver and cocked it. Achilles raised his eyebrows.

"I say, this is not the place for such jokes!"

"Why shouldn't it be the place?"

"Because it isn't."

"Well, brother, I don't mind that. It's a good place. When you are asked, you just say he was going, he said, to America."

He put the revolver to his right temple.

"You can't do it here, it's not the place," cried Achilles, rousing himself, his eyes growing bigger and bigger.

Svidrigaïlov pulled the trigger.

7

The same day, about seven o'clock in the evening, Raskolnikov was on his way to his mother's and sister's lodging—the lodging in Bakaleyev's house which Razumihin had found for them. The stairs went up from the street. Raskolnikov walked with lagging steps, as though still hesitating whether to go or not. But nothing would have turned him back: his decision was taken.

"Besides, it doesn't matter, they still know nothing," he thought, "and they are used to thinking of me as eccentric."

He was appallingly dressed: his clothes torn and dirty, soaked with a night's rain. His face was almost distorted from fatigue, exposure, the inward conflict that had lasted for twenty-four hours. He had spent all the previous night alone, God knows where. But anyway he had reached a decision.

He knocked at the door which was opened by his mother. Dounia was not at home. Even the servant happened to be out. At first Pulcheria Alexandrovna was speechless with joy and surprise; then she took him by the hand and drew him into the room.

"Here you are!" she began, faltering with joy. "Don't be angry with me, Rodya, for welcoming you so foolishly with tears: I am laughing, not crying. Did you think I was crying? No, I am delighted, but I've got into such a stupid habit of shedding tears. I've been like that ever since your father's death. I cry for anything. Sit down, dear boy, you must be tired; I see you are. Ah, how muddy you are."

"I was in the rain yesterday, mother. . . ." Raskolnikov began.

"No, no," Pulcheria Alexandrovna hurriedly interrupted, "you thought I was going to cross-question you in the womanish way I used to; don't be anxious, I understand, I understand it all: now I've learned the ways here and truly I see for myself that they are better. I've made up my mind once for all: how could I understand your plans and expect you to give an account of them? God knows what concerns and plans you may have, or what ideas you are hatching; so it's not for me to keep nudging your elbow, asking you what you are thinking about. But, my goodness! why am I running to and fro as though I were crazy . . . ? I am reading your article in the magazine for the third time, Rodya. Dmitri Prokofitch brought it to me. Directly I saw it I cried out to myself, there, foolish one, I thought, that's what he is busy about; that's the solution of the mystery! Learned people are always like that. He may have some new ideas in his head just now; he is thinking them over and I worry him and upset him. I read it, my dear, and of course there was a great deal I did not understand; but that's only natural—how should I?"

"Show me, mother."

Raskolnikov took the magazine and glanced at his article. Incongruous as it was with his mood and his circumstances, he felt that strange and bitter sweet sensation that every author experiences the first time he sees himself in print; besides, he was only twenty-three. It lasted only a moment. After reading a few lines he frowned and his heart throbbed with anguish. He recalled all the inward conflict of the preceding months. He flung the article on the table with disgust and anger.

"But, however foolish I may be, Rodya, I can see for myself

that you will very soon be one of the leading—if not the leading man—in the world of Russian thought. And they dared to think you were mad! You don't know, but they really thought that. Ah, the despicable creatures, how could they understand genius! And Dounia, Dounia was all but believing it—what do you say to that! Your father sent twice to magazines—the first time poems (I've got the manuscript and will show you) and the second time a whole novel (I begged him to let me copy it out) and how we prayed that they should be taken—they weren't! I was breaking my heart, Rodya, six or seven days ago over your food and your clothes and the way you are living. But now I see again how foolish I was, for you can attain any position you like by your intellect and talent. No doubt you don't care about that for the present and you are occupied with much more important matters. . . ."

"Dounia's not at home, mother?"

"No, Rodya. I often don't see her; she leaves me alone. Dmitri Prokofitch comes to see me, it's so good of him, and he always talks about you. He loves and respects you, my dear. I don't say that Dounia is very wanting in consideration. I am not complaining. She has her ways and I have mine; she seems to have got some secrets of late and I never have any secrets from you two. Of course, I am sure that Dounia has far too much sense, and besides she loves you and me . . . but I don't know what it will all lead to. You've made me so happy by coming now, Rodya, but she has missed you by going out; when she comes in I'll tell her: your brother came in while you were out. Where have you been all this time? You mustn't spoil me, Rodya, you know; come when you can, but if you can't, it doesn't matter, I can wait. I shall know, anyway, that you are fond of me, that will be enough for me. I shall read what you write, I shall hear about you from every one, and sometimes you'll come yourself to see me. What could be better? Here you've come now to comfort your mother, I see that."

Here Pulcheria Alexandrovna began to cry.

"Here I am again! Don't mind my foolishness. My goodness, why am I sitting here?" she cried, jumping up. "There is coffee and I don't offer you any. Ah, that's the selfishness of old age. I'll get it at once!"

"Mother, don't trouble, I am going at once. I haven't come for that. Please listen to me."

Pulcheria Alexandrovna went up to him timidly.

"Mother, whatever happens, whatever you hear about me, whatever you are told about me, will you always love me as you do now?" he asked suddenly from the fulness of his heart, as though not thinking of his words and not weighing them.

"Rodya, Rodya, what is the matter? How can you ask me such a question? Why, who will tell me anything about you? Besides, I shouldn't believe any one, I should refuse to listen."

"I've come to assure you that I've always loved you and I am glad that we are alone, even glad Dounia is out," he went on with the same impulse. "I have come to tell you that though you will be unhappy, you must believe that your son loves you now more than himself, and that all you thought about me, that I was cruel and didn't care about you, was all a mistake. I shall never cease to love you. . . . Well, that's enough: I thought I must do this and begin with this. . . ."

Pulcheria Alexandrovna embraced him in silence, pressing him to her bosom and weeping gently.

"I don't know what is wrong with you, Rodya," she said at last. "I've been thinking all this time that we were simply boring you and now I see that there is a great sorrow in store for you, and that's why you are miserable. I've foreseen it a long time, Rodya. Forgive me for speaking about it. I keep thinking about it and lie awake at nights. Your sister lay talking in her sleep all last night, talking of nothing but you. I caught something, but I couldn't make it out. I felt all the morning as though I were going to be hanged, waiting for something, expecting something, and now it has come! Rodya, Rodya, where are you going? You are going away somewhere?"

"Yes."

"That's what I thought! I can come with you, you know, if you need me. And Dounia, too; she loves you, she loves you dearly—and Sofya Semyonovna may come with us if you like.

You see, I am glad to look upon her as a daughter even. . . . Dmitri Prokofitch will help us to go together. But . . . where . . . are you going?"

"Good-bye, mother."

"What, to-day?" she cried, as though losing him for ever.

"I can't stay, I must go now. . . ."

"And can't I come with you?"

"No, but kneel down and pray to God for me. Your prayer perhaps will reach Him."

"Let me bless you and sign you with the cross. That's right, that's right. Oh, God, what are we doing?"

Yes, he was glad, he was very glad that there was no one there, that he was alone with his mother. For the first time after all those awful months his heart was softened. He fell down before her, he kissed her feet and both wept, embracing. And she was not surprised and did not question him this time. For some days she had realised that something awful was happening to her son and that now some terrible minute had come for him.

"Rodya, my darling, my first born," she said sobbing, "now you are just as when you were little. You would run like this to me and hug me and kiss me. When your father was living and we were poor, you comforted us simply by being with us and when I buried your father, how often we wept together at his grave and embraced, as now. And if I've been crying lately, it's that my mother's heart had a foreboding of trouble. The first time I saw you, that evening you remember, as soon as we arrived here, I guessed simply from your eyes. My heart sank at once, and to-day when I opened the door and looked at you, I thought the fatal hour had come. Rodya, Rodya, you are not going away to-day?"

"No!"

"You'll come again?"

"Yes . . . I'll come."

"Rodya, don't be angry, I don't dare to question you. I know I mustn't. Only say two words to me—is it far where you are going?"

"Very far."

"What is awaiting you there? Some post or career for you?"

"What God sends . . . only pray for me." Raskolnikov went to the door, but she clutched him and gazed despairingly into his eyes. Her face worked with terror.

"Enough, mother," said Raskolnikov, deeply regretting that he had come.

"Not for ever, it's not yet for ever? You'll come, you'll come to-morrow?"

"I will, I will, good-bye." He tore himself away at last.

It was a warm, fresh, bright evening; it had cleared up in the morning. Raskolnikov went to his lodgings; he made haste. He wanted to finish all before sunset. He did not want to meet any one till then. Going up the stairs he noticed that Nastasya rushed from the samovar to watch him intently. "Can any one have come to see me?" he wondered. He had a disgusted vision of Porfiry. But opening his door he saw Dounia. She was sitting alone, plunged in deep thought, and looked as though she had been waiting a long time. He stopped short in the doorway. She rose from the sofa in dismay and stood up facing him. Her eyes fixed upon him, betrayed horror and infinite grief. And from those eyes alone he saw at once that she knew.

"Am I to come in or go away?" he asked uncertainly.

"I've been all day with Sofya Semyonovna. We were both waiting for you. We thought that you would be sure to come there."

Raskolnikov went into the room and sank exhausted on a chair.

"I feel weak, Dounia, I am very tired; and I should have liked at this moment to be able to control myself."

He glanced at her mistrustfully.

"Where were you all night?"

"I don't remember clearly. You see, sister, I wanted to make up my mind once for all, and several times I walked by the Neva, I remember that I wanted to end it all there, but . . . I couldn't make up my mind," he whispered, looking at her mistrustfully again.

"Thank God! That was just what we were afraid of, Sofya

Semyonovna and I. Then you still have faith in life? Thank God, thank God!"

Raskolnikov smiled bitterly.

"I haven't faith, but I have just been weeping in mother's arms; I haven't faith, but I have just asked her to pray for me. I don't know how it is, Dounia, I don't understand it."

"Have you been at mother's? Have you told her?" cried Dounia, horror-stricken. "Surely you haven't done that?"

"No, I didn't tell her . . . in words; but she understood a great deal. She heard you talking in your sleep. I am sure she half understands it already. Perhaps I did wrong in going to see her. I don't know why I did go. I am a contemptible person, Dounia."

"A contemptible person, but ready to face suffering! You are, aren't you?"

"Yes, I am going. At once. Yes, to escape the disgrace I thought of drowning myself, Dounia, but as I looked into the water, I thought that if I had considered myself strong till now I'd better not be afraid of disgrace," he said, hurrying on. "It's pride, Dounia."

"Pride, Rodya."

There was a gleam of fire in his lustreless eyes; he seemed to be glad to think that he was still proud.

"You don't think, sister, that I was simply afraid of the water?" he asked, looking into her face with a sinister smile.

"Oh, Rodya, hush!" cried Dounia bitterly. Silence lasted for two minutes. He sat with his eyes fixed on the floor; Dounia stood at the other end of the table and looked at him with anguish. Suddenly he got up.

"You doubted it?"

"It's late, it's time to go! I am going at once to give myself up. But I don't know why I am going to give myself up."

Big tears fell down her cheeks.

"You are crying, sister, but can you hold out your hand to me?"

"You doubted it?"

She threw her arms round him.

"Aren't you half expiating your crime by facing the suffering!" she cried, holding him close and kissing him.

"Crime? What crime?" he cried in sudden fury. "That I killed a vile noxious insect, an old pawnbroker woman, of use to no one! . . . Killing her was atonement for forty sins. She was sucking the life out of poor people. Was that a crime? I am not thinking of it and I am not thinking of expiating it, and why are you all rubbing it in on all sides? 'A crime! a crime!' Only now I see clearly the imbecility of my cowardice, now that I have decided to face this superfluous disgrace. It's simply because I am contemptible and have nothing in me that I have decided to, perhaps too for my advantage, as that . . . Porfiry . . . suggested!"

"Brother, brother, what are you saying! Why, you have shed blood!" cried Dounia in despair.

"Which all men shed," he put in almost frantically, "which flows and has always flowed in streams, which is spilt like champagne, and for which men are crowned in the Capitol and are called afterwards benefactors of mankind. Look into it more carefully and understand it! I too wanted to do good to men and would have done hundreds, thousands of good deeds to make up for that one piece of stupidity, not stupidity even, simply clumsiness, for the idea was by no means so stupid as it seems now that it has failed. . . . (Everything seems stupid when it fails.) By that stupidity I only wanted to put myself into an independent position, to take the first step, to obtain means, and then everything would have been smoothed over by benefits immeasurable in comparison. . . . But I . . . I couldn't carry out even the first step, because I am contemptible, that's what's the matter! And yet I won't look at it as you do. If I had succeeded I should have been crowned with glory, but now I'm trapped."

"But that's not so, not so! Brother, what are you saying?"

"Ah, it's not picturesque, not aesthetically attractive! I fail to understand why bombarding people by regular siege is more honourable. The fear of appearances is the first symptom of impotence. I've never, never recognised this more clearly than now, and I am further than ever from seeing that what I did was a crime. I've never, never been stronger and more convinced than now."

The colour had rushed into his pale exhausted face, but as he uttered his last explanation, he happened to meet Dounia's eyes and he saw such anguish in them that he could not help being checked. He felt that he had any way made these two poor women miserable, that he was any way the cause. . . .

"Dounia darling, if I am guilty forgive me (though I cannot be forgiven if I am guilty). Good-bye! We won't dispute. It's time, high time to go. Don't follow me, I beseech you, I have somewhere else to go. . . . But you go at once and sit with mother. I entreat you to! It's my last request of you. Don't leave her at all; I left her in a state of anxiety, that she is not fit to bear; she will die or go out of her mind. Be with her! Razumihin will be with you. I've been talking to him. . . . Don't cry about me: I'll try to be honest and manly all my life, even if I am a murderer. Perhaps I shall some day make a name. I won't disgrace you, you will see; I'll still show. . . . Now good-bye for the present," he concluded hurriedly, noticing again a strange expression in Dounia's eyes at his last words and promises. "Why are you crying? Don't cry, don't cry: we are not parting for ever! Ah, yes! Wait a minute, I'd forgotten!"

He went to the table, took up a thick dusty book, opened it and took from between the pages a little water-colour portrait on ivory. It was the portrait of his landlady's daughter, who had died of fever, that strange girl who had wanted to be a nun. For a minute he gazed at the delicate expressive face of his betrothed, kissed the portrait and gave it to Dounia.

"I used to talk a great deal about it to her, only to her," he said thoughtfully. "To her heart I confided much of what has since been so hideously realised. Don't be uneasy," he returned to Dounia, "she was as much opposed to it as you, and I am glad that she is gone. The great point is that everything now is going to be different, is going to be broken in two," he cried, suddenly returning to his dejection. "Everything, everything, and am I prepared for it? Do I want it myself? They say it is necessary for me to suffer! What's the object of these senseless sufferings? shall I

know any better what they are for, when I am crushed by hardships and idiocy, and weak as an old man after twenty years' penal
servitude? And what shall I have to live for then? Why am I
consenting to that life now? Oh, I knew I was contemptible when
I stood looking at the Neva at daybreak to-day!"

At last they both went out. It was hard for Dounia, but she
loved him. She walked away, but after going fifty paces she turned
round to look at him again. He was still in sight. At the corner
he too turned and for the last time their eyes met; but noticing
that she was looking at him, he motioned her away with impatience and even vexation, and turned the corner abruptly.

"I am wicked, I see that," he thought to himself, feeling
ashamed a moment later of his angry gesture to Dounia. "But
why are they so fond of me if I don't deserve it? Oh, if only I were
alone and no one loved me and I too had never loved any one!
Nothing of all this would have happened. But I wonder shall I
in those fifteen or twenty years grow so meek that I shall humble
myself before people and whimper at every word that I am a
criminal. Yes, that's it, that's it, that's what they are sending me
there for, that's what they want. Look at them running to and fro
about the streets, every one of them a scoundrel and a criminal
at heart and, worse still, an idiot. But try to get me off and they'd
be wild with righteous indignation: Oh, how I hate them all!"

He fell to musing by what process it could come to pass, that
he could be humbled before all of them, indiscriminately—humbled by conviction. And yet why not? It must be so. Would not
twenty years of continual bondage crush him utterly? Water
wears out a stone. And why, why should he live after that? Why
should he go now when he knew that it would be so? It was the
hundredth time perhaps that he had asked himself that question
since the previous evening, but still he went.

8

When he went into Sonia's room, it was already getting dark.
All day Sonia had been waiting for him in terrible anxiety.

Dounia had been waiting with her. She had come to her that morning, remembering Svidrigaïlov's words that Sonia knew. We will not describe the conversation and tears of the two girls, and how friendly they became. Dounia gained one comfort at least from that interview, that her brother would not be alone. He had gone to her, Sonia, first with his confession; he had gone to her for human fellowship when he needed it; she would go with him wherever fate might send him. Dounia did not ask, but she knew it was so. She looked at Sonia almost with reverence and at first almost embarrassed her by it. Sonia was almost on the point of tears. She felt herself, on the contrary, hardly worthy to look at Dounia. Dounia's gracious image when she had bowed to her so attentively and respectfully at their first meeting in Raskolnikov's room had remained in her mind as one of the fairest visions of her life.

Dounia at last became impatient and, leaving Sonia, went to her brother's room to await him there; she kept thinking that he would come there first. When she had gone, Sonia began to be tortured by the dread of his committing suicide, and Dounia too feared it. But they had spent the day trying to persuade each other that that could not be, and both were less anxious while they were together. As soon as they parted, each thought of nothing else. Sonia remembered how Svidrigaïlov had said to her the day before that Raskolnikov had two alternatives—Siberia or . . . Besides she knew his vanity, his pride and his lack of faith.

"Is it possible that he has nothing but cowardice and fear of death to make him live?" she thought at last in despair.

Meanwhile the sun was setting. Sonia was standing in dejection, looking intently out of the window, but from it she could see nothing but the unwhitewashed blank wall of the next house. At last when she began to feel sure of his death—he walked into the room.

She gave a cry of joy, but looking carefully into his face she turned pale.

"Yes," said Raskolnikov, smiling. "I have come for your cross, Sonia. It was you told me to go to the cross roads; why is it you are frightened now it's come to that?"

Sonia gazed at him astonished. His tone seemed strange to her; a cold shiver ran over her, but in a moment she guessed that the tone and the words were a mask. He spoke to her looking away, as though to avoid meeting her eyes.

"You see, Sonia, I've decided that it will be better so. There is one fact. . . . But it's a long story and there's no need to discuss it. But do you know what angers me? It annoys me that all those stupid brutish faces will be gaping at me directly, pestering me with their stupid questions, which I shall have to answer—they'll point their fingers at me. . . . Tfoo! You know I am not going to Porfiry, I am sick of him. I'd rather go to my friend, the Explosive Lieutenant; how I shall surprise him, what a sensation I shall make! But I must be cooler; I've become too irritable of late. You know I was nearly shaking my fist at my sister just now, because she turned to take a last look at me. It's a brutal state to be in! Ah! what am I coming to! Well, where are the crosses?"

He seemed hardly to know what he was doing. He could not stay still or concentrate his attention on anything; his ideas seemed to gallop after one another, he talked incoherently, his hands trembled slightly.

Without a word Sonia took out of the drawer two crosses, one of cypress wood and one of copper. She made the sign of the cross over herself and over him, and put the wooden cross on his neck.

"It's the symbol of my taking up the cross," he laughed. "As though I had not suffered much till now! The wooden cross, that is the peasant one; the copper one, that is Lizaveta's—you will wear yourself, show me! So she had it on . . . at that moment? I remember two things like these too, a silver one and a little ikon. I threw them back on the old woman's neck. Those would be appropriate now, really, those are what I ought to put on now. . . . But I am talking nonsense and forgetting what matters; I'm somehow forgetful. . . . You see I have come to warn you, Sonia, so that you might know . . . that's all—that's all I came for. But I thought I had more to say. You wanted me to go yourself. Well, now I am going to prison and you'll have your wish. Well, what

are you crying for? You too? Don't. Leave off! Oh, how I hate
it all!"

But his feeling was stirred; his heart ached, as he looked at
her. "Why is she grieving too?" he thought to himself. "What am
I to her? Why does she weep? Why is she looking after me, like
my mother or Dounia? She'll be my nurse."

"Cross yourself, say at least one prayer," Sonia begged in a
timid broken voice.

"Oh certainly, as much as you like! And sincerely, Sonia,
sincerely. . . ."

But he wanted to say something quite different.

He crossed himself several times. Sonia took up her shawl
and put it over her head. It was the green *drap de dames* shawl
of which Marmeladov had spoken, "the family shawl." Raskolnikov thought of that looking at it, but he did not ask. He began
to feel himself that he was certainly forgetting things and was
disgustingly agitated. He was frightened at this. He was suddenly
struck too by the thought that Sonia meant to go with him.

"What are you doing? Where are you going? Stay here, stay!
I'll go alone," he cried in cowardly vexation, and almost resent-
ful, he moved towards the door. "What's the use of going in
procession!" he muttered going out.

Sonia remained standing in the middle of the room. He had
not even said good-bye to her; he had forgotten her. A poignant
and rebellious doubt surged in his heart.

"Was it right, was it right, all this?" he thought again as he
went down the stairs. "Couldn't he stop and retract it all
. . . and not go?"

But still he went. He felt suddenly once for all that he
mustn't ask himself questions. As he turned into the street he
remembered that he had not said good-bye to Sonia, that he had
left her in the middle of the room in her green shawl, not daring
to stir after he had shouted at her, and he stopped short for a
moment. At the same instant, another thought dawned upon him,
as though it had been lying in wait to strike him then.

"Why, with what object did I go to her just now? I told
her—on business; on what business? I had no sort of business! To

tell her I was *going;* but where was the need? Do I love her? No, no, I drove her away just now like a dog. Did I want her crosses? Oh, how low I've sunk! No, I wanted her tears, I wanted to see her terror, to see how her heart ached! I had to have something to cling to, something to delay me, some friendly face to see! And I dared to believe in myself, to dream of what I would do! I am a beggarly contemptible wretch, contemptible!''

He walked along the canal bank, and he had not much further to go. But on reaching the bridge he stopped and turning out of his way along it went to the Hay Market.

He looked eagerly to right and left, gazed intently at every object and could not fix his attention on anything; everything slipped away. "In another week, another month I shall be driven in a prison van over this bridge, how shall I look at the canal then? I should like to remember this!" slipped into his mind. "Look at this sign! How shall I read those letters then? It's written here 'Campany,' that's a thing to remember, that letter *a,* and to look at it again in a month—how shall I look at it then? What shall I be feeling and thinking then? . . . How trivial it all must be, what I am fretting about now! Of course it must all be interesting . . . in its way . . . (Ha-ha-ha! What am I thinking about?) I am becoming a baby, I am showing off to myself; why am I ashamed? Foo, how people shove! that fat man—a German he must be— who pushed against me, does he know whom he pushed? There's a peasant woman with a baby, begging. It's curious that she thinks me happier than she is. I might give her something, for the incongruity of it. Here's a five copeck piece left in my pocket, where did I get it? Here, here . . . take it, my good woman!"

"God bless you," the beggar chanted in a lachrymose voice.

He went into the Hay Market. It was distasteful, very distasteful to be in a crowd, but he walked just where he saw most people. He would have given anything in the world to be alone; but he knew himself that he would not have remained alone for a moment. There was a man drunk and disorderly in the crowd; he kept trying to dance and falling down. There was a ring round him. Raskolnikov squeezed his way through the crowd, stared for some minutes at the drunken man and suddenly gave a short jerky laugh. A minute later he had forgotten him and did not see him, though he still stared. He moved away at last, not remembering where he was; but when he got into the middle of the square an emotion suddenly came over him, overwhelming him body and mind.

He suddenly recalled Sonia's words, "Go to the cross roads, bow down to the people, kiss the earth, for you have sinned against it too, and say aloud to the whole world, 'I am a murderer.'" He trembled, remembering that. And the hopeless misery and anxiety of all that time, especially of the last hours, had weighed so heavily upon him that he positively clutched at the chance of this new unmixed, complete sensation. It came over him like a fit; it was like a single spark kindled in his soul and spreading fire through him. Everything in him softened at once and the tears started into his eyes. He fell to the earth on the spot.
. . .

He knelt down in the middle of the square, bowed down to the earth, and kissed that filthy earth with bliss and rapture. He got up and bowed down a second time.

"He's boozed," a youth near him observed.

There was a roar of laughter.

"He's going to Jerusalem, brothers, and saying good-bye to his children and his country. He's bowing down to all the world and kissing the great city of St. Petersburg and its pavement," added a workman who was a little drunk.

"Quite a young man, too!" observed a third.

"And a gentleman," some one observed soberly.

"There's no knowing who's a gentleman and who isn't nowadays."

These exclamations and remarks checked Raskolnikov, and the words, "I am a murderer," which were perhaps on the point of dropping from his lips, died away. He bore these remarks quietly, however, and without looking round, he turned down a street leading to the police office. He had a glimpse of something on the way which did not surprise him; he had felt that it must be so. The second time he bowed down in the Hay Market, he saw standing fifty paces from him on the left Sonia. She was hiding from him behind one of the wooden shanties in the market-place. She had followed him then on his painful way! Raskolnikov at that moment felt and knew once for all that Sonia was with him for ever and would follow him to the ends of the earth, wherever fate might take him. It wrung his heart . . . but he was just reaching the fatal place.

He went into the yard fairly resolutely. He had to mount to the third storey. "I shall be some time going up," he thought. He felt as though the fateful moment was still far off, as though he had plenty of time left for consideration.

Again the same rubbish, the same eggshells lying about on the spiral stairs, again the open doors of the flats, again the same kitchens and the same fumes and stench coming from them. Raskolnikov had not been here since that day. His legs were numb and gave way under him, but still they moved forward. He stopped for a moment to take breath, to collect himself, so as to enter *like a man.* "But why? what for?" he wondered, reflecting. "If I must drink the cup what difference does it make? The more revolting the better." He imagined for an instant the figure of the "explosive lieutenant," Ilya Petrovitch. Was he actually going to him? Couldn't he go to some one else? To Nikodim Fomitch? Couldn't he turn back and go straight to Nikodim Fomitch's lodgings? At least then it would be done privately. . . . No, no! To the "explosive lieutenant"! If he must drink it, drink it off at once.

Turning cold and hardly conscious, he opened the door of the office. There were very few people in it this time—only a house porter and a peasant. The doorkeeper did not even peep out from behind his screen. Raskolnikov walked into the next room. "Perhaps I still need not speak," passed through his mind. Some sort of clerk not wearing a uniform was settling himself at a bureau to write. In a corner another clerk was seating himself. Zametov was not there, nor, of course, Nikodim Fomitch.

"No one in?" Raskolnikov asked, addressing the person at the bureau.

"Whom do you want?"

"A-ah! Not a sound was heard, not a sight was seen, but I

scent the Russian . . . how does it go on in the fairy tale
. . . I've forgotten! At your service!" a familiar voice cried suddenly.

Raskolnikov shuddered. The Explosive Lieutenant stood
before him. He had just come in from the third room. "It is the
hand of fate," thought Raskolnikov. "Why is he here?"

"You've come to see us? What about?" cried Ilya Petrovitch.
He was obviously in an exceedingly good humour and perhaps
a trifle exhilarated. "If it's on business you are rather early.* It's
only a chance that I am here . . . however I'll do what I can. I must
admit, I . . . what is it, what is it? Excuse me. . . ."

"Raskolnikov."

"Of course, Raskolnikov. You didn't imagine I'd forgotten?
Don't think I am like that . . . Rodion Ro——Ro——Ro-
dionovitch, that's it, isn't it?"

"Rodion Romanovitch."

"Yes, yes, of course, Rodion Romanovitch! I was just getting
at it. I made many inquiries about you. I assure you I've been
genuinely grieved since that . . . since I behaved like that
. . . it was explained to me afterwards that you were a literary man
. . . and a learned one too . . . and so to say the first steps
. . . Mercy on us! What literary or scientific man does not begin
by some originality of conduct! My wife and I have the greatest
respect for literature, in my wife it's a genuine passion! Literature
and art! If only a man is a gentleman, all the rest can be gained
by talents, learning, good sense, genius. As for a hat—well, what
does a hat matter? I can buy a hat as easily as I can a bun; but
what's under the hat, what the hat covers, I can't buy that! I was
even meaning to come and apologise to you, but thought maybe
you'd . . . But I am forgetting to ask you, is there anything you
want really? I hear your family have come?"

"Yes, my mother and sister."

"I've even had the honour and happiness of meeting your
sister—a highly cultivated and charming person. I confess I was

* Dostoyevsky appears to have forgotten that it is after sunset, and that the last time Raskolnikov visited the
police office at two in the afternoon, he was reproached for coming too late.

sorry I got so hot with you. There it is! But as for my looking suspiciously at your fainting fit,—that affair has been cleared up splendidly! Bigotry and fanaticism! I understand your indignation. Perhaps you are changing your lodging on account of your family's arriving?"

"No, I only looked in . . . I came to ask . . . I thought that I should find Zametov here."

"Oh, yes! Of course, you've made friends, I heard. Well, no, Zametov is not here. Yes, we've lost Zametov. He's not been here since yesterday . . . he quarrelled with every one on leaving . . . in the rudest way. He is a feather-headed youngster, that's all; one might have expected something from him, but there, you know what they are, our brilliant young men. He wanted to go in for some examination, but it's only to talk and boast about it, it will go no further than that. Of course it's a very different matter with you or Mr. Razumihin there, your friend. Your career is an intellectual one and you won't be deterred by failure. For you, one may say, all the attractions of life *nihil est*—you are an ascetic, a monk, a hermit! . . . A book, a pen behind your ear, a learned research—that's where your spirit soars! I am the same way myself. . . . Have you read Livingstone's Travels?"

"No."

"Oh, I have. There are a great many Nihilists about nowadays, you know, and indeed it is not to be wondered at. What sort of days are they? I ask you. But we thought . . . you are not a Nihilist of course? Answer me openly, openly!"

"N-no. . . ."

"Believe me, you can speak openly to me as you would to yourself! Official duty is one thing but . . . you are thinking I meant to say *friendship* is quite another? No, you're wrong! It's not friendship, but the feeling of a man and a citizen, the feeling of humanity and of love for the Almighty. I may be an official, but I am always bound to feel myself a man and a citizen. . . . You were asking about Zametov. Zametov will make a scandal in the French style in a house of bad reputation, over a glass of champagne . . . that's all your Zametov is good for! While I'm perhaps, so to speak, burning with devotion and lofty feelings, and besides

I have rank, consequence, a post! I am married and have children, I fulfil the duties of a man and a citizen, but who is he, may I ask? I appeal to you as a man ennobled by education . . . Then these midwives, too, have become extraordinarily numerous."

Raskolnikov raised his eyebrows inquiringly. The words of Ilya Petrovitch, who had obviously been dining, were for the most part a stream of empty sounds for him. But some of them he understood. He looked at him inquiringly, not knowing how it would end.

"I mean those crop-headed wenches," the talkative Ilya Petrovitch continued. "Midwives is my name for them. I think it a very satisfactory one, ha-ha! They go to the Academy, study anatomy. If I fall ill, am I to send for a young lady to treat me? What do you say? Ha-ha!" Ilya Petrovitch laughed, quite pleased with his own wit. "It's an immoderate zeal for education, but once you're educated, that's enough. Why abuse it? Why insult honourable people, as that scoundrel Zametov does? Why did he insult me, I ask you? Look at these suicides, too, how common they are, you can't fancy! People spend their last halfpenny and kill themselves, boys and girls and old people. Only this morning we heard about a gentleman who had just come to town. Nil Pavlitch, I say, what was the name of that gentleman who shot himself?"

"Svidrigaïlov," some one answered from the other room with drowsy listlessness.

Raskolnikov started.

"Svidrigaïlov! Svidrigaïlov has shot himself!" he cried.

"What, do you know Svidrigaïlov?"

"Yes . . . I knew him. . . . He hadn't been here long."

"Yes, that's so. He had lost his wife, was a man of reckless habits and all of a sudden shot himself, and in such a shocking way. . . . He left in his notebook a few words; that he dies in full possession of his faculties and that no one is to blame for his death. He had money, they say. How did you come to know him?"

"I . . . was acquainted . . . my sister was governess in his family."

"Bah-bah-bah! Then no doubt you can tell us something about him. You had no suspicion?"

"I saw him yesterday . . . he . . . was drinking wine; I knew nothing."

Raskolnikov felt as though something had fallen on him and was stifling him.

"You've turned pale again. It's so stuffy here. . . ."

"Yes, I must go," muttered Raskolnikov. "Excuse my troubling you. . . ."

"Oh, not at all, as often as you like. It's a pleasure to see you and I am glad to say so."

Ilya Petrovitch held out his hand.

"I only wanted . . . I came to see Zametov."

"I understand, I understand, and it's a pleasure to see you."

"I . . . am very glad . . . good-bye," Raskolnikov smiled.

He went out; he reeled, he was overtaken with giddiness and did not know what he was doing. He began going down the stairs, supporting himself with his right hand against the wall. He fancied that a porter pushed past him on his way upstairs to the police office, that a dog in the lower storey kept up a shrill barking and that a woman flung a rolling-pin at it and shouted. He went down and out into the yard. There, not far from the entrance, stood Sonia, pale and horror-stricken. She looked wildly at him. He stood still before her. There was a look of poignant agony, of despair, in her face. She clasped her hands. His lips worked in an ugly, meaningless smile. He stood still a minute, grinned and went back to the police office.

Ilya Petrovitch had sat down and was rummaging among some papers. Before him stood the same peasant who had pushed by on the stairs.

"Hulloa! Back again! have you left something behind? What's the matter?"

Raskolnikov, with white lips and staring eyes, came slowly nearer. He walked right to the table, leaned his hand on it, tried to say something, but could not; only incoherent sounds were audible.

"You are feeling ill, a chair! Here, sit down! Some water!"

Raskolnikov dropped on to a chair, but he kept his eyes fixed on the face of Ilya Petrovitch which expressed unpleasant surprise. Both looked at one another for a minute and waited. Water was brought.

"It was I . . ." began Raskolnikov.

"Drink some water."

Raskolnikov refused the water with his hand, and softly and brokenly, but distinctly said:

"It was I killed the old pawnbroker woman and her sister Lizaveta with an axe and robbed them."

Ilya Petrovitch opened his mouth. People ran up on all sides. Raskolnikov repeated his statement.

EPILOGUE—

1

Siberia. On the banks of a broad solitary river stands a town, one of the administrative centres of Russia; in the town there is a fortress, in the fortress there is a prison. In the prison the second-class convict Rodion Raskolnikov has been confined for nine months. Almost a year and a half has passed since his crime.

There had been little difficulty about his trial. The criminal adhered exactly, firmly, and clearly to his statement. He did not confuse nor misrepresent the facts, nor soften them in his own interest, nor omit the smallest detail. He explained every incident of the murder, the secret of *the pledge* (the piece of wood with a strip of metal) which was found in the murdered woman's hand. He described minutely how he had taken her keys, what they were like, as well as the chest and its contents; he explained the mystery of Lizaveta's murder; described how Koch and, after him, the student knocked, and repeated all they had said to one another; how he afterwards had run downstairs and heard Nikolay and Dmitri shouting; how he had hidden in the empty flat and afterwards gone home. He ended by indicating the stone in the yard off the Voznesensky Prospect under which the purse and the trinkets were found. The whole thing, in fact, was perfectly clear.

The lawyers and the judges were very much struck, among other things, by the fact that he had hidden the trinkets and the purse under a stone, without making use of them, and that, what was more, he did not now remember what the trinkets were like, or even how many there were. The fact that he had never opened the purse and did not even know how much was in it seemed incredible. There turned out to be in the purse three hundred and seventeen roubles and sixty copecks. From being so long under the stone, some of the most valuable notes lying uppermost had suffered from the damp. They were a long while trying to discover why the accused man should tell a lie about this, when about everything else he had made a truthful and straightforward confession. Finally some of the lawyers more versed in psychology admitted that it was possible he had really not looked into the purse, and so didn't know what was in it when he hid it under the stone. But they immediately drew the deduction that the crime could only have been committed through temporary mental derangement, through homicidal mania, without object or the pursuit of gain. This fell in with the most recent fashionable theory of temporary insanity, so often applied in our days in criminal cases. Moreover Raskolnikov's hypochondriacal condition was proved by many witnesses, by Dr. Zossimov, his former fellow students, his landlady and her servant. All this pointed strongly to the conclusion that Raskolnikov was not quite like an ordinary murderer and robber, but that there was another element in the case.

To the intense annoyance of those who maintained this opinion, the criminal scarcely attempted to defend himself. To the decisive question as to what motive impelled him to the murder and the robbery, he answered very clearly with the coarsest frankness that the cause was his miserable position, his poverty and helplessness, and his desire to provide for his first steps in life by the help of the three thousand roubles he had reckoned on finding. He had been led to the murder through his shallow and cowardly nature, exasperated moreover by privation and failure. To the question what led him to confess, he answered that it was his heartfelt repentance. All this was almost coarse. . . .

The sentence however was more merciful than could have been expected, perhaps partly because the criminal had not tried to justify himself, but had rather shown a desire to exaggerate his guilt. All the strange and peculiar circumstances of the crime were taken into consideration. There could be no doubt of the abnormal and poverty-stricken condition of the criminal at the time. The fact that he had made no use of what he had stolen was put down partly to the effect of remorse, partly to his abnormal mental condition at the time of the crime. Incidentally the murder of Lizaveta served indeed to confirm the last hypothesis: a man commits two murders and forgets that the door is open! Finally, the confession, at the very moment when the case was hopelessly muddled by the false evidence given by Nikolay through melancholy and fanaticism, and when, moreover, there were no proofs against the real criminal, no suspicions even (Porfiry Petrovitch fully kept his word)—all this did much to soften the sentence. Other circumstances, too, in the prisoner's favour came out quite unexpectedly. Razumihin somehow discovered and proved that while Raskolnikov was at the university he had helped a poor consumptive fellow student and had spent his last penny on supporting him for six months, and when this student died, leaving a decrepit old father whom he had maintained almost from his thirteenth year, Raskolnikov had got the old man into a hospital and paid for his funeral when he died. Raskolnikov's landlady bore witness, too, that when they had lived in another house at Five Corners, Raskolnikov had rescued two little children from a house on fire and was burnt in doing so. This was investigated and fairly well confirmed by many witnesses. These facts made an impression in his favour.

And in the end the criminal was in consideration of extenuating circumstances condemned to penal servitude in the second class for a term of eight years only.

At the very beginning of the trial Raskolnikov's mother fell ill. Dounia and Razumihin found it possible to get her out of Petersburg during the trial. Razumihin chose a town on the railway not far from Petersburg, so as to be able to follow every step of the trial and at the same time to see Avdotya Romanovna as

often as possible. Pulcheria Alexandrovna's illness was a strange
nervous one and was accompanied by a partial derangement of
her intellect.

When Dounia returned from her last interview with her
brother, she had found her mother already ill, in feverish delirium. That evening Razumihin and she agreed what answers they
must make to her mother's questions about Raskolnikov and
made up a complete story for her mother's benefit of his having
to go away to a distant part of Russia on a business commission,
which would bring him in the end money and reputation.

But they were struck by the fact that Pulcheria Alexandrovna
never asked them anything on the subject, neither then nor thereafter. On the contrary, she had her own version of her son's
sudden departure; she told them with tears how he had come to
say good-bye to her, hinting that she alone knew many mysterious
and important facts, and that Rodya had many very powerful
enemies, so that it was necessary for him to be in hiding. As for
his future career, she had no doubt that it would be brilliant when
certain sinister influences could be removed. She assured Razumihin that her son would be one day a great statesman, that his
article and brilliant literary talent proved it. This article she was
continually reading, she even read it aloud, almost took it to bed
with her, but scarcely asked where Rodya was, though the subject
was obviously avoided by the others, which might have been
enough to awaken her suspicions.

They began to be frightened at last at Pulcheria Alexandrovna's strange silence on certain subjects. She did not, for instance,
complain of getting no letters from him, though in previous years
she had only lived on the hope of letters from her beloved Rodya.
This was the cause of great uneasiness to Dounia; the idea occurred to her that her mother suspected that there was something
terrible in her son's fate and was afraid to ask, for fear of hearing
something still more awful. In any case, Dounia saw clearly that
her mother was not in full possession of her faculties.

It happened once or twice, however, that Pulcheria Alexandrovna gave such a turn to the conversation that it was impossible
to answer her without mentioning where Rodya was, and on

receiving unsatisfactory and suspicious answers she became at once gloomy and silent, and this mood lasted for a long time. Dounia saw at last that it was hard to deceive her and came to the conclusion that it was better to be absolutely silent on certain points; but it became more and more evident that the poor mother suspected something terrible. Dounia remembered her brother's telling her that her mother had overheard her talking in her sleep on the night after her interview with Svidrigaïlov and before the fatal day of the confession: had not she made out something from that? Sometimes days and even weeks of gloomy silence and tears would be succeeded by a period of hysterical animation, and the invalid would begin to talk almost incessantly of her son, of her hopes of his future. . . . Her fancies were sometimes very strange. They humoured her, pretended to agree with her (she saw perhaps that they were pretending), but she still went on talking.

Five months after Raskolnikov's confession, he was sentenced. Razumihin and Sonia saw him in prison as often as it was possible. At last the moment of separation came. Dounia swore to her brother that the separation should not be for ever, Razumihin did the same. Razumihin, in his youthful ardour, had firmly resolved to lay the foundations at least of a secure livelihood during the next three or four years, and saving up a certain sum, to emigrate to Siberia, a country rich in every natural resource and in need of workers, active men and capital. There they would settle in the town where Rodya was and all together would begin a new life. They all wept at parting.

Raskolnikov had been very dreamy for a few days before. He asked a great deal about his mother and was constantly anxious about her. He worried so much about her that it alarmed Dounia. When he heard about his mother's illness he became very gloomy. With Sonia he was particularly reserved all the time. With the help of the money left to her by Svidrigaïlov, Sonia had long ago made her preparations to follow the party of convicts in which he was despatched to Siberia. Not a word passed between Raskolnikov and her on the subject, but both knew it would be so. At the final leave-taking he smiled strangely at his sister's and

Razumihin's fervent anticipations of their happy future together when he should come out of prison. He predicted that their mother's illness would soon have a fatal ending. Sonia and he at last set off.

Two months later Dounia was married to Razumihin. It was a quiet and sorrowful wedding; Porfiry Petrovitch and Zossimov were invited however. During all this period Razumihin wore an air of resolute determination. Dounia put implicit faith in his carrying out his plans and indeed she could not but believe in him. He displayed a rare strength of will. Among other things he began attending university lectures again in order to take his degree. They were continually making plans for the future; both counted on settling in Siberia within five years at least. Till then they rested their hopes on Sonia.

Pulcheria Alexandrovna was delighted to give her blessing to Dounia's marriage with Razumihin; but after the marriage she became even more melancholy and anxious. To give her pleasure Razumihin told her how Raskolnikov had looked after the poor student and his decrepit father and how a year ago he had been burnt and injured in rescuing two little children from a fire. These two pieces of news excited Pulcheria Alexandrovna's disordered imagination almost to ecstasy. She was continually talking about them, even entering into conversation with strangers in the street, though Dounia always accompanied her. In public conveyances and shops, wherever she could capture a listener, she would begin the discourse about her son, his article, how he had helped the student, how he had been burnt at the fire, and so on! Dounia did not know how to restrain her. Apart from the danger of her morbid excitement, there was the risk of some one's recalling Raskolnikov's name and speaking of the recent trial. Pulcheria Alexandrovna found out the address of the mother of the two children her son had saved and insisted on going to see her.

At last her restlessness reached an extreme point. She would sometimes begin to cry suddenly and was often ill and feverishly delirious. One morning she declared that by her reckoning Rodya ought soon to be home, that she remembered when he said good-bye to her he said that they must expect him back in nine months. She began to prepare for his coming, began to do up her room for him, to clean the furniture, to wash and put up new hangings and so on. Dounia was anxious, but said nothing and helped her to arrange the room. After a fatiguing day spent in continual fancies, in joyful day dreams and tears, Pulcheria Alexandrovna was taken ill in the night and by morning she was feverish and delirious. It was brain fever. She died within a fortnight. In her delirium she dropped words which showed that she knew a great deal more about her son's terrible fate than they had supposed.

For a long time Raskolnikov did not know of his mother's death, though a regular correspondence had been maintained from the time he reached Siberia. It was carried on by means of Sonia, who wrote every month to the Razumihins and received an answer with unfailing regularity. At first they found Sonia's letters dry and unsatisfactory, but later on they came to the conclusion that the letters could not be better, for from these letters they received a complete picture of their unfortunate brother's life. Sonia's letters were full of the most matter of fact detail, the simplest and clearest description of all Raskolnikov's surroundings as a convict. There was no word of her own hopes, no conjecture as to the future, no description of her feelings. Instead of any attempt to interpret his state of mind and inner life, she gave the simple facts—that is, his own words, an exact account of his health, what he asked for at their interviews, what commission he gave her and so on. All these facts she gave with extraordinary minuteness. The picture of their unhappy brother stood out at last with great clearness and precision. There could be no mistake, because nothing was given but facts.

But Dounia and her husband could get little comfort out of the news, especially at first. Sonia wrote that he was constantly sullen and not ready to talk, that he scarcely seemed interested in the news she gave him from their letters, that he sometimes asked after his mother and that when, seeing that he had guessed the truth, she told him at last of her death, she was surprised to find that he did not seem greatly affected by it, not externally at any rate. She told them that, although he seemed so wrapped up in himself and, as it were, shut himself off from every one—he took a very direct and simple view of his new life; that he understood his position, expected nothing better for the time, had no ill-founded hopes (as is so common in his position) and scarcely seemed surprised at anything in his surroundings, so unlike anything he had known before. She wrote that his health was satisfactory; he did his work without shirking or seeking to do more; he was almost indifferent about food, but except on Sundays and holidays the food was so bad that at last he had been glad to accept some money from her, Sonia, to have his own tea every day. He begged her not to trouble about anything else, declaring that all this fuss about him only annoyed him. Sonia wrote further that in prison he shared the same room with the rest, that she had not seen the inside of their barracks, but concluded that they were crowded, miserable and unhealthy; that he slept on a plank bed with a rug under him and was unwilling to make any other arrangement. But that he lived so poorly and roughly, not from any plan or design, but simply from inattention and indifference.

Sonia wrote simply that he had at first shown no interest in her visits, had almost been vexed with her indeed for coming, unwilling to talk and rude to her. But that in the end these visits had become a habit and almost a necessity for him, so that he was positively distressed when she was ill for some days and could not visit him. She used to see him on holidays at the prison gates or in the guard-room, to which he was brought for a few minutes to see her. On working days she would go to see him at work either at the workshops or at the brick kilns, or at the sheds on the banks of the Irtish.

About herself, Sonia wrote that she had succeeded in making some acquaintances in the town, that she did sewing and, as there was scarcely a dressmaker in the town, she was looked upon as an indispensable person in many houses. But she did not mention that the authorities were, through her, interested in Raskolnikov; that his task was lightened and so on.

At last the news came (Dounia had indeed noticed signs of alarm and uneasiness in the preceding letters) that he held aloof from every one, that his fellow prisoners did not like him, that he kept silent for days at a time and was becoming very pale. In the last letter Sonia wrote that he had been taken very seriously ill and was in the convict ward of the hospital.

2

He was ill a long time. But it was not the horrors of prison life, not the hard labour, the bad food, the shaven head, or the patched clothes that crushed him. What did he care for all those trials and hardships! he was even glad of the hard work. Physically exhausted, he could at least reckon on a few hours of quiet sleep. And what was the food to him—the thin cabbage soup with beetles floating in it? In the past as a student he had often not had even that. His clothes were warm and suited to his manner of life. He did not even feel the fetters. Was he ashamed of his shaven head and parti-coloured coat? Before whom? Before Sonia? Sonia was afraid of him, how could he be ashamed before her? And yet he was ashamed even before Sonia, whom he tortured because of it with his contemptuous rough manner. But it was not his shaven head and his fetters he was ashamed of: his pride had been stung to the quick. It was wounded pride that made him ill. Oh, how happy he would have been if he could have blamed himself! He could have borne anything then, even shame and disgrace. But he judged himself severely, and his exasperated conscience found no particularly terrible fault in his past, except a simple *blunder* which might happen to any one. He was ashamed just because he, Raskolnikov, had so hopelessly, stupidly come to grief through some decree of blind fate, and must humble himself and submit to "the idiocy" of a sentence, if he were anyhow to be at peace.

Vague and objectless anxiety in the present, and in the future a continual sacrifice leading to nothing—that was all that lay before him. And what comfort was it to him that at the end of eight years he would only be thirty-two and able to begin a new life! What had he to live for? What had he to look forward to? Why should he strive? To live in order to exist? Why, he had been ready a thousand times before to give up existence for the sake of an idea, for a hope, even for a fancy. Mere existence had always been too little for him; he had always wanted more. Perhaps it was just because of the strength of his desires that he had thought himself a man to whom more was permissible than to others.

And if only fate would have sent him repentance—burning repentance that would have torn his heart and robbed him of sleep, that repentance, the awful agony of which brings visions of hanging or drowning! Oh, he would have been glad of it! Tears and agonies would at least have been life. But he did not repent of his crime.

At least he might have found relief in raging at his stupidity, as he had raged at the grotesque blunders that had brought him to prison. But now in prison, *in freedom,* he thought over and criticised all his actions again and by no means found them so blundering and so grotesque as they had seemed at the fatal time.

"In what way," he asked himself, "was my theory stupider than others that have swarmed and clashed from the beginning of the world? One has only to look at the thing quite independently, broadly, and uninfluenced by commonplace ideas, and my idea will by no means seem so . . . strange. Oh, sceptics and halfpenny philosophers, why do you halt half-way!"

"Why does my action strike them as so horrible?" he said to himself. "Is it because it was a crime? What is meant by crime? My conscience is at rest. Of course, it was a legal crime, of course, the letter of the law was broken and blood was shed. Well, punish me for the letter of the law . . . and that's enough. Of course, in that case many of the benefactors of mankind who snatched power for themselves instead of inheriting it ought to have been punished at their first steps. But those men succeeded and so *they were right,* and I didn't, and so I had no right to have taken that step."

It was only in that that he recognised his criminality, only in the fact that he had been unsuccessful and had confessed it.

He suffered too from the question: why had he not killed himself? Why had he stood looking at the river and preferred to confess? Was the desire to live so strong and was it so hard to overcome it? Had not Svidrigaïlov overcome it, although he was afraid of death?

In misery he asked himself this question, and could not understand that, at the very time he had been standing looking into the river, he had perhaps been dimly conscious of the fundamental falsity in himself and his convictions. He didn't understand that that consciousness might be the promise of a future crisis, of a new view of life and of his future resurrection.

He preferred to attribute it to the dead weight of instinct which he could not step over, again through weakness and meanness. He looked at his fellow prisoners and was amazed to see how they all loved life and prized it. It seemed to him that they loved and valued life more in prison than in freedom. What terrible agonies and privations some of them, the tramps for instance, had endured! Could they care so much for a ray of sunshine, for the primeval forest, the cold spring hidden away in some unseen spot, which the tramp had marked three years before, and longed to see again, as he might to see his sweetheart, dreaming of the green grass round it and the bird singing in the bush? As he went on he saw still more inexplicable examples.

In prison, of course, there was a great deal he did not see and did not want to see; he lived as it were with downcast eyes. It was loathsome and unbearable for him to look. But in the end there was much that surprised him and he began, as it were involuntarily, to notice much that he had not suspected before. What surprised him most of all was the terrible impossible gulf that lay between him and all the rest. They seemed to be a different species, and he looked at them and they at him with distrust and hostility. He felt and knew the reasons of his isolation, but he would never had admitted till then that those reasons were so deep and strong. There were some Polish exiles, political prisoners, among them. They simply looked down upon all the rest as ignorant churls; but Raskolnikov could not look upon them like that. He saw that these ignorant men were in many respects far wiser than the Poles. There were some Russians who were just as contemptuous, a former officer and two seminarists. Raskolnikov saw their mistake as clearly. He was disliked and avoided by every one; they even began to hate him at last,—why, he could not tell. Men who had been far more guilty despised and laughed at his crime.

"You're a gentleman," they used to say. "You shouldn't hack about with an axe; that's not a gentleman's work."

The second week in Lent, his turn came to take the sacrament with his gang. He went to church and prayed with the others. A quarrel broke out one day, he did not know how. All fell on him at once in a fury.

"You're an infidel! You don't believe in God," they shouted. "You ought to be killed."

He had never talked to them about God nor his belief, but they wanted to kill him as an infidel. He said nothing. One of the prisoners rushed at him in a perfect frenzy. Raskolnikov awaited him calmly and silently; his eyebrows did not quiver, his face did not flinch. The guard succeeded in intervening between him and his assailant, or there would have been bloodshed.

There was another question he could not decide: why were they all so fond of Sonia? She did not try to win their favour; she rarely met them, sometimes only she came to see him at work for a moment. And yet everybody knew her, they knew that she had come out to follow *him,* knew how and where she lived. She never gave them money, did them no particular services. Only once at Christmas she sent them all presents of pies and rolls. But by degrees closer relations sprang up between them and Sonia. She would write and post letters for them to their relations. Relations of the prisoners who visited the town, at their instructions, left with Sonia presents and money for them. Their wives and sweethearts knew her and used to visit her. And when she visited Raskolnikov at work, or met a party of the prisoners on the road, they all took off their hats to her. "Little mother Sofya Semyonovna, you are our dear, good little mother," coarse branded criminals said to that frail little creature. She would smile and bow to them and every one was delighted when she smiled. They even admired her gait and turned round to watch her walking; they admired her too for being so little, and, in fact, did not know what to admire her most for. They even came to her for help in their illnesses.

He was in the hospital from the middle of Lent till after Easter. When he was better, he remembered the dreams he had had while he was feverish and delirious. He dreamt that the whole world was condemned to a terrible new strange plague that had come to Europe from the depths of Asia. All were to be destroyed except a very few chosen. Some new sorts of microbes were attacking the bodies of men, but these microbes were endowed with intelligence and will. Men attacked by them became at once mad and furious. But never had men considered themselves so intellectual and so completely in possession of the truth as these sufferers, never had they considered their decisions, their scientific conclusions, their moral convictions so infallible. Whole villages, whole towns and peoples went mad from the infection. All were excited and did not understand one another. Each thought that he alone had the truth and was wretched looking at the others, beat himself on the breast, wept, and wrung his hands. They did not know how to judge and could not agree what to consider evil and what good; they did not know whom to blame, whom to justify. Men killed each other in a sort of senseless spite. They gathered together in armies against one another, but even on the march the armies would begin attacking each other, the ranks would be broken and the soldiers would fall on each other, stabbing and cutting, biting and devouring each other. The alarm bell was ringing all day long in the towns; men rushed together, but why they were summoned and who was summoning them no one knew. The most ordinary trades were abandoned, because every one proposed his own ideas, his own improvements, and they could not agree. The land too was abandoned. Men met in groups, agreed on something, swore to keep together, but at once began on something quite different from what they had proposed. They accused one another, fought and killed each other. There were conflagrations and famine. All men and all things were involved in destruction. The plague spread and moved further and further. Only a few men could be saved in the whole world. They were a pure chosen people, destined to found a new race and a new life, to renew and purify the earth, but no one had seen these men, no one had heard their words and their voices.

Raskolnikov was worried that this senseless dream haunted his memory so miserably, the impression of this feverish delirium persisted so long. The second week after Easter had come. There were warm bright spring days; in the prison ward the grating windows under which the sentinel paced were opened. Sonia had only been able to visit him twice during his illness; each time she had to obtain permission, and it was difficult. But she often used to come to the hospital yard, especially in the evening, sometimes only to stand a minute and look up at the windows of the ward.

One evening, when he was almost well again, Raskolnikov fell asleep. On waking up he chanced to go to the window, and at once saw Sonia in the distance at the hospital gate. She seemed to be waiting for some one. Something stabbed him to the heart at that minute. He shuddered and moved away from the window. Next day Sonia did not come, nor the day after; he noticed that he was expecting her uneasily. At last he was discharged. On reaching the prison he learnt from the convicts that Sofya Semyonovna was lying ill at home and was unable to go out.

He was very uneasy and sent to inquire after her; he soon learnt that her illness was not dangerous. Hearing that he was anxious about her, Sonia sent him a pencilled note, telling him that she was much better, that she had a slight cold and that she would soon, very soon come and see him at his work. His heart throbbed painfully as he read it.

Again it was a warm bright day. Early in the morning, at six o'clock, he went off to work on the river bank, where they used to pound alabaster and where there was a kiln for baking it in a shed. There were only three of them sent. One of the convicts went with the guard to the fortress to fetch a tool; the other began getting the wood ready and laying it in the kiln, Raskolnikov came out of the shed on to the river bank, sat down on a heap of logs by the shed and began gazing at the wide deserted river. From the high bank a broad landscape opened before him, the sound of singing floated faintly audible from the other bank. In the vast steppe, bathed in sunshine, he could just see, like black specks, the nomads' tents. There there was freedom, there other men were living, utterly unlike those here; there time itself seemed to stand still, as though the age of Abraham and his flocks had not passed. Raskolnikov sat gazing, his thoughts passed into day-dreams, into contemplation; he thought of nothing, but a vague restlessness excited and troubled him. Suddenly he found Sonia beside him; she had come up noiselessly and sat down at his side. It was still quite early; the morning chill was still keen. She wore her poor old burnous and the green shawl; her face still showed signs of illness, it was thinner and paler. She gave him a joyful smile of welcome, but held out her hand with her usual timidity. She was always timid of holding out her hand to him and sometimes did not offer it at all, as though afraid he would repel it. He always took her hand as though with repugnance, always seemed vexed to meet her and was sometimes obstinately silent throughout her visit. Sometimes she trembled before him and went away deeply grieved. But now their hands did not part. He stole a rapid glance at her and dropped his eyes on the ground without speaking. They were alone, no one had seen them. The guard had turned away for the time.

How it happened he did not know. But all at once something seemed to seize him and fling him at her feet. He wept and threw his arms round her knees. For the first instant she was terribly frightened and she turned pale. She jumped up and looked at him trembling. But at the same moment she understood, and a light of infinite happiness came into her eyes. She knew and had no doubt that he loved her beyond everything and that at last the moment had come. . . .

They wanted to speak, but could not; tears stood in their eyes. They were both pale and thin; but those sick pale faces were bright with the dawn of a new future, of a full resurrection into a new life. They were renewed by love; the heart of each held infinite sources of life for the heart of the other.

They resolved to wait and be patient. They had another seven years to wait, and what terrible suffering and what infinite happiness before them! But he had risen again and he knew it and felt it in all his being, while she—she only lived in his life.

On the evening of the same day, when the barracks were locked, Raskolnikov lay on his plank bed and thought of her. He had even fancied that day that all the convicts who had been his enemies looked at him differently; he had even entered into talk with them and they answered him in a friendly way. He remembered that now, and thought it was bound to be so. Wasn't everything now bound to be changed?

He thought of her. He remembered how continually he had tormented her and wounded her heart. He remembered her pale and thin little face. But these recollections scarcely troubled him now; he knew with what infinite love he would now repay all her sufferings. And what were all, *all* the agonies of the past! Everything, even his crime, his sentence and imprisonment, seemed to him now in the first rush of feeling an external, strange fact with which he had no concern. But he could not think for long together of anything that evening, and he could not have analysed anything consciously; he was simply feeling. Life had stepped into the place of theory and something quite different would work itself out in his mind.

Under his pillow lay the New Testament. He took it up mechanically. The book belonged to Sonia; it was the one from which she had read the raising of Lazarus to him. At first he was afraid that she would worry him about religion, would talk about the gospel and pester him with books. But to his great surprise she had not once approached the subject and had not even offered him the Testament. He had asked her for it himself not long before his illness and she brought him the book without a word. Till now he had not opened it.

He did not open it now, but one thought passed through his mind: "Can her convictions not be mine now? Her feelings, her aspirations at least. . . ."

She too had been greatly agitated that day, and at night she was taken ill again. But she was so happy—and so unexpectedly happy—that she was almost frightened of her happiness. Seven years, *only* seven years! At the beginning of their happiness at some moments they were both ready to look on those seven years as though they were seven days. He did not know that the new life would not be given him for nothing, that he would have to pay dearly for it, that it would cost him great striving, great suffering.

But that is the beginning of a new story—the story of the gradual renewal of a man, the story of his gradual regeneration, of his passing from one world into another, of his initiation into a new unknown life. That might be the subject of a new story, but our present story is ended.

FATHERS AND SONS

BY

IVAN TURGENEV

THE NAMES OF THE CHARACTERS IN THE BOOK.

NIKOLÁI PETRÓVITCH KIRSÁNOV.
PÁVEL PETRÓVITCH KIRSÁNOV.
ARKÁDY (ARKÁSHA) NIKOLÁ-EVITCH (*or* NIKOLÁ-ITCH).
YEVGÉNY (ÉNYUSHA) VASSÍL-YEVITCH (*or* VASSÍL-YITCH) BAZÁROV.
VASSÍLY IVÁNOVITCH (*or* IVÁNITCH).
ARÍNA VLÁSYEVNA.
FEDÓS-YA (FÉNITCHKA) NIKOLÁ-EVNA.
ÁNNA SÉRG-YEVNA ODÍNTSOV.
KÁTYA SÉRG-YEVNA.
PORFÍRY PLATÓNITCH.
MATVÝ ÍL-YITCH KOLYÁZIN.
EVDÓKS-YA (*or* AVDÓTYA) NIKÍTISHNA KÚKSHIN.
VÍKTOR SÍTNIKOV.
PIOTR (*pron.* P-*yotr*).
PROKÓFITCH.
DUN-YÁSHA.
MÍT-YA.
TIMÓFEITCH.

In transcribing the Russian names into English—

    a has the sound of *a* in *father.*
    e   "   "   *a* in *pane.*
    i "   ,,   *ee.*
    u "   "   *oo.*
    y is always consonantal except when it is the last letter of the
        word.
    g is always hard.

I

"Well, Piotr, not in sight yet?" was the question asked on May the 20th, 1859, by a gentleman of a little over forty, in a dusty coat and checked trousers, who came out without his hat on to the low steps of the posting station at S———. He was addressing his servant, a chubby young fellow, with whitish down on his chin, and little, lack-lustre eyes.

The servant, in whom everything—the turquoise ring in his ear, the streaky hair plastered with grease, and the civility of his movements—indicated a man of the new, improved generation, glanced with an air of indulgence along the road, and made answer:

"No, sir; not in sight."

"Not in sight?" repeated his master.

"No, sir," responded the man a second time.

His master sighed, and sat down on a little bench. We will introduce him to the reader while he sits, his feet tucked under him, gazing thoughtfully round.

His name was Nikolai Petrovitch Kirsanov. He had, twelve miles from the posting station, a fine property of two hundred souls, or, as he expressed it—since he had arranged the division of his land with the peasants, and started "a farm"—of nearly five thousand acres. His father, a general in the army, who served in 1812, a coarse, half-educated, but not ill-natured man, a typical Russian, had been in harness all his life, first in command of a brigade, and then of a division, and lived constantly in the provinces, where, by virtue of his rank, he played a fairly important part. Nikolai Petrovitch was born in the south of Russia like his elder brother, Pavel, of whom more hereafter. He was educated at home till he was fourteen, surrounded by cheap tutors, free-and-easy but toadying adjutants, and all the usual regimental and staff set. His mother, one of the Kolyazin family, as a girl called Agathe, but as a general's wife Agathokleya Kuzminishna Kirsanov, was one of those military ladies who take their full share of the duties and dignities of office. She wore gorgeous caps and rustling silk dresses; in church she was the first to advance to the cross; she talked a great deal in a loud voice, let her children kiss her hand in the morning, and gave them her blessing at night—in fact, she got everything out of life she could. Nikolai Petrovitch, as a general's son—though so far from being distinguished by courage that he even deserved to be called "a funk"—was intended, like his brother Pavel, to enter the army; but he broke his leg on the very day when the news of his commission came, and, after being two months in bed, retained a slight limp to the end of his days. His father gave him up as a bad job, and let him go into the civil service. He took him to Petersburg directly he was eighteen, and placed him in the university. His brother happened about the same time to be made an officer in the Guards. The young men started living together in one set of rooms, under the remote supervision of a cousin on their mother's side, Ilya Kolyazin, an official of high rank. Their father returned to his division and his wife, and only rarely sent his sons large sheets of grey paper, scrawled over in a bold clerkly hand. At the bottom of these sheets stood in letters, enclosed carefully in scroll-work, the words, "Piotr Kirsanov, General-Major." In 1835 Nikolai Petrovitch left the university, a graduate, and in the same year General Kirsanov was put on to the retired list after an unsuccessful review, and came to Petersburg with his wife to live. He was about to take a house in the Tavrichesky Gardens, and had joined the English club, but he died suddenly of an apoplectic fit. Agathokleya Kuzminishna soon followed him; she could not accustom herself to a dull life in the capital; she was consumed by the ennui of existence away from the regiment. Meanwhile Nikolai Petrovitch had already, in his parents' lifetime and to their no slight chagrin, had time to fall in love with the daughter of his landlord, a petty official, Prepolovensky. She was a pretty and, as it is called, "advanced" girl; she used to read the serious articles in the "Science" column of the journals. He married her directly the term of mourning was over; and leaving the civil service in which his father had by favour procured him a post, was perfectly blissful with his Masha, first in a country villa near the Lyesny Institute, afterwards in town in a pretty little flat with a clean staircase and a draughty drawing-room, and then in the country, where he settled finally, and where in a short time a son, Arkady, was born to him. The young couple lived very happily and peacefully; they were scarcely ever apart; they read together, sang and played duets together on the piano; she tended her flowers and looked after the poultry-yard; he sometimes went hunting, and busied himself with the estate, while Arkady grew and grew in the same happy and peaceful way. Ten years passed like a dream. In 1847 Kirsanov's wife died. He almost succumbed to this blow; in a few weeks his hair was grey; he was getting ready to go abroad, if possible to distract his mind . . . but then came the year 1848. He returned unwillingly to the country, and, after a rather prolonged period of inactivity, began to take an interest in improvements in the management of his land. In 1855 he brought his son to the university; he spent three winters with him in Petersburg, hardly going out anywhere, and trying to make acquaintance with Arkady's young companions. The last winter he had not been able to go, and here we have seen him in the May of 1859, already quite grey, stoutish, and rather bent, waiting for his son, who had just taken his degree, as once he had taken it himself.

The servant, from a feeling of propriety, and perhaps, too, not anxious to remain under the master's eye, had gone to the gate, and was smoking a pipe. Nikolai Petrovitch bent his head, and began staring at the crumbling steps; a big mottled fowl walked sedately towards him, treading firmly with its great yellow legs; a muddy cat gave him an unfriendly look, twisting herself coyly round the railing. The sun was scorching; from the half-dark passage of the posting station came an odour of hot rye-bread.

Nikolai Petrovitch fell to dreaming. "My son . . . a graduate
. . . Arkasha . . ." were the ideas that continually came round again
and again in his head; he tried to think of something else, and
again the same thoughts returned. He remembered his dead wife.
. . . "She did not live to see it!" he murmured sadly. A plump,
dark-blue pigeon flew into the road, and hurriedly went to drink
in a puddle near the well. Nikolai Petrovitch began looking at it,
but his ear had already caught the sound of approaching wheels.

"It sounds as if they're coming sir," announced the servant,
popping in from the gateway.

Nikolai Petrovitch jumped up, and bent his eyes on the road.
A carriage appeared with three posting-horses harnessed abreast;
in the carriage he caught a glimpse of the blue band of a student's
cap, the familiar outline of a dear face.

"Arkasha! Arkasha!" cried Kirsanov, and he ran waving his
hands. . . . A few instants later, his lips were pressed to the
beardless, dusty, sunburnt cheek of the youthful graduate.

II

"Let me shake myself first, daddy," said Arkady, in a voice
tired from travelling, but boyish and clear as a bell, as he gaily
responded to his father's caresses; "I am covering you with dust."

"Never mind, never mind," repeated Nikolai Petrovitch,
smiling tenderly, and twice he struck the collar of his son's cloak
and his own greatcoat with his hand. "Let me have a look at you;
let me have a look at you," he added, moving back from him, but
immediately he went with hurried steps towards the yard of the
station, calling, "This way, this way; and horses at once."

Nikolai Petrovitch seemed far more excited than his son; he
seemed a little confused, a little timid. Arkady stopped him.

"Daddy," he said, "let me introduce you to my great friend,
Bazarov, about whom I have so often written to you. He has been
so good as to promise to stay with us."

Nikolai Petrovitch went back quickly, and going up to a tall man in a long, loose, rough coat with tassels, who had only just got out of the carriage, he warmly pressed the ungloved red hand, which the latter did not at once hold out to him.

"I am heartily glad," he began, "and very grateful for your kind intention of visiting us. . . . Let me know your name, and your father's."

"Yevgeny Vassilyev," answered Bazarov, in a lazy but manly voice; and turning back the collar of his rough coat, he showed Nikolai Petrovitch his whole face. It was long and lean, with a broad forehead, a nose flat at the base and sharper at the end, large greenish eyes, and drooping whiskers of a sandy colour; it was lighted up by a tranquil smile, and showed self-confidence and intelligence.

"I hope, dear Yevgeny Vassilyitch, you won't be dull with us," continued Nikolai Petrovitch.

Bazarov's thin lips moved just perceptibly, though he made no reply, but merely took off his cap. His long, thick hair did not hide the prominent bumps on his head.

"Then, Arkady," Nikolai Petrovitch began again, turning to his son, "shall the horses be put to at once? or would you like to rest?"

"We will rest at home, daddy; tell them to harness the horses."

At once, at once," his father assented. "Hey, Piotr, do you hear? Get things ready, my good boy; look sharp."

Piotr, who as a modernised servant had not kissed the young master's hand, but only bowed to him from a distance, again vanished through the gateway.

"I came here with the carriage, but there are three horses for your coach too," said Nikolai Petrovitch fussily, while Arkady drank some water from an iron dipper brought him by the woman in charge of the station, and Bazarov began smoking a pipe and went up to the driver, who was taking out the horses; "there are only two seats in the carriage, and I don't know how your friend" . . .

"He will go in the coach," interposed Arkady in an under-

tone. "You must not stand on ceremony with him, please. He's
a splendid fellow, so simple—you will see."

Nikolai Petrovitch's coachman brought the horses round.

"Come, hurry up, bushy beard!" said Bazarov, addressing
the driver.

"Do you hear, Mityuha," put in another driver, standing by
with his hands thrust behind him into the opening of his sheepskin
coat, "what the gentleman called you? It's a bushy beard you are
too."

Mityuha only gave a jog to his hat and pulled the reins off
the heated shaft-horse.

"Look sharp, look sharp, lads, lend a hand," cried Nikolai
Petrovitch; "there'll be something to drink our health with!"

In a few minutes the horses were harnessed; the father and
son were installed in the carriage; Piotr climbed up on to the box;
Bazarov jumped into the coach, and nestled his head down into
the leather cushion; and both the vehicles rolled away.

III

"So here you are, a graduate at last, and come home again,"
said Nikolai Petrovitch, touching Arkady now on the shoulder,
now on the knee. "At last!"

"And how is uncle? quite well?" asked Arkady who, in spite
of the genuine, almost childish delight filling his heart, wanted as
soon as possible to turn the conversation from the emotional into
a commonplace channel.

"Quite well. He was thinking of coming with me to meet
you, but for some reason or other he gave up the idea."

"And how long have you been waiting for me?" inquired
Arkady.

"Oh, about five hours."

"Dear old dad!"

Arkady turned round quickly to his father, and gave him a

sounding kiss on the cheek. Nikolai Petrovitch gave vent to a low chuckle.

"I have got such a capital horse for you!" he began. "You will see. And your room has been fresh papered."

"And is there a room for Bazarov?

"We will find one for him too."

"Please, dad, make much of him. I can't tell you how I prize his friendship."

"Have you made friends with him lately?"

"Yes, quite lately."

"Ah, that's how it is I did not see him last winter. What does he study?"

"His chief subject is natural science. But he knows everything. Next year he wants to take his doctor's degree."

"Ah! he's in the medical faculty," observed Nikolai Petrovitch, and he was silent for a little. "Piotr," he went on, stretching out his hand, "aren't those our peasants driving along?"

Piotr looked where his master was pointing. Some carts harnessed with unbridled horses were moving rapidly along a narrow by-road. In each cart there were one or two peasants in sheepskin coats, unbuttoned.

"Yes, sir," replied Piotr.

"Where are they going,—to the town?"

"To the town, I suppose. To the gin-shop," he added contemptuously, turning slightly towards the coachman, as though he would appeal to him. But the latter did not stir a muscle; he was a man of the old stamp, and did not share the modern views of the younger generation.

"I have had a lot of bother with the peasants this year," pursued Nikolai Petrovitch, turning to his son. "They won't pay their rent. What is one to do?"

"But do you like your hired labourers?"

"Yes," said Nikolai Petrovitch between his teeth. "They're being set against me, that's the mischief; and they don't do their best. They spoil the tools. But they have tilled the land pretty fairly. When things have settled down a bit, it will be all right. Do you take an interest in farming now?"

"You've no shade; that's a pity," remarked Arkady, without answering the last question.

"I have had a great awning put up on the north side over the balcony," observed Nikolai Petrovitch; "now we can have dinner even in the open air."

"It'll be rather too like a summer villa. . . . Still, that's all nonsense. What air though here! How delicious it smells! Really I fancy there's nowhere such fragrance in the world as in the meadows here! And the sky too."

Arkady suddenly stopped short, cast a stealthy look behind him, and said no more.

"Of course," observed Nikolai Petrovitch, "you were born here, and so everything is bound to strike you in a special ——"

"Come, dad, that makes no difference where a man is born."

"Still——"

"No; it makes absolutely no difference."

Nikolai Petrovitch gave a sidelong glance at his son, and the carriage went on half-a-mile further before the conversation was renewed between them.

"I don't recollect whether I wrote to you," began Nikolai Petrovitch, "your old nurse, Yegorovna, is dead."

"Really? Poor thing! Is Prokofitch still living?"

"Yes, and not a bit changed. As grumbling as ever. In fact, you won't find many changes at Maryino."

"Have you still the same bailiff?"

"Well, to be sure there is a change there. I decided not to keep about me any freed serfs, who have been house servants, or, at least, not to intrust them with duties of any responsibility." (Arkady glanced towards Piotr.) *"Il est libre, en effet,"* observed Nikolai Petrovitch in an undertone; "but, you see, he's only a valet. Now I have a bailiff, a townsman; he seems a practical fellow. I pay him two hundred and fifty roubles a year. But," added Nikolai Petrovitch, rubbing his forehead and eyebrows with his hand, which was always an indication with him of inward embarrassment, "I told you just now that you would not find changes at Maryino. . . . That's not quite correct. I think it my duty to prepare you, though . . ."

He hesitated for an instant, and then went on in French.

"A severe moralist would regard my openness as improper; but, in the first place, it can't be concealed, and secondly, you are aware I have always had peculiar ideas as regards the relation of father and son. Though, of course, you would be right in blaming me. At my age. . . . In short . . . that . . . that girl, about whom you have probably heard already . . ."

"Fenitchka?" asked Arkady easily.

Nikolai Petrovitch blushed. "Don't mention her name aloud, please. . . . Well . . . she is living with me now. I have installed her in the house . . . there were two little rooms there. But that can all be changed."

"Goodness, daddy, what for?"

"Your friend is going to stay with us . . . it would be awkward . . ."

"Please, don't be uneasy on Bazarov's account. He's above all that."

Well, but you too," added Nikolai Petrovitch. "The little lodge is so horrid—that's the worst of it."

"Goodness, dad," interposed Arkady, "it's as if you were apologising; I wonder you're not ashamed."

"Of course, I ought to be ashamed," answered Nikolai Petrovitch, flushing more and more.

"Nonsense, dad, nonsense; please don't!" Arkady smiled affectionately. "What a thing to apologise for!" he thought to himself, and his heart was filled with a feeling of condescending tenderness for his kind, soft-hearted father, mixed with a sense of secret superiority. "Please, stop," he repeated once more, instinctively revelling in a consciousness of his own advanced and emancipated condition.

Nikolai Petrovitch glanced at him from under the fingers of the hand with which he was still rubbing his forehead, and there was a pang in his heart. . . . But at once he blamed himself for it.

"Here are our meadows at last," he said after a long silence.

"And that in front is our forest, isn't it?" asked Arkady.

"Yes. Only I have sold the timber. This year they will cut it down.

"Why did you sell it?"

"The money was needed; besides, that land is to go to the peasants."

"Who don't pay you their rent?"

"That's their affair; besides, they will pay it some day."

"I am sorry about the forest," observed Arkady, and he began to look about him.

The country through which they were driving could not be called picturesque. Fields upon fields stretched all along to the very horizon, now sloping gently upwards, then dropping down again; in some places woods were to be seen, and winding ravines, planted with low, scanty bushes, recalling vividly the representation of them on the old-fashioned maps of the times of Catherine. They came upon little streams too with hollow banks; and tiny lakes with narrow dykes; and little villages, with low hovels under dark and often tumble-down roofs, and slanting barns with walls woven of brushwood and gaping doorways beside neglected threshing-floors; and churches, some brick-built, with stucco peeling off in patches, others wooden, with crosses fallen askew, and overgrown grave-yards. Slowly Arkady's heart sank. To complete the picture, the peasants they met were all in tatters and on the sorriest little nags; the willows, with their trunks stripped of bark, and broken branches, stood like ragged beggars along the roadside; cows lean and shaggy and looking pinched up by hunger, were greedily tearing at the grass along the ditches. They looked as though they had just been snatched out of the murderous clutches of some threatening monster; and the piteous state of the weak, starved beasts in the midst of the lovely spring day, called up, like a white phantom, the endless, comfortless winter with its storms, and frosts, and snows. . . . "No," thought Arkady, "this is not a rich country; it does not impress one by plenty or industry; it can't, it can't go on like this, reforms are absolutely necessary . . . but how is one to carry them out, how is one to begin?"

Such were Arkady's reflections; . . . but even as he reflected, the spring regained its sway. All around was golden green, all—trees, bushes, grass—shone and stirred gently in wide waves under the soft breath of the warm wind; from all sides flooded the endless trilling music of the larks; the peewits were calling as they hovered over the low-lying meadows, or noiselessly ran over the tussocks of grass; the rooks strutted among the half-grown short spring-corn, standing out black against its tender green; they disappeared in the already whitening rye, only from time to time their heads peeped out amid its grey waves. Arkady gazed and gazed, and his reflections grew slowly fainter and passed away. . . . He flung off his cloak and turned to his father, with a face so bright and boyish, that the latter gave him another hug.

"We're not far off now," remarked Nikolai Petrovitch; "we have only to get up this hill, and the house will be in sight. We shall get on together splendidly, Arkasha; you shall help me in farming the estate, if only it isn't a bore to you. We must draw close to one another now, and learn to know each other thoroughly, mustn't we!"

"Of course," said Arkady; "but what an exquisite day it is to-day!"

"To welcome you, my dear boy. Yes, it's spring in its full loveliness. Though I agree with Pushkin—do you remember in *Yevgeny Onyegin*—

> "To me how sad thy coming is,
> Spring, spring, sweet time of love!
> What . . ."

"Arkady!" called Bazarov's voice from the coach, "send me a match; I've nothing to light my pipe with."

Nikolai Petrovitch stopped, while Arkady, who had begun listening to him with some surprise, though with sympathy too, made haste to pull a silver matchbox out of his pocket, and sent it to Bazarov by Piotr.

"Will you have a cigar?" shouted Bazarov again.

"Thanks," answered Arkady.

Piotr returned to the carriage, and handed him with the

match-box a thick black cigar, which Arkady began to smoke promptly, diffusing about him such a strong and pungent odour of cheap tobacco, that Nikolai Petrovitch, who had never been a smoker from his youth up, was forced to turn away his head, as imperceptibly as he could for fear of wounding his son.

A quarter of an hour later, the two carriages drew up before the steps of a new wooden house, painted grey, with a red iron roof. This was Maryino, also known as New-Wick, or, as the peasants had nicknamed it, Poverty Farm.

IV

No crowd of house-serfs ran out on to the steps to meet the gentlemen; a little girl of twelve years old made her appearance alone. After her there came out of the house a young lad, very like Piotr, dressed in a coat of grey livery, with white armorial buttons, the servant of Pavel Petrovitch Kirsanov. Without speaking, he opened the door of the carriage, and unbuttoned the apron of the coach. Nikolai Petrovitch with his son and Bazarov walked through a dark and almost empty hall, from behind the door of which they caught a glimpse of a young woman's face, into a drawing room furnished in the most modern style.

"Here we are at home," said Nikolai Petrovitch, taking off his cap, and shaking back his hair. "That's the great thing; now we must have supper and rest."

"A meal would not come amiss, certainly," observed Bazarov, stretching, and he dropped on to a sofa.

"Yes, yes, let us have supper, supper directly." Nikolai Petrovitch with no apparent reason stamped his foot. "And here just at the right moment comes Prokofitch."

A man about sixty entered, white-haired, thin, and swarthy, in a cinnamon-coloured dress-coat with brass buttons, and a pink neckerchief. He smirked, went up to kiss Arkady's hand, and bowing to the guest retreated to the door, and put his hands behind him.

"Here he is, Prokofitch," began Nikolai Petrovitch; "he's come back to us at last. . . . Well, how do you think him looking?"

"As well as could be," said the old man, and was grinning again, but he quickly knitted his bushy brows. "You wish supper to be served?" he said impressively.

"Yes, yes, please. But won't you like to go to your room first, Yevgeny Vassilyitch?"

"No, thanks; I don't care about it. Only give orders for my little box to be taken there, and this garment, too," he added, taking off his frieze overcoat.

"Certainly. Prokofitch, take the gentleman's coat." (Prokofitch, with an air of perplexity, picked up Bazarov's "garment" in both hands, and holding it high above his head, retreated on tiptoe.) "And you, Arkady, are you going to your room for a minute?"

"Yes, I must wash," answered Arkady, and was just moving towards the door, but at that instant there came into the drawing-room a man of medium height, dressed in a dark English suit, a fashionable low cravat, and kid shoes, Pavel Petrovitch Kirsanov. He looked about forty-five: his close-cropped, grey hair shone with a dark lustre, like new silver; his face, yellow but free from wrinkles, was exceptionally regular and pure in line, as though carved by a light and delicate chisel, and showed traces of remarkable beauty; specially fine were his clear, black, almond-shaped eyes. The whole person of Arkady's uncle, with its aristocratic elegance, had preserved the gracefulness of youth and that air of striving upwards, away from earth, which for the most part is lost after the twenties are past.

Pavel Petrovitch took out of his trouser pocket his exquisite hand with its long tapering pink nails, a hand which seemed still more exquisite from the snowy whiteness of the cuff, buttoned with a single, big opal, and gave it to his nephew. After a preliminary handshake in the European style, he kissed him thrice after the Russian fashion, that is to say, he touched his cheek three times with his perfumed moustaches, and said, "Welcome."

Nikolai Petrovitch presented him to Bazarov; Pavel Petrovitch greeted him with a slight inclination of his supple figure, and a slight smile, but he did not give him his hand, and even put it back into his pocket.

"I had begun to think you were not coming to-day," he began in a musical voice, with a genial swing and shrug of the shoulders, as he showed his splendid white teeth. "Did anything happen on the road?"

"Nothing happened," answered Arkady; "we were rather slow. But we're as hungry as wolves now. Hurry up Prokofitch, dad; and I'll be back directly."

"Stay, I'm coming with you," cried Bazarov pulling himself up suddenly from the sofa. Both the young men went out.

"Who is he?" asked Pavel Petrovitch.

"A friend of Arkasha's; according to him, a very clever fellow."

"Is he going to stay with us?"

"Yes."

"That unkempt creature?"

"Why, yes."

Pavel Petrovitch drummed with his finger tips on the table. "I fancy Arkady *s'est dégourdi,*" he remarked. "I'm glad he has come back."

At supper there was little conversation. Bazarov especially said nothing, but he ate a great deal. Nikolai Petrovitch related various incidents in what he called his career as a farmer, talked about the impending government measures, about committees, deputations, the necessity of introducing machinery, etc. Pavel Petrovitch paced slowly up and down the dining-room (he never ate supper), sometimes sipping at a wineglass of red wine, and less often uttering some remark or rather exclamation, of the nature of "Ah! aha! hm!" Arkady told some news from Petersburg, but he was conscious of a little awkwardness, that awkwardness, which usually overtakes a youth when he has just ceased to be a child, and has come back to a place where they are accustomed to regard him and treat him as a child. He made his sentences quite unnecessarily long, avoided the word "daddy," and even sometimes replaced it by the word "father," mumbled, it is true, between his teeth; with an exaggerated carelessness he poured into his glass far more wine than he really wanted, and drank it all off. Prokofitch did not take his eyes off him, and kept chewing his lips. After supper they all separated at once.

"Your uncle's a queer fish," Bazarov said to Arkady, as he sat in his dressing-gown by his bedside, smoking a short pipe. "Only fancy such style in the country! His nails, his nails—you ought to send them to an exhibition!"

"Why, of course, you don't know," replied Arkady. "He was a great swell in his own day, you know. I will tell you his story one day. He was very handsome, you know, used to turn all the women's heads."

"Oh, that's it, is it? So he keeps it up in memory of the past. It's a pity there's no one for him to fascinate here though. I kept staring at his exquisite collars. They're like marble, and his chin's shaved simply to perfection. Come, Arkady Nikolaitch, isn't that ridiculous?"

"Perhaps it is; but he's a splendid man, really."

"An antique survival! But your father's a capital fellow. He wastes his time reading poetry, and doesn't know much about farming but he's a good-hearted fellow."

"My father's a man in a thousand.

"Did you notice how shy and nervous he is?"

Arkady shook his head as though he himself were not shy and nervous.

"It's something astonishing," pursued Bazarov, "these old idealists, they develop their nervous systems till they break down . . . so balance is lost. But good-night. In my room there's an English washstand, but the door won't fasten. Anyway that ought to be encouraged—an English washstand stands for progress!"

Bazarov went away, and a sense of great happiness came over Arkady. Sweet it is to fall asleep in one's own home, in the familiar bed, under the quilt worked by loving hands, perhaps a dear nurse's hands, those kind, tender, untiring hands. Arkady remembered Yegorovna, and sighed and wished her peace in heaven. . . . For himself he made no prayer.

Both he and Bazarov were soon asleep, but others in the house were awake long after. His son's return had agitated Nikolai Petrovitch. He lay down in bed, but did not put out the candles, and his head propped on his hand, he fell into long reveries. His brother was sitting long after midnight in his study, in a wide armchair before the fireplace, on which there smouldered some faintly glowing embers. Pavel Petrovitch was not undressed, only some red Chinese slippers had replaced the kid shoes on his feet. He held in his hand the last number of *Galignani,* but he was not reading; he gazed fixedly into the grate, where a bluish flame flickered, dying down, then flaring up again. . . . God knows where his thoughts were rambling, but they were not rambling in the past only; the expression of his face was concentrated and surly, which is not the way when a man is absorbed solely in recollections. In a small back room there sat, on a large chest, a young woman in a blue dressing jacket with a white kerchief thrown over her dark hair, Fenitchka. She was half listening, half dozing, and often looked across towards the open door through which a child's cradle was visible, and the regular breathing of a sleeping baby could be heard.

V

The next morning Bazarov woke up earlier than any one and went out of the house. "Oh, my!" he thought, looking about him, "the little place isn't much to boast of!" When Nikolai Petrovitch had divided the land with his peasants, he had had to build his new manor-house on four acres of perfectly flat and barren land. He had built a house, offices, and farm buildings, laid out a garden, dug a pond, and sunk two wells; but the young trees had not done well, very little water had collected in the pond, and that in the wells tasted brackish. Only one arbour of lilac and acacia had grown fairly well; they sometimes had tea and dinner in it. In a few minutes Bazarov had traversed all the little paths of the garden; he went into the cattle-yard and the stable, routed out two farm-boys, with whom he made friends at once, and set off with them to a small swamp about a mile from the house to look for frogs.

"What do you want frogs for, sir?" one of the boys asked him.

"I'll tell you what for," answered Bazarov, who possessed the special faculty of inspiring confidence in people of a lower class, though he never tried to win them, and behaved very casually with them; "I shall cut the frog open, and see what's going on in his inside, and then, as you and I are much the same as frogs, only that we walk on legs, I shall know what's going on inside us too."

"And what do you want to know that for?"

"So as not to make a mistake, if you're taken ill, and I have to cure you."

"Are you a doctor then?"

"Yes."

"Vaska, do you hear, the gentleman says you and I are the same as frogs, that's funny!"

"I'm afraid of frogs," observed Vaska, a boy of seven, with a head as white as flax, and bare feet, dressed in a grey smock with a stand-up collar.

"What is there to be afraid of? Do they bite?"

"There, paddle into the water, philosophers," said Bazarov.

Meanwhile Nikolai Petrovitch too had waked up, and gone in to see Arkady, whom he found dressed. The father and son went out on to the terrace under the shelter of the awning; near the balustrade, on the table, among great bunches of lilac, the samovar was already boiling. A little girl came up, the same who had been the first to meet them at the steps on their arrival the evening before. In a shrill voice she said—

"Fedosya Nikolaevna is not quite well, she cannot come; she gave orders to ask you, will you please to pour out tea yourself, or should she send Dunyasha?"

"I will pour out myself, myself," interposed Nikolai Petrovitch hurriedly. "Arkady, how do you take your tea, with cream, or with lemon?"

"With cream," answered Arkady; and after a brief silence, he uttered interrogatively, "Daddy?"

Nikolai Petrovitch in confusion looked at his son.

"Well?" he said.

Arkady dropped his eyes.

"Forgive me, dad, if my question seems unsuitable to you," he began, "but you yourself, by your openness yesterday, encourage me to be open . . . you will not be angry . . .?"

"Go on."

"You give me confidence to ask you. . . . Isn't the reason, Fen . . . isn't the reason she will not come here to pour out tea, because I'm here?"

Nikolai Petrovitch turned slightly away.

Perhaps," he said, at last, "she supposes . . . is ashamed."

Arkady turned a rapid glance on his father.

"She has no need to be ashamed. In the first place, you are aware of my views" (it was very sweet to Arkady to utter that word); "and secondly, could I be willing to hamper your life, your habits in the least thing? Besides, I am sure you could not make a bad choice; if you have allowed her to live under the same roof with you, she must be worthy of it; in any case, a son cannot judge his father,—least of all, I, and least of all such a father who, like you, has never hampered my liberty in anything."

Arkady's voice had been shaky at the beginning; he felt himself magnanimous, though at the same time he realised he was delivering something of the nature of a lecture to his father; but the sound of one's own voice has a powerful effect on any man, and Arkady brought out his last words resolutely, even with emphasis.

"Thanks, Arkasha," said Nikolai Petrovitch thickly, and his fingers again strayed over his eyebrows and forehead. "Your suppositions are just in fact. Of course, if this girl had not deserved. . . . It is not a frivolous caprice. It's not easy for me to talk to you about this; but you will understand that it is difficult for her to come here, in your presence, especially the first day of your return."

"In that case I will go to her," cried Arkady, with a fresh rush of magnanimous feeling, and he jumped up from his seat. "I will explain to her that she has no need to be ashamed before me."

Nikolai Petrovitch too got up.

"Arkady," he began, "be so good . . . how can . . . there . . . I have not told you yet . . ."

But Arkady did not listen to him, and ran off the terrace. Nikolai Petrovitch looked after him, and sank into his chair overcome by confusion. His heart began to throb. Did he at that moment realise the inevitable strangeness of the future relations between him and his son? Was he conscious that Arkady would perhaps have shown him more respect if he had never touched on this subject at all? Did he reproach himself for weakness?—it is hard to say; all these feelings were within him, but in the state of sensations—and vague sensations—while the flush did not leave his face, and his heart throbbed.

There was the sound of hurrying footsteps, and Arkady came on to the terrace. "We have made friends, dad!" he cried, with an expression of a kind of affectionate and good-natured triumph on his face. "Fedosya Nikolaevna is not quite well to-day really, and she will come a little later. But why didn't you tell me I had a brother? I should have kissed him last night, as I have kissed him just now."

Nikolai Petrovitch tried to articulate something, tried to get up and open his arms. Arkady flung himself on his neck.

"What's this? embracing again?" sounded the voice of Pavel Petrovitch behind them.

Father and son were equally rejoiced at his appearance at that instant; there are positions, genuinely affecting, from which one longs to escape as soon as possible.

"Why should you be surprised at that?" said Nikolai Petrovitch gaily. "Think what ages I have been waiting for Arkasha. I've not had time to get a good look at him since yesterday."

"I'm not at all surprised," observed Pavel Petrovitch; "I feel not indisposed to be embracing him myself."

Arkady went up to his uncle, and again felt his cheeks caressed by his perfumed moustache. Pavel Petrovitch sat down to the table. He wore an elegant morning suit in the English style, and a gay little fez on his head. This fez and the carelessly tied little cravat carried a suggestion of the freedom of country life, but the stiff collars of his shirt—not white, it is true, but striped, as is correct in morning dress—stood up as inexorably as ever against his well-shaved chin.

"Where's your new friend?" he asked Arkady.

"He's not in the house; he usually gets up early and goes off somewhere. The great thing is, we mustn't pay any attention to him; he doesn't like ceremony."

"Yes, that's obvious." Pavel Petrovitch began deliberately spreading butter on his bread. "Is he going to stay long with us?"

"Perhaps. He came here on the way to his father's."

"And where does his father live?"

"In our province, sixty-four miles from here. He has a small property there. He was formerly an army doctor."

"Tut, tut, tut! To be sure, I kept asking myself, "Where have I heard that name, Bazarov?" Nikolai, do you remember, in our father's division there was a surgeon Bazarov?"

"I believe there was."

"Yes, yes, to be sure. So that surgeon was his father. Hm!" Pavel Petrovitch pulled his moustaches. "Well, and what is Mr. Bazarov, himself?" he asked, deliberately.

"What is Bazarov?" Arkady smiled. "Would you like me, uncle, to tell you what he really is?"

"If you will be so good, nephew."

"He's a nihilist."

"Eh?" inquired Nikolai Petrovitch, while Pavel Petrovitch lifted a knife in the air with a small piece of butter on its tip, and remained motionless.

"He's a nihilist," repeated Arkady.

"A nihilist," said Nikolai Petrovitch. "That's from the Latin, *nihil, nothing,* as far as I can judge; the word must mean a man who . . . who accepts nothing?"

"Say, 'who respects nothing,' " put in Pavel Petrovitch, and he set to work on the butter again.

"Who regards everything from the critical point of view," observed Arkady.

"Isn't that just the same thing?" inquired Pavel Petrovitch.

"No, it's not the same thing. A nihilist is a man who does not bow down before any authority, who does not take any principle on faith, whatever reverence that principle may be enshrined in."

"Well, and is that good?" interrupted Pavel Petrovitch.

"That depends, uncle. Some people it will do good to, but some people will suffer for it."

"Indeed. Well, I see it's not in our line. We are old-fashioned people; we imagine that without principles, taken as you say on faith, there's no taking a step, no breathing. *Vous avez changé tout cela.* God give you good health and the rank of a general, while we will be content to look on and admire, worthy . . . what was it?"

"Nihilists," Arkady said, speaking very distinctly.

"Yes. There used to be Hegelists, and now there are nihilists. We shall see how you will exist in void, in vacuum; and now ring, please, brother Nikolai Petrovitch; it's time I had my cocoa."

Nikolai Petrovitch rang the bell and called, "Dunyasha!" But instead of Dunyasha, Fenitchka herself came on to the terrace. She was a young woman about three-and-twenty, with a white soft skin, dark hair and eyes, red, childishly-pouting lips, and little delicate hands. She wore a neat print dress; a new blue kerchief lay lightly on her plump shoulders. She carried a large cup of cocoa, and setting it down before Pavel Petrovitch, she was overwhelmed with confusion; the hot blood rushed in a wave of crimson over the delicate skin of her pretty face. She dropped her eyes, and stood at the table, leaning a little on the very tips of her fingers. It seemed as though she were ashamed of having come in, and at the same time felt that she had a right to come.

Pavel Petrovitch knitted his brows severely, while Nikolai Petrovitch looked embarrassed.

"Good morning, Fenitchka," he muttered through his teeth.

"Good morning," she replied in a voice not loud but resonant, and with a sidelong glance at Arkady, who gave her a friendly smile, she went gently away. She walked with a slightly rolling gait, but even that suited her.

For some minutes silence reigned on the terrace. Pavel Petrovitch sipped his cocoa; suddenly he raised his head. "Here is Sir Nihilist coming towards us," he said in an undertone.

Bazarov was in fact approaching through the garden, stepping over the flower-beds. His linen coat and trousers were besmeared with mud; clinging marsh weed was twined round the crown of his old round hat; in his right hand he held a small bag; in the bag something alive was moving. He quickly drew near the terrace, and said with a nod, "Good morning, gentlemen; sorry I was late for tea; I'll be back directly; I must just put these captives away."

"What have you there—leeches?" asked Pavel Petrovitch.

"No, frogs."

"Do you eat them—or keep them?"

"For experiment," said Bazarov indifferently, and he went off into the house.

"So he's going to cut them up," observed Pavel Petrovitch. "He has no faith in principles, but he has faith in frogs."

Arkady looked compassionately at his uncle; Nikolai Petrovitch shrugged his shoulders stealthily. Pavel Petrovitch himself felt that his epigram was unsuccessful, and began to talk about husbandry and the new bailiff, who had come to him the evening before to complain that a labourer, Foma, "was deboshed," and quite unmanageable. "He's such an *Æ*sop," he said among other things; "in all places he has protested himself a worthless fellow; he's not a man to keep his place; he'll walk off in a huff like a fool."

VI

Bazarov came back, sat down to the table, and began hastily drinking tea. The two brothers looked at him in silence, while Arkady stealthily watched first his father and then his uncle.

"Did you walk far from here?" Nikolai Petrovitch asked at last.

"Where you've a little swamp near the aspen wood. I started some half-dozen snipe; you might slaughter them, Arkady."

"Aren't you a sportsman then?"

"No."

"Is your special study physics?" Pavel Petrovitch in his turn inquired.

"Physics, yes; and natural science in general."

"They say the Teutons of late have had great success in that line."

"Yes; the Germans are our teachers in it," Bazarov answered carelessly.

The word Teutons instead of Germans, Pavel Petrovitch had used with ironical intention; none noticed it however.

"Have you such a high opinion of the Germans?" said Pavel Petrovitch, with exaggerated courtesy. He was beginning to feel a secret irritation. His aristocratic nature was revolted by Bazarov's absolute nonchalance. This surgeon's son was not only not overawed, he even gave abrupt and indifferent answers, and in the tone of his voice there was something churlish, almost insolent.

"The scientific men there are a clever lot."

"Ah, ah. To be sure, of Russian scientific men you have not such a flattering opinion, I dare say?"

"That's very likely,"

"That's very praiseworthy self-abnegation," Pavel Petrovitch declared, drawing himself up, and throwing his head back. "But how is this? Arkady Nikolaitch was telling us just now that you accept no authorities? Don't you believe in *them?*"

"And how am I accepting them? And what am I to believe in? They tell me the truth, I agree, that's all."

"And do all Germans tell the truth?" said Pavel Petrovitch, and his face assumed an expression as unsympathetic, as remote, as if he had withdrawn to some cloudy height.

"Not all," replied Bazarov, with a short yawn. He obviously did not care to continue the discussion.

Pavel Petrovitch glanced at Arkady, as though he would say to him, "Your friend's polite, I must say." "For my own part," he began again, not without some effort, "I am so unregenerate as not to like Germans. Russian Germans I am not speaking of now; we all know what sort of creatures they are. But even German Germans are not to my liking. In former days there were some here and there; they had—well, Schiller, to be sure, Goethe ... my brother—he takes a particularly favourable view of them. ... But now they have all turned chemists and materialists ..."

"A good chemist is twenty times as useful as any poet," broke in Bazarov.

"Oh, indeed," commented Pavel Petrovitch, and, as though falling asleep, he faintly raised his eyebrows. "You don't acknowledge art then, I suppose?"

"The art of making money or of advertising pills!" cried Bazarov, with a contemptuous laugh.

"Ah, ah. You are pleased to jest, I see. You reject all that, no doubt? Granted. Then you believe in science only?"

"I have already explained to you that I don't believe in anything; and what is science—science in the abstract? There are sciences, as there are trades and crafts; but abstract science doesn't exist at all."

"Very good. Well, and in regard to the other traditions accepted in human conduct, do you maintain the same negative attitude?"

"What's this, an examination?" asked Bazarov.

Pavel Petrovitch turned slightly pale. . . . Nikolai Petrovitch thought it his duty to interpose in the conversation.

"We will converse on this subject with you more in detail some day, dear Yevgeny Vassilyitch; we will hear your views, and express our own. For my part, I am heartily glad you are studying the natural sciences. I have heard that Liebig has made some wonderful discoveries in the amelioration of soils. You can be of assistance to me in my agricultural labours; you can give me some useful advice."

"I am at your service, Nikolai Petrovitch; but Liebig's miles over our heads! One has first to learn the a b c, and then begin to read, and we haven't set eyes on the alphabet yet."

"You are certainly a nihilist, I see that," thought Nikolai

Petrovitch. "Still, you will allow me to apply to you on occasion," he added aloud. "And now I fancy, brother, it's time for us to be going to have a talk with the bailiff."

Pavel Petrovitch got up from his seat.

"Yes," he said, without looking at any one; "it's a misfortune to live five years in the country like this, far from mighty intellects! You turn into a fool directly. You may try not to forget what you've been taught, but—in a snap!—they'll prove all that's rubbish, and tell you that sensible men have nothing more to do with such foolishness, and that you, if you please, are an antiquated old fogey. What's to be done? Young people, of course, are cleverer than we are!"

Pavel Petrovitch turned slowly on his heels, and slowly walked away; Nikolai Petrovitch went after him.

"Is he always like that?" Bazarov coolly inquired of Arkady, directly the door had closed behind the two brothers.

"I must say, Yevgeny, you weren't nice to him," remarked Arkady. "You have hurt his feelings."

"Well, am I going to consider them, these provincial aristocrats! Why, it's all vanity, dandy habits, fatuity. He should have continued his career in Petersburg, if that's his bent. But there, enough of him! I've found a rather rare species of a water-beetle, *Dytiscus marginatus;* do you know it? I will show you."

"I promised to tell you his story," began Arkady.

"The story of the beetle?"

"Come, don't, Yevgeny. The story of my uncle. You will see he's not the sort of man you fancy. He deserves pity rather than ridicule."

"I don't dispute it; but why are you worrying over him?"

"One ought to be just, Yevgeny."

"How does that follow?"

"No; listen . . ."

And Arkady told him his uncle's story. The reader will find it in the following chapter.

VII

Pavel Petrovitch Kirsanov was educated first at home, like younger brother, and afterwards in the Corps of Pages. From childhood he was distinguished by remarkable beauty; moreover he was self-confident, somewhat ironical, and had a rather biting humour; he could not fail to please. He began to be seen everywhere, directly he had received his commission as an officer. He was much admired in society, and he indulged every whim, even every caprice and every folly, and gave himself airs, but that too was attractive in him. Women went out of their senses over him; men called him a coxcomb, and were secretly jealous of him. He lived, as has been related already, in the same apartments as his brother, whom he loved sincerely, though he was not at all like him. Nikolai Petrovitch was a little lame, he had small, pleasing features of a rather melancholy cast, small, black eyes, and thin, soft hair; he liked being lazy, but he also liked reading, and was timid in society. Pavel Petrovitch did not spend a single evening at home, prided himself on his ease and audacity (he was just bringing gymnastics into fashion among young men in society), and had read in all some five or six French books. At twenty-eight he was already a captain; a brilliant career awaited him. Suddenly everything was changed.

At that time, there was sometimes seen in Petersburg society a woman who has even yet not been forgotten, Princess R——. She had a well-educated, well-bred, but rather stupid husband, and no children. She used suddenly to go abroad, and suddenly to return to Russia, and led an eccentric life in general. She had the reputation of being a frivolous coquette, abandoned herself eagerly to every sort of pleasure, danced to exhaustion, laughed and jested with young men, whom she received in the dim light of her drawing-room before dinner; while at night she wept and prayed, found no peace in anything, and often paced her room till morning, wringing her hands in anguish, or sat, pale and chill, over a psalter. Day came, and she was transformed again into a grand lady; again she went out, laughed, chattered, and simply flung herself headlong into anything which could afford her the slightest distraction. She was marvellously well-proportioned, her hair coloured like gold and heavy as gold hung below her knees, but no one would have called her a beauty; in her whole face the only good point was her eyes, and even her eyes were not good—they were grey, and not large—but their glance was swift and deep, unconcerned to the point of audacity, and thoughtful to the point of melancholy—an enigmatic glance. There was a light of something extraordinary in them, even while her tongue was lisping the emptiest of inanities. She dressed with elaborate care. Pavel Petrovitch met her at a ball, danced a mazurka with her, in the course of which she did not utter a single rational word, and fell passionately in love with her. Being accustomed to make conquests, in this instance, too, he soon attained his object, but his easy success did not damp his ardour. On the contrary, he was in still more torturing, still closer bondage to this woman, in whom, even at the very moment when she surrendered herself utterly, there seemed always something still mysterious and unattainable, to which none could penetrate. What was hidden in that soul—God knows! It seemed as though she were in the power of mysterious forces, incomprehensible even to herself; they seemed to play on her at will; her intellect was not powerful enough to master their caprices. Her whole behaviour presented a series of inconsistencies; the only letters which could have awakened her husband's just suspicions, she wrote to a man who was almost a stranger to her, whilst her love had always an element of melancholy; with a man she had chosen as a lover, she ceased to laugh and to jest, she listened to him, and gazed at him with a look of bewilderment. Sometimes, for the most part suddenly, this bewilderment passed into chill horror; her face took a wild, death-like expression; she locked herself up in her bedroom, and her maid, putting her ear to the keyhole, could hear her smothered sobs. More than once, as he went home after a tender interview, Kirsanov felt within him that heartrending, bitter vexation which follows on a total failure.

"What more do I want?" he asked himself, while his heart

was heavy. He once gave her a ring with a sphinx engraved on the stone.

"What's that?" she asked; "a sphinx?"

"Yes," he answered, "and that sphinx is you."

"I?" she queried, and slowly raising her enigmatical glance upon him. "Do you know that's awfully flattering?" she added with a meaningless smile, while her eyes still kept the same strange look.

Pavel Petrovitch suffered even while Princess R—— loved him; but when she grew cold to him, and that happened rather quickly, he almost went out of his mind. He was on the rack, and he was jealous; he gave her no peace, followed her about everywhere; she grew sick of his pursuit of her, and she went abroad. He resigned his commission in spite of the entreaties of his friends and the exhortations of his superiors, and followed the princess; four years he spent in foreign countries, at one time pursuing her, at another time intentionally losing sight of her. He was ashamed of himself, he was disgusted with his own lack of spirit . . . . but nothing availed. Her image, that incomprehensible, almost meaningless, but bewitching image, was deeply rooted in his heart. At Baden he once more regained his old footing with her; it seemed as though she had never loved him so passionately . . . but in a month it was all at an end: the flame flickered up for the last time and went out for ever. Foreseeing inevitable separation, he wanted at least to remain her friend, as though friendship with such a woman was possible. . . . She secretly left Baden, and from that time steadily avoided Kirsanov. He returned to Russia, and tried to live his former life again; but he could not get back into the old groove. He wandered from place to place like a man possessed; he still went into society; he still retained the habits of a man of the world; he could boast of two or three fresh conquests; but he no longer expected anything much of himself or of others, and he undertook nothing. He grew old and grey; spending all his evenings at the club, jaundiced and bored, and arguing in bachelor society became a necessity for him—a bad sign, as we all know. Marriage, of course, he did not even think of. Ten years passed in this way; they passed by colourless and fruitless—and quickly, fearfully quickly. Nowhere does time fly past as in Russia; in prison they say it flies even faster. One day at dinner at the club, Pavel Petrovitch heard of the death of the Princess R——. She had died at Paris in a state bordering on insanity. He got up from the table, and a long time he paced about the rooms of the club, or stood stockstill near the card-players, but he did not go home earlier than usual. Some time later he received a packet addressed to him; in it was the ring he had given the princess. She had drawn lines in the shape of a cross over the sphinx and sent him word that the solution of the enigma—was the cross.

This happened at the beginning of the year 1848, at the very time when Nikolai Petrovitch came to Petersburg, after the loss of his wife. Pavel Petrovitch had scarcely seen his brother since the latter had settled in the country; the marriage of Nikolai Petrovitch had coincided with the very first days of Pavel Petrovitch's acquaintance with the princess. When he came back from abroad, he had gone to him with the intention of staying a couple of months with him, in sympathetic enjoyment of his happiness, but he had only succeeded in standing a week of it. The difference in the positions of the two brothers was too great. In 1848, this difference had grown less; Nikolai Petrovitch had lost his wife, Pavel Petrovitch had lost his memories; after the death of the princess he tried not to think of her. But to Nikolai, there remained the sense of a well-spent life, his son was growing up under his eyes; Pavel, on the contrary, a solitary bachelor, was entering upon that indefinite twilight period of regrets that are akin to hopes, and hopes that are akin to regrets, when youth is over, while old age has not yet come.

This time was harder for Pavel Petrovitch than for another man; in losing his past, he lost everything.

"I will not invite you to Maryino now," Nikolai Petrovitch said to him one day, (he had called his property by that name in honour of his wife); "you were dull there in my dear wife's time, and now I think you would be bored to death."

"I was stupid and fidgety then," answered Pavel Petrovitch;

"since then I have grown quieter, if not wiser. On the contrary, now, if you will let me, I am ready to settle with you for good."

For all answer Nikolai Petrovitch embraced him; but a year and a half passed after this conversation, before Pavel Petrovitch made up his mind to carry out his intention. When he was once settled in the country, however, he did not leave it, even during the three winters which Nikolai Petrovitch spent in Petersburg with his son. He began to read, chiefly English; he arranged his whole life, roughly speaking, in the English style, rarely saw the neighbours, and only went out to the election of marshals, where he was generally silent, only occasionally annoying and alarming landowners of the old school by his liberal sallies, and not associating with the representatives of the younger generation. Both the latter and the former considered him "stuck up"; and both parties respected him for his fine aristocratic manners; for his reputation for successes in love; for the fact that he was very well dressed and always stayed in the best room in the best hotel; for the fact that he generally dined well, and had once even dined with Wellington at Louis Philippe's table; for the fact that he always took everywhere with him a real silver dressing-case and a portable bath; for the fact that he always smelt of some exceptionally "good form" scent; for the fact that he played whist in masterly fashion, and always lost; and lastly, they respected him also for his incorruptible honesty. Ladies considered him enchantingly romantic, but he did not cultivate ladies' acquaintance.
. . .

"So you see, Yevgeny," observed Arkady, as he finished his story, "how unjustly you judge of my uncle! To say nothing of his having more than once helped my father out of difficulties, given him all his money—the property, perhaps you don't know, wasn't divided—he's glad to help any one, among other things he always sticks up for the peasants; it's true, when he talks to them he frowns and sniffs eau de cologne." . . .

"His nerves, no doubt," put in Bazarov.

"Perhaps; but his heart is very good. And he's far from being stupid. What useful advice he has given me especially . . . especially in regard to relations with women."

"Aha! a scalded dog fears cold water, we know that!"

"In short," continued Arkady, "he's profoundly unhappy, believe me; it's a sin to despise him."

"And, who does despise him?" retorted Bazarov. "Still, I must say that a fellow who stakes his whole life on one card—a woman's love—and when that card fails, turns sour, and lets himself go till he's fit for nothing, is not a man, but a male. You say he's unhappy; you ought to know best; to be sure, he's not got rid of all his fads. I'm convinced that he solemnly imagines himself a superior creature because he reads that wretched *Galignani,* and once a month saves a peasant from a flogging."

"But remember his education, the age in which he grew up," observed Arkady.

"Education?" broke in Bazarov. "Every man must educate himself, just as I've done, for instance. . . . And as for the age, why should I depend on it? Let it rather depend on me. No, my dear fellow, that's all shallowness, want of backbone! And what stuff it all is, about these mysterious relations between a man and woman? We physiologists know what these relations are. You study the anatomy of the eye; where does the enigmatical glance you talk about come in there? That's all romantic, nonsensical, aesthetic rot. We had much better go and look at the beetle."

And the two friends went off to Bazarov's room, which was already pervaded by a sort of medico-surgical odour, mingled with the smell of cheap tobacco.

VIII

Pavel Petrovitch did not long remain present at his brother's interview with his bailiff, a tall, thin man with a sweet consumptive voice and knavish eyes, who to all Nikolai Petrovitch's remarks answered, "Certainly, sir," and tried to make the peasants out to be thieves and drunkards. The estate had only recently been put on to the new reformed system, and the new mechanism worked, creaking like an ungreased wheel, warping and cracking like home-made furniture of unseasoned wood. Nikolai Petrovitch did not lose heart, but often he sighed, and was gloomy; he felt that the thing could not go on without money, and his money was almost all spent. Arkady had spoken the truth; Pavel Petrovitch had more than once helped his brother; more than once, seeing him struggling and cudgelling his brains, at a loss which way to turn, Pavel Petrovitch moved deliberately to the window, and with his hands thrust into his pockets, muttered between his teeth, *"mais je puis vous donner de l'argent,"* and gave him money; but to-day he had none himself, and he preferred to go away. The petty details of agricultural management worried him; besides, it constantly struck him that Nikolai Petrovitch, for all his zeal and industry, did not set about things in the right way, though he would not have been able to point out precisely where Nikolai Petrovitch's mistake lay. "My brother's not practical enough," he reasoned to himself; "they impose upon him." Nikolai Petrovitch, on the other hand, had the highest opinion of Pavel Petrovitch's practical ability, and always asked his advice. "I'm a soft, weak fellow, I've spent my life in the wilds," he used to say; "while you haven't seen so much of the world for nothing, you see through people; you have an eagle eye." In answer to which Pavel Petrovitch only turned away, but did not contradict his brother.

Leaving Nikolai Petrovitch in his study, he walked along the corridor, which separated the front part of the house from the back; when he had reached a low door, he stopped in hesitation, then pulling his moustaches, he knocked at it.

"Who's there? Come in," sounded Fenitchka's voice.

"It's I," said Pavel Petrovitch, and he opened the door.

Fenitchka jumped up from the chair on which she was sitting with her baby, and giving him into the arms of a girl, who at once carried him out of the room, she put straight her kerchief hastily.

"Pardon me, if I disturb you," began Pavel Petrovitch, not looking at her; "I only wanted to ask you . . . they are sending into the town to-day, I think . . . please let them buy me some green tea."

"Certainly," answered Fenitchka; "how much do you desire them to buy?"

"Oh, half a pound will be enough, I imagine. You have made a change here, I see," he added, with a rapid glance round him, which glided over Fenitchka's face too. "The curtains here," he explained, seeing she did not understand him.

"Oh, yes, the curtains; Nikolai Petrovitch was so good as to make me a present of them; but they have been put up a long while now."

"Yes, and it's a long while since I have been to see you. Now it is very nice here."

"Thanks to Nikolai Petrovitch's kindness," murmured Fenitchka.

"You are more comfortable here than in the little lodge you used to have?" inquired Pavel Petrovitch urbanely, but without the slightest smile.

"Certainly, it's more comfortable."

"Who has been put in your place now?"

"The laundry-maids are there now."

"Ah!"

Pavel Petrovitch was silent. "Now he is going," thought Fenitchka; but he did not go, and she stood before him motionless.

"What did you send your little one away for?" said Pavel Petrovitch at last. "I love children; let me see him."

Fenitchka blushed all over with confusion and delight. She was afraid of Pavel Petrovitch; he had scarcely ever spoken to her.

"Dunyasha," she called; "will you bring Mitya, please." (Fenitchka did not treat any one in the house familiarly.) "But wait a minute he must have a frock on," Fenitchka was going towards the door.

"That doesn't matter," remarked Pavel Petrovitch.

"I will be back directly," answered Fenitchka, and she went out quickly.

Pavel Petrovitch was left alone, and he looked round this time with special attention. The small low-pitched room in which he found himself was very clean and snug. It smelt of the freshly

painted floor and of camomile. Along the walls stood chairs with
lyre-shaped backs, bought by the late general on his campaign in
Poland; in one corner was a little bedstead under a muslin canopy
beside an iron-clamped chest with a convex lid. In the opposite
corner a little lamp was burning before a big dark picture of St.
Nikolai the wonder-worker; a tiny porcelain egg hung by a red
ribbon from the protruding gold halo down to the saint's breast;
by the windows greenish glass jars of last year's jam carefully tied
down could be seen; on their paper covers Fenitchka herself had
written in big letters "Gooseberry"; Nikolai Petrovitch was particularly fond of that preserve. On a long cord from the ceiling
a cage hung with a short-tailed siskin in it; he was constantly
chirping and hopping about, the cage was constantly shaking and
swinging, while hempseeds fell with a light tap on to the floor.
On the wall just above a small chest of drawers hung some rather
bad photographs of Nikolai Petrovitch in various attitudes, taken
by an itinerant photographer; there too hung a photograph of
Fenitchka herself, which was an absolute failure; it was an eyeless
face wearing a forced smile, in a dingy frame, nothing more could
be made out; while above Fenitchka, General Yermolov, in a
Circassian cloak, scowled menacingly upon the Caucasian mountains in the distance, from beneath a little silk shoe for pins which
fell right on to his brows.

Five minutes passed; bustling and whispering could be heard
in the next room. Pavel Petrovitch took up from the chest of
drawers a greasy book, an odd volume of Masalsky's *Musketeer,*
and turned over a few pages. . . . The door opened, and Fenitchka
came in with Mitya in her arms. She had put on him a little red
smock with embroidery on the collar, had combed his hair and
washed his face; he was breathing heavily, his whole body working, and his little hands waving in the air, as is the way with all
healthy babies; but his smart smock obviously impressed him, an
expression of delight was reflected in every part of his little fat
person. Fenitchka had put her own hair too in order, and had
arranged her kerchief; but she might well have remained as she
was. And really is there anything in the world more captivating
than a beautiful young mother with a healthy baby in her arms?

"What a chubby fellow!" said Pavel Petrovitch graciously, and he tickled Mitya's little double chin with the tapering nail of his forefinger. The baby stared at the siskin, and chuckled.

"That's uncle," said Fenitchka, bending her face down to him and slightly rocking him, while Dunyasha quietly set in the window a smouldering perfumed stick, putting a half-penny under it.

"How many months old is he?" asked Pavel Petrovitch.

"Six months; it will soon be seven, on the eleventh."

"Isn't it eight, Fedosya Nikolaevna?" put in Dunyasha, with some timidity.

"No, seven; what an idea!" The baby chuckled again, stared at the chest, and suddenly caught hold of his mother's nose and mouth with all his five little fingers. "Saucy mite," said Fenitchka, not drawing her face away.

"He's like my brother," observed Pavel Petrovitch.

"Who else should he be like?" thought Fenitchka.

"Yes," continued Pavel Petrovitch, as though speaking to himself; "there's an unmistakable likeness." He looked attentively, almost mournfully, at Fenitchka.

"That's uncle," she repeated, in a whisper this time.

"Ah! Pavel! so you're here!" was heard suddenly the voice of Nikolai Petrovitch.

Pavel Petrovitch turned hurriedly round, frowning; but his brother looked at him with such delight, such gratitude, that he could not help responding to his smile.

"You've a splendid little cherub," he said, and looking at his watch. "I came in here to speak about some tea."

And, assuming an expression of indifference, Pavel Petrovitch at once went out of the room.

"Did he come of himself?" Nikolai Petrovitch asked Fenitchka.

"Yes; he knocked and came in."

"Well, and has Arkasha been in to see you again?"

"No. Hadn't I better move into the lodge, Nikolai Petrovitch?"

"Why so?"

"I wonder whether it wouldn't be best just for the first."

"N . . no," Nikolai Petrovitch brought out hesitatingly, rubbing his forehead. "We ought to have done it before. . . . How are you, fatty?" he said, suddenly brightening, and going up to the baby, he kissed him on the cheek; then he bent a little and pressed his lips to Fenitchka's hand, which lay white as milk upon Mitya's little red smock.

"Nikolai Petrovitch! what are you doing?" she whispered, dropping her eyes, then slowly raised them. Very charming was the expression of her eyes when she peeped, as it were, from under her lids, and smiled tenderly and a little foolishly.

Nikolai Petrovitch had made Fenitchka's acquaintance in the following manner. He had once happened three years before to stay a night at an inn in a remote district town. He was agreeably struck by the cleanness of the room assigned to him, the freshness of the bed-linen. Surely the woman of the house must be a German? was the idea that occurred to him; but she proved to be a Russian, a woman of about fifty, neatly dressed, of a good-looking, sensible countenance and discreet speech. He entered into conversation with her at tea; he liked her very much. Nikolai Petrovitch had at that time only just moved into his new home, and not wishing to keep serfs in the house, he was on the look-out for wage-servants; the woman of the inn on her side complained of the small number of visitors to the town, and the hard times; he proposed to her to come into his house in the capacity of housekeeper; she consented. Her husband had long been dead, leaving her an only daughter, Fenitchka. Within a fortnight Arina Savishna (that was the new housekeeper's name) arrived with her daughter at Maryino and installed herself in the little lodge. Nikolai Petrovitch's choice proved a successful one. Arina brought order into the household. As for Fenitchka, who was at that time seventeen, no one spoke of her, and scarcely any one saw her; she lived quietly and sedately, and only on Sundays Nikolai Petrovitch noticed in the church somewhere in a side place the delicate profile of her white face. More than a year passed thus.

One morning, Arina came into his study, and bowing low as usual, she asked him if he could do anything for her daughter, who had got a spark from the stove in her eye. Nikolai Petrovitch, like all stay-at-home people, had studied doctoring and even compiled a homoeopathic guide. He at once told Arina to bring the patient to him. Fenitchka was much frightened when she heard the master had sent for her; however, she followed her mother. Nikolai Petrovitch led her to the window and took her head in his two hands. After thoroughly examining her red and swollen eye, he prescribed a fomentation, which he made up himself at once, and tearing his handkerchief in pieces, he showed her how it ought to be applied. Fenitchka listened to all he had to say, and then was going. "Kiss the master's hand, silly girl," said Arina. Nikolai Petrovitch did not give her his hand, and in confusion himself kissed her bent head on the parting of her hair. Fenitchka's eye was soon well again, but the impression she had made on Nikolai Petrovitch did not pass away so quickly. He was for ever haunted by that pure, delicate, timidly raised face; he felt on the palms of his hands that soft hair, and saw those innocent, slightly parted lips, through which pearly teeth gleamed with moist brilliance in the sunshine. He began to watch her with great attention in church, and tried to get into conversation with her. At first she was shy of him, and one day meeting him at the approach of evening in a narrow footpath through a field of rye, she ran into the tall thick rye, overgrown with cornflowers and wormwood, so as not to meet him face to face. He caught sight of her little head through a golden network of ears of rye, from which she was peeping out like a little animal, and called affectionately to her—

"Good-evening, Fenitchka! I don't bite."

"Good-evening," she whispered, not coming out of her ambush.

By degrees she began to be more at home with him, but was still shy in his presence, when suddenly her mother, Arina, died of cholera. What was to become of Fenitchka? She inherited from her mother a love for order, regularity, and respectability; but she was so young, so alone. Nikolai Petrovitch was himself so good and considerate. . . . It's needless to relate the rest . . .

"So my brother came in to see you?" Nikolai Petrovitch questioned her. "He knocked and came in?"

"Yes."

"Well, that's a good thing. Let me give Mitya a swing."

And Nikolai Petrovitch began tossing him almost up to the ceiling, to the huge delight of the baby, and to the considerable uneasiness of the mother, who every time he flew up stretched her arms up towards his little bare legs.

Pavel Petrovitch went back to his artistic study, with its walls covered with handsome bluish-grey hangings, with weapons hanging upon a variegated Persian rug nailed to the wall; with walnut furniture, upholstered in dark green velveteen, with a *renaissance* bookcase of old black oak, with bronze statuettes on the magnificent writing-table, with an open hearth. He threw himself on the sofa, clasped his hands behind his head, and remained without moving, looking with a face almost of despair at the ceiling. Whether he wanted to hide from the very walls that which was reflected in his face, or for some other reason, he got up, drew the heavy window curtains, and again threw himself on the sofa.

IX

On the same day Bazarov made acquaintance with Fenitchka. He was walking with Arkady in the garden, and explaining to him why some of the trees, especially the oaks, had not done well.

"You ought to have planted silver poplars here by preference, and spruce firs, and perhaps limes, giving them some loam. The arbour there has done well," he added, "because it's acacia and lilac; they're accommodating good fellows, those trees, they don't want much care. But there's some one in here."

In the arbour was sitting Fenitchka, with Dunyasha and Mitya. Bazarov stood still, while Arkady nodded to Fenitchka like an old friend.

"Who's that?" Bazarov asked him directly they had passed by. "What a pretty girl!"

"Whom are you speaking of?"

"You know; only one of them was pretty."

Arkady, not without embarrassment, explained to him briefly who Fenitchka was.

"Aha!" commented Bazarov; "your father's got good taste, one can see. I like him, your father, ay, ay! He's a jolly fellow. We must make friends though," he added, and turned back towards the arbour.

"Yevgeny!" Arkady cried after him in dismay; "mind what you are about, for mercy's sake."

"Don't worry yourself," said Bazarov; "I know how to behave myself—I'm not a booby."

Going up to Fenitchka, he took off his cap.

"Allow me to introduce myself," he began, with a polite bow. "I'm a harmless person, and a friend of Arkady Nikola-evitch's."

Fenitchka got up from the garden seat and looked at him without speaking.

"What a splendid baby!" continued Bazarov; "don't be uneasy, my praises have never brought ill-luck yet. Why is it his cheeks are so flushed? Is he cutting his teeth?"

"Yes," said Fenitchka; "he has cut four teeth already, and now the gums are swollen again."

"Show me, and don't be afraid, I'm a doctor."

Bazarov took the baby up in his arms, and to the great astonishment both of Fenitchka and Dunyasha the child made no resistance, and was not frightened.

"I see, I see. . . . It's nothing, everything's as it should be; he will have a good set of teeth. If anything goes wrong, tell me. And are you quite well yourself?"

"Quite, thank God."

"Thank God, indeed—that's the great thing. And you?" he added, turning to Dunyasha.

Dunyasha, a girl very prim in the master's house, and a romp outside the gates, only giggled in answer.

"Well, that's all right. Here's your gallant fellow."

Fenitchka received the baby in her arms.

"How good he was with you!" she commented in an undertone.

"Children are always good with me," answered Bazarov; "I have a way with them."

"Children know who loves them," remarked Dunyasha.

"Yes, they certainly do," Fenitchka said. "Why, Mitya will not go to some people for anything."

"Will he come to me?" asked Arkady, who, after standing in the distance for some time, had gone up to the arbour.

He tried to entice Mitya to come to him, but Mitya threw his head back and screamed, to Fenitchka's great confusion.

"Another day, when he's had time to get used to me," said Arkady indulgently, and the two friends walked away.

"What's her name?" asked Bazarov.

"Fenitchka . . . Fedosya," answered Arkady.

"And her father's name? One must know that too."

"Nikolaevna."

"*Bene.* What I like in her is that she's not too embarrassed. Some people, I suppose, would think ill of her for it. What nonsense! What is there to embarrass her? She's a mother—she's all right."

"She's all right," observed Arkady,—"but my father."

"And he's right too," put in Bazarov.

"Well, no, I don't think so."

"I suppose an extra heir's not to your liking?"

"I wonder you're not ashamed to attribute such ideas to me!" retorted Arkady hotly; "I don't consider my father wrong from that point of view; I think he ought to marry her."

"Hoity-toity!" responded Bazarov tranquilly. "What magnanimous fellows we are! You still attach significance to marriage; I did not expect that of you."

The friends walked a few paces in silence.

"I have looked at all your father's establishment," Bazarov began again. "The cattle are inferior, the horses are broken down; the buildings aren't up to much, and the workmen look confirmed loafers; while the superintendent is either a fool, or a knave, I haven't quite found out which yet."

"You are rather hard on everything to-day, Yevgeny Vassilyevitch."

"And the dear good peasants are taking your father in to a dead certainty. You know the Russian proverb, "The Russian peasant will cheat God Himself.' "

"I begin to agree with my uncle," remarked Arkady; "you certainly have a poor opinion of Russians."

"As though that mattered! The only good point in a Russian is his having the lowest possible opinion of himself. What does matter is that two and two make four, and the rest is all foolery."

"And is nature foolery?" said Arkady, looking pensively at the bright-coloured fields in the distance, in the beautiful soft light of the sun, which was not yet high up in the sky.

"Nature, too, is foolery in the sense you understand it. Nature's not a temple, but a workshop, and man's the workman in it."

At that instant, the long drawn notes of a violoncello floated out to them from the house. Some one was playing Schubert's *Expectation* with much feeling, though with an untrained hand, and the melody flowed with honey sweetness through the air.

"What's that?" cried Bazarov in amazement.

"It's my father."

"Your father plays the violoncello?"

"Yes."

"And how old is your father?"

"Forty-four."

Bazarov suddenly burst into a roar of laughter.

"What are you laughing at?"

"Upon my word, a man of forty-four, a *paterfamilias* in this out-of-the-way district, playing on the violoncello!"

Bazarov went on laughing; but much as he revered his master, this time Arkady did not even smile.

X

About a fortnight passed by. Life at Maryino went on its accustomed course, while Arkady was lazy and enjoyed himself, and Bazarov worked. Every one in the house had grown used to him, to his careless manners, and his curt and abrupt speeches. Fenitchka, in particular, was so far at home with him that one night she sent to wake him up; Mitya had had convulsions; and he had gone, and, half joking, half-yawning as usual, he stayed two hours with her and relieved the child. On the other hand Pavel Petrovitch had grown to detest Bazarov with all the strength of his soul; he regarded him as stuck-up, impudent, cynical, and vulgar; he suspected that Bazarov had no respect for him, that he had all but a contempt for him—him, Pavel Kirsanov! Nikolai Petrovitch was rather afraid of the young "nihilist," and was doubtful whether his influence over Arkady was for the good; but he was glad to listen to him, and was glad to be present at his scientific and chemical experiments. Bazarov had brought with him a microscope, and busied himself for hours together with it. The servants, too, took to him, though he made fun of them; they felt, all the same, that he was one of themselves, not a master. Dunyasha was always ready to giggle with him, and used to cast significant and stealthy glances at him when she skipped by like a rabbit; Piotr, a man vain and stupid to the last degree, for ever wearing an affected frown on his brow, a man whose whole merit consisted in the fact that he looked civil, could spell out a page of reading, and was diligent in brushing his coat—even he smirked and brightened up directly Bazarov paid him any attention; the boys on the farm simply ran after the "doctor" like puppies. The old man Prokofitch was the only one who did not like him; he handed him the dishes at table with a surly face, called him a "butcher" and "an upstart," and declared that with his great whiskers he looked like a pig in a stye. Prokofitch in his own way was quite as much of an aristocrat as Pavel Petrovitch.

The best days of the year had come—the first days of June. The weather kept splendidly fine; in the distance, it is true, the cholera was threatening, but the inhabitants of that province had had time to get used to its visits. Bazarov used to get up very early and go out for two or three miles, not for a walk—he couldn't bear walking without an object—but to collect specimens of plants and insects. Sometimes he took Arkady with him. On the way home an argument usually sprang up, and Arkady was usually vanquished in it, though he said more than his companion.

One day they had lingered rather late; Nikolai Petrovitch went to meet them in the garden, and as he reached the arbour he suddenly heard the quick steps and voices of the two young men. They were walking on the other side of the arbour, and could not see him.

"You don't know my father well enough," said Arkady.

"Your father's a nice chap," said Bazarov, "but he's behind the times; his day is done."

Nikolai Petrovitch listened intently. . . . Arkady made no answer.

The man whose day was done remained two minutes motionless, and stole slowly home.

"The day before yesterday I saw him reading Pushkin," Bazarov was continuing meanwhile. "Explain to him, please, that that's no earthly use. He's not a boy, you know; it's time to throw up that rubbish. And what an idea to be a romantic at this time of day! Give him something sensible to read."

"What ought I to give him?" asked Arkady.

"Oh, I think Büchner's *Stoff und Kraft* to begin with."

"I think so too," observed Arkady approvingly, *"Stoff und Kraft* is written in popular language. . . ."

"So it seems," Nikolai Petrovitch said the same day after dinner to his brother, as he sat in his study, "you and I are behind the times, our day's over. Well, well. Perhaps Bazarov is right; but one thing I confess, makes me feel sore; I did so hope, precisely now, to get on to such close intimate terms with Arkady, and it turns out I'm left behind, and he has gone forward, and we can't understand one another."

"How has he gone forward? And in what way is he so superior to us already?" cried Pavel Petrovitch impatiently. "It's that high and mighty gentleman, that nihilist, who's knocked all that into his head. I hate that doctor fellow; in my opinion, he's simply a quack; I'm convinced, for all his tadpoles, he's not got very far even in medicine."

"No, brother, you mustn't say that; Bazarov is clever, and knows his subject."

"And his conceit's something revolting," Pavel Petrovitch broke in again.

"Yes," observed Nikolai Petrovitch, "he is conceited. But there's no doing without that, it seems; only that's what I did not take into account. I thought I was doing everything to keep up with the times; I have started a model farm; I have done well by the peasants, so that I am positively called a "Red Radical" all over the province; I read, I study, I try in every way to keep abreast with the requirements of the day—and they say my day's over. And, brother, I begin to think that it is."

"Why so?"

"I'll tell you why. This morning I was sitting reading Pushkin. . . . I remember, it happened to be *The Gipsies* . . . all of a sudden Arkady came up to me, and, without speaking, with such a kindly compassion on his face, as gently as if I were a baby, took the book away from me, and laid another before me—a German book . . . smiled, and went away, carrying Pushkin off with him."

"Upon my word! What book did he give you?"

"This one here."

And Nikolai Petrovitch pulled the famous treatise of Büchner, in the ninth edition, out of his coat-tail pocket.

Pavel Petrovitch turned it over in his hands. "Hm!" he growled. "Arkady Nikolaevitch is taking your education in hand. Well, did you try reading it?"

"Yes, I tried it."

"Well, what did you think of it?"

"Either I'm stupid, or its all—nonsense. I must be stupid, I suppose."

"Haven't you forgotten your German?" queried Pavel Petrovitch.

"Oh, I understand the German."

Pavel Petrovitch again turned the book over in his hands, and glanced from under his brows at his brother. Both were silent.

"Oh, by the way," began Nikolai Petrovitch, obviously wishing to change the subject, "I've got a letter from Kolyazin."

"Matvy Ilyitch?"

"Yes. He has come to——to inspect the province. He's quite a bigwig now; and writes to me that, as a relation, he should like to see us again, and invites you and me and Arkady to the town."

"Are you going?" asked Pavel Petrovitch.

"No; are you?"

"No, I shan't go either. Much object there would be in dragging oneself over forty miles on a wild-goose chase. *Mathieu* wants to show himself in all his glory. Damn him! he will have the whole province doing him homage; he can get on without the likes of us. A grand dignity, indeed, a privy councillor! If I had stayed in the service, if I had drudged on in official harness, I should have been a general-adjutant by now. Besides, you and I are behind the times, you know."

"Yes, brother; it's time, it seems, to order a coffin and cross one's arms on one's breast," remarked Nikolai Petrovitch, with a sigh.

"Well, I'm not going to give in quite so soon," muttered his brother. "I've got a tussle with that doctor fellow before me, I feel sure of that."

A tussle came off that same day at evening tea. Pavel Petrovitch came into the drawing-room, all ready for the fray, irritable and determined. He was only waiting for an excuse to fall upon the enemy; but for a long while an excuse did not present itself. As a rule, Bazarov said little in the presence of the "old Kirsanovs" (that was how he spoke of the brothers), and that evening he felt out of humour, and drank off cup after cup of tea without a word. Pavel Petrovitch was all aflame with impatience; his wishes were fulfilled at last.

The conversation turned on one of the neighbouring land-owners. "Rotten aristocratic snob," observed Bazarov indifferently. He had met him in Petersburg.

"Allow me to ask you," began Pavel Petrovitch, and his lips were trembling, "according to your ideas, have the words "rotten" and "aristocrat" the same meaning?"

"I said "aristocratic snob,' " replied Bazarov, lazily swallowing a sip of tea.

"Precisely so; but I imagine you have the same opinion of aristocrats as of aristocratic snobs. I think it my duty to inform you that I do not share that opinion. I venture to assert that every one knows me for a man of liberal ideas and devoted to progress; but, exactly for that reason, I respect aristocrats—real aristocrats. Kindly remember, sir" (at these words Bazarov lifted his eyes and looked at Pavel Petrovitch), "kindly remember, sir," he repeated, with acrimony—"the English aristocracy. They do not abate one iota of their rights, and for that reason they respect the rights of others; they demand the performance of what is due to them, and for that reason they perform their own duties. The aristocracy has given freedom to England, and maintains it for her."

"We've heard that story a good many times" replied Bazarov; "but what are you trying to prove by that?"

"I am tryin' to prove by that, sir" (when Pavel Petrovitch was angry he intentionally clipped his words in this way, though, of course, he knew very well that such forms are not strictly grammatical. In this fashionable whim could be discerned a survival of the habits of the times of Alexander. The exquisites of those days, on the rare occasions when they spoke their own language, made use of such slipshod forms; as much as to say, "We, of course, are born Russians, at the same time we are great swells, who are at liberty to neglect the rules of scholars"); "I am tryin' to prove by that, sir, that without the sense of personal dignity, without self-respect—and these two sentiments are well developed in the aristocrat—there is no secure foundation for the social . . . *bien public* . . . the social fabric. Personal character, sir—that is the chief thing; a man's personal character must be firm as a rock, since everything is built on it. I am very well aware, for instance, that you are pleased to consider my habits, my dress, my refinements, in fact, ridiculous; but all that proceeds from a sense of self-respect, from a sense of duty—yes, indeed, of duty.

I live in the country, in the wilds, but I will not lower myself. I respect the dignity of man in myself."

"Let me ask you, Pavel Petrovitch," commented Bazarov; "you respect yourself, and sit with your hands folded; what sort of benefit does that do to the *bien public?* If you didn't respect yourself, you'd do just the same."

Pavel Petrovitch turned white. "That's a different question. Its absolutely unnecessary for me to explain to you now why I sit with folded hands, as you are pleased to express yourself. I wish only to tell you that aristocracy is a principle, and in our days none but immoral or silly people can live without principles. I said that to Arkady the day after he came home, and I repeat it now. Isn't it, Nikolai?"

Nikolai Petrovitch nodded his head. "Aristocracy, Liberalism, progress, principles," Bazarov was saying meanwhile; "if you think of it, what a lot of foreign . . . and useless words! To a Russian they're good for nothing."

"What is good for something according to you? If we listen to you, we shall find ourselves outside humanity, outside its laws. Come—the logic of history demands . . ."

"But what's that logic to us? We can get on without that too."

"How do you mean?"

"Why, this. You don't need logic, I hope, to put a bit of bread in your mouth when you're hungry. What's the object of these abstractions to us?"

Pavel Petrovitch raised his hands in horror.

"I don't understand you, after that. You insult the Russian people. I don't understand how it's possible not to acknowledge principles, rules. By virtue of what do you act then?"

"I've told you already, uncle, that we don't accept any authorities," put in Arkady.

"We act by virtue of what we recognise as beneficial," observed Bazarov. "At the present time, negation is the most beneficial of all—and we deny——"

"Everything?"

"Everything!"

"What? not only art and poetry . . . but even . . . horrible to say . . ."

"Everything," repeated Bazarov, with indescribable composure.

Pavel Petrovitch stared at him. He had not expected this; while Arkady fairly blushed with delight.

"Allow me, though," began Nikolai Petrovitch. "You deny everything; or, speaking more precisely, you destroy everything. . . . But one must construct too, you know."

"That's not our business now. . . . The ground wants clearing first."

"The present condition of the people requires it," added Arkady, with dignity; "we are bound to carry out these requirements, we have no right to yield to the satisfaction of our personal egoism."

This last phrase obviously displeased Bazarov; there was a flavour of philosophy, that is to say, romanticism about it, for Bazarov called philosophy, too, romanticism, but he did not think it necessary to correct his young disciple.

No, no!" cried Pavel Petrovitch, with sudden energy. "I'm not willing to believe that you, young men, know the Russian people really, that you are the representatives of their requirements, their efforts! No; the Russian people is not what you imagine it. Tradition it holds sacred; it is a patriarchal people; it cannot live without faith . . ."

"I'm not going to dispute that," Bazarov interrupted. "I'm even ready to agree that in that you're right."

"But if I am right . . ."

"And, all the same, that proves nothing."

"It just proves nothing," repeated Arkady, with the confidence of a practised chess-player, who has foreseen an apparently dangerous move on the part of his adversary, and so is not at all taken aback by it.

"How does it prove nothing?" muttered Pavel Petrovitch, astounded. "You must be going against the people then?"

"And what if we are?" shouted Bazarov. "The people imagine that, when it thunders, the prophet Ilya's riding across the sky in his chariot. What then? Are we to agree with them? Besides, the people's Russian; but am I not Russian too?"

"No, you are not Russian, after all you have just been saying! I can't acknowledge you as Russian."

"My grandfather ploughed the land," answered Bazarov with haughty pride. "Ask any one of your peasants which of us—you or me—he'd more readily acknowledge as a fellow-countryman. You don't even know how to talk to them."

"While you talk to him and despise him at the same time."

"Well, suppose he deserves contempt. You find fault with my attitude, but how do you know that I have got it by chance, that it's not a product of that very national spirit, in the name of which you wage war on it?"

"What an idea! Much use in nihilists!"

"Whether they're of use or not, is not for us to decide. Why, even you suppose you're not a useless person."

"Gentlemen, gentlemen, no personalities, please!" cried Nikolai Petrovitch, getting up.

Pavel Petrovitch smiled, and laying his hand on his brother's shoulder, forced him to sit down again.

"Don't be uneasy," he said; "I shall not forget myself, just through that sense of dignity which is made fun of so mercilessly by our friend—our friend, the doctor. Let me ask," he resumed, turning again to Bazarov; "you suppose, possibly, that your doctrine is a novelty? That is quite a mistake. The materialism you advocate has been more than once in vogue already, and has always proved insufficient . . ."

"A foreign word again!" broke in Bazarov. He was beginning to feel vicious, and his face assumed a peculiar coarse coppery hue. "In the first place, we advocate nothing; that's not our way."

"What do you do, then?"

"I'll tell you what we do. Not long ago we used to say that our officials took bribes, that we had no roads, no commerce, no real justice . . ."

"Oh, I see, you are reformers—that's what that's called, I fancy. I too should agree to many of your reforms, but . . ."

"Then we suspected that talk, perpetual talk, and nothing but talk, about our social diseases, was not worth while, that it all led to nothing but superficiality and pedantry; we saw that our leading men, so-called advanced people and reformers, are no good; that we busy ourselves over foolery, talk rubbish about art, unconscious creativeness, parliamentarism, trial by jury, and the deuce knows what all; while, all the while, it's a question of getting bread to eat, while we're stifling under the grossest superstition, while all our enterprises come to grief, simply because there aren't honest men enough to carry them on, while the very emancipation our Government's busy upon will hardly come to any good, because peasants are glad to rob even themselves to get drunk at the gin-shop."

"Yes," interposed Pavel Petrovitch, "yes; you were convinced of all this, and decided not to undertake anything seriously, yourselves."

"We decided not to undertake anything," repeated Bazarov grimly. He suddenly felt vexed with himself for having, without reason, been so expansive before this gentleman.

"But to confine yourselves to abuse?"

"To confine ourselves to abuse."

"And that is called nihilism?"

"And that's called nihilism," Bazarov repeated again, this time with peculiar rudeness.

Pavel Petrovitch puckered up his face a little. "So that's it!" he observed in a strangely composed voice. "Nihilism is to cure all our woes, and you, you are our heroes and saviours. But why do you abuse others, those reformers even? Don't you do as much talking as every one else?"

"Whatever faults we have, we do not err in that way," Bazarov muttered between his teeth.

"What, then? Do you act, or what? Are you preparing for action?"

Bazarov made no answer. Something like a tremor passed over Pavel Petrovitch, but he at once regained control of himself.

"Hm! . . . Action, destruction . . ." he went on. "But how destroy without even knowing why?"

"We shall destroy, because we are a force," observed Arkady.

Pavel Petrovitch looked at his nephew and laughed.

"Yes, a force is not to be called to account," said Arkady, drawing himself up.

"Unhappy boy!" wailed Pavel Petrovitch, he was positively incapable of maintaining his firm demeanour any longer. "If you could only realise what it is you are doing for your country. No; it's enough to try the patience of an angel! Force! There's force in the savage Kalmuck, in the Mongolian; but what is it to us? What is precious to us is civilisation; yes, yes, sir, its fruits are precious to us. And don't tell me those fruits are worthless; the poorest dauber, *un barbouilleur,* the man who plays dance music for five farthings an evening, is of more use than you, because they are the representatives of civilisation, and not of brute Mongolian force! You fancy yourselves advanced people, and all the while you are only fit for the Kalmuck's hovel! Force! And recollect, you forcible gentlemen, that you're only four men and a half, and the others are millions, who won't let you trample their sacred traditions under foot, who will crush you and walk over you!"

"If we're crushed, serve us right," observed Bazarov. "But that's an open question. We are not so few as you suppose."

"What? You seriously suppose you will come to terms with a whole people?"

"All Moscow was burnt down, you know, by a farthing dip," answered Bazarov.

"Yes, yes. First a pride almost Satanic, then ridicule—that, that's what it is attracts the young, that's what gains an ascendancy over the inexperienced hearts of boys! Here's one of them sitting beside you, ready to worship the ground under your feet. Look at him! (Arkady turned away and frowned.) And this plague has spread far already. I have been told that in Rome our artists never set foot in the Vatican. Raphael they regard as almost a fool, because, if you please, he's an authority; while they're all the while most disgustingly sterile and unsuccessful, men whose imagination does not soar beyond "Girls at a Fountain," however

they try! And the girls even out of drawing. They are fine fellows
to your mind, are they not?"

"To my mind," retorted Bazarov, "Raphael's not worth a
brass farthing; and they're no better than he."

"Bravo! bravo! Listen, Arkady . . . that's how young men of
to-day ought to express themselves! And if you come to think of
it, how could they fail to follow you! In old days, young men had
to study; they didn't want to be called dunces, so they had to work
hard whether they liked it or not. But now, they need only say,
"Everything in the world is foolery!" and the trick's done. Young
men are delighted. And, to be sure, they were simply geese
before, and now they have suddenly turned nihilists."

"Your praiseworthy sense of personal dignity has given
way," remarked Bazarov phlegmatically, while Arkady was hot
all over, and his eyes were flashing. "Our argument has gone too
far; it's better to cut it short, I think. I shall be quite ready to agree
with you," he added, getting up, "when you bring forward a
single institution in our present mode of life, in family or in social
life, which does not call for complete and unqualified destruction."

"I will bring forward millions of such institutions," cried
Pavel Petrovitch—"millions! Well—the Mir, for instance."

A cold smile curved Bazarov's lips. "Well, as regards the
Mir," he commented; "you had better talk to your brother. He
has seen by now, I should fancy, what sort of thing the Mir is in
fact—its common guarantee, its sobriety, and other features of the
kind."

"The family, then, the family as it exists among our peasants!" cried Pavel Petrovitch.

"And that subject, too, I imagine, it will be better for yourselves not to go into in detail. Don't you realise all the advantages
of the head of the family choosing his daughters-in-law? Take my
advice, Pavel Petrovitch, allow yourself two days to think about
it; you're not likely to find anything on the spot. Go through all
our classes, and think well over each, while I and Arkady will
. . ."

"Will go on turning everything into ridicule," broke in Pavel Petrovitch.

"No, will go on dissecting frogs. Come, Arkady; good-bye for the present, gentlemen!"

The two friends walked off. The brothers were left alone, and at first they only looked at one another.

"So that," began Pavel Petrovitch, "so that's what our young men of this generation are! They are like that—our successors!"

"Our successors!" repeated Nikolai Petrovitch, with a dejected smile. He had been sitting on thorns, all through the argument, and had done nothing but glance stealthily, with a sore heart, at Arkady. "Do you know what I was reminded of, brother? I once had a dispute with our poor mother; she stormed, and wouldn't listen to me. At last I said to her, "Of course, you can't understand me; we belong," I said, "to two different generations." She was dreadfully offended, while I thought, "There's no help for it. It's a bitter pill, but she has to swallow it." You see, now, our turn has come, and our successors can say to us, "You are not of our generation; swallow your pill.'"

"You are beyond everything in your generosity and modesty," replied Pavel Petrovitch. "I'm convinced, on the contrary, that you and I are far more in the right than these young gentlemen, though we do perhaps express ourselves in old-fashioned language, *vieilli,* and have not the same insolent conceit. . . . And the swagger of the young men nowadays! You ask one, "Do you take red wine or white?" "It is my custom to prefer red!" he answers in a deep bass, with a face as solemn as if the whole universe had its eyes on him at that instant. . . ."

"Do you care for any more tea?" asked Fenitchka, putting her head in at the door; she had not been able to make up her mind to come into the drawing-room while there was the sound of voices in dispute there.

"No, you can tell them to take the samovar," answered Nikolai Petrovitch, and he got up to meet her. Pavel Petrovitch said *"bon soir"* to him abruptly, and went away to his study.

XI

Half an hour later Nikolai Petrovitch went into the garden to his favourite arbour. He was overtaken by melancholy thoughts. For the first time he realised clearly the distance between him and his son; he foresaw that every day it would grow wider and wider. In vain, then, had he spent whole days sometimes in the winter at Petersburg over the newest books; in vain had he listened to the talk of the young men; in vain had he rejoiced when he succeeded in putting in his word too in their heated discussions. "My brother says we are right," he thought, "and apart from all vanity, I do think myself that they are further from the truth than we are, though at the same time I feel there is something behind them we have not got, some superiority over us. . . . Is it youth? No; not only youth. Doesn't their superiority consist in there being fewer traces of the slaveowner in them than in us?"

Nikolai Petrovitch's head sank despondently, and he passed his hand over his face.

"But to renounce poetry?" he thought again; "to have no feeling for art, for nature . . ."

And he looked round, as though trying to understand how it was possible to have no feeling for nature. It was already evening; the sun was hidden behind a small copse of aspens which lay a quarter of a mile from the garden; its shadow stretched indefinitely across the still fields. A peasant on a white nag went at a trot along the dark, narrow path close beside the copse; his whole figure was clearly visible even to the patch on his shoulder, in spite of his being in the shade; the horse's hoofs flew along bravely. The sun's rays from the farther side fell full on the copse, and piercing through its thickets, threw such a warm light on the aspen trunks that they looked like pines, and their leaves were almost a dark blue, while above them rose a pale blue sky, faintly tinged by the glow of sunset. The swallows flew high; the wind had quite died away, belated bees hummed slowly and drowsily among the lilac blossom; a swarm of midges hung like a cloud over a solitary branch which stood out against the sky. "How beautiful, my God!" thought Nikolai Petrovitch, and his favourite verses were almost on his lips; he remembered Arkady's *Stoff und Kraft*—and was silent, but still he sat there, still he gave himself up to the sorrowful consolation of solitary thought. He was fond of dreaming; his country life had developed the tendency in him. How short a time ago, he had been dreaming like this, waiting for his son at the posting station, and what a change already since that day; their relations that were then undefined, were defined now—and how defined! Again his dead wife came back to his imagination, but not as he had known her for many years, not as the good domestic housewife, but as a young girl with a slim figure, innocently inquiring eyes, and a tight twist of hair on her childish neck. He remembered how he had seen her for the first time. He was still a student then. He had met her on the staircase of his lodgings, and, jostling by accident against her, he tried to apologise, and could only mutter, *"Pardon, monsieur,"* while she bowed, smiled, and suddenly seemed frightened, and ran away, though at the bend of the staircase she had glanced rapidly at him, assumed a serious air, and blushed. Afterwards, the first timid visits, the half-words, the half-smiles, and embarrassment; and melancholy, and yearnings, and at last that breathing rapture. . . . Where had it all vanished? She had been his wife, he had been happy as few on earth are happy. . . . "But," he mused, "these sweet first moments, why could one not live an eternal, undying life in them?"

He did not try to make his thought clear to himself; but he felt that he longed to keep that blissful time by something stronger than memory; he longed to feel his Marya near him again to have the sense of her warmth and breathing, and already he could fancy that over him. . . .

"Nikolai Petrovitch," came the sound of Fenitchka's voice close by him; "where are you?"

He started. He felt no pang, no shame. He never even admitted the possibility of comparison between his wife and Fenitchka, but he was sorry she had thought of coming to look for

him. Her voice had brought back to him at once his grey hairs,
his age, his reality. . . .

The enchanted world into which he was just stepping, which
was just rising out of the dim mists of the past, was shaken—and
vanished.

"I'm here," he answered; "I'm coming, run along." "There
it is, the traces of the slave owner," flashed through his mind.
Fenitchka peeped into the arbour at him without speaking, and
disappeared; while he noticed with astonishment that the night
had come on while he had been dreaming. Everything around
was dark and hushed. Fenitchka's face had glimmered so pale and
slight before him. He got up, and was about to go home; but the
emotion stirred in his heart could not be soothed at once, and he
began slowly walking about the garden, sometimes looking at the
ground at his feet, and then raising his eyes towards the sky where
swarms of stars were twinkling. He walked a great deal, till he was
almost tired out, while the restlessness within him, a kind of
yearning, vague, melancholy restlessness, still was not appeased.
Oh, how Bazarov would have laughed at him, if he had known
what was passing within him then! Arkady himself would have
condemned him. He, a man forty-four years old, an agriculturist
and a farmer, was shedding tears, causeless tears; this was a hundred times worse than the violoncello.

Nikolai Petrovitch continued walking, and could not make
up his mind to go into the house, into the snug peaceful nest,
which looked out at him so hospitably from all its lighted windows; he had not the force to tear himself away from the darkness,
the garden, the sense of the fresh air in his face, from that melancholy, that restless craving.

At a turn in the path, he was met by Pavel Petrovitch.
"What's the matter with you?" he asked Nikolai Petrovitch; "you
are as white as a ghost; you are not well; why don't you go to
bed?"

Nikolai Petrovitch explained to him briefly his state of feeling and moved away. Pavel Petrovitch went to the end of the
garden, and he too grew thoughtful, and he too raised his eyes
towards the heavens. But in his beautiful dark eyes, nothing was

reflected but the light of the stars. He was not born an idealist, and his fastidiously dry and sensuous soul, with its French tinge of cynicism was not capable of dreaming.

"Do you know what?" Bazarov was saying to Arkady the same night. "I've got a splendid idea. Your father was saying to-day that he'd had an invitation from your illustrious relative. Your father's not going; let us be off to X——; you know the worthy man invites you too. You see what fine weather it is; we'll stroll about and look at the town. We'll have five or six days' outing, and enjoy ourselves."

"And you'll come back here again?"

"No; I must go to my father's. You know, he lives about twenty-five miles from X——. I've not seen him for a long while, and my mother too; I must cheer the old people up. They've been good to me, especially my father; he's awfully funny. I'm their only one too."

"And will you be long with them?"

"I don't suppose so. It will be dull, of course."

"And you'll come to us on your way back?"

"I don't know . . . I'll see. Well, what do you say? Shall we go?"

"If you like," observed Arkady languidly.

In his heart he was highly delighted with his friend's suggestion, but he thought it a duty to conceal his feeling. He was not a nihilist for nothing!

The next day he set off with Bazarov to X——. The younger part of the household at Maryino were sorry at their going; Dunyasha even cried . . . but the old folks breathed more easily.

XII

The town of X—— to which our friends set off was in the jurisdiction of a governor who was a young man, and at once a progressive and a despot, as often happens with Russians. Before the end of the first year of his government, he had managed to

quarrel not only with the marshal of nobility, a retired officer of
the guards, who kept open house and a stud of horses, but even
with his own subordinates. The feuds arising from this cause
assumed at last such proportions that the ministry in Petersburg
had found it necessary to send down a trusted personage with a
commission to investigate it all on the spot. The choice of the
authorities fell upon Matvy Ilyitch Kolyazin, the son of the Kolyazin, under whose protection the brothers Kirsanov had once
found themselves. He, too, was a "young man"; that is to say, he
had not long passed forty, but he was already on the high road
to becoming a statesman, and wore a star on each side of his
breast—one, to be sure, a foreign star, not of the first magnitude.
Like the governor, whom he had come down to pass judgment
upon, he was reckoned a progressive; and though he was already
a bigwig, he was not like the majority of bigwigs. He had the
highest opinion of himself, his vanity knew no bounds, but he
behaved simply, looked affable, listened condescendingly, and
laughed so good-naturedly, that on a first acquaintance he might
even be taken for "a jolly good fellow." On important occasions,
however, he knew, as the saying is, how to make his authority felt.
"Energy is essential," he used to say then, *"l'énergie est la pre-
mière qualité d'un homme d'état;"* and for all that, he was usually
taken in, and any moderately experienced official could turn him
round his finger. Matvy Ilyitch used to speak with great respect
of Guizot, and tried to impress every one with the idea that he
did not belong to the class of *routiniers* and high-and-dry bureau-
crats, that not a single phenomenon of social life passed unnoticed
by him. . . . All such phrases were very familiar to him. He even
followed, with dignified indifference, it is true, the development
of contemporary literature; so a grown-up man who meets a
procession of small boys in the street will sometimes walk after
it. In reality, Matvy Ilyitch had not got much beyond those political men of the days of Alexander, who used to prepare for an
evening party at Madame Svyetchin's by reading a page of Con-
dillac; only his methods were different, more modern. He was an
adroit courtier, a great hypocrite, and nothing more; he had no
special aptitude for affairs, and no intellect, but he knew how to

manage his own business successfully; no one could get the better of him there, and, to be sure, that's the principal thing.

Matvy Ilyitch received Arkady with the good-nature, we might even call it playfulness, characteristic of the enlightened higher official. He was astonished, however, when he heard that the cousins he had invited had remained at home in the country. "Your father was always a queer fellow," he remarked, playing with the tassels of his magnificent velvet dressing-gown, and suddenly turning to a young official in a discreetly buttoned-up uniform, he cried, with an air of concentrated attention, "What?" The young man, whose lips were glued together from prolonged silence, got up and looked in perplexity at his chief. But, having nonplussed his subordinate, Matvy Ilyitch paid him no further attention. Our higher officials are fond as a rule of nonplussing their subordinates; the methods to which they have recourse to attain that end are rather various. The following means, among others, is in great vogue, *"is quite a favourite,"* as the English say; a high official suddenly ceases to understand the simplest words, assuming total deafness. He will ask, for instance, "What's to-day?"

He is respectfully informed, "To-day's Friday, your Ex-s-s-s-lency."

"Eh? What? What's that? What do you say?" the great man repeats with intense attention.

"To-day's Friday, your Ex—s—s—lency."

"Eh? What? What's Friday? What Friday?"

"Friday, your Ex—s—s—s—lency, the day of the week."

"What, do you pretend to teach me, eh?"

Matvy Ilyitch was a higher official all the same, though he was reckoned a liberal.

"I advise you, my dear boy, to go and call on the Governor," he said to Arkady; "you understand, I don't advise you to do so because I adhere to old-fashioned ideas of the necessity of paying respect to authorities, but simply because the Governor's a very decent fellow; besides, you probably want to make acquaintance with the society here. . . . You're not a bear, I hope? And he's giving a great ball the day after to-morrow."

"Will you be at the ball?" inquired Arkady.

"He gives it in my honour," answered Matvy Ilyitch, almost pityingly. "Do you dance?"

"Yes; I dance, but not well."

"That's a pity! There are pretty girls here, and it's a disgrace for a young man not to dance. Again, I don't say that through any old-fashioned ideas; I don't in the least imagine that a man's wit lies in his feet, but Byronism is ridiculous, *il a fait son temps.*"

"But, uncle, it's not through Byronism, I . . ."

"I will introduce you to the ladies here; I will take you under my wing," interrupted Matvy Ilyitch, and he laughed complacently. "You'll find it warm, eh?"

A servant entered and announced the arrival of the superintendent of the Crown domains, a mild-eyed old man, with deep creases round his mouth, who was excessively fond of nature, especially on a summer day, when, in his words, "every little busy bee takes a little bribe from every little flower." Arkady withdrew.

He found Bazarov at the tavern where they were staying, and was a long while persuading him to go with him to the Governor's. "Well, there's no help for it," said Bazarov at last. "It's no good doing things by halves. We came to look at the gentry; let's look at them!"

The Governor received the young men affably, but he did not ask them to sit down, nor did he sit down himself. He was in an everlasting fuss and hurry; in the morning he used to put on a tight uniform and an excessively stiff cravat; he never ate or drank enough; he was for ever making arrangements. He invited Kirsanov and Bazarov to his ball, and within a few minutes invited them a second time, regarding them as brothers, and calling them Kisarov.

They were on their way home from the Governor's, when suddenly a short man, in a Slavophil national dress, leaped out of a trap that was passing them, and crying, "Yevgeny Vassilyitch!" dashed up to Bazarov.

"Ah! it's you, Herr Sitnikov," observed Bazarov, still stepping along on the pavement; "by what chance did you come here?"

"Fancy, absolutely by chance," he replied, and returning to the trap, he waved his hand several times, and shouted, "Follow, follow us! My father had business here," he went on, hopping across the gutter, "and so he asked me. . . . I heard to-day of your arrival, and have already been to see you. . . . (The friends did, in fact, on returning to their room, find there a card, with the corners turned down, bearing the name of Sitnikov, on one side in French, on the other in Slavonic characters.) "I hope you are not coming from the Governor's?"

"It's no use to hope; we come straight from him."

"Ah! in that case I will call on him too. . . . Yevgeny Vassilyitch, introduce me to your . . . to the . . ."

"Sitnikov, Kirsanov," mumbled Bazarov, not stopping.

"I am greatly flattered," began Sitnikov, walking sidewise, smirking, and hurriedly pulling off his really over-elegant gloves. "I have heard so much. . . . I am an old acquaintance of Yevgeny Vassilyitch, and, I may say—his disciple. I am indebted to him for my regeneration. . . ."

Arkady looked at Bazarov's disciple. There was an expression of excitement and dulness imprinted on the small but pleasant features of his well-groomed face; his small eyes, that seemed squeezed in, had a fixed and uneasy look, and his laugh, too, was uneasy—a sort of short, wooden laugh.

"Would you believe it," he pursued, "when Yevgeny Vassilyitch for the first time said before me that it was not right to accept any authorities, I felt such enthusiasm . . . as though my eyes were opened! Here, I thought, at last I have found a man! By the way, Yevgeny Vassilyitch, you positively must come to know a lady here, who is really capable of understanding you, and for whom your visit would be a real festival; you have heard of her, I suppose?"

"Who is it?" Bazarov brought out unwillingly.

"Kukshina, *Eudoxie*, Evdoksya Kukshin. She's a remarkable nature, *émancipée* in the true sense of the word, an advanced woman. Do you know what? We'll all go together to see her now.

She lives only two steps from here. We will have lunch there. I suppose you have not lunched yet?"

"No; not yet."

"Well, that's capital. She has separated, you understand, from her husband; she is not dependent on any one."

"Is she pretty?" Bazarov cut in.

"N . . . no, one couldn't say that."

"Then, what the devil are you asking us to see her for?"

"Fie; you must have your joke. . . . She will give us a bottle of champagne."

"Oh, that's it. One can see the practical man at once. By the way, is your father still in the gin business?"

"Yes," said Sitnikov, hurriedly, and he gave a shrill spasmodic laugh. "Well? Will you come?"

"I don't really know."

"You wanted to see people, go along," said Arkady in an undertone.

"And what do you say to it, Mr. Kirsanov Sitnikov put in. "You must come too; can't go without you."

"But how can we burst in upon her all at once?"

"That's no matter. Kukshina's a brick!"

"There will be a bottle of champagne?" asked Bazarov.

"Three!" cried Sitnikov; "that I answer for."

"What with?"

"My own head."

"Your father's purse would be better. However, we are coming."

XIII

The small gentleman's house in the Moscow style, in which Avdotya Nikitishna, otherwise Evdoksya, Kukshin, lived, was in one of the streets of X——, which had been lately burnt down; it is well known that our provincial towns are burnt down every five years. At the door, above a visiting card nailed on all askew, there was a bell-handle to be seen, and in the hall the visitors were met by some one, not exactly a servant, nor exactly a companion, in a cap—unmistakable tokens of the progressive tendencies of the lady of the house. Sitnikov inquired whether Avdotya Nikitishna was at home.

"Is that you, *Victor?*" sounded a shrill voice from the adjoining room. "Come in."

The woman in the cap disappeared at once.

"I'm not alone," observed Sitnikov, with a sharp look at Arkady and Bazarov as he briskly pulled off his overcoat, beneath which appeared something of the nature of a coachman's velvet jacket.

"No matter," answered the voice. *"Entrez."*

The young men went in. The room into which they walked was more like a working study than a drawing-room. Papers, letters, fat numbers of Russian journals, for the most part uncut, lay at random on the dusty tables; white cigarette ends lay scattered in every direction. On a leather-covered sofa, a lady, still young, was half reclining. Her fair hair was rather dishevelled; she wore a silk gown, not perfectly tidy, heavy bracelets on her short arms, and a lace handkerchief on her head. She got up from the sofa, and carelessly drawing a velvet cape trimmed with yellowish ermine over her shoulders, she said languidly, "Goodmorning, *Victor,*" and pressed Sitnikov's hand.

"Bazarov, Kirsanov," he announced abruptly in imitation of Bazarov.

"Delighted," answered Madame Kukshin, and fixing on Bazarov a pair of round eyes, between which was a forlorn little turned-up red nose, "I know you," she added, and pressed his hand too.

Bazarov scowled. There was nothing repulsive in the little plain person of the emancipated woman; but the expression of her face produced a disagreeable effect on the spectator. One felt impelled to ask her, "What's the matter; are you hungry? Or bored? Or shy? What are you in a fidget about?" Both she and Sitnikov had always the same uneasy air. She was extremely unconstrained, and at the same time awkward; she obviously regarded herself as a good-natured, simple creature, and all the while, whatever she did, it always struck one that it was not just what she wanted to do; everything with her seemed, as children say, done on purpose, that's to say, not simply, not naturally.

"Yes, yes, I know you, Bazarov," she repeated. (She had the habit—peculiar to many provincial and Moscow ladies—of calling men by their surnames from the first day of acquaintance with them.) "Will you have a cigar?"

"A cigar's all very well," put in Sitnikov, who by now was lolling in an armchair, his legs in the air; "but give us some lunch. We're awfully hungry; and tell them to bring us up a little bottle of champagne."

"Sybarite," commented Evdoksya, and she laughed. (When she laughed the gum showed above her upper teeth.) "Isn't it true, Bazarov; he's a Sybarite?"

"I like comfort in life," Sitnikov brought out, with dignity. "That does not prevent my being a Liberal."

"No, it does; it does prevent it!" cried Evdoksya. She gave directions, however, to her maid, both as regards the lunch and the champagne.

"What do you think about it?" she added, turning to Bazarov. "I'm persuaded you share my opinion."

"Well, no," retorted Bazarov; "a piece of meat's better than a piece of bread even from the chemical point of view."

"You are studying chemistry? That is my passion. I've even invented a new sort of composition myself."

"A composition? You?"

"Yes. And do you know for what purpose? To make dolls' heads so that they shouldn't break. I'm practical, too, you see. But everything's not quite ready yet. I've still to read Liebig. By the way, have you read Kislyakov's article on Female Labour, in the *Moscow Gazette?* Read it, please. You're interested in the woman question, I suppose? And in the schools too? What does your friend do? What is his name?"

Madame Kukshin shed her questions one after another with affected negligence, not waiting for an answer; spoilt children talk so to their nurses.

"My name's Arkady Nikolaitch Kirsanov, said Arkady, "and I'm doing nothing."

Evdoksya giggled. "How charming! What, don't you smoke? Victor, do you know, I'm very angry with you."

"What for?"

"They tell me you've begun singing the praises of George Sand again. A retrograde woman, and nothing else! How can people compare her with Emerson! She hasn't an idea on education, nor physiology, nor anything. She'd never, I'm persuaded, heard of embryology, and in these days—what can be done without that?" (Evdoksya even threw up her hands.) "Ah, what a wonderful article Elisyevitch has written on that subject! He's a gentleman of genius." (Evdoksya constantly made use of the word "gentleman" instead of the word "man.") "Bazarov, sit by me on the sofa. You don't know, perhaps, I'm awfully afraid of you."

"Why so? Allow me to ask."

"You're a dangerous gentleman; you're such a critic. Good God! yes! why, how absurd, I'm talking like some country lady. I really am a country lady, though. I manage my property myself; and only fancy, my bailiff Erofay's a wonderful type, quite like Cooper's Pathfinder; something in him so spontaneous! I've come to settle here finally; it's an intolerable town, isn't it? But what's one to do?"

"The town's like every town," Bazarov remarked coolly.

"All its interests are so petty, that's what's so awful! I used to spend the winters in Moscow . . . but now my lawful spouse, Monsieur Kukshin's residing there. And besides, Moscow nowadays . . . there, I don't know—it's not the same as it was. I'm thinking of going abroad; last year I was on the point of setting off."

"To Paris, I suppose?" queried Bazarov.

"To Paris and to Heidelberg."

"Why to Heidelberg?"

"How can you ask? Why, Bunsen's there!"

To this Bazarov could find no reply.

"*Pierre* Sapozhnikov . . . do you know him?"

"No, I don't."

"Not know *Pierre* Sapozhnikov . . . he's always at Lidia Hestatov's."

"I don't know her either."

"Well, it was he undertook to escort me. Thank God, I'm independent; I've no children. . . . What was that I said: *thank God!* It's no matter though."

Evdoksya rolled a cigarette up between her fingers, which were brown with tobacco stains, put it to her tongue, licked it up, and began smoking. The maid came in with a tray.

"Ah, here's lunch! Will you have an appetiser first? Victor, open the bottle; that's in your line."

"Yes, it's in my line," muttered Sitnikov, and again he gave vent to the same convulsive laugh.

"Are there any pretty women here?" inquired Bazarov, as he drank off a third glass.

"Yes, there are," answered Evdoksya; "but they're all such empty-headed creatures. *Mon amie,* Odintsova, for instance, is nice-looking. It's a pity her reputation's rather doubtful. . . . That wouldn't matter, though, but she's no independence in her views, no width, nothing . . . of all that. The whole system of education wants changing. I've thought a great deal about it; our women are very badly educated."

"There's no doing anything with them," put in Sitnikov; "one ought to despise them, and I do despise them fully and completely!" (The possibility of feeling and expressing contempt was the most agreeable sensation to Sitnikov; he used to attack women in especial, never suspecting that it was to be his fate a few months later to be cringing before his wife merely because she had been born a princess Durdoleosov.) "Not a single one of them would be capable of understanding our conversation; not a single one deserves to be spoken of by serious men like us!"

"But there's not the least need for them to understand our conversation," observed Bazarov.

"Whom do you mean?" put in Evdoksya.

"Pretty women."

"What? Do you adopt Proudhon's ideas, then?"

Bazarov drew himself up haughtily. "I don't adopt any one's ideas; I have my own."

"Damn all authorities!" shouted Sitnikov, delighted to have a chance of expressing himself boldly before the man he slavishly admired.

"But even Macaulay," Madame Kukshin was beginning . . .

"Damn Macaulay," thundered Sitnikov. "Are you going to stand up for the silly hussies?"

"For silly hussies, no, but for the rights of women, which I have sworn to defend to the last drop of my blood."

"Damn!"—but here Sitnikov stopped. "But I don't deny them," he said.

"No, I see you're a Slavophil."

"No, I'm not a Slavophil, though, of course . . ."

"No, no, no! You are a Slavophil. You're an advocate of patriarchal despotism. You want to have the whip in your hand!"

"A whip's an excellent thing," remarked Bazarov; "but we've got to the last drop."

"Of what?" interrupted Evdoksya.

"Of champagne, most honoured Avdotya Nikitishna, of champagne—not of your blood."

"I can never listen calmly when women are attacked," pursued Evdoksya. "It's awful, awful. Instead of attacking them, you'd better read Michelet's book, *De l'amour.* That's exquisite! Gentlemen, let us talk of love," added Evdoksya, letting her arm fall languidly on the rumpled sofa cushion.

A sudden silence followed. "No, why should we talk of love," said Bazarov; "but you mentioned just now a Madame Odintsov . . . That was what you called her, I think? Who is that lady?"

"She's charming, charming!" piped Sitnikov. "I will introduce you. Clever, rich, a widow. It's a pity, she's not yet advanced enough; she ought to see more of our Evdoksya. I drink to your health, *Evdoxie!* Let us clink glasses! *Et toc, et toc, et tin-tin-tin! Et toc, et toc, et tin-tin-tin! ! !*"

"Victor, you're a wretch."

The lunch dragged on a long while. The first bottle of champagne was followed by another, a third, and even a fourth. . . . Evdoksya chattered without pause; Sitnikov seconded her. They had much discussion upon the question whether marriage was a prejudice or a crime, and whether men were born equal or not, and precisely what individuality consists in. Things came at last to Evdoksya, flushed from the wine she had drunk, tapping with her flat finger-tips on the keys of a discordant piano, and beginning to sing in a hoarse voice, first gipsy songs, and then Seymour Schiff's song, "Granada lies slumbering"; while Sitnikov tied a scarf round his head, and represented the dying lover at the words—

> "And thy lips to mine
> In burning kiss entwine."

Arkady could not stand it at last. "Gentlemen, it's getting something like Bedlam," he remarked aloud. Bazarov, who had at rare intervals put in an ironical word in the conversation—he paid more attention to the champagne—gave a loud yawn, got up, and, without taking leave of their hostess, he walked off with Arkady. Sitnikov jumped up and followed them.

"Well, what do you think of her?" he inquired, skipping obsequiously from right to left of them. "I told you, you see, a remarkable personality! If we only had more women like that! She is, in her own way, an expression of the highest morality."

"And is that establishment of your governor's an expression of the highest morality too?" observed Bazarov, pointing to a ginshop which they were passing at that instant.

Sitnikov again went off into a shrill laugh. He was greatly ashamed of his origin, and did not know whether to feel flattered or offended at Bazarov's unexpected familiarity.

XIV

A few days later the ball at the Governor's took place. Matvy Ilyitch was the real "hero of the occasion." The marshal of nobility declared to all and each that he had come simply out of respect for him; while the Governor, even at the ball, even while he remained perfectly motionless, was still "making arrangements." The affability of Matvy Ilyitch's demeanour could only be equalled by its dignity. He was gracious to all, to some with a shade of disgust, to others with a shade of respect; he was all bows and smiles *"en vrai chevalier français"* before the ladies, and was continually giving vent to a hearty, sonorous, unshared laugh, such as befits a high official. He slapped Arkady on the back, and called him loudly "nephew"; vouchsafed Bazarov—who was attired in a rather old evening coat—a sidelong glance in passing— absent but condescending—and an indistinct but affable grunt, in which nothing could be distinguished but "I . . ." and "very much"; gave Sitnikov a finger and a smile, though with his head already averted; even to Madame Kukshin, who made her appearance at the ball with dirty gloves, no crinoline, and a bird of Paradise in her hair, he said *"enchanté."* There were crowds of people, and no lack of dancing men; the civilians were for the most part standing close along the walls, but the officers danced assiduously, especially one of them who had spent six weeks in Paris, where he had mastered various daring interjections of the kind of—*"zut,"* *"Ah, fichtr-re,"* *"pst, pst, mon bibi,"* and such. He pronounced them to perfection with genuine Parisian *chic,* and at the same time he said *"si j'aurais"* for *"si j'avais,"* *"absolument"* in the sense of "absolutely," expressed himself, in fact, in that Great Russo-French jargon which the French ridicule so when they have no reason for assuring us that we speak French like angels, *"comme des anges."*

Arkady, as we are aware, danced badly, while Bazarov did not dance at all; they both took up their position in a corner; Sitnikov joined himself on to them, with an expression of contemptuous scorn on his face, and giving vent to spiteful comments, he looked insolently about him, and seemed to be really enjoying himself. Suddenly his face changed, and turning to Arkady, he said, with some show of embarrassment it seemed, "Odintsova is here!"

Arkady looked round, and saw a tall woman in a black dress

standing at the door of the room. He was struck by the dignity
of her carriage. Her bare arms lay gracefully beside her slender
waist; gracefully some light sprays of fuchsia drooped from her
shining hair on to her sloping shoulders; her clear eyes looked out
from under a rather overhanging white brow, with a tranquil and
intelligent expression—tranquil it was precisely, not pensive—
and on her lips was a scarcely perceptible smile. There was a kind
of gracious and gentle force about her face.

"Do you know her?" Arkady asked Sitnikov.

"Intimately. Would you like me to introduce you?"

"Please . . . after this quadrille."

Bazarov's attention, too, was directed to Madame Odintsov.

"That's a striking figure," he remarked. "Not like the other
females."

After waiting till the end of the quadrille, Sitnikov led Arkady up to Madame Odintsov; but he hardly seemed to be intimately acquainted with her; he was embarrassed in his sentences,
while she looked at him in some surprise. But her face assumed
an expression of pleasure when she heard Arkady's surname. She
asked him whether he was not the son of Nikolai Petrovitch.

"Yes."

"I have seen your father twice, and have heard a great deal
about him," she went on; "I am glad to make your acquaintance."

At that instant some adjutant flew up to her and begged for
a quadrille. She consented.

"Do you dance then?" asked Arkady respectfully.

"Yes, I dance. Why do you suppose I don't dance? Do you
think I am too old?"

"Really, how could I possibly. . . . But in that case, let me
ask you for a mazurka."

Madame Odintsov smiled graciously. "Certainly," she said,
and she looked at Arkady, not exactly with an air of superiority,
but as married sisters look at very young brothers. Madame
Odintsov was a little older than Arkady—she was twenty-nine—
but in her presence he felt himself a schoolboy, a little student,
so that the difference in age between them seemed of more consequence. Matvy Ilyitch approached her with a majestic air and

ingratiating speeches. Arkady moved away, but he still watched her; he could not take his eyes off her even during the quadrille. She talked with equal ease to her partner and to the grand official, softly turned her head and eyes, and twice laughed softly. Her nose—like almost all Russian noses—was a little thick; and her complexion was not perfectly clear; Arkady made up his mind, for all that, that he had never before met such an attractive woman. He could not get the sound of her voice out of his ears; the very folds of her dress seemed to hang upon her differently from all the rest—more gracefully and amply—and her movements were distinguished by a peculiar smoothness and naturalness.

Arkady felt some timidity in his heart when at the first sounds of the mazurka he began to sit it out beside his partner; he had prepared to enter into a conversation with her, but he only passed his hand through his hair, and could not find a single word to say. But his timidity and agitation did not last long; Madame Odintsov's tranquillity gained upon him too; before a quarter of an hour had passed he was telling her freely about his father, his uncle, his life in Petersburg and in the country. Madame Odintsov listened to him with courteous sympathy, slightly opening and closing her fan; his talk was broken off when partners came for her; Sitnikov, among others, twice asked her. She came back, sat down again, took up her fan, and her bosom did not even heave more rapidly, while Arkady fell to chattering again, filled through and through by the happiness of being near her, talking to her, looking at her eyes, her lovely brow, all her sweet, dignified, clever face. She said little, but her words showed a knowledge of life; from some of her observations, Arkady gathered that this young woman had already felt and thought much. . . .

"Who is that you were standing with?" she asked him, "when Mr. Sitnikov brought you to me?"

"Did you notice him?" Arkady asked in his turn. "He has a splendid face, hasn't he? That's Bazarov, my friend."

Arkady fell to discussing "his friend." He spoke of him in such detail, and with such enthusiasm, that Madame Odintsov turned towards him and looked attentively at him. Meanwhile, the mazurka was drawing to a close. Arkady felt sorry to part from his partner; he had spent nearly an hour so happily with her! He had, it is true, during the whole time continually felt as though she were condescending to him, as though he ought to be grateful to her . . . but young hearts are not weighed down by that feeling.

The music stopped. *"Merci,"* said Madame Odintsov, getting up. "You promised to come and see me; bring your friend with you. I shall be very curious to see the man who has the courage to believe in nothing."

The Governor came up to Madame Odintsov, announced that supper was ready, and, with a careworn face, offered her his arm. As she went away, she turned to give a last smile and bow to Arkady. He bowed low, looked after her (how graceful her figure seemed to him, draped in the greyish lustre of the black silk!), and thinking, "This minute she has forgotten my existence," was conscious of an exquisite humility in his soul.

"Well?" Bazarov questioned him, directly he had gone back to him in the corner. "Did you have a good time? A gentleman has just been talking to me about that lady; he said, "She's—oh, fie! fie!" but I fancy the fellow was a fool. What do you think, what is she?—oh, fie! fie!"

"I don't quite understand that definition," answered Arkady.

"Oh, my! What innocence!"

"In that case, I don't understand the gentleman you quote. Madame Odintsov is very sweet, no doubt, but she behaves so coldly and severely, that . . ."

"Still waters . . . you know!" put in Bazarov. "That's just what gives it piquancy. You like ices, I expect?"

"Perhaps," muttered Arkady. "I can't give an opinion about that. She wishes to make your acquaintance, and has asked me to bring you to see her."

"I can imagine how you've described me! But you did very well. Take me. Whatever she may be—whether she's simply a provincial lioness, or "advanced" after Kukshina's fashion—any way she's got a pair of shoulders such as I've not set eyes on for a long while."

Arkady was wounded by Bazarov's cynicism, but—as often

happens—he reproached his friend not precisely for what he did not like in him . . .

"Why are you unwilling to allow freethinking in women?" he said in a low voice.

"Because, my boy, as far as my observations go, the only freethinkers among women are frights."

The conversation was cut short at this point. Both the young men went away immediately after supper. They were pursued by a nervously malicious, but somewhat faint-hearted laugh from Madame Kukshin; her vanity had been deeply wounded by neither of them having paid any attention to her. She stayed later than any one at the ball, and at four o'clock in the morning she was dancing a polka-mazurka with Sitnikov in the Parisian style. This edifying spectacle was the final event of the Governor's ball.

XV

"Let's see what species of mammalia this specimen belongs to," Bazarov said to Arkady the following day, as they mounted the staircase of the hotel in which Madame Odintsov was staying. "I scent out something wrong here."

"I'm surprised at you!" cried Arkady. "What? You, you, Bazarov, clinging to the narrow morality, which . . ."

"What a funny fellow you are!" Bazarov cut him short, carelessly. "Don't you know that "something wrong" means "something right" in my dialect and for me? It's an advantage for me, of course. Didn't you tell me yourself this morning that she made a strange marriage, though, to my mind, to marry a rich old man is by no means a strange thing to do, but, on the contrary, very sensible. I don't believe the gossip of the town; but I should like to think, as our cultivated Governor says, that it's well-grounded."

Arkady made no answer, and knocked at the door of the apartments. A young servant in livery conducted the two friends into a large room, badly furnished, like all rooms in Russian hotels, but filled with flowers. Soon Madame Odintsov herself appeared in a simple morning dress. She seemed still younger by the light of the spring sunshine. Arkady presented Bazarov, and noticed with secret amazement that he seemed embarrassed, while Madame Odintsov remained perfectly tranquil, as she had been the previous day. Bazarov himself was conscious of being embarrassed, and was irritated by it. "Here's a go!—frightened of a petticoat!" he thought, and lolling, quite like Sitnikov, in an easy-chair, he began talking with an exaggerated appearance of ease, while Madame Odintsov kept her clear eyes fixed on him.

Anna Sergyevna Odintsov was the daughter of Sergay Nikolaevitch Loktev, notorious for his personal beauty, his speculations, and his gambling propensities, who after cutting a figure and making a sensation for fifteen years in Petersburg and Moscow, finished by ruining himself completely at cards, and was forced to retire to the country, where, however, he soon after died, leaving a very small property to his two daughters—Anna, a girl of twenty, and Katya, a child of twelve. Their mother, who came of an impoverished line of princes—the H——s—had died at Petersburg when her husband was in his heyday. Anna's position after her father's death was very difficult. The brilliant education she had received in Petersburg had not fitted her for putting up with the cares of domestic life and economy,—for an obscure existence in the country. She knew positively no one in the whole neighbourhood, and there was no one she could consult. Her father had tried to avoid all contact with the neighbours; he despised them in his way, and they despised him in theirs. She did not lose her head, however, and promptly sent for a sister of her mother's, Princess Avdotya Stepanovna H——, a spiteful and arrogant old lady, who, on installing herself in her niece's house, appropriated all the best rooms for her own use, scolded and grumbled from morning till night, and would not go a walk even in the garden unattended by her one serf, a surly footman in a threadbare pea-green livery with light blue trimming and a three-cornered hat. Anna put up patiently with all her aunt's whims, gradually set to work on her sister's education, and was, it seemed, already getting reconciled to the idea of wasting her life in the wilds. . . . But destiny had decreed another fate for her. She chanced to be seen by Odintsov, a very wealthy man of forty-six, an eccentric hypochondriac, stout, heavy, and sour, but not stupid, and not ill-natured; he fell in love with her, and offered her his hand. She consented to become his wife, and he lived six years with her, and on his death settled all his property upon her. Anna Sergyevna remained in the country for nearly a year after his death; then she went abroad with her sister, but only stopped in Germany; she got tired of it, and came back to live at her favourite Nikolskoe, which was nearly thirty miles from the town of X——. There she had a magnificent, splendidly furnished house and a beautiful garden, with conservatories; her late husband had spared no expense to gratify his fancies. Anna Sergyevna went very rarely to the town, generally only on business, and even then she did not stay long. She was not liked in the province; there had been a fearful outcry at her marriage with Odintsov, all sorts of fictions were told about her; it was asserted that she had helped her father in his cardsharping tricks, and even that she had gone abroad for excellent reasons, that it had been necessary to conceal the lamentable consequences . . . "You understand?" the indignant gossips would wind up. "She has gone through the fire," was said of her; to which a noted provincial wit usually added: "And through all the other elements?" All this talk reached her; but she turned a deaf ear to it; there was much independence and a good deal of determination in her character.

Madame Odintsov sat leaning back in her easy-chair, and listened with folded hands to Bazarov. He, contrary to his habit, was talking a good deal, and obviously trying to interest her—again a surprise for Arkady. He could not make up his mind whether Bazarov was attaining his object. It was difficult to conjecture from Anna Sergyevna's face what impression was being made on her; it retained the same expression, gracious and refined; her beautiful eyes were lighted up by attention, but by quiet attention. Bazarov's bad manners had impressed her unpleasantly for the first minutes of the visit like a bad smell or a discordant sound; but she saw at once that he was nervous, and that even flattered her. Nothing was repulsive to her but vulgarity, and no one could have accused Bazarov of vulgarity. Arkady was fated to meet with surprises that day. He had expected that Bazarov would talk to a clever woman like Madame Odintsov about his opinions and his views; she had herself expressed a desire to listen to the man "who dares to have no belief in anything"; but, instead of that, Bazarov talked about medicine, about homoeopathy, and about botany. It turned out that Madame Odintsov had not wasted her time in solitude; she had read a good many excellent books, and spoke herself in excellent Russian. She turned the conversation upon music; but noticing that Bazarov did not appreciate art, she quietly brought it back to botany, even though Arkady was just launching into a discourse upon the significance of national melodies. Madame Odintsov treated him as though he were a younger brother; she seemed to appreciate his good-nature and youthful simplicity—and that was all. For over three hours, a lively conversation was kept up, ranging freely over various subjects.

The friends at last got up and began to take leave. Anna Sergyevna looked cordially at them, held out her beautiful, white hand to both, and, after a moment's thought, said with a doubtful but delightful smile, "If you are not afraid of being dull, gentlemen, come and see me at Nikolskoe."

"Oh, Anna Sergyevna," cried Arkady, "I shall think it the greatest happiness . . ."

"And you, Monsieur Bazarov?"

Bazarov only bowed, and a last surprise was in store for Arkady; he noticed that his friend was blushing.

"Well?" he said to him in the street; "are you still of the same opinion—that she's . . ."

"Who can tell? See how correct she is!" retorted Bazarov; and after a brief pause he added, "She's a perfect grand-duchess, a royal personage. She only needs a train on behind, and a crown on her head."

"Our grand-duchesses don't talk Russian like that," remarked Arkady.

"She's seen ups and downs, my dear boy; she's known what it is to be hard up!"

"Any way, she's charming," observed Arkady.

"What a magnificent body!" pursued Bazarov. "Shouldn't I like to see it on the dissecting-table."

"Hush, for mercy's sake, Yevgeny! that's beyond everything."

"Well, don't get angry, you baby. I meant it's first-rate. We must go to stay with her."

"When?"

"Well, why not the day after to-morrow. What is there to do here? Drink champagne with Kukshina. Listen to your cousin, the Liberal dignitary? . . . Let's be off the day after to-morrow. By the way, too—my father's little place is not far from there. This Nikolskoe's on the S—— road, isn't it?"

"Yes."

"Optime why hesitate? leave that to fools and prigs! I say, what a splendid body!"

Three days later the two friends were driving along the road to Nikolskoe. The day was bright, and not too hot, and the sleek posting-horses trotted smartly along, switching their tied and plaited tails. Arkady looked at the road, and not knowing why, he smiled.

"Congratulate me," cried Bazarov suddenly, "to-day's the 22nd of June, my guardian angel's day. Let's see how he will watch over me. To-day they expect me home," he added, dropping his voice. . . . "Well, they can go on expecting. . . . What does it matter!"

XVI

The country-house in which Anna Sergyevna lived stood on an exposed hill at no great distance from a yellow stone church with a green roof, white columns, and a fresco over the principal entrance representing the "Resurrection of Christ" in the "Italian" style. Sprawling in the foreground of the picture was a swarthy warrior in a helmet, specially conspicuous for his rotund contours. Behind the church a long village stretched in two rows, with chimneys peeping out here and there above the thatched roofs. The manor-house was built in the same style as the church, the style known among us as that of Alexander; the house too was painted yellow, and had a green roof, and white columns, and a pediment with an escutcheon on it. The architect had designed both buildings with the approval of the deceased Odintsov, who could not endure—as he expressed it—idle and arbitrary innovations. The house was enclosed on both sides by the dark trees of an old garden; an avenue of lopped pines led up to the entrance.

Our friends were met in the hall by two tall footmen in livery; one of them at once ran for the steward. The steward, a stout man in a black dress coat, promptly appeared and led the visitors by a staircase covered with rugs to a special room, in which two bedsteads were already prepared for them with all necessaries for the toilet. It was clear that order reigned supreme in the house; everything was clean, everywhere there was a peculiar delicate fragrance, just as there is in the reception rooms of ministers.

"Anna Sergyevna asks you to come to her in half-an-hour," the steward announced; "will there be orders to give meanwhile?"

"No orders," answered Bazarov; "perhaps you will be so good as to trouble yourself to bring me a glass of vodka."

"Yes, sir," said the steward, looking in some perplexity, and he withdrew, his boots creaking as he walked.

"What *grand genre!*" remarked Bazarov. "That's what it's called in your set, isn't it? She's a grand-duchess, and that's all about it."

"A nice grand-duchess," retorted Arkady, "at the very first meeting she invited such great aristocrats as you and me to stay with her."

"Especially me, a future doctor, and a doctor's son, and a village sexton's grandson. . . . You know, I suppose, I'm the grandson of a sexton? Like the great Speransky," added Bazarov after a brief pause, contracting his lips. "At any rate she likes to be comfortable; oh, doesn't she, this lady! Oughtn't we to put on evening dress?"

Arkady only shrugged his shoulders . . . but he too was conscious of a little nervousness.

Half-an-hour later Bazarov and Arkady went together into the drawing-room. It was a large lofty room, furnished rather luxuriously but without particularly good taste. Heavy, expensive furniture stood in the ordinary stiff arrangement along the walls, which were covered with cinnamon-coloured paper with gold flowers on it; Odintsov had ordered the furniture from Moscow through a friend and agent of his, a spirit merchant. Over a sofa in the centre of one wall hung a portrait of a faded light-haired man—and it seemed to look with displeasure at the visitors. "It must be the late lamented," Bazarov whispered to Arkady, and turning up his nose, he added, "Hadn't we better bolt . . .?" But at that instant the lady of the house entered. She wore a light barège dress; her hair smoothly combed back behind her ears gave a girlish expression to her pure and fresh face.

"Thank you for keeping your promise," she began. "You must stay a little while with me; it's really not bad here. I will introduce you to my sister; she plays the piano well. That is a matter of indifference to you, Monsieur Bazarov; but you, I think, Monsieur Kirsanov, are fond of music. Besides my sister I have an old aunt living with me, and one of our neighbours comes in sometimes to play cards; that makes up all our circle. And now let us sit down."

Madame Odintsov delivered all this little speech with peculiar precision, as though she had learned it by heart; then she turned to Arkady. It appeared that her mother had known Arkady's mother, and had even been her confidante in her love for Nikolai Petrovitch. Arkady began talking with great warmth of his dead mother; while Bazarov fell to turning over albums. "What a tame cat I'm getting!" he was thinking to himself.

A beautiful greyhound with a blue collar on, ran into the drawing-room, tapping on the floor with his paws, and after him entered a girl of eighteen, black-haired and dark-skinned, with a rather round but pleasing face, and small dark eyes. In her hands she held a basket filled with flowers.

"This is my Katya," said Madame Odintsov, indicating her with a motion of her head. Katya made a slight curtsey, placed herself beside her sister, and began picking out flowers. The greyhound, whose name was Fifi, went up to both of the visitors, in turn wagging his tail and thrusting his cold nose into their hands.

"Did you pick all that yourself?" asked Madame Odintsov.

"Yes," answered Katya.

"Is auntie coming to tea?"

"Yes."

When Katya spoke, she had a very charming smile, sweet, timid, and candid, and looked up from under her eyebrows with a sort of humorous severity. Everything about her was still young and undeveloped; the voice, and the bloom on her whole face, and the rosy hands, with white palms, and the rather narrow shoulders. . . . She was constantly blushing and getting out of breath.

Madame Odintsov turned to Bazarov. "You are looking at pictures from politeness, Yevgeny Vassilyitch," she began. "That does not interest you. You had better come nearer to us, and let us have a discussion about something."

Bazarov went closer. "What subject have you decided upon for discussion?" he said.

"What you like. I warn you, I am dreadfully argumentative."

"You?"

"Yes. That seems to surprise you. Why?"

"Because, as far as I can judge, you have a calm, cool character, and one must be impulsive to be argumentative."

"How can you have had time to understand me so soon? In the first place, I am impatient and obstinate—you should ask Katya; and secondly, I am very easily carried away."

Bazarov looked at Anna Sergyevna. "Perhaps; you must know best. And so you are inclined for a discussion—by all means. I was looking through the views of the Saxon mountains in your album, and you remarked that that couldn't interest me.

You said so, because you suppose me to have no feeling for art, and as a fact I haven't any; but these views might be interesting to me from a geological standpoint, for the formation of the mountains, for instance."

"Excuse me; but as a geologist, you would sooner have recourse to a book, to a special work on the subject, and not to a drawing."

"The drawing shows me at a glance what would be spread over ten pages in a book."

Anna Sergyevna was silent for a little.

"And so you haven't the least artistic feeling?" she observed, putting her elbow on the table, and by that very action bringing her face nearer to Bazarov. "How can you get on without it?"

"Why, what is it wanted for, may I ask?"

"Well, at least to enable one to study and understand men."

Bazarov smiled. "In the first place, experience of life does that; and in the second, I assure you, studying separate individuals is not worth the trouble. All people are like one another, in soul as in body; each of us has brain, spleen, heart, and lungs made alike; and the so-called moral qualities are the same in all; the slight variations are of no importance. A single human specimen is sufficient to judge of all by. People are like trees in a forest; no botanist would think of studying each individual birch-tree."

Katya, who was arranging the flowers, one at a time in a leisurely fashion, lifted her eyes to Bazarov with a puzzled look, and meeting his rapid and careless glance, she crimsoned up to her ears. Anna Sergyevna shook her head.

"The trees in a forest," she repeated. "Then according to you there is no difference between the stupid and the clever person, between the good-natured and ill-natured?"

"No, there is a difference, just as between the sick and the healthy. The lungs of a consumptive patient are not in the same condition as yours and mine, though they are made on the same plan. We know approximately what physical diseases come from; moral diseases come from bad education, from all the nonsense people's heads are stuffed with from childhood up, from the defective state of society; in short, reform society, and there will be no diseases."

Bazarov said all this with an air, as though he were all the while thinking to himself, "Believe me or not, as you like, it's all one to me!" He slowly passed his fingers over his whiskers, while his eyes strayed about the room.

"And you conclude," observed Anna Sergyevna, "that when society is reformed, there will be no stupid nor wicked people?"

"At any rate, in a proper organisation of society, it will be absolutely the same whether a man is stupid or clever, wicked or good."

"Yes, I understand; they will all have the same spleen."

"Precisely so, madam."

Madame Odintsov turned to Arkady. "And what is your opinion, Arkady Nikolaevitch?"

"I agree with Yevgeny," he answered.

Katya looked up at him from under her eyelids.

"You amaze me, gentlemen," commented Madame Odintsov, "but we will have more talk together. But now I hear my aunt coming in to tea; we must spare her."

Anna Sergyevna's aunt, Princess H——, a thin little woman with a pinched-up face, drawn together like a fist, and staring ill-natured-looking eyes under a grey front, came in, and, scarcely bowing to the guests, she dropped into a wide velvet covered arm-chair, upon which no one but herself was privileged to sit. Katya put a foot-stool under her feet; the old lady did not thank her, did not even look at her, only her hands shook under the yellow shawl, which almost covered her feeble body. The Princess liked yellow; her cap, too, had bright yellow ribbons.

"How have you slept, aunt? inquired Madame Odintsov, raising her voice.

"That dog in here again," the old lady muttered in reply, and noticing Fifi was making two hesitating steps in her direction, she cried, "Ss . . . ss!"

Katya called Fifi and opened the door for him.

Fifi rushed out delighted, in the expectation of being taken out for a walk; but when he was left alone outside the door, he began scratching and whining. The princess scowled. Katya was about to go out. . . .

"I expect tea is ready," said Madame Odintsov.

"Come, gentlemen; aunt, will you go in to tea?"

The princess got up from her chair without speaking and led the way out of the drawing-room. They all followed her into the dining-room. A little page in livery drew back, with a scraping sound, from the table, an arm-chair covered with cushions, devoted to the princess's use; she sank into it; Katya in pouring out the tea, handed her first a cup emblazoned with a heraldic crest. The old lady put some honey in her cup (she considered it both sinful and extravagant to drink tea with sugar in it, though she never spent a farthing herself on anything), and suddenly asked in a hoarse voice, "And what does Prince Ivan write?"

No one made her any reply. Bazarov and Arkady soon guessed that they paid no attention to her though they treated her respectfully.

"Because of her grand family," thought Bazarov. . . .

After tea, Anna Sergyevna suggested they should go out for a walk; but it began to rain a little, and the whole party, with the exception of the princess, returned to the drawing-room. The neighbour, the devoted card-player, arrived; his name was Porfiry Platonitch, a stoutish, greyish man with short, spindly legs, very polite and ready to be amused. Anna Sergyevna, who still talked principally with Bazarov, asked him whether he'd like to try a contest with them in the old-fashioned way at preference? Bazarov assented, saying "that he ought to prepare himself beforehand for the duties awaiting him as a country doctor."

"You must be careful," observed Anna Sergyevna; "Porfiry Platonitch and I will beat you. And you, Katya," she added, "play something to Arkady Nikolaevitch; he is fond of music, and we can listen, too."

Katya went unwillingly to the piano; and Arkady, though he certainly was fond of music, unwillingly followed her; it seemed to him that Madame Odintsov was sending him away, and already, like every young man at his age, he felt a vague and oppressive emotion surging up in his heart, like the forebodings of love. Katya raised the top of the piano, and not looking at Arkady, she said in a low voice—

"What am I to play you?"

"What you like," answered Arkady indifferently.

"What sort of music do you like best?" repeated Katya, without changing her attitude.

"Classical," Arkady answered in the same tone of voice.

"Do you like Mozart?"

"Yes, I like Mozart."

Katya pulled out Mozart's Sonata-Fantasia in C minor. She played very well, though rather over correctly and precisely. She sat upright and immovable, her eyes fixed on the notes, and her lips tightly compressed, only at the end of the sonata her face glowed, her hair came loose, and a little lock fell on to her dark brow.

Arkady was particularly struck by the last part of the sonata, the part in which, in the midst of the bewitching gaiety of the careless melody, the pangs of such mournful, almost tragic suffering, suddenly break in. . . . But the ideas stirred in him by Mozart's music had no reference to Katya. Looking at her, he simply thought, "Well, that young lady doesn't play badly, and she's not bad-looking either."

When she had finished the sonata, Katya, without taking her hands from the keys, asked, "Is that enough?" Arkady declared that he could not venture to trouble her again, and began talking to her about Mozart; he asked her whether she had chosen that sonata herself, or some one had recommended it to her. But Katya answered him in monosyllables; she withdrew into herself, went back into her shell. When this happened to her, she did not very quickly come out again; her face even assumed at such times an obstinate, almost stupid expression. She was not exactly shy, but diffident, and rather overawed by her sister, who had educated her, and who had no suspicion of the fact. Arkady was reduced at last to calling Fifi to him, and with an affable smile patting him on the head to give himself an appearance of being at home.

Katya set to work again upon her flowers.

Bazarov meanwhile was losing and losing. Anna Sergyevna

played cards in masterly fashion; Porfiry Platonitch, too, could hold his own in the game. Bazarov lost a sum which, though trifling in itself, was not altogether pleasant for him. At supper Anna Sergyevna again turned the conversation on botany.

"We will go for a walk to-morrow morning," she said to him; "I want you to teach me the Latin names of the wild flowers and their species."

"What use are the Latin names to you?" asked Bazarov.

"Order is needed in everything," she answered.

"What an exquisite woman Anna Sergyevna is!" cried Arkady, when he was alone with his friend in the room assigned to them.

"Yes," answered Bazarov, "a female with brains. Yes, and she's seen life too."

"In what sense do you mean that, Yevgeny Vassilitch?"

"In a good sense, a good sense, my dear friend, Arkady Nikolaitch! I'm convinced she manages her estate capitally too. But what's splendid is not her, but her sister."

"What, that little dark thing?"

"Yes, that little dark thing. She now is fresh and untouched, and shy and silent, and anything you like. She's worth educating and developing. You might make something fine out of her; but the other's—a stale loaf."

Arkady made no reply to Bazarov, and each of them got into bed with rather singular thoughts in his head.

Anna Sergyevna, too, thought of her guests that evening. She liked Bazarov for the absence of gallantry in him, and even for his sharply defined views. She found in him something new, which she had not chanced to meet before, and she was curious.

Anna Sergyevna was a rather strange creature. Having no prejudices of any kind, having no strong convictions even, she never gave way or went out of her way for anything. She had seen many things very clearly; she had been interested in many things, but nothing had completely satisfied her; indeed, she hardly desired complete satisfaction. Her intellect was at the same time inquiring and indifferent; her doubts were never soothed to forgetfulness, and they never grew strong enough to distract her.

Had she not been rich and independent, she would perhaps have thrown herself into the struggle, and have known passion. But life was easy for her, though she was bored at times, and she went on passing day after day with deliberation, never in a hurry, placid, and only rarely disturbed. Dreams sometimes danced in rainbow colours before her eyes even, but she breathed more freely when they died away, and did not regret them. Her imagination indeed overstepped the limits of what is reckoned permissible by conventional morality; but even then her blood flowed as quietly as ever in her fascinatingly graceful, tranquil body. Sometimes coming out of her fragrant bath all warm and enervated, she would fall to musing on the nothingness of life, the sorrow, the labour, the malice of it. . . . Her soul would be filled with sudden daring, and would flow with generous ardour, but a draught would blow from a half-closed window, and Anna Sergyevna would shrink into herself, and feel plaintive and almost angry, and there was only one thing she cared for at that instant—to get away from that horrid draught.

Like all women who have not succeeded in loving, she wanted something, without herself knowing what. Strictly speaking, she wanted nothing; but it seemed to her that she wanted everything. She could hardly endure the late Odintsov (she had married him from prudential motives, though probably she would not have consented to become his wife if she had not considered him a good sort of man), and had conceived a secret repugnance for all men, whom she could only figure to herself as slovenly, heavy, drowsy, and feebly importunate creatures. Once, somewhere abroad, she had met a handsome young Swede, with a chivalrous expression, with honest blue eyes under an open brow; he had made a powerful impression on her, but it had not prevented her from going back to Russia.

"A strange man this doctor!" she thought as she lay in her luxurious bed on lace pillows under a light silk coverlet. . . . Anna Sergyevna had inherited from her father a little of his inclination for splendour. She had fondly loved her sinful but good-natured father, and he had idolised her, used to joke with her in a friendly way as though she were an equal, and to confide in her fully, to ask her advice. Her mother she scarcely remembered.

"This doctor is a strange man!" she repeated to herself. She stretched, smiled, clasped her hands behind her head, then ran her eyes over two pages of a stupid French novel, dropped the book—and fell asleep, all pure and cold, in her pure and fragrant linen.

The following morning Anna Sergyevna went off botanising with Bazarov directly after lunch, and returned just before dinner; Arkady did not go off anywhere, and spent about an hour with Katya. He was not bored with her; she offered of herself to repeat the sonata of the day before; but when Madame Odintsov came back at last, when he caught sight of her, he felt an instantaneous pang at his heart. She came through the garden with a rather tired step; her cheeks were glowing and her eyes shining more brightly than usual under her round straw hat. She was twirling in her fingers the thin stalk of a wildflower, a light mantle had slipped down to her elbows, and the wide gray ribbons of her hat were clinging to her bosom. Bazarov walked behind her, self-confident and careless as usual, but the expression of his face, cheerful and even friendly as it was, did not please Arkady. Muttering between his teeth, "Good-morning!" Bazarov went away to his room, while Madame Odintsov shook Arkady's hand abstractedly, and also walked past him.

"Good-morning!" thought Arkady . . . "As though we had not seen each other already to-day!"

XVII

Time, it is well known, sometimes flies like a bird, sometimes crawls like a worm; but man is wont to be particularly happy when he does not even notice whether it passes quickly or slowly. It was in that way Arkady and Bazarov spent a fortnight at Madame Odintsov's. The good order she had established in her house and in her life partly contributed to this result. She adhered strictly to this order herself, and forced others to submit to it. Everything during the day was done at a fixed time. In the morning, precisely at eight o'clock, all the party assembled for tea; from morning-tea till lunch-time every one did what he pleased, the hostess herself was engaged with her bailiff (the estate was on the rent-system), her steward, and her head housekeeper. Before dinner the party met again for conversation or reading; the evening was devoted to walking, cards, and music; at half-past ten Anna Sergyevna retired to her own room, gave her orders for the following day, and went to bed. Bazarov did not like this measured, somewhat ostentatious punctuality in daily life, "like moving along rails," he pronounced it to be; the footmen in livery, the decorous stewards, offended his democratic sentiments. He declared that if one went so far, one might as well dine in the English style at once—in tail-coats and white ties. He once spoke plainly upon the subject to Anna Sergyevna. Her attitude was such that no one hesitated to speak his mind freely before her. She heard him out; and then her comment was, "From your point of view, you are right—and perhaps, in that respect, I am too much of a lady; but there's no living in the country without order, one would be devoured by ennui," and she continued to go her own way. Bazarov grumbled, but the very reason life was so easy for him and Arkady at Madame Odintsov's was that everything in the house "moved on rails." For all that, a change had taken place in both the young men since the first days of their stay at Nikolskoe. Bazarov, in whom Anna Sergyevna was obviously interested, though she seldom agreed with him, began to show signs of an unrest, unprecedented in him; he was easily put out of temper, and unwilling to talk, he looked irritated, and could not sit still in one place, just as though he were possessed by some secret longing; while Arkady, who had made up his mind conclusively that he was in love with Madame Odintsov, had begun to yield to a gentle melancholy. This melancholy did not, however, prevent him from becoming friendly with Katya; it even impelled him to get into friendly, affectionate terms with her. "*She* does not appreciate me? So be it! . . . But here is a good creature, who does not repulse me," he thought, and his heart again knew the sweetness of magnanimous emotions. Katya vaguely realised that he was seeking a sort of consolation in her company, and did not deny him or herself the innocent pleasure of a half-shy, half-confidential friendship. They did not talk to each other in Anna Sergyevna's presence; Katya always shrank into herself under her sister's sharp eyes; while Arkady, as befits a man in love, could pay attention to nothing else when near the object of his passion; but he was happy with Katya alone. He was conscious that he did not possess the power to interest Madame Odintsov; he was shy and at a loss when he was left alone with her, and she did not know what to say to him, he was too young for her. With Katya, on the other hand, Arkady felt at home; he treated her condescendingly, encouraged her to express the impressions made on her by music, reading novels, verses, and other such trifles, without noticing or realising that these trifles were what interested him too. Katya, on her side, did not try to drive away melancholy. Arkady was at his ease with Katya, Madame Odintsov with Bazarov, and thus it usually came to pass that the two couples, after being a little while together, went off on their separate ways, especially during the walks. Katya adored nature, and Arkady loved it, though he did not dare to acknowledge it; Madame Odintsov was, like Bazarov, rather indifferent to the beauties of nature. The almost continual separation of the two friends was not without its consequences; the relations between them began to change. Bazarov gave up talking to Arkady about Madame Odintsov, gave up even abusing her "aristocratic ways"; Katya, it is true, he praised as before, and only advised him to restrain her sentimental tendencies, but his praises were hurried, his advice dry, and in general he talked less to Arkady than before . . . he seemed to avoid him, seemed ill at ease with him.

Arkady observed it all, but he kept his observations to himself.

The real cause of all this "newness" was the feeling inspired in Bazarov by Madame Odintsov, a feeling which tortured and maddened him, and which he would at once have denied, with scornful laughter and cynical abuse, if any one had ever so remotely hinted at the possibility of what was taking place in him.

Bazarov had a great love for women and for feminine beauty; but love in the ideal, or, as he expressed it, romantic sense, he called lunacy, unpardonable imbecility; he regarded chivalrous sentiments as something of the nature of deformity or disease, and had more than once expressed his wonder that Toggenburg and all the minnesingers and troubadours had not been put into a lunatic asylum. "If a woman takes your fancy," he used to say, "try and gain your end; but if you can't—well, turn your back on her— there are lots of good fish in the sea." Madame Odintsov had taken his fancy; the rumours about her, the freedom and independence of her ideas, her unmistakable liking for him, all seemed to be in his favour, but he soon saw that with her he would not "gain his ends," and to turn his back on her he found, to his own bewilderment, beyond his power. His blood was on fire directly if he merely thought of her; he could easily have mastered his blood, but something else was taking root in him, something he had never admitted, at which he had always jeered, at which all his pride revolted. In his conversations with Anna Sergyevna he expressed more strongly than ever his calm contempt for everything idealistic; but when he was alone, with indignation he recognised idealism in himself. Then he would set off to the forest and walk with long strides about it, smashing the twigs that came in his way, and cursing under his breath both her and himself; or he would get into the hay-loft in the barn, and, obstinately closing his eyes, try to force himself to sleep, in which, of course, he did not always succeed. Suddenly his fancy would bring before him those chaste hands twining one day about his neck, those proud lips responding to his kisses, those intellectual eyes dwelling with tenderness—yes, with tenderness—on his, and his head went round, and he forgot himself for an instant, till indignation boiled up in him again. He caught himself in all sorts of "shameful" thoughts, as though he were driven on by a devil mocking him. Sometimes he fancied that there was a change taking place in Madame Odintsov too; that there were signs in the expression of her face of something special; that, perhaps ... but at that point he would stamp, or grind his teeth, and clench his fists.

Meanwhile Bazarov was not altogether mistaken. He had struck Madame Odintsov's imagination; he interested her, she thought a great deal about him. In his absence, she was not dull, she was not impatient for his coming, but she always grew more lively on his appearance; she liked to be left alone with him, and she liked talking to him, even when he irritated her or offended her taste, her refined habits. She was, as it were, eager at once to sound him and to analyse herself.

One day walking in the garden with her, he suddenly announced, in a surly voice, that he intended going to his father's place very soon. . . . She turned white, as though something had given her a pang, and such a pang, that she wondered and pondered long after, what could be the meaning of it. Bazarov had spoken of his departure with no idea of putting her to the test, of seeing what would come of it; he never "fabricated." On the morning of that day he had an interview with his father's bailiff, who had taken care of him when he was a child, Timofeitch. This Timofeitch, a little old man of much experience and astuteness, with faded yellow hair, a weather-beaten red face, and tiny teardrops in his shrunken eyes, unexpectedly appeared before Bazarov, in his shortish overcoat of stout greyish-blue cloth, girt with a strip of leather, and in tarred boots.

"Hullo, old man; how are you?" cried Bazarov.

"How do you do, Yevgeny Vassilyitch?" began the little old man, and he smiled with delight, so that his whole face was all at once covered with wrinkles.

"What have you come for? They sent for me, eh?"

"Upon my word, sir, how could we?" mumbled Timofeitch. (He remembered the strict injunctions he had received from his master on starting.) "We were sent to the town on business, and we'd heard news of your honour, so here we turned off on our way, that's to say—to have a look at your honour . . . as if we could think of disturbing you!"

"Come, don't tell lies!" Bazarov cut him short. "Is this the road to the town, do you mean to tell me?" Timofeitch hesitated, and made no answer. "Is my father well?"

"Thank God, yes."

"And my mother?"

"Anna Vlasyevna too, glory be to God."

"They are expecting me, I suppose?"

The little old man held his tiny head on one side.

"Ah, Yevgeny Vassilyitch, it makes one's heart ache to see them; it does really."

"Come, all right, all right! shut up! Tell them I'm coming soon."

"Yes, sir," answered Timofeitch, with a sigh.

As he went out of the house, he pulled his cap down on his head with both hands, clambered into a wretched-looking racing droshky, and went off at a trot, but not in the direction of the town.

On the evening of the same day, Madame Odintsov was sitting in her own room with Bazarov, while Arkady walked up and down the hall listening to Katya's playing. The princess had gone upstairs to her own room; she could not bear guests as a rule, and "especially this new riff-raff lot," as she called them. In the common rooms she only sulked; but she made up for it in her own room by breaking out into such abuse before her maid that the cap danced on her head, wig and all. Madame Odintsov was well aware of all this.

"How is it you are proposing to leave us?" she began; "how about your promise?"

Bazarov started. "What promise?"

"Have you forgotten? You meant to give me some lessons in chemistry."

"It can't be helped! My father expects me; I can't loiter any longer. However, you can read Pelouse et Frémy, *Notions générales de Chimie;* it's a good book, and clearly written. You will find everything you need in it."

"But do you remember; you assured me a book cannot take the place of . . . I've forgotten how you put it, but you know what I mean . . . do you remember?"

"It can't be helped!" repeated Bazarov.

"Why go away?" said Madame Odintsov, dropping her voice.

He glanced at her. Her head had fallen on to the back of her easy-chair, and her arms, bare to the elbow, were folded on her bosom. She seemed paler in the light of the single lamp covered with a perforated paper shade. An ample white gown hid her completely in its soft folds; even the tips of her feet, also crossed, were hardly seen.

"And why stay?" answered Bazarov.

Madame Odintsov turned her head slightly. "You ask why. Have you not enjoyed yourself with me? Or do you suppose you will not be missed here?"

"I am sure of it."

Madame Odintsov was silent a minute. "You are wrong in thinking that. But I don't believe you. You could not say that seriously." Bazarov still sat immovable. "Yevgeny Vassilyitch, why don't you speak?"

"Why, what am I to say to you? People are not generally worth being missed, and I less than most."

"Why so?"

"I'm a practical, uninteresting person. I don't know how to talk."

"You are fishing, Yevgeny Vassilyitch."

"That's not a habit of mine. Don't you know yourself that I've nothing in common with the elegant side of life, the side you prize so much?"

Madame Odintsov bit the corner of her handkerchief.

"You may think what you like, but I shall be dull when you go away."

"Arkady will remain," remarked Bazarov. Madame Odintsov shrugged her shoulders slightly. "I shall be dull," she repeated.

"Really? In any case you will not feel dull for long."

"What makes you suppose that?"

"Because you told me yourself that you are only dull when your regular routine is broken in upon. You have ordered your existence with such unimpeachable regularity that there can be no place in it for dulness or sadness . . . for any unpleasant emotions."

"And do you consider I am so unimpeachable . . . that's to say, that I have ordered my life with such regularity?"

"I should think so. Here's an example; in a few minutes it will strike ten, and I know beforehand that you will drive me away."

"No; I'm not going to drive you away, Yevgeny Vassilyitch. You may stay. Open that window. . . . I feel half-stifled."

Bazarov got up and gave a push to the window. It flew up with a loud crash. . . . He had not expected it to open so easily; besides, his hands were shaking. The soft, dark night looked in to the room with its almost black sky, its faintly rustling trees, and the fresh fragrance of the pure open air.

"Draw the blind and sit down," said Madame Odintsov; "I want to have a talk with you before you go away. Tell me something about yourself; you never talk about yourself."

"I try to talk to you upon improving subjects, Anna Sergyevna."

"You are very modest. . . . But I should like to know something about you, about your family, about your father, for whom you are forsaking us."

"Why is she talking like that?" thought Bazarov.

"All that's not in the least interesting," he uttered aloud, "especially for you; we are obscure people. . . ."

"And you regard me as an aristocrat?"

Bazarov lifted his eyes to Madame Odintsov.

"Yes," he said, with exaggerated sharpness.

She smiled. "I see you know me very little, though you do maintain that all people are alike, and it's not worth while to study them. I will tell you my life some time or other . . . but first you tell me yours."

"I know you very little," repeated Bazarov. "Perhaps you are right; perhaps, really, every one is a riddle. You, for instance; you avoid society, you are oppressed by it, and you have invited two students to stay with you. What makes you, with your intellect, with your beauty, live in the country?"

"What? What was it you said?" Madame Odintsov interposed eagerly. "With my . . . beauty?"

Bazarov scowled. "Never mind that," he muttered; "I meant to say that I don't exactly understand why you have settled in the country?"

"You don't understand it. . . . But you explain it to yourself in some way?"

"Yes . . . I assume that you remain continually in the same place because you indulge yourself, because you are very fond of comfort and ease, and very indifferent to everything else."

Madame Odintsov smiled again. "You would absolutely refuse to believe that I am capable of being carried away by anything?"

Bazarov glanced at her from under his brows.

"By curiosity, perhaps; but not otherwise."

"Really? Well, now I understand why we are such friends; you are just like me, you see."

"We are such friends . . ." Bazarov articulated in a choked voice.

"Yes! . . . Why, I'd forgotten you wanted to go away."

Bazarov got up. The lamp burnt dimly in the middle of the dark, luxurious, isolated room; from time to time the blind was shaken, and there flowed in the freshness of the insidious night; there was heard its mysterious whisperings. Madame Odintsov did not move in a single limb; but she was gradually possessed by concealed emotion.

It communicated itself to Bazarov. He was suddenly conscious that he was alone with a young and lovely woman. . . .

"Where are you going?" she said slowly.

He answered nothing, and sank into a chair.

"And so you consider me a placid, pampered, spoiled creature," she went on in the same voice, never taking her eyes off the window. "While I know so much about myself, that I am unhappy.

"You unhappy? What for? Surely you can't attach any importance to idle gossip?"

Madame Odintsov frowned. It annoyed her that he had given such a meaning to her words.

"Such gossip does not even affect me, Yevgeny Vassilyevitch, and I am too proud to allow it to disturb me. I am unhappy because . . . I have no desires, no passion for life. You look at me incredulously; you think that's said by an "aristocrat," who is all in lace, and sitting in a velvet armchair. I don't conceal the fact: I love what you call comfort, and at the same time I have little desire to live. Explain that contradiction as best you can. But all that's romanticism in your eyes."

Bazarov shook his head. "You are in good health, independent, rich; what more would you have? What do you want?"

"What do I want," echoed Madame Odintsov, and she sighed. "I am very tired, I am old, I feel as if I have had a very long life. Yes, I am old," she added, softly drawing the ends of her lace over her bare arms. Her eyes met Bazarov's eyes, and she faintly blushed. "Behind me I have already so many memories: my life in Petersburg, wealth, then poverty, then my father's death, marriage, then the inevitable tour in due order. . . . So many memories, and nothing to remember, and before me, before me—a long, long road, and no goal. . . . I have no wish to go on."

"Are you so disillusioned?" queried Bazarov.

"No, but I am dissatisfied," Madame Odintsov replied, dwelling on each syllable. "I think if I could interest myself strongly in something. . . ."

"You want to fall in love," Bazarov interrupted her, "and you can't love; that's where your unhappiness lies."

Madame Odintsov began to examine the sleeve of her lace.

"Is it true I can't love?" she said.

"I should say not! Only I was wrong in calling that an unhappiness. On the contrary, any one's more to be pitied when such a mischance befalls him."

"Mischance, what?"

"Falling in love."

"And how do you come to know that?"

"By hearsay," answered Bazarov angrily.

"You're flirting," he thought; "you're bored, and teasing me for want of something to do, while I . . ." His heart really seemed as though it were being torn to pieces.

"Besides, you are perhaps too exacting," he said, bending his whole frame forward and playing with the fringe of the chair.

"Perhaps. My idea is everything or nothing. A life for a life. Take mine, give up thine, and that without regret or turning back. Or else better have nothing."

"Well?" observed Bazarov; "that's fair terms, and I'm surprised that so far you . . . have not found what you wanted."

"And do you think it would be easy to give oneself up wholly to anything whatever?"

"Not easy, if you begin reflecting, waiting and attaching value to yourself, prizing yourself, I mean; but to give oneself up without reflection is very easy."

"How can one help prizing oneself? If I am of no value, who could need my devotion?"

"That's not my affair; that's the other's business to discover what is my value. The chief thing is to be able to devote oneself."

Madame Odintsov bent forward from the back of her chair. "You speak," she began, "as though you had experienced all that."

"It happened to come up, Anna Sergyevna; all that, as you know, is not in my line."

"But you could devote yourself?"

"I don't know. I shouldn't like to boast."

Madame Odintsov said nothing, and Bazarov was mute. The sounds of the piano floated up to them from the drawing-room.

"How is it Katya is playing so late?" observed Madame Odintsov.

Bazarov got up. "Yes, it is really late now; it's time for you to go to bed."

"Wait a little; why are you in a hurry? . . . I want to say one word to you."

"What is it?"

"Wait a little," whispered Madame Odintsov. Her eyes rested on Bazarov; it seemed as though she were examining him attentively.

He walked across the room, then suddenly went up to her, hurriedly said "Good-bye," squeezed her hand so that she almost screamed, and was gone. She raised her crushed fingers to her lips, breathed on them, and suddenly, impulsively getting up from her low chair, she moved with rapid steps towards the door, as though she wished to bring Bazarov back. . . . A maid came into the room with a decanter on a silver tray. Madame Odintsov stood still, told her she could go, and sat down again, and again sank into thought. Her hair slipped loose and fell in a dark coil down her shoulders. Long after the lamp was still burning in Anna Sergyevna's room, and for long she stayed without moving, only from time to time chafing her hands, which ached a little from the cold of the night.

Bazarov went back two hours later to his bedroom with his boots wet with dew, dishevelled and ill-humoured. He found Arkady at the writing-table with a book in his hands, his coat buttoned up to the throat.

"You're not in bed yet?" he said, in a tone, it seemed, of annoyance.

"You stopped a long while with Anna Sergyevna this evening," remarked Arkady, not answering him.

"Yes, I stopped with her all the while you were playing the piano with Katya Sergyevna."

"I did not play . . ." Arkady began, and he stopped. He felt the tears were coming into his eyes, and he did not like to cry before his sarcastic friend.

XVIII

The following morning when Madame Odintsov came down to morning tea, Bazarov sat a long while bending over his cup, then suddenly he glanced up at her. . . . She turned to him as though he had struck her a blow, and he fancied that her face was a little paler since the night before. She quickly went off to her own room, and did not appear till lunch. It rained from early morning; there was no possibility of going for a walk. The whole company assembled in the drawing-room. Arkady took up the new number of a journal and began reading it aloud. The princess, as was her habit, tried to express her amazement in her face, as though he were doing something improper, then glared angrily at him; but he paid no attention to her.

"Yevgeny Vassilyevitch," said Anna Sergyevna, "come to my room. . . . I want to ask you. . . . You mentioned a text-book yesterday . . ."

She got up and went to the door. The princess looked round with an expression that seemed to say, "Look at me; see how shocked I am!" and again glared at Arkady; but he raised his voice, and exchanging glances with Katya, near whom he was sitting, he went on reading.

Madame Odintsov went with rapid steps to her study. Bazarov followed her quickly, not raising his eyes, and only with his ears catching the delicate swish and rustle of her silk gown gliding before him. Madame Odintsov sank into the same easy-chair in which she had sat the previous evening, and Bazarov took up the same position as before.

"What was the name of that book?" she began, after a brief silence.

"Pelouse et Frémy, *Notions générales,*" answered Bazarov. "I might though recommend you also Ganot, *Traité élémentaire de physique expérimentale.* In that book the illustrations are clearer, and in general it's a text-book."

Madame Odintsov stretched out her hand. "Yevgeny Vassilyitch, I beg your pardon, but I didn't invite you in here to discuss text-books. I wanted to continue our conversation of last night. You went away so suddenly. . . . It will not bore you . . ."

"I am at your service, Anna Sergyevna. But what were we talking about last night?"

Madame Odintsov flung a sidelong glance at Bazarov.

"We were talking of happiness, I believe. I told you about myself. By the way, I mentioned the word "happiness." Tell me why it is that even when we are enjoying music, for instance, or a fine evening, or a conversation with sympathetic people, it all seems an intimation of some measureless happiness existing apart somewhere rather than actual happiness—such, I mean, as we ourselves are in possession of? Why is it? Or perhaps you have no feeling like that?"

"You know the saying, "Happiness is where we are not,' " replied Bazarov; "besides, you told me yesterday you are discontented. I certainly never have such ideas come into my head."

"Perhaps they seem ridiculous to you?"

"No; but they don't come into my head."

"Really? Do you know, I should very much like to know what you do think about?"

"What? I don't understand."

"Listen; I have long wanted to speak openly to you. There's no need to tell you—you are conscious of it yourself—that you are not an ordinary man; you are still young—all life is before you. What are you preparing yourself for? What future is awaiting you? I mean to say—what object do you want to attain? What are you going forward to? What is in your heart? in short, who are you? What are you?"

"You surprise me, Anna Sergyevna. You are aware that I am studying natural science, and who I . . .'"

"Well, who are you?"

"I have explained to you already that I am going to be a district doctor."

Anna Sergyevna made a movement of impatience.

"What do you say that for? You don't believe it yourself. Arkady might answer me in that way, but not you."

"Why, in what is Arkady . . .'"

"Stop! Is it possible you could content yourself with such a humble career, and aren't you always maintaining yourself that you don't believe in medicine? You—with your ambition—a district doctor! You answer me like that to put me off, because you have no confidence in me. But, do you know, Yevgeny Vassilyitch, that I could understand you; I have been poor myself, and ambitious, like you; I have been perhaps through the same trials as you."

"That is all very well, Anna Sergyevna, but you must pardon me for . . . I am not in the habit of talking freely about myself at any time as a rule, and between you and me there is such a gulf . . ."

"What sort of gulf? You mean to tell me again that I am an aristocrat? No more of that, Yevgeny Vassilyitch; I thought I had proved to you . . ."

"And even apart from that," broke in Bazarov, "what could induce one to talk and think about the future, which for the most part does not depend on us? If a chance turns up of doing something—so much the better; and if it doesn't turn up—at least one will be glad one didn't gossip idly about it beforehand."

"You call a friendly conversation idle gossip? . . . Or perhaps you consider me as a woman unworthy of your confidence? I know you despise us all."

"I don't despise you, Anna Sergyevna, and you know that."

"No, I don't know anything . . . but let us suppose so. I understand your disinclination to talk of your future career; but as to what is taking place within you now . . ."

"Taking place!" repeated Bazarov, "as though I were some sort of government or society! In any case, it is utterly uninteresting; and besides, can a man always speak of everything that "takes place" in him?"

"Why, I don't see why you can't speak freely of everything you have in your heart."

"Can *you?*" asked Bazarov.

"Yes," answered Anna Sergyevna, after a brief hesitation. Bazarov bowed his head. "You are more fortunate than I am."

Anna Sergyevna looked at him questioningly. "As you please," she went on, "but still something tells me that we have not come together for nothing; that we shall be great friends. I am sure this—what should I say, constraint, reticence in you will vanish at last."

"So you have noticed reticence . . . as you expressed it . . . constraint?"

"Yes."

Bazarov got up and went to the window. "And would you like to know the reason of this reticence? Would you like to know what is passing within me?"

"Yes," repeated Madame Odintsov, with a sort of dread she did not at the time understand.

"And you will not be angry?"

"No."

"No?" Bazarov was standing with his back to her. "Let me tell you then that I love you like a fool, like a madman. . . . There, you've forced it out of me."

Madame Odintsov held both her hands out before her; but Bazarov was leaning with his forehead pressed against the window pane. He breathed hard; his whole body was visibly trembling. But it was not the tremor of youthful timidity, not the sweet alarm of the first declaration that possessed him; it was passion struggling in him, strong and painful—passion not unlike hatred, and perhaps akin to it. . . . Madame Odintsov felt both afraid and sorry for him.

"Yevgeny Vassilyitch!" she said, and there was the ring of unconscious tenderness in her voice.

He turned quickly, flung a searching look on her, and snatching both her hands, he drew her suddenly to his breast.

She did not at once free herself from his embrace, but an instant later, she was standing far away in a corner, and looking from there at Bazarov. He rushed at her . . .

"You have misunderstood me," she whispered hurriedly, in alarm. It seemed if he had made another step she would have screamed. . . . Bazarov bit his lips, and went out.

Half-an-hour after, a maid gave Anna Sergyevna a note from Bazarov; it consisted simply of one line: "Am I to go to-day, or can I stop till to-morrow?"

"Why should you go? I did not understand you—you did not understand me," Anna Sergyevna answered him, but to herself she thought: "I did not understand myself either."

She did not show herself till dinner-time, and kept walking to and fro in her room, stopping sometimes at the window, sometimes at the looking-glass, and slowly rubbing her handkerchief over her neck, on which she still seemed to feel a burning spot. She asked herself what had induced her to "force" on Bazarov's words, his confidence, and whether she had suspected nothing . . . "I am to blame," she decided aloud, "but I could not have foreseen this." She fell to musing, and blushed crimson, remembering Bazarov's almost animal face when he had rushed at her. . . .

"Or?" she uttered suddenly aloud, and she stopped short and shook back her curls. . . . She caught sight of herself in the glass; her head thrown back, with a mysterious smile on the half-closed, half-opened eyes and lips, told her, it seemed, in a flash something at which she herself was confused. . . .

"No," she made up her mind at last. "God knows what it would lead to; he couldn't be played with; peace is anyway the best thing in the world."

Her peace of mind was not shaken; but she felt gloomy, and even shed a few tears once, though she could not have said why—certainly not for the insult done her. She did not feel insulted; she was more inclined to feel guilty. Under the influence of various vague emotions, the sense of life passing by, the desire of novelty, she had forced herself to go up to a certain point, forced herself to look behind herself, and had seen behind her not even an abyss, but what was empty . . . or revolting.

XIX

Great as was Madame Odintsov's self-control, and superior as she was to every kind of prejudice, she felt awkward when she went into the dining-room to dinner. The meal went off fairly successfully, however. Porfiry Platonovitch made his appearance and told various anecdotes; he had just come back from the town. Among other things, he informed them that the governor had ordered his secretaries on special commissions to wear spurs, in case he might send them off anywhere for greater speed on horseback. Arkady talked in an undertone to Katya, and dip-

lomatically attended to the princess's wants. Bazarov maintained a grim and obstinate silence. Madame Odintsov looked at him twice, not stealthily, but straight in the face, which was bilious and forbidding, with downcast eyes, and contemptuous determination stamped on every feature, and thought: "No . . . no . . . no."
. . . After dinner, she went with the whole company into the garden, and seeing that Bazarov wanted to speak to her, she took a few steps to one side and stopped. He went up to her, but even then did not raise his eyes, and said hoarsely—

"I have to apologise to you, Anna Sergyevna. You must be in a fury with me."

"No, I'm not angry with you, Yevgeny Vassilyitch," answered Madame Odintsov; "but I am sorry."

"So much the worse. Any way, I'm sufficiently punished. My position, you will certainly agree, is most foolish. You wrote to me, 'Why go away?' But I cannot stay, and don't wish to. To-morrow I shall be gone."

"Yevgeny Vassilyitch, why are you . . ."

"Why am I going away?"

"No; I didn't mean to say that."

"There's no recalling the past, Anna Sergyevna . . . and this was bound to come about sooner or later. Consequently I must go. I can only conceive of one condition upon which I could remain; but that condition will never be. Excuse my impertinence, but you don't love me, and you never will love me, I suppose?"

Bazarov's eyes glittered for an instant under their dark brows.

Anna Sergyevna did not answer him. "I'm afraid of this man," flashed through her brain.

"Good-bye, then," said Bazarov, as though he guessed her thought, and he went back into the house.

Anna Sergyevna walked slowly after him, and calling Katya to her, she took her arm. She did not leave her side till quite evening. She did not play cards, and was constantly laughing, which did not at all accord with her pale and perplexed face. Arkady was bewildered, and looked on at her as all young people look on—that's to say, he was constantly asking himself, "What is the meaning of that?" Bazarov shut himself up in his room; he came back to tea, however. Anna Sergyevna longed to say some friendly word to him, but she did not know how to address him. . . .

An unexpected incident relieved her from her embarrassment; a steward announced the arrival of Sitnikov.

It is difficult to do justice in words to the strange figure cut by the young apostle of progress as he fluttered into the room. Though, with his characteristic impudence, he had made up his mind to go into the country to visit a woman whom he hardly knew, who had never invited him; but with whom, according to information he had gathered, such talented and intimate friends were staying, he was nevertheless trembling to the marrow of his bones; and instead of bringing out the apologies and compliments he had learned by heart beforehand, he muttered some absurdity about Evdoksya Kukshin having sent him to inquire after Anna Sergyevna's health, and Arkady Nicolaevitch's too, having always spoken to him in the highest terms. . . . At this point he faltered and lost his presence of mind so completely that he sat down on his own hat. However, since no one turned him out, and Anna Sergyevna even presented him to her aunt and her sister, he soon recovered himself and began to chatter volubly. The introduction of the commonplace is often an advantage in life; it relieves over-strained tension, and sobers too self-confident or self-sacrificing emotions by recalling its close kinship with them. With Sitnikov's appearance everything became somehow duller and simpler; they all even ate a more solid supper, and retired to bed half-an-hour earlier than usual.

"I might now repeat to you," said Arkady, as he lay down in bed, to Bazarov, who was also undressing, what you once said to me, "Why are you so melancholy? One would think you had fulfilled some sacred duty." For some time past a sort of pretence of free-and-easy banter had sprung up between the two young men, which is always an unmistakable sign of secret displeasure or unexpressed suspicions.

"I'm going to my father's to-morrow," said Bazarov.

Arkady raised himself and leaned on his elbow. He felt both surprised, and for some reason or other pleased. "Ah!" he commented, "and is that why you're sad?"

Bazarov yawned. "You'll get old if you know too much."

"And Anna Sergyevna?" persisted Arkady.

"What about Anna Sergyevna?"

"I mean, will she let you go?"

"I'm not her paid man."

Arkady grew thoughtful, while Bazarov lay down and turned with his face to the wall.

Some minutes went by in silence. "Yevgeny?" cried Arkady suddenly.

"Well?"

"I will leave with you to-morrow too."

Bazarov made no answer.

"Only I will go home," continued Arkady. "We will go together as far as Hohlovsky, and there you can get horses at Fedot's. I should be delighted to make the acquaintance of your people, but I'm afraid of being in their way and yours. You are coming to us again later, of course?"

"I've left all my things with you," Bazarov said, without turning round.

"Why doesn't he ask me why I am going," and just as suddenly as he?" thought Arkady. "In reality, why am I going, and why is he going?" he pursued his reflections. He could find no satisfactory answer to his own question, though his heart was filled with some bitter feeling. He felt it would be hard to part from this life to which he had grown so accustomed; but for him to remain alone would be rather odd. "Something has passed between them," he reasoned to himself; "what good would it be for me to hang on after he's gone? She's utterly sick of me; I'm losing the last that remained to me." He began to imagine Anna Sergyevna to himself, then other features gradually eclipsed the lovely image of the young widow.

"I'm sorry to lose Katya too!" Arkady whispered to his pillow, on which a tear had already fallen.... All at once he shook back his hair and said aloud—

"What the devil made that fool of a Sitnikov turn up here?"

Bazarov at first stirred a little in his bed, then he uttered the following rejoinder: "You're still a fool, my boy, I see. Sitnikovs are indispensable to us. I—do you understand? I need dolts like him. It's not for the gods to bake bricks, in fact!" . . .

"Oho!" Arkady thought to himself, and then in a flash all the fathomless depths of Bazarov's conceit dawned upon him. "Are you and I gods then? at least, you're a god; am not I a dolt then?"

"Yes," repeated Bazarov; "you're still a fool."

Madame Odintsov expressed no special surprise when Arkady told her the next day that he was going with Bazarov; she seemed tired and absorbed. Katya looked at him silently and seriously; the princess went so far as to cross herself under her shawl so that he could not help noticing it. Sitnikov, on the other hand, was completely disconcerted. He had only just come in to lunch in a new and fashionable get-up, not on this occasion of a Slavophil cut; the evening before he had astonished the man told off to wait on him by the amount of linen he had brought with him, and now all of a sudden his comrades were deserting him! He took a few tiny steps, doubled back like a hunted hare at the edge of a copse, and abruptly, almost with dismay, almost with a wail, announced that he proposed going too. Madame Odintsov did not attempt to detain him.

"I have a very comfortable carriage," added the luckless young man, turning to Arkady; "I can take you, while Yevgeny Vassilyitch can take your coach, so it will be even more convenient."

"But, really, it's not at all in your way, and it's a long way to my place."

"That's nothing, nothing; I've plenty of time; besides, I have business in that direction."

"Gin-selling?" asked Arkady, rather too contemptuously.

But Sitnikov was reduced to such desperation that he did not even laugh as usual. "I assure you, my carriage is exceedingly comfortable," he muttered; "and there will be room for all."

"Don't wound Monsieur Sitnikov by a refusal," commented Anna Sergyevna.

Arkady glanced at her, and bowed his head significantly.

The visitors started off after lunch. As she said good-bye to Bazarov, Madame Odintsov held out her hand to him, and said, "We shall meet again, shan't we?"

"As you command," answered Bazarov.

"In that case, we shall."

Arkady was the first to descend the steps; he got into Sitnikov's carriage. A steward tucked him in respectfully, but he could have killed him with pleasure, or have burst into tears. Bazarov took his seat in the coach. When they reached Hohlovsky, Arkady waited till Fedot, the keeper of the posting-station, had put in the horses, and going up to the coach, he said, with his old smile, to Bazarov, "Yevgeny, take me with you; I want to come to you."

"Get in," Bazarov brought out through his teeth.

Sitnikov, who had been walking to and fro round the wheels of his carriage, whistling briskly, could only gape when he heard these words; while Arkady coolly pulled his luggage out of the carriage, took his seat beside Bazarov, and bowing politely to his former fellow-traveller, he called, "Whip up!" The coach rolled away, and was soon out of sight. . . . Sitnikov, utterly confused, looked at his coachman, but the latter was flicking his whip about the tail of the off horse. Then Sitnikov jumped into the carriage, and growling at two passing peasants, "Put on your caps, idiots!" he drove to the town, where he arrived very late, and where, next day, at Madame Kukshin's, he dealt very severely with two "disgusting stuck-up churls."

When he was seated in the coach by Bazarov, Arkady pressed his hand warmly, and for a long while he said nothing. It seemed as though Bazarov understood and appreciated both the pressure and the silence. He had not slept all the previous night, and had not smoked, and had eaten scarcely anything for several days. His profile, already thinner, stood out darkly and sharply under his cap, which was pulled down to his eyebrows.

"Well, brother," he said at last, "give us a cigarette. But look, I say, is my tongue yellow?"

"Yes, it is," answered Arkady.

"Hm . . . and the cigarette's tasteless. The machine's out of gear."

"You look changed lately certainly," observed Arkady.

"It's nothing! we shall soon be all right. One thing's a bother —my mother's so tender-hearted; if you don't grow as round as a tub, and eat ten times a day, she's quite upset. My father's all right, he's known all sorts of ups and downs himself. No, I can't smoke," he added, and he flung the cigarette into the dust of the road.

"Do you think it's twenty miles?" asked Arkady.

"Yes. But ask this sage here." He indicated the peasant sitting on the box, a labourer of Fedot's.

But the sage only answered, "Who's to know—miles hereabout aren't measured," and went on swearing in an undertone at the shaft horse for "kicking with her head-piece," that is, shaking with her head down.

"Yes, yes," began Bazarov; "it's a lesson to you, my young friend, an instructive example. God knows, what rot it is? Every man hangs on a thread, the abyss may open under his feet any minute, and yet he must go and invent all sorts of discomforts for himself, and spoil his life."

"What are you alluding to?" asked Arkady.

"I'm not alluding to anything; I'm saying straight out that we've both behaved like fools. What's the use of talking about it! Still, I've noticed in hospital practice, the man who's furious at his illness—he's sure to get over it."

"I don't quite understand you," observed Arkady; "I should have thought you had nothing to complain of."

"And since you don't quite understand me, I'll tell you this— to my mind, it's better to break stones on the highroad than to let a woman have the mastery of even the end of one's little finger. That's all . . ." Bazarov was on the point of uttering his favourite word, "romanticism," but he checked himself, and said, "rubbish. You don't believe me now, but I tell you; you and I have been in feminine society, and very nice we found it; but to throw up society like that is for all the world like a dip in cold water on a hot day. A man hasn't time to attend to such trifles; a man ought not to be tame, says an excellent Spanish proverb. Now, you, I suppose, my sage friend," he added, turning to the peasant sitting on the box—you've a wife?"

The peasant showed both the friends his dull blear-eyed face.

"A wife? Yes. Every man has a wife."

"Do you beat her?"

"My wife? Everything happens sometimes. We don't beat her without good reason!"

"That's excellent. Well, and does she beat you?"

The peasant gave a tug at the reins. "That's a strange thing to say, sir. You like your joke." . . . He was obviously offended.

"You hear, Arkady Nikolaevitch! But we have taken a beating . . . that's what comes of being educated people."

Arkady gave a forced laugh, while Bazarov turned away, and did not open his mouth again the whole journey.

The twenty miles seemed to Arkady quite forty. But at last, on the slope of some rising ground, appeared the small hamlet where Bazarov's parents lived. Beside it, in a young birch copse, could be seen a small house with a thatched roof. Two peasants stood with their hats on at the first hut, abusing each other. "You're a great sow," said one; "and worse than a little sucking pig."

"And your wife's a witch," retorted the other.

"From their unconstrained behavior," Bazarov remarked to Arkady, "and the playfulness of their retorts, you can guess that my father's peasants are not too much oppressed. Why, there he is himself coming out on the steps of his house. They must have heard the bells. It's he; it's he—I know his figure. Ay, ay! how grey he's grown though, poor chap!"

XX

Bazarov leaned out of the coach, while Arkady thrust his head out behind his companion's back, and caught sight on the steps of the little manor-house of a tall, thinnish man with dishevelled hair, and a thin hawk nose, dressed in an old military coat not buttoned up. He was standing, his legs wide apart, smoking a long pipe and screwing up his eyes to keep the sun out of them.

The horses stopped.

"Arrived at last," said Bazarov's father, still going on smoking though the pipe was fairly dancing up and down between his fingers. "Come, get out; get out; let me hug you."

He began embracing his son . . . "Enyusha, Enyusha," was heard a trembling woman's voice. The door was flung open, and in the doorway was seen a plump, short, little old woman in a white cap and a short striped jacket. She moaned, staggered, and would certainly have fallen, had not Bazarov supported her. Her plump little hands were instantly twined round his neck, her head was pressed to his breast, and there was a complete hush. The only sound heard was her broken sobs.

Old Bazarov breathed hard and screwed his eyes up more than ever.

"There, that's enough, that's enough, Arisha! give over," he said, exchanging a glance with Arkady, who remained motionless in the coach, while the peasant on the box even turned his head away; "that's not at all necessary, please give over."

"Ah, Vassily Ivanitch," faltered the old woman, "for what ages, my dear one, my darling, Enyusha," . . . and, not unclasping her hands, she drew her wrinkled face, wet with tears and working with tenderness, a little away from Bazarov, and gazed at him with blissful and comic-looking eyes, and again fell on his neck.

"Well, well, to be sure, that's all in the nature of things," commented Vassily Ivanitch, "only we'd better come indoors. Here's a visitor come with Yevgeny. You must excuse it," he added, turning to Arkady, and scraping with his foot; "you understand, a woman's weakness; and well, a mother's heart . . ."

His lips and eyebrows too were twitching, and his beard was quivering . . . but he was obviously trying to control himself and appear almost indifferent.

"Let's come in, mother, really," said Bazarov, and he led the enfeebled old woman into the house. Putting her into a comfortable armchair, he once more hurriedly embraced his father and introduced Arkady to him.

"Heartily glad to make your acquaintance," said Vassily Ivanovitch, "but you mustn't expect great things; everything here in my house is done in a plain way, on a military footing. Arina Vlasyevna, calm yourself, pray; what weakness! The gentleman our guest will think ill of you."

"My dear sir," said the old lady through her tears, "your name and your father's I haven't the honour of knowing . . ."

"Arkady Nikolaitch," put in Vassily Ivanitch solemnly, in a low voice.

"You must excuse a silly old woman like me." The old woman blew her nose, and bending her head to right and to left, carefully wiped one eye after the other. "You must excuse me. You see, I thought I should die, that I should not live to see my da . . arling."

"Well, here we have lived to see him, madam," put in Vassily Ivanovitch. "Tanyushka," he turned to a bare-legged little girl of thirteen in a bright red cotton dress, who was timidly peeping in at the door, "bring your mistress a glass of water—on a tray, do you hear?—and you, gentlemen," he added, with a kind of old-fashioned playfulness, "let me ask you into the study of a retired old veteran."

"Just once more let me embrace you, Enyusha," moaned Arina Vlasyevna. Bazarov bent down to her. "Why, what a handsome fellow you have grown!"

"Well, I don't know about being handsome," remarked Vassily Ivanovitch, "but he's a man as the saying is, *ommfay*. And now I hope, Arina Vlasyevna, that having satisfied your maternal heart, you will turn your thoughts to satisfying the appetites of our dear guests, because, as you're aware, even nightingales can't be fed on fairy tales."

The old lady got up from her chair. "This minute, Vassily Ivanovitch, the table shall be laid. I will run myself to the kitchen and order the samovar to be brought in; everything shall be ready, everything. Why, I have not seen him, not given him food or drink these three years; is that nothing?"

"There, mind, good mother, bustle about; don't put us to shame; while you, gentlemen, I beg you to follow me. Here's Timofeitch come to pay his respects to you, Yevgeny. He, too, I daresay, is delighted, the old dog. Eh, aren't you delighted, old dog? Be so good as to follow me."

And Vassily Ivanovitch went bustling forward, scraping and flapping with his slippers trodden down at heel.

His whole house consisted of six tiny rooms. One of them— the one to which he led our friends—was called the study. A thick-legged table, littered over with papers black with the accumulation of ancient dust as though they had been smoked, occupied all the space between the two windows; on the walls hung Turkish firearms, whips, a sabre, two maps, some anatomical diagrams, a portrait of Hoffland, a monogram woven in hair in a blackened frame, and a diploma under glass; a leather sofa, torn and worn into hollows in parts, was placed between two huge cupboards of birchwood; on the shelves books, boxes, stuffed birds, jars, and phials were huddled together in confusion; in one corner stood a broken galvanic battery.

"I warned you, my dear Arkady Nikolaitch," began Vassily Ivanitch, "that we live, so to say, bivouacking . . ."

"There, stop that, what are you apologising for?" Bazarov interrupted. "Kirsanov knows very well we're not Croesuses, and that you have no butler. Where are we going to put him, that's the question?"

"To be sure, Yevgeny; I have a capital room there in the little lodge; he will be very comfortable there."

"Have you had a lodge put up then?"

"Why, where the bath-house is," put in Timofeitch.

"That is next to the bathroom," Vassily Ivanitch added hurriedly. "It's summer now . . . I will run over there at once, and make arrangements; and you, Timofeitch, meanwhile bring in their things. You, Yevgeny, I shall of course offer my study. *Suum cuique.*"

"There you have him! A comical old chap, and very good-

natured," remarked Bazarov, directly Vassily Ivanitch had gone.
"Just such a queer fish as yours, only in another way. He chatters
too much."

"And your mother seems an awfully nice woman," observed
Arkady.

"Yes, there's no humbug about her. You'll see what a dinner
she'll give us."

"They didn't expect you to-day, sir; they've not brought any
beef?" observed Timofeitch, who was just dragging in Bazarov's
box.

"We shall get on very well without beef. It's no use crying
for the moon. Poverty, they say, is no vice."

"How many serfs has your father?" Arkady asked suddenly.

"The estate's not his, but mother's; there are fifteen serfs, if
I remember."

"Twenty-two in all," Timofeitch added, with an air of displeasure.

The flapping of slippers was heard, and Vassily Ivanovitch
reappeared. "In a few minutes your room will be ready to receive
you," he cried triumphantly. Arkady . . . Nikolaitch? I think that
is right? And here is your attendant," he added, indicating a
short-cropped boy, who had come in with him in a blue full-
skirted coat with ragged elbows and a pair of boots which did not
belong to him. "His name is Fedka. Again, I repeat, even though
my son tells me not to, you mustn't expect great things. He knows
how to fill a pipe, though. You smoke, of course?"

"I generally smoke cigars," answered Arkady.

"And you do very sensibly. I myself give the preference to
cigars, but in these solitudes it is exceedingly difficult to obtain
them."

"There, that's enough humble pie," Bazarov interrupted
again. "You'd much better sit here on the sofa and let us have a
look at you."

Vassily Ivanovitch laughed and sat down. He was very like
his son in face, only his brow was lower and narrower, and his
mouth rather wider, and he was for ever restless, shrugging up
his shoulder as though his coat cut him under the armpits, blink-

ing, clearing his throat, and gesticulating with his fingers, while his son was distinguished by a kind of nonchalant immobility.

"Humble-pie!" repeated Vassily Ivanovitch. "You must not imagine, Yevgeny, I want to appeal, so to speak, to our guest's sympathies by making out we live in such a wilderness. Quite the contrary, I maintain that for a thinking man nothing is a wilderness. At least, I try as far as possible not to get rusty, so to speak, not to fall behind the age."

Vassily Ivanovitch drew out of his pocket a new yellow silk handkerchief, which he had had time to snatch up on the way to Arkady's room, and flourishing it in the air, he proceeded: "I am not now alluding to the fact that, for example, at the cost of sacrifices not inconsiderable for me, I have put my peasants on the rent-system and given up my land to them on half profits. I regarded that as my duty; common sense itself enjoins such a proceeding, though other proprietors do not even dream of it; I am alluding to the sciences, to culture."

"Yes; I see you have here *The Friend of Health* for 1855," remarked Bazarov.

"It's sent me by an old comrade out of friendship," Vassily Ivanovitch made haste to answer; "but we have, for instance, some idea even of phrenology," he added, addressing himself principally, however, to Arkady, and pointing to a small plaster head on the cupboard, divided into numbered squares; "we are not unacquainted even with Schenlein and Rademacher."

"Why do people still believe in Rademacher in this province?" asked Bazarov.

Vassily Ivanovitch cleared his throat. "In this province. . . . Of course, gentlemen, you know best; how could we keep pace with you? You are here to take our places. In my day, too, there was some sort of a Humouralist school, Hoffmann, and Brown too with his vitalism—they seemed very ridiculous to us, but, of course, they too had been great men at one time or other. Some one new has taken the place of Rademacher with you; you bow down to him, but in another twenty years it will be his turn to be laughed at."

"For your consolation I will tell you," observed Bazarov,

"that nowadays we laugh at medicine altogether, and don't bow down to any one."

"How's that? Why, you're going to be a doctor, aren't you?"

"Yes, but the one fact doesn't prevent the other."

Vassily Ivanovitch poked his third finger into his pipe, where a little smouldering ash was still left. "Well, perhaps, perhaps—I am not going to dispute. What am I? A retired army-doctor, *volla-too;* now fate has made me take to farming. I served in your grandfather's brigade," he addressed himself again to Arkady; "yes, yes, I have seen many sights in my day. And I was thrown into all kinds of society, brought into contact with all sorts of people! I myself, the man you see before you now, have felt the pulse of Prince Wittgenstein and of Zhukovsky! They were in the southern army, in the fourteenth, you understand" (and here Vassily Ivanovitch pursed his mouth up significantly). "Well, well, but my business was on one side; stick to your lancet, and let everything else go hang! Your grandfather was a very honourable man, a real soldier."

"Confess, now, he was rather a blockhead," remarked Bazarov lazily.

"Ah, Yevgeny, how can you use such an expression! Do consider. . . . Of course, General Kirsanov was not one of the . . ."

"Come, drop him," broke in Bazarov; "I was pleased as I was driving along here to see your birch copse; it has shot up capitally."

Vassily Ivanovitch brightened up. "And you must see what a little garden I've got now! I planted every tree myself. I've fruit, and raspberries, and all kinds of medicinal herbs. However clever you young gentlemen may be, old Paracelsus spoke the holy truth: *in herbis, verbis et lapidibus.* . . . I've retired from practice, you know, of course, but two or three times a week it will happen that I'm brought back to my old work. They come for advice—I can't drive them away. Sometimes the poor have recourse to me for help. And indeed there are no doctors here at all. There's one of the neighbours here, a retired major, only fancy, he doctors the people too. I asked the question, "Has he studied medicine?"

And they told me, "No, he's not studied; he does it more from philanthropy." . . . Ha! ha! ha! from philanthropy! What do you think of that? Ha! ha! ha!"

"Fedka, fill me a pipe!" said Bazarov rudely.

"And there's another doctor here who just got to a patient," Vassily Ivanovitch persisted in a kind of desperation, "when the patient had gone *ad patres;* the servant didn't let the doctor speak; you're no longer wanted, he told him. He hadn't expected this, got confused, and asked, "Why, did your master hiccup before his death?" "Yes." "Did he hiccup much?" "Yes." "Ah, well, that's all right," and off he set back again. Ha! ha! ha!"

The old man was alone in his laughter; Arkady forced a smile on his face. Bazarov simply stretched. The conversation went on in this way for about an hour; Arkady had time to go to his room, which turned out to be the anteroom attached to the bathroom, but was very snug and clean. At last Tanyusha came in and announced that dinner was ready.

Vassily Ivanovitch was the first to get up. "Come, gentlemen. You must be magnanimous and pardon me if I've bored you. I daresay my good wife will give you more satisfaction."

The dinner, though prepared in haste, turned out to be very good, even abundant; only the wine was not quite up to the mark; it was almost black sherry, bought by Timofeitch in the town at a well-known merchant's, and had a faint coppery, resinous taste, and the flies were a great nuisance. On ordinary days a serf-boy used to keep driving them away with a large green branch; but on this occasion Vassily Ivanovitch had sent him away through dread of the criticism of the younger generation. Arina Vlasyevna had had time to dress; she had put on a high cap with silk ribbons and a pale blue flowered shawl. She broke down again directly she caught sight of her Enyusha, but her husband had no need to admonish her; she made haste to wipe away her tears herself, for fear of spotting her shawl. Only the young men ate anything; the master and mistress of the house had dined long ago. Fedka waited at table, obviously encumbered by having boots on for the first time; he was assisted by a woman of a masculine cast of face and one eye, by name Anfisushka, who performed the duties of housekeeper, poultry-woman, and laundress. Vassily Ivanovitch walked up and down during the whole of dinner, and with a perfectly happy, positively beatific countenance, talked about the serious anxiety he felt at Napoleon's policy, and the intricacy of the Italian question. Arina Vlasyevna took no notice of Arkady. She did not press him to eat; leaning her round face, to which the full cherry-coloured lips and the little moles on the cheeks and over the eyebrows gave a very simple good-natured expression, on her little closed fist, she did not take her eyes off her son, and kept constantly sighing, she was dying to know for how long he had come, but she was afraid to ask him.

"What if he says for two days," she thought, and her heart sank. After the roast Vassily Ivanovitch disappeared for an instant, and returned with an opened half-bottle of champagne. "Here," he cried, "though we do live in the wilds, we have something to make merry with on festive occasions!" He filled three champagne glasses and a little wineglass, proposed the health of "our inestimable guests," and at once tossed off his glass in military fashion; while he made Arina Vlasyevna drink her wineglass to the last drop. When the time came in due course for preserves, Arkady, who could not bear anything sweet, thought it his duty, however, to taste four different kinds which had been freshly made, all the more as Bazarov flatly refused them and began at once smoking a cigarette. Then tea came on the scene with cream, butter, and cracknels; then Vassily Ivanovitch took them all into the garden to admire the beauty of the evening. As they passed a garden seat he whispered to Arkady—

"At this spot I love to meditate, as I watch the sunset; it suits a recluse like me. And there, a little farther off, I have planted some of the trees beloved of Horace."

"What trees?" asked Bazarov, overhearing.

"Oh . . . acacias."

Bazarov began to yawn.

"I imagine it's time our travellers were in the arms of Morpheus," observed Vassily Ivanovitch.

"That is, it's time for bed," Bazarov put in. "That's a correct idea. It is time, certainly."

As he said good-night to his mother, he kissed her on the forehead, while she embraced him, and stealthily behind his back she gave him her blessing three times. Vassily Ivanovitch conducted Arkady to his room, and wished him "as refreshing repose as I enjoyed at your happy years." And Arkady did as a fact sleep excellently in his bath-house; there was a smell of mint in it, and two crickets behind the stove rivalled each other in their drowsy chirping. Vassily Ivanovitch went from Arkady's room to his study, and perching on the sofa at his son's feet, he was looking forward to having a chat with him; but Bazarov at once sent him away, saying he was sleepy, and did not fall asleep till morning. With wide open eyes he stared vindictively into the darkness; the memories of childhood had no power over him; and besides, he had not yet had time to get rid of the impression of his recent bitter emotions. Arina Vlasyevna first prayed to her heart's content, then she had a long, long conversation with Anfisushka, who stood stockstill before her mistress, and fixing her solitary eye upon her, communicated in a mysterious whisper all her observations and conjectures in regard to Yevgeny Vassilyevitch. The old lady's head was giddy with happiness and wine and tobacco smoke: her husband tried to talk to her, but with a wave of his hand gave it up in despair.

Arina Vlasyevna was a genuine Russian gentlewoman of the olden times; she ought to have lived two centuries before, in the old Moscow days. She was very devout and emotional; she believed in fortune-telling, charms, dreams, and omens of every possible kind; she believed in the prophecies of crazy people, in house-spirits, in wood-spirits, in unlucky meetings, in the evil eye, in popular remedies, she ate specially prepared salt on Holy Thursday, and believed that the end of the world was at hand; she believed that if on Easter Sunday the lights did not go out at vespers, then there would be a good crop of buckwheat, and that a mushroom will not grow after it has been looked on by the eye of man; she believed that the devil likes to be where there is water, and that every Jew has a blood-stained patch on his breast; she was afraid of mice, of snakes, of frogs, of sparrows, of leeches, of thunder, of cold water, of draughts, of horses, of goats, of

red-haired people, and black cats, and she regarded crickets and
dogs as unclean beasts; she never ate veal, doves, crayfishes,
cheese, asparagus, artichokes, hares, nor water-melons, because a
cut water-melon suggested the head of John the Baptist, and of
oysters she could not speak without a shudder; she was fond of
eating—and fasted rigidly; she slept ten hours out of the twenty-
four—and never went to bed at all if Vassily Ivanovitch had so
much as a headache; she had never read a single book except
Alexis or the Cottage in the Forest; she wrote one, or at the most
two letters in a year, but was great in housewifery, preserving,
and jam-making, though with her own hands she never touched
a thing, and was generally disinclined to move from her place.
Arina Vlasyevna was very kindhearted, and in her way not at all
stupid. She knew that the world is divided into masters whose
duty it is to command, and simple folk whose duty it is to serve
them—and so she felt no repugnance to servility and prostrations
to the ground; but she treated those in subjection to her kindly
and gently, never let a single beggar go away empty-handed, and
never spoke ill of any one, though she was fond of gossip. In her
youth she had been pretty, had played the clavichord, and spoken
French a little; but in the course of many years' wanderings with
her husband, whom she had married against her will, she had
grown stout, and forgotten music and French. Her son she loved
and feared unutterably; she had given up the management of the
property to Vassily Ivanovitch—and now did not interfere in
anything; she used to groan, wave her handkerchief, and raise her
eyebrows higher and higher with horror directly her old husband
began to discuss the impending government reforms and his own
plans. She was apprehensive, and constantly expecting some great
misfortune, and began to weep directly she remembered anything
sorrowful. . . . Such women are not common nowadays. God
knows whether we ought to rejoice!

XXI

On getting up Arkady opened the window, and the first object that met his view was Vassily Ivanovitch. In an Oriental dressing-gown girt round the waist with a pocket-handkerchief he was industriously digging in his garden. He perceived his young visitor, and leaning on his spade, he called, "The best of health to you! How have you slept?"

"Capitally," answered Arkady.

"Here am I, as you see, like some Cincinnatus, marking out a bed for late turnips. The time has come now—and thank God for it!—when every one ought to obtain his sustenance with his own hands; it's useless to reckon on others; one must labour oneself. And it turns out that Jean Jacques Rousseau is right. Half an hour ago, my dear young gentleman, you might have seen me in a totally different position. One peasant woman, who complained of looseness—that's how they express it, but in our language, dysentery—I . . . how can I express it best? I administered opium; and for another I extracted a tooth. I proposed an anaesthetic to her . . . but she would not consent. All that I do *gratis—anamatyer (en amateur).* I'm used to it, though; you see, I'm a plebeian, *homo novus*—not one of the old stock, not like my spouse. . . . Wouldn't you like to come this way into the shade, to breathe the morning freshness a little before tea?"

Arkady went out to him.

"Welcome once again," said Vassily Ivanovitch, raising his hand in a military salute to the greasy skull-cap which covered his head. "You, I know, are accustomed to luxury, to amusements, but even the great ones of this world do not disdain to spend a brief space under a cottage roof."

"Good heavens," protested Arkady, "as though I were one of the great ones of this world! And I'm not accustomed to luxury."

"Pardon me, pardon me," rejoined Vassily Ivanovitch with a polite simper. "Though I am laid on the shelf now, I have knocked about the world too—I can tell a bird by its flight. I am something of a psychologist too in my own way, and a physiogno-mist. If I had not, I will venture to say, been endowed with that gift, I should have come to grief long ago; I should have stood no chance, a poor man like me. I tell you without flattery, I am sincerely delighted at the friendship I observe between you and my son. I have just seen him; he got up as he usually does—no doubt you are aware of it—very early, and went a ramble about the neighbourhood. Permit me to inquire—have you known my son long?"

"Since last winter."

"Indeed. And permit me to question you further—but hadn't we better sit down? Permit me, as a father, to ask without reserve, What is your opinion of my Yevgeny?"

"Your son is one of the most remarkable men I have ever met," Arkady answered emphatically.

Vassily Ivanovitch's eyes suddenly grew round, and his cheeks were suffused with a faint flush. The spade fell out of his hand.

"And so you expect," he began . . .

"I'm convinced," Arkady put in, "that your son has a great future before him; that he will do honour to your name. I've been certain of that ever since I first met him."

"How . . . how was that?" Vassily Ivanovitch articulated with an effort. His wide mouth was relaxed in a triumphant smile, which would not leave it.

"Would you like me to tell you how we met?"

"Yes . . . and altogether. . . ."

Arkady began to tell his tale, and to talk of Bazarov with even greater warmth, even greater enthusiasm than he had done on the evening when he danced a mazurka with Madame Odintsov.

Vassily Ivanovitch listened and listened, blinked, and rolled his handkerchief up into a ball in both his hands, cleared his throat, ruffled up his hair, and at last could stand it no longer; he bent down to Arkady and kissed him on his shoulder. "You have made me perfectly happy," he said, never ceasing to smile. "I ought to tell you, I . . . idolise my son; my old wife I won't speak of—we all know what mothers are!—but I dare not show my feelings before him, because he doesn't like it. He is averse to every kind of demonstration of feeling; many people even find fault with him for such firmness of character, and regard it as a proof of pride or lack of feeling, but men like him ought not to be judged by the common standard, ought they? And here, for example, many another fellow in his place would have been a constant drag on his parents; but he, would you believe it? has never from the day he was born taken a farthing more than he could help, that's God's truth!''

"He is a disinterested, honest man,'' observed Arkady.

"Exactly so; he is disinterested. And I don't only idolise him, Arkady Nikolaitch, I am proud of him, and the height of my ambition is that some day there will be the following lines in his biography: 'The son of a simple army-doctor, who was, however, capable of divining his greatness betimes, and spared nothing for his education . . .' '' The old man's voice broke.'

Arkady pressed his hand.

"What do you think,'' inquired Vassily Ivanovitch, after a short silence, "will it be in the career of medicine that he will attain the celebrity you anticipate for him?''

"Of course, not in medicine, though even in that department he will be one of the leading scientific men.''

"In what then, Arkady Nikolaitch?

"It would be hard to say now, but he will be famous.''

"He will be famous!'' repeated the old man, and he sank into a reverie.

"Arina Vlasyevna sent me to call you in to tea,'' announced Anfisushka, coming by with an immense dish of ripe raspberries.

Vassily Ivanovitch started. "And will there be cooled cream for the raspberries?''

"Yes.''

"Cold now, mind! Don't stand on ceremony, Arkady Nikolaitch; take some more. How is it, Yevgeny doesn't come?''

"I'm here,'' was heard Bazarov's voice from Arkady's room.

Vassily Ivanovitch turned round quickly. "Aha! you wanted to pay a visit to your friend; but you were too late, *amice,* and we have already had a long conversation with him. Now we must go in to tea, mother summons us. By the way, I want to have a little talk with you."

"What about?"

"There's a peasant here; he's suffering from icterus. . . ."

"You mean jaundice?"

"Yes, a chronic and very obstinate case of icterus. I have prescribed him centaury and St. John's wort, ordered him to eat carrots, given him soda; but all that's merely palliative measures; we want some more decided treatment. Though you do laugh at medicine, I am certain you can give me practical advice. But we will talk of that later. Now come in to tea."

Vassily Ivanovitch jumped up briskly from the garden seat, and hummed from *Robert le Diable*—

> "The rule, the rule we set ourselves,
>   To live, to live for pleasure!"

"Singular vitality!" observed Bazarov, going away from the window.

It was midday. The sun was burning hot behind a thin veil of unbroken whitish clouds. Everything was hushed; there was no sound but the cocks crowing irritably at one another in the village, producing in every one who heard them a strange sense of drowsiness and ennui; and somewhere, high up in a tree-top, the incessant plaintive cheep of a young hawk. Arkady and Bazarov lay in the shade of a small haystack, putting under themselves two armfuls of dry and rustling, but still greenish and fragrant grass.

"That aspen-tree," began Bazarov, "reminds me of my childhood; it grows at the edge of the clay-pits where the bricks were dug, and in those days I believed firmly that that clay-pit and aspen-tree possessed a peculiar talismanic power; I never felt dull near them. I did not understand then that I was not dull, because I was a child. Well, now I'm grown up, the talisman's lost its power."

"How long did you live here altogether?" asked Arkady.

"Two years on end; then we travelled about. We led a roving life, wandering from town to town for the most part."

"And has this house been standing long?"

"Yes. My grandfather built it—my mother's father."

"Who was he—your grandfather?"

"Devil knows. Some second-major. He served with Suvorov, and was always telling stories about the crossing of the Alps —inventions probably.

"You have a portrait of Suvorov hanging in the drawing-room. I like these dear little houses like yours; they're so warm and old-fashioned; and there's always a special sort of scent about them."

"A smell of lamp-oil and clover," Bazarov remarked, yawning. "And the flies in those dear little houses. . . . Faugh!"

"Tell me," began Arkady, after a brief pause, "were they strict with you when you were a child?"

"You can see what my parents are like. They're not a severe sort."

"Are you fond of them, Yevgeny?"

"I am, Arkady."

"How fond they are of you!"

Bazarov was silent for a little. "Do you know what I'm thinking about?" he brought out at last, clasping his hands behind his head.

"No. What is it?"

"I'm thinking life is a happy thing for my parents. My father at sixty is fussing around, talking about "palliative" measures, doctoring people, playing the bountiful master with the peasants —having a festive time, in fact; and my mother's happy too; her day's so chockful of duties of all sorts, and sighs and groans that she's no time even to think of herself; while I . . . ."

"While you?"

"I think; here I lie under a haystack. . . . The tiny space I occupy is so infinitely small in comparison with the rest of space, in which I am not, and which has nothing to do with me; and the period of time in which it is my lot to live is so petty beside the eternity in which I have not been, and shall not be. . . . And in this atom, this mathematical point, the blood is circulating, the brain is working and wanting something. . . . Isn't it loathsome? Isn't it petty?"

"Allow me to remark that what you're saying applies to men in general."

"You are right," Bazarov cut in. "I was going to say that they now—my parents, I mean—are absorbed and don't trouble themselves about their own nothingness; it doesn't sicken them . . . while I . . . I feel nothing but weariness and anger."

"Anger? why anger?

"Why? How can you ask why? Have you forgotten?"

"I remember everything, but still I don't admit that you have any right to be angry. You're unlucky, I'll allow, but . . ."

"Pooh! then you, Arkady Nikolaevitch, I can see, regard love like all modern young men; cluck, cluck, cluck you call to the hen, but if the hen comes near you, you run away. I'm not like that. But that's enough of that. What can't be helped, it's shameful to talk about." He turned over on his side. "Aha! there goes a valiant ant dragging off a half-dead fly. Take her, brother, take her! Don't pay attention to her resistance; it's your privilege as an animal to be free from the sentiment of pity—make the most of it—not like us conscientious self-destructive animals!"

"You shouldn't say that, Yevgeny! When have you destroyed yourself?

Bazarov raised his head. "That's the only thing I pride myself on. I haven't crushed myself, so a woman can't crush me. Amen! It's all over! You shall not hear another word from me about it."

Both the friends lay for some time in silence.

"Yes," began Bazarov, "man's a strange animal. When one gets a side view from a distance of the dead-alive life our "fathers" lead here, one thinks, What could be better? You eat and drink, and know you are acting in the most reasonable, most judicious manner. But if not, you're devoured by ennui. One wants to have to do with people if only to abuse them."

"One ought so to order one's life that every moment in it should be of significance," Arkady affirmed reflectively.

"I dare say! What's of significance is sweet, however mistaken; one could make up one's mind to what's insignificant even. But pettiness, pettiness, that's what's insufferable."

"Pettiness doesn't exist for a man so long as he refuses to recognise it."

"H'm . . . what you've just said is a commonplace reversed."

"What? What do you mean by that term?"

"I'll tell you: saying, for instance, that education is beneficial, that's a commonplace; but to say that education is injurious, that's a commonplace turned upside down. There's more style about it, so to say, but in reality it's one and the same."

"And the truth is—where, which side?"

"Where? Like an echo I answer, "Where?""

"You're in a melancholy mood to-day, Yevgeny."

"Really? The sun must have softened my brain, I suppose, and I can't stand so many raspberries either."

"In that case, a nap's not a bad thing," observed Arkady.

"Certainly; only don't look at me; every man's face is stupid when he's asleep."

"But isn't it all the same to you what people think of you?"

"I don't know what to say to you. A real man ought not to care; a real man is one whom it's no use thinking about, whom one must either obey or hate."

"It's funny! I don't hate anybody," observed Arkady, after a moment's thought.

"And I hate so many. You are a soft-hearted, mawkish creature; how could you hate any one? . . . You're timid; you don't rely on yourself much."

"And you," interrupted Arkady, "do you expect much of yourself? Have you a high opinion of yourself?"

Bazarov paused. "When I meet a man who can hold his own beside me," he said, dwelling on every syllable, "then I'll change my opinion of myself. Yes, hatred! You said, for instance, to-day as we passed our bailiff Philip's cottage—it's the one that's so nice and clean—well, you said, Russia will come to perfection when the poorest peasant has a house like that, and every one of us ought to work to bring it about. . . . And I felt such a hatred for this poorest peasant, this Philip or Sidor, for whom I'm to be ready to jump out of my skin, and who won't even thank me for it . . . and why should he thank me? Why, suppose he does live in a clean house, while the nettles are growing out of me,—well what do I gain by it?"

"Hush, Yevgeny . . . if one listened to you to-day one would be driven to agreeing with those who reproach us for want of principles."

"You talk like your uncle. There are no general principles—you've not made out that even yet! There are feelings. Everything depends on them."

"How so?"

"Why, I, for instance, take up a negative attitude, by virtue of my sensations; I like to deny—my brain's made on that plan, and that's all about it! Why do I like chemistry? Why do you like apples?—by virtue of our sensations. It's all the same thing. Deeper than that men will never penetrate. Not every one will tell you that, and, in fact, I shan't tell you so another time."

"What? and is honesty a matter of the senses?"

"I should rather think so."

"Yevgeny!" Arkady was beginning in a dejected voice . . .

"Well? What? Isn't it to your taste?" broke in Bazarov. "No, brother. If you've made up your mind to mow down everything, don't spare your own legs. But we've talked enough metaphysics. 'Nature breathes the silence of sleep,' said Pushkin."

"He never said anything of the sort," protested Arkady.

"Well, if he didn't, as a poet he might have—and ought to have said it. By the way, he must have been a military man."

"Pushkin never was a military man!"

"Why, on every page of him there's, 'To arms! to arms! for Russia's honour!' "

"Why, what stories you invent! I declare, it's positive calumny."

"Calumny? That's a mighty matter! What a word he's found to frighten me with! Whatever charge you make against a man, you may be certain he deserves twenty times worse than that in reality."

"We had better go to sleep," said Arkady, in a tone of vexation.

"With the greatest pleasure," answered Bazarov. But neither of them slept. A feeling almost of hostility had come over both the young men. Five minutes later, they opened their eyes and glanced at one another in silence.

"Look," said Arkady suddenly, "a dry maple leaf has come off and is falling to the earth; its movement is exactly like a butterfly's flight. Isn't it strange? Gloom and decay—like brightness and life."

"Oh, my friend, Arkady Nikolaitch!" cried Bazarov, "one thing I entreat of you; no fine talk."

"I talk as best I can. . . . And, I declare, it's perfect despotism. An idea came into my head; why shouldn't I utter it?"

"Yes; and why shouldn't I utter my ideas? I think that fine talk's positively indecent."

"And what is decent? Abuse?"

"Ha! ha! you really do intend, I see, to walk in your uncle's footsteps. How pleased that worthy imbecile would have been if he had heard you!"

"What did you call Pavel Petrovitch?"

"I called him, very justly, an imbecile."

"But this is unbearable!" cried Arkady.

"Aha! family feeling spoke there," Bazarov commented coolly. "I've noticed how obstinately it sticks to people. A man's ready to give up everything and break with every prejudice; but to admit that his brother, for instance, who steals handkerchiefs, is a thief—that's too much for him. And when one comes to think of it: my brother, mine—and no genius . . . that's an idea no one can swallow."

"It was a simple sense of justice spoke in me and not in the least family feeling," retorted Arkady passionately. "But since that's a sense you don't understand, since you haven't that sensation, you can't judge of it."

"In other words, Arkady Kirsanov is too exalted for my comprehension. I bow down before him and say no more."

"Don't, please, Yevgeny; we shall really quarrel at last."

"Ah, Arkady! do me a kindness. I entreat you, let us quarrel for once in earnest. . . ."

"But then perhaps we should end by . . ."

"Fighting?" put in Bazarov. "Well? Here, on the hay, in these idyllic surroundings, far from the world and the eyes of men, it wouldn't matter. But you'd be no match for me. I'd have you by the throat in a minute."

Bazarov spread out his long, cruel fingers. . . . Arkady turned round and prepared, as though in jest, to resist. . . . But his friend's face struck him as so vindictive—there was such menace in grim earnest in the smile that distorted his lips, and in his glittering eyes, that he felt instinctively afraid.

"Ah! so this is where you have got to!" the voice of Vassily Ivanovitch was heard saying at that instant, and the old army-doctor appeared before the young men, garbed in a home-made linen pea-jacket, with a straw hat, also home-made, on his head. "I've been looking everywhere for you. . . . Well, you've picked out a capital place, and you're excellently employed. Lying on the "earth, gazing up to heaven." Do you know, there's a special significance in that?"

"I never gaze up to heaven except when I want to sneeze," growled Bazarov, and turning to Arkady he added in an undertone. "Pity he interrupted us."

"Come, hush!" whispered Arkady, and he secretly squeezed his friend's hand. But no friendship can long stand such shocks.

"I look at you, my youthful friends," Vassily Ivanovitch was saying meantime, shaking his head, and leaning his folded arms on a rather cunningly bent stick of his own carving, with a Turk's figure for a top,—"I look, and I cannot refrain from admiration. You have so much strength, such youth and bloom, such abilities, such talents! Positively, a Castor and Pollux!"

"Get along with you—going off into mythology!" commented Bazarov. "You can see at once that he was a great Latinist in his day! Why, I seem to remember, you gained the silver medal for Latin prose—didn't you?"

"The Dioscuri, the Dioscuri!" repeated Vassily Ivanovitch.

"Come, shut up, father; don't show off."

"Once in a way it's surely permissible," murmured the old man. "However, I have not been seeking for you, gentlemen, to pay you compliments; but with the object, in the first place, of announcing to you that we shall soon be dining; and secondly, I wanted to prepare you, Yevgeny. . . . You are a sensible man, you know the world, and you know what women are, and consequently you will excuse. . . . Your mother wished to have a Te Deum sung on the occasion of your arrival. You must not imagine that I am inviting you to attend this thanksgiving—it is over indeed now; but Father Alexey . . ."

"The village parson?"

"Well, yes, the priest; he . . . is to dine . . . with us. . . . I did not anticipate this, and did not even approve of it . . . but it somehow came about . . . he did not understand me. . . . And, well . . . Arina Vlasyevna . . . Besides, he's a worthy, reasonable man."

"He won't eat my share at dinner, I suppose?" queried Bazarov.

Vassily Ivanovitch laughed. "How you talk!"

"Well, that's all I ask. I'm ready to sit down to table with any man."

Vassily Ivanovitch set his hat straight. "I was certain before I spoke," he said, "that you were above any kind of prejudice. Here am I, an old man at sixty-two, and I have none." (Vassily Ivanovitch did not dare to confess that he had himself desired the thanksgiving service. He was no less religious than his wife.) "And Father Alexey very much wanted to make your acquaintance. You will like him, you'll see. He's no objection even to cards, and he sometimes—but this is between ourselves . . . positively smokes a pipe."

"All right. We'll have a round of whist after dinner, and I'll clean him out."

"He! he! he! We shall see! That remains to be seen."

"I know you're an old hand," said Bazarov, with a peculiar emphasis.

Vassily Ivanovitch's bronzed cheeks were suffused with an uneasy flush.

"For shame, Yevgeny. . . . Let bygones be bygones. Well, I'm ready to acknowledge before this gentleman I had that passion in my youth; and I have paid for it too! How hot it is, though! Let me sit down with you. I shan't be in your way, I hope?"

"Oh, not at all," answered Arkady.

Vassily Ivanovitch lowered himself, sighing, into the hay. "Your present quarters remind me, my dear sirs," he began, "of my military bivouacking existence, the ambulance halts, somewhere like this under a haystack, and even for that we were thankful." He sighed. "I have had many, many experiences in my life. For example, if you will allow me, I will tell you a curious episode of the plague in Bessarabia."

"For which you got the Vladimir cross?" put in Bazarov. "We know, we know.... By the way, why is it you're not wearing it?"

"Why, I told you that I have no prejudices," muttered Vassily Ivanovitch (he had only the evening before had the red ribbon unpicked off his coat), and he proceeded to relate the episode of the plague. "Why, he's fallen asleep," he whispered all at once to Arkady, pointing to Yevgeny, and winking good-naturedly. "Yevgeny! get up," he went on aloud. "Let's go in to dinner."

Father Alexey, a good-looking stout man with thick, carefully-combed hair, with an embroidered girdle round his lilac silk cassock, appeared to be a man of much tact and adaptability. He made haste to be the first to offer his hand to Arkady and Bazarov, as though understanding beforehand that they did not want his blessing, and he behaved himself in general without constraint. He neither derogated from his own dignity, nor gave offence to others; he vouchsafed a passing smile at the seminary Latin, and stood up for his bishop; drank two small glasses of wine, but refused a third; accepted a cigar from Arkady, but did not proceed to smoke it, saying he would take it home with him. The only thing not quite agreeable about him was a way he had of constantly raising his hand with care and deliberation to catch the flies on his face, sometimes succeeding in smashing them. He took his seat at the green table, expressing his satisfaction at so doing in measured terms, and ended by winning from Bazarov two roubles and a half in paper money; they had no idea of even reckoning in silver in the house of Arina Vlasyevna.... She was sitting, as before, near her son (she did not play cards), her cheek, as before, propped on her little fist; she only got up to order some new dainty to be served. She was afraid to caress Bazarov, and he gave her no encouragement, he did not invite her caresses; and besides, Vassily Ivanovitch had advised her not to "worry" him too much. "Young men are not fond of that sort of thing," he declared to her. (It's needless to say what the dinner was like that day; Timofeitch in person had galloped off at early dawn for beef; the bailiff had gone off in another direction for turbot, gremille, and crayfish; for mushrooms alone forty-two farthings had been paid the peasant women in copper); but Arina Vlasyevna's eyes, bent steadfastly on Bazarov, did not express only devotion and tenderness; in them was to be seen sorrow also, mingled with awe and curiosity; there was to be seen too a sort of humble reproach-fulness.

Bazarov, however, was not in a humour to analyse the exact expression of his mother's eyes; he seldom turned to her, and then only with some short question. Once he asked her for her hand "for luck"; she gently laid her soft, little hand on his rough, broad palm.

"Well," she asked, after waiting a little, "has it been any use?"

"Worse luck than ever," he answered, with a careless laugh.

"He plays too rashly," pronounced Father Alexey, as it were compassionately, and he stroked his beard.

"Napoleon's rule, good Father, Napoleon's rule," put in Vassily Ivanovitch, leading an ace.

"It brought him to St. Helena, though, observed Father Alexey, as he trumped the ace.

"Wouldn't you like some currant tea, Enyusha?" inquired Arina Vlasyevna.

Bazarov merely shrugged his shoulders.

"No!" he said to Arkady the next day, "I'm off from here to-morrow. I'm bored; I want to work, but I can't work here. I will come to your place again; I've left all my apparatus there too. In your house one can at any rate shut oneself up. While here my father repeats to me, "My study is at your disposal—nobody shall interfere with you," and all the time he himself is never a yard away. And I'm ashamed somehow to shut myself away from him. It's the same thing too with mother. I hear her sighing the other side of the wall, and if one goes in to her, one's nothing to say to her."

"She will be very much grieved," observed Arkady, "and so will he."

"I shall come back again to them."

"When?"

"Why, when on my way to Petersburg."

"I feel sorry for your mother particularly."

"Why's that? Has she won your heart with strawberries, or what?"

Arkady dropped his eyes. "You don't understand your mother, Yevgeny. She's not only a very good woman, she's very clever really. This morning she talked to me for half-an-hour, and so sensibly, interestingly."

"I suppose she was expatiating upon me all the while?"

"We didn't talk only about you."

"Perhaps; lookers-on see most. If a woman can keep up half-an-hour's conversation, it's always a hopeful sign. But I'm going, all the same."

"It won't be very easy for you to break it to them. They are always making plans for what we are to do in a fortnight's time."

"No; it won't be easy. Some demon drove me to tease my father to-day; he had one of his rent-paying peasants flogged the other day, and quite right too—yes, yes, you needn't look at me in such horror—he did quite right, because he's an awful thief and drunkard; only my father had no idea that I, as they say, was cognisant of the facts. He was greatly perturbed, and now I shall have to upset him more than ever. . . . Never mind! Never say die! He'll get over it!"

Bazarov said, "Never mind"; but the whole day passed before he could make up his mind to inform Vassily Ivanovitch of his intentions. At last, when he was just saying good-night to him in the study, he observed, with a feigned yawn—

"Oh . . . I was almost forgetting to tell you. . . . Send to Fedot's for our horses to-morrow."

Vassily Ivanovitch was dumfoundered. "Is Mr. Kirsanov leaving us, then?"

"Yes; and I'm going with him."

Vassily Ivanovitch positively reeled. "You are going?"

"Yes . . . I must. Make the arrangements about the horses, please."

"Very good. . . ." faltered the old man; to Fedot's . . . very good . . . only . . . only. . . . How is it?"

"I must go to stay with him for a little time. I will come back here again later."

"Ah! For a little time . . . very good." Vassily Ivanovitch drew out his handkerchief, and, blowing his nose, doubled up almost to the ground. "Well . . . everything shall be done. I had thought you were to be with us . . . a little longer. Three days. . . . After three years, it's rather little; rather little, Yevgeny!"

"But, I tell you, I'm coming back directly. It's necessary for me to go."

"Necessary. . . . Well! Duty before everything. So the horses shall be in readiness. Very good. Arina and I, of course, did not anticipate this. She has just begged some flowers from a neighbour; she meant to decorate the room for you." (Vassily Ivanovitch did not even mention that every morning almost at dawn he took counsel with Timofeitch, standing with his bare feet in his slippers, and pulling out with trembling fingers one dog's-eared rouble note after another, charged him with various purchases, with special reference to good things to eat, and to red wine, which, as far as he could observe, the young men liked extremely.) "Liberty . . . is the great thing; that's my rule. . . . I don't want to hamper you . . . not . . .

He suddenly ceased, and made for the door.

"We shall soon see each other again, father, really."

But Vassily Ivanovitch, without turning round, merely waved his hand and was gone. When he got back to his bedroom he found his wife in bed, and began to say his prayers in a whisper, so as not to wake her up. She woke, however. "Is that you, Vassily Ivanovitch?" she asked.

"Yes, mother."

"Have you come from Enyusha? Do you know, I'm afraid of his not being comfortable on that sofa. I told Anfisushka to put him your travelling mattress and the new pillows; I should have given him our feather-bed, but I seem to remember he doesn't like too soft a bed. . . ."

"Never mind, mother; don't worry yourself. He's all right. Lord, have mercy on me, a sinner," he went on with his prayer in a low voice. Vassily Ivanovitch was sorry for his old wife; he did not mean to tell her over night what a sorrow there was in store for her.

Bazarov and Arkady set off the next day. From early morning all was dejection in the house; Anfisushka let the tray slip out of her hands; even Fedka was bewildered, and was reduced to taking off his boots. Vassily Ivanitch was more fussy than ever; he was obviously trying to put a good face on it, talked loudly, and stamped with his feet, but his face looked haggard, and his eyes were continually avoiding his son. Arina Vlasyevna was crying quietly; she was utterly crushed, and could not have controlled herself at all if her husband had not spent two whole hours early in the morning exhorting her. When Bazarov, after repeated promises to come back certainly not later than in a month's time, tore himself at last from the embraces detaining him, and took his seat in the coach; when the horses had started, the bell was ring-ing, and the wheels were turning round, and when it was no longer any good to look after them, and the dust had settled, and Timofeitch, all bent and tottering as he walked, had crept back to his little room; when the old people were left alone in their little house, which seemed suddenly to have grown shrunken and decrepit too, Vassily Ivanovitch, after a few more moments of hearty waving of his handkerchief on the steps, sank into a chair, and his head dropped on to his breast. "He has cast us off; he has forsaken us," he faltered; "forsaken us; he was dull with us. Alone, alone!" he repeated several times. Then Arina Vlasyevna went up to him, and, leaning her grey head against his grey head, said, "There's no help for it, Vasya! A son is a separate piece cut off. He's like the falcon that flies home and flies away at his pleasure; while you and I are like funguses in the hollow of a tree, we sit side by side, and don't move from our place. Only I am left you unchanged for ever, as you for me."

Vassily Ivanovitch took his hands from his face and clasped his wife, his friend, as warmly as he had never clasped in youth; she comforted him in his grief.

XXII

In silence, only rarely exchanging a few insignificant words, our friends travelled as far as Fedot's. Bazarov was not altogether pleased with himself. Arkady was displeased with him. He was feeling, too, that causeless melancholy which is only known to very young people. The coachman changed the horses, and getting up on to the box, inquired, "To the right or to the left?"

Arkady started. The road to the right led to the town, and from there home; the road to the left led to Madame Odintsov's.

He looked at Bazarov.

"Yevgeny," he queried; "to the left?"

Bazarov turned away. "What folly is this?" he muttered.

"I know it's folly," answered Arkady.... "but what does that matter? It's not the first time."

Bazarov pulled his cap down over his brows. "As you choose," he said at last. "Turn to the left," shouted Arkady.

The coach rolled away in the direction of Nikolskoe. But having resolved on the folly, the friends were even more obstinately silent than before, and seemed positively ill-humoured.

Directly the steward met them on the steps of Madame Odintsov's house, the friends could perceive that they had acted injudiciously in giving way so suddenly to a passing impulse. They were obviously not expected. They sat rather a long while, looking rather foolish, in the drawing-room. Madame Odintsov came in to them at last. She greeted them with her customary politeness, but was surprised at their hasty return; and, so far as could be judged from the deliberation of her gestures and words, she was not over pleased at it. They made haste to announce that they had only called on their road, and must go on farther, to the town, within four hours. She confined herself to a slight exclamation, begged Arkady to remember her to his father, and sent for her aunt. The princess appeared very sleepy, which gave her wrinkled old face an even more ill-natured expression. Katya was not well; she did not leave her room. Arkady suddenly realised that he was at least as anxious to see Katya as Anna Sergyevna herself. The four hours were spent in insignificant discussion of one thing and another; Anna Sergyevna both listened and spoke without a smile. It was only quite at parting that her former friendliness seemed, as it were, to revive.

"I have an attack of spleen just now," she said; "but you must not pay attention to that, and come again—I say this to both of you—before long."

Both Bazarov and Arkady responded with a silent bow, took their seats in the coach, and without stopping again anywhere, went straight home to Maryino, where they arrived safely on the evening of the following day. During the whole course of the journey neither one nor the other even mentioned the name of Madame Odintsov; Bazarov, in particular, scarcely opened his mouth, and kept staring in a side direction away from the road, with a kind of exasperated intensity.

At Maryino every one was exceedingly delighted to see them. The prolonged absence of his son had begun to make Nikolai Petrovitch uneasy; he uttered a cry of joy, and bounced about on the sofa, dangling his legs, when Fenitchka ran to him with sparkling eyes, and informed him of the arrival of the "young gentlemen"; even Pavel Petrovitch was conscious of some degree of agreeable excitement, and smiled condescendingly as he shook hands with the returned wanderers. Talk, questions followed; Arkady talked most, especially at supper, which was prolonged long after midnight. Nikolai Petrovitch ordered up some bottles of porter which had only just been sent from Moscow, and partook of the festive beverage till his cheeks were crimson, and he kept laughing a half-childish, half-nervous little chuckle. Even the servants were infected by the general gaiety. Dunyasha ran up and down like one possessed, and was continually slamming doors; while Piotr was, at three o'clock in the morning, still attempting to strum a Cossack waltz on the guitar. The strings gave forth a sweet and plaintive sound in the still air; but with the exception of a small preliminary flourish, nothing came of the cultured valet's efforts; nature had given him no more musical talent than all the rest of the world.

But meanwhile things were not going over harmoniously at Maryino, and poor Nikolai Petrovitch was having a bad time of it. Difficulties on the farm sprang up every day—senseless, distressing difficulties. The troubles with the hired labourers had become insupportable. Some asked for their wages to be settled, or for an increase of wages, while others made off with the wages they had received in advance; the horses fell sick; the harness fell to pieces as though it were burnt; the work was carelessly done; a threshing machine that had been ordered from Moscow turned out to be useless from its great weight, another was ruined the first time it was used; half the cattle sheds were burnt down through an old blind woman on the farm going in windy weather with a burning brand to fumigate her cow . . . the old woman, it is true, maintained that the whole mischief could be traced to the master's plan of introducing new-fangled cheeses and milk-products. The overseer suddenly turned lazy, and began to grow fat, as every Russian grows fat when he gets a snug berth. When he caught sight of Nikolai Petrovitch in the distance, he would fling a stick at a passing pig, or threaten a half-naked urchin, to show his zeal, but the rest of the time he was generally asleep. The peasants who had been put on the rent system did not bring their money at the time due, and stole the forest-timber; almost every night the keepers caught peasants' horses in the meadows of the "farm," and sometimes forcibly bore them off. Nikolai Petrovitch would fix a money fine for damages, but the matter usually ended after the horses had been kept a day or two on the master's forage by their returning to their owners. To crown all, the peasants began quarrelling among themselves; brothers asked for a division of property, their wives could not get on together in one house; all of a sudden the squabble, as though at a given signal, came to a head, and at once the whole village came running to the counting-house steps, crawling to the master often drunken and with battered face, demanding justice and judgment; then arose an uproar and clamour, the shrill wailing of the women mixed with the curses of the men. Then one had to examine the contending parties, and shout oneself hoarse, knowing all the while that one could never anyway arrive at a just decision. . . . There were not hands enough for the harvest; a neighbouring small owner, with the most benevolent countenance, contracted to supply him with reapers for a commission of two roubles an acre, and cheated him in the most shameless fashion; his peasant women demanded unheardof sums, and the corn meanwhile went to waste; and here they were not getting on with the mowing, and there the Council of Guardians threatened and demanded prompt payment, in full, of interest due. . . .

"I can do nothing!" Nikolai Petrovitch cried more than once in despair. "I can't flog them myself; and as for calling in the police captain, my principles don't allow of it, while you can do nothing with them without the fear of punishment!"

"Du calme, du calme," Pavel Petrovitch would remark upon this, but even he hummed to himself, knitted his brows, and tugged at his moustache.

Bazarov held aloof from these matters, and indeed as a guest it was not for him to meddle in other people's business. The day after his arrival at Maryino, he set to work on his frogs, his infusoria, and his chemical experiments, and was for ever busy with them. Arkady, on the contrary, thought it his duty, if not to help his father, at least to make a show of being ready to help him. He gave him a patient hearing, and once offered him some advice, not with any idea of its being acted upon, but to show his interest. Farming details did not arouse any aversion in him; he used even to dream with pleasure of work on the land, but at this time his brain was swarming with other ideas. Arkady, to his own astonishment, thought incessantly of Nikolskoe; in former days he would simply have shrugged his shoulders if any one had told him that he could ever feel dull under the same roof as Bazarov—and that roof his father's! but he actually was dull and longed to get away. He tried going long walks till he was tired, but that was no use. In conversation with his father one day, he found out that Nikolai Petrovitch had in his possession rather interesting letters, written by Madame Odintsov's mother to his wife, and he gave him no rest till he got hold of the letters, for which Nikolai Petrovitch had to rummage in twenty drawers and boxes. Having gained possession of these half-crumbling papers, Arkady felt, as it were, soothed, just as though he had caught a glimpse of the goal towards which he ought now to go. "I mean that for both of you," he was constantly whispering—she had added that herself! "I'll go, I'll go, hang it all!" But he recalled the last visit, the cold reception, and his former embarrassment, and timidity got the better of him. The "go-ahead" feeling of youth, the secret desire to try his luck, to prove his powers in solitude, without the protection of any one whatever, gained the day at last. Before ten days had passed after his return to Maryino, on the pretext of studying the working of the Sunday schools, he galloped off to the town again, and from there to Nikolskoe. Urging the driver on without intermission, he flew along, like a young officer riding to battle; and he felt both frightened and light-hearted, and was breathless with impatience. "The great thing is—one mustn't think," he kept repeating to himself. His driver happened to be a lad of spirit; he halted before every public house, saying, "A drink or not a drink?" but, to make up for it, when he had drunk he did not spare his horses. At last the lofty roof of the familiar house came in sight. . . . "What am I to do?" flashed through Arkady's head. "Well, there's no turning back now!" The three horses galloped in unison; the driver whooped and whistled at them. And now the bridge was groaning under the hoofs and wheels, and now the avenue of lopped pines seemed running to meet them. . . . There was a glimpse of a woman's pink dress against the dark green, a young face peeped out from under the light fringe of a parasol. . . . He recognised Katya, and she recognised him. Arkady told the driver to stop the galloping horses, leaped out of the carriage, and went up to her. "It's you!"

she cried, gradually flushing all over; "let us go to my sister, she's here in the garden; she will be pleased to see you."

Katya led Arkady into the garden. His meeting with her struck him as a particularly happy omen; he was delighted to see her, as though she were of his own kindred. Everything had happened so splendidly; no steward, no formal announcement. At a turn in the path he caught sight of Anna Sergyevna. She was standing with her back to him. Hearing footsteps, she turned slowly round.

Arkady felt confused again, but the first words she uttered soothed him at once. "Welcome back, runaway!" she said in her even, caressing voice, and came to meet him, smiling and frowning to keep the sun and wind out of her eyes. "Where did you pick him up, Katya?"

"I have brought you something, Anna Sergyevna," he began, "which you certainly don't expect."

"You have brought yourself; that's better than anything."

XXIII

Having seen Arkady off with ironical compassion, and given him to understand that he was not in the least deceived as to the real object of his journey, Bazarov shut himself up in complete solitude; he was overtaken by a fever for work. He did not dispute now with Pavel Petrovitch, especially as the latter assumed an excessively aristocratic demeanour in his presence, and expressed his opinions more in inarticulate sounds than in words. Only on one occasion Pavel Petrovitch fell into a controversy with the *nihilist* on the subject of the question then much discussed of the rights of the nobles of the Baltic province; but suddenly he stopped of his own accord, remarking with chilly politeness, "However, we cannot understand one another; I, at least, have not the honour of understanding you."

"I should think not!" cried Bazarov. "A man's capable of understanding anything—how the ether vibrates, and what's going on in the sun—but how any other man can blow his nose differently from him, that he's incapable of understanding."

"What, is that an epigram?" observed Pavel Petrovitch inquiringly, and he walked away.

However, he sometimes asked permission to be present at Bazarov's experiments, and once even placed his perfumed face, washed with the very best soap, near the microscope to see how a transparent infusoria swallowed a green speck and busily munched it with two very rapid sort of clappers which were in its throat. Nikolai Petrovitch visited Bazarov much oftener than his brother; he would have come every day, as he expressed it, to "study," if his worries on the farm had not taken off his attention. He did not hinder the young man in his scientific researches; he used to sit down somewhere in a corner of the room and look on attentively, occasionally permitting himself a discreet question. During dinner and supper-time he used to try to turn the conversation upon physics, geology, or chemistry, seeing that all other topics, even agriculture, to say nothing of politics, might lead, if not to collisions, at least to mutual unpleasantness. Nikolai Petrovitch surmised that his brother's dislike for Bazarov was no less. An unimportant incident, among many others, confirmed his surmises. The cholera began to make its appearance in some places in the neighbourhood, and even "carried off" two persons from Maryino itself. In the night Pavel Petrovitch happened to have rather severe symptoms. He was in pain till the morning, but did not have recourse to Bazarov's skill. And when he met him the following day, in reply to his question, "Why he had not sent for him?" answered, still quite pale, but scrupulously brushed and shaved, "Why, I seem to recollect you said yourself you didn't believe in medicine." So the days went by. Bazarov went on obstinately and grimly working . . . and meanwhile there was in Nikolai Petrovitch's house one creature to whom, if he did not open his heart, he at least was glad to talk. . . . That creature was Fenitchka.

He used to meet her for the most part early in the morning, in the garden, or the farmyard; he never used to go to her room to see her, and she had only once been to his door to inquire—

ought she to let Mitya have his bath or not? It was not only that she confided in him, that she was not afraid of him—she was positively freer and more at her ease in her behaviour with him than with Nikolai Petrovitch himself. It is hard to say how it came about; perhaps it was because she unconsciously felt the absence in Bazarov of all gentility, of all that superiority which at once attracts and overawes. In her eyes he was both an excellent doctor and a simple man. She looked after her baby without constraint in his presence; and once when she was suddenly attacked with giddiness and headache—she took a spoonful of medicine from his hand. Before Nikolai Petrovitch she kept, as it were, at a distance from Bazarov; she acted in this way not from hypocrisy, but from a kind of feeling of propriety. Pavel Petrovitch she was more afraid of than ever; for some time he had begun to watch her, and would suddenly make his appearance, as though he sprang out of the earth behind her back, in his English suit, with his immovable vigilant face, and his hands in his pockets. "It's like a bucket of cold water on one," Fenitchka complained to Dunyasha, and the latter sighed in response, and thought of another "heartless" man. Bazarov, without the least suspicion of the fact, had become the *cruel tyrant* of her heart.

Fenitchka liked Bazarov; but he liked her too. His face was positively transformed when he talked to her; it took a bright, almost kind expression, and his habitual nonchalance was replaced by a sort of jesting attentiveness. Fenitchka was growing prettier every day. There is a time in the life of young women when they suddenly begin to expand and blossom like summer roses; this time had come for Fenitchka. Dressed in a delicate white dress, she seemed herself slighter and whiter; she was not tanned by the sun; but the heat, from which she could not shield herself, spread a slight flush over her cheeks and ears, and, shedding a soft indolence over her whole body, was reflected in a dreamy languor in her pretty eyes. She was almost unable to work; her hands seem to fall naturally into her lap. She scarcely walked at all, and was constantly sighing and complaining with comic helplessness.

"You should go oftener to bathe, Nikolai Petrovitch told

her. He had made a large bath covered in with an awning in the
one of his ponds which had not yet quite disappeared.

"Oh, Nikolai Petrovitch! But by the time one gets to the
pond, one's utterly dead, and, coming back, one's dead again.
You see, there's no shade in the garden."

"That's true, there's no shade," replied Nikolai Petrovitch,
rubbing his forehead.

One day at seven o'clock in the morning Bazarov, returning
from a walk, came upon Fenitchka in the lilac arbour, which was
long past flowering, but was still thick and green. She was sitting
on the garden seat, and had as usual thrown a white kerchief over
her head; near her lay a whole heap of red and white roses still
wet with dew. He said good morning to her.

"Ah! Yevgeny Vassilyitch!" she said, and lifted the edge of
her kerchief a little to look at him, in doing which her arm was
left bare to the elbow.

"What are you doing here?" said Bazarov, sitting down
beside her. "Are you making a nosegay?"

"Yes, for the table at lunch. Nikolai Petrovitch likes it."

"But it's a long while yet to lunch time. What a heap of
flowers!"

"I gathered them now, for it will be hot then, and one can't
go out. One can only just breathe now. I feel quite weak with the
heat. I'm really afraid whether I'm not going to be ill."

"What an idea! Let me feel your pulse." Bazarov took her
hand, felt for the evenly-beating pulse, but did not even begin to
count its throbs. "You'll live a hundred years!" he said, dropping
her hand.

"Ah, God forbid!" she cried.

"Why? Don't you want a long life?"

"Well, but a hundred years! There was an old woman near
us eighty-five years old—and what a martyr she was! Dirty and
deaf and bent and coughing all the time; nothing but a burden
to herself. That's a dreadful life!"

"So it's better to be young?"

"Well, isn't it?"

"But why is it better? Tell me!"

"How can you ask why? Why, here I now, while I'm young, I can do everything—go and come and carry, and needn't ask any one for anything. . . . What can be better?"

"And to me it's all the same whether I'm young or old."

"How do you mean—it's all the same? It's not possible what you say."

"Well, judge for yourself, Fedosya Nikolaevna, what good is my youth to me. I live alone, a poor lonely creature . . ."

"That always depends on you."

"It doesn't at all depend on me! At least, some one ought to take pity on me."

Fenitchka gave a sidelong look at Bazarov, but said nothing. "What's this book you have?" she asked after a short pause.

"That? That's a scientific book, very difficult."

"And are you still studying? And don't you find it dull? You know everything already I should say."

"It seems not everything. You try to read a little."

"But I don't understand anything here. Is it Russian?" asked Fenitchka, taking the heavily bound book in both hands. "How thick it is!"

"Yes, it's Russian."

"All the same, I shan't understand anything."

"Well, I didn't give it you for you to understand it. I wanted to look at you while you were reading. When you read, the end of your little nose moves so nicely."

Fenitchka, who had set to work to spell out in a low voice the article on "Creosote" she had chanced upon, laughed and threw down the book . . . it slipped from the seat on to the ground.

"I like it too when you laugh," observed Bazarov.

"Nonsense!"

"I like it when you talk. It's just like a little brook babbling."

Fenitchka turned her head away. "What a person you are to talk!" she commented, picking the flowers over with her finger. "And how can you care to listen to me? You have talked with such clever ladies."

"Ah, Fedosya Nikolaevna! believe me; all the clever ladies in the world are not worth your little elbow."

"Come, there's another invention!" murmured Fenitchka, clasping her hands.

Bazarov picked the book up from the ground.

"That's a medical book; why do you throw it away?"

"Medical?" repeated Fenitchka, and she turned to him again. "Do you know, ever since you gave me those drops—do you remember?—Mitya has slept so well! I really can't think how to thank you; you are so good, really."

"But you have to pay doctors," observed Bazarov with a smile. "Doctors, you know yourself, are grasping people."

Fenitchka raised her eyes, which seemed still darker from the whitish reflection cast on the upper part of her face, and looked at Bazarov. She did not know whether he was joking or not.

"If you please, we shall be delighted. . . . I must ask Nikolai Petrovitch . . ."

"Why, do you think I want money?" Bazarov interposed. "No; I don't want money from you."

"What then?" asked Fenitchka.

"What?" repeated Bazarov. "Guess!"

"A likely person I am to guess!"

"Well, I will tell you; I want . . . one of those roses."

Fenitchka laughed again, and even clapped her hands, so amusing Bazarov's request seemed to her. She laughed, and at the same time felt flattered. Bazarov was looking intently at her.

"By all means," she said at last; and, bending down to the seat, she began picking over the roses. "Which will you have—a red or a white one?"

"Red, and not too large."

She sat up again. "Here, take it," she said, but at once drew back her outstretched hand, and, biting her lips, looked towards the entrance of the arbour, then listened.

"What is it?" asked Bazarov. "Nikolai Petrovitch?"

"No . . . Mr. Kirsanov has gone to the fields . . . besides, I'm not afraid of him . . . but Pavel Petrovitch . . . I fancied . . ."

"What?"

"I fancied he was coming here. No . . . it was no one. Take it." Fenitchka gave Bazarov the rose.

"On what grounds are you afraid of Pavel Petrovitch?"

"He always scares me. And I know you don't like him. Do you remember, you always used to quarrel with him? I don't know what your quarrel was about, but I can see you turn him about like this and like that."

Fenitchka showed with her hands how in her opinion Bazarov turned Pavel Petrovitch about.

Bazarov smiled. "But if he gave me a beating," he asked, "would you stand up for me?"

"How could I stand up for you? but no, no one will get the better of you."

"Do you think so? But I know a hand which could overcome me if it liked."

"What hand?"

"Why, don't you know, really? Smell, how delicious this rose smells you gave me."

Fenitchka stretched her little neck forward, and put her face close to the flower. . . . The kerchief slipped from her head on to her shoulders; her soft mass of dark, shining, slightly ruffled hair was visible.

"Wait a minute; I want to smell it with you," said Bazarov. He bent down and kissed her vigorously on her parted lips.

She started, pushed him back with both her hands on his breast, but pushed feebly, and he was able to renew and prolong his kiss.

A dry cough was heard behind the lilac bushes. Fenitchka instantly moved away to the other end of the seat. Pavel Petrovitch showed himself, made a slight bow, and saying with a sort of malicious mournfulness, "You are here," he retreated. Fenitchka at once gathered up all her roses and went out of the arbour. "It was wrong of you, Yevgeny Vassilyevitch," she whispered as she went. There was a note of genuine reproach in her whisper.

Bazarov remembered another recent scene, and he felt both shame and contemptuous annoyance. But he shook his head directly, ironically congratulated himself "on his final assumption of the part of the gay Lothario," and went off to his own room.

Pavel Petrovitch went out of the garden, and made his way with deliberate steps to the copse. He stayed there rather a long while; and when he returned to lunch, Nikolai Petrovitch inquired anxiously whether he were quite well—his face looked so gloomy.

"You know, I sometimes suffer with my liver," Pavel Petrovitch answered tranquilly.

XXIV

Two hours later he knocked at Bazarov's door.

"I must apologise for hindering you in your scientific pursuits," he began, seating himself on a chair in the window, and leaning with both hands on a handsome walking-stick with an ivory knob (he usually walked without a stick), "but I am constrained to beg you to spare me five minutes of your time . . . no more."

"All my time is at your disposal," answered Bazarov, over whose face there passed a quick change of expression directly Pavel Petrovitch crossed the threshold.

"Five minutes will be enough for me. I have come to put a single question to you."

"A question? What is it about?"

"I will tell you, if you will kindly hear me out. At the commencement of your stay in my brother's house, before I had renounced the pleasure of conversing with you, it was my fortune to hear your opinions on many subjects; but so far as my memory serves, neither between us, nor in my presence, was the subject of single combats and duelling in general broached. Allow me to hear what are your views on that subject?"

Bazarov, who had risen to meet Pavel Petrovitch, sat down on the edge of the table and folded his arms.

"My view is," he said, "that from the theoretical standpoint, duelling is absurd; from the practical standpoint, now—it's quite a different matter."

"That is, you mean to say, if I understand you right, that whatever your theoretical views on duelling, you would not in practice allow yourself to be insulted without demanding satisfaction?"

"You have guessed my meaning absolutely."

"Very good. I am very glad to hear you say so. Your words relieve me from a state of incertitude."

"Of uncertainty, you mean to say."

"That is all the same; I express myself so as to be understood; I . . . am not a seminary rat. Your words save me from a rather deplorable necessity. I have made up my mind to fight you."

Bazarov opened his eyes wide. "Me?"

"Undoubtedly."

"But what for, pray?"

"I could explain the reason to you," began Pavel Petrovitch, "but I prefer to be silent about it. To my idea your presence here is superfluous; I cannot endure you; I despise you; and if that is not enough for you . . ."

Pavel Petrovitch's eyes glittered . . . Bazarov's too were flashing.

"Very good," he assented. "No need of further explanations. You've a whim to try your chivalrous spirit upon me. I might refuse you this pleasure, but—so be it!"

"I am sensible of my obligation to you," replied Pavel Petrovitch; "and may reckon then on your accepting my challenge without compelling me to resort to violent measures."

"That means, speaking without metaphor, to that stick?" Bazarov remarked coolly. "That is precisely correct. It's quite unnecessary for you to insult me. Indeed, it would not be a perfectly safe proceeding. You can remain a gentleman. . . . I accept your challenge, too, like a gentleman."

"That is excellent," observed Pavel Petrovitch, putting his stick in the corner. "We will say a few words directly about the conditions of our duel; but I should like first to know whether you think it necessary to resort to the formality of a trifling dispute, which might serve as a pretext for my challenge?"

"No; it's better without formalities."

"I think so myself. I presume it is also out of place to go into the real grounds of our difference. We cannot endure one another. What more is necessary?"

"What more, indeed?" repeated Bazarov ironically.

"As regards the conditions of the meeting itself, seeing that we shall have no seconds—for where could we get them?"

"Exactly so; where could we get them?"

"Then I have the honour to lay the following proposition before you: The combat to take place early to-morrow, at six, let us say, behind the copse, with pistols, at a distance of ten paces. . . ."

"At ten paces? that will do; we hate one another at that distance."

"We might have it eight," remarked Pavel Petrovitch.

"We might."

"To fire twice; and, to be ready for any result, let each put a letter in his pocket, in which he accuses himself of his end."

"Now, that I don't approve of at all," observed Bazarov. "There's a slight flavour of the French novel about it, something not very plausible."

"Perhaps. You will agree, however, that it would be unpleasant to incur a suspicion of murder?"

"I agree as to that. But there is a means of avoiding that painful reproach. We shall have no seconds, but we can have a witness."

"And whom, allow me to inquire?"

"Why, Piotr."

"What Piotr?"

"Your brother's valet. He's a man who has attained to the acme of contemporary culture, and he will perform his part with all the *comilfo (comme il faut)* necessary in such cases."

"I think you are joking, sir."

"Not at all. If you think over my suggestion, you will be convinced that it's full of commonsense and simplicity. You can't hide a candle under a bushel; but I'll undertake to prepare Piotr in a fitting manner, and bring him on to the field of battle."

"You persist in jesting still," Pavel Petrovitch declared, getting up from his chair. "But after the courteous readiness you have shown me, I have no right to pretend to lay down. . . . And so, everything is arranged. . . . By the way, perhaps you have no pistols?"

"How should I have pistols, Pavel Petrovitch? I'm not in the army."

"In that case, I offer you mine. You may rest assured that it's five years now since I shot with them."

"That's a very consoling piece of news."

Pavel Petrovitch took up his stick. . . . "And now, my dear sir, it only remains for me to thank you and to leave you to your studies. I have the honour to take leave of you."

"Till we have the pleasure of meeting again, my dear sir," said Bazarov, conducting his visitor to the door.

Pavel Petrovitch went out, while Bazarov remained standing a minute before the door, and suddenly exclaimed, "Pish, well, I'm dashed! how fine, and how foolish! A pretty farce we've been through! Like trained dogs dancing on their hind-paws. But to decline was out of the question; why, I do believe he'd have struck me, and then . . ." (Bazarov turned white at the very thought; all his pride was up in arms at once)—"then it might have come to my strangling him like a cat." He went back to his microscope, but his heart was beating, and the composure necessary for taking observations had disappeared. "He caught sight of us to-day," he thought; "but would he really act like this on his brother's account? And what a mighty matter is it—a kiss? There must be something else in it. Bah! isn't he perhaps in love with her himself? To be sure, he's in love; it's as clear as day. What a complication. It's a nuisance!" he decided at last; "it's a bad job, look at it which way you will. In the first place, to risk a bullet through one's brains, and in any case to go away; and then Arkady . . . and that dear innocent pussy, Nikolai Petrovitch. It's a bad job, an awfully bad job."

The day passed in a kind of peculiar stillness and languor.

Fenitchka gave no sign of her existence; she sat in her little room like a mouse in its hole. Nikolai Petrovitch had a careworn air. He had just heard that blight had begun to appear in his wheat, upon which he had in particular rested his hopes. Pavel Petrovitch overwhelmed every one, even Prokofitch, with his icy courtesy. Bazarov began a letter to his father, but tore it up, and threw it under the table.

"If I die," he thought," "they will find it out; but I'm not going to die. No, I shall struggle along in this world a good while yet." He gave Piotr orders to come to him on important business the next morning directly it was light. Piotr imagined that he wanted to take him to Petersburg with him. Bazarov went late to bed, and all night long he was harassed by disordered dreams. . . . Madame Odintsov kept appearing in them, now she was his mother, and she was followed by a kitten with black whiskers, and this kitten seemed to be Fenitchka; then Pavel Petrovitch took the shape of a great wood, with which he had yet to fight. Piotr waked him up at four o'clock; he dressed at once, and went out with him.

It was a lovely, fresh morning; tiny flecked clouds hovered overhead in little curls of foam on the pale clear blue; a fine dew lay in drops on the leaves and grass, and sparkled like silver on the spiders' webs; the damp, dark earth seemed still to keep traces of the rosy dawn; from the whole sky the songs of larks came pouring in showers. Bazarov walked as far as the copse, sat down in the shade at its edge, and only then disclosed to Piotr the nature of the service he expected of him. The refined valet was mortally alarmed; but Bazarov soothed him by the assurance that he would have nothing to do but stand at a distance and look on, and that he would not incur any sort of responsibility. "And meantime," he added, "only think what an important part you have to play!" Piotr threw up his hands, looked down, and leaned against a birch-tree, looking green with terror.

The road from Maryino skirted the copse; a light dust lay on it, untouched by wheel or foot since the previous day. Bazarov unconsciously stared along this road, picked and gnawed a blade of grass, while he kept repeating to himself, "What a piece of foolery!" The chill of the early morning made him shiver twice.

. . . Piotr looked at him dejectedly, but Bazarov only smiled; he was not afraid.

The tramp of horses' hoofs was heard along the road. . . . A peasant came into sight from behind the trees. He was driving before him two horses hobbled together, and as he passed Bazarov he looked at him rather strangely, without touching his cap, which it was easy to see disturbed Piotr, as an unlucky omen. "There's some one else up early too," thought Bazarov; "but he at least has got up for work, while we . . ."

"Fancy the gentleman's coming," Piotr faltered suddenly.

Bazarov raised his head and saw Pavel Petrovitch. Dressed in a light check jacket and snow-white trousers, he was walking rapidly along the road; under his arm he carried a box wrapped up in green cloth.

"I beg your pardon, I believe I have kept you waiting," he observed, bowing first to Bazarov, then to Piotr, whom he treated respectfully at that instant, as representing something in the nature of a second. "I was unwilling to wake my man."

"It doesn't matter," answered Bazarov; "we've only just arrived ourselves."

"Ah! so much the better!" Pavel Petrovitch took a look round. "There's no one in sight; no one hinders us. We can proceed?"

"Let us proceed."

"You do not, I presume, desire any fresh explanations?"

"No, I don't."

"Would you like to load?" inquired Pavel Petrovitch, taking the pistols out of the box.

"No; you load, and I will measure out the paces. My legs are longer," added Bazarov with a smile. "One, two, three."

"Yevgeny Vassilyevitch," Piotr faltered with an effort (he was shaking as though he were in a fever), "say what you like, I am going farther off."

"Four . . . five. . . . Good. Move away, my good fellow, move away; you may get behind a tree even, and stop up your ears, only don't shut your eyes; and if any one falls, run and pick him up. Six . . . seven . . . eight . . ." Bazarov stopped. "Is that enough?"

he said, turning to Pavel Petrovitch; "or shall I add two paces
more?"

"As you like," replied the latter, pressing down the second
bullet.

"Well, we'll make it two paces more." Bazarov drew a line
on the ground with the toe of his boot. "There's the barrier then.
By the way, how many paces may each of us go back from the
barrier? That's an important question too. That point was not
discussed yesterday."

"I imagine, ten," replied Pavel Petrovitch, handing Bazarov
both pistols. "Will you be so good as to choose?"

"I will be so good. But, Pavel Petrovitch, you must admit
our combat is singular to the point of absurdity. Only look at the
countenance of our second."

"You are disposed to laugh at everything," answered Pavel
Petrovitch. "I acknowledge the strangeness of our duel, but I
think it my duty to warn you that I intend to fight seriously. *A bon
entendeur, salut!*"

"Oh! I don't doubt that we've made up our minds to make
away with each other; but why not laugh too and unite *utile dulci?*
You talk to me in French, while I talk to you in Latin."

"I am going to fight in earnest," repeated Pavel Petrovitch,
and he walked off to his place. Bazarov on his side counted off
ten paces from the barrier, and stood still.

"Are you ready?" asked Pavel Petrovitch.

"Perfectly."

"We can approach one another."

Bazarov moved slowly forward, and Pavel Petrovitch, his
left hand thrust in his pocket, walked towards him, gradually
raising the muzzle of his pistol. . . . "He's aiming straight at my
nose," thought Bazarov, "and doesn't he blink down it carefully,
the ruffian! Not an agreeable sensation though. I'm going to look
at his watch chain."

Something whizzed sharply by his very ear, and at the same
instant there was the sound of a shot. "I heard it, so it must be
all right," had time to flash through Bazarov's brain. He took one
more step, and without taking aim, pressed the spring.

Pavel Petrovitch gave a slight start, and clutched at his thigh.
A stream of blood began to trickle down his white trousers.

Bazarov flung aside the pistol, and went up to his antagonist.
"Are you wounded?" he said.

"You had the right to call me up to the barrier," said Pavel
Petrovitch, "but that's of no consequence. According to our
agreement, each of us has the right to one more shot."

"All right, but, excuse me, that'll do another time," answered Bazarov, catching hold of Pavel Petrovitch, who was
beginning to turn pale. "Now, I'm not a duellist, but a doctor,
and I must have a look at your wound before anything else. Piotr!
come here, Piotr! where have you got to?"

"That's all nonsense. . . . I need no one's aid," Pavel Petrovitch declared jerkily, "and . . . we must . . . again . . ." He
tried to pull at his moustaches, but his hand failed him, his eyes
grew dim, and he lost consciousness.

"Here's a pretty pass! A fainting fit! What next!" Bazarov
cried unconsciously, as he laid Pavel Petrovitch on the grass.
"Let's have a look what's wrong." He pulled out a handkerchief,
wiped away the blood, and began feeling round the wound.
. . . "The bone's not touched," he muttered through his teeth;
"the ball didn't go deep; one muscle, *vastus externus,* grazed.
He'll be dancing about in three weeks! . . . And to faint! Oh, these
nervous people, how I hate them! My word, what a delicate skin!"

"Is he killed?" the quaking voice of Piotr came rustling
behind his back.

Bazarov looked round. "Go for some water as quick as you
can, my good fellow, and he'll outlive us yet."

But the modern servant seemed not to understand his words,
and he did not stir. Pavel Petrovitch slowly opened his eyes. "He
will die!" whispered Piotr, and he began crossing himself.

"You are right. . . . What an imbecile countenance!" remarked the wounded gentleman with a forced smile.

"Well, go for the water, damn you!" shouted Bazarov.

"No need. . . . It was a momentary *vertigo.* . . . Help me to
sit up . . . there, that's right. . . . I only need something to bind
up this scratch, and I can reach home on foot, or else you can send

a droshky for me. The duel, if you are willing, shall not be renewed. You have behaved honourably . . . to-day, to-day—observe."

"There's no need to recall the past," rejoined Bazarov; "and as regards the future, it's not worth while for you to trouble your head about that either, for I intend being off without delay. Let me bind up your leg now; your wound's not serious, but it's always best to stop bleeding. But first I must bring this corpse to his senses."

Bazarov shook Piotr by the collar, and sent him for a droshky.

"Mind you don't frighten my brother," Pavel Petrovitch said to him; "don't dream of informing him."

Piotr flew off; and while he was running for a droshky, the two antagonists sat on the ground and said nothing. Pavel Petrovitch tried not to look at Bazarov; he did not want to be reconciled to him in any case; he was ashamed of his own haughtiness, of his failure; he was ashamed of the whole position he had brought about, even while he felt it could not have ended in a more favourable manner. "At any rate, there will be no scandal," he consoled himself by reflecting, "and for that I am thankful." The silence was prolonged, a silence distressing and awkward. Both of them were ill at ease. Each was conscious that the other understood him. That is pleasant to friends, and always very unpleasant to those who are not friends, especially when it is impossible either to have things out or to separate.

"Haven't I bound up your leg too tight?" inquired Bazarov at last.

"No, not at all; it's capital," answered Pavel Petrovitch; and after a brief pause, he added, "There's no deceiving my brother; we shall have to tell him we quarrelled over politics."

"Very good," assented Bazarov. "You can say I insulted all anglomaniacs."

"That will do capitally. What do you imagine that man thinks of us now?" continued Pavel Petrovitch, pointing to the same peasant, who had driven the hobbled horses past Bazarov a few

minutes before the duel, and going back again along the road,
took off his cap at the sight of the "gentlefolk."

"Who can tell!" answered Bazarov; "it's quite likely he
thinks nothing. The Russian peasant is that mysterious unknown
about whom Mrs. Radcliffe used to talk so much. Who is to
understand him! He doesn't understand himself!"

"Ah! so that's your idea!" Pavel Petrovitch began; and suddenly he cried, "Look what your fool of a Piotr has done! Here's
my brother galloping up to us!"

Bazarov turned round and saw the pale face of Nikolai Petrovitch, who was sitting in the droshky. He jumped out of it
before it had stopped, and rushed up to his brother.

"What does this mean?" he said in an agitated voice.
"Yevgeny Vassilyitch, pray, what is this?"

"Nothing," answered Pavel Petrovitch; "they have alarmed
you for nothing. I had a little dispute with Mr. Bazarov, and I
have had to pay for it a little."

"But what was it all about, mercy on us!"

"How can I tell you? Mr. Bazarov alluded disrespectfully to
Sir Robert Peel. I must hasten to add that I am the only person
to blame in all this, while Mr. Bazarov has behaved most honourably. I called him out."

"But you're covered with blood, good Heavens!"

"Well, did you suppose I had water in my veins? But this
blood-letting is positively beneficial to me. Isn't that so, doctor?
Help me to get into the droshky, and don't give way to melancholy. I shall be quite well to-morrow. That's it; capital. Drive on,
coachman."

Nikolai Petrovitch walked after the droshky; Bazarov was
remaining where he was. . . .

"I must ask you to look after my brother," Nikolai Petrovitch said to him, "till we get another doctor from the town."

Bazarov nodded his head without speaking. In an hour's time
Pavel Petrovitch was already lying in bed with a skilfully ban-
daged leg. The whole house was alarmed; Fenitchka fainted.
Nikolai Petrovitch kept stealthily wringing his hands, while Pavel
Petrovitch laughed and joked, especially with Bazarov; he had

put on a fine cambric night-shirt, an elegant morning wrapper, and a fez, did not allow the blinds to be drawn down, and humorously complained of the necessity of being kept from food.

Towards night, however, he began to be feverish; his head ached. The doctor arrived from the town. (Nikolai Petrovitch would not listen to his brother, and indeed Bazarov himself did not wish him to; he sat the whole day in his room, looking yellow and vindictive, and only went in to the invalid for as brief a time as possible; twice he happened to meet Fenitchka, but she shrank away from him with horror.) The new doctor advised a cooling diet; he confirmed, however, Bazarov's assertion that there was no danger. Nikolai Petrovitch told him his brother had wounded himself by accident, to which the doctor responded, "Hm!" but having twenty-five silver roubles slipped into his hand on the spot, he observed, "You don't say so! Well, it's a thing that often happens, to be sure."

No one in the house went to bed or undressed. Nikolai Petrovitch kept going in to his brother on tiptoe, retreating on tiptoe again; the latter dozed, moaned a little, told him in French, *Couchez-vous,* and asked for drink. Nikolai Petrovitch sent Fenitchka twice to take him a glass of lemonade; Pavel Petrovitch gazed at her intently, and drank off the glass to the last drop. Towards morning the fever had increased a little; there was slight delirium. At first Pavel Petrovitch uttered incoherent words; then suddenly he opened his eyes, and seeing his brother near his bed bending anxiously over him, he said, "Don't you think, Nikolai, Fenitchka has something in common with Nellie?"

"What Nellie, Pavel dear?"

"How can you ask? Princess R——. Especially in the upper part of the face. *C'est de la même famille.*"

Nikolai Petrovitch made no answer, while inwardly he marvelled at the persistence of old passions in man. "It's like this when it comes to the surface," he thought.

"Ah, how I love that light-headed creature!" moaned Pavel Petrovitch, clasping his hands mournfully behind his head. "I can't bear any insolent upstart to dare to touch . . ." he whispered a few minutes later.

Nikolai Petrovitch only sighed; he did not even suspect to whom these words referred.

Bazarov presented himself before him at eight o'clock the next day. He had already had time to pack, and to set free all his frogs, insects, and birds.

"You have come to say good-bye to me?" said Nikolai Petrovitch, getting up to meet him.

"Yes."

"I understand you, and approve of you fully. My poor brother, of course, is to blame; and he is punished for it. He told me himself that he made it impossible for you to act otherwise. I believe that you could not avoid this duel, which . . . which to some extent is explained by the almost constant antagonism of your respective views." (Nikolai Petrovitch began to get a little mixed up in his words.) "My brother is a man of the old school, hot-tempered and obstinate. . . . Thank God that it has ended as it has. I have taken every precaution to avoid publicity."

"I'm leaving you my address, in case there's any fuss," Bazarov remarked casually.

"I hope there will be no fuss, Yevgeny Vassilyitch. . . . I am very sorry your stay in my house should have such a . . . such an end. It is the more distressing to me through Arkady's . . ."

"I shall be seeing him, I expect," replied Bazarov, in whom "explanations" and "protestations" of every sort always aroused a feeling of impatience; "in case I don't, I beg you to say good-bye to him for me, and accept the expression of my regret."

"And I beg . . ." answered Nikolai Petrovitch. But Bazarov went off without waiting for the end of his sentence.

When he heard of Bazarov's going, Pavel Petrovitch expressed a desire to see him, and shook his hand. But even then he remained as cold as ice; he realised that Pavel Petrovitch wanted to play the magnanimous. He did not succeed in saying good-bye to Fenitchka; he only exchanged glances with her at the window. Her face struck him as looking dejected. "She'll come to grief, perhaps," he said to himself. . . . "But who knows? she'll pull through somehow, I daresay!" Piotr, however, was so overcome that he wept on his shoulder, till Bazarov damped him by asking if he'd a constant supply laid on in his eyes; while Dunya-sha was obliged to run away into the wood to hide her emotion. The originator of all this woe got into a light cart, smoked a cigar, and when at the third mile, at the bend in the road, the Kirsanovs' farm, with its new house, could be seen in a long line, he merely spat, and muttering, "Cursed snobs!" wrapped himself closer in his cloak.

Pavel Petrovitch was soon better; but he had to keep his bed about a week. He bore his captivity, as he called it, pretty patient-ly, though he took great pains over his toilette, and had every-thing scented with eau-de-cologne. Nikolai Petrovitch used to read him the journals; Fenitchka waited on him as before, brought him lemonade, soup, boiled eggs, and tea; but she was overcome with secret dread whenever she went into his room. Pavel Petrovitch's unexpected action had alarmed every one in the house, and her more than any one; Prokofitch was the only person not agitated by it; he discoursed upon how gentlemen in his day used to fight, but only with real gentlemen; low curs like that they used to order a horsewhipping in the stable for their insolence.

Fenitchka's conscience scarcely reproached her; but she was tormented at times by the thought of the real cause of the quarrel; and Pavel Petrovitch too looked at her so strangely . . . that even when her back was turned, she felt his eyes upon her. She grew thinner from constant inward agitation, and, as is always the way, became still more charming.

One day—the incident took place in the morning—Pavel Petrovitch felt better, and moved from his bed to the sofa, while Nikolai Petrovitch, having satisfied himself he was better, went off to the threshing-floor. Fenitchka brought him a cup of tea, and setting it down on a little table, was about to withdraw. Pavel Petrovitch detained her.

"Where are you going in such a hurry, Fedosya Nikolaev-na?" he began; "are you busy?"

"No . . . I have to pour out tea."

"Dunyasha will do that without you; sit a little while with a poor invalid. By the way, I must have a little talk with you."

Fenitchka sat down on the edge of an easy-chair, without speaking.

"Listen," said Pavel Petrovitch, tugging at his moustaches; "I have long wanted to ask you something; you seem somehow afraid of me?"

"I?"

"Yes, you. You never look at me, as though your conscience were not at rest."

Fenitchka crimsoned, but looked at Pavel Petrovitch. He impressed her as looking strange, and her heart began throbbing slowly.

"Is your conscience at rest?" he questioned her.

"Why should it not be at rest?" she faltered.

"Goodness knows why! Besides, whom can you have wronged? Me? That is not likely. Any other people in the house here? That, too, is something incredible. Can it be my brother? But you love him, don't you?"

"I love him."

"With your whole soul, with your whole heart?"

"I love Nikolai Petrovitch with my whole heart."

"Truly? Look at me, Fenitchka." (It was the first time he had called her that name.) "You know, it's a great sin telling lies!"

"I am not telling lies, Pavel Petrovitch. Not love Nikolai Petrovitch—I shouldn't care to live after that."

"And will you never give him up for any one?"

"For whom could I give him up?"

"For whom indeed! Well, how about that gentleman who has just gone away from here?"

Fenitchka got up. "My God, Pavel Petrovitch, what are you torturing me for? What have I done to you? How can such things be said?" . . .

"Fenitchka," said Pavel Petrovitch, in a sorrowful voice, "you know I saw . . ."

"What did you see?"

"Well, there . . . in the arbour."

Fenitchka crimsoned to her hair and to her ears. "How was I to blame for that?" she articulated with an effort.

Pavel Petrovitch raised himself up. "You were not to blame? No? Not at all?"

"I love Nikolai Petrovitch, and no one else in the world, and I shall always love him!" cried Fenitchka with sudden force, while her throat seemed fairly breaking with sobs. "As for what you saw, at the dreadful day of judgment I will say I'm not to blame, and wasn't to blame for it, and I would rather die at once if people can suspect me of such a thing against my benefactor, Nikolai Petrovitch."

But here her voice broke, and at the same time she felt that Pavel Petrovitch was snatching and pressing her hand. . . . She looked at him, and was fairly petrified. He had turned even paler than before; his eyes were shining, and what was most marvellous of all, one large solitary tear was rolling down his cheek.

"Fenitchka!" he was saying in a strange whisper; "love him, love my brother! Don't give him up for any one in the world; don't listen to any one else! Think what can be more terrible than to love and not be loved! Never leave my poor Nikolai!"

Fenitchka's eyes were dry, and her terror had passed away, so great was her amazement. But what were her feelings when Pavel Petrovitch, Pavel Petrovitch himself, put her hand to his lips and seemed to pierce into it without kissing it, and only heaving convulsive sighs from time to time. . . .

"Goodness," she thought, "isn't it some attack coming on him?" . . .

At that instant his whole ruined life was stirred up within him.

The staircase creaked under rapidly approaching footsteps. . . . He pushed her away from him, and let his head drop back on the pillow. The door opened, and Nikolai Petrovitch entered, cheerful, fresh, and ruddy. Mitya, as fresh and ruddy as his father, in nothing but his little shirt, was frisking on his shoulder, catching the big buttons of his rough country coat with his little bare toes.

Fenitchka simply flung herself upon him, and clasping him and her son together in her arms, dropped her head on his shoulder. Nikolai Petrovitch was surprised; Fenitchka, the reserved

and staid Fenitchka, had never given him a caress in the presence
of a third person.

"What's the matter?" he said, and, glancing at his brother,
he gave her Mitya. "You don't feel worse?" he inquired, going
up to Pavel Petrovitch.

He buried his face in a cambric handkerchief. "No . . . not
at all . . . on the contrary, I am much better."

"You were in too great a hurry to move on to the sofa.
Where are you going?" added Nikolai Petrovitch, turning round
to Fenitchka; but she had already closed the door behind her. "I
was bringing in my young hero to show you; he's been crying for
his uncle. Why has she carried him off? What's wrong with you,
though? Has anything passed between you, eh?"

"Brother!" said Pavel Petrovitch solemnly.

Nikolai Petrovitch started. He felt dismayed, he could not
have said why himself.

"Brother," repeated Pavel Petrovitch, "give me your word
that you will carry out my one request."

"What request? Tell me."

"It is very important; the whole happiness of your life, to my
idea, depends on it. I have been thinking a great deal all this time
over what I want to say to you now. . . . Brother, do your duty,
the duty of an honest and generous man; put an end to the scandal
and bad example you are setting—you, the best of men!"

"What do you mean, Pavel?"

"Marry Fenitchka. . . . She loves you; she is the mother of
your son."

Nikolai Petrovitch stepped back a pace, and flung up his
hands. "Do you say that, Pavel? you whom I have always regarded as the most determined opponent of such marriages! You say
that? Don't you know that it has simply been out of respect for
you that I have not done what you so rightly call my duty?"

"You were wrong to respect me in that case," Pavel Petrovitch responded, with a weary smile. "I begin to think Bazarov
was right in accusing me of snobbishness. No, dear brother, don't
let us worry ourselves about appearances and the world's opinion
any more; we are old folks and humble now; it's time we laid aside

vanity of all kinds. Let us, just as you say, do our duty; and mind, we shall get happiness that way into the bargain."

Nikolai Petrovitch rushed to embrace his brother.

"You have opened my eyes completely!" he cried. "I was right in always declaring you the wisest and kindest-hearted fellow in the world, and now I see you are just as reasonable as you are noble-hearted."

"Quietly, quietly," Pavel Petrovitch interrupted him; "don't hurt the leg of your reasonable brother, who at close upon fifty has been fighting a duel like an ensign. So, then, it's a settled matter; Fenitchka is to be my . . . *belle soeur.*"

"My dearest Pavel! But what will Arkady say?"

"Arkady? he'll be in ecstasies, you may depend upon it! Marriage is against his principles, but then the sentiment of equality in him will be gratified. And, after all, what sense have class distinctions *au dix-neuvième siècle?*"

"Ah, Pavel, Pavel! let me kiss you once more! Don't be afraid, I'll be careful."

The brothers embraced each other.

"What do you think, should you not inform her of your intention now?" queried Pavel Petrovitch.

"Why be in a hurry?" responded Nikolai Petrovitch. "Has there been any conversation between you?"

"Conversation between us? *Quelle idée!*"

"Well, that is all right then. First of all, you must get well, and meanwhile there's plenty of time. We must think it over well, and consider . . ."

"But your mind is made up, I suppose?"

"Of course, my mind is made up, and I thank you from the bottom of my heart. I will leave you now; you must rest; any excitement is bad for you. . . . But we will talk it over again. Sleep well, dear heart, and God bless you!"

"What is he thanking me like that for?" thought Pavel Petrovitch, when he was left alone. "As though it did not depend on him! I will go away directly he is married, somewhere a long way off—to Dresden or Florence, and will live there till I
____"

Pavel Petrovitch moistened his forehead with eau de cologne, and closed his eyes. His beautiful, emaciated head, the glaring daylight shining full upon it, lay on the white pillow like the head of a dead man. . . . And indeed he was a dead man.

XXV

At Nikolskoe Katya and Arkady were sitting in the garden on a turf seat in the shade of a tall ash tree; Fifi had placed himself on the ground near them, giving his slender body that graceful curve, which is known among dog-fanciers as "the hare bend." Both Arkady and Katya were silent; he was holding a half-open book in his hands, while she was picking out of a basket the few crumbs of bread left in it, and throwing them to a small family of sparrows, who with the frightened impudence peculiar to them were hopping and chirping at her very feet. A faint breeze stirring in the ash leaves kept slowly moving pale-gold flecks of sunlight up and down over the path and Fifi's tawny back; a patch of unbroken shade fell upon Arkady and Katya; only from time to time a bright streak gleamed on her hair. Both were silent, but the very way in which they were silent, in which they were sitting together, was expressive of confidential intimacy; each of them seemed not even to be thinking of his companion, while secretly rejoicing in his presence. Their faces, too, had changed since we saw them last; Arkady looked more tranquil, Katya brighter and more daring.

"Don't you think," began Arkady, "that the ash has been very well named in Russian *yasen;* no other tree is so lightly and brightly transparent *(yasno)* against the air as it is."

Katya raised her eyes to look upward, and assented, "Yes"; while Arkady thought, "Well, she does not reproach me for *talking finely.*"

"I don't like Heine," said Katya, glancing towards the book which Arkady was holding in his hands, "either when he laughs or when he weeps; I like him when he's thoughtful and melancholy."

"And I like him when he laughs," remarked Arkady.

"That's the relics left in you of your old satirical tendencies." "(Relics!" thought Arkady—"if Bazarov had heard that?") "Wait a little; we shall transform you."

"Who will transform me? You?"

"Who?—my sister; Porfiry Platonovitch, whom you've given up quarrelling with; auntie, whom you escorted to church the day before yesterday."

"Well, I couldn't refuse! And as for Anna Sergyevna, she agreed with Yevgeny in a great many things, you remember?"

"My sister was under his influence then, just as you were."

"As I was? Do you discover, may I ask, that I've shaken off his influence now?"

Katya did not speak.

"I know," pursued Arkady, "you never liked him."

"I can have no opinion about him."

"Do you know, Katerina Sergyevna, every time I hear that answer I disbelieve it. . . . There is no man that every one of us could not have an opinion about! That's simply a way of getting out of it."

"Well, I'll say, then, I don't. . . . It's not exactly that I don't like him, but I feel that he's of a different order from me, and I am different from him . . . and you too are different from him."

"How's that?"

"How can I tell you. . . . He's a wild animal, and you and I are tame."

"Am I tame too?"

Katya nodded.

Arkady scratched his ear. "Let me tell you, Katerina Sergyevna, do you know, that's really an insult?"

"Why, would you like to be a wild——

"Not wild, but strong, full of force."

"It's no good wishing for that. . . . Your friend, you see, doesn't wish for it, but he has it."

"Hm! So you imagine he had a great influence on Anna Sergyevna?"

"Yes. But no one can keep the upper hand of her for long," added Katya in a low voice.

"Why do you think that?"

"She's very proud. . . . I didn't mean that . . . she values her independence a great deal."

"Who doesn't value it?" asked Arkady, and the thought flashed through his mind, "What good is it?" "What good is it?" it occurred to Katya to wonder too. When young people are often together on friendly terms, they are constantly stumbling on the same ideas.

Arkady smiled, and, coming slightly closer to Katya, he said in a whisper, "Confess that you are a little afraid of her."

"Of whom?"

"Her," repeated Arkady significantly.

"And how about you?" Katya asked in her turn.

"I am too, observe I said, I am *too.*"

Katya threatened him with her finger. "I wonder at that," she began; "my sister has never felt so friendly to you as just now; much more so than when you first came."

"Really!"

"Why, haven't you noticed it? Aren't you glad of it?"

Arkady grew thoughtful.

"How have I succeeded in gaining Anna Sergyevna's good opinion? Wasn't it because I brought her your mother's letters?"

"Both that and other causes, which I shan't tell you."

"Why?"

"I shan't say."

"Oh! I know; you're very obstinate."

"Yes, I am."

"And observant."

Katya gave Arkady a sidelong look. "Perhaps so; does that irritate you? What are you thinking of?"

"I am wondering how you have come to be as observant as in fact you are. You are so shy so reserved; you keep every one at a distance."

"I have lived a great deal alone; that drives one to reflection. But do I really keep every one at a distance?"

Arkady flung a grateful glance at Katya.

"That's all very well," he pursued; "but people in your position—I mean in your circumstances—don't often have that faculty; it is hard for them, as it is for sovereigns, to get at the truth."

"But, you see, I am not rich."

Arkady was taken aback, and did not at once understand Katya. "Why, of course, the property's all her sister's!" struck him suddenly; the thought was not unpleasing to him. "How nicely you said that!" he commented.

"What?"

"You said it nicely, simply, without being ashamed or making a boast of it. By the way, I imagine there must always be something special, a kind of pride of a sort in the feeling of any man, who knows and says he is poor."

"I have never experienced anything of that sort, thanks to my sister. I only referred to my position just now because it happened to come up."

"Well; but you must own you have a share of that pride I spoke of just now."

"For instance?"

"For instance, you—forgive the question—you wouldn't marry a rich man, I fancy, would you?"

"If I loved him very much. . . . No, I think even then I wouldn't marry him."

"There! you see!" cried Arkady, and after a short pause he added, "And why wouldn't you marry him?"

"Because even in the ballads unequal matches are always unlucky."

"You want to rule, perhaps, or . . ."

"Oh, no! why should I? On the contrary, I am ready to obey; only inequality is intolerable. To respect one's self and obey, that I can understand, that's happiness; but a subordinate existence . . . No, I've had enough of that as it is."

"Enough of that as it is," Arkady repeated after Katya. "Yes,

yes," he went on, "you're not Anna Sergyevna's sister for nothing; you're just as independent as she is; but you're more reserved. I'm certain you wouldn't be the first to give expression
to your feeling, however strong and holy it might be . . ."

"Well, what would you expect?" asked Katya.

"You're equally clever; and you've as much, if not more,
character than she."

"Don't compare me with my sister, please," interposed
Katya hurriedly; "that's too much to my disadvantage. You seem
to forget my sister's beautiful and clever, and . . . you in particular,
Arkady Nikolaevitch, ought not to say such things, and with such
a serious face too."

"What do you mean by "you in particular"—and what makes
you suppose I am joking?"

"Of course, you are joking."

"You think so? But what if I'm persuaded of what I say? if
I believe I have not put it strongly enough even?"

"I don't understand you."

"Really? Well, now I see; I certainly took you to be more
observant than you are."

"How?"

Arkady made no answer, and turned away, while Katya
looked for a few more crumbs in the basket, and began throwing
them to the sparrows; but she moved her arm too vigorously, and
they flew away, without stopping to pick them up.

"Katerina Sergyevna!" began Arkady suddenly; "it's of no
consequence to you, probably; but, let me tell you, I put you not
only above your sister, but above every one in the world."

He got up and went quickly away, as though he were frightened at the words that had fallen from his lips.

Katya let her two hands drop together with the basket on to
her lap, and with bent head she stared a long while after Arkady.
Gradually a crimson flush came faintly out upon her cheeks; but
her lips did not smile, and her dark eyes had a look of perplexity
and some other, as yet undefined, feeling.

"Are you alone?" she heard the voice of Anna Sergyevna
near her; "I thought you came into the garden with Arkady."

Katya slowly raised her eyes to her sister (elegantly, even elaborately dressed, she was standing in the path and tickling Fifi's ears with the tip of her open parasol), and slowly replied. "Yes, I'm alone."

"So I see," she answered with a smile; "I suppose he has gone to his room."

"Yes."

"Have you been reading together?"

"Yes."

Anna Sergyevna took Katya by the chin and lifted her face up.

"You have not been quarrelling, I hope?"

"No," said Katya, and she quietly removed her sister's hand.

"How solemnly you answer! I expected to find him here, and meant to suggest his coming on a walk with me. That's what he is always asking for. They have sent you some shoes from the town; go and try them on; I noticed only yesterday your old ones are quite shabby. You never think enough about it, and you have such charming little feet! Your hands are nice too . . . though they're large; so you must make the most of your little feet. But you're not vain."

Anna Sergyevna went farther along the path with a light rustle of her beautiful gown; Katya got up from the grass, and, taking Heine with her, went away too—but not to try on her shoes.

"Charming little feet!" she thought, as she slowly and lightly mounted the stone steps of the terrace, which were burning with the heat of the sun; "charming little feet you call them. . . . Well, he shall be at them."

But all at once a feeling of shame came upon her, and she ran swiftly upstairs.

Arkady had gone along the corridor to his room; a steward had overtaken him, and announced that Mr. Bazarov was in his room.

"Yevgeny!" murmured Arkady, almost with dismay; "has he been here long?"

"Mr. Bazarov arrived this minute, sir, and gave orders not

to announce him to Anna Sergyevna, but to show him straight up to you."

"Can any misfortune have happened at home?" thought Arkady, and running hurriedly up the stairs, he at once opened the door. The sight of Bazarov at once reassured him, though a more experienced eye might very probably have discerned signs of inward agitation in the sunken, though still energetic face of the unexpected visitor. With a dusty cloak over his shoulders, with a cap on his head, he was sitting at the window; he did not even get up when Arkady flung himself with noisy exclamations on his neck.

"This is unexpected! What good luck brought you?" he kept repeating, bustling about the room like one who both imagines himself and wishes to show himself delighted. "I suppose everything's all right at home; every one's well, eh?"

"Everything's all right, but not every one's well," said Bazarov. "Don't be a chatterbox, but send for some kvass for me, sit down, and listen while I tell you all about it in a few, but, I hope, pretty vigorous sentences."

Arkady was quiet while Bazarov described his duel with Pavel Petrovitch. Arkady was very much surprised, and even grieved, but he did not think it necessary to show this; he only asked whether his uncle's wound was really not serious; and on receiving the reply that it was most interesting, but not from a medical point of view, he gave a forced smile, but at heart he felt both wounded and as it were ashamed. Bazarov seemed to understand him.

"Yes, my dear fellow," he commented, "you see what comes of living with feudal personages. You turn a feudal personage yourself, and find yourself taking part in knightly tournaments. Well, so I set off for my father's," Bazarov wound up, "and I've turned in here on the way . . . to tell you all this, I should say, if I didn't think a useless lie a piece of foolery. No, I turned in here—the devil only knows why. You see, it's sometimes a good thing for a man to take himself by the scruff of the neck and pull himself up, like a radish out of its bed; that's what I've been doing of late. . . . But I wanted to have one more look at what I'm giving up, at the bed where I've been planted."

"I hope those words don't refer to me," responded Arkady with some emotion; "I hope you don't think of giving me up?"

Bazarov turned an intent, almost piercing look upon him.

"Would that be such a grief to you? It strikes me *you* have given me up already, you look so fresh and smart. . . . Your affair with Anna Sergyevna must be getting on successfully."

"What do you mean by my affair with Anna Sergyevna?"

"Why, didn't you come here from the town on her account, chicken? By the way, how are those Sunday schools getting on? Do you mean to tell me you're not in love with her? Or have you already reached the stage of discretion?"

"Yevgeny, you know I have always been open with you; I can assure you, I will swear to you, you're making a mistake."

"Hm! That's another story," remarked Bazarov in an undertone. "But you needn't be in a taking, it's a matter of absolute indifference to me. A sentimentalist would say, 'I feel that our paths are beginning to part,' but I will simply say that we're tired of each other."

"Yevgeny . . ."

"My dear soul, there's no great harm in that. One gets tired of much more than that in this life. And now I suppose we'd better say good-bye, hadn't we? Ever since I've been here I've had such a loathsome feeling, just as if I'd been reading Gogol's effusions to the governor of Kalouga's wife. By the way, I didn't tell them to take the horses out."

"Upon my word, this is too much!"

"Why?"

"I'll say nothing of myself; but that would be discourteous to the last degree to Anna Sergyevna, who will certainly wish to see you."

"Oh, you're mistaken there."

"On the contrary, I am certain I'm right," retorted Arkady. "And what are you pretending for? If it comes to that, haven't you come here on her account yourself?"

"That may be so, but you're mistaken any way."

But Arkady was right. Anna Sergyevna desired to see Baza-rov, and sent a summons to him by a steward. Bazarov changed his clothes before going to her; it turned out that he had packed his new suit so as to be able to get it out easily.

Madame Odintsov received him not in the room where he had so unexpectedly declared his love to her, but in the drawing-room. She held her finger tips out to him cordially, but her face betrayed an involuntary sense of tension.

"Anna Sergyevna," Bazarov hastened to say, "before every-thing else I must set your mind at rest. Before you is a poor mortal, who has come to his senses long ago, and hopes other people too have forgotten his follies. I am going away for a long while; and though, as you will allow, I'm by no means a very soft creature, it would be anything but cheerful for me to carry away with me the idea that you remember me with repugnance."

Anna Sergyevna gave a deep sigh like one who has just climbed up a high mountain, and her face was lighted up by a smile. She held out her hand a second time to Bazarov, and responded to his pressure.

"Let bygones be bygones," she said. "I am all the readier to do so because, speaking from my conscience, I was to blame then too for flirting or something. In a word, let us be friends as before. That was a dream, wasn't it? And who remembers dreams?"

"Who remembers them? And besides, love . . . you know, is a purely imaginary feeling."

"Really? I am very glad to hear that."

So Anna Sergyevna spoke, and so spoke Bazarov; they both supposed they were speaking the truth. Was the truth, the whole truth, to be found in their words? They could not themselves have said, and much less could the author. But a conversation followed between them precisely as though they completely believed one another.

Anna Sergyevna asked Bazarov, among other things, what he had been doing at the Kirsanovs'. He was on the point of telling her about his duel with Pavel Petrovitch, but he checked himself with the thought that she might imagine he was trying to make himself interesting, and answered that he had been at work all the time.

"And I," observed Anna Sergyevna, "had a fit of depression at first, goodness knows why; I even made plans for going abroad, fancy! . . . Then it passed off, your friend Arkady Nikolaitch came, and I fell back into my old routine, and took up my real part again."

"What part is that, may I ask?"

"The character of aunt, guardian, mother—call it what you like. By the way, do you know I used not quite to understand your close friendship with Arkady Nikolaitch; I thought him rather insignificant. But now I have come to know him better, and to see that he is clever. . . . And he's young, he's young . . . that's the great thing . . . not like you and me, Yevgeny Vassilyitch."

"Is he still as shy in your company?" queried Bazarov.

"Why, was he?" . . . Anna Sergyevna began, and after a brief pause she went on: "He has grown more confiding now; he talks to me. He used to avoid me before. Though, indeed, I didn't seek his society either. He's more friends with Katya."

Bazarov felt irritated. "A woman can't help humbugging, of course!" he thought. "You say he used to avoid you," he said aloud, with a chilly smile; "but it is probably no secret to you that he was in love with you?"

"What! he too?" fell from Anna Sergyevna's lips.

"He too," repeated Bazarov, with a submissive bow. "Can it be you didn't know it, and I've told you something new?"

Anna Sergyevna dropped her eyes. "You are mistaken, Yevgeny Vassilyitch."

"I don't think so. But perhaps I ought not to have mentioned it." "And don't you try telling me lies again for the future," he added to himself.

"Why not? But I imagine that in this too you are attributing too much importance to a passing impression. I begin to suspect you are inclined to exaggeration."

"We had better not talk about it, Anna Sergyevna."

"Oh, why?" she retorted; but she herself led the conversation into another channel. She was still ill at ease with Bazarov, though she had told him, and assured herself that everything was forgotten. While she was exchanging the simplest sentences with him, even while she was jesting with him, she was conscious of a faint spasm of dread. So people on a steamer at sea talk and laugh carelessly, for all the world as though they were on dry land; but let only the slightest hitch occur, let the least sign be seen of anything out of the common, and at once on every face there comes out an expression of peculiar alarm, betraying the constant consciousness of constant danger.

Anna Sergyevna's conversation with Bazarov did not last long. She began to seem absorbed in thought, answered abstractedly, and suggested at last that they should go into the hall, where they found the princess and Katya. "But where is Arkady Nikolaitch?" inquired the lady of the house; and on hearing that he had not shown himself for more than an hour, she sent for him. He was not very quickly found; he had hidden himself in the very thickest part of the garden, and with his chin propped on his folded hands, he was sitting lost in meditation. They were deep and serious meditations, but not mournful. He knew Anna Sergyevna was sitting alone with Bazarov, and he felt no jealousy, as once he had; on the contrary, his face slowly brightened; he seemed to be at once wondering and rejoicing, and resolving on something.

XXVI

The deceased Odintsov had not liked innovations, but he had tolerated "the fine arts within a certain sphere," and had in consequence put up in his garden, between the hothouse and the lake, an erection after the fashion of a Greek temple, made of Russian brick. Along the dark wall at the back of this temple or gallery were placed six niches for statues, which Odintsov had proceeded to order from abroad. These statues were to represent Solitude, Silence, Meditation, Melancholy, Modesty, and Sensibility. One of them, the goddess of Silence, with her finger on her lip, had been sent and put up; but on the very same day some boys on the farm had broken her nose; and though a plasterer of the neighbourhood undertook to make her a new nose "twice as good as the old one," Odintsov ordered her to be taken away, and she was still to be seen in the corner of the threshing barn, where she had stood many long years, a source of superstitious terror to the peasant women. The front part of the temple had long ago been overgrown with thick bushes; only the pediments of the columns could be seen above the dense green. In the temple itself it was cool even at mid-day. Anna Sergyevna had not liked visiting this place ever since she had seen a snake there; but Katya often came and sat on the wide stone seat under one of the niches. Here, in the midst of the shade and coolness, she used to read and work, or to give herself up to that sensation of perfect peace, known, doubtless, to each of us, the charm of which consists in the half-unconscious, silent listening to the vast current of life that flows for ever both around us and within us.

The day after Bazarov's arrival Katya was sitting on her favourite stone seat, and beside her again was sitting Arkady. He had besought her to come with him to the "temple."

There was about an hour still to lunch-time; the dewy morning had already given place to a sultry day. Arkady's face retained the expression of the preceding day; Katya had a preoccupied look. Her sister had, directly after their morning tea, called her into her room, and after some preliminary caresses, which always scared Katya a little, she had advised her to be more guarded in her behaviour with Arkady, and especially to avoid solitary talks with him, as likely to attract the notice of her aunt and all the household. Besides this, even the previous evening Anna Sergyevna had not been herself; and Katya herself had felt ill at ease, as though she were conscious of some fault in herself. As she yielded to Arkady's entreaties, she said to herself that it was for the last time.

"Katerina Sergyevna," he began with a sort of bashful easiness, "since I've had the happiness of living in the same house with you, I have discussed a great many things with you; but meanwhile there is one, very important . . . for me . . . one question, which I have not touched upon up till now. You remarked yesterday that I have been changed here," he went on, at once catching and avoiding the questioning glance Katya was turning upon him. "I have changed certainly a great deal, and you know that better than any one else—you to whom I really owe this change."

"I? . . . Me? . . ." said Katya.

"I am not now the conceited boy I was when I came here," Arkady went on. "I've not reached twenty-three for nothing; as before, I want to be useful, I want to devote all my powers to the truth; but I no longer look for my ideals where I did; they present themselves to me . . much closer to hand. Up till now I did not understand myself; I set myself tasks which were beyond my powers. . . . My eyes have been opened lately, thanks to one feeling. . . . I'm not expressing myself quite clearly, but I hope you understand me."

Katya made no reply, but she ceased looking at Arkady.

"I suppose," he began again, this time in a more agitated voice, while above his head a chaffinch sang its song unheeding among the leaves of the birch—"I suppose it's the duty of every one to be open with those . . . with those people who . . . in fact, with those who are near to him, and so I . . . I resolved . . ."

But here Arkady's eloquence deserted him; he lost the thread, stammered, and was forced to be silent for a moment. Katya still did not raise her eyes. She seemed not to understand what he was leading up to in all this, and to be waiting for something.

"I foresee I shall surprise you," began Arkady, pulling himself together again with an effort, "especially since this feeling relates in a way . . . in a way, notice . . . to you. You reproached me, if you remember, yesterday with a want of seriousness," Arkady went on, with the air of a man who has got into a bog, feels that he is sinking further and further in at every step, and yet hurries onwards in the hope of crossing it as soon as possible; "that reproach is often aimed . . . often falls . . . on young men even when they cease to deserve it; and if I had more self-confidence . . ." ("Come, help me, do help me!" Arkady was thinking, in desperation; but, as before, Katya did not turn her head.) "If I could hope . . ."

"If I could feel sure of what you say," was heard at that instant the clear voice of Anna Sergyevna.

Arkady was still at once, while Katya turned pale. Close by the bushes that screened the temple ran a little path. Anna Sergyevna was walking along it escorted by Bazarov. Katya and Arkady could not see them, but they heard every word, the rustle of their clothes, their very breathing. They walked on a few steps, and, as though on purpose, stood still just opposite the temple.

"You see," pursued Anna Sergyevna, "you and I made a mistake; we are both past our first youth, I especially so; we have seen life, we are tired; we are both—why affect not to know it?—clever; at first we interested each other, curiosity was aroused . . . and then . . ."

"And then I grew stale," put in Bazarov.

"You know that was not the cause of our misunderstanding. But, however, it was to be, we had no need of one another, that's the chief point; there was too much . . . what shall I say? . . . that was alike in us. We did not realise it all at once. Now, Arkady . . ."

"Do you need him?" queried Bazarov.

"Hush, Yevgeny Vassilyitch. You tell me he is not indifferent to me, and it always seemed to me he liked me. I know that I might well be his aunt, but I don't wish to conceal from you that I have come to think more often of him. In such youthful, fresh feeling there is a special charm . . ."

"The word *fascination* is most usual in such cases," Bazarov interrupted; the effervescence of his spleen could be heard in his choked though steady voice. "Arkady was mysterious over something with me yesterday, and didn't talk either of you or of your sister. . . . That's a serious symptom."

"He is just like a brother with Katya," commented Anna Sergyevna, "and I like that in him, though, perhaps, I ought not to have allowed such intimacy between them."

"That idea is prompted by . . . your feelings as a sister?" Bazarov brought out, drawling.

"Of course . . . but why are we standing still? Let us go on. What a strange talk we are having, aren't we? I could never have believed I should talk to you like this. You know, I am afraid of you . . . and at the same time I trust you, because in reality you are so good."

"In the first place, I am not in the least good; and in the second place, I have lost all significance for you, and you tell me I am good. . . . It's like laying a wreath of flowers on the head of a corpse."

"Yevgeny Vassilyitch, we are not responsible . . ." Anna Sergyevna began; but a gust of wind blew across, set the leaves rustling, and carried away her words. "Of course, you are free . . ." Bazarov declared after a brief pause. Nothing more could be distinguished; the steps retreated . . . everything was still.

Arkady turned to Katya. She was sitting in the same position, but her head was bent still lower. "Katerina Sergyevna," he said with a shaking voice, and clasping his hands tightly together, "I love you for ever and irrevocably, and I love no one but you. I wanted to tell you this, to find out your opinion of me, and to ask for your hand, since I am not rich, and I feel ready for any sacrifice. . . . You don't answer me? You don't believe me? Do you think I speak lightly? But remember these last days! Surely for a long time past you must have known that everything—understand me—everything else has vanished long ago and left no trace? Look at me, say one word to me . . . I love . . . I love you . . . believe me!"

Katya glanced at Arkady with a bright and serious look, and after long hesitation, with the faintest smile, she said, "Yes."

Arkady leapt up from the stone seat. "Yes! You said Yes, Katerina Sergyevna! What does that word mean? Only that I do love you, that you believe me . . . or . . . or . . . I daren't go on . . ."

"Yes," repeated Katya, and this time he understood her. He snatched her large beautiful hands, and, breathless with rapture, pressed them to his heart. He could scarcely stand on his feet, and could only repeat, "Katya, Katya . . ." while she began weeping in a guileless way, smiling gently at her own tears. No one who has not seen those tears in the eyes of the beloved, knows yet to what a point, faint with shame and gratitude, a man may be happy on earth.

The next day, early in the morning, Anna Sergyevna sent to summon Bazarov to her boudoir, and with a forced laugh handed him a folded sheet of notepaper. It was a letter from Arkady; in it he asked for her sister's hand.

Bazarov quickly scanned the letter, and made an effort to control himself, that he might not show the malignant feeling which was instantaneously aflame in his breast.

"So that's how it is," he commented; "and you, I fancy, only yesterday imagined he loved Katerina Sergyevna as a brother. What are you intending to do now?"

"What do you advise me?" asked Anna Sergyevna, still laughing.

"Well, I suppose," answered Bazarov, also with a laugh, though he felt anything but cheerful, and had no more inclination to laugh than she had; "I suppose you ought to give the young people your blessing. It's a good match in every respect; Kirsanov's position is passable, he's the only son, and his father's a good-natured fellow, he won't try to thwart him."

Madame Odintsov walked up and down the room. By turns her face flushed and grew pale. "You think so," she said. "Well, I see no obstacles . . . I am glad for Katya. . . . and for Arkady Nikolaevitch too. Of course, I will wait for his father's answer. I will send him in person to him. But it turns out, you see, that I was right yesterday when I told you we were both old people. . . . How was it I saw nothing? That's what amazes me!" Anna Sergyevna laughed again, and quickly turned her head away.

"The younger generation have grown awfully sly," remarked Bazarov, and he too laughed. "Good-bye," he began again after a short silence. "I hope you will bring the matter to the most satisfactory conclusion; and I will rejoice from a distance."

Madame Odintsov turned quickly to him. "You are not going away? Why should you not stay *now?* Stay . . . it's exciting talking to you . . . one seems walking on the edge of a precipice.

At first one feels timid, but one gains courage as one goes on. Do stay."

"Thanks for the suggestion, Anna Sergyevna, and for your flattering opinion of my conversational talents. But I think I have already been moving too long in a sphere which is not my own. Flying fishes can hold out for a time in the air, but soon they must splash back into the water; allow me, too, to paddle in my own element."

Madame Odintsov looked at Bazarov. His pale face was twitching with a bitter smile. "This man did love me!" she thought, and she felt pity for him, and held out her hand to him with sympathy.

But he too understood her. "No!" he said, stepping back a pace. "I'm a poor man, but I've never taken charity so far. Goodbye, and good luck to you."

"I am certain we are not seeing each other for the last time," Anna Sergyevna declared with an unconscious gesture.

"Anything may happen!" answered Bazarov, and he bowed and went away.

"So you are thinking of making yourself a nest?" he said the same day to Arkady, as he packed his box, crouching on the floor. "Well, it's a capital thing. But you needn't have been such a humbug. I expected something from you in quite another quarter. Perhaps, though, it took you by surprise yourself?"

"I certainly didn't expect this when I parted from you," answered Arkady; "but why are you a humbug yourself, calling it 'a capital thing,' as though I didn't know your opinion of marriage."

"Ah, my dear fellow," said Bazarov, "how you talk! You see what I'm doing; there seems to be an empty space in the box, and I am putting hay in; that's how it is in the box of our life; we would stuff it up with anything rather than have a void. Don't be offended, please; you remember, no doubt, the opinion I have always had of Katerina Sergyevna. Many a young lady's called clever simply because she can sigh cleverly; but yours can hold her own, and, indeed, she'll hold it so well that she'll have you under her thumb—to be sure, though, that's quite as it ought to be." He slammed the lid to, and got up from the floor. "And now, I say again, good-bye, for it's useless to deceive ourselves—we are parting for good, and you know that yourself . . . you have acted sensibly; you're not made for our bitter, rough, lonely existence. There's no dash, no hate in you, but you've the daring of youth and the fire of youth. Your sort, you gentry, can never get beyond refined submission or refined indignation, and that's no good. You won't fight—and yet you fancy yourselves gallant chaps—but we mean to fight. Oh well! Our dust would get into your eyes, our mud would bespatter you, but yet you're not up to our level, you're admiring yourselves unconsciously, you like to abuse yourselves; but we're sick of that—we want something else! we want to smash other people! You're a capital fellow; but you're a sugary, liberal snob for all that—*ay volla-too,* as my parent is fond of saying."

"You are parting from me for ever, Yevgeny," responded Arkady mournfully; "and have you nothing else to say to me?"

Bazarov scratched the back of his head. "Yes, Arkady, yes, I have other things to say to you, but I'm not going to say them, because that's sentimentalism—that means, mawkishness. And you get married as soon as you can; and build your nest, and get children to your heart's content. They'll have the wit to be born in a better time than you and me. Aha! I see the horses are ready. Time's up! I've said good-bye to every one. . . . What now? embracing, eh?"

Arkady flung himself on the neck of his former leader and friend, and the tears fairly gushed from his eyes.

"That's what comes of being young!" Bazarov commented calmly. "But I rest my hopes on Katerina Sergyevna. You'll see how quickly she'll console you! Good-bye, brother!" he said to Arkady when he had got into the light cart, and, pointing to a pair of jackdaws sitting side by side on the stable roof, he added, "That's for you! follow that example."

"What does that mean?" asked Arkady.

"What? Are you so weak in natural history, or have you forgotten that the jackdaw is a most respectable family bird? An example to you! . . . Good-bye!"

The cart creaked and rolled away.

Bazarov had spoken truly. In talking that evening with Katya, Arkady completely forgot about his former teacher. He already began to follow her lead, and Katya was conscious of this, and not surprised at it. He was to set off the next day for Maryino, to see Nikolai Petrovitch. Anna Sergyevna was not disposed to put any constraint on the young people, and only on account of the proprieties did not leave them by themselves for too long together. She magnanimously kept the princess out of their way; the latter had been reduced to a state of tearful frenzy by the news of the proposed marriage. At first Anna Sergyevna was afraid the sight of their happiness might prove rather trying to herself, but it turned out quite the other way; this sight not only did not distress her, it interested her, it even softened her at last. Anna Sergyevna felt both glad and sorry at this. "It is clear that Bazarov was right," she thought; "it has been curiosity, nothing but curiosity, and love of ease, and egoism . . ."

"Children," she said aloud, "what do you say, is love a purely imaginary feeling?"

But neither Katya nor Arkady even understood her. They were shy with her; the fragment of conversation they had involuntarily overheard haunted their minds. But Anna Sergyevna soon set their minds at rest; and it was not difficult for her—she had set her own mind at rest.

XXVII

Bazarov's old parents were all the more overjoyed by their son's arrival, as it was quite unexpected. Arina Vlasyevna was greatly excited, and kept running backwards and forwards in the house, so that Vassily Ivanovitch compared her to a "hen partridge"; the short tail of her abbreviated jacket did, in fact, give her something of a birdlike appearance. He himself merely growled and gnawed the amber mouthpiece of his pipe, or, clutching his neck with his fingers, turned his head round, as though he were trying whether it were properly screwed on, then all at once he opened his wide mouth and went off into a perfectly noiseless chuckle.

"I've come to you for six whole weeks, governor," Bazárov said to him. "I want to work, so please don't hinder me now."

"You shall forget my face completely, if you call that hindering you!" answered Vassily Ivanovitch.

He kept his promise. After installing his son as before in his study, he almost hid himself away from him, and he kept his wife from all superfluous demonstrations of tenderness. "On Enyusha's first visit, my dear soul," he said to her, "we bothered him a little; we must be wiser this time." Arina Vlasyevna agreed with her husband, but that was small compensation since she saw her son only at meals, and was now absolutely afraid to address him. "Enyushenka," she would say sometimes—and before he had time to look round, she was nervously fingering the tassels of her reticule and faltering, "Never mind, never mind, I only——" and afterwards she would go to Vassily Ivanovitch and, her cheek in her hand, would consult him: "If you could only find out, darling, which Enyusha would like for dinner to-day—cabbage-broth or beetroot-soup?"—"But why didn't you ask him yourself?"— "Oh, he will get sick of me!" Bazárov, however, soon ceased to shut himself up; the fever of work fell away, and was replaced by dreary boredom or vague restlessness. A strange weariness began to show itself in all his movements; even his walk, firm, bold and strenuous, was changed. He gave up walking in solitude, and began to seek society; he drank tea in the drawing-room, strolled about the kitchen-garden with Vassily Ivanovitch, and smoked with him in silence; once even asked after Father Alexey. Vassily Ivanovitch at first rejoiced at this change, but his joy was not long-lived. "Enyusha's breaking my heart," he complained in secret to his wife: "it's not that he's discontented or angry—that would be nothing; he's sad, he's sorrowful—that's what's so terrible. He's always silent. If he'd only abuse us; he's growing thin, he's lost his colour."—"Mercy on us, mercy on us!" whispered the old woman; "I would put an amulet on his neck, but, of course, he won't allow it." Vassily Ivanovitch several times at-

tempted in the most circumspect manner to question Bazarov
about his work, about his health, and about Arkady. . . . But
Bazarov's replies were reluctant and casual; and, once noticing
that his father was trying gradually to lead up to something in
conversation, he said to him in a tone of vexation: "Why do you
always seem to be walking round me on tiptoe? That way's worse
than the old one."—"There, there, I meant nothing!" poor Vassily Ivanovitch answered hurriedly. So his diplomatic hints remained fruitless. He hoped to awaken his son's sympathy one day
by beginning, *à propos* of the approaching emancipation of the
peasantry, to talk about progress; but the latter responded indifferently: "Yesterday I was walking under the fence, and I heard
the peasant boys here, instead of some old ballad, bawling a street
song. That's what progress is."

Sometimes Bazarov went into the village, and in his usual
bantering tone entered into conversation with some peasant:
"Come," he would say to him, "expound your views on life to
me, brother; you see, they say all the strength and future of Russia
lies in your hands, a new epoch in history will be started by
you—you give us our real language and our laws."

The peasant either made no reply, or articulated a few words
of this sort, "Well, we'll try . . . because, you see, to be sure.
. . ."

"You explain to me what your *mir* is," Bazarov interrupted;
"and is it the same *mir* that is said to rest on three fishes?"

"That, little father, is the earth that rests on three fishes," the
peasant would declare soothingly, in a kind of patriarchal, simple-
hearted sing-song; "and over against ours, that's to say, the *mir,*
we know there's the master's will; wherefore you are our fathers.
And the stricter the master's rule, the better for the peasant."

After listening to such a reply one day, Bazarov shrugged his
shoulders contemptuously and turned away, while the peasant
sauntered slowly homewards.

"What was he talking about?" inquired another peasant of
middle age and surly aspect, who at a distance from the door of
his hut had been following his conversation with Bazarov.—"Arrears? eh?"

"Arrears, no indeed, mate!" answered the first peasant, and now there was no trace of patriarchal singsong in his voice; on the contrary, there was a certain scornful gruffness to be heard in it: "Oh, he clacked away about something or other; wanted to stretch his tongue a bit. Of course, he's a gentleman; what does he understand?"

"What should he understand!" answered the other peasant, and jerking back their caps and pushing down their belts, they proceeded to deliberate upon their work and their wants. Alas! Bazarov, shrugging his shoulders contemptuously, Bazarov, who knew how to talk to peasants (as he had boasted in his dispute with Pavel Petrovitch), did not in his self-confidence even suspect that in their eyes he was all the while something of the nature of a buffooning clown.

He found employment for himself at last, however. One day Vassily Ivanovitch bound up a peasant's wounded leg before him, but the old man's hands trembled, and he could not manage the bandages; his son helped him, and from time to time began to take a share in his practice, though at the same time he was constantly sneering both at the remedies he himself advised and at his father, who hastened to make use of them. But Bazarov's jeers did not in the least perturb Vassily Ivanovitch; they were positively a comfort to him. Holding his greasy dressing-gown across his stomach with two fingers, and smoking his pipe, he used to listen with enjoyment to Bazarov; and the more malicious his sallies, the more good-humouredly did his delighted father chuckle, showing every one of his black teeth. He used even to repeat these sometimes flat or pointless retorts, and would, for instance, for several days constantly without rhyme or reason, reiterate, "Not a matter of the first importance!" simply because his son, on hearing he was going to matins, had made use of that expression. "Thank God! he has got over his melancholy!" he whispered to his wife; "how he gave it to me to-day, it was splendid!" Moreover, the idea of having such an assistant excited him to ecstasy, filled him with pride. "Yes, yes," he would say to some peasant woman in a man's cloak, and a cap shaped like a horn, as he handed her a bottle of Goulard's extract or a box of white ointment, "you ought to be thanking God, my good woman, every minute that my son is staying with me; you will be treated now by the most scientific, most modern method. Do you know what that means? The Emperor of the French, Napoleon, even, has no better doctor." And the peasant woman, who had come to complain that she felt so sort of queer all over (the exact meaning of these words she was not able, however, herself to explain), merely bowed low and rummaged in her bosom, where four eggs lay tied up in the corner of a towel.

Bazarov once even pulled out a tooth for a passing pedlar of cloth; and though this tooth was an average specimen, Vassily Ivanovitch preserved it as a curiosity, and incessantly repeated, as he showed it to Father Alexey, "Just look, what a fang! The force Yevgeny has! The pedlar seemed to leap into the air. If it had been an oak, he'd have rooted it up!"

"Most promising!" Father Alexey would comment at last, not knowing what answer to make, and how to get rid of the ecstatic old man.

One day a peasant from a neighbouring village brought his brother to Vassily Ivanovitch, ill with typhus. The unhappy man, lying flat on a truss of straw, was dying; his body was covered with dark patches, he had long ago lost consciousness. Vassily Ivanovitch expressed his regret that no one had taken steps to procure medical aid sooner, and declared there was no hope. And, in fact, the peasant did not get his brother home again; he died in the cart.

Three days later Bazarov came into his father's room and asked him if he had any caustic.

"Yes; what do you want it for?"

"I must have some . . . to burn a cut."

"For whom?"

"For myself."

"What, yourself? Why is that? What sort of a cut? Where is it?"

"Look here, on my finger. I went to-day to the village, you know, where they brought that peasant with typhus fever. They were just going to open the body for some reason or other, and I've had no practice of that sort for a long while."

"Well?"

"Well, so I asked the district doctor about it; and so I dissected it."

Vassily Ivanovitch all at once turned quite white, and, without uttering a word, rushed to his study, from which he returned at once with a bit of caustic in his hand. Bazarov was about to take it and go away.

"For mercy's sake," said Vassily Ivanovitch, "let me do it myself."

Bazarov smiled. "What a devoted practitioner!"

"Don't laugh, please. Show me your finger. The cut is not a large one. Do I hurt?"

"Press harder; don't be afraid."

Vassily Ivanovitch stopped. "What do you think, Yevgeny; wouldn't it be better to burn it with hot iron?"

"That ought to have been done sooner; the caustic even is useless, really, now. If I've taken the infection, it's too late now."

"How . . . too late . . ." Vassily Ivanovitch could scarcely articulate the words.

"I should think so! It's more than four hours ago."

Vassily Ivanovitch burnt the cut a little more. "But had the district doctor no caustic?"

"No."

"How was that, good Heavens? A doctor not have such an indispensable thing as that!"

"You should have seen his lancets," observed Bazarov as he walked away.

Up till late that evening, and all the following day, Vassily Ivanovitch kept catching at every possible excuse to go into his son's room; and though far from referring to the cut—he even tried to talk about the most irrelevant subjects—he looked so persistently into his face, and watched him in such trepidation, that Bazarov lost patience and threatened to go away. Vassily Ivanovitch gave him a promise not to bother him, the more readily as Arina Vlasyevna, from whom, of course, he kept it all secret, was beginning to worry him as to why he did not sleep, and what had come over him. For two whole days he held himself

in, though he did not at all like the look of his son, whom he kept
watching stealthily, . . . but on the third day, at dinner, he could
bear it no longer. Bazarov sat with downcast looks, and had not
touched a single dish.

"Why don't you eat, Yevgeny?" he inquired, putting on an
expression of the most perfect carelessness. "The food, I think,
is very nicely cooked."

"I don't want anything, so I don't eat."

"Have you no appetite? And your head?" he added timidly;
"does it ache?"

"Yes. Of course, it aches."

Arina Vlasyevna sat up and was all alert.

"Don't be angry, please, Yevgeny," continued Vassily
Ivanovitch; "won't you let me feel your pulse?"

Bazarov got up. "I can tell you without feeling my pulse; I'm
feverish."

"Has there been any shivering?"

"Yes, there has been shivering too. I'll go and lie down, and
you can send me some lime-flower tea. I must have caught cold."

"To be sure, I heard you coughing last night," observed
Arina Vlasyevna.

"I've caught cold," repeated Bazarov, and he went away.

Arina Vlasyevna busied herself about the preparation of the
decoction of lime-flowers, while Vassily Ivanovitch went into the
next room and clutched at his hair in silent desperation.

Bazarov did not get up again that day, and passed the whole
night in heavy, half-unconscious torpor. At one o'clock in the
morning, opening his eyes with an effort, he saw by the light of
a lamp his father's pale face bending over him, and told him to
go away. The old man begged his pardon, but he quickly came
back on tiptoe, and half-hidden by the cupboard door, he gazed
persistently at his son. Arina Vlasyevna did not go to bed either,
and leaving the study door just open a very little, she kept coming
up to it to listen "how Enyusha was breathing," and to look at
Vassily Ivanovitch. She could see nothing but his motionless bent
back, but even that afforded her some faint consolation. In the
morning Bazarov tried to get up; he was seized with giddiness,

his nose began to bleed; he lay down again. Vassily Ivanovitch waited on him in silence. Arina Vlasyevna went in to him and asked him how he was feeling. He answered, "Better," and turned to the wall. Vassily Ivanovitch gesticulated at his wife with both hands; she bit her lips so as not to cry, and went away. The whole house seemed suddenly darkened; every one looked gloomy; there was a strange hush; a shrill cock was carried away from the yard to the village, unable to comprehend why he should be treated so. Bazarov still lay, turned to the wall. Vassily Ivanovitch tried to address him with various questions, but they fatigued Bazarov, and the old man sank into his arm-chair, motionless, only cracking his finger-joints now and then. He went for a few minutes into the garden, stood there like a statue, as though overwhelmed with unutterable bewilderment (the expression of amazement never left his face all through), and went back again to his son, trying to avoid his wife's questions. She caught him by the arm at last, and passionately, almost menacingly, said, "What is wrong with him?" Then he came to himself, and forced himself to smile at her in reply; but to his own horror, instead of a smile, he found himself taken somehow by a fit of laughter. He had sent at daybreak for a doctor. He thought it necessary to inform his son of this, for fear he should be angry. Bazarov suddenly turned over on the sofa, bent a fixed dull look on his father, and asked for drink.

Vassily Ivanovitch gave him some water, and as he did so felt his forehead. It seemed on fire.

"Governor," began Bazarov, in a slow, drowsy voice; "I'm in a bad way; I've got the infection, and in a few days you'll have to bury me."

Vassily Ivanovitch staggered back, as though some one had aimed a blow at his legs.

"Yevgeny!" he faltered; "what do you mean! . . . God have mercy on you! You've caught cold!"

"Hush!" Bazarov interposed deliberately. "A doctor can't be allowed to talk like that. There's every symptom of infection; you know yourself."

"Where are the symptoms . . . of infection Yevgeny? . . . Good Heavens!"

"What's this?" said Bazarov, and, pulling up his shirt-sleeve, he showed his father the ominous red patches coming out on his arm.

Vassily Ivanovitch was shaking and chill with terror.

"Supposing," he said at last, "even supposing . . . if even there's something like . . . infection . . ."

"Pyaemia," put in his son.

"Well, well . . . something of the epidemic . . ."

"Pyaemia," Bazarov repeated sharply and distinctly; "have you forgotten your text-books?"

"Well, well—as you like. . . . Anyway, we will cure you!"

"Come, that's humbug. But that's not the point. I didn't expect to die so soon; it's a most unpleasant incident, to tell the truth. You and mother ought to make the most of your strong religious belief; now's the time to put it to the test." He drank off a little water. "I want to ask you about one thing . . . while my head is still under my control. To-morrow or next day my brain, you know, will send in its resignation. I'm not quite certain even now whether I'm expressing myself clearly. While I've been lying here, I've kept fancying red dogs were running round me, while you were making them point at me, as if I were a woodcock. Just as if I were drunk. Do you understand me all right?"

"I assure you, Yevgeny, you are talking perfectly correctly."

"All the better. You told me you'd sent for the doctor. You did that to comfort yourself . . . comfort me too; send a messenger . . ."

"To Arkady Nikolaitch?" put in the old man.

"Who's Arkady Nikolaitch?" said Bazarov, as though in doubt. . . . "Oh, yes! that chicken! No, let him alone; he's turned jackdaw now. Don't be surprised; that's not delirium yet. You send a messenger to Madame Odintsov, Anna Sergyevna; she's a lady with an estate. . . . Do you know?" (Vassily Ivanovitch nodded.) "Yevgeny Bazarov, say, sends his greetings, and sends word he is dying. Will you do that?"

"Yes, I will do it. . . . But is it a possible thing for you to die,

Yevgeny? . . . Think only! Where would divine justice be after that?"

"I know nothing about that; only you send the messenger."

"I'll send this minute, and I'll write a letter myself."

"No, why? Say I sent greetings; nothing more is necessary. And now I'll go back to my dogs. Strange! I want to fix my thoughts on death, and nothing comes of it. I see a kind of blur . . . and nothing more."

He turned painfully back to the wall again; while Vassily Ivanovitch went out of the study, and struggling as far as his wife's bedroom, simply dropped down on to his knees before the holy pictures.

"Pray, Arina, pray for us!" he moaned; "our son is dying."

The doctor, the same district doctor who had had no caustic, arrived, and after looking at the patient, advised them to persevere with a cooling treatment, and at that point said a few words of the chance of recovery.

"Have you ever chanced to see people in my state *not* set off for Elysium?" asked Bazarov, and suddenly snatching the leg of a heavy table that stood near his sofa, he swung it round, and pushed it away. "There's strength, there's strength," he murmured; "everything's here still, and I must die! . . . An old man at least has time to be weaned from life, but I . . . Well, go and try to disprove death. Death will disprove you, and that's all! Who's crying there?" he added, after a short pause.—"Mother? Poor thing! Whom will she feed now with her exquisite beetroot-soup? You, Vassily Ivanovitch, whimpering too, I do believe! Why, if Christianity's no help to you, be a philosopher, a Stoic, or what not! Why, didn't you boast you were a philosopher?"

"Me a philosopher!" wailed Vassily Ivanovitch, while the tears fairly streamed down his cheeks.

Bazarov got worse every hour; the progress of the disease was rapid, as is usually the way in cases of surgical poisoning. He still had not lost consciousness, and understood what was said to him; he was still struggling. "I don't want to lose my wits," he muttered, clenching his fists; "what rot it all is!" And at once he would say, "Come, take ten from eight, what remains?" Vassily

Ivanovitch wandered about like one possessed, proposed first one remedy, then another, and ended by doing nothing but cover up his son's feet. "Try cold pack . . . emetic . . . mustard plasters on the stomach . . . bleeding," he would murmur with an effort. The doctor, whom he had entreated to remain, agreed with him, ordered the patient lemonade to drink, and for himself asked for a pipe and something "warming and strengthening"—that's to say, brandy. Arina Vlasyevna sat on a low stool near the door, and only went out from time to time to pray. A few days before, a looking-glass had slipped out of her hands and been broken, and this she had always considered an omen of evil; even Anfisushka could say nothing to her. Timofeitch had gone off to Madame Odintsov's.

The night passed badly for Bazarov. . . . He was in the agonies of high fever. Towards morning he was a little easier. He asked for Arina Vlasyevna to comb his hair, kissed her hand, and swallowed two gulps of tea. Vassily Ivanovitch revived a little.

"Thank God!" he kept declaring; "the crisis is coming, the crisis is at hand!"

"There, to think now!" murmured Bazarov; "what a word can do! He's found it; he's said 'crisis,' and is comforted. It's an astounding thing how man believes in words. If he's told he's a fool, for instance, though he's not thrashed, he'll be wretched; call him a clever fellow, and he'll be delighted if you go off without paying him."

This little speech of Bazarov's, recalling his old retorts, moved Vassily Ivanovitch greatly.

"Bravo! well said, very good!" he cried, making as though he were clapping his hands.

Bazarov smiled mournfully.

"So what do you think," he said; "is the crisis over, or coming?"

"You are better, that's what I see, that's what rejoices me," answered Vassily Ivanovitch.

"Well, that's good; rejoicings never come amiss. And to her, do you remember? did you send?"

"To be sure I did."

The change for the better did not last long. The disease resumed its onslaughts. Vassily Ivanovitch was sitting by Bazarov. It seemed as though the old man were tormented by some special anguish. He was several times on the point of speaking—and could not.

"Yevgeny!" he brought out at last; "my son, my one, dear son!"

This unfamiliar mode of address produced an effect on Bazarov. He turned his head a little, and, obviously trying to fight against the load of oblivion weighing upon him, he articulated: "What is it, father?"

"Yevgeny," Vassily Ivanovitch went on, and he fell on his knees before Bazarov, though the latter had closed his eyes and could not see him. "Yevgeny, you are better now; please God, you will get well, but make use of this time, comfort your mother and me, perform the duty of a Christian! What it means for me to say this to you, it's awful; but still more awful . . . for ever and ever, Yevgeny . . . think a little, what . . ."

The old man's voice broke, and a strange look passed over his son's face, though he still lay with closed eyes.

"I won't refuse, if that can be any comfort to you," he brought out at last; "but it seems to me there's no need to be in a hurry. You say yourself I am better."

"Oh, yes, Yevgeny, better certainly; but who knows, it is all in God's hands, and in doing the duty . . ."

"No, I will wait a bit," broke in Bazarov. "I agree with you that the crisis has come. And if we're mistaken, well! they give the sacrament to men who're unconscious, you know."

"Yevgeny, I beg."

"I'll wait a little. And now I want to go to sleep. Don't disturb me." And he laid his head back on the pillow.

The old man rose from his knees, sat down in the armchair, and, clutching his beard, began biting his own fingers . . .

The sound of a light carriage on springs, that sound which is peculiarly impressive in the wilds of the country, suddenly struck upon his hearing. Nearer and nearer rolled the light wheels; now even the neighing of the horses could be heard.

. . . Vassily Ivanovitch jumped up and ran to the little window. There drove into the courtyard of his little house a carriage with seats for two, with four horses harnessed abreast. Without stopping to consider what it could mean, with a rush of a sort of senseless joy, he ran out on to the steps. . . . A groom in livery was opening the carriage doors; a lady in a black veil and a black mantle was getting out of it . . .

"I am Madame Odintsov," she said. "Yevgeny Vassilyitch is still living? You are his father? I have a doctor with me."

"Benefactress!" cried Vassily Ivanovitch, and snatching her hand, he pressed it convulsively to his lips, while the doctor brought by Anna Sergyevna, a little man in spectacles, of German physiognomy, stepped very deliberately out of the carriage. "Still living, my Yevgeny is living, and now he will be saved! Wife! wife! . . . An angel from heaven has come to us. . . ."

"What does it mean, good Lord!" faltered the old woman, running out of the drawing-room; and, comprehending nothing, she fell on the spot in the passage at Anna Sergyevna's feet, and began kissing her garments like a mad woman.

"What are you doing!" protested Anna Sergyevna; but Arina Vlasyevna did not heed her, while Vassily Ivanovitch could only repeat, "An angel! an angel!"

"*Wo ist der Kranke?* and where is the patient?" said the doctor at last, with some impatience.

Vassily Ivanovitch recovered himself. "Here, here, follow me, würdigster Herr Collega," he added through old associations.

"Ah!" articulated the German, grinning sourly.

Vassily Ivanovitch led him into the study. "The doctor from Anna Sergyevna Odintsov," he said, bending down quite to his son's ear, "and she herself is here."

Bazarov suddenly opened his eyes. "What did you say?"

"I say that Anna Sergyevna is here, and has brought this gentleman, a doctor, to you."

Bazarov moved his eyes about him. "She is here. . . . I want to see her."

"You shall see her, Yevgeny; but first we must have a little talk with the doctor. I will tell him the whole history of your illness since Sidor Sidoritch" (this was the name of the district doctor) "has gone, and we will have a little consultation."

Bazarov glanced at the German. "Well, talk away quickly, only not in Latin; you see, I know the meaning of *jam moritur*."

"*Der Herr scheint des Deutschen mächtig zu sein*," began the new follower of Æsculapius, turning to Vassily Ivanovitch.

"*Ich . . . gabe . . .* We had better speak Russian," said the old man.

"Ah, ah! so that's how it is . . . . To be sure . . ." And the consultation began.

Half-an-hour later Anna Sergyevna, conducted by Vassily Ivanovitch, came into the study. The doctor had had time to whisper to her that it was hopeless even to think of the patient's recovery.

She looked at Bazarov . . . and stood still in the doorway, so greatly was she impressed by the inflamed, and at the same time deathly face, with its dim eyes fastened upon her. She felt simply dismayed, with a sort of cold and suffocating dismay; the thought that she would not have felt like that if she had really loved him flashed instantaneously through her brain.

"Thanks," he said painfully, "I did not expect this. It's a deed of mercy. So we have seen each other again, as you promised."

"Anna Sergyevna has been so kind," began Vassily Ivanovitch . . .

"Father, leave us alone. Anna Sergyevna, you will allow it, I fancy, now?"

With a motion of his head, he indicated his prostrate helpless frame.

Vassily Ivanovitch went out.

"Well, thanks," repeated Bazarov. "This is royally done. Monarchs, they say, visit the dying too."

"Yevgeny Vassilyitch, I hope——"

"Ah, Anna Sergyevna, let us speak the truth. It's all over with me. I'm under the wheel. So it turns out that it was useless to think of the future. Death's an old joke, but it comes fresh to every one. So far I'm not afraid . . . but there, senselessness is coming, and then it's all up!——" he waved his hand feebly. "Well, what had I to say to you . . . I loved you! there was no sense in that even before, and less than ever now. Love is a form, and my own form is already breaking up. Better say how lovely you are! And now here you stand, so beautiful . . ."

Anna Sergyevna gave an involuntary shudder.

"Never mind, don't be uneasy. . . . Sit down there. . . . Don't come close to me; you know, my illness is catching."

Anna Sergyevna swiftly crossed the room, and sat down in the armchair near the sofa on which Bazarov was lying.

"Noble-hearted!" he whispered. "Oh, how near, and how young, and fresh, and pure . . . in this loathsome room! . . . Well, good-bye! live long, that's the best of all, and make the most of it while there is time. You see what a hideous spectacle; the worm half-crushed, but writhing still. And, you see, I thought too: I'd break down so many things, I wouldn't die, why should I! there were problems to solve, and I was a giant! And now all the problem for the giant is how to die decently, though that makes no difference to any one either. . . . Never mind; I'm not going to turn tail."

Bazarov was silent, and began feeling with his hand for the glass. Anna Sergyevna gave him some drink, not taking off her glove, and drawing her breath timorously.

"You will forget me," he began again; "the dead's no companion for the living. My father will tell you what a man Russia is losing. . . . That's nonsense, but don't contradict the old man. Whatever toy will comfort the child . . . you know. And be kind to mother. People like them aren't to be found in your great world if you look by daylight with a candle. . . . I was needed by Russia. . . . No, it's clear, I wasn't needed. And who is needed? The shoemaker's needed, the tailor's needed, the butcher . . . gives us meat . . . the butcher . . . wait a little, I'm getting mixed. . . . There's a forest here . . ."

Bazarov put his hand to his brow.

Anna Sergyevna bent down to him. "Yevgeny Vassilyitch, I am here . . ."

He at once took his hand away, and raised himself.

"Good-bye," he said with sudden force, and his eyes gleamed with their last light. "Good-bye. . . . Listen . . . you know I didn't kiss you then. . . . Breathe on the dying lamp, and let it go out . . ."

Anna Sergyevna put her lips to his forehead.

"Enough!" he murmured, and dropped back on to the pillow. "Now . . darkness . . ."

Anna Sergyevna went softly out. "Well?" Vassily Ivanovitch asked her in a whisper.

"He has fallen asleep," she answered, hardly audibly. Bazarov was not fated to awaken. Towards evening he sank into complete unconsciousness, and the following day he died. Father Alexey performed the last rites of religion over him. When they anointed him with the last unction, when the holy oil touched his breast, one eye opened, and it seemed as though at the sight of the priest in his vestments, the smoking censers, the light before the image, something like a shudder of horror passed over the death-stricken face. When at last he had breathed his last, and there arose a universal lamentation in the house, Vassily Ivanovitch was seized by a sudden frenzy. "I said I should rebel," he shrieked hoarsely, with his face inflamed and distorted, shaking his fist in the air, as though threatening some one; "and I rebel, I rebel!" But Arina Vlasyevna, all in tears, hung upon his neck, and both fell on their faces together. "Side by side," Anfisushka related afterwards in the servants' room, "they drooped their poor heads like lambs at noonday . . ."

But the heat of noonday passes, and evening comes and night, and then, too, the return to the kindly refuge, where sleep is sweet for the weary and heavy laden. . . .

XXVIII

Six months had passed by. White winter had come with the cruel stillness of unclouded frosts, the thick-lying, crunching snow, the rosy rime on the trees, the pale emerald sky, the wreaths of smoke above the chimneys, the clouds of steam rushing out of the doors when they are opened for an instant, with the fresh faces, that look stung by the cold, and the hurrying trot of the chilled horses. A January day was drawing to its close; the cold of evening was more keen than ever in the motionless air, and a lurid sunset was rapidly dying away. There were lights burning in the windows of the house at Maryino; Prokofitch in a black frockcoat and white gloves, with a special solemnity, laid the table for seven. A week before in the small parish church two weddings had taken place quietly, and almost without witnesses— Arkady and Katya's, and Nikolai Petrovitch and Fenitchka's; and on this day Nikolai Petrovitch was giving a farewell dinner to his brother, who was going away to Moscow on business. Anna Sergyevna had gone there also directly after the ceremony was over, after making very handsome presents to the young people.

Precisely at three o'clock they all gathered about the table. Mitya was placed there too; with him appeared a nurse in a cap of glazed brocade. Pavel Petrovitch took his seat between Katya and Fenitchka; the "husbands" took their places beside their wives. Our friends had changed of late; they all seemed to have grown stronger and better looking; only Pavel Petrovitch was thinner, which gave even more of an elegant and "grand seigneur" air to his expressive features. . . . And Fenitchka too was different. In a fresh silk gown, with a wide velvet head-dress on her hair, with a gold chain round her neck, she sat with deprecating immobility, respectful towards herself and everything surrounding her, and smiled as though she would say, "I beg your pardon; I'm not to blame." And not she alone—all the others smiled, and also seemed apologetic; they were all a little awkward, a little sorry, and in reality very happy. They all helped one another with humorous attentiveness, as though they had all agreed to rehearse a sort of artless farce. Katya was the most composed of all; she looked confidently about her, and it could be seen that Nikolai Petrovitch was already devotedly fond of her. At the end of dinner he got up, and, his glass in his hand, turned to Pavel Petrovitch.

"You are leaving us . . . you are leaving us, dear brother,"

he began; "not for long, to be sure; but still, I cannot help express-
ing what I . . . what we . . . how much I . . . how much we
. . . There, the worst of it is, we don't know how to make speeches.
Arkady, you speak."

"No, daddy, I've not prepared anything."

"As though I were so well prepared! Well, brother, I will
simply say, let us embrace you, wish you all good luck, and come
back to us as quick as you can!"

Pavel Petrovitch exchanged kisses with every one, of course
not excluding Mitya; in Fenitchka's case, he kissed also her hand,
which she had not yet learned to offer properly, and drinking off
the glass which had been filled again, he said with a deep sigh,
"May you be happy, my friends! *Farewell!*" This English finale
passed unnoticed; but all were touched.

"To the memory of Bazarov," Katya whispered in her husband's ear, as she clinked glasses with him. Arkady pressed her
hand warmly in response, but he did not venture to propose this
toast aloud.

The end, would it seem? But perhaps some one of our readers would care to know what each of the characters we have
introduced is doing in the present, the actual present. We are
ready to satisfy him.

Anna Sergyevna has recently made a marriage, not of love
but of good sense, with one of the future leaders of Russia, a very
clever man, a lawyer, possessed of vigorous practical sense, a
strong will, and remarkable fluency—still young, good-natured,
and cold as ice. They live in the greatest harmony together, and
will live perhaps to attain complete happiness . . . perhaps love.
The Princess K—— is dead, forgotten the day of her death. The
Kirsanovs, father and son, live at Maryino; their fortunes are
beginning to mend. Arkady has become zealous in the management of the estate, and the "farm" now yields a fairly good
income. Nikolai Petrovitch has been made one of the mediators
appointed to carry out the emancipation reforms, and works with
all his energies; he is for ever driving about over his district;
delivers long speeches (he maintains the opinion that the peasants
ought to be "brought to comprehend things," that is to say, they

ought to be reduced to a state of quiescence by the constant repetition of the same words); and yet, to tell the truth, he does not give complete satisfaction either to the refined gentry, who talk with *chic,* or depression of the *emancipation* (pronouncing it as though it were French), nor of the uncultivated gentry, who unceremoniously curse "the damned *"mancipation."* He is too soft-hearted for both sets. Katerina Sergyevna has a son, little Nikolai, while Mitya runs about merrily and talks fluently. Fenitchka, Fedosya Nikolaevna, after her husband and Mitya, adores no one so much as her daughter-in-law, and when the latter is at the piano, she would gladly spend the whole day at her side. A passing word of Piotr. He has grown perfectly rigid with stupidity and dignity, but he too is married and received a respectable dowry with his bride, the daughter of a market-gardener of the town, who had refused two excellent suitors, only because they had no watch; while Piotr had not only a watch—he had a pair of kid shoes.

In the Brühl Terrace in Dresden, between two and four o'clock—the most fashionable time for walking—you may meet a man about fifty, quite grey, and looking as though he suffered from gout, but still handsome, elegantly dressed, and with that special stamp, which is only gained by moving a long time in the higher strata of society. That is Pavel Petrovitch. From Moscow he went abroad for the sake of his health, and has settled for good at Dresden, where he associates most with English and Russian visitors. With English people he behaves simply, almost modestly, but with dignity; they find him rather a bore, but respect him for being, as they say, *"a perfect gentleman."* With Russians he is more free and easy, gives vent to his spleen, and makes fun of himself and them, but that is done by him with great amiability, negligence, and propriety. He holds Slavophil views; it is well known that in the highest society this is regarded as *très distingué!* He reads nothing in Russian, but on his writing table there is a silver ashpan in the shape of a peasant's plaited shoe. He is much run after by our tourists. Matvy Ilyitch Kolyazin, happening to be in temporary opposition, paid him a majestic visit; while the natives, with whom, however, he is very little seen, positively grovel before him. No one can so readily and quickly obtain a ticket for the court chapel, for the theatre, and such things as *der Herr Baron von Kirsanoff*. He does everything good-naturedly that he can; he still makes some little noise in the world; it is not for nothing that he was once a great society lion;—but life is a burden to him . . . a heavier burden than he suspects himself. One need but glance at him in the Russian church, when, leaning against the wall on one side, he sinks into thought, and remains long without stirring, bitterly compressing his lips, then suddenly recollects himself, and begins almost imperceptibly crossing himself. . . .

Madame Kukshin, too, went abroad. She is in Heidelberg, and is now studying not natural science, but architecture, in which, according to her own account, she has discovered new laws. She still fraternises with students, especially with the young Russians studying natural science and chemistry, with whom Heidelberg is crowded, and who, astounding the naïve German professors at first by the soundness of their views of things, astound the same professors no less in the sequel by their complete inefficiency and absolute idleness. In company with two or three such young chemists, who don't know oxygen from nitrogen, but are filled with scepticism and self-conceit, and, too, with the great Elisyevitch, Sitnikov roams about Petersburg, also getting ready to be great, and in his own conviction continues the "work" of Bazarov. There is a story that some one recently gave him a beating; but he was avenged upon him; in an obscure little article, hidden in an obscure little journal, he has hinted that the man who beat him was a coward. He calls this irony. His father bullies him as before, while his wife regards him as a fool . . . and a literary man.

There is a small village graveyard in one of the remote corners of Russia. Like almost all our graveyards, it presents a wretched appearance; the ditches surrounding it have long been overgrown; the grey wooden crosses lie fallen and rotting under their once painted gables; the stone slabs are all displaced, as though some one were pushing them up from behind; two or three bare trees give a scanty shade; the sheep wander unchecked among the tombs . . . But among them is one untouched by man, untrampled by beast, only the birds perch upon it and sing at daybreak. An iron railing runs round it; two young fir-trees have been planted, one at each end. Yevgeny Bazarov is buried in this tomb. Often from the little village not far off, two quite feeble old people come to visit it—a husband and wife. Supporting one another, they move to it with heavy steps; they go up to the railing, fall down, and remain on their knees, and long and bitterly they weep, and yearn and intently they gaze at the dumb stone, under which their son is lying; they exchange some brief word, wipe away the dust from the stone, set straight a branch of a fir-tree, and pray again, and cannot tear themselves from this place, where they seem to be nearer to their son, to their memories of him . . . Can it be that their prayers, their tears are fruitless? Can it be that love, sacred, devoted love, is not all-powerful? Oh, no! However passionate, sinning, and rebellious the heart hidden in the tomb, the flowers growing over it peep serenely at us with their innocent eyes; they tell us not of eternal peace alone, of that great peace of "indifferent" nature; they tell us too of eternal reconciliation and of life without end.

THE END

TOLSTOY'S SHORT STORIES

BY LEO TOLSTOY

THE INVADERS.

A VOLUNTEER'S NARRATIVE.

I.

On the 24th of July, Captain Khlopof in epaulets and cap—a style of dress in which I had not seen him since my arrival in the Caucasus—entered the low door of my earth-hut.

"I'm just from the colonel's," he said in reply to my questioning look; "to-morrow our battalion is to move."

"Where?" I asked.

"To N——. The troops have been ordered to muster at that place."

"And probably some expedition will be made from there?"

"Of course."

"In what direction, think you?"

"I don't think. I tell you all I know. Last night a Tatar from the general came galloping up,—brought orders for the battalion to march, taking two days' rations. But whither, why, how long, isn't for them to ask. Orders are to go—that's enough."

"Still, if they are going to take only two days' rations, it's likely the army will not stay longer."

"That's no argument at all."

"And how is that?" I asked with astonishment.

"This is the way of it: When they went against Dargi they took a week's rations, but they spent almost a month."

"And can I go with you?" I asked, after a short silence.

"Yes, you *can* go; but my advice is—better not. Why run the risk?"

"No, allow me to disregard your advice. I have been spending a whole month here for this very purpose,—of having a chance to see action,—and you want me to let it have the go-by!"

"All right, come with us; only isn't it true that it would be better for you to stay behind? You could wait for us here, you could go hunting. But as to us,—God knows what will become of us! . . . And that would be first-rate," he said in such a convincing tone that it seemed to me at the first moment that it would actually be first-rate. Nevertheless, I said resolutely that I wouldn't stay behind for any thing.

"And what have you to see there?" said the captain, still trying to dissuade me. "If you want to learn how battles are fought, read Mikhaïlovski Danilevski's 'Description of War,' a charming book; there it's all admirably described,—where every corps stands, and how battles are fought."

"On the contrary, that does not interest me," I replied.

"Well, now, how is this? It simply means that you want to see how men kill each other, doesn't it? . . . Here in 1832 there was a man like yourself, not in the regular service,—a Spaniard, I think he was. He went on two expeditions with us, . . . in a blue mantle or something of the sort, and so the young fellow was killed. Here, *bátiushka,* one is not surprised at any thing."

Ashamed as I was at the captain's manifest disapprobation of my project, I did not attempt to argue him down.

"Well, he was brave, wasn't he?"

"God knows as to that. He always used to ride at the front. Wherever there was firing, there he was."

"So he must have been brave, then," said I.

"No, that doesn't signify bravery,—his putting himself where he wasn't called."

"What do you call bravery, then?"

"Bravery, bravery?" repeated the captain with the expression of a man to whom such a question presents itself for the first time. "A brave man is one who conducts himself as he ought," said he after a brief consideration.

I remembered that Plato defined bravery as the knowledge of what one ought and what one ought not to fear; and in spite of the triteness and obscurity in the terminology of the captain's definition, I thought that the fundamental conception of both was not so unlike as might at first sight appear, and that the captain's definition was even more correct than the Greek philosopher's, for the reason, that, if he could have expressed himself as Plato did, he would in all probability have said that that man is brave who fears only what he ought to fear and not what there is no need of fearing.

I was anxious to explain my thought to the captain.

"Yes," I said, "it seems to me that in every peril there is an alternative, and the alternative adopted under the influence of, say, the sentiment of duty, is bravery, but the alternative adopted under the influence of a lower sentiment is cowardice; therefore it is impossible to call a man brave who risks his life out of vanity or curiosity or greediness, and, *vice versa,* the man who under the influence of the virtuous sentiment of family obligation, or simply from conviction, avoids peril, cannot be called a coward."

The captain looked at me with a queer sort of expression while I was talking.

"Well, now, I don't know how to reason this out with you," said he, filling his pipe, "but we have with us a junker, and he likes to philosophize. You talk with him. He also writes poetry."

I had only become intimate with the captain in the Caucasus, but I had known him before in Russia. His mother, Márya Ivánovna Khlópova, the owner of a small landed estate, lives about two versts[1] from my home. Before I went to the Caucasus I visited her. The old lady was greatly delighted that I was going to see her Páshenka[2] (thus she called the old gray-haired captain), and, like a living letter, could tell him about her circumstances and give him a little message. Having made me eat my fill of a glorious pie and roast chicken, Márya Ivánovna went to her sleeping-room

[1] One and a third miles.
[2] An affectionate diminished diminutive: Pavel (Paul), Pasha, Pashenka.

and came back with a rather large black relic-bag,[3] to which was attached some kind of silken ribbon.

"Here is this image of our Mother-Intercessor from the September festival," she said, kissing the picture of the divine Mother attached to the cross, and putting it into my hand. "Please give it to him, *bátiushka*. You see, when he went to the Kaikaz, I had a Te Deum sung, and made a vow, that if he should be safe and sound, I would order this image of the divine Mother. And here it is seventeen years that the *Mátushka* and the saints have had him in their keeping; not once has he been wounded, and what battles he has been in, as it seems! . . . When Mikháilo, who was with him, told me about it, my hair actually stood on end. You see, all that I know about him I have to hear from others; he never writes me any thing about his doings, my dove,—he is afraid of frightening me."

(I had already heard in the Caucasus, but not from the captain himself, that he had been severely wounded four times; and, as was to be expected, he had not written his mother about his wounds any more than about his campaigns.)

"Now let him wear this holy image," she continued. "I bless him with it. The most holy Intercessor protect him, especially in battle may she always look after him! And so tell him, my dear friend,[4] that thy mother gave thee this message."

I promised faithfully to fulfil her commission.

"I know you will be fond of him, of my *Páshenka*," the old lady continued,—"he is such a splendid fellow! Would you believe me, not a year goes by without his sending me money, and he also helps Annushka my daughter, and all from his wages alone. Truly I shall always thank God," she concluded with tears in her eyes, "that he has given me such a child."

"Does he write you often?" I asked.

"Rarely, *bátiushka*,—not more than once a year; and sometimes when he sends money he writes a little word, and sometimes he doesn't. 'If I don't write you, *mámenka*,' he says, 'it

---

[3] *ládanka*, the bag containing sacred things worn by the pious, together with the baptismal cross.
[4] *moï bátiushka*.

means that I'm alive and well; but if any thing should happen,—which God forbid,—then they will write you for me.' "

When I gave the captain his mother's gift (it was in my room), he asked me for some wrapping-paper, carefully tied it up, and put it away. I gave him many details of his mother's life: the captain was silent. When I had finished, he went into a corner, and took a very long time in filling his pipe.

"Yes, she's a fine old lady," said he from the corner, in a rather choked voice: "God grant that we may meet again!"

Great love and grief were expressed in these simple words.

"Why do you serve here?" I asked.

"Have to serve," he replied with decision. "And double pay means a good deal for our brother, who is a poor man."

The captain lived economically; he did not play cards, he rarely drank to excess, and he smoked ordinary tobacco, which from some inexplicable reason he did not call by its usual name, but *sambrotalicheski tabák*. The captain had pleased me even before this. He had one of those simple, calm Russian faces, and looked you straight in the eye agreeably and easily. But after this conversation I felt a genuine respect for him.

II.

At four o'clock on the morning of the next day, the captain came riding up to my door. He had on an old well-worn coat without epaulets, wide Lesghian trousers, a round white Circassian cap, with drooping lambskin dyed yellow, and an ugly-looking Asiatic sabre across his shoulder. The little white horse on which he rode came with head down, and mincing gait, and kept switching his slender tail. In spite of the fact that the good captain's figure was neither very warlike nor very handsome, yet there was in it such an expression of good-will toward every one around him, that it inspired involuntary respect.

I did not keep him waiting a minute, but immediately mounted, and we rode off together from the gate of the fortress.

The battalion was already two hundred *sazhens*[5] ahead of us, and had the appearance of some black, solid body in motion. It was possible to make out that it was infantry, only from the circumstance that while the bayonets appeared like long, dense needles, occasionally there came to the ear the sounds of a soldier's song, the drum, and a charming tenor, the leader of the sixth company,—a song which I had more than once enjoyed at the fort.

The road ran through the midst of a deep, wide ravine, or *balka* as it is called in the Caucasian dialect, along the banks of a small river, which at this time was *playing,* that is, was having a freshet. Flocks of wild pigeons hovered around it, now settling on the rocky shore, now wheeling about in mid-air in swift circles and disappearing from sight.

The sun was not yet visible, but the summit of the balka on the right began to grow luminous. The gray and white colored crags, the greenish-yellow moss wet with dew, the clumps of different kinds of wild thorn,[6] stood out extraordinarily distinct and rotund in the pellucid golden light of the sunrise.

On the other hand, the ravine, hidden in thick mist which rolled up like smoke in varying volumes, was damp, and dark, and gave the impression of an indistinguishable mixture of colors—pale lilac, almost purple, dark green, and white.

Directly in front of us, against the dark blue of the horizon, with startling distinctness appeared the dazzling white, silent masses of the snow-capped mountains with their marvellous shadows and outlines exquisite even in the smallest details. Crickets, grasshoppers, and a thousand other insects, were awake in the tall grass, and filled the air with their sharp, incessant clatter: it seemed as though a numberless multitude of tiny bells were jingling in our very ears. The atmosphere was alive with waters, with foliage, with mist; in a word, had all the life of a beautiful early summer morning.

The captain struck a light, and began to puff at his pipe; the

[5] Fourteen hundred feet.
[6] Paliurus, box-thorn, and *karachag.*

fragrance of *sambrotalicheski tabák* and of the punk struck me as extremely pleasant.

We rode along the side of the road so as to overtake the infantry as quickly as possible. The captain seemed more serious than usual; he did not take his Daghestan pipe from his mouth, and at every step he dug his heels into his horse's legs as the little beast, capering from one side to the other, laid out a scarcely noticeable dark green track through the damp, tall grass. Up from under his very feet, with its shrill cry,[7] and that drumming of the wings that is so sure to startle the huntsman in spite of himself, flew the pheasant, and slowly winged its flight on high. The captain paid him not the slightest attention.

We had almost overtaken the battalion, when behind us was heard the sound of a galloping horse, and in an instant there rode by us a very handsome young fellow in an officer's coat, and a tall white Circassian cap.[8] As he caught up with us he smiled, bowed to the captain, and waved his whip. . . . I only had time to notice that he sat in the saddle and held the bridle with peculiar grace, and that he had beautiful dark eyes, a finely cut nose, and a mustache just beginning to grow. I was particularly attracted by the way in which he could not help smiling, as if to impress it upon us that we were friends of his. If by nothing else than his smile, one would have known that he was still very young.

"And now where is he going?" grumbled the captain with a look of dissatisfaction, not taking his pipe from his mouth.

"Who is that?" I asked.

"Ensign Alánin, a subaltern officer of my company. . . . Only last month he came from the School of Cadets."

"This is the first time that he is going into action, I suppose?" said I.

"And so he is overjoyed," replied the captain thoughtfully, shaking his head; "it's youth."

"And why shouldn't he be glad? I can see that for a young officer this must be very interesting."

[7] *tordokan'yé.*
[8] *papákha.*

The captain said nothing for two minutes.

"And that's why I say 'it's youth,' " he continued in a deep tone. "What is there to rejoice in, when there's nothing to see? Here when one goes often, one doesn't find any pleasure in it. Here, let us suppose there are twenty of us officers going: some of us will be either killed or wounded; that's likely. Today my turn, to-morrow his, the next day somebody else's. So what is there to rejoice in?"

III.

Scarcely had the bright sun risen above the mountains, and begun to shine into the valley where we were riding, when the undulating clouds of mist scattered, and it grew warm. The soldiers with guns and knapsacks on their backs marched slowly along the dusty road. In the ranks were frequently heard Malo-Russian dialogues and laughter. A few old soldiers in white linen coats—for the most part non-commissioned officers—marched along the roadside with their pipes, engaged in earnest conversation. The triple rows of heavily laden wagons advanced step by step, and raised a thick dust, which hung motionless.

The mounted officers rode in advance; a few *jiggited,* as they say in the Caucasus;[9] that is, applying the whip to their horses, they spurred them on to make four or five leaps, and then reined them in suddenly, pulling the head back. Others listened to the song-singers, who notwithstanding the heat and the oppressive air indefatigably tuned up one song after another.

A hundred *sazhens* in advance of the infantry, on a great white horse, surrounded by mounted Tatars, rode a tall, handsome officer in Asiatic costume, known to the regiment as a man of reckless valor, one who cuts *any one straight in the eyes!*[10] He wore a black Tatar half-coat or *beshmét* trimmed with silver

---

[9] *jigit* or *djigit* in the Kumuits dialect signifies valiant. The Russians make from it the verb *jigitovat.*
[10] That is, known for telling the plain truth.

braid, similar trousers, new leggings[11] closely laced with *chirazui* as they call galloons in the Caucasus, and a tall, yellow Cherkessian cap worn jauntily on the back of his head. On his breast and back were silver lacings. His powder-flask and pistol were hung at his back; another pistol, and a dagger in a silver sheath, depended from his belt. Besides all this was buckled on a sabre in a red morocco sheath adorned with silver; and over the shoulder hung his musket in a black case.

By his garb, his carriage, his manner, and indeed by every motion, it was manifest that his ambition was to ape the Tatars. He was just saying something, in a language that I did not understand, to the Tatars who rode with him; but from the doubtful, mocking glances which these latter gave each other, I came to the conclusion that they did not understand him either.

This was one of our young officers of the dare-devil, *jigit* order, who get themselves up à la Marlinski and Lermontof. These men look upon the Caucasus, as it were, through the prism of the "Heroes of our Time," Mulla-Nurof[12] and others, and in all their activities are directed not by their own inclinations but by the example of these models.

This lieutenant, for instance, was very likely fond of the society of well-bred women and men of importance, generals, colonels, adjutants,—I may even go so far as to believe that he was very fond of this society, because he was in the highest degree vainglorious,—but he considered it his unfailing duty to show his rough side to all important people, although he offended them always more or less; and when any lady made her appearance at the fortress, then he considered it his duty to ride by her windows with his cronies, or *kunaki* as they are called in the dialect of the Caucasus, dressed in a red shirt and nothing but *chuviaki* on his bare legs, and shouting and swearing at the top of his voice—but all this not only with the desire to insult her, but also to show her what handsome white legs he had, and how easy it would be to fall in love with him if only he himself were willing. Or he often

[11] *chuviaki.*
[12] The name of a character in one of Marlinski's novels.

went by at night with two or three friendly Tatars to the mountains into ambush by the road so as to take by surprise and kill
hostile Tatars coming along; and though more than once his heart
told him that there was nothing brave in such a deed, yet he felt
himself under obligations to inflict suffering upon people in
whom he thought that he was disappointed, and whom he affected
to hate and despise. He always carried two things,—an immense
holy image around his neck, and a dagger above his shirt. He
never took them off, but even went to bed with them. He firmly
believed that enemies surrounded him. It was his greatest delight
to argue that he was under obligations to wreak vengeance on
some one and wash out insults in blood. He was persuaded that
spite, vengeance, and hatred of the human race were the highest
and most poetical of feelings. But his mistress,—a Circassian girl
of course,—whom I happened afterwards to meet, said that he
was the mildest and gentlest of men, and that every evening he
wrote in his gloomy diary, cast up his accounts on ruled paper,
and got on his knees to say his prayers. And how much suffering
he endured, to seem to himself only what he desired to be,
because his comrades and the soldiers could not comprehend him
as he desired!

Once, in one of his nocturnal expeditions with his Tatar
friends, it happened that he put a bullet into the leg of a hostile
Tchetchenets, and took him prisoner. This Tchetchenets for
seven weeks thereafter lived with the lieutenant; the lieutenant
dressed his wound, waited on him as though he were his nearest
friend, and when he was cured sent him home with gifts. Afterwards, during an expedition when the lieutenant was retreating
from the post, having been repulsed by the enemy, he heard some
one call him by name, and his wounded *kunák* strode out from
among the hostile Tatars, and by signs asked him to do the same.
The lieutenant went to meet his *kunák,* and shook hands with
him. The mountaineers stood at some little distance, and refrained from firing; but, as soon as the lieutenant turned his horse
to go back, several shot at him, and one bullet grazed the small
of his back.

Another time I myself saw a fire break out by night in the

fortress, and two companies of soldiers were detailed to put it out. Amid the crowd, lighted up by the ruddy glare of the fire, suddenly appeared the tall form of the man on a coal-black horse. He forced his way through the crowd, and rode straight to the fire. As soon as he came near, the lieutenant leaped from his horse, and hastened into the house, which was all in flames on one side. At the end of five minutes he emerged with singed hair and burned sleeves, carrying in his arms two doves which he had rescued from the flames.

His name was Rosenkranz; but he often spoke of his ancestry, traced it back to the Varangians, and clearly showed that he and his forefathers were genuine Russians.

IV.

The sun had travelled half its course, and was pouring down through the glowing atmosphere its fierce rays upon the parched earth. The dark blue sky was absolutely clear; only the bases of the snow-capped mountains began to clothe themselves in pale lilac clouds. The motionless atmosphere seemed to be full of some impalpable dust; it became intolerably hot.

When the army came to a small brook that had overflowed half the road, a halt was called. The soldiers, stacking their arms, plunged into the stream. The commander of the battalion sat down in the shade, on a drum, and, showing by his broad countenance the degree of his rank, made ready, in company with a few officers, to take lunch. The captain lay on the grass under the company's transport-wagon; the gallant lieutenant Rosenkranz and some other young officers, spreading out their Caucasian mantles, or *burki,* threw themselves down, and began to carouse as was manifest by the flasks and bottles scattered around them and by the extraordinary liveliness of their singers, who, standing in a half-circle behind them, gave an accompaniment to the Caucasian dance-song sung by a Lesghian girl:—

> Shamyl resolved to make a league
> In the years gone by,

Traï-raï, rattat-taï,
In the years gone by.

Among these officers was also the young ensign who had passed us in the morning. He was very entertaining: his eyes gleamed, his tongue never grew weary. He wanted to greet every one, and show his good-will to them all. Poor lad! he did not know that in acting this way he might be ridiculous, that his frankness and the gentleness which he showed to every one might win for him, not the love which he so much desired, but ridicule; he did not know this either, that when at last, thoroughly heated, he threw himself down on his *burka,* and leaned his head on his hand, letting his thick black curls fall over, he was a very picture of beauty.

Two officers crouched under a wagon, and were playing cards on a hamper.

I listened with curiosity to the talk of the soldiers and officers, and attentively watched the expression of their faces; but, to tell the truth, in not one could I discover a shadow of that anxiety which I myself felt; jokes, laughter, anecdotes, expressed the universal carelessness, and indifference to the coming peril. How impossible to suppose that it was not fated for some never again to pass that road!

V.

At seven o'clock in the evening, dusty and weary, we entered the wide, fortified gate of Fort N——. The sun was setting, and shed oblique rosy rays over the picturesque batteries and lofty-walled gardens that surrounded the fortress, over the fields yellow for the harvest, and over the white clouds which, gathering around the snow-capped mountains, simulated their shapes, and formed a chain no less wonderful and beauteous. A young half moon, like a translucent cloud, shone above the horizon. In the native village or *aul,* situated near the gate, a Tatar on the roof of a hut was calling the faithful to prayer. The singers broke out with new zeal and energy.

After resting and making my toilet I set out to call upon an adjutant who was an acquaintance of mine, to ask him to make my intention known to the general. On the way from the suburb where I was quartered, I chanced to see a most unexpected spectacle in the fortress of N——. I was overtaken by a handsome two-seated vehicle in which I saw a stylish bonnet, and heard French spoken. From the open window of the commandant's house came floating the sounds of some "Lízanka" or "Kátenka" polka played upon a wretched piano, out of tune. In the tavern which I was passing were sitting a number of clerks over their glasses of wine, with cigarettes in their hands, and I overheard one saying to another,—

"Excuse me, but taking politics into consideration, Márya Grigór'yevna is our first lady."

A humpbacked Jew of sickly countenance, dressed in a dilapidated coat, was creeping along with a shrill, broken-down hand-organ; and over the whole suburb echoed the sounds of the finale of "Lucia."

Two women in rustling dresses, with silk kerchiefs around their necks and bright-colored sun-shades in their hands, hastened past me on the plank sidewalk. Two girls, one in pink, the other in a blue dress, with uncovered heads, were standing on the terrace of a small house, and affectedly laughing with the obvious intention of attracting the notice of some passing officers. Officers in new coats, white gloves, and glistening epaulets, were parading up and down the streets and boulevards.

I found my acquaintance on the lower floor of the general's house. I had scarcely had time to explain to him my desire, and have his assurance that it could most likely be gratified, when the handsome carriage, which I had before seen, rattled past the window where I was sitting. From the carriage descended a tall, slender man, in uniform of the infantry service and major's epaulets, and came up to the general's rooms.

"*Akh!* pardon me, I beg of you," said the adjutant, rising from his place: "it's absolutely necessary that I tell the general."

"Who is it that just came?" I asked.

"The countess," he replied, and donning his uniform coat hastened up-stairs.

In the course of a few minutes there appeared on the steps a short but very handsome man in a coat without epaulets, and a white cross in his button-hole. Behind him came the major, the adjutant, and two other officers.

In his carriage, his voice, in all his motions, the general showed that he had a very keen appreciation of his high importance.

"*Bon soir, Madame la Comtesse,*" he said, extending his hand through the carriage window.

A dainty little hand in dog-skin glove took his hand, and a pretty, smiling little visage under a yellow bonnet appeared in the window.

From the conversation which lasted several minutes, I only heard, as I went by, the general saying in French with a smile,—

"You know that I have vowed to fight the infidels; beware of becoming one!"

A laugh rang from the carriage.

"*Adieu donc, cher général.*"

"*Non, à revoir,*" said the general, returning to the steps of the staircase; "don't forget that I have invited myself for to-morrow evening."

The carriage drove away.

"Here is a man," said I to myself as I went home, "who has every thing that Russians strive after,—rank, wealth, society,— and this man, before a battle the outcome of which God only knows, jests with a pretty little woman, and promises to drink tea with her on the next day, just as though he had met her at a ball!"

There at that adjutant's I became acquainted with a man who still more surprised me; it was the young lieutenant of the K. regiment, who was distinguished for his almost feminine mildness and cowardice. He came to the adjutant to pour out his peevishness and ill humor against those men who, he thought, were intriguing against him to keep him from taking part in the matter in hand.

He declared that it was hateful to be treated so, that it was not doing as comrades ought, that he would remember him, and so forth.

As soon as I saw the expression of his face, as soon as I heard the sound of his voice, I could not escape the conviction that he was not only not putting it on, but was deeply stirred and hurt because he was not allowed to go against the Cherkess, and expose himself to their fire: he was as much hurt as a child is hurt who is unjustly punished. I could not understand it at all.

VI.

At ten o'clock in the evening the troops were ordered to march. At half-past nine I mounted my horse, and started off to find the general; but on reflecting that he and his adjutant must be busy, I remained in the street, and, tying my horse to a fence, sat down on the terrace to wait until the general should come.

The heat and glare of the day had already vanished in the fresh night air; and the obscure light of the young moon, which, infolding around itself a pale gleaming halo against the dark blue of the starry sky, was beginning to decline. Lights shone in the windows of the houses and in the chinks of the earth huts. The gracefully proportioned poplars in the gardens, standing out against the horizon from behind the earth huts, whose reed-thatched roofs gleamed pale in the moonlight, seemed still taller and blacker.

The long shadows of the houses, of the trees, of the fences, lay beautifully across the white dusty road. . . . In the river rang incessantly the voice of the frogs;[13] in the streets were heard hurrying steps, and sounds of voices, and the galloping of horses. From the suburb came floating, now and again, the strains of the hand-organ; now the popular Russian air, "The winds are blowing," now one of the Aurora waltzes.

I will not tell what my thoughts were: in the first place,

---

[13] The frogs in the Caucasus make a sound entirely different from the *Kvakan'ye* of the Russian frogs.

because I should be ashamed to confess to the melancholy ideas which without cessation arose in my mind, while all around me I perceived only gayety and mirth; and, in the second place, because they have nothing to do with my story.

I was so deeply engrossed in thought, that I did not notice that the bell was ringing for eleven o'clock, and the general was riding past me with his suite.

The rearguard was just at the fortress gate. I galloped at full speed across the bridge, amid a crush of cannon, caissons, military wagons, and commanding officers shouting at the top of their voices. After reaching the gate, I rode at a brisk trot for almost a verst, past the army stretched out and silently moving through the darkness, and overtook the general. As I made my way past the mounted artillery dragging their ordnance, amid the cannon and officers, a German voice, like a disagreeable dissonance interrupting soft and majestic harmony, struck my ear. It screamed, "Agkhtingkhist,[14] bring a linstock."

And a soldier's voice replied, quick as a flash, "Chevchenko! the lieutenant asks for a light!"

The greater part of the sky had become enveloped in long steel-gray clouds: here and there gleamed from between them the lustreless stars. The moon was now sinking behind the near horizon of dark mountains which were on the right; and it shed on their summits a feeble, waning, half light, which contrasted sharply with the impenetrable darkness that marked their bases.

The air was mild, and so still, that not a single grass-blade, not a single mist-wreath, moved. It became so dark, that it was impossible to distinguish objects, even though very near at hand. On the side of the road, there seemed to me sometimes to be rocks, sometimes animals, sometimes strange men; and I knew that they were bushes only when I heard them rustle, and felt the coolness of the dew with which they were covered. In front of me I saw a dense, waving black shadow, behind which followed a few moving spots; this was the van-guard of cavalry, and the general

---

[14] German mispronunciation for *Antichrist*, the accent of which in Russian falls on the penult.

with his suite. Between us moved another similar black mass, but this was not as high as the first; this was the infantry.

Such silence reigned in the whole detachment, that there could be plainly distinguished all the harmonious voices of the night, full of mysterious charm. The distant melancholy howls of jackals, sometimes like the wails of despair, sometimes like laughter; the monotonous ringing song of the cricket, the frog, the quail; a gradually approaching murmur, the cause of which I could not make clear to my own mind; and all those nocturnal, almost audible motions of nature, which it is so impossible either to comprehend or define,—unite into one complete, beautiful harmony which we call silent night.

This silence was broken, or rather was unified, by the dull thud of the hoofs, and the rustling of the tall grass through which the division was slowly moving.

Occasionally, however, was heard in the ranks the ring of a heavy cannon, the sound of clashing bayonets, stifled conversation, and the snorting of a horse.

Nature breathed peacefully in beauty and power.

Is it possible that people find no room to live together in this beautiful world, under this boundless starry heaven? Is it possible that amid this bewitching nature, the soul of man can harbor the sentiments of hatred and revenge, or the passion for inflicting destruction upon his kind? All ugly feelings in the heart of man ought, it would seem, to vanish away in this intercourse with nature,—with this immediate expression of beauty and goodness!

VII.

We had now been marching more than two hours. I began to feel chilly, and to be overcome with drowsiness. In the darkness the same indistinct objects dimly appeared: at a little distance, the same black shadow, the same moving spots. Beside me was the crupper of a white horse, which switched his tail and swung his hind-legs in wide curves. I could see a back in a white Circassian shirt, against which was outlined a carbine in its black case, and the handle of a pistol in an embroidered holster: the glow of a cigarette casting a gleam on a reddish mustache, a fur collar, and a hand in a chamois-skin glove.

I leaned over my horse's neck, closed my eyes, and lost myself for a few minutes: then suddenly the regular hoof-beat[15] and rustling came into my consciousness again. I looked around, and it seemed to me as though I were standing still in one spot, and that the black shadow in front of me was moving down upon me; or else that the shadow stood still, and I was rapidly riding down upon it.

At one such moment I was more strongly than ever impressed by that incessantly approaching sound, the cause of which I could not fathom: it was the roar of water. We were passing though a deep gulch, and coming close to a mountain river, which at that season was in full flood.[16] The roaring became louder, the damp grass grew taller and thicker, bushes were encountered in denser clumps, and the horizon narrowed itself down to closer limits. Now and then, in different places in the dark hollows of the mountains, bright fires flashed out and were immediately extinguished.

"Tell me, please, what are those fires," I asked in a whisper of the Tatar riding at my side.

"Don't you really know?" was his reply.

"No," said I.

"That is mountain straw tied to a pole,[17] and the light is waved."

"What for?"

"So that every man may know the Russian is coming. Now in the Auls," he added with a smile, "*ai, aï!* the *tomásha*[18] are flying about; every sort of *khurda-murda*[19] will be hurried into the ravines."

[15] *tópot.*
[16] In the Caucasus the freshets take place in the month of July.
[17] *tayak* in the Caucasian dialect.
[18] *tomásha* means slaves in the ordinary dialect invented for intercourse between Russians and Tatars. There are many words in this strange dialect, the roots of which are not to be found either in Russian or Tatar.—AUTHOR'S NOTE.
[19] Goods and chattels in the same dialect.

"How do they know so soon in the mountains that the expedition is coming?" I asked.

"*Ei!* How can they help knowing? It's known everywhere: that's the kind of people we are."

"And so Shamyl is now getting ready to march out?" I asked.

"*Yok* (no)," he replied, shaking his head as a sign of negation, "Shamyl will not march out. Shamyl will send his *naïbs,*[20] and he himself will look down from up yonder through his glass."

"But doesn't he live a long way off?"

"Not a long way off. Here, at your left, about ten *versts* he will be."

"How do you know that?" I inquired. "Have you been there?"

"I've been there. All of us in the mountains have."

"And you have seen Shamyl?"

"*Píkh!* Shamyl is not to be seen by us. A hundred, three hundred, a thousand *murids*[21] surround him. Shamyl will be in the midst of them," he said with an expression of fawning servility.

Looking up in the air, it was possible to make out that the sky which had become clear again was lighter in the east, and the Pleiades were sinking down into the horizon. But in the gulch through which we were passing, it was humid and dark.

Suddenly, a little in advance of us, from out the darkness flashed a number of lights; at the same instant, with a ping some bullets whizzed by, and from out the silence that surrounded us from afar arose the heavy, o'ermastering roar of the guns. This was the vanguard of the enemy's pickets. The Tatars, of which it was composed, set up their war-cry, shot at random, and fled in all directions.

Every thing became silent again. The general summoned his interpreter. The Tatar in a white Circassian dress hastened up to

---

[20] *naïb* ordinarily means a Mohammedan judge or high religious officer, in Turkey and the Caucasus; here it means an officer whom the great Circassian chieftain Shamyl endowed with special authority.
[21] The word *murid* has many significations, but in the sense here employed it means something between adjutant and body-guard.—AUTHOR'S NOTE.

him, and the two held a rather long conversation in a sort of whisper and with many gestures.

"Colonel Khasánof! give orders to scatter the enemy," said the general in a low, deliberate, but distinct tone of voice.

The division went down to the river. The black mountains stood back from the pass; it was beginning to grow light. The arch of heaven, in which the pale, lustreless stars were barely visible, seemed to come closer; the dawn began to glow brightly in the east; a cool, penetrating breeze sprang up from the west, and a bright mist like steam arose from the foaming river.

VIII.

The guide pointed out the ford; and the vanguard of cavalry, with the general and his suite immediately in its rear, began to cross the river. The water, which reached the horses' breasts, rushed with extraordinary violence among the white bowlders which in some places came to the top, and formed foaming, gurgling whirlpools around the horses' legs. The horses were frightened at the roar of the water, lifted their heads, pricked up their ears, but slowly and carefully picked their way against the stream along the uneven bottom. The riders held up their legs and fire-arms. The foot-soldiers, literally in their shirts alone, lifting above the water their muskets to which were fastened their bundles of clothing, struggled against the force of the stream by clinging together, a score of men at a time, showing noticeable determination on their excited faces. The artillery-men on horseback, with a loud shout, put their horses into the water at full trot. The cannon and green-painted caissons, over which now and then the water came pouring, plunged with a clang over the rocky bottom; but the noble Cossack horses pulled with united effort, made the water foam, and with dripping tails and manes emerged on the farther shore.

As soon as the crossing was effected, the general's face suddenly took on an expression of deliberation and seriousness; he wheeled his horse around, and at full gallop rode across the wide forest-surrounded field which spread before us. The Cossack horses were scattered along the edge of the forest.

In the forest appears a man in Circassian dress and round cap; then a second and a third . . . one of the officers shouts, "Those are Tatars!" At this instant a puff of smoke came from behind a tree . . . a report—another. The quick volleys of our men drown out those of the enemy. Only occasionally a bullet, with long-drawn ping like the hum of a bee, flies by, and is the only proof that not all the shots are ours.

Here the infantry at double quick, and with fixed bayonets, dash against the chain; one can hear the heavy reports of the guns, the metallic clash of grapeshot, the whiz of rockets, the crackling of musketry. The cavalry, the infantry, converge from all sides on the wide field. The smoke from the guns, rockets, and fire-arms, unites with the early mist arising from the dew-covered grass.

Colonel Khasánof gallops up to the general, and reins in his horse while at full tilt.

"Your Excellency," says he, lifting his hand to his cap, "give orders for the cavalry to advance. The standards are coming,"[22] and he points with his whip to mounted Tatars, at the head of whom rode two men on white horses with red and blue streamers on their lances.

"All right,[23] Iván Mikháïlovitch," says the general.

The colonel wheels his horse round on the spot, draws his sabre, and shouts "Hurrah!"

"Hurrah! hurrah! hurrah!" echoes from the ranks, and the cavalry dash after him.

All look on with excitement: there is a standard; another; a third; a fourth! . . .

The enemy, not waiting the assault, fly into the forest, and open a musket fire from behind the trees. The bullets fly more and more thickly.

"*Quel charmant coup d'oeil!*" exclaimed the general as he

---

[22] *znatchki.* This word among the mountaineers has almost the signification of banner, with this single distinction, that each jigit can make a standard for himself and carry it.—AUTHOR'S NOTE.
[23] *S Bógom,* literally "with God," but a mere phrase.

easily rose in English fashion on his coal-black, slender-limbed little steed.

"*Charmant,*" replies the major, who rolls his *r's* like a Frenchman, and whipping up his horse dashes after the general. "It's a genuine pleasure to carry on war in such a fine country," says he.[24]

"And above all in good company," adds the general still in French, with a pleasant smile.

The major bowed.

At this time a cannon-ball from the enemy comes flying by with a swift, disagreeable whiz, and strikes something; immediately is heard the groan of a wounded man. This groan impresses me so painfully that the martial picture instantly loses for me all its fascination: but no one beside myself seems to be affected in the same way; the major smiles apparently with the greatest satisfaction; another officer with perfect equanimity repeats the opening words of a speech; the general looks in the opposite direction, and with the most tranquil smile says something in French.

"Will you give orders to reply to their heavy guns?" asks the commander of the artillery, galloping up. "Yes, scare them a little," says the general carelessly, lighting a cigar.

The battery is unlimbered, and the cannonade begins. The ground shakes under the report; the firing continues without cessation; and the smoke in which it is scarcely possible to distinguish those attending the guns, blinds the eyes.

The aul is battered down. Again Colonel Khasánof dashes up, and at the general's command darts off to the aul. The war-cry is heard again, and the cavalry disappears in the cloud of its own dust.

The spectacle was truly grandiose. One thing only spoiled the general impression for me as a man who had no part in the affair, and was wholly unwonted to it; and this was that there was too much of it,—the motion and the animation and the shouts. Involuntarily the comparison occurred to me of a man who in his haste would cut the air with a hatchet.

----

[24] *C'est un vrai plaisir, que la guerre dans un aussi beau pays.*

IX.

The aul was already in the possession of our men, and not a soul of the enemy remained in it when the general with his suite, to which I had joined myself, entered it.

The long neat huts or *saklí,* with their flat earthen roofs and red chimneys, were situated on rough, rocky hills, between which ran a small river. On one side were seen the green gardens, shining in the clear sunlight, with monstrous pear-trees, and the plum-trees, called *luitcha.* The other side bristled with strange shadows, where stood the high perpendicular stones of a cemetery, and the tall wooden poles adorned at the ends with balls and variegated banners. These were the tombs of jigits.

The army stood drawn up within the gates.

After a moment the dragoons, the Cossacks, the infantry, with evident joy were let loose through the crooked streets, and the empty aul suddenly teemed with life. Here a roof is crushed in; the axe rings on the tough trees, and the plank door is broken down; there hay-ricks, fences, and huts are burning, and the dense smoke arises like a tower in the clear air. Here a Cossack is carrying off sacks of flour, and carpets; a soldier with a gay face lugs from a hut a tin basin and a dish-clout; another with outstretched arms is trying to catch a couple of hens, which cackling furiously fly about the yard; a third is going somewhere with a monstrous *kumgan* or pitcher of milk, and drinking as he goes, and when he has had his fill smashes it on the ground with a loud laugh.

The battalion which I had accompanied from Fort N—— was also in the aul. The captain was sitting on the roof of a hut, and was puffing from his short little pipe clouds of smoke of *sambrotalicheski tabák* with such an indifferent expression of countenance that when I saw him I forgot that I was in a hostile aul, and it seemed to me that I was actually at home with him.

"Ah! and here you are?" he said as he caught sight of me.

The tall form of Lieutenant Rosenkranz flashed here and there through the aul. Without a moment's pause he was engaged in carrying out orders, and he had the appearance of a man who had all he could do. I saw him coming out of a hut, his face full of triumph; behind him two soldiers were dragging an old Tatar with his arms tied. The old man, whose garb consisted merely of a many-colored *beshmét* torn in tatters, and ragged drawers, was so feeble that it seemed as if his bony arms, tightly tied behind his misshapen back, were almost falling from his shoulders; and his crooked bare legs moved with difficulty. His face, and even a part of his shaven head, were covered with deep wrinkles; his distorted toothless mouth, encircled by gray clipped mustache and beard, incessantly mumbled as though whispering something; but his handsome eyes, from which the lashes were gone, still gleamed with fire, and clearly expressed an old man's indifference to life.

Rosenkranz through an interpreter asked him why he had not gone with the others.

"Where should I go?" he replied, calmly looking away.

"Where the rest have gone," suggested some one.

"The jigits have gone to fight with the Russians, and I am an old man."

"Aren't you afraid of the Russians?"

"What will the Russians do to me? I am an old man," he repeated, carelessly glancing at the circle surrounding him.

On the way back, I saw this old man without a hat, with his hands still tied, jolting behind a mounted Cossack, and he was looking about him with the same expression of unconcern. He was necessary in an exchange of prisoners.

I went to the staircase, and crept up to where the captain was.

"Not many of the enemy, it seems," I said to him, wishing to obtain his opinion about the affair.

"The enemy," he repeated with surprise, "there weren't any at all. Do you call these enemies? . . . Here when evening comes, you will see how we shall retreat; you will see how they will go with us! Won't they show themselves there?" he added, pointing with his pipe to the forest which we had passed in the morning.

"What is that?" I asked anxiously, interrupting the captain, and drawing his attention to some Don Cossacks who were grouped around some one not far from us.

Among them was heard something like the weeping of a child, and the words,—

"Eh! don't cut—hold on—you will be seen—here's a knife—give him the knife."

"They are up to some mischief, the brutes," said the captain indifferently.

But at this very instant, suddenly from around the corner came the handsome ensign with burning, horror-stricken face, and waving his hands rushed among the Cossacks.

"Don't you move! don't kill him!" he cried in his boyish treble.

When the Cossacks saw the officer they started back, and allowed a little white goat to escape from their hands. The young ensign was wholly taken aback, began to mutter something, and stood before them full of confusion. When he caught sight of the captain and me on the roof, he grew still redder in the face, and springing up the steps joined us.

"I thought they were going to kill a child," he said with a timid smile.

X.

The general had gone on ahead with the cavalry. The battalion with which I had come from Fort N—— remained in the rear-guard. The companies under command of Captain Khlopof and Lieutenant Rosenkranz were retreating together.

The captain's prediction was fully justified: as soon as we had reached the narrow forest of which he had spoken, from both sides the mountaineers, mounted and on foot, began to show themselves incessantly, and so near that I could very distinctly see many crouching down, with muskets in their hands, and running from tree to tree.

The captain took off his hat, and piously made the sign of the cross; a few old soldiers did the same. In the forest were heard shouts, the words, *"iáï! Giaur! Urús! iáï!"*

Dry, short musket reports followed in quick succession, and

bullets whizzed from both sides. Our men silently replied with rapid fire; only occasionally in the ranks were heard exclamations in the guise of directions: "He [25] has stopped shooting there;" "He has a good chance behind the trees;" "We ought to have cannon," and such expressions.

The cannon were brought to bear on the range, and after a few discharges of grape the enemy apparently gave way; but after a little their fire became more and more violent with each step that the army took, and the shouts and war-cries increased.

We were scarcely three hundred *sazhens*[26] from the aul when the enemy's shot began to hail down upon us. I saw a ball with a thud strike one soldier dead . . . but why relate details of this terrible spectacle, when I myself would give much to forget it?

Lieutenant Rosenkranz was firing his musket without a moment's cessation; with animating voice he was shouting to the soldiers, and galloping at full speed from one end of the line to the other. He was slightly pale, and this was decidedly becoming to his martial countenance.

The handsome ensign was in his element: his beautiful eyes gleamed with resolution, his mouth was slightly parted with a smile; he was constantly riding up to the captain, and asking permission to charge.[27]

"We'll drive them back," he said impulsively,—"we'll drive them back surely."

"No need of it," replied the captain gently: "we must get out of here."

The captain's company occupied the edge of the forest, and was fully exposed to the enemy's fire. The captain in his well-worn coat and tattered cap, slackening the reins for his white trotter and clinging by his short stirrups, silently staid in one place. (The soldiers were so well trained, and did their work so accurately, that there was no need of giving commands to them.) Only now

[25] *On*—he—the collective expression by which the soldiers in the Caucasus indicate the enemy.—AUTHOR'S NOTE.
[26] 2,100 feet.
[27] *brosítsa na urá*—to rush with a hurrah!

and then he raised his voice, and shouted to those who exposed their heads. The captain's face was very far from martial; but such truth and simplicity were manifest in it, that it impressed me profoundly.

"There is some one who is truly brave," I said to myself involuntarily.

He was almost exactly the same as I had always seen him; the same tranquil motions, the same even voice, the same expression of frankness on his homely but honest face; but by his more than ordinarily keen glance it was possible to recognize him as a man who infallibly knew his business. It is easy to say *the same as always;* but how different were the traits brought out in others! one tried to seem calmer, another rougher, a third gayer, than usual; but by the captain's face it was manifest that he did not even understand *how to seem.*

The Frenchman who at Waterloo said, *La garde meurt, mais ne se rend pas,* and other heroes, especially among the French, who have uttered notable sayings, were brave, and really uttered notable sayings; but between their bravery, and the bravery of the captain, is this difference, that if a great saying in regard to any subject came into my hero's mind, I believe that he would not have uttered it; in the first place, because he would have feared that in saying something great he might spoil a great deed, and, secondly, because when a man is conscious within himself of the power to do a great deed, there is no need of saying any thing at all. This, in my opinion, is the especial and lofty character of Russian bravery; and how, henceforth, can it fail to wound the Russian heart when among our young warriors one hears French platitudes which have their vogue because they were the stock phrases of the old French nobility? . . .

Suddenly, from the direction in which the handsome ensign with his division was stationed, was heard a faint hurrah from the enemy. Turning round at this shouting I saw thirty soldiers who with muskets in their hands and knapsacks on their shoulders were going at double-quick across the ploughed field. They stumbled, but still pushed ahead and shouted. Leading them galloped the young ensign, waving his sabre.

All were lost to sight in the forest.

At the end of a few moments of shouting and clash of arms, a frightened horse came dashing out of the woods, and just at the edge soldiers were seen bearing the killed and wounded. Among the latter was the young ensign. Two soldiers carried him in their arms. He was pale as a sheet, and his graceful head, where could be now detected only the shadow of that martial enthusiasm which inspired him but a moment before, was strangely drawn down between his shoulders and rested on his breast. On his white shirt under his coat, which was torn open, could be seen a small blood-stain.

"Akh! what a pity!" I said in spite of myself, as I turned away from this heart-rending spectacle.

"Indeed it's too bad," said an old soldier who with gloomy face stood beside me leaning on his musket. "He wasn't afraid of any thing! How is this possible?" he added, looking steadily at the wounded lad. "Always foolish! and now he has to pay for it!"

"And aren't you afraid?" I asked.

"No, indeed!"

XI.

Four soldiers bore the ensign on a litter; behind them followed a soldier from the suburb, leading a lean, foundered horse laden with two green chests in which were the surgeon's implements. They were expecting the doctor. The officers hurried up to the litter, and tried to encourage and comfort the wounded lad.

"Well, brother Alánin, it'll be some time before you dance and make merry again," said Lieutenant Rosenkranz coming up with a smile.

He probably intended these words to sustain the handsome ensign's courage; but as could be easily seen from the coldly mournful expression in the eyes of the latter, these words did not produce the wished-for effect.

The captain also came up. He gazed earnestly at the wound-

ed young fellow, and his always cold, calm face expressed heartfelt pity.

"How is it, my dear Anatoli Ivánuitch?" said he in a tone
which rang with a deeper sympathy than I had expected from him:
"we see it's as God wills."

The wounded lad looked up; his pale face was lighted with
a mournful smile.

"Yes, I disobeyed you."

"Say rather, it was God's will," replied the captain.

The doctor, who had now arrived, took from his chest, bandages, probes, and other instruments, and, rolling up his sleeves
with a re-assuring smile, approached the sufferer.

"So it seems they have been making a little hole through
you," he said in a tone of jesting unconcern. "Let us have a look
at the place."

The ensign listened, but in the gaze which he fixed on the
jolly doctor were expressed surprise and reproachfulness which
the latter did not expect. He began to probe the wound and
examine it from all sides; but at last the sufferer, losing his patience, pushed away his hand with a heavy groan.

"Let me be," he said in an almost inaudible voice: "it makes
no difference; I am dying." With these words he fell on his back;
and five minutes later when I joined the group gathered about
him, and asked a soldier, "How is the ensign?" I was told, *"He
has gone."*

XII.

It was late when the expedition, deploying in a broad column, entered the fortress with songs. The sun had set behind the
snow-covered mountain crest, and was throwing its last rosy rays
on the long delicate clouds which stretched across the bright
pellucid western sky. The snow-capped mountains began to
clothe themselves in purple mist; only their upper outlines were
marked with extraordinary distinctness against the violet light of

the sunset. The clear moon, which had long been up, began to shed its light through the dark blue sky. The green of the grass and of the trees changed to black, and grew wet with dew. The dark masses of the army, with gradually increasing tumult, advanced across the field; from different sides were heard the sounds of cymbals, drums, and merry songs. The leader of the sixth company sang out with full strength, and full of feeling and power the clear chest-notes of the tenor were borne afar through the translucent evening air.

AN OLD ACQUAINTANCE.

PRINCE NEKHILUDOF RELATES HOW, DURING AN EXPEDITION IN THE CAUCASUS, HE MET AN ACQUAINTANCE FROM MOSCOW.

Our division had been out in the field.

The work in hand was accomplished: we had cut a way through the forest, and each day we were expecting from headquarters orders for our return to the fort. Our division of field-pieces was stationed at the top of a steep mountain-crest which was terminated by the swift mountain river Mechík, and had to command the plain that stretched before us. Here and there on this picturesque plain, out of the reach of gunshot, now and then, especially at evening, groups of mounted mountaineers showed themselves, attracted by curiosity to ride up and view the Russian camp.

The evening was clear, mild, and fresh, as it is apt to be in December in the Caucasus; the sun was setting behind the steep chain of the mountains at the left, and threw rosy rays upon the tents scattered over the slope, upon the soldiers moving about, and upon our two guns, which seemed to crane their necks as they rested motionless on the earthwork two paces from us. The infantry picket, stationed on the knoll at the left, stood in perfect silhouette against the light of the sunset; no less distinct were the stacks of muskets, the form of the sentry, the groups of soldiers, and the smoke of the smouldering camp-fire.

At the right and left of the slope, on the black, sodden earth, the tents gleamed white; and behind the tents, black stood the bare trunks of the platane forest, which rang with the incessant sound of axes, the crackling of the bonfires, and the crashing of the trees as they fell under the axes. The bluish smoke arose from tobacco-pipes on all sides, and vanished in the transparent blue of the frosty sky. By the tents and on the lower ground around the arms rushed the Cossacks, dragoons, and artillerists, with great galloping and snorting of horses as they returned from getting water. It began to freeze; all sounds were heard with extraordinary distinctness, and one could see an immense distance across the plain through the clear, rare atmosphere. The groups of the enemy, their curiosity at seeing the soldiers satisfied, quietly galloped off across the fields, still yellow with the golden corn-stubble, toward their *auls* or villages, which were visible beyond the forest, with the tall posts of the cemeteries and the smoke rising in the air.

Our tent was pitched not far from the guns on a place high and dry, from which we had a remarkably extended view. Near the tent, on a cleared space, around the battery itself, we had our games of skittles, or *chushki*. The obliging soldiers had made for us rustic benches and tables. On account of all these amusements, the artillery officers, our comrades, and a few infantry men liked to gather of an evening around our battery, and the place came to be called the club.

As the evening was fine, the best players had come, and we were amusing ourselves with skittles. Ensign D., Lieutenant O., and myself had played two games in succession; and to the common satisfaction and amusement of all the spectators, officers, soldiers, and servants who were watching us from their tents, we had twice carried the winning party on our backs from one end of the ground to the other. Especially droll was the situation of the huge fat Captain S., who, puffing and smiling good-naturedly, with legs dragging on the ground, rode pickapack on the feeble little Lieutenant O.

When it grew somewhat later, the servants brought three glasses of tea for the six men of us, and not a spoon; and we who had finished our game came to the plaited settees.

There was standing near them a small bow-legged man, a stranger to us, in a sheepskin jacket, and a *papákha,* or Circassian cap, with long overhanging white crown. As soon as we came near where he stood, he took a few irresolute steps, and put on his cap; and several times he seemed to make up his mind to come to meet us, and then stopped again. But after deciding, probably, that it was impossible to remain irresolute, the stranger took off his cap, and, going in a circuit around us, approached Captain S.

"Ah, Guskantini, how is it, old man?" said S., still smiling good-naturedly, under the influence of his ride.

Guskantini, as S. called him, instantly replaced his cap, and made a motion as though to thrust his hands into the pockets of his jacket; but on the side toward me there was no pocket in the jacket, and his small red hand fell into an awkward position. I felt a strong desire to make out who this man was (was he a yunker, or a degraded officer?) and, not realizing that my gaze (that is, the gaze of a strange officer) disconcerted him, I continued to stare at his dress and appearance.

I judged that he was about thirty. His small, round, gray eyes had a sleepy expression, and at the same time gazed calmly out from under the dirty white lambskin of his cap, which hung down over his face. His thick, irregular nose, standing out between his sunken cheeks, gave evidence of emaciation that was the result of illness, and not natural. His restless lips, barely covered by a sparse, soft, whitish mustache, were constantly changing their shape, as though they were trying to assume now one expression, now another. But all these expressions seemed to be endless, and his face retained one predominating expression of timidity and fright. Around his thin neck, where the veins stood out, was tied a green woollen scarf tucked into his jacket. His fur jacket, or *polushúbok,* was worn bare, short, and had dog-fur sewed on the collar and on the false pockets. The trousers were checkered, of ash-gray color, and his *sapogi* had short, unblacked military boot-legs.

"I beg of you, do not disturb yourself," said I when he for the second time, timidly glancing at me, had taken off his cap.

He bowed to me with an expression of gratitude, replaced his hat, and, drawing from his pocket a dirty chintz tobacco-pouch with lacings, began to roll a cigarette.

I myself had not been long a yunker, an elderly yunker; and as I was incapable, as yet, of being good-naturedly serviceable to my younger comrades, and without means, I well knew all the moral difficulties of this situation for a proud man no longer young, and I sympathized with all men who found themselves in such a situation, and I endeavored to make clear to myself their character and rank, and the tendencies of their intellectual peculiarities, in order to judge of the degree of their moral sufferings. This yunker or degraded officer, judging by his restless eyes and that intentionally constant variation of expression which I noticed in him, was a man very far from stupid, and extremely egotistical, and therefore much to be pitied.

Captain S. invited us to play another game of skittles, with the stakes to consist, not only of the usual pickapack ride of the winning party, but also of a few bottles of red wine, rum, sugar, cinnamon, and cloves for the mulled wine which that winter, on account of the cold, was greatly popular in our division.

Guskantini, as S. again called him, was also invited to take part; but before the game began, the man, struggling between gratification because he had been invited and a certain timidity, drew Captain S. aside, and began to say something in a whisper. The good-natured captain punched him in the ribs with his big, fat hand, and replied, loud enough to be heard,—

"Not at all, old fellow,[1] I assure you."

When the game was over, and that side in which the stranger whose rank was so low had taken part, had come out winners, and it fell to his lot to ride on one of our officers, Ensign D., the ensign

---

[1] *bátenka,* Malo-Russian diminutive, little father.

grew red in the face: he went to the little divan and offered the stranger a cigarette by way of a compromise.

While they were ordering the mulled wine, and in the steward's tent were heard assiduous preparations on the part of Nikíta, who had sent an orderly for cinnamon and cloves, and the shadow of his back was alternately lengthening and shortening on the dingy sides of the tent, we men, seven in all, sat around on the benches; and while we took turns in drinking tea from the three glasses, and gazed out over the plain, which was now beginning to glow in the twilight, we talked and laughed over the various incidents of the game.

The stranger in the fur jacket took no share in the conversation, obstinately refused to drink the tea which I several times offered him, and as he sat there on the ground in Tatar fashion, occupied himself in making cigarettes of fine-cut tobacco, and smoking them one after another, evidently not so much for his own satisfaction as to give himself the appearance of a man with something to do. When it was remarked that the summons to return was expected on the morrow, and that there might be an engagement, he lifted himself on his knees, and, addressing Captain B. only, said that he had been at the adjutant's, and had himself written the order for the return on the next day. We all said nothing while he was speaking; and notwithstanding the fact that he was so bashful, we begged him to repeat this most interesting piece of news. He repeated what he had said, adding only that he had been staying at the adjutant's (since he made it his home there) when the order came.

"Look here, old fellow, if you are not telling us false, I shall have to go to my company and give some orders for to-morrow," said Captain S.

"No . . . why . . . it may be, I am sure" . . . stammered the stranger, but suddenly stopped, and, apparently feeling himself affronted, contracted his brows, and, muttering something between his teeth, again began to roll a cigarette. But the fine-cut tobacco in his chintz pouch began to show signs of giving out, and he asked S. to lend him a little cigarette.[2]

We kept on for a considerable time with that monotonous military chatter which every one who has ever been on an expedition will appreciate; all of us, with one and the same expression, complaining of the dullness and length of the expedition, in one and the same fashion sitting in judgment on our superiors, and all of us likewise, as we had done many times before, praising one comrade, pitying another, wondering how much this one had gained, how much that one had lost, and so on, and so on.

"Here, fellows, this adjutant of ours is completely broken up," said Captain S. "At headquarters he was everlastingly on the winning side; no matter whom he sat down with, he'd rake in every thing: but now for two months past he has been losing all the time. The present expedition hasn't been lucky for him. I think he has got away with two thousand silver rubles and five hundred rubles' worth of articles,—the carpet that he won at Mukhin's, Nikitin's pistols, Sada's gold watch which Vorontsof gave him. He has lost it all."

"The truth of the matter in his case," said Lieutenant O., "was that he used to cheat everybody; it was impossible to play with him."

"He cheated every one, but now it's all gone up in his pipe;" and here Captain S. laughed good-naturedly. "Our friend Guskof here lives with him. He hasn't quite lost *him* yet: that's so, isn't it, old fellow?" he asked, addressing Guskof.

Guskof tried to laugh. It was a melancholy, sickly laugh, which completely changed the expression of his countenance. Till this moment it had seemed to me that I had seen and known this man before; and, besides, the name Guskof, by which Captain S. called him, was familiar to me; but how and when I had seen and known him, I actually could not remember.

"Yes," said Guskof, incessantly putting his hand to his mustaches, but instantly dropping it again without touching them. "Pavel Dmitriévitch's luck has been against him in this expedi-

---

[2] *papirósotchka*, diminished diminutive of *papiróska*, from *papiros*.

tion, such a *veine de malheur,*" he added in a careful but pure French pronunciation, again giving me to think that I had seen him, and seen him often, somewhere. "I know Pavel Dmitriévitch very well. He has great confidence in me," he proceeded to say; "he and I are old friends; that is, he is fond of me," he explained, evidently fearing that it might be taken as presumption for him to claim old friendship with the adjutant. "Pavel Dmitriévitch plays admirably; but now, strange as it may seem, it's all up with him, he is just about perfectly ruined; *la chance a tourné,*" he added, addressing himself particularly to me.

At first we had listened to Guskof with condescending attention; but as soon as he made use of that second French phrase, we all involuntarily turned from him.

"I have played with him a thousand times, and we agreed then that it was strange," said Lieutenant O., with peculiar emphasis on the word *strange.*[3] "I never once won a ruble from him. Why was it, when I used to win of others?"

"Pavel Dimitriévitch plays admirably: I have known him for a long time," said I. In fact, I had known the adjutant for several years; more than once I had seen him in the full swing of a game, surrounded by officers, and I had remarked his handsome, rather gloomy and always passionless calm face, his deliberate Malo-Russian pronunciation, his handsome belongings and horses, his bold, manly figure, and above all his skill and self-restraint in carrying on the game accurately and agreeably. More than once, I am sorry to say, as I looked at his plump white hands with a diamond ring on the index-finger, passing out one card after another, I grew angry with that ring, with his white hands, with the whole of the adjutant's person, and evil thoughts on his account arose in my mind. But as I afterwards reconsidered the matter coolly, I persuaded myself that he played more skilfully than all with whom he happened to play: the more so, because as I heard his general observations concerning the game,—how one ought not to back out when one had laid the smallest stake, how one ought not to leave off in certain cases as the first rule for

---

[3] *stránno.*

honest men, and so forth, and so forth,—it was evident that he was always on the winning side merely from the fact that he played more sagaciously and coolly than the rest of us. And now it seemed that this self-reliant, careful player had been stripped not only of his money but of his effects, which marks the lowest depths of loss for an officer.

"He always had devilish good luck with me," said Lieutenant O. "I made a vow never to play with him again."

"What a marvel you are, old fellow!" said S., nodding at me, and addressing O. "You lost three hundred silver rubles, that's what you lost to him."

"More than that," said the lieutenant savagely.

"And now you have come to your senses; it is rather late in the day, old man, for the rest of us have known for a long time that he was the cheat of the regiment," said S., with difficulty restraining his laughter, and feeling very well satisfied with his fabrication. "Here is Guskof right here,—he *fixes* his cards for him. That's the reason of the friendship between them, old man"[4] ... and Captain S., shaking all over, burst out into such a hearty "ha, ha, ha!" that he spilt the glass of mulled wine which he was holding in his hand. On Guskof's pale emaciated face there showed something like a color; he opened his mouth several times, raised his hands to his mustaches and once more dropped them to his side where the pockets should have been, stood up, and then sat down again, and finally in an unnatural voice said to S.,—

"It's no joke, Nikolai Ivánovitch, for you to say such things before people who don't know me and who see me in this unlined jacket ... because"— His voice failed him, and again his small red hands with their dirty nails went from his jacket to his face, touching his mustache, his hair, his nose, rubbing his eyes, or needlessly scratching his cheek.

"As to saying that, everybody knows it, old fellow," continued S., thoroughly satisfied with his jest, and not heeding Guskof's complaint. Guskof was still trying to say something; and

---

4 *bátenka moi.*

placing the palm of his right hand on his left knee in a most unnatural position, and gazing at S., he had an appearance of smiling contemptuously.

"No," said I to myself, as I noticed that smile of his, "I have not only seen him, but have spoken with him somewhere."

"You and I have met somewhere," said I to him when, under the influence of the common silence, S.'s laughter began to calm down. Guskof's mobile face suddenly lighted up, and his eyes, for the first time with a truly joyous expression, rested upon me.

"Why, I recognized you immediately," he replied in French. "In '48 I had the pleasure of meeting you quite frequently in Moscow at my sister's."

I had to apologize for not recognizing him at first in that costume and in that new garb. He arose, came to me, and with his moist hand irresolutely and weakly seized my hand, and sat down by me. Instead of looking at me, though he apparently seemed so glad to see me, he gazed with an expression of unfriendly bravado at the officers.

Either because I recognized in him a man whom I had met a few years before in a dress-coat in a parlor, or because he was suddenly raised in his own opinion by the fact of being recognized,—at all events it seemed to me that his face and even his motions completely changed: they now expressed lively intelligence, a childish self-satisfaction in the consciousness of such intelligence, and a certain contemptuous indifference; so that I confess, notwithstanding the pitiable position in which he found himself, my old acquaintance did not so much excite sympathy in me as it did a sort of unfavorable sentiment.

I now vividly remembered our first meeting. In 1848, while I was staying at Moscow, I frequently went to the house of Ivá-shin, who from childhood had been an old friend of mine. His wife was an agreeable hostess, a charming woman, as everybody said; but she never pleased me. . . . The winter that I knew her, she often spoke with hardly concealed pride of her brother, who had shortly before completed his course, and promised to be one of the most fashionable and popular young men in the best society of Petersburg. As I knew by reputation the father of the Guskofs, who was very rich and had a distinguished position, and as I knew also the sister's ways, I felt some prejudice against meeting the young man. One evening when I was at Iváshin's, I saw a short, thoroughly pleasant-looking young man, in a black coat, white vest and necktie. My host hastened to make me acquainted with him. The young man, evidently dressed for a ball, with his cap in his hand, was standing before Iváshin, and was eagerly but politely arguing with him about a common friend of ours, who had distinguished himself at the time of the Hungarian campaign. He said that this acquaintance was not at all a hero or a man born for war, as was said of him, but was simply a clever and cultivated man. I recollect, I took part in the argument against Guskof, and went to the extreme of declaring also that intellect and cultivation always bore an inverse relation to bravery; and I recollect how Guskof pleasantly and cleverly pointed out to me that bravery was necessarily the result of intellect and a decided degree of development,—a statement which I, who considered myself an intellectual and cultivated man, could not in my heart of hearts agree with.

I recollect that towards the close of our conversation Madame Iváshina introduced me to her brother; and he, with a condescending smile, offered me his little hand on which he had not yet had time to draw his kid gloves, and weakly and irresolutely pressed my hand as he did now. Though I had been prejudiced against Guskof, I could not help granting that he was in the right, and agreeing with his sister that he was really a clever and agreeable young man, who ought to have great success in society. He was extraordinarily neat, beautifully dressed, and fresh, and had affectedly modest manners, and a thoroughly youthful, almost childish appearance, on account of which, you could not help excusing his expression of self-sufficiency, though it modified the impression of his high-mightiness caused by his intellectual face and especially his smile. It was said that he had great success that winter with the high-born ladies of Moscow. As I saw him at his sister's I could only infer how far this was true by the feeling of pleasure and contentment constantly excited in me by his youthful appearance and by his sometimes indiscreet anecdotes. He and I met half a dozen times, and talked a good deal; or, rather, he talked a good deal, and I listened. He spoke for the most part in French, always with a good accent, very fluently and ornately; and he had the skill of drawing others gently and politely into the conversation. As a general thing, he behaved toward all, and toward me, in a somewhat supercilious manner, and I felt that he was perfectly right in this way of treating people. I always feel that way in regard to men who are firmly convinced that they ought to treat me superciliously, and who are comparative strangers to me.

Now, as he sat with me, and gave me his hand, I keenly recalled in him that same old haughtiness of expression; and it seemed to me that he did not properly appreciate his position of official inferiority, as, in the presence of the officers, he asked me what I had been doing in all that time, and how I happened to be there. In spite of the fact that I invariably made my replies in Russian, he kept putting his questions in French, expressing himself as before in remarkably correct language. About himself he said fluently that after his unhappy, wretched story (what the story was, I did not know, and he had not yet told me), he had been three months under arrest, and then had been sent to the Caucasus to the N. regiment, and now had been serving three years as a soldier in that regiment.

"You would not believe," said he to me in French,[5] "how much I have to suffer in these regiments from the society of the officers. Still it is a pleasure to me, that I used to know the adjutant of whom we were just speaking: he is a good man—it's a fact," he remarked condescendingly. "I live with him, and that's something of a relief for me. Yes, my dear, the days fly by, but they aren't all alike," he added; and suddenly hesitated, reddened, and stood up, as he caught sight of the adjutant himself coming toward us.

"It is such a pleasure to meet such a man as you," said Guskof to me in a whisper as he turned from me. "I should like very, very much, to have a long talk with you."

I said that I should be very happy to talk with him, but in

[5] *Oui, mon cher, les jours se suivent, mais ne se ressemblent pas:* in French in the original.

reality I confess that Guskof excited in me a sort of dull pity that was not akin to sympathy.

I had a presentiment that I should feel a constraint in a private conversation with him; but still I was anxious to learn from him several things, and, above all, why it was, when his father had been so rich, that he was in poverty, as was evident by his dress and appearance.

The adjutant greeted us all, including Guskof, and sat down by me in the seat which the cashiered officer had just vacated. Pavel Dmitriévitch, who had always been calm and leisurely, a genuine gambler, and a man of means, was now very different from what he had been in the flowery days of his success; he seemed to be in haste to go somewhere, kept constantly glancing at everybody, and it was not five minutes before he proposed to Lieutenant O., who had sworn off from playing, to set up a small faro-bank. Lieutenant O. refused, under the pretext of having to attend to his duties, but in reality because, as he knew that the adjutant had few possessions and little money left, he did not feel himself justified in risking his three hundred rubles against a hundred or even less which the adjutant might stake.

"Well, Pavel Dmitriévitch," said the lieutenant, anxious to avoid a repetition of the invitation, "is it true, what they tell us, that we return to-morrow?"

"I don't know," replied the adjutant. "Orders came, to be in readiness; but if it's true, then you'd better play a game. I would wager my Kabarda cloak."

"No, to-day already" . . .

"It's a gray one, never been worn; but if you prefer, play for money. How is that?"

"Yes, but . . . I should be willing—pray don't think that" . . . said Lieutenant O., answering the implied suspicion; "but as there may be a raid or some movement, I must go to bed early."

The adjutant stood up, and, thrusting his hands into his pockets, started to go across the grounds. His face assumed its ordinary expression of coldness and pride, which I admired in him.

"Won't you have a glass of mulled wine?" I asked him.

"That might be acceptable," and he came back to me; but Guskof politely took the glass from me, and handed it to the adjutant, striving at the same time not to look at him. But as he did not notice the tent-rope, he stumbled over it, and fell on his hand, dropping the glass.

"What a bungler!" exclaimed the adjutant, still holding out his hand for the glass. Everybody burst out laughing, not excepting Guskof, who was rubbing his hand on his sore knee, which he had somehow struck as he fell. "That's the way the bear waited on the hermit," continued the adjutant. "It's the way he waits on me every day. He has pulled up all the tent-pins; he's always tripping up."

Guskof, not hearing him, apologized to us, and glanced toward me with a smile of almost noticeable melancholy as though saying that I alone could understand him. He was pitiable to see; but the adjutant, his protector, seemed, on that very account, to be severe on his messmate, and did not try to put him at his ease.

"Well, you're a graceful lad! Where did you think you were going?"

"Well, who can help tripping over these pins, Pavel Dmitriévitch?" said Guskof. "You tripped over them yourself the other day."

"I, old man,[6]—I am not of the rank and file, and such gracefulness is not expected of me."

"He can be lazy," said Captain S., keeping the ball rolling, "but low-rank men have to make their legs fly."

"Ill-timed jest," said Guskof almost in a whisper, and casting down his eyes. The adjutant was evidently vexed with his messmate; he listened with inquisitive attention to every word that he said.

"He'll have to be sent out into ambuscade again," said he, addressing S., and pointing to the cashiered officer.

"Well, there'll be some more tears," said S., laughing. Guskof no longer looked at me, but acted as though he were going

6 *bâtiushka.*

to take some tobacco from his pouch, though there had been none there for some time.

"Get ready for the ambuscade, old man," said S., addressing him with shouts of laughter. "To-day the scouts have brought the news, there'll be an attack on the camp to-night, so it's necessary to designate the trusty lads." Guskof's face showed a fleeting smile as though he were preparing to make some reply, but several times he cast a supplicating look at S.

"Well, you know I have been, and I'm ready to go again if I am sent," he said hastily.

"Then you'll be sent."

"Well, I'll go. Isn't that all right?"

"Yes, as at Arguna, you deserted the ambuscade and threw away your gun," said the adjutant; and turning from him he began to tell us the orders for the next day.

As a matter of fact, we expected from the enemy a cannonade of the camp that night, and the next day some sort of diversion. While we were still chatting about various subjects of general interest, the adjutant, as though from a sudden and unexpected impulse, proposed to Lieutenant O. to have a little game. The lieutenant most unexpectedly consented; and, together with S. and the ensign, they went off to the adjutant's tent, where there was a folding green table with cards on it. The captain, the commander of our division, went to our tent to sleep; the other gentlemen also separated, and Guskof and I were left alone. I was not mistaken, it was really very uncomfortable for me to have a *tête-à-tête* with him; I arose involuntarily, and began to promenade up and down on the battery. Guskof walked in silence by my side, hastily and awkwardly wheeling around so as not to delay or incommode me.

"I do not annoy you?" he asked in a soft, mournful voice. So far as I could see his face in the dim light, it seemed to me deeply thoughtful and melancholy.

"Not at all," I replied; but as he did not immediately begin to speak, and as I did not know what to say to him, we walked in silence a considerably long time.

The twilight had now absolutely changed into dark night;

over the black profile of the mountains gleamed the bright evening heat-lightning; over our heads in the light-blue frosty sky twinkled the little stars; on all sides gleamed the ruddy flames of the smoking watch-fires; near us, the white tents stood out in contrast to the frowning blackness of our earth-works. The light from the nearest watch-fire, around which our servants, engaged in quiet conversation, were warming themselves, occasionally flashed on the brass of our heavy guns, and fell on the form of the sentry, who, wrapped in his cloak, paced with measured tread along the battery.

"You cannot imagine what a delight it is for me to talk with such a man as you are," said Guskof, although as yet he had not spoken a word to me. "Only one who had been in my position could appreciate it."

I did not know how to reply to him, and we again relapsed into silence, although it was evident that he was anxious to talk and have me listen to him.

"Why were you . . . why did you suffer this?" I inquired at last, not being able to invent any better way of breaking the ice.

"Why, didn't you hear about this wretched business from Metenin?"

"Yes, a duel, I believe; I did not hear much about it," I replied. "You see, I have been for some time in the Caucasus."

"No, it wasn't a duel, but it was a stupid and horrid story. I will tell you all about it, if you don't know. It happened, that the same year that I met you at my sister's, I was living at Petersburg. I must tell you I had then what they call *une position dans le monde,*—a position good enough if it was not brilliant. *Mon père me donnait* ten thousand *par an.* In '49 I was promised a place in the embassy at Turin; my uncle on my mother's side had influence, and was always ready to do a great deal for me. That sort of thing is all past now. *J'étais reçu dans la meilleure société de Pétersbourg;* I might have aspired to any girl in the city. I was well educated, as we all are who come from the school, but was not especially cultivated; to be sure, I read a good deal afterwards, *mais j'avais surtout,* you know, *ce jargon du monde,* and, however it came about, I was looked upon as a leading light among the young men of Petersburg. What raised me more than all in common estimation, *c'est cette liaison avec Madame D.,* about which a great deal was said in Petersburg: but I was frightfully young at that time, and did not prize these advantages very highly. I was simply young and stupid. What more did I need? Just then that Metenin had some notoriety"—

And Guskof went on in the same fashion to relate to me the history of his misfortunes, which I will omit, as it would not be at all interesting.

"Two months I remained under arrest," he continued, "absolutely alone; and what thoughts did I not have during that time? But, you know, when it was all over, as though every tie had been broken with the past, then it became easier for me. *Mon père,* —you have heard tell of him, of course, a man of iron will and strong convictions,—*il m'a désherité,* and broken off all intercourse with me. According to his convictions he had to do as he did, and I don't blame him at all. He was consistent. Consequently I have not taken a step to induce him to change his mind. My sister was abroad. Madame D. is the only one who wrote to me when I was released, and she sent me assistance; but you understand that I could not accept it, so that I had none of those little things which make one's position a little easier, you know,—books, linen, food, nothing at all. At this time I thought things over and over, and began to look at life with different eyes. For instance, this noise, this society gossip about me in Petersburg, did not interest me, did not flatter me: it all seemed to me ridiculous. I felt that I myself had been to blame; I was young and indiscreet; I had spoiled my career, and I only thought how I might get into the right track again. And I felt that I had strength and energy enough for it. After my arrest, as I told you, I was sent here to the Caucasus to the N. regiment.

"I thought," he went on to say, all the time becoming more and more animated,—"I thought that here in the Caucasus, *la vie de camp,* the simple, honest men with whom I should associate, and war and danger, would all admirably agree with my mental state, so that I might begin a new life. They will see me under fire.[7] I shall make myself liked; I shall be respected for my real self,—the cross—non-commissioned officer; they will relieve me of my fine; and I shall get up again, *et vous savez avec ce prestige du malheur!* But, *quel désenchantement!* You can't imagine how I have been deceived! You know what sort of men the officers of our regiment are."

He did not speak for some little time, waiting, as it appeared, for me to tell him that I knew the society of our officers here was bad; but I made him no reply. It went against my grain that he should expect me, because I knew French, forsooth, to be obliged to take issue with the society of the officers, which, during my long residence in the Caucasus, I had had time enough to appreciate fully, and for which I had far higher respect than for the society from which Mr. Guskof had sprung. I wanted to tell him so, but his position constrained me.

"In the N. regiment the society of the officers is a thousand times worse than it is here," he continued. "I hope that it is saying a good deal; *j'espère que c'est beaucoup dire;* that is, you cannot imagine what it is. I am not speaking of the yunkers and the soldiers, That is horrible, it is so bad. At first they received me very kindly, that is absolutely the truth; but when they saw that I could not help despising them, you know, in these inconceivably small circumstances, they saw that I was a man absolutely different, standing far above them, they got angry with me, and began to put various little humiliations on me. You haven't an idea what I had to suffer.[8] Then this forced relationship with the yunkers, and especially with the small means that I had—I lacked every thing;[9] I had only what my sister used to send me. And here's a proof for you! As much as it made me suffer, I with my character, *avec ma fierté, j'ai écris à mon père,* begged him to send me something. I understand how living four years of such a life may make a man like our cashiered Dromof who drinks with soldiers, and writes notes to all the officers asking them to *loan* him three

---

[7] *On me verra au feu.*
[8] *Ce que j'ai eu à souffrir vous ne vous faites pas une idée.*
[9] *Avec les petits moyens que j'avais, je manquais de tout.*

rubles, and signing it, *tout à vous, Dromof.* One must have such a character as I have, not to be mired in the least by such a horrible position."

For some time he walked in silence by my side.

"Have you a cigarette?"[10] he asked me.

"And so I staid right where I was? Yes. I could not endure it physically, because, though we were wretched, cold, and ill-fed, I lived like a common soldier, but still the officers had some sort of consideration for me. I had still some *prestige* that they regarded. I wasn't sent out on guard nor for drill. I could not have stood that. But morally my sufferings were frightful; and especially because I didn't see any escape from my position. I wrote my uncle, begged him to get me transferred to my present regiment, which, at least, sees some service; and I thought that here Pavel Dmitriévitch, *qui est le fils de l'intendant de mon père,* might be of some use to me. My uncle did this for me; I was transferred. After that regiment this one seemed to me a collection of chamberlains. Then Pavel Dmitriévitch was here; he knew who I was, and I was splendidly received. At my uncle's request—a Guskof, *vous savez;* but I forgot that with these men without cultivation and undeveloped,—they can't appreciate a man, and show him marks of esteem, unless he has that aureole of wealth, of friends; and I noticed how, little by little, when they saw that I was poor, their behavior to me showed more and more indifference until they have come almost to despise me. It is horrible, but it is absolutely the truth.

"Here I have been in action, I have fought, they have seen me under fire,"[11] he continued; "but when will it all end? I think, never. And my strength and energy have already begun to flag. Then I had imagined *la guerre, la vie de camp;* but it isn't at all what I see, in a sheepskin jacket, dirty linen, soldier's boots, and you go out in ambuscade, and the whole night long lie in the ditch with some Antónof reduced to the ranks for drunkenness, and any minute from behind the bush may come a rifle-shot and hit you

---

[10] *"Avez-vous un papiros?"*
[11] *On m'a vu au feu.*

or Antónof,—it's all the same which. That is not bravery: it's horrible, *c'est affreux,* it's killing!"[12]

"Well, you can be promoted a non-commissioned officer for this campaign, and next year an ensign," said I.

"Yes, it may be: they promised me that in two years, and it's not up yet. What would those two years amount to, if I knew any one! You can imagine this life with Pavel Dmitriévitch; cards, low jokes, drinking all the time; if you wish to tell any thing that is weighing on your mind, you would not be understood, or you would be laughed at; they talk with you, not for the sake of sharing a thought, but to get something funny out of you. Yes, and so it has gone—in a brutal, beastly way, and you are always conscious that you belong to the rank and file; they always make you feel that. Hence you can't realize what an enjoyment it is to talk *à coeur ouvert* to such a man as you are."

I had never imagined what kind of a man I was, and consequently I did not know what answer to make him.

"Will you have your lunch now?" asked Nikíta at this juncture, approaching me unseen in the darkness, and, as I could perceive, vexed at the presence of a guest. "Nothing but curd dumplings, there's none of the roast beef left."

"Has the captain had his lunch yet?"

"He went to bed long ago," replied Nikíta gruffly. "According to my directions, I was to bring you lunch here and your brandy." He muttered something else discontentedly, and sauntered off to his tent. After loitering a while longer, he brought us, nevertheless, a lunch-case; he placed a candle on the lunch-case, and shielded it from the wind with a sheet of paper. He brought a saucepan, some mustard in a jar, a tin dipper with a handle, and a bottle of absinthe. After arranging these things, Nikíta lingered around us for some moments, and looked on as Guskof and I were drinking the liquor, and it was evidently very distasteful to him. By the feeble light shed by the candle through the paper, amid the encircling darkness, could be seen the seal-skin cover of the lunch-case, the supper arranged upon it, Gu-

[12] *Ça tue.*

skof's sheepskin jacket, his face, and his small red hands which he used in lifting the patties from the pan. Every thing around us was black; and only by straining the sight could be seen the dark battery, the dark form of the sentry moving along the breastwork, on all sides the watch-fires, and on high the ruddy stars.

Guskof wore a melancholy, almost guilty smile, as though it were awkward for him to look into my face after his confession. He drank still another glass of liquor, and ate ravenously, emptying the saucepan.

"Yes; for you it must be a relief all the same," said I, for the sake of saying something,—"your acquaintance with the adjutant. He is a very good man, I have heard."

"Yes," replied the cashiered officer, "he is a kind man; but he can't help being what he is, with his education, and it is useless to expect it."

A flush seemed suddenly to cross his face. "You remarked his coarse jest this evening about the ambuscade;" and Guskof, though I tried several times to interrupt him, began to justify himself before me, and to show that he had not run away from the ambuscade, and that he was not a coward as the adjutant and Capt. S. tried to make him out.

"As I was telling you," he went on to say, wiping his hands on his jacket, "such people can't show any delicacy toward a man, a common soldier, who hasn't much money either. That's beyond their strength. And here recently, while I haven't received any thing at all from my sister, I have been conscious that they have changed toward me. This sheepskin jacket, which I bought of a soldier, and which hasn't any warmth in it, because it's all worn off " (and here he showed me where the wool was gone from the inside), "it doesn't arouse in him any sympathy or consideration for my unhappiness, but scorn, which he does not take pains to hide. Whatever my necessities may be, as now when I have nothing to eat except soldiers' gruel, and nothing to wear," he continued, casting down his eyes, and pouring out for himself still another glass of liquor, "he does not even offer to lend me some money, though he knows perfectly well that I would give it back to him; but he waits till I am obliged to ask him for it. But you appreciate how it is for me to go to *him*. In your case I should say, square and fair, *Vous êtes au dessus de cela, mon cher, je n'ai pas le sou*. And you know," said he, looking straight into my eyes with an expression of desperation, "I am going to tell you, square and fair, I am in a terrible situation: *pouvez-vous me prêter dix rubles argent?* My sister ought to send me some by the next mail, *et mon père*"—

"Why, most willingly," said I, although, on the contrary, it was trying and unpleasant, especially because the evening before, having lost at cards, I had left only about five rubles in Nikíta's care. "In a moment," said I, arising, "I will go and get it at the tent."

"No, by and by: *ne vous dérangez pas*."

Nevertheless, not heeding him, I hastened to the closed tent, where stood my bed, and where the captain was sleeping.

"Alekséi Ivánuitch, let me have ten rubles, please, for rations," said I to the captain, shaking him.

"What! have you been losing again? But this very evening, you were not going to play any more," murmured the captain, still half asleep.

"No, I have not been playing; but I want the money; let me have it, please."

"Makatiuk!" shouted the captain to his servant, "hand me my bag with the money."

"Hush, hush!" said I, hearing Guskof's measured steps near the tent.

"What? Why hush?"

"Because that cashiered fellow has asked to borrow it of me. He's right there."

"Well, if you knew him, you wouldn't let him have it," remarked the captain. "I have heard about him. He's a dirty, low-lived fellow."

Nevertheless, the captain gave me the money, ordered his man to put away the bag, pulled the flap of the tent neatly to, and, again saying, "If you only knew him, you wouldn't let him have it," drew his head down under the coverlet. "Now you owe me thirty-two, remember," he shouted after me.

When I came out of the tent, Guskof was walking near the settees; and his slight figure, with his crooked legs, his shapeless cap, his long white hair, kept appearing and disappearing in the darkness, as he passed in and out of the light of the candles. He made believe not to see me.

I handed him the money. He said *"Merci,"* and, crumpling the bank-bill, thrust it into his trousers pocket.

"Now I suppose the game is in full swing at the adjutant's," he began immediately after this.

"Yes, I suppose so."

"He's a wonderful player, always bold, and never backs out. When he's in luck, it's fine; but when it does not go well with him, he can lose frightfully. He has given proof of that. During this expedition, if you reckon his valuables, he has lost more than fifteen hundred rubles. But, as he played discreetly before, that officer of yours seemed to have some doubts about his honor."

"Well, that's because he . . . Nikíta, haven't we any of that red Kavkas wine[13] left?" I asked, very much enlivened by Guskof's conversational talent. Nikíta still kept muttering; but he brought us the red wine, and again looked on angrily as Guskof drained his glass. In Guskof's behavior was noticeable his old freedom from constraint. I wished that he would go as soon as possible; it seemed as if his only reason for not going was because he did not wish to go immediately after receiving the money. I said nothing.

"How could you, who have means, and were under no necessity, simply *de gaiété de coeur,* make up your mind to come and serve in the Caucasus? That's what I don't understand," said he to me.

I endeavored to explain this act of renunciation, which seemed so strange to him.

"I can imagine how disagreeable the society of these officers —men without any comprehension of culture—must be for you. You could not understand each other. You see, you might live

---

[13] *chikír.*

ten years, and not see any thing, and not hear about any thing, except cards, wine, and gossip about rewards and campaigns."

It was unpleasant for me, that he wished me to put myself on a par with him in his position; and, with absolute honesty, I assured him that I was very fond of cards and wine, and gossip about campaigns, and that I did not care to have any better comrades than those with whom I was associated. But he would not believe me.

"Well, you may say so," he continued; "but the lack of women's society,—I mean, of course, *femmes comme il faut,*—is that not a terrible deprivation? I don't know what I would give now to go into a parlor, if only for a moment, and to have a look at a pretty woman, even though it were through a crack."

He said nothing for a little, and drank still another glass of the red wine.

"Oh, my God, my God![14] If it only might be our fate to meet again, somewhere in Petersburg, to live and move among men, among ladies!"

He drank up the dregs of the wine still left in the bottle, and when he had finished it he said, "*Akh! pardon,* maybe you wanted some more. It was horribly careless of me. However, I suppose I must have taken too much, and my head isn't very strong.[15] There was a time when I lived on Morskaïa Street, *au rez-de-chaussée,* and had marvellous apartments, furniture, you know, and I was able to arrange it all beautifully, not so very expensively though; my father, to be sure, gave me porcelains, flowers, and silver,—a wonderful lot. *Le matin je sortais,* visits, *à 5 heures régulièrement.* I used to go and dine with *her;* often she was alone. *Il faut avouer que c'était une femme ravissante!* You didn't know her at all, did you?"

"No."

"You see, there was such a high degree of womanliness in her, and such tenderness, and what love! Lord! I did not know how to appreciate my happiness then. We would return after the

[14] *Akh, Bozhe moi, Bozhe moi!*
[15] *Et je n'ai pas la tête forte.*

theatre, and have a little supper together. It was never dull where she was, *toujours gaie, toujours aimante.* Yes, and I had never imagined what rare happiness it was. *Et j'ai beaucoup à me reprocher* in regard to her. *Je l'ai fait souffrir et souvent.* I was outrageous. *Akh!* What a marvellous time that was! Do I bore you?"

"No, not at all."

"Then I will tell you about our evenings. I used to go—that stairway, every flower-pot I knew,—the door-handle, all was so lovely, so familiar; then the vestibule, her room . . . No, it will never, never come back to me again! Even now she writes to me: if you will let me, I will show you her letters. But I am not what I was; I am ruined; I am no longer worthy of her. . . . Yes, I am ruined forever. *Je suis cassé.* There's no energy in me, no pride, nothing—nor even any rank.[16] . . . Yes, I am ruined; and no one will ever appreciate my sufferings. Every one is indifferent. I am a lost man. Never any chance for me to rise, because I have fallen morally . . . into the mire—I have fallen." . . .

At this moment there was evident in his words a genuine, deep despair: he did not look at me, but sat motionless.

"Why are you in such despair?" I asked.

"Because I am abominable. This life has degraded me, all that was in me, all is crushed out. It is not by pride that I hold out, but by abjectness: there's no *dignité dans le malheur.* I am humiliated every moment; I endure it all; I got myself into this abasement. This mire has soiled me. I myself have become coarse; I have forgotten what I used to know; I can't speak French any more; I am conscious that I am base and low. I cannot tear myself away from these surroundings, indeed I cannot. I might have been a hero: give me a regiment, gold epaulets, a trumpeter, but to march in the ranks with some wild Anton Bondarenko or the like, and feel that between me and him there was no difference at all—that he might be killed or I might be killed—all the same, that thought is maddening. You understand how horrible it is to think that some ragamuffin may kill me, a man who has thoughts

---

[16] *blagorodstva,* noble birth, nobility.

and feelings, and that it would make no difference if alongside of me some Antónof were killed,—a being not different from an animal—and that it might easily happen that I and not this Antónof were killed, which is always *une fatalité* for every lofty and good man. I know that they call me a coward: grant that I am a coward, I certainly am a coward, and can't be any thing else. Not only am I a coward, but I am in my way a low and despicable man. Here I have just been borrowing money of you, and you have the right to despise me. No, take back your money." And he held out to me the crumpled bank-bill. "I want you to have a good opinion of me." He covered his face with his hands, and burst into tears. I really did not know what to say or do.

"Calm yourself," I said to him. "You are too sensitive; don't take every thing so to heart; don't indulge in self-analysis, look at things more simply. You yourself say that you have character. Keep up good heart, you won't have long to wait," I said to him, but not very consistently, because I was much stirred both by a feeling of sympathy and a feeling of repentance, because I had allowed myself mentally to sin in my judgment of a man truly and deeply unhappy.

"Yes," he began, "if I had heard even once, at the time when I was in that hell, one single word of sympathy, of advice, of friendship—one humane word such as you have just spoken, perhaps I might have calmly endured all; perhaps I might have struggled, and been a soldier. But now this is horrible. . . . When I think soberly, I long for death. Why should I love my despicable life and my own self, now that I am ruined for all that is worth while in the world? And at the least danger, I suddenly, in spite of myself, begin to pray for my miserable life, and to watch over it as though it were precious, and I cannot, *je ne puis pas,* control myself.—That is, I could," he continued again after a minute's silence, "but this is too hard work for me, a monstrous work, when I am alone. With others, under special circumstances, when you are going into action, I am brave, *j'ai fait mes épreuves,* because I am vain and proud: that is my failing, and in presence of others. . . . Do you know, let me spend the night with you: with us, they will play all night long; it makes no difference, anywhere, on the ground."

While Nikíta was making the bed, we got up, and once more began to walk up and down in the darkness on the battery. Certainly Guskof's head must have been very weak, because two glasses of liquor and two of wine made him dizzy. As we got up and moved away from the candles, I noticed that he again thrust the ten-ruble bill into his pocket, trying to do so without my seeing it. During all the foregoing conversation, he had held it in his hand. He continued to reiterate how he felt that he might regain his old station if he had a man such as I were to take some interest in him.

We were just going into the tent to go to bed when suddenly a cannon-ball whistled over us, and buried itself in the ground not far from us. So strange it was,—that peacefully sleeping camp, our conversation, and suddenly the hostile cannon-ball which flew from God knows where, into the midst of our tents,—so strange that it was some time before I could realize what it was. Our sentinel, Andréief, walking up and down on the battery, moved toward me.

"Ha! he's crept up to us. It was the fire here that he aimed at," said he.

"We must rouse the captain," said I, and gazed at Guskof.

He stood cowering close to the ground, and stammered, trying to say, "Th-that's th-the ene-my's . . . f-f-fire—th-that's—hidi—." Further he could not say a word, and I did not see how and where he disappeared so instantaneously.

In the captain's tent a candle gleamed; his cough, which always troubled him when he was awake, was heard; and he himself soon appeared, asking for a linstock to light his little pipe.

"What does this mean, old man?"[17] he asked with a smile. "Aren't they willing to give me a little sleep to-night? First it's you with your cashiered friend, and then it's Shamyl. What shall we do, answer him or not? There was nothing about this in the instructions, was there?"

---

[17] bátiushka.

"Nothing at all. There he goes again," said I. "Two of them!"

Indeed, in the darkness, directly in front of us, flashed two fires, like two eyes; and quickly over our heads flew one cannon-ball and one heavy shell. It must have been meant for us, coming with a loud and penetrating hum. From the neighboring tents the soldiers hastened. You could hear them hawking and talking and stretching themselves.

"Hist! the fuse sings like a nightingale," was the remark of the artillerist.

"Send for Nikíta," said the captain with his perpetually benevolent smile. "Nikíta, don't hide yourself, but listen to the mountain nightingales."

"Well, your honor,"[18] said Nikíta, who was standing near the captain, "I have seen them—these nightingales. I am not afraid of 'em; but here was that stranger who was here, he was drinking up your red wine. When he heard how that shot dashed by our tents, and the shell rolled by, he cowered down like some wild beast."

"However, we must send to the commander of the artillery," said the captain to me in a serious tone of authority, "and ask whether we shall reply to the fire or not. It will probably be nothing at all, but still it may. Have the goodness to go and ask him. Have a horse saddled. Do it as quickly as possible, even if you take my Polkan."

In five minutes they brought me a horse, and I galloped off to the commander of the artillery. "Look you, return on foot," whispered the punctilious captain, "else they won't let you through the lines."

It was half a verst to the artillery commander's, the whole road ran between the tents. As soon as I rode away from our fire, it became so black that I could not see even the horse's ears, but only the watch-fires, now seeming very near, now very far off, as they gleamed into my eyes. After I had ridden some distance,

[18] *vashe vuisokoblagoródie*. German, *hochwohlgeborener*, high-well born; regulation title of officers from major to general.

trusting to the intelligence of the horse whom I allowed free rein, I began to distinguish the white four-cornered tents and then the black tracks of the road. After a half-hour, having asked my way three times, and twice stumbled over the tent-stakes, causing each time a volley of curses from the tents, and twice been detained by the sentinels, I reached the artillery commander's. While I was on the way, I heard two more cannon shot in the direction of our camp; but the projectiles did not reach to the place where the headquarters were. The artillery commander ordered not to reply to the firing, the more as the enemy did not remain in the same place; and I went back, leading the horse by the bridle, making my way on foot between the infantry tents. More than once I delayed my steps, as I went by some soldier's tent where a light was shining, and some merry-andrew was telling a story; or I listened to some educated soldier reading from some book while the whole division overflowed the tent, or hung around it, sometimes interrupting the reading with various remarks; or I simply listened to the talk about the expedition, about the fatherland, or about their chiefs.

As I came around one of the tents of the third battalion, I heard Guskof's rough voice: he was speaking hilariously and rapidly. Young voices replied to him, not those of soldiers, but of gay gentlemen. It was evidently the tent of some yunker or sergeant-major. I stopped short.

"I've known him a long time," Guskof was saying. "When I lived in Petersburg, he used to come to my house often; and I went to his. He moved in the best society."

"Whom are you talking about?" asked a drunken voice.

"About the prince," said Guskof. "We were relatives, you see, but, more than all, we were old friends.It's a mighty good thing, you know, gentlemen, to have such an acquaintance. You see, he's fearfully rich. To him a hundred silver rubles is a mere bagatelle. Here, I just got a little money out of him, enough to last me till my sister sends."

"Let's have some."

"Right away.—Savelitch, my dear," said Guskof, coming to the door of the tent, "here's ten rubles for you: go to the sutler, get two bottles of Kakhetinski. Any thing else, gentlemen? What do you say?" and Guskof, with unsteady gait, with dishevelled hair, without his hat, came out of the tent. Throwing open his jacket, and thrusting his hands into the pockets of his trousers, he stood at the door of the tent. Though he was in the light, and I in darkness, I trembled with fear lest he should see me, and I went on, trying to make no noise.

"Who goes there?" shouted Guskof after me in a thoroughly drunken voice. Apparently, the cold took hold of him. "Who the devil is going off with that horse?"

I made no answer, and silently went on my way.

LOST ON THE STEPPE; OR, THE SNOWSTORM.

A TALE.

I.

At seven o'clock in the evening, having taken my tea, I started from a station, the name of which I have quite forgotten, though I remember that it was somewhere in the region of the Don Cossacks, not far from Novocherkask. It was already dark when I took my seat in the sledge next to Alyoshka, and wrapped myself in my fur coat and the robes. Back of the station-house it seemed warm and calm. Though it was not snowing, not a single star was to be seen overhead, and the sky seemed remarkably low and black, in contrast with the clear snowy expanse stretching out before us.

We had scarcely passed by the black forms of the windmills, one of which was awkwardly waving its huge wings, and had left the station behind us, when I perceived that the road was growing rougher and more drifted; the wind began to blow more fiercely on the left, and to toss the horses' manes and tails to one side, and obstinately to lift and carry away the snow stirred up by the runners and hoofs. The little bell rang with a muffled sound; a draught of cold air forced its way through the opening in my sleeves, to my very back; and the inspector's advice came into my head, that I had better not go farther, lest I wander all night, and freeze to death on the road.

"Won't you get us lost?" said I to the driver,[1] but, as I got no answer, I put the question more explicitly: "Say, shall we reach the station, driver? We sha'n't lose our way?"

"God knows," was his reply; but he did not turn his head. "You see what kind of going we have. No road to be seen. Great heavens!"[2]

"Be good enough to tell me, do you hope to reach the station, or not?" I insisted. "Shall we get there?"

"Must get there," said the driver; and he muttered something else, which I could not hear for the wind.

I did not wish to turn about, but the idea of wandering all night in the cold and snow over the perfectly shelterless steppe, which made up this part of the Don Cossack land, was very unpleasant. Moreover, notwithstanding the fact that I could not, by reason of the darkness, see him very well, my driver, somehow, did not please me, nor inspire any confidence. He sat exactly in the middle, with his legs in, and not on one side; his stature was too great; his voice expressed indolence; his cap, not like those usually worn by his class, was large and loose on all sides. Besides, he did not manage his horses in the proper way, but held the reins in both hands, just like the lackey who sat on the box behind the coachman; and, chiefly, I did not believe in him, because he had his ears wrapped up in a handkerchief. In a word, he did not please me; and it seemed as if that crooked, sinister back looming before me boded nothing good.

"In my opinion, it would be better to turn about," said Alyoshka to me: "fine thing it would be to be lost!"

---

[1] *yamshchik.*
[2] *gospodi-bátiushka!* Literally, Lord, little father.

"Great heavens! see what a snowstorm's coming! No road in sight. It blinds one's eyes. Great heavens!" repeated the driver.

We had not been gone a quarter of an hour when the driver stopped the horses, handed the reins to Alyoshka, awkwardly liberated his legs from the seat, and went to search for the road, crunching over the snow in his great boots.

"What is it? Where are you going? Are we lost?" I asked, but the driver made no reply, but, turning his face away from the wind, which cut his eyes, marched off from the sledge.

"Well, how is it?" I repeated, when he returned.

"Nothing at all," said he to me impatiently and with vexation, as though I were to blame for his missing the road; and again slowly wrapping up his big legs in the robe, he gathered the reins in his stiffened mittens.

"What's to be done?" I asked as we started off again.

"What's to be done? We shall go as God leads."

And we drove along in the same dog-trot over what was evidently an untrodden waste, sometimes sinking in deep, mealy snow, sometimes gliding over crisp, unbroken crust.

Although it was cold, the snow kept melting quickly on my collar. The low-flying snow-clouds increased, and occasionally the dry snowflakes began to fall.

It was clear that we were going out of our way, because, after keeping on for a quarter of an hour more, we saw no sign of a verst-post.

"Well, what do you think about it now?" I asked of the driver once more. "Shall we get to the station?"

"Which one? We should go back if we let the horses have their way: they will take us. But, as for the next one, that's a problem. . . . Only we might perish."

"Well, then, let us go back," said I. "And indeed"—

"How is it? Shall we turn about?" repeated the driver.

"Yes, yes: turn back."

The driver shook the reins. The horses started off more rapidly; and, though I did not notice that we had turned around, the wind changed, and soon through the snow appeared the windmills. The driver's good spirits returned, and he began to be communicative.

"Lately," said he, "in just such a snowstorm some people coming from that same station lost their way. Yes: they spent the night in the hayricks, and barely managed to get here in the morning. Thanks to the hayricks, they were rescued. If it had not been for them, they would have frozen to death, it was so cold. And one froze his foot, and died three weeks afterwards."

"But now, you see, it's not cold; and it's growing less windy," I said. "Couldn't we go on?"

"It's warm enough, but it's snowing. Now going back, it seems easier. But it's snowing hard. Might go on, if you were a cou *l*ier or something; but this is for your own sake. What kind of a joke would that be if a passenger froze to death? How, then, could I be answerable to your grace?"

II.

At this moment we heard behind us the bells of a troïka which was rapidly overtaking us.

"A cou *l*ier's bell," said my driver. "There's one such for every station."

And, in fact, the bell of the courier's troïka, the sound of which now came clearly to me on the wind, was peculiarly beautiful,—clear, sonorous, deep, and jangling a little. As I then knew, this was a huntsman's team; three bells,—one large one in the centre, with the *crimson* tone, as it is called, and two small ones tuned in thirds. The sound of this triad and the tinkling fifth, ringing through the air, was extraordinarily effective and strangely pleasant in this dark desert steppe.

"The posht is coming," said my driver when the foremost of the three troïkas drew up in line with ours. "Well, how is the road? is it possible to go on?" he cried to the last of the drivers. But the yamshchík only shouted to his horses, and made no reply.

The sound of the bells quickly died away on the wind, almost as soon as the post-team passed us.

Of course my driver felt ashamed.

"Well, you shall go, barin," he said to me. "People have made their way through, now their tracks will be fresh."

I agreed; and once more we faced the wind, and began to crawl along on the deep snow. I kept my eyes on one side on the road, so that we should not get off the track that had been made by the other sledges. For two versts the tracks were clearly visible, then there began to be only a slight irregularity where the runners had gone; and soon I really could no longer distinguish whether it was the track, or merely a layer of snow heaped up. My eyes grew weary of gazing at the monotonous stretch of snow under the runners, and I began to look ahead. The third verst-post we had already seen, but the fourth we could not find at all. As before, we went in the teeth of the wind, and with the wind, and to the right and to the left; and finally we reached such a state that the driver declared that we must have turned off to the right. I declared that we must have turned off to the left, and Alyoshka was sure that we ought to go back. Again we stopped a number of times, the driver uncoiled his long legs, and crawled along trying to find the road. But all in vain. I also got out once to see whether it were the road or something else that attracted my attention. But I had scarcely taken six steps with difficulty against the wind, and convinced myself that we were surrounded by the same monotonous white heaps of snow, and that the road existed only in my imagination, when I lost sight of the sledge. I shouted, "Yamshchík! Alyoshka!" but my voice,—I felt how the wind tore it right out of my mouth, and carried it in a twinkling far from me. I went in the direction where the sledge had been—the sledge was not there. I went to the right—not there either. I am ashamed to recollect what a loud, penetrating, and even rather despairing voice, I summoned to shout once more, "Yamshchík!" and there he was two steps away. His black figure, with his whip, and his huge cap hanging down on one side, suddenly loomed up before me. He led me to the sledge.

"Thank the Lord, it's still warm!" said he. "To perish with

the cold—awful! Great heavens!"[3]

"Let the horses find their own way, let us turn back," said I, as I took my place in the sledge. "Won't they take us back? hey, driver?"

"They ought to."

He gave the horses the reins, cracked his whip three times over the saddle of the shaft-horse, and again we started off at hap-hazard. We went for half an hour. Suddenly before us again I heard the well-known bell of the hunting establishment, and the other two. But now they were coming toward us. It was the same three troïkas, which had already deposited the mail, and, with a change of horses attached behind, were returning to the station. The courier's troïka, with powerful horses with the hunting-bell, quickly dashed ahead. A single driver sat in it on the driver's seat, and was shouting vigorously. Behind him, in the middle one of the empty troïkas, were two other drivers; and their loud and hilarious talk could be heard. One of them was smoking a pipe; and the spark, brightened by the wind, lighted up a part of his face.

As I looked at them, I felt ashamed that I was afraid to go on; and my driver doubtless had the same feeling, because we both said with one voice, "Let us follow them."

III.

My driver, without waiting for the last troïka to pass, began awkwardly to turn around; and the thills hit the horses attached behind. One of the troïka teams shied, tore away the reins, and galloped off.

"Hey there, you squint-eyed devil! Don't you see where you are turning? Running people down, you devil!" in a hoarse, discordant voice scolded one of the drivers, a short, little old man, as I judged by his voice and expression. He sprang hastily out of the hindmost sledge where he had been sitting, and started to run

---

[3] *gospodi-bátiushka.*

after the horses, still continuing roughly and violently to vilify my yamshchík.

But the horses did not come back. The driver ran after them, and in one instant both horses and driver were lost from sight in the white mist of the storm.

"Vasí-í-í-li! bring the bay horse here. Can't ketch him, so-o-o," echoed his voice in the distance.

One of the drivers, a very tall fellow, got out of his sledge, silently unhitched his troïka, mounted one of the horses by the breeching, and crunching over the snow in a clumsy gallop, disappeared in the same direction.

Our own troïka, with the two others, followed on over the steppe, behind the courier's which dashed ahead in full trot, jingling its bell.

"How is it? He'll get 'em?" said my driver, referring to the one who had gone to catch the horses. "If that mare didn't find the horses she wouldn't be good for much, you know: she'd wander off, so that—she'd get lost."

From the moment that my driver had the company of other teams he became more hilarious and talkative; and, as I had no desire to sleep, I did not fail, as a matter of course, to make the most of it. I took pains to ask him about his home and his family, and soon learned that he was a fellow-countryman of mine from Tula,—a peasant, belonging to a noble family from the village of Kirpitchnoé; that they had very little land, and the grain had entirely ceased to grow, owing to the cholera; that he and one of his brothers had staid at home, and a third had gone as a soldier; that since Christmas they had lacked bread, and had been obliged to work out; that his younger brother had kept the farm because he was married, but that he himself was a widower; that his villagers every year came here to exercise the trade of yamshchík, or driver; that, though he had not come as a regular driver, yet he was in the postal-service, so as to help his brother; that he earned there, thanks to God, a hundred and twenty paper rubles a year, of which he sent a hundred to his family; and that it would be good living, "but the couliers were very wild beasts, and the people here were impudent."

"Now, what was that driver scolding about? Great heavens![4] did I mean to lose his horses for him? Did I treat him in a mean way? And why did he go galloping off after 'em? They'd have come in of their own accord. Anyway, 'twould be better for the horses to freeze to death than for him to get lost," said the pious muzhík.

"What is that black thing I see coming?" I asked, pointing to some dark object in front of us.

"That's a baggage-train. Splendid wheeling!" he added, as he came up with the huge mat-covered vans on wheels, following one after the other. "See, not a soul to be seen—all asleep. The wise horse knows: you won't drive her from the road, never. . . . We've driven in that same way—so we know," he added.

It was indeed strange to see the huge vans covered with snow from the matted tops to the wheels, moving along, absolutely alone. Only the front corner of the snow-covered mat would be lifted by two fingers; and, for a moment, a cap would peer out as our bells jingled past the train. A great piebald horse, stretching out his neck, and straining his back, walked with measured pace over the drifted road, monotonously shaking his shaggy head under the whitened bell-bow,[5] and pricking up one snow-covered ear as we went by.

After we had gone still another half-hour, the driver once more turned to me,—

"Well, what do you think, bárin? Are we getting along well?"

"I don't know," I said.

"Before, the wind blew in our faces, but now we go right along with it. No, we sha'n't get there: we are off the track," he said in conclusion, with perfect equanimity.

It was evident, that, though he was very timid, yet, as "death in company with others is pleasant," he was perfectly content to die now that there were a number of us, and he was not obliged to take the lead, and be responsible. He coolly made observations

---

[4] *gospodi-bátiushka.*
[5] *dugá,* the distinctive part of the Russian harness, rising high above the horse, and carrying the bells.

on the mistakes of the head driver, as though it were not of the least consequence to himself. In fact, I had noticed that sometimes the front troïka appeared on my right, and again on my left. It seemed to me, too, that we were making a circle in very small space. However, it might be that it was an ocular deception, just as sometimes it seemed as if the front troïka were climbing up a mountain or were going along a slope or down a mountain, even when the steppe was everywhere perfectly level.

After we had gone on a little while longer, I saw, as it seemed to me, at a distance, on the very horizon, a long black, moving line; but it quickly became plain to me that it was the same baggage-train which we had passed. In exactly the same way, the snow covered the creaking wheels, several of which did not turn; in exactly the same way, the men were sleeping under the matted tops; and likewise the piebald leader, swelling out his nostrils, snuffed out the road, and pricked back his ears.

"See, we've gone round in a circle; we've gone round in a circle! Here's the same baggage-train again!" exclaimed my driver in a discontented tone. "The coulier's horses are good ones, so it makes no difference to him, even if he does go on a wild-goose chase. But ours will get tired out if we have to spend the whole night here."

He had an attack of coughing.

"Should we go back, bárin, owing to the mistake?"

"No! Why? We shall come out somewhere."

"Come out where? We shall have to spend the night in the steppe. How it's snowing! . . . Great heavens!"[6]

Although it was clear to me that the head driver had lost both the road and the direction, and yet was not hunting for the road, but was singing at the top of his voice, and letting his horses take their own speed; and so I did not like to part company from them.

"Follow them," said I.

The yamshchík drove on, but followed them less willingly than before, and no longer had any thing to say to me.

---

[6] *gospodi-bátiushka.*

IV.

The storm became more and more violent, and the snow fell dry and fine; it seemed as if we were in danger of freezing. My nose and cheeks began to tingle; more frequently the draught of cold air insinuated itself under my furs, and it became necessary to bundle up warmer. Sometimes the sledges bumped on the bare, icy crust from which the snow had been blown away. As I had already gone six hundred versts without sleeping under roof, and though I felt great interest in the outcome of our wanderings, my eyes closed in spite of me, and I drowsed. Once when I opened my eyes, I was struck, as it seemed to me at the first moment, by a bright light, gleaming over the white plain: the horizon widened considerably, the lowering black sky suddenly lifted up on all sides, the white slanting lines of the falling snow became visible, the shapes of the head troïkas stood out clearly; and when I looked up, it seemed to me at the first moment that the clouds had scattered, and that only the falling snow veiled the stars. At the moment that I awoke from my drowse, the moon came out, and cast through the tenuous clouds and the falling snow her cold bright beams. I saw clearly my sledge, horses, driver, and the three troïkas, ploughing on in front: the first, the courier's, in which still sat on the box the one yamshchík driving at a hard trot; the second, in which rode the two drivers, who let the horses go at their own pace, and had made a shelter out of a camel's-hair coat[7] behind which they still smoked their pipes as could be seen by the sparks glowing in their direction; and the third, in which no one was visible, for the yamshchík was comfortably sleeping in the middle. The leading driver, however, while I was napping had several times halted his horses, and attempted to find the road. Then while we stopped the howling of the wind became more audible, and the monstrous heaps of snow piling through the atmosphere seemed more tremendous. By the aid of the moonlight which made its way through the storm, I could see the driver's short figure, whip in hand, examining the snow

---

[7] *armyák.*

before him, moving back and forth in the misty light, again coming back to the sledge, and springing sidewise on the seat; and then again I heard above the monotonous whistling of the wind, the comfortable, clear jingling and melody of the bells. When the head driver crept out to find the marks of the road or the hayricks, each time was heard the lively, self-confident voice of one of the yamshchíks in the second sledge shouting, "Hey, Ignashka![8] you turned off too much to the left. Strike off to the right into the storm." Or, "Why are you going round in a circle? keep straight ahead as the snow flies. Follow the snow, then you'll hit it." Or, "Take the right, take the right, old man.[9] There's something black, it must be a post." Or, "What are you getting lost for? why are you getting lost? Unhitch the piebald horse, and let him find the road for you. He'll do it every time. That would be the best way."

The man who was so free with his advice not only did not offer to unhitch his off-horse, or go himself across the snow to hunt for the road, but did not even put his nose outside of his shelter-coat; and when Ignashka the leader, in reply to one of his proffers of advice, shouted to him to come and take the forward place since he knew the road so well, the mentor replied that when he came to drive a courier's sledge, then he would take the lead, and never once miss the road. "But our horses wouldn't go straight through a snowdrift," he shouted: "they ain't the right kind."

"Then don't you worry yourselves," replied Ignashka, gayly whistling to his horses.

The yamshchík who sat in the same sledge with the mentor said nothing at all to Ignashka, and paid no attention to the difficulty, though he was not yet asleep, as I concluded by his pipe which still glowed, and because, when we halted, I heard his measured voice in uninterrupted flow. He was telling a story. Once only, when Ignashka for the sixth or seventh time came to

---

[8] diminished diminutive of Ignat.
[9] *bratets tui moi*, literally, "thou brother mine."

a stop, it seemed to vex him because his comfort in travelling was disturbed, and he shouted,—

"Stopping again? He's missing the road on purpose. Call this a snowstorm! The surveyor himself could not find the road! he would let the horses find it. We shall freeze to death here; just let him go on regardless!"

"What! Don't you know a poshtellion froze to death last winter?" shouted my driver.

All this time the driver of the third troïka had not been heard from. But once while we were stopping, the mentor shouted, "Filipp! ha! Filipp!" and not getting any response remarked,—

"Can he have frozen to death? Ignashka, you go and look."

Ignashka, who was responsible for all, went to his sledge, and began to shake the sleeper.

"See what drink has done for him! Tell us if you are frozen to death!" said he, shaking him.

The sleeper grunted a little, and then began to scold.

"Live enough, fellows!" said Ignashka, and again started ahead, and once more we drove on; and with such rapidity that the little brown off-horse, in my three-span, which was constantly whipping himself with his tail, did not once interrupt his awkward gallop.

V.

It was already about midnight, I judge, when the little old man and Vasíli, who had gone in search of the runaway horses, rejoined us. They had caught the horses, and had now overtaken us; but how in the world they had accomplished this in the thick, blinding snowstorm, in the midst of the bare steppe, was more than I could comprehend. The little old man, with his elbows and legs flying, came trotting up on the shaft-horse (the two other horses he had caught by the collars; it was impossible to lead them in the snowstorm). When they had caught up with me, he began to scold at my driver.

"You see, you cross-eyed devil! you"—

"O Uncle Mitritch,"[10] cried the talkative fellow in the second sledge, "you alive? Come along where we are!"

The old man did not answer him, but continued to scold. When he had satisfied himself, he rejoined the second sledge.

"Get em all?" was asked him.

"Why, of course we did."

And his small figure leaped up and down on the horse's back as he went off at full trot; then he sprang down into the snow, and without stopping caught up with the sledge, and sat in it with his legs hanging over the side. The tall Vasíli, just as before, took his place in perfect silence in the front sledge with Ignashka; and then the two began to look for the road together.

"What a spitfire! Great heavens!" muttered my driver.

For a long time after this we drove on without stopping, over the white waste, in the cold, pellucid, and wavering light of the snowstorm. When I opened my eyes, there before me rose the same clumsy, snow-covered cap; the same low *dugá* or bell-bow, under which, between the leathern reins tightly stretched, there moved always at the same distance the head of the shaft-horse with the black mane blown to one side by the wind. And I could see, above his back, the brown off-horse on the right, with his short braided tail, and the whiffletree sometimes knocking against the dasher of the sleigh. If I looked below, then I saw the scurrying snow stirred up by the runners, and constantly tossed and borne by the wind to one side. In front of me, always at the same distance, glided the other troïkas. To left and right, all was white and bewildering. Vainly the eye sought for any new object: neither verst-post, nor hayrick, nor fence was to be seen; nothing at all. Everywhere, all was white, white and fluctuating. Now the horizon seems to be indistinguishably distant, then it comes down within two steps on every side; now suddenly a high white wall grows up on the right, and accompanies the course of the sledges, then it suddenly vanishes, and grows up in front, only to glide on in advance, farther and farther away, and disappear again.

As I look up, it seems light. At the first moment, I imagine

---

[10] Condensed form for Dmitriyévitch, "son of Dmitri." The peasants often call each other by the patronymic.

that through the mist I see the stars; but the stars, as I gaze, flee
into deeper and deeper depths, and I see only the snow falling
into face and eyes, and the collar of my fur coat;[11] the sky has
everywhere one tone of light, one tone of white,—colorless,
monotonous, and constantly shifting. The wind seems to vary: at
one moment it blows into my face, and flings the snow into my
eyes; the next it goes to one side, and peevishly tosses the collar
of my shuba over my head, and insultingly slaps me in the face
with it; then it finds some crevice behind, and plays a tune upon
it. I hear the soft, unceasing crunching of the hoofs and the
runners on the snow, and the muffled tinkling of the bells, as we
speed over the deep snow. Only occasionally when we drive
against the wind, and glide over the bare frozen crust, I can
clearly distinguish Ignat's energetic whistling, and the full chords
of the chime, with the resounding jarring fifth; and these sounds
break suddenly and comfortingly upon the melancholy character
of the desert; and then again rings monotonously, with unendurable fidelity of execution, the whole of that motive which involuntarily coincides with my thoughts.

One of my feet began to feel cold, and when I turned round
so as to protect it better, the snow which covered my collar and
my cap sifted down my neck, and made me shiver; but still I was,
for the most, comfortable in my warm shuba, and drowsiness
overcame me.

VI.

Things remembered and things conceived mixed and mingled with wonderful quickness in my imagination.

"The mentor who is always shouting from the second sledge,
what kind of a man must he be? Probably red-haired, thick-set,
with short legs, a man somewhat like Feódor Filíppuitch our old
butler," is what I say to myself.

And here I see the staircase of our great house, and five of

---

[11] *shuba.*

the house-servants who with towels, with heavy steps, carry the
pianoforte from the L; I see Feódor Filíppuitch with the sleeves
of his nankeen coat tucked up, carrying one of the pedals, and
going in advance, unbolting the door, taking hold of the door-
knob here, there pushing a little, now crawling under the legs; he
is here, there, and everywhere, crying with an anxious voice
continually, "Look out, take more weight, you there in front! Be
careful, you there at the tail-end! Up—up—up—don't hit the
door. There, there!"

"Excuse me, Feódor Filíppuitch! There ain't enough of us,"
says the gardener timidly, crushed up against the balustrade, and
all red with exertion, lifting one end of the grand with all his
remaining strength. But Feódor Filíppuitch does not hold his
peace.

"And what does it mean?" I ask myself. "Does he think that
he is of any use, that he is indispensable for the work in hand?
or is he simply glad that God has given him this self-confident
persuasive eloquence, and takes enjoyment in squandering it?"

And I somehow see the pond, the weary servants, who, up
to their knees in the water, drag the heavy net; and again Feódor
Filíppuitch, shouting to everybody, walking up and down on the
bank, and only now and then venturing to the brink, taking with
his hand the golden carp, and letting the dirty water run out from
his watering-pot, so as to fill it up with fresh.

But here it is midday, in the month of July. Across the newly
mown turf of the lawn, under the burning perpendicular rays of
the sun, I seem to be going somewhere. I am still very young; I
am free from yearnings, free from desires. I am going to the pond,
to my own favorite spot between the rose-bushes and the birch-
tree alley; and I shall lie down and nap. Keen is the sensation that
I have, as I lie down, and look across the red thorny stems of the
rose-bushes upon the dark ground with its dry grass and on the
gleaming bright-blue mirror of the pond. It is a sensation of a
peculiarly simple self-contentment and melancholy. All around
me is so lovely, and this loveliness has such a powerful effect upon
me, that it seems to me as if I myself were good; and the one thing
that vexes me is, that no one is there to admire me.

It is hot. I try to go to sleep for comfort's sake; but the flies, the unendurable flies, even here, give me no rest. They begin to swarm around me, and obstinately, insolently as it were, heavy as cherry-stones, jump from my forehead to my hands. A bee buzzes near me in the sunbeam. Yellow-winged butterflies fly wearily from flower to flower.

I gaze up. It pains my eyes. The sun shines too bright through the light foliage of the bushy birch-tree, gracefully waving its branches high above my head, and it grows hotter still. I cover my face with my handkerchief. It becomes stifling; and the flies seem to stick to my hands, on which the perspiration stands. In the rose-bush the sparrows twitter under the thick leaves. One hops to the ground almost within my reach, makes two or three feints to peck energetically at the ground, and after making the little twigs crackle, and chirping gayly, flies away from the bushes; another also hops to the ground, wags his little tail, looks around, and, like an arrow, flies off twittering after the first. At the pond are heard the blows of the pounder on the wet clothes; and the noise re-echoes, and is carried far away down along the shore. I hear laughter and talking, and the splashing of bathers. The breath of the wind sweeps the tops of the birches far above my head, and bends them down again. I hear it moving the grass, and now the leaves of the rose-bushes toss and rustle on their stems. And now, lifting the corner of my handkerchief, it tickles my sweaty face, and pours in upon me in a cooling current. Through the opening where the handkerchief is lifted a fly finds his way, and timidly buzzes around my moist mouth. A dry twig begins to make itself felt under my back. No: it becomes unendurable; I must get it out. But now, around the clump of bushes, I hear the sound of footsteps, and the frightened voice of a woman:—

"Mercy on me![12] what's to be done? And no man anywhere!"

"What's the matter?" I ask, running out into the sun, as a serving-woman, screaming, hurries past me. She merely glances at me, wrings her hands, and hurries along faster. And here comes

[12] akh, bátiushki!

also the seventy-year-old Matryóna, holding her handkerchief to her head, with her hair all in disorder, and hopping along with her lame leg in woollen stockings. Two girls come running, hand in hand; and a ten-year-old boy in his father's jacket runs behind, clinging to the linen petticoat of one of them.

"What has happened?" I ask of them.

"A muzhík drowned!"

"Where?"

"In the pond."

"Who is he? one of ours?"

"No, a tramp."

The coachman Iván, bustling about in his big boots over the mown grass, and the fat overseer[13] Yakof, all out of breath, come hurrying to the pond; and I follow after them.

I experience the feeling which says to me, "Now jump in, and pull the muzhík out, and save him; and all will admire you," which was exactly what I wanted.

"Where is he? where?" I asked of the throng of domestics gathered on the shore.

"Over there in the deepest part, on the other shore, almost at the baths," says the laundress, stowing away the wet linen on her yoke. . . . "I see him dive; there he comes up again, then he sinks a second time, and comes up again, and then he cries, 'I'm drowning, help!' And then he goes down again—and then a lot of bubbles. And while I am looking on, the muzhík gets drowned. And so I give the alarm: 'Help! a muzhík is drowning!'"

And the laundress, lifting the yoke upon her shoulder, turning to one side, goes along the narrow footpath away from the pond.

"See! what a shame," says Yakof Ivánof the overseer, in a despairing voice; "now there'll be a rumpus with the police court[14]—we'll have enough of it."

One muzhík with a scythe makes his way through the throng of peasant women, children, and old men gathered round the

---

[13] *prikáshchik.*
[14] *zemski sūt.*

shore, and, hanging the scythe on the limb of a willow, leisurely takes off his clothes.

"Where was it? where was he drowned?" I keep asking, having still the desire to jump in, and do something extraordinary.

They point out to me the smooth surface of the pond, which is now and then just ruffled by the puffs of the breeze. It is incomprehensible how he came to drown; for the water lies so smooth, beautiful and calm above him, shining golden in the midday sun, and it seems to me that I could not do any thing or surprise any one, the more as I am a very poor swimmer; but the muzhík is now pulling his shirt over his head, and instantly throws himself into the water. All look at him with hope and anxiety. After going into the water up to his neck, the muzhík turns back, and puts on his shirt again: he knows not how to swim.

People keep coming down to the shore; the throng grows larger and larger; the women cling to each other: but no one brings any help. Those who have just come, offer advice, and groan; fear and despair are stamped on all faces. Of those who had come first, some have sat down, or stand wearily on the grass, others have gone back to their work. The old Matryóna asks her daughter whether she shut the oven-door. The small boy in his father's jacket industriously flings stones into the water.

And now from the house down the hill comes Trezorka, the butler's dog, barking, and looking at the stupid people. And lo! there is Feódor's tall figure hurrying from the hill-top, and shouting something as he comes out from behind the rose-bushes.

"What are you standing there for?" he shouts, taking off his coat as he runs. "A man drowning, and there you are standing around! Give us a rope."

All look at Feódor with hope and fear while he, leaning his hand on the shoulder of one of the men-servants, pries off his left boot with the toe of the right.

"There it was, where the people are standing, there at the right of the willows, Feódor Filíppuitch, right there," says some one to him.

"I know it," he replies; and knitting his brows, probably as a rebuke to the manifestations of modesty visible among the women, he takes off his shirt and baptismal cross, handing them to the gardener-boy who stands officiously near him, and then stepping energetically across the mown grass comes to the pond.

Trezorka, unable to explain the reason for his master's rapid motions, stands irresolute near the crowd, and noisily eats a few grass-blades on the shore, then looks questioningly at his master, and suddenly with a joyous bark plunges after him into the water. At first nothing can be seen except foam, and splashing water, which reached even to us. But soon the butler, gracefully spreading his arms in long strokes, and with regular motion lifting and sinking his back, swims across to the other shore. Trezorka, however, gurgling in the water, hastily returns, shakes himself near the crowd, and rolls over on his back upon the shore.

While the butler is swimming to the other side, two coachmen hasten to the willows with a net fastened to a stake. The butler for some reason lifts up his hands, dives once, twice, three times, each time spewing from his mouth a stream of water, gracefully shaking his long hair, and paying no heed to the questions which are showered upon him from all sides. At last he comes to the shore, and, so far as I can see, arranges for the disposition of the net.

They haul out the net, but it contains nothing except slime and a few small carp flopping in it. They have just cast the net once more as I reach that side.

The voice of the butler giving directions, the water dripping from the wet rope, and the sighs of dismay, alone break the silence. The wet rope stretches to the right wing, covers up more and more of the grass, slowly emerges farther and farther out of the water.

"Now pull all together, friends, once more!" cries the butler's voice. The net appears, dripping with water.

"There's something! it comes heavy, fellows," says some one's voice.

And here the wings with two or three carp flapping in them, wetting and crushing down the grass, are drawn to shore. And through the delicate strata of the agitated depths of the waters, something white gleams in the tightly stretched net. Not loud, but plainly audible amid the dead silence, a sigh of horror passes over the throng.

"Pull it up on the dry land! pull it up, friends!" says the butler's resolute voice; and the drowned man is pulled up across the mown burdocks and other weeds, to the shelter of the willows.

And here I see my good old auntie in her silk dress. I see her lilac sunshade with its fringe,—which somehow is incongruous with this picture of death terrible in its very simplicity,—and her face ready this moment to be convulsed with sobs. I realize the disappointment expressed on her face, because it is impossible to use the arnica; and I recall the sickening melancholy feeling that I have when she says with the simple egoism of love, "Come, my dear. Ah! how terrible this is! And here you always go in swimming by yourself."

I remember how bright and hot the sun shines on the dry ground, crumpling under the feet; how it gleams on the mirror of the pond; how the plump carp flap on the bank; how the schools of fish stir the smooth surface in the middle of the pond; how high in the air a hawk hangs, watching the ducklings which, quacking and spattering, swim through the reeds toward the centre; how the white tumulous thunder-clouds gather on the horizon; how the mud, brought up by the net, is scattered over the bank; and how, as I come to the dike, I again hear the blows of the clothes-pounders at work along the pond.

But the clothes-pounder has a ringing sound; two clothes-pounders, as it were, ring together, making a chord; and this sound torments, pains me, the more as I know that this clothes-pounder is a bell, and Feódor Filíppuitch does not cease to ring it. And this clothes-pounder, like an instrument of torture, squeezes my leg, which is freezing.—I fall into deep sleep.

I was waked by what seemed to me our very rapid progress, and by two voices speaking close to me.

"Say, Ignat, Ignat," says the voice of my driver. "You take my passenger; you've got to go anyway; it's only wasted labor for me: you take him."

Ignat's voice near me replies, "What fun would it be for me to answer for a passenger? . . . Will you treat me to a half-pint of brandy?"

"Now! a half-pint! Call it a glass."

"The idea, a glass!" cries the other voice; "bother my horses for a glass of vodka!"

I open my eyes. Still the same unendurable whirling snow-flakes dazzling me, the same drivers and horses, but next me I see some sledge or other. My driver has caught up with Ignat, and for some time we have been going side by side.

Notwithstanding the fact that the voice from the other sledge advises not to take less than the half-pint, Ignat suddenly reins up his troïka.

"Change the things; just your good luck! You'll give me the brandy when we meet to-morrow. Have you got much luggage?"

My driver, with unwonted liveliness, leaps into the snow, makes me a bow, and begs me to change into Ignat's sledge. I am perfectly willing. But evidently the pious little muzhík is so delighted that he must needs express to every one his gratefulness and pleasure. He bows to me, to Alyoshka, to Ignashka, and thanks us.

"Well, now, thank the Lord! What a scheme this is! Heavens and earth![15] we have been going half the night. Don't know ourselves where we are. He will take you, sir;[16] but my horses are all beat out."

And he transfers the luggage with vigorous activity.

When it was moved, I got into the other sledge in spite of the wind which almost carried me away. The sledge, especially on that side toward which was spread the coat as a protection against the wind, for the two yamshchíks, was quarter buried in the snow; but behind the coat, it was warm and cosey. The little old man was lying with his legs hanging over, and the story-teller was still spinning his yarn: "At that very same time when the general in the king's name, you know, comes to Marya, you know, in the

[15] gospodi-bátiushka.
[16] bátiushka-bárin.

darkness, at this same time, Marya says to him, 'General, I do not need you, and I cannot love you; and, you know, you are not my lover, but my lover is the prince himself'—At this very time," he was going on to say; but, catching sight of me, he kept silence for a time, and began to puff at his pipe.

"Well, bárin, you missed the story, didn't you?" said the other, whom I have called the mentor.

"Yes; but you are finely provided for behind here," said I.

"Out of sheer dulness,—have to keep ourselves from thinking."

"But, say, don't you know where we are now?"

This question, as it seemed to me, did not please the yamshchíks.

"Who can tell where we are? Maybe we are going to the Kalmucks," replied the mentor.

"But what are we going to do?" I asked.

"What are we going to do? Well, we are going, and will keep on going," he said in a fretful tone.

"Well, what will keep us from getting lost? Besides, the horses will get tired in the snow. What then?"

"Well, nothing."

"But we may freeze to death."

"Of course we may, because we don't see any hayricks just now; but we may come, you know, to the Kalmucks. First thing, we must look at the snow."

"But you aren't afraid of freezing to death, are you, bárin?" asked the little old man with quavering voice.

Notwithstanding that he was making sport of me, as it were, it was plain that he was trembling all over.

"Yes: it is growing very cold," I replied.

"Ekh! bárin! You ought to do like me. No, no: stamp up and down,—that will warm you up."

"Do it the first thing when you get to the sledge," said the mentor.

VII.

"If you please: all ready!" shouted Alyoshka from the front sledge.

The storm was so violent that only by violent exertion, leaning far forward and holding down the folds of my cloak with both hands, was I able to make my way through the whirling snow, drifting before the wind under my very feet, over the short distance between me and the sledge. My former driver was still on his knees in the middle of the empty sledge; but when he saw me going he took off his big cap, the wind angrily tossing up his hair, and asked me for a fee. Apparently he did not expect me to give it to him, because my refusal did not affront him in the least. He even thanked me, waved his cap, and said, "Well, good luck to you, sir!"[17] and picking up the reins, and clucking to the horses, turned from us.

Immediately Ignashka straightened his back, and shouted to his horses. Again the sound of crunching hoofs, voices, bells, took the place of the howling wind which was chiefly audible when we stood still. For a quarter of an hour after my transfer I did not sleep, and I diverted my mind by contemplating the form of my new driver and horses. Ignashka was youthful in appearance, was constantly jumping up, cracking his whip over the horses, shouting out, changing from one leg to the other, and leaning forward to fix the breeching for the shaft-horse, which was always slipping to one side. The man was not tall in stature, but well built as it seemed. Over his unlined sheepskin coat[18] he wore an ungirdled cloak, the collar of which was turned back, leaving his neck perfectly bare; his boots were of leather, not felt; and he wore a small cap which he constantly took off and straightened. In all his motions was manifest not only energy, but much more, as it seemed to me, the desire to keep his energy alive. Moreover, the farther we went, the more frequently he settled himself on his seat, changed the position of his legs, and addressed himself to Alyoshka and me: it seemed to me that he was afraid of losing his

---

[17] *Nu, daï Bog vam, bárin.*
[18] *polushubka;* a garment of tanned sheepskin, the wool inwards, and reaching to the knees or even the ankles.

spirits. And there was good reason: though the horses were excellent, the road at each step grew heavier and heavier, and it was noticeable that the horses' strength was flagging. It was already necessary to use the whip; and the shaft-horse, a good big, shaggy animal, stumbled once or twice, though immediately, as if frightened, it sprang forward and tossed up its shaggy head almost to the bell itself. The right off-horse, which I could not help watching, had a long leather breeching adorned with tassels, slipping and sliding to the left, and kept dropping the traces, and required the whip; but, being naturally a good and even zealous horse, seemed to be vexed at his own weakness, and angrily tossed his head, as if asking to be driven. Indeed, it was terrible to see how, as the storm and cold increased, the horses grew weak, the road became worse; and we really did not know where we were, or where we were going, whether to a station or to any shelter whatsoever. And strange and ridiculous it was to hear the bells jingling so merrily and carelessly, and Ignatka shouting so energetically and delightfully as though it were a sunny Christmas noon, and we were hurrying to a festival along the village street; and stranger than all it was to think that we were always riding and riding rapidly away from the place where we had been.

Ignat began to sing some song in a horrible falsetto, but so loud and with such stops, during which he whistled, that it was weird to listen to, and made one melancholy.

"Hey-y-y! Why are you splitting your throat, Ignat? Hold on a bit!" said the voice of the mentor.

"What?"

"Hold o-o-o-o-n!"

Ignat reined up. Again silence only broken by the wailing and whistling of the wind, while the snow began to pile up, rustling on the sledge. The mentor drove up to us.

"Well, what is it?"

"Say![19] where are you going?"

"Who knows?"

"Are your feet frozen, that you stamp so?"

---

[19] *da chto!*

"They're frozen off."

"Well, you ought to go this way. The way you were going means starvation,—not even a Kalmuck there. Get out, and it will warm your legs."

"All right. Hold the horses—there."

And Ignat stumped off in the direction indicated.

"Have to keep looking all the time, have to get out and hunt; then you find the way. But this way's a crazy way to go," said the mentor. "See how tired the horses are."

All the time that Ignat was gone, and it was so long that I actually began to be afraid that he had lost his way, the mentor kept talking to me in a self-confident, easy tone, telling me how it was necessary to behave in a snowstorm; how much better it was to unhitch one of the horses, and let her go as God Almighty should direct; how sometimes you can see the stars occasionally; and how, if he had taken the front place, we should have been at the station long before.

"Well, how is it?" he asked, as Ignat came back, ploughing with difficulty knee-deep in snow.

"Not so bad. I found a Kalmuck camp," replied the driver, out of breath. "Still I don't know where we are. It must be that we have been going toward Prolgovsky forest. We must turn to the left."

"Why worry? It must be the camp just behind our station," replied the mentor.

"I tell you it isn't."

"Well, I've seen it, and so I know. If it isn't that, then it's Tamuishevskoé. You must turn to the right; and soon we'll be on the big bridge,—eight versts."

"Say what you will, 'tain't so. I have seen it," said Ignat angrily.

"Eh! what's that? I am a yamshchík as much as you are."

"Fine yamshchík! you go ahead, then."

"Why should I go ahead? But I know."

Ignat was evidently angry. Without replying, he climbed to his seat, and drove on.

"You see how cold one's feet get. No way to warm them,"

said he to Alyoshka, pounding his feet more and more frequently, and brushing and shaking off the snow which had got into his boot-legs.

I felt an uncontrollable desire to sleep.

VIII.

"Can it be that I am going to freeze to death?" I asked myself, as I dropped off. "Death, they say, always begins with drowsiness. It's much better to drown than freeze to death, then they would pull me out of the net. However, it makes no difference whether one drowns or freezes to death. If only this stake did not stick into my back so, I might forget myself."

For a second I lost consciousness.

"How will all this end?" I suddenly ask myself in thought, for a moment opening my eyes, and gazing at the white expanse, —"how will it end? If we don't find some hayricks, and the horses get winded, as it seems likely they will be very soon, we shall all freeze to death."

I confess, that, though I was afraid, I had a desire for something extraordinarily tragic to happen to us; and this was stronger than the small fear. It seemed to me that it would not be unpleasant if at morning the horses themselves should bring us, half-frozen, to some far-off, unknown village, where some of us might even perish of the cold.

And while I have this thought, my imagination works with extraordinary clearness and rapidity. The horses become weary, the snow grows deeper and deeper, and now only the ears and the bell-bow are visible; but suddenly Ignashka appears on horseback, driving his troïka past us. We beseech him, we shout to him to take us: but the wind carries away our voices; we have no voices left. Ignashka laughs at us, shouts to his horses, whistles, and passes out of our sight in some deep snow-covered ravine. A little old man climbs upon a horse, flaps his elbows, and tries to gallop after him; but he cannot stir from the place. My old driver, with his great cap, throws himself upon him, drags him to the ground, and tramples him into the snow. "You're a wizard!" he cries. "You're a spitfire. We are all lost on your account." But the little old man flings a snowball at his head. He is no longer a little old man, but only a hare, and bounds away from us. All the dogs bound after him. The mentor, who is now the butler, tells us to sit around in a circle, that nothing will happen to us if we protect ourselves with snow: it will be warm.

In fact, it is warm and cosey: our only trouble is thirst. I get out my travelling-case; I offer every one rum and sugar, and drink myself with great satisfaction. The story-teller spins some yarn about the rainbow, and over our heads is a roof of snow and a rainbow.

"Now each of you," I say, "make a chamber in the snow, and go to sleep." The snow is soft and warm like wool. I make myself a room, and am just going into it; but Feódor Filíppuitch, who has caught a glimpse of my money in my travelling-case, says, "Hold! give me your money, you won't need it when you're dead," and seizes me by the leg. I hand him the money, asking him only to let me go; but they will not believe that it is all my money, and they are going to kill me. I seize the old man's hand, and with indescribable pleasure kiss it: the old man's hand is tender and soft. At first he takes it away from me, but afterwards he lets me have it, and even caresses me with his other hand. Nevertheless, Feódor Filíppuitch comes near and threatens me. I hasten to my chamber; it is not a chamber, but a long white corridor, and some one pulls back on my leg. I tear myself away. In the hand of the man who holds me back, remain my trousers and a part of my skin; but I feel only cold and ashamed,—all the more ashamed because my auntie with her sunshade, and homeopathic pellets, comes arm in arm with the drowned man to meet me. They smile, but do not understand the signs that I make to them. I fling myself after the sledge; my feet glide over the snow, but the little old man follows after me, flapping his elbows. He comes close to me. But I hear just in front of me two church-bells, and I know that I shall be safe when I reach them. The church-bells ring nearer and nearer; but the little old man has caught up with me, and falls with his body across my face, so that I can scarcely hear the bells.

Once more I seize his hand, and begin to kiss it; but the little old man is no longer the little old man, but the drowned man, and he cries,—

"Ignashka, hold on! here are Akhmet's hayricks! just look!"

That is strange to hear! no, I would rather wake up.

I open my eyes. The wind is flapping the tails of Alyoshka's cloak into my face; my knees are uncovered. We are going over the bare crust, and the triad of the bells rings pleasantly through the air with its dominant fifth.

I look, expecting to see the hayricks; but instead of hayricks, now that my eyes are wide open, I see something like a house with a balcony, and the crenellated walls of a fortress. I feel very little interest in seeing this house and fortress; my desire is much stronger to see the white corridor where I had been walking, to hear the sound of the church-bells, and to kiss the little old man's hand. Again I close my eyes and sleep.

IX.

I sleep sound. But all the time I can hear the chords of the bells, and in my dream I can see a dog barking and jumping after me; then the organ, one stop of which I seem to draw out; then the French poem which I am composing. Then it seems to me that this triad is some instrument of torture with which my right foot is constantly compressed. This was so severe that I woke up, and opening my eyes I rubbed my leg. It was beginning to grow numb with cold.

The night was, as before, light, melancholy, white. The sledge and its passengers were still shaken by the same motion; there was Ignashka sitting on one side and stamping his feet. There was the off-horse as before, straining her neck, lifting her feet, as she trotted over the deep snow; the tassel slipping along the reins, and whipping against the horse's belly; the head of the shaft-horse, with the waving mane, alternately pulling and loosening the reins attached to the bell-bow as it nodded up and down. But all this was covered and hidden with snow far more than before. The snow was whirled about in front of us, and covered up our runners, and reached above the horses' knees, and fell thick and fast on our collars and caps. The wind blew now from the right, now from the left, and played with the collar and tails of Ignashka's cloak, the mane of the horses, and howled above the bell-bow and the shafts.

It had become fearfully cold; and I had scarcely lifted my head out of my collar ere the frosty dry snow made its way, rustling, into my eyelids, nose, and mouth, and ran down my neck. Looking around, all was white, light, and snowy; nothing anywhere except a melancholy light and the snow. I felt a sensation of real terror. Alyoshka was sitting cross-legged in the very depths of the sledge; his whole back was covered with a thick deposit of snow.

Ignashka still kept up his spirits; he kept constantly pulling at the reins, stamping and pounding his feet. The bell also sounded strange. The horses sometimes snorted, but plunged along more quietly, though they stumbled more and more often. Ignashka again sprang up, swung his mittens, and began to sing in his clear, strong voice. Not ceasing to sing, he stopped the troïka, tossed the reins on the dasher, and got out. The wind howled madly; the snow, as though shovelled down, was dashed upon the folds of my furs.

I looked around. The third troïka was nowhere to be seen (it had stopped somewhere). Next the second troïka, in a mist of snow, could be seen the little old man making his way with long strides. Ignashka went three steps from the sledge, sat down in the snow, took off his girdle, and began to remove his boots.

"What are you going to do?" I asked.

"Must change my boots: this leg is frozen solid," he replied, and went on with his work.

It was cold for me to keep my neck out of my collar to watch what he was doing. I sat straight, looking at the off-horse, which, with legs spread, stood feebly switching its snow-covered tail. The thump which Ignat gave the sledge as he clambered to his place startled me.

"Well, where are we now?" I asked. "Are we getting any-where in the world?"

"Don't you worry. We shall get there," he replied. "Now my feet are thoroughly warm, since I changed them."

And he drove on; the bells jingled, the sledge again began to rock, and the wind whistled under the runners, and once more we struggled to swim through the limitless ocean of snow.

X.

I sunk into a sound sleep. When Alyoshka awoke me by punching me in the leg, and I opened my eyes, it was morning. It seemed even colder than it had been during the night. There was nothing to be seen but snow; but a strong dry wind still swept the powdery snow across the field, and especially under the hoofs of the horses, and the runners of the sledge. The sky on the right toward the east was of a deep purple color, but the bright reddish-orange rays of the sunrise kept growing more and more clearly defined in it; above our heads, between the hurrying white clouds, scarcely tinged as yet, gleamed the sickly blue of the sky; in the west the clouds were bright, light, and fluctuating. Every-where around, as far as the eye could see, lay the snow, white and deep, in sharply defined strata. Everywhere could be seen gray hillocks where lay the fine, dry, powdery snow. Nothing was to be seen,—not even the shadow of a sledge, nor of a human being, nor of a beast. The outline and color of the driver's back, and of the horses, began to stand out clear and sharp against the white background. The rim of Ignashka's dark-blue cap, his collar, his hair, and even his boots, were white. The sledge was perfectly covered. The whole right side and the mane of the brown shaft-horse were plastered with snow. The legs of my off-horse were thick with it up to the knee, and the whole of the shaggy right flank had the same sticky covering. The tassel leaped up and down in some sort of rhythm, the structure of which it would not be easy to represent; and the off-horse also kept to it in her gait: only by the gaunt belly rising and sinking, and by the hanging ears, could it be seen how tired she was.

Only one new object attracted the attention: this was a verst-post, from which the snow had been blown away, leaving it clear to the ground, and making a perfect mountain on one side; while the wind was still sweeping it across, and drifting it from one side to the other.

It was odd to me to think that we had gone the whole night without change of horses, not knowing for twelve hours where we were, and not coming to our destination, and yet not really missing the road. Our bells seemed to sound more cheerful than ever. Ignat buttoned his coat up, and began to shout again. Behind us snorted the horses, and jingled the bells, of the troïka that carried the little old man and the mentor; but the one who was asleep had wandered away from us somewhere on the steppe.

After going half a verst farther, we came upon the fresh, and as yet unobliterated, traces of a sledge and troïka; and occasionally drops of blood, caused by the whip on the horses' side, could be seen.

"That was Filipp. See, he's got in ahead of us," said Ignashka.

And here appears a little house with a sign, alone by itself, near the road, standing in the midst of the snow which covers it almost to the roof. Near the inn stands a troïka of gray horses, their hair rough with sweat, with wide-spread legs and drooping heads. At the door, the snow is shovelled away, and the shovel is standing in it; but it still falls from the roof, and the roaring wind whirls the snow around.

Out from the door at the sound of our bells comes a big ruddy, red-headed driver, with a glass of wine in his hand, and shouts something. Ignashka turns to me, and asks permission to stop. Then for the first time I fairly see his face.

XI.

His features were not dark, dry, and regular, as I had reason to expect from his hair and build. His face was round, jolly, with a snub nose and a big mouth, and clear-shining eyes, blue and round. His cheeks and neck were like well-worn cloth. His eyebrows, his long eyelashes, and the beard which evenly covered the lower part of his face, were crusted thick with snow, and perfectly white.

The distance to the station was all of a half-verst, and we stopped.

"Only be quick about it," I said.

"Just a minute," replied Ignashka, springing down from his seat, and going up to Filipp.

"Let us have it, brother," said he, taking the glass in his right hand; and throwing his mitten and whip down on the snow, tipping back his head, he drank down at a gulp the glass of vodka.

The inn-keeper, who must have been a discharged Cossack, came, with a bottle in his hand, out of the door.

"Who have you got there?" he asked.

The tall Vasíli, a lean, blond muzhík with a goatee, and the fat mentor, with white eyebrows, and a thick white beard framing his ruddy face, came up and also drank a glass. The little old man joined the group of drinkers; but no one offered him any thing, and he went off again to his horses, fastened behind, and began to stroke one of them on the back and side.

The little old man was pretty much what I had imagined him to be; small, ugly, with wrinkled, strongly marked features, a thin little beard, a sharp nose, and worn yellow teeth. He wore a driver's cap, perfectly new; but his sheepskin jacket[20] was old, soiled with oil, and torn on the shoulders and flaps, and did not cover his knees or his hempen trousers tucked into his huge felt boots. He himself was bent, and frowned all the time, and, with trembling lips and limbs, tramped around his sledge in his efforts to keep warm.

"Well, Mitritch, you ought to have a drink; it would warm you up," said the mentor to him.

Mitritch gave a start. He arranged the horses' harness, straightened the bell-bow, and then came to me.

---

[20] *polushúbchishka.*

"Say, bárin," said he, taking his cap off from his white hair and bowing very low, "all night long we have been wandering together; we have found the road. We would seem to deserve a bit of a drink. Isn't that so, sir, your eminence?[21] just enough to get warmed," he added with an obsequious smile.

I gave him a quarter-ruble. The inn-keeper brought out a glass of vodka, and handed it to the old man. He laid aside his mitten and whip, and took the glass in his small, dark hand, bony and somewhat bluish; but strangely enough he could not control his thumb. Before he had lifted the glass to his lips, he dropped it in the snow, spilling the wine.

All the drivers burst out laughing.

"See, Mitritch-to is half-frozen like; he can't hold his wine."

But Mitritch was greatly vexed because he had spilt the wine.

They brought him, however, another glass, and poured it into his mouth. He immediately became jolly, went into the inn, lighted his pipe, began to show his yellow worn teeth, and to scold at every word. After they had taken their last drinks, the drivers came back to their troïkas, and we set off.

The snow kept growing whiter and brighter, till it made one's eyes ache to look at it. The orange-colored reddish streaks stretched brighter and brighter, higher and higher, across the heavens; now the red circle of the sun appeared on the horizon through the bluish clouds; the blue sky came out in constantly increasing brilliancy and depth. On the road around the station the tracks were clear, distinct, and yellow; in some places were cradle-holes. In the frosty, bracing atmosphere, there was a pleasant exhilaration and freshness.

My troïka glided along very swiftly. The head of the shaft-horse, and the neck with the mane tossing up to the bell-bow, constantly made the same quick, swinging motions under the hunting-bell, the tongue of which no longer struck, but scraped around the rim. The good side-horses, in friendly rivalry tugging at the frozen twisted traces, energetically galloped on, the tassels striking against their ribs and necks. Occasionally the off-horse

---

[21] bátiushka, váshe siyátelstvo.

would plunge into some drift, and kick up the snow, filling the eyes with the fine powder. Ignashka kept shouting in his gay tenor. The runners creaked over the dry, frosty snow. Behind us, with a loud festival sound, rang the two sledge-chimes; and the voices of the drivers, made jolly by wine, could be heard.

I looked back: the gray shaggy side-horses arching their necks, regularly puffing out the breath, with their curved bits, galloped over the snow. Filipp was flourishing his whip and adjusting his cap. The little old man, with his legs hanging out, was reclining as before in the middle of his sledge.

At the end of two minutes the sledge scraped against the boards of the well-cleared entrance of the station-house; and Ignashka turned to me, his jolly face covered with snow, where his breath had turned to ice, and said,—

"Here we are, bárin!"

CHEKHOV'S SHORT STORIES
BY ANTON CHEKHOV

VANKA

Vanka Zhukov, a nine-year-old boy, who had been apprenticed to Alyahin the shoemaker these three months, did not go to bed on Christmas Eve. After his master and mistress and the journeymen had gone to midnight Mass, he got an inkpot and a penholder with a rusty nib out of the master's cupboard and having spread out a crumpled sheet of paper, began writing. Before he formed the first letter he looked fearfully at the doors and windows several times, shot a glance at the dark icon, at either side of which stretched shelves filled with lasts, and heaved a broken sigh. He was kneeling before a bench on which his paper lay.

"Dear Granddaddy, Konstantin Makarych," he wrote. "And I am writing you a letter. I wish you a merry Christmas and everything good from the Lord God. I have neither father nor mother, you alone are left me."

Vanka shifted his glance to the dark window on which flickered the reflection of his candle and vividly pictured his grandfather to himself. Employed as a watchman by the Zhivaryovs, he was a short, thin, but extraordinarily lively and nimble old man of about sixty-five whose face was always crinkled with laughter and who had a toper's eyes. By day he slept in the servants' kitchen or cracked jokes with the cook; at night, wrapped in an ample sheepskin coat, he made the rounds of the estate, shaking his clapper. The old bitch, Brownie, and the dog called Wriggles, who had a black coat and a long body like a weasel's, followed him with hanging heads. This Wriggles was extraordinarily deferential and demonstrative, looked with equally friendly eyes both at his masters and at strangers, but did not enjoy a good reputation. His deference and meekness concealed the most Jesuitical spite. No one knew better than he how to creep up behind you and suddenly snap at your leg, how to slip into the icehouse, or how to steal a hen from a peasant. More than once his hind legs had been all but broken, twice he had been hanged, every week he was whipped till he was half dead, but he always managed to revive.

At the moment Grandfather was sure to be standing at the gates, screwing up his eyes at the bright-red windows of the church, stamping his felt boots, and cracking jokes with the servants. His clapper was tied to his belt. He was clapping his hands, shrugging with the cold, and, with a senile titter, pinching now the housemaid, now the cook.

"Shall we have a pinch of snuff?" he was saying, offering the women his snuffbox.

They each took a pinch and sneezed. Grandfather, indescribably delighted, went off into merry peals of laughter and shouted:

"Peel it off, it has frozen on!"

The dogs too are given a pinch of snuff. Brownie sneezes, wags her head, and walks away offended. Wriggles is too polite to sneeze and only wags his tail. And the weather is glorious. The air is still, clear, and fresh. The night is dark, but one can see the whole village with its white roofs and smoke streaming out of the chimneys, the trees silvery with hoarfrost, the snowdrifts. The entire sky is studded with gaily twinkling stars and the Milky Way is as distinctly visible as though it had been washed and rubbed with snow for the holiday. . . .

Vanka sighed, dipped his pen into the ink and went on writing:

"And yesterday I got it hot. The master pulled me out into the courtyard by the hair and gave me a hiding with a knee-strap because I was rocking the baby in its cradle and happened to fall asleep. And last week the mistress ordered me to clean a herring and I began with the tail, and she took the herring and jabbed me in the mug with it. The helpers make fun of me, send me to the pothouse for vodka and tell me to steal pickles for them from the master, and the master hits me with anything that comes handy. And there is nothing to eat. In the morning they give me bread, for dinner porridge, and in the evening bread again. As for tea or cabbage soup, the master and mistress bolt it all themselves. And they tell me to sleep in the entry, and when the baby cries I don't sleep at all, but rock the cradle. Dear Granddaddy, for God's sake have pity on me, take me away from here, take me home to the village, it's more than I can bear. I bow down at your feet and I will pray to God for you forever, take me away from here or I'll die."

Vanka puckered his mouth, rubbed his eyes with his black fist, and gave a sob.

"I will grind your snuff for you," he continued, "I will pray to God for you, and if anything happens, you may thrash me all you like. And if you think there's no situation for me, I will beg the manager for Christ's sake to let me clean boots, or I will take Fedka's place as a shepherd boy. Dear Granddaddy, it's more than I can bear, it will simply be the death of me. I thought of running away to the village, but I have no boots and I am afraid of the frost. And in return for this when I grow big, I will feed you and won't let anybody do you any harm, and when you die I will pray for the repose of your soul, just as for my Mom's.

"Moscow is a big city. The houses are all the kind the gentry live in, and there are lots of horses, but no sheep, and the dogs are not fierce. The boys here don't go caroling, carrying the star at Christmas, and they don't let anyone sing in the choir, and once in a shop window I saw fishing-hooks for sale all fitted up with a line, for every kind of fish, very fine ones, there was even one hook that will hold a forty-pound sheatfish. And I saw shops where there are all sorts of guns, like the master's at home, so maybe each one of them is a hundred rubles. And in butchers' shops there are woodcocks and partridge and hares, but where they shoot them the clerks won't tell.

"Dear Granddaddy, when they have a Christmas tree with presents at the master's, do get a gilt walnut and put it away in the little green chest. Ask the young lady, Olga Ignatyevna, for it, say it's for Vanka."

Vanka heaved a broken sigh and again stared at the window. He recalled that it was his grandfather who always went to the forest to get the Christmas tree for the master's family and that he would take his grandson with him. It was a jolly time! Grandfather grunted, the frost crackled, and, not to be outdone, Vanka too made a cheerful noise in his throat. Before chopping down the Christmas tree, Grandfather would smoke a pipe, slowly take a pinch of snuff, and poke fun at Vanka who looked chilled to the bone. The young firs draped in hoarfrost stood still, waiting to see which of them was to die. Suddenly, coming out of nowhere, a hare would dart across the snowdrifts like an arrow. Grandfather could not keep from shouting: "Hold him, hold him, hold him! Ah, the bob-tailed devil!"

When he had cut down the fir tree, Grandfather would drag it to the master's house, and there they would set to work decorating it. The young lady, Olga Ignatyevna, Vanka's favorite, was the busiest of all. When Vanka's mother, Pelageya, was alive and a chambermaid in the master's house, the young lady used to give him goodies, and, having nothing with which to occupy herself, taught him to read and write, to count up to a hundred, and even to dance the quadrille. When Pelageya died, Vanka had been relegated to the servants' kitchen to stay with his grandfather, and from the kitchen to the shoemaker's.

"Do come, dear Granddaddy," Vanka went on. "For Christ's sake, I beg you, take me away from here. Have pity on me, an unhappy orphan, here everyone beats me, and I am terribly hungry, and I am so blue, I can't tell you how, I keep crying. And the other day the master hit me on the head with a last, so that I fell down and it was a long time before I came to. My life is miserable, worse than a dog's—I also send greetings to Alyona, one-eyed Yegorka and the coachman, and don't give my harmonica to anyone. I remain, your grandson, Ivan Zhukov, dear Granddaddy, do come."

Vanka twice folded the sheet covered with writing and put it into an envelope he had bought for a kopeck the previous day.

He reflected a while, then dipped the pen into the ink and wrote the address:

To Grandfather in the village

Then he scratched himself, thought a little, and added: *Konstantin Makarych.* Glad that no one had interrupted him at his writing, he put on his cap and, without slipping on his coat, ran out into the street with nothing over his shirt.

The clerks at the butchers' whom he had questioned the day before had told him that letters were dropped into letter boxes and from the boxes they were carried all over the world in troikas with ringing bells and drunken drivers. Vanka ran to the nearest letter box and thrust the precious letter into the slit.

An hour later, lulled by sweet hopes, he was fast asleep. In his dream he saw the stove. On the stove sat grandfather, his bare legs hanging down, and read the letter to the cooks. Near the stove was Wriggles, wagging his tail.

1886

PEASANTS

Nikolay Chikildeyev, a waiter in the Moscow hotel, Slavyansky Bazar, had been taken ill. His legs went numb and his gait became unsteady, so that one day as he was going along the corridor, carrying an order of ham and peas on a tray, he stumbled and fell. He had to give up his job. Whatever money he and his wife had was spent on doctors and medicines; they had nothing left to live on; idleness weighed heavily upon him and he decided to go back to the village from which he had come. It was easier to be ill at home, and it was cheaper living there; and not for nothing is it said that there is help in the walls of home.

He arrived in his native Zhukovo toward evening. In his childhood the house in which he was born figured as a bright, cosy, comfortable place. But now, going into the log cabin, he was positively frightened: it was so dark and crowded and squalid. His wife Olga and his daughter Sasha, who had come with him, stared in bewilderment at the big dirty stove, which occupied almost half the room and was black with soot and flies. What a lot of flies! The stove was lopsided, the logs in the walls sloped, and it looked as though the cabin were about to collapse. In the corner, near the icons, bottle labels and scraps of newspaper were pasted on the walls instead of pictures. The poverty, the poverty! None of the grown-ups were at home; all were at work, reaping. On the stove sat a flaxen-haired girl of eight, unwashed, apathetic; she did not even look up at the newcomers. Below, a white cat was rubbing itself against the oven fork.

"Pussy, pussy!" Sasha called to it coaxingly. "Pussy!"

"It can't hear," said the little girl; "it's gone deaf."

"Why?"

"Oh, it was hit."

Nikolay and Olga realized at first glance what life was like here, but said nothing to each other; silently they put down their bundles, and silently went out into the village street. Their cabin was the third from the end and seemed the poorest and oldest-looking; the second was not much better; but the last one had an iron roof and curtains at the windows. That cottage stood apart, and was not enclosed; it was a tavern. The cabins were all in a single row, and the entire little village—quiet and pensive, with willows, elders, and mountain ash peeping out from the court-yards—had a pleasant look.

Behind the peasant homesteads the ground sloped down to the river steeply and precipitously, so that huge boulders jutted out here and there through the clay. On the steep slope paths wound among the stones and pits dug by the potters; pieces of broken pottery, brown and red, lay about in heaps, and below there stretched a broad, level, bright-green meadow, already mown, over which the peasants' cattle were now wandering. The river, two thirds of a mile from the village, ran, twisting and turning, between beautiful wooded banks. Beyond it was another broad meadow, a herd of cattle, long files of white geese; then, just as on the hither side, there was a steep rise, and at the top of it, on a ridge, a village with a church that had five domes, and, at a little distance, a manor house.

"It's nice here!" said Olga, crossing herself at the sight of the church. "Lord, what space!"

Just at that moment the bells began ringing for vespers (it was Saturday evening). Two little girls, down below, who were carrying a pail of water, looked round at the church to listen to the chimes.

"About this time they are serving the dinners at the Slavyansky Bazar," said Nikolay dreamily.

Sitting on the edge of the ravine, Nikolay and Olga watched the sunset, and saw how the gold and crimson sky was reflected in the river, in the church windows, and in the very air, which was soft and still and inexpressibly pure, as it never was in Moscow. And when the sun had set, the herds went past, bleating and bellowing; geese flew across from the other side of the river, and then all was hushed; the soft light faded from the air, and dusk began its rapid descent.

Meanwhile Nikolay's father and mother, two gaunt, bent, toothless old people, of the same height, had returned. The daughters-in-law, Marya and Fyokla, who had been working on the estate across the river, came home, too. Marya, the wife of Nikolay's brother Kiryak, had six children, and Fyokla, the wife of his brother Denis, who was in the army, had two; and when Nikolay, stepping into the cabin, saw the whole family, all those bodies big and little stirring on the sleeping platforms, in the cradles and in all the corners, and when he saw the greed with which his old father and the women ate the black bread, dipping it in water, it was borne in upon him that he had made a mistake in coming here, sick, penniless, and with a family, too—a mistake!

"And where is brother Kiryak?" he asked, when they had greeted each other.

"He works as a watchman for a merchant," answered his father; "he stays there in the woods. He ain't a bad worker, but he's too fond of the drink."

"He's no breadwinner," said the old woman tearfully. "Our men are a poor lot; they bring nothing into the house, but take plenty out. Kiryak drinks, and the old man too knows his way to the tavern—it's no use hiding the sin. The wrath of the Queen of Heaven is on us."

On account of the guests they heated the samovar. The tea smelt of fish; the sugar was gray and had been nibbled; cockroaches ran about over the bread and the crockery. It was disgusting to drink the tea, and the conversation was disgusting, too—about nothing but poverty and sickness. And before they had emptied their first cups there came a loud, long-drawn-out, drunken shout from the courtyard:

"Ma-arya!"

"Looks like Kiryak's coming," said the old man. "Talk of the devil—"

Silence fell. And after a little while, the shout sounded again, coarse and long-drawn-out, as though it came from under the ground:

"Ma-arya!"

Marya, the elder daughter-in-law, turned pale and huddled against the stove, and it was odd to see the look of terror on the face of this strong, broad-shouldered, homely woman. Her daughter, the apathetic-looking little girl who had been sitting on the stove, suddenly broke into loud weeping.

"What are you bawling for, you pest?" Fyokla, a handsome woman, also strong and broad-shouldered, shouted at her. "He won't kill her, no fear!"

From the old man Nikolay learned that Marya was afraid to live in the woods with Kiryak, and that whenever he was drunk he came for her, raised Cain, and beat her mercilessly.

"Ma-arya!" the shout sounded at the very door.

"Help me, for Christ's sake, good people," stammered Marya, breathing as though she were being plunged into icy water. "Help me, good people—,"

All the children in the cabin began crying, and affected by their example, Sasha, too, began to cry. A drunken cough was heard, and a tall, black-bearded peasant wearing a winter cap came into the cabin, and because his face could not be seen in the dim light of the little lamp, he looked terrifying. It was Kiryak.

Going up to his wife, he swung his arm and punched her in the face; stunned by the blow, she did not utter a sound, but sank down, and her nose instantly began bleeding.

"What a shame! What a shame!" muttered the old man, clambering up onto the stove. "Before guests, too! What a sin!"

The old woman sat silent, hunched, lost in thought; Fyokla rocked the cradle.

Evidently aware of inspiring terror, and pleased by it, Kiryak seized Marya by the arm, dragged her toward the door, and growled like a beast in order to seem still more terrible; but at that moment he suddenly caught sight of the guests and halted.

"Oh, they have come . . ." he said, letting go of his wife; "my own brother with his family . . ."

Staggering and opening his blood-shot, drunken eyes wide, he muttered a prayer before the icon and went on:

"My dear brother and his family, come to the parental house —from Moscow, I mean. The ancient capital city of Moscow, I mean, mother of cities—Excuse me."

He sank down on the bench near the samovar and began drinking tea, sipping it loudly from the saucer amid general silence. He drank a dozen cups, then lay down on the bench and began to snore.

They started going to bed. Nikolay, being ill, was to sleep on the stove with the old man; Sasha lay down on the floor, while Olga went into the shed with the other women.

"Now, now, dearie," she said, lying down on the hay beside Marya; "tears won't help. Bear your cross, that's all. It says in Scripture: 'Whosoever shall smite thee on thy right cheek, turn to him the other also.' . . . Now, now, dearie."

Then, speaking under her breath in a singsong, she told them about Moscow, about her life, how she had been a chambermaid in furnished rooms.

"And in Moscow the houses are big, made of stone," she said; "and there are many, many churches, forty times forty, dearie; and in the houses they're all gentry, so goodlooking and so proper!"

Marya said that not only had she never been to Moscow, but

had not even been in their own district town; she could neither read nor write, and knew no prayers, not even "Our Father." Both she and Fyokla, her sister-in-law, who was sitting a little way off listening, were exceedingly backward and dull-witted. They both disliked their husbands; Marya was afraid of Kiryak, and whenever he stayed with her she shook with fear, and always got a headache from the fumes of vodka and tobacco of which he reeked. And in response to the question whether she did not miss her husband, Fyokla replied sourly:

"Deuce take him!"

They talked a while and then grew silent.

It was cool, and a cock was crowing at the top of his voice near the shed, interfering with sleep. When the bluish morning light was already showing through every crack, Fyokla got up quietly and went out, and then they heard her hurry off somewhere, her bare feet thumping as she ran.

II

Olga went to church, and took Marya with her. As they went down the path toward the meadow both were cheerful. Olga liked the open country, and Marya felt that in her sister-in-law she had found someone near and dear to her. The sun was rising. Low over the meadow hovered a drowsy hawk; the river looked dull; wisps of mist were floating here and there, but on the farther shore a streak of light already lay across the hill; the church was shining, and in the garden attached to the manor the rooks were cawing frantically.

"The old man ain't bad," Marya told her, "but Granny is strict, and is free with her hand. Our own flour lasted till Carnival, and now we buy it at the tavern; so she's cross; she says we eat too much."

"Now, now, dearie! Bear your cross, that's all. It's written: 'Come unto me, all ye that labor and are heavy laden.' "

Olga spoke sedately, in a singsong, and her gait was that of a pilgrim woman, rapid and fidgety. Every day she read the gospel, read it aloud like a deacon; a great deal of it she did not understand, but the sacred phrases moved her to tears, and such words as "behold" and "whosoever" she pronounced with a sweet faintness at her heart. She believed in God, in the Holy Virgin, in the saints; she believed that it was wrong to harm anyone—whether simple folk, or Germans, or gypsies, or Jews— and that misfortune awaited even those who did not pity animals. She believed that this was written in the Scriptures; and so when she pronounced words from Holy Writ, even though she did not understand them, her face softened with emotion, grew compassionate and radiant.

"Where do you come from?" Marya asked her.

"I am from the province of Vladimir. But I was taken to Moscow long ago, when I was eight years old."

They reached the river. On the other side a woman stood at the water's edge, taking off her clothes.

"That's our Fyokla," said Marya, recognizing her. "She's been across the river to the manor yard. She's been with the squire's men. She's a hussy and foul-mouthed—she is that!"

Black-browed Fyokla, her hair undone, still young and with the firm flesh of a girl, jumped off the bank and began thrashing the water with her feet, sending waves in all directions.

"A hussy—she is that!" repeated Marya.

The river was spanned by a rickety little bridge of logs, and below in the clean, clear water shoals of broad-headed chub were swimming. The dew was glistening on the green shrubs that were mirrored in the water. Then the air grew warmer; it was pleasant. What a glorious morning it was! And how glorious life would probably be in this world, were it not for want, horrible, inescapable want, from which you cannot hide anywhere! Only to look round at the village was to remember all that had happened the day before, and the spell of the happiness that they thought they felt around them vanished instantly.

They went into the church. Marya stood in the entrance and did not dare to go farther. Nor did she dare to sit down either, though they only began ringing for Mass after eight o'clock. She remained standing the whole time.

While the gospel was being read the crowd suddenly parted to make way for the squire's family. Two young ladies in white frocks and wide-brimmed hats walked in, and with them was a chubby, rosy boy in a sailor suit. Their appearance moved Olga; she concluded at first glance that they were decent, elegant, cultivated people. But Marya glared at them from under her brows, sullenly, dejectedly, as though they were not human beings but monsters who might crush her if she did not move aside.

And every time the deacon intoned in his bass voice, she imagined that she heard the cry, "Ma-arya!" and she shuddered.

III

The arrival of the guests became known in the village, and directly after Mass a great many people assembled in the cabin. The Leonychevs and the Matveichevs and the Ilyichovs came to make inquiries about relatives of theirs who had situations in Moscow. All the lads of Zhukovo who could read and write were packed off to Moscow and hired out as bellboys or waiters (just as the lads from the village on the other side of the river all apprenticed to bakers), and this had been the custom from the days of serfdom, long ago, when a certain Luka Ivanych, a peasant from Zhukovo, now a legendary figure, who had been a bartender in one of the Moscow clubs, would take none but his fellow villagers into his service, and these in turn, as they got up in the world, sent for their kinsfolk and found jobs for them in taverns and restaurants; and from that time on the village of Zhukovo was known throughout the countryside round about as Flunkeyville or Toadytown. Nikolay had been taken to Moscow when he was eleven, and gotten a situation by Ivan Makarych, a Matveichev, who was then an attendant at the Hermitage garden restaurant. And now, addressing the Matveichevs, Nikolay said unctuously:

"Ivan Makarych is my benefactor, and I am bound to pray for him day and night, because it was he who set me on the right path."

"God bless you!" a tall old woman, the sister of Ivan Makarych, said tearfully, "and not a word have we heard about him, the dear man."

"Last winter he was in service at Omon's, and there was a rumor that this season he was somewhere out of town, in a garden restaurant. He has aged! Why, it used to be that he would bring home as much as ten rubles a day in the summertime, but now things are very quiet everywhere. It's hard on the old man."

The women and the old crones looked at Nikolay's feet, shod in felt boots, and at his pale face, and said mournfully:

"You're no breadwinner, Nikolay Osipych; you're no breadwinner! No, indeed!"

And they all fondled Sasha. She was going on eleven, but she was small and very thin, and she looked no more than seven. Among the other little girls, with their sunburnt faces and roughly cropped hair, and their long, faded shifts, she, with her pallor, her big dark eyes and the red ribbon in her hair, looked droll, as though she were some little wild thing that had been caught in the fields and brought into the cabin.

"She can read, too," said Olga, looking tenderly at her daughter and showing her off. "Read a little, child!" she said, taking the Gospels from the corner. "You read, and the good Christian folk will listen."

It was an old, heavy volume in a leather binding with dog-eared edges, and it gave off a smell as though monks had come into the house. Sasha raised her eyebrows and began in a loud singsong:

" 'And when they were departed, behold, the angel of the Lord . . . appeareth to Joseph in a dream, saying, Arise, and take the young child and his mother . . .' "

" 'The young child and his mother,' " Olga repeated, and flushed all over with emotion.

" 'And flee into Egypt, and be thou there until I bring thee word: for Herod will seek the young child, to destroy him . . .' "

At these words Olga could not contain herself and burst into tears. Affected by her example, Marya began to whimper, and then Ivan Makarych's sister followed suit. The old man coughed and bustled about looking for a present for his granddaughter, but finding nothing, gave it up with a wave of his hand. And when the reading was over the neighbors dispersed to their homes, deeply moved and very much pleased with Olga and Sasha.

Because of the holiday, the family stayed home all day. The old woman, whom her husband, her daughters-in-law, her grand-children, all alike called Granny, always tried to do everything herself; she lit the stove and heated the samovar with her own hands, even carried the midday meal to the men in the fields, and then complained that she was worn out with work. And all the time she fretted for fear that someone should eat a bite too much or that her husband and daughters-in-law should sit idle. Now she would hear the tavernkeeper's geese making for her kitchen gar-den by the back way, and she would run out of the cabin with a long stick and spend half an hour screaming beside her cabbages which were as meager and flabby as herself; again she would imagine that a crow was after her chickens and would rush at it with loud words of abuse. She was cross and full of complaints from morning till night, and often raised such a hubbub that passers-by stopped in the street.

She treated the old man roughly, calling him a lazybones and a plague. He was a shiftless, undependable man, and perhaps if she had not been prodding him continually he would not have worked at all, but would just have sat on the stove and talked. He told his son at great length about certain enemies of his, com-plained of the injuries he suffered every day at the hands of the neighbors, and it was tedious to listen to him.

"Yes," he would hold forth, with his arms akimbo, "yes—A week after the Exaltation of the Cross I sold my hay at thirty kopecks a pood, of my own free will. Yes, well and good. So you see I was taking the hay in the morning of my own free will; I wasn't doing no one no harm. In an unlucky hour I see the village headman, Antip Sedelnikov, coming out of the tavern. 'Where are you taking it, you blank blank?' says he, and fetches me a box on the ear."

Kiryak had a terrible hangover and was ashamed to face his brother.

"What vodka will do! Oh, my God!" he muttered as he

shook his throbbing head. "For Christ's sake, forgive me, dear brother and sister; I'm not happy about it myself."

Because it was a holiday, they bought a herring at the tavern and made a soup of the herring head. At midday they sat down to have tea and went on drinking it until they were all perspiring; they looked actually swollen with tea; and then they attacked the soup, all helping themselves out of one pot. The herring itself Granny hid away.

In the evening a potter was firing pots on the slope. Down below in the meadow the girls got up a round dance and sang songs. Someone played an accordion. On the other side of the river, too, one kiln was going, and the girls sang songs, and in the distance the singing sounded soft and melodious. In and about the tavern the peasants were making a racket. They sang with drunken voices, discordantly, and swore at one another so filthily that Olga could only shudder and repeat:

"Oh, holy saints!"

What amazed her was that the swearing was incessant, and that the old men who were near their end were the loudest and most persistent in using this foul language. And the girls and children listened to the swearing without turning a hair; it was evident that they had been used to it from their cradles.

It got to be past midnight, the fire in the kilns on both sides of the river died down, but in the meadow below and in the tavern the merrymaking continued. The old man and Kiryak, both drunk, walking arm in arm, their shoulders jostling, went up to the shed where Olga and Marya were lying.

"Let her be," the old man pleaded; "let her be—She's a harmless woman—It's a sin—"

"Ma-arya!" shouted Kiryak.

"Let her be—It's a sin—She's not a bad woman."

Both stood there for a minute and then went on.

"I lo-ove the flowers of the fi-ield," the old man burst forth in a high, piercing tenor. "I lo-ove to pick them in the meadows!"

Then he spat, swore filthily, and went into the cabin.

IV

Granny stationed Sasha near her kitchen garden and ordered her to see to it that the geese did not get in. It was a hot August day. The tavernkeeper's geese could get into the kitchen garden by the back way, but at the moment they were seriously engaged: they were picking up oats near the tavern, peacefully chatting together, and only the gander craned his neck as though to see if the old woman were not coming with a stick. Other geese from down below might have trespassed, but they were now feeding far away on the other side of the river, stretching across the meadow in a long white garland. Sasha stood about a while, grew bored, and, seeing that the geese were not coming, went up to the brink of the slope.

There she saw Marya's eldest daughter Motka, who was standing motionless on a huge boulder, staring at the church. Marya had been brought to bed thirteen times, but she had only six living children, all girls, not one boy, and the eldest was eight. Motka, barefoot and wearing a long shift, was standing in the full sunshine; the sun was blazing down right on her head, but she did not notice it, and seemed as though turned to stone. Sasha stood beside her and said, looking at the church:

"God lives in the church. People have lamps and candles, but God has little green and red and blue iconlamps like weeny eyes. At night God walks about the church, and with Him the Holy Mother of God and Saint Nicholas—clump, clump, clump they go! And the watchman is scared, so scared! Now, now, dearie," she added, imitating her mother. "And when the end of the world comes, all the churches will fly up to heaven."

"With the be-elfri-ies?" Motka asked in a deep voice, drawling the syllables.

"With the belfries. And when the end of the world comes, the good people will go to Paradise, but the wicked will burn in fire eternal and unquenchable, dearie. To my mama and to Marya, too, God will say: 'You never harmed anyone, and so you go to the right, to Paradise'; but to Kiryak and Granny He will say: 'You go to the left, into the fire.' And the ones who ate forbidden food on fast days will be sent into the fire, too.''

She looked up at the sky, opening her eyes wide, and said: "Look at the sky and don't blink and you will see angels."

Motka began looking at the sky, too, and a minute passed in silence.

"Do you see them?" asked Sasha.

"I don't," said Motka in her deep voice.

"But I do. Little angels are flying about the sky and go flap, flap with their little wings like midges."

Motka thought for a while, with her eyes on the ground, and asked:

"Will Granny burn?"

"She will, dearie."

From the boulder down to the very bottom there was a smooth, gentle slope, covered with soft green grass, which one longed to touch with one's hands or to lie upon.

Sasha lay down and rolled to the bottom. Motka, with a grave, stern face, and breathing heavily, followed suit, and as she did so, her shift rolled up to her shoulders.

"What fun!" said Sasha, delighted.

They walked up to the top to roll down again, but just then they heard the familiar, shrill voice. Oh, how awful it was! Granny, toothless, bony, hunched, her short gray hair flying in the wind, was driving the geese out of the kitchen garden with a long stick, screaming.

"They have trampled all the cabbages, the cursed creatures! May you croak, you thrice accursed plagues! Why don't the devil take you!"

She saw the little girls, threw down the stick, picked up a switch, and, seizing Sasha by the neck with her fingers, dry and hard as spikes, began whipping her. Sasha cried with pain and fear, while the gander, waddling and craning his neck, went up to the old woman and hissed something, and when he went back to his flock all the geese greeted him approvingly with a "Ga-ga-ga!" Then Granny proceeded to whip Motka, and so Motka's shift was rolled up again. In despair and crying loudly, Sasha went to the cabin to complain. Motka followed her; she, too, was crying, but on a deeper note, without wiping her tears, and her face as wet as though it had been dipped in water.

"Holy Fathers!" cried Olga, dismayed, as the two came into the cabin. "Queen of Heaven!"

Sasha began telling her story, when Granny walked in with shrill cries and abuse; then Fyokla got angry, and there was a hubbub in the house.

"Never mind, never mind!" Olga, pale and distressed, tried to comfort the children, stroking Sasha's head. "She's your grandmother; it's a sin to be cross with her. Never mind, child."

Nikolay, who was already worn out by the continual clamor, the hunger, the sickening fumes, the stench, who already hated and despised the poverty, who was ashamed of his father and mother before his wife and daughter, swung his legs off the stove and said to his mother in an irritable, tearful voice:

"You shouldn't beat her! You have no right to beat her!"

"You're ready to croak there on the stove, you loafer!" Fyokla snapped at him spitefully. "The devil has brought you here, you spongers!"

Sasha and Motka and all the little girls in the household huddled into a corner on top of the stove behind Nikolay's back, and from there listened to all this in silence and terror, and one could hear the beating of their little hearts. When there is someone in a family who has long been ill, and hopelessly ill, there come terrible moments when all those close to him timidly, secretly, at the bottom of their hearts wish for his death, and only the children fear the death of someone close to them, and always feel horrified at the thought of it. And now the little girls, with bated breath and a mournful look on their faces, stared at Nikolay and thought that he would soon die; and they wanted to cry and to say something friendly and compassionate to him.

He was pressing close to Olga, as though seeking her protection, and saying to her softly in a shaking voice:

"Olya dear, I can't bear it here any longer. I haven't the strength. For Christ's sake, for the sake of God in heaven, write to your sister, Klavdia Abramovna. Let her sell and pawn everything she has; let her send us the money, and we'll go away from here. Oh, Lord," he went on with anguish, "to have one peep at Moscow! To see mother Moscow, if only in my dreams!"

And when evening came, and it was dark in the cabin, it got so dismal that it was hard to bring out a word. Granny, cross as ever, soaked some crusts of rye bread in a cup, and was a whole hour sucking at them. Marya, having milked the cow, brought in a pail of milk and set it on a bench; then Granny poured it from the pail into jugs slowly and deliberately, evidently pleased that it was now the Fast of Assumption, so that no one would drink milk and all of it would be left untouched. And she only poured out just a little into a saucer for Fyokla's baby. When she and Marya carried the jugs down to the cellar, Motka suddenly came to life, slipped down from the stove, and going to the bench where the wooden cup full of crusts was standing, splashed some milk from the saucer into it.

Granny, coming back into the cabin, attacked her soaked crusts again, while Sasha and Motka sat on the stove, staring at her, and were glad that she had taken forbidden food and now was sure to go to hell. They were comforted and lay down to sleep, and as she dozed off, Sasha pictured the Last Judgment to herself: a fire was burning in a stove something like a potter's kiln, and the Evil One, with horns like a cow's and black all over, was driving Granny into the fire with a long stick, just as Granny herself had driven the geese.

V

On the Feast of Assumption, after ten o'clock at night, the girls and boys who were making merry down in the meadow suddenly began to scream and shout, and ran in the direction of the village; and those who were sitting on the brink of the slope at first could not make out what was the matter.

"Fire! Fire!" desperate shouts sounded from below. "The place is on fire!"

Those who were sitting above looked back and a terrible and

extraordinary spectacle presented itself to them. From the thatched roof of one of the last cabins in the village rose a pillar of flame, seven feet high, which coiled and scattered sparks in all directions as though it were a fountain playing. And all at once the whole roof burst into bright flame, and the crackling of the fire was heard.

The moonlight was dimmed, and now the whole village was enveloped in a quivering red glow: black shadows moved over the ground, there was a smell of burning, and those who ran up from below were all gasping and trembling so that they could not speak; they jostled each other, fell down, and, unaccustomed to the bright light, could hardly see and did not recognize each other. It was terrifying. What was particularly frightening was that pigeons were flying in the smoke above the flames, and that in the tavern, where they did not yet know of the fire, people were still singing and playing the accordion as though nothing was wrong.

"Uncle Semyon's place is on fire," someone shouted in a loud, coarse voice.

Marya was rushing about near her cabin, weeping and wringing her hands, her teeth chattering, though the fire was a long way off, at the other end of the village. Nikolay came out in felt boots, the children ran about in their little shifts. Near the village policeman's cabin an iron sheet was struck. Boom, boom, boom! floated through the air, and this rapid, incessant sound sent a pang to the heart and turned one cold. The old women stood about, holding the icons. Sheep, calves, cows were driven out of the courtyards into the street; chests, sheepskins, tubs were carried out. A black stallion, that was kept apart from the drove of horses because he kicked and injured them, was set free and ran back and forth through the village once or twice, neighing and pawing the ground, then suddenly stopped short near a cart and started kicking it with his hind legs.

The bells in the church on the other side of the river began ringing.

Near the burning cabin it was so hot and so bright that every blade of grass on the ground was distinctly visible. On one of the chests that they had managed to carry out sat Semyon, a carrot-haired peasant with a long nose, wearing a jacket and a cap pulled down over his ears; his wife was lying face down, unconscious and moaning. A little old man of eighty with a big beard, who looked like a gnome, a stranger to the village, but apparently connected in some way with the fire, walked about near it, bareheaded, with a white bundle in his arms. The flames were reflected on his bald spot. The village headman, Antip Sedelnikov, as swarthy and black-haired as a gypsy, went up to the cabin with an ax, and hacked out the windows one after another—no one knew why— and then began chopping up the porch.

"Women, water!" he shouted. "Bring the engine! Shake a leg!"

The peasants who had just been carousing in the tavern were dragging up the engine. They were all drunk; they kept stumbling and falling down, and all had a helpless expression and tears in their eyes.

"Girls, water!" shouted the headman, who was drunk, too. "Shake a leg, girls!"

The women and the girls ran downhill to a spring, and hauled pails and tubs of water up the hill, and, after pouring it into the engine, ran down again. Olga and Marya and Sasha and Motka, too, all carried water. The women and the boys pumped the water; the hose hissed, and the headman, directing it now at the door, now at the windows, held back the stream with his finger, which made it hiss yet more sharply.

"He's a top-notcher, Antip is!" voices shouted approvingly. "Keep it up!"

Antip dove into the burning cabin and shouted from within.

"Pump! Lend a hand, good Orthodox folk, on the occasion of such a terrible accident!"

The peasants stood round in a crowd, doing nothing and staring at the fire. No one knew what to do, no one knew how to do anything, and there were stacks of grain and hay, piles of faggots, and sheds all about. Kiryak and old Osip, his father, both tipsy, stood there, too. And, as though to justify his inaction, old Osip said to the woman lying on the ground:

"Why carry on so, friend? The cabin's insured—why worry?"

Semyon, addressing himself now to one person, now to another, kept telling how the fire had started.

"That same old man, the one with the bundle, a house-serf of General Zhukov's—He was cook at our general's, God rest his soul! He came over this evening: 'Let me stay the night,' says he. Well, we had a glass, to be sure. The wife got busy with the samovar—we were going to give the old man some tea, and in an unlucky hour she set the samovar in the entry. And the sparks from the chimney blew straight up to the thatch; well, that's how it was. We were nearly burnt up ourselves. And the old man's cap got burnt up; it's a shame!"

And the sheet of iron was struck tirelessly, and the bells of the church on the other side of the river kept ringing. Ruddy with the glow, and breathless, Olga, looking with horror at the red sheep and at the pink pigeons flying through the smoke, kept running down the slope and up again. It seemed to her that the ringing had entered her soul like a sharp thorn, that the fire would never be over, that Sasha was lost. . . . And when the ceiling of the cabin fell in with a crash, the thought that now the whole village was sure to burn down made her faint, and she could no longer go on carrying water, but sat down on the edge of the slope, setting the buckets near her; beside her and below her, the peasant women sat wailing as though at a wake.

Then, from the village across the river, came men in two carts, bringing a fire-engine with them. A very young student, his white tunic wide open, rode up on horseback. There was the sound of axes. A ladder was placed against the burning frame of the house, and five men ran up it at once, led by the student, who was red in the face and shouted in a harsh, hoarse voice, and in the tone of one who was used to putting out fires. They pulled the house to pieces, a log at a time; they took apart the stable and the wattled fence, and removed the near-by stack of hay.

"Don't let them smash things!" cried stern voices in the crowd. "Don't let them."

Kiryak made his way to the cabin with a resolute air, as

though he meant to prevent the newcomers from smashing things, but one of the workmen turned him round and hit him on the neck. There was the sound of laughter, the workman struck him again, Kiryak fell and crawled back into the crowd on all fours.

Two pretty girls in hats, probably the student's sisters, came from the other side of the river. They stood at a distance, looking at the fire. The logs that had been pulled away were no longer burning, but were smoking badly; the student, who was working the hose, turned the stream first on the logs, then on the peasants, then on the women who were hauling the water.

"Georges!" the girls called to him reproachfully and anxiously, "Georges!"

The fire was over. And only when the crowd began to disperse they noticed that day was breaking, that all were pale and rather dark in the face, as people always appear in the early morning when the last stars are fading. As they separated, the peasants laughed and cracked jokes about General Zhukov's cook and his cap which had been burnt; they already wanted to turn the fire into a jest, and even seemed sorry that it had been put out so soon.

"You were good at putting out the fire, sir!" said Olga to the student. "You ought to come to us in Moscow: there we have a fire 'most every day."

"Why, do you come from Moscow?" asked one of the young ladies.

"Yes, miss. My husband was employed at the Slavyansky Bazar. And this is my daughter," she said, pointing to Sasha, who was chilly and huddled up to her. "She is a Moscow girl, too."

The two young ladies said something in French to the student and he gave Sasha a twenty-kopeck piece.

Old Osip noticed this, and a gleam of hope came into his face.

"We must thank God, your honor, there was no wind," he said, addressing the student, "or else we should have been all burnt out in no time. Your honor, kind gentlefolk," he added, with embarrassment in a lower tone, "the dawn's chilly . . .

something to warm a man . . . half a bottle to your honor's health."

He was given nothing, and clearing his throat, he shuffled off towards home. Afterwards Olga stood on the edge of the slope and watched the two carts fording the river and the gentlefolk walking across the meadow; a carriage was waiting for them on the other side of the river. Going into the cabin, she said to her husband with enthusiasm:

"Such kind people! And so good-looking! The young ladies were like cherubs!"

"May they burst!" Fyokla, who was sleepy, said spitefully.

VI

Marya thought herself unhappy, and often said that she longed to die; Fyokla, on the contrary, found everything in this life to her taste: the poverty, the filth, the incessant cursing. She ate whatever was given her indiscriminately, slept anywhere and on whatever came to hand. She would empty the slops just at the porch, would splash them out from the doorsill, and then walk barefoot through the puddle. And from the very first day she conceived a hatred for Olga and Nikolay just because they did not like this life.

"I'll see what you'll eat here, you Moscow gentry!" she would say maliciously. "I'll see!"

One morning at the beginning of September Fyokla, vigorous, good-looking, and rosy from the cold, brought up two pails of water from down below on a yoke; Marya and Olga were just then sitting at the table, having tea.

"Enjoy your tea!" said Fyokla sarcastically. "The fine ladies!" she added, setting down the pails. "They've gotten into the habit of tea every day. You'd better look out you don't swell up with your tea-drinking," she went on, looking at Olga with hatred. "She's come by her fat mug in Moscow, the tub of lard!"

She swung the yoke and hit Olga a blow on the shoulder so

that the two sisters-in-law could only strike their hands together
and say:

"Oh, holy saints!"

Then Fyokla went down to the river to wash the clothes,
swearing all the time so loudly that she could be heard in the
house.

The day passed and then came the long autumn evening.
They wound silk in the cabin; everyone did it except Fyokla; she
had gone across the river. They got the silk from a factory near
by, and the whole family working together earned a mere trifle,
some twenty kopecks a week.

"Under the masters things were better," said the old man as
he wound silk. "You worked and ate and slept, everything in its
turn. At dinner you had *shchi* and *kasha,* and at supper the same
again. Cucumbers and cabbage galore: you could eat to your
heart's content, as much as you liked. And there was more strict-
ness. Everyone knew his place."

The cabin was lighted by a single little lamp, which burned
dimly and smoked. When someone stood in front of the lamp and
a large shadow fell across the window, one noticed the bright
moonlight. Speaking unhurriedly, old Osip related how people
used to live before the Emancipation; how in these very parts,
where life was now so poverty-striken and dreary, they used to
hunt with harriers, greyhounds, and specially trained stalkers, and
the peasants who were employed as beaters got vodka; how caravans loaded with slaughtered fowls were sent to Moscow for the
young masters; how the serfs that were bad were beaten with rods
or sent off to the Tver estate, while those who were good were
rewarded. And Granny, too, had something to tell. She remembered everything, absolutely everything. She told about her mistress, a kind, God-fearing woman, whose husband was a boozer
and a rake, and all of whose daughters made wretched marriages:
one married a drunkard, another a commoner, a third eloped
(Granny herself, a young girl at the time, had helped with the
elopement), and they had all three soon died of grief, as did their
mother. And remembering all this, Granny actually shed a tear.

Suddenly someone knocked at the door, and they all started.

"Uncle Osip, put me up for the night."

The little bald old man, General Zhukov's cook, the very one whose cap had been burnt, walked in. He sat down and listened. Then he, too, began to reminisce and tell stories. Nikolay, sitting on the stove with his legs hanging down, listened and asked questions about the dishes that were prepared for the gentry in the old days. They talked about chops, cutlets, various soups and sauces, and the cook, who remembered everything very well, mentioned dishes that are no longer prepared; there was one, for instance—a dish made of bulls' eyes, that was called "Waking up in the morning."

"And did you have cutlets *maréchal* then?" asked Nikolay.

"No."

Nikolay shook his head scornfully and said:

"Ah-h! Fine cooks you were!"

The little girls, who were sitting or lying on the stove, stared down without blinking; there seemed to be a lot of them, like cherubs in the clouds. They liked the stories; they sighed and shuddered and turned pale with rapture or terror, and to Granny, whose stories were the most interesting of all, they listened breathlessly, afraid to stir.

They lay down to sleep in silence; and the old people, stirred up and troubled by their reminiscences, thought what a fine thing it was to be young: youth, whatever it may have been like, left nothing in the memory but what was buoyant, joyful, touching; and death, they thought, how terribly cold was death, which was not far off—better not think of it! The little lamp went out. The darkness, and the two little windows brightly lit by the moon, and the stillness and the creak of the cradle, for some reason made them think of nothing but that life was over and that there was no way of bringing it back. You doze off, you sink into obliviousness, and suddenly someone touches your shoulder or breathes on your cheek—and sleep is gone; your body feels numb, as though circulation had stopped, and thoughts of death keep coming into your head. You turn on the other side: you forget about death, but old, dull, dismal thoughts of want, of fodder, of how dear flour is getting, stray through the mind, and a little later you remember again that life is over and there is no way of bringing it back. . . .

"Oh, Lord!" sighed the cook.

Someone rapped gently, ever so gently, at the window. It must have been Fyokla, come back. Olga got up, and yawning and whispering a prayer, unlocked the door, then pulled the bolt of the outer door. But no one came in; only there was a cold draft of air from the street and the entry suddenly grew bright with moonlight. Through the open door could be seen the silent, deserted street, and the moon itself floating across the sky.

"Who's there?" called Olga.

"Me," came the answer, "it's me."

Near the door, hugging the wall, stood Fyokla, stark naked. She was shivering with cold, her teeth were chattering, and in the bright moonlight she looked very pale, strange, and beautiful. The shadows and the bright spots of moonlight on her skin stood out sharply, and her dark eyebrows and firm, young breasts were defined with peculiar distinctness.

"The ruffians over there stripped me and turned me out like this," she muttered. "I had to go home without my clothes— mother-naked. Bring me something to put on."

"But come inside," Olga said softly, beginning to shiver, too.

"I don't want the old folks to see." Granny was, in fact, already stirring and grumbling, and the old man asked: "Who's there?" Olga brought out her own shift and skirt, dressed Fyokla, and then both went softly into the house, trying to close the door noiselessly.

"Is that you, you slick one?" Granny grumbled angrily, guessing who it was. "Curse you, you nightwalker! Why don't the devil take you!"

"It's all right, it's all right," whispered Olga, wrapping Fyokla up; "it's all right, dearie."

All was quiet again. They always slept badly; each one was kept awake by something nagging and persistent: the old man by the pain in his back, Granny by anxiety and malice, Marya by fear, the children by itch and hunger. Now, too, their sleep was restless; they kept turning from one side to the other, they talked in their sleep, they got up for a drink.

Fyokla suddenly burst out into a loud, coarse howl, but checked herself at once, and only sobbed from time to time, her sobs growing softer and more muffled until she was still. Occasionally from the other side of the river came the sound of the striking of the hours; but the clock struck oddly—first five and then three.

"Oh, Lord!" sighed the cook.

Looking at the windows, it was hard to tell whether the moon was still shining or whether it was already dawn. Marya got up and went out, and could be heard milking the cows and saying, "Stea-dy!" Granny went out, too. It was still dark in the cabin, but already one could distinguish all the objects in it.

Nikolay, who had not slept all night, got down from the stove. He took his dress-coat out of a green chest, put it on, and going to the window, stroked the sleeves, fingered the coat-tails— and smiled. Then he carefully removed the coat, put it away in the chest, and lay down again.

Marya came in again and started to light the stove. She was evidently half asleep and was waking up on her feet. She must have had some dream, or perhaps the stories of the previous night came into her mind, for she stretched luxuriously before the stove and said:

"No, freedom is better!"

VII

"The master" arrived—that was what they called the district police inspector. When he would come and what he was coming for had been known for a week. There were only forty households in Zhukovo, but they had accumulated more than two thousand rubles of arrears in Zemstvo and other taxes.

The police inspector stopped at the tavern. There he drank two glasses of tea, and then went on foot to the headman's house, near which a crowd of tax defaulters stood waiting. The headman,

Antip Sedelnikov, in spite of his youth—he was only a little over thirty—was strict and always sided with the authorities, though he himself was poor and remiss in paying his taxes. Apparently he enjoyed being headman, and liked the sense of power, which he could only display by harshness. At the village meetings he was feared and obeyed. Occasionally he would pounce on a drunken man in the street or near the tavern, tie his hands behind him, and put him in jail. Once he even put Granny under arrest and kept her in the lock-up for a whole day and a night because, coming to the village meeting instead of Osip, she started to curse. He had never lived in a city or read a book, but somewhere or other he had picked up various bookish expressions, and loved to employ them in conversation, and people respected him for this although they did not always understand him.

When Osip came into the headman's cabin with his tax book, the inspector, a lean old man with long gray side-whiskers, who wore a gray tunic, was sitting at a table in a corner writing something down. The cabin was clean; all the walls were bright with pictures clipped from magazines, and in the most conspicuous place near the icons there was a portrait of Prince Battenberg of Bulgaria. Beside the table stood Antip Sedelnikov with his arms folded.

"He owes one hundred and nineteen rubles, Your Honor," he said, when Osip's turn came. "Before Easter he paid a ruble, and he's not paid a kopeck since."

The inspector looked up at Osip and asked:

"Why is this, brother?"

"Show heavenly mercy, Your Honor," began Osip, growing agitated. "Allow me to say, last year the master from Lutoretzk said to me, 'Osip,' says he, 'sell me your hay . . . you sell it,' says he. Well, why not? I had a hundred *poods*[1] for sale; the women mowed it on the water-meadow. Well, we struck a bargain. It was all right and proper."

He complained of the headman, and kept turning round to

---

[1] *Pood* is a unit of weight, a little over 36 pounds.

the peasants as though inviting them to bear witness; his face got red and sweaty and his eyes grew sharp and angry.

"I don't know why you're saying all this," said the inspector. "I am asking you—I am asking you why you don't pay your arrears. You don't pay, any of you, and am I to answer for you?"

"I just can't."

"These words are of no consequence, Your Honor," said the headman. "The Chikildeyevs certainly are of the needy class, but please just inquire of the others, the root of it all is vodka, and they are a disorderly lot. With no understanding at all."

The inspector wrote something down, and then said to Osip quietly, in an even tone, as though he were asking him for a drink of water:

"Get out."

Soon he drove off; and as he was climbing into his cheap buggy, coughing as he did so, it could be seen from the very look of his long lean back that he no longer remembered Osip or the village headman or the Zhukovo arrears, but was thinking of his own affairs. Before he had gone two thirds of a mile Antip was already carrying off the samovar from the Chikildeyevs' cabin, while Granny followed him, screaming shrilly, straining her lungs:

"I won't let you have it! I won't let you have it, goddamn you!"

He walked rapidly with long strides, and she ran after him, panting, almost falling down, a hunched infuriated creature; her kerchief slipped onto her shoulders, her gray hair with a greenish tint to it blew in the wind. She suddenly stood still, and like a real insurgent, fell to thumping her breast with her fists and shouting louder than ever in a singsong voice, seeming to sob:

"Christians, all you who believe in God! Dear friends, they have wronged me! Darlings, they're trampling on me! Oh, oh, darlings, come and help me!"

"Granny, Granny!" said the village headman sternly, "get some sense into your head!"

With no samovar it was hopelessly dismal in the Chikildeyevs' cabin. There was something humiliating in this deprivation, something insulting, as though the honor of the house were lost. It would have been better, had the headman carried off the table, all the benches, all the pots—the place would not have seemed so bare. Granny screamed, Marya cried, and the little girls, seeing her tears, cried too. The old man, feeling guilty, sat in the corner, silent, with hanging head. Nikolay too was silent. Granny loved him and was sorry for him, but now, forgetting her pity, she fell upon him with abuse, with reproaches, shaking her fist right in his face. She screamed that it was all his fault; indeed, why had he sent them so little when he bragged in his letters that he was earning fifty rubles a month at the Slavyansky Bazar? Why had he come, and with his family, too? If he died, where would the money come from for his funeral? And it was pitiful to look at Nikolay, Olga, and Sasha.

The old man sighed hoarsely, took his cap, and went off to the headman. It was getting dark. Antip was soldering something by the stove, puffing out his cheeks; the air was full of fumes. His children, thin and unwashed, no better than the Chikildeyev brood, were scrambling about on the floor; his wife, an ugly, freckled, big-bellied woman, was winding silk. They were a wretched, unlucky family, and Antip was the only one who looked sturdy and handsome. On a bench stood five samovars in a row. The old man muttered a prayer to Battenberg and then said:

"Antip, show heavenly mercy, give me back the samovar! For Christ's sake!"

"Bring three rubles, then you can have it."

"I just can't."

Antip puffed out his cheeks, the fire hummed and hissed, and was reflected in the samovars. The old man kneaded his cap and said after a moment's thought:

"You give it back to me."

The dark-skinned headman looked quite black and resembled a magician; he turned round to Osip and said sternly, speaking rapidly:

"It all depends on the district magistrate. On the twenty-sixth instant you can state the grounds of your dissatisfaction before the administrative session, verbally or in writing."

Osip did not understand a word, but he was satisfied with that and went home.

Some ten days later the police inspector came again, stayed for an hour and drove away. During those days it had been cold and windy; the river had been frozen for a long time, but still there was no snow, and people were worn to a frazzle because the roads were impassable. On the eve of a holiday some of the neighbors came in to Osip's to sit and have a chat. They talked in the dark, because it was a sin to work and so they did not light the lamp. There were some scraps of news, all rather unpleasant. In two or three households hens had been taken for the arrears and had been sent to the district office, and there they had died because no one had fed them; sheep had been taken, and while they were being carted away tied to one another, and shifted into another cart at each village, one of them had died. And now the question was being discussed: who was to blame?

"The Zemstvo," said Osip. "Who else?"

"Of course, the Zemstvo."

The Zemstvo was blamed for everything—for the arrears, the unjust exactions, the failure of the crops, though no one of them knew what was meant by the Zemstvo. And this dated from the time when well-to-do peasants who had factories, shops, and inns of their own served as members of the Zemstvo boards, were dissatisfied with them, and took to berating the Zemstvos in their factories and taverns.

They talked about how God was not sending the snow; wood had to be hauled for fuel, yet there was no driving or walking over the frozen ruts. In former days, fifteen to twenty years ago, talk had been much more interesting in Zhukovo. In those days every old man looked as though he were guarding some secret; as though he knew something and were waiting for something. They used to talk about a charter with a golden seal, about the division of acreage, about new lands, about treasure troves; they hinted at something. Now the folk of Zhukovo had no secrets at all; their whole life lay bare and clear to all, as though on the palm

of your hand, and they could talk of nothing but want, food and
fodder, the absence of snow.

There was a lull. Then they recalled the hens again, and the
sheep, and began arguing once more as to who was at fault.

"The Zemstvo," said Osip dejectedly. "Who else?"

VIII

The parish church was nearly four miles away at Kosogoro-
vo, and the peasants only attended it when they had to do so, for
christenings, weddings, or funerals; for regular services they went
to the church across the river. On holidays in fine weather the
girls dressed up in their best and went to Mass in a crowd, and
it was a cheering sight to see them walk across the meadow in
their red, yellow, and green frocks; when the weather was bad
they all stayed home. To confess and to take the communion, they
went to the parish church. The priest, making the round of the
cabins with the cross at Easter, took fifteen kopecks from each of
those who had not managed to take the sacrament during Lent.

The old man did not believe in God, for he had hardly ever
given Him a thought; he acknowledged the supernatural, but felt
that it could be of concern to women only, and when religion or
miracles were discussed in his presence, and a question about
these matters was put to him, he would say reluctantly, scratching
himself:

"Who can tell!"

Granny did believe, but somehow her faith was hazy; everything was mixed up in her memory, and no sooner did she begin
to think of sins, of death, of the salvation of the soul, than want
and cares took possession of her mind, and she instantly forgot
what she had started to think about. She remembered no prayers
at all, and usually in the evenings, before lying down to sleep, she
would stand before the icons and whisper:

"Virgin Mother of Kazan, Virgin Mother of Smolensk, Virgin Mother of the Three Arms. . . ."

Marya and Fyokla crossed themselves regularly, fasted, and

took communion every year, but quite ignorantly. The children were not taught any prayers, nothing was told them about God, and no moral precepts were given them; they were merely forbidden to take certain foods on fast days. In other families it was much the same: there were few who believed, few who had any understanding. At the same time all loved the Holy Scripture, loved it tenderly, reverently; but they had no books, there was no one to read the Bible and explain it, and because Olga sometimes read them the Gospels, they respected her, and they all addressed her and Sasha in the deferential second-person plural.

For local holidays and special services Olga often went to neighboring villages and to the county seat, in which there were two monasteries and twenty-seven churches. She was abstracted, and when she went on these pilgrimages she quite forgot her family, and only when she was on her way home would suddenly make the joyful discovery that she had a husband and daughter, and then she would say, smiling and radiant:

"God has blessed me!"

What went on in the village seemed to her revolting and was a source of torment to her. On St. Elijah's Day they drank, at the Assumption they drank, at the Exaltation of the Cross they drank. The Feast of the Intercession was the parish holiday for Zhukovo, and on that occasion the peasants drank for three days on end; they drank up fifty rubles belonging to the communal fund, and on top of that collected money for vodka from each household. On the first day the Chikildeyevs slaughtered a sheep and ate mutton in the morning, at noon, and in the evening; they ate large amounts of it, and the children got up at night to eat some more. Those three days Kiryak was fearfully drunk; he drank up all his belongings, even his cap and boots, and beat Marya so terribly that they had to pour water over her to revive her. Afterwards they were all ashamed and felt sick.

However, even in Zhukovo, in this "Flunkeyville," once a year there was a genuine religious event. It was in August, when they carried the icon of the Life-Bearing Mother of God from village to village throughout the district. The day on which it was expected at Zhukovo was windless and the sky was overcast. The girls, in their bright holiday frocks, set off in the morning to meet the icon, and they brought it to the village towards evening, in solemn procession, singing, while the bells pealed in the church across the river. A huge crowd of villagers and strangers blocked the street; there was noise, dust, a crush of people. . . . The old man and Granny and Kiryak all stretched out their hands to the icon, gazed at it greedily and cried, weeping:

"Intercede for us! Mother! Intercede!"

All seemed suddenly to grasp that there was no void between earth and heaven, that the rich and powerful had not seized everything, that there was still protection from abuse, from bondage, from crushing, unbearable want, from the terrible vodka.

"Intercede for us! Mother!" sobbed Marya. "Mother!"

But the service ended, the icon was carried away, and everything went on as before; and again the sound of coarse, drunken voices came from the tavern.

Only the well-to-do peasants were afraid of death; the richer they grew the less they believed in God and in the salvation of the soul, and only through fear of their earthly end did they light candles and have Masses said, in order to be on the safe side. The poorer peasants did not fear death. The old man and Granny were told to their faces that they had lived too long, that it was time they were dead, and they did not mind. They did not scruple to tell Fyokla in Nikolay's presence that when Nikolay died her husband Denis would be discharged from the army and return home. And Marya, far from dreading death, regretted that it was so long in coming, and was glad when her children died.

Death they did not fear, but they had an exaggerated terror of every disease. The merest trifle—an upset stomach, a slight chill, and Granny would lie down on the stove, wrap herself up, and start moaning loudly and incessantly: "I am dy-ing!" The old man would hurry off for the priest, and Granny would receive the sacrament and extreme unction. They often talked of colds, of worms, of tumors that shifted about in the stomach and moved up close to the heart. Most of all they feared catching cold, and so dressed in heavy clothes even in summer and warmed themselves on the stove. Granny was fond of doctoring herself and often drove to the dispensary, where she always said she was fifty-eight instead of seventy; she supposed that if the doctor knew her real age he would not treat her, but would say it was time she died instead of doctoring herself. She usually went to the dispensary early in the morning, taking with her two or three of the little girls, and came back in the evening, hungry and cross, with drops for herself and salves for the little girls. Once she had Nikolay go along with her, too, and for a fortnight afterwards he took drops, and said he felt better.

Granny knew all the doctors, medical assistants, and quacks for twenty miles round, and not one of them she liked. At the Feast of the Intercession, when the priest made the round of the cabins with the cross, the deacon told her that in the town near the prison lived an old man who had been an army surgeon's assistant and who worked many cures, and advised her to turn to him. Granny took his advice. After the first snowfall she drove to the town and fetched a little bearded old man, in a long coat, a converted Jew, whose face was covered with a network of tiny blue veins. Just then there were people working in the house: an old tailor, in terrifying spectacles, was cutting a waistcoat out of some rags, and two young men were making felt boots out of wool; Kiryak, who had been sacked for drunkenness and now lived at home, was sitting beside the tailor mending a horse-collar. And the place was crowded, stuffy, and evil-smelling. The converted Jew examined Nikolay and said that it was necessary to cup the patient.

He put on the cups, and the old tailor, Kiryak, and the little girls stood round and looked on, and it seemed to them that they saw the disease coming out of Nikolay; and Nikolay, too, watched how the cups sucking at his breast gradually filled with dark blood, and felt as though there really were something coming out of him, and smiled with pleasure.

"That's fine," said the tailor. "Please God, it will do you good."

The convert put on twelve cups and then another twelve, had tea, and drove away. Nikolay began shivering; his face took on a drawn look, and, as the women put it, shrank up into a little fist;

his fingers turned blue. He wrapped himself up in a quilt and a sheepskin coat, but felt colder and colder. Towards evening he began to feel very ill, asked to be laid on the floor, begged the tailor not to smoke; then he grew quiet under the coat, and towards morning he died.

IX

Oh, what a hard, what a long, winter it was!

Already by Christmas their own flour had given out and they started buying flour. Kiryak, who lived at home now, was disorderly in the evenings, terrifying everyone, and in the mornings he was tormented by headache and shame, and it was pitiful to look at him. Day and night the bellowing of the starved cow came from the barn—breaking the hearts of Granny and Marya. And as though out of spite, the frosts were bitter the whole time and the snowdrifts high; and the winter dragged on. At Annunciation there was a regular blizzard, and snow fell at Easter.

But after all, the winter did end. At the beginning of April there were warm days and frosty nights; winter would not yield, but one warm day overpowered it at last, and the streams began to flow and the birds to sing. The whole meadow and the shrubs that fringed the river were submerged by the spring floods, and the area between Zhukovo and the farther bank was one vast sheet of water, from which wild ducks rose up in flocks here and there. Every evening a fiery spring sunset, with superb clouds, offered new, extraordinary, incredible sights, just the sort of thing that one does not credit afterwards, when one sees those very colors and those very clouds in a painting.

The cranes flew swiftly, swiftly, uttering mournful sounds, and there seemed to be a summoning note in their cries. Standing on the edge of the slope, Olga stared for a long time at the flooded meadow, at the sunshine, at the church, which looked bright and rejuvenated, as it were; and her tears flowed and she gasped for breath: so passionate was her longing to go away, anywhere, to the end of the world. It was already decided that she should return to Moscow to go into service as a chambermaid, and that Kiryak should set off with her to get a job as a gatekeeper or something of the sort. Oh, to get away quickly!

As soon as the ground was dry and it was warm, they made ready to leave. Olga and Sasha, with bundles on their backs and sandals of plaited bast on their feet, left at daybreak: Marya came out, too, to see them off. Kiryak was not well and remained at home for another week. For the last time Olga, looking at the church, crossed herself and murmured a prayer; thought of her husband, and though she did not cry, her face puckered up and turned ugly, like an old woman's. During the winter she had grown thinner and plainer, her hair had gone a little gray, and instead of her former attractive appearance and pleasant smile, her face now had the sad, resigned expression left by the sorrows she had experienced, and there was something obtuse and wooden about her gaze, as though she were deaf.

She was sorry to leave the village and the peasants. She kept remembering how they had carried Nikolay down the street, and how a Mass for the repose of his soul had been said at every cabin, and how all had wept in sympathy with her grief. During the summer and the winter there had been hours and days when it seemed as though these people lived worse than cattle, and it was terrible to be with them; they were coarse, dishonest, dirty, and drunken; they did not live at peace with one another but quarreled continually, because they feared, suspected, and despised each other. Who keeps the tavern and encourages drunkenness? The peasant. Who embezzles and drinks up the funds that belong to the community, the schools, the church? The peasant. Who steals from his neighbors, sets fire to their property, bears false witness at court for a bottle of vodka? At meetings of the Zemstvo and other local bodies, who is the first to raise his voice against the peasants? The peasant. Yes, to live with them was terrible; but yet, they were human beings, they suffered and wept like human beings, and there was nothing in their lives for which one could not find justification. Crushing labor that made the whole body ache at night, cruel winters, scanty crops, overcrowding; and no help, and nowhere to look for help. Those who were stronger and better-off could give no assistance, as they were themselves coarse, dishonest, drunken, and swore just as foully. The most insignificant little clerk or official treated the peasants as though they were tramps, and addressed even the village elders and church wardens as inferiors, and as though they had a right to do so. And indeed, can any sort of help or good example be given by lazy, grasping, greedy, dissolute men who only visit the village in order to outrage, to despoil, to terrorize? Olga recalled the wretched, humiliated look of the old folks when in the winter Kiryak had been led off to be flogged. . . . And now she felt sorry for all these people, it hurt her, and as she walked on she kept looking back at the cabins.

After walking two miles with them Marya said good-by, then she knelt, and pressing her face against the earth, began wailing:

"Again I am left alone. Poor me! poor unhappy soul that I am!"

And for a long time she went on wailing like this, and for a long time Olga and Sasha could see her still on her knees, as she kept bowing sideways, clutching her head in her hands, while the rooks flew over her.

The sun rose high; it turned hot. Zhukovo was left far behind. Walking was pleasant; Olga and Sasha soon forgot both the village and Marya; they were cheerful and everything entertained them: an ancient burial-mound; a row of telegraph posts marching one after another into the distance and disappearing on the horizon, the wires humming mysteriously; a farmhouse, half hidden by green foliage, and with a scent of dampness and hemp coming from it, a place that for some reason seemed inhabited by happy people; a horse's skeleton making a lonely white spot in the open fields. And the larks trilled tirelessly, quails called to one another, and the corncrake cawed as though someone were jerking an old cramp-iron.

At noon Olga and Sasha came to a large village. There on the broad street they encountered the little old man who had been General Zhukov's cook. He was hot, and his red, perspiring bald spot shone in the sun. At first he and Olga failed to recognize each other, then they looked round at the same moment, did recognize each other, and went their separate ways without saying a word. Stopping before the open windows of a cottage which looked newer and more prosperous than the rest, Olga bowed down and said in a loud, thin, singsong voice:

"Orthodox Christians, give alms, for Christ's sake, as much as you can, and in the Kingdom of Heaven may your parents know peace eternal."

"Orthodox Christians," Sasha echoed her chant, "give alms, for Christ's sake, as much as you can, and in the Kingdom of Heaven. . . ."

1897

THE MAN IN A SHELL

On the outskirts of the village of Mironositzkoe two belated huntsmen had settled for the night in the barn belonging to the Elder, Prokofy. They were the veterinary, Ivan Ivanych, and the high school teacher, Burkin. Ivan Ivanych had a rather queer double surname—Chimsha-Himalaisky—which did not suit him at all, and he was known as Ivan Ivanych all over the province. He lived on a stud-farm near the town, and had gone out shooting to breathe some fresh air. As for Burkin, the high school teacher, he spent every summer at Count P——'s, and had long been thoroughly at home in the district.

They did not sleep. Ivan Ivanych, a tall, spare old man with long mustaches, was sitting outside the door, smoking a pipe in the moonlight. Burkin was lying inside on the hay, and could not be seen for the darkness.

They were telling each other stories. Among other things, they spoke of the Elder's wife, Mavra, a healthy and by no means stupid woman, observing that she had never been beyond her native village, had never seen a city or a railway in her life, and had spent the last ten years hugging the stove and only going out into the street at night.

"There's nothing remarkable about that!" said Burkin. "There are not a few people in the world, temperamentally unsociable, who try to withdraw into a shell like a hermit crab or a snail. Perhaps it is a manifestation of atavism, a return to the time when man's ancestor was not yet a gregarious animal and lived alone in his lair, or perhaps it is only one of the varieties of human character—who knows? I am no naturalist, and it is not my business to settle such questions; I only mean to say that people like Mavra are by no means rare. Why, not to go far afield, there was Belikov, a colleague of mine, a teacher of Greek, who died in our town two months ago. You have heard of him, no doubt. The curious thing about him was that he wore rubbers, and a warm coat with an interlining, and carried an umbrella even in the finest weather. And he kept his umbrella in its cover and his watch in a gray chamois case, and when he took out his penknife to sharpen his pencil, his penknife, too, was in a little case; and his face seemed to be in a case too, because it was always hidden in his turned-up collar. He wore dark spectacles and a sweater, stuffed his ears with cotton-wool, and when he got into a cab always told the driver to put up the hood. In short, the man showed a constant and irrepressible inclination to keep a covering about himself, to create for himself a membrane, as it were, which would isolate him and protect him from outside influences. Actuality irritated him, frightened him, kept him in a state of continual agitation, and, perhaps to justify his timidity, his aversion for the present, he would always laud the past and things that had never existed, and the dead languages that he taught were in effect for him the same rubbers and umbrella in which he sought concealment from real life.

" 'Oh, how sonorous, how beautiful the Greek language is!' he would say, with a saccharine expression; and as though to prove his point, he would screw up his eyes and, raising one finger, utter: 'Anthropos!'

"His thoughts, too, Belikov tried to tuck away in a sheath. The only things that were clear to him were Government regulations and newspaper notices in which something was forbidden. When some ruling prohibited high school students from appearing on the streets after nine o'clock at night, or some article censured carnal love, this he found clear and definite: it was forbidden, and that was that. But there was always a doubtful element for him, something vague and not fully expressed in any sanction or permission. When a dramatic club or a reading-room or a teahouse was licensed in the town, he would shake his head and say in a low voice:

" 'Of course, it's all very well, but you can't tell what may come of it.'

"Any infringement of the rules, any deviation or departure from them, plunged him into gloom, though one would have thought it was no concern of his. If one of his colleagues was late for the thanksgiving service, or if rumors reached him of some prank of the high school boys, or if one of the female members of the staff had been seen late in the evening in the company of an officer, he would become very much agitated and keep saying that one couldn't tell what might come of it. At faculty meetings he simply crushed us with his cautiousness, his suspiciousness, and his typical remarks to the effect that the young people in the girls' as well as in the boys' high school were unruly, that there was much noise in the classrooms, that it might reach the ears of the authorities, that one couldn't tell what might come of it, and that it would be a good thing if Petrov were expelled from the second form and Yegorov from the fourth. And what do you think, with his sighs, his moping, the dark spectacles on his pale little face, a little face like a polecat's, you know, he weighed us all down, and we submitted, reduced Petrov's and Yegorov's marks for conduct, detained them, and in the end expelled them both.

"He had a peculiar habit of visiting our lodgings. He would call on some teacher, would sit down, and remain silently staring, as though he were trying to detect something. He would sit like this in silence for an hour or two and then leave. This he called 'maintaining good relations with his colleagues'; and it was obvious that making these calls and sitting there like that was painful to him, and that he went to see us simply because he considered it his duty to his colleagues. We teachers were afraid of him. And even the principal was afraid of him. Would you believe it, our

teachers were all thoughtful, decent people, brought up on Turgenev and Shchedrin, yet this little man, who always wore rubbers and carried an umbrella, had the whole high school under
his thumb for fully fifteen years! The high school? The whole
town! Our ladies did not get up private theatricals on Saturdays
for fear he should find it out, and the clergy dared not eat meat
in Lent or play cards in his presence. Under the influence of
people like Belikov the whole town spent ten to fifteen frightened
years. We were afraid to speak out loud, to write letters, to make
acquaintances, to read books, to help the poor, to teach people
how to read and write. . . ."

Ivan Ivanych coughed, as a preliminary to making some
remark, but first lighted his pipe, gazed at the moon, and then
said, between pauses:

"Yes, thoughtful, decent people, readers of Shchedrin and
Turgenev, of Buckle and all the rest of them, yet they knuckled
under and put up with it—that's just how it is."

"Belikov and I lived in the same house," Burkin went on,
"on the same floor, his door facing mine; we often saw each other,
and I was acquainted with his domestic arrangements. It was the
same story: dressing-gown, nightcap, blinds, bolts, prohibitions
and restrictions of all sorts, and, 'Oh, you can't tell what may
come of it!' Lenten fare didn't agree with him, yet he could not
eat meat, as people might say that Belikov did not keep the fasts,
and he ate perch fried in butter—not a Lenten dish, yet one could
not call it meat. He did not keep a female servant for fear people
might think evil of him, but instead employed an old man of sixty,
called Afanasy, half-witted and given to drinking, who had once
been an orderly and could cook after a fashion. This Afanasy was
usually standing at the door with folded arms; he would sigh
deeply and always mutter the same thing:

" 'The likes of *them* is thick as hops hereabouts!'

"Belikov's bedroom was tiny and boxlike; his bed was cur-
tained. When he went to bed he drew the bedclothes over his
head; it was hot and stuffy; the wind rattled the closed doors; a
humming noise came from the stove and the sound of sighs from
the kitchen, ominous sighs—And he lay under the quilt, terrified.

He was afraid that something might happen, that Afanasy would murder him, that thieves would break in, and he had bad dreams all night long, and in the morning when we went to school together, he was downcast and pale, and it was plain that the place, swarming with people, towards which he was going, filled his whole being with dread and aversion, and that walking beside me was disagreeable to a man of his unsociable temperament.

" 'How noisy the classrooms are,' he used to say, as though trying to find an explanation for his distress. 'It's an outrage.'

"And imagine, this teacher of Greek—this man in a shell— came near to getting married."

Ivan Ivanych glanced rapidly into the barn, and said, "You are joking!"

"Yes, strange as it seems, he nearly got married. A new teacher of geography and history, a certain Mihail Savvich Kovalenko, a Ukrainian, was assigned to our school. He did not come alone, but with his sister, Varenka. He was a tall, dark young man with huge hands, and one could see from his face that he spoke in a deep voice, and, in fact, his voice seemed to come out of a barrel: 'Boom, boom, boom!' She was not so young, about thirty, but she too was tall, well built, with black eyebrows and red cheeks—in a word, she was not a girl but a peach, and so lively, so noisy; she was always singing Little Russian songs and laughing. At the least provocation, she would go off into ringing laughter: 'Ha-ha-ha!' We first got well acquainted with the Kovalenkos, I remember, at the principal's name-day party. Among the morose, emphatically dull pedagogues who attend even a name-day party as a duty, we suddenly saw a new Aphrodite risen from the foam; she walked with her arms akimbo, laughed, sang, danced. She sang with feeling 'The Winds Are Blowing' and then another Ukrainian song and another, and she fascinated us all, all, even Belikov. He sat down beside her and said with a saccharine smile:

" 'The Little Russian tongue reminds one of ancient Greek in its softness and agreeable sonority.'

"That flattered her, and she began telling him with feeling and persuasiveness that they had a farm in the Gadyach district, and that her Mummy lived there, and that they had such pears, such melons, such *kabaki!* The Little Russians call a pumpkin *kabak* [Russian for tavern], while their taverns they call *shinki,* and they make a *borshch* with tomatoes and eggplant in it, 'which is so delicious—ever so delicious!'

"We listened, and listened, and suddenly the same idea occurred to all of us:

" 'It would be a good thing to marry them off,' the principal's wife whispered to me.

"For some reason we all recalled that our friend Belikov was unmarried, and it seemed strange to us now that we had failed to notice it before, and in fact had completely lost sight of so important a detail in his life. What was his attitude towards women? How had he settled for himself this vital problem? Until then we had had no interest in the matter; perhaps we had not even admitted the idea that a man who wore rubbers in all weathers and slept behind curtains was capable of love.

" 'He is way past forty and she is thirty,' the principal's wife clarified her idea. 'I believe she would marry him.'

"What isn't done in the provinces out of boredom, how many useless and foolish things! And that is because what is necessary isn't done at all. What need was there, for instance, for us to make a match for this Belikov, whom one could not even imagine as a married man? The principal's wife, the inspector's wife, and all our high school ladies, grew livelier and even better looking, as though they had suddenly found an object in life. The principal's wife would take a box at the theater, and lo and behold! Varenka would be sitting in it, fanning herself, beaming and happy, and beside her would be Belikov, a twisted little man, looking as though he had been pulled out of his lodging by pincers. I would give an evening party and the ladies would insist on my inviting Belikov and Varenka. In short, the machine was set in motion. It turned out that Varenka was not averse to matrimony. Her life with her brother was not very cheerful: they did nothing but argue and quarrel with one another for days on end. Here is a typical scene: Kovalenko strides down the street, a tall, husky fellow, in an embroidered shirt, a lock of hair falling over his forehead from under his cap, in one hand a bundle of books, in the other a thick, knotted stick; he is followed by his sister, also carrying books.

" 'But you haven't read it, Mihailik!' she is arguing loudly. 'I tell you, I swear you haven't read it at all!'

" 'And I tell you I have read it,' bellows Kovalenko, banging his stick on the sidewalk.

" 'Oh, my goodness, Mihailik, why are you so cross? We are only discussing principles.'

" 'I tell you that I have read it!' Kovalenko shouts, more loudly than ever.

"And at home, if there was an outsider present, there was sure to be a fusillade. She must have been fed up with such a life and longed for a home of her own. Besides, there was her age; there was no time left to pick and choose; she was apt to marry anybody, even a teacher of Greek. Come to think of it, most of our young ladies don't care whom they marry so long as they do marry. Be that as it may, Varenka began to show an unmistakable inclination for Belikov.

"And Belikov? He used to call on Kovalenko just as he did on the rest of us. He would arrive, sit down, and go on sitting there in silence. He would sit quietly, and Varenka would sing to him 'The Winds Are Blowing' or would stare at him pensively with her dark eyes, or would suddenly go off into a peal of laughter—'Ha-ha-ha!'

"In amorous affairs and in marrying, suggestion plays a great part. Everybody—both his colleagues and the ladies—began assuring Belikov that he ought to get married, that there was nothing left for him in life but to get married; we all felicitated him, and with solemn faces delivered ourselves of various platitudes, such as 'Marriage is a serious step.' Besides, Varenka was good-looking and attractive; she was the daughter of a civil councilor, and she owned a farm; above all, she was the first woman who had treated him cordially and affectionately. His head was turned, and he decided that he really ought to get married."

"Well, at that point," said Ivan Ivanych, "you should have taken away his rubbers and umbrella."

"Just fancy, that proved to be impossible. He put Varenka's portrait on his table, kept calling on me and talking about Varenka, and about family life, saying that marriage was a serious step. He went frequently to the Kovalenkos, but he did not alter his habits in the least. On the contrary, his decision to get married seemed to have a deleterious effect on him. He grew thinner and paler and seemed to retreat further into his shell.

" 'I like Varvara Savvishna,' he would say to me, with a faint and crooked smile, 'and I know that everyone ought to get married, but—you know, all this has happened so suddenly—One must think it over a little.'

" 'What is there to think over?' I would say to him. 'Get married—that's all.'

" 'No; marriage is a serious step; one must first weigh the impending duties and responsibilities—so that nothing untoward may come of it. It worries me so much that I don't sleep nights. And I must confess I am afraid: she and her brother have such a peculiar way of thinking; they reason so strangely, you know, and she has a very impetuous disposition. You get married, and then, there is no telling, you may get into trouble.'

"And he did not propose; he kept putting it off, to the great vexation of the principal's wife and all our ladies; he kept weighing his future duties and responsibilities, and meanwhile he went for a walk with Varenka almost every day—possibly he thought that this was the proper thing under the circumstances—and came to see me to talk about family life. And in all probability he would have ended by proposing to her, and would have made one of those needless, stupid marriages thousands of which are made among us out of sheer boredom and idleness, if it had not been for a *kolossalischer Skandal.*

"I must tell you that Varenka's brother conceived a hatred of Belikov from the first day of their acquaintance and couldn't endure him.

" 'I don't understand,' he used to say to us, shrugging his shoulders, 'I don't understand how you can put up with that informer, that nasty mug. Ugh! how can you live here? The atmosphere you breathe is vile, stifling! Are you pedagogues, teachers? No, you are piddling functionaries; yours is not a temple of learning but a police station, and it has the same sour smell. No, brothers, I will stay with you for a while, and then I will go to my farm and catch crayfish there and teach Ukrainian brats. I will go, and you can stay here with your Judas—blast him!'

"Or he would laugh till tears came to his eyes, his laughter now deep, now shrill, and ask me, throwing up his hands, 'What does he come here for? What does he want? He sits and stares.'

"He even gave Belikov a nickname, 'The Spider.' Of course, we avoided talking to him about his sister's planning to marry 'The Spider.' And when, on one occasion, the principal's wife hinted to him what a good thing it would be if his sister settled down with such a substantial, universally respected man as Belikov, he frowned and grumbled:

" 'It's none of my business; let her marry a viper if she likes. I don't care to meddle in other people's affairs.'

"Now listen to what happened next. Some wag drew a caricature of Belikov walking along under his umbrella, wearing his rubbers, his trousers tucked up, with Varenka on his arm; below there was the legend 'Anthropos in love.' The artist got the expression admirably, you know. He must have worked more than one night, for the teachers of both the boys' and the girls' high schools, the teachers of the theological seminary, and the government officials all received copies. Belikov received one, too. The caricature made a very painful impression on him.

"We left the house together; it was the first of May, a Sunday, and all of us, the boys and the teachers, had agreed to meet at the high school and then to walk to a grove on the outskirts of the town. We set off, and he was green in the face and gloomier than a thundercloud.

" 'What wicked, malicious people there are!' he said, and his lips quivered.

"I couldn't help feeling sorry for him. We were walking along, and all of a sudden—imagine!—Kovalenko came rolling along on a bicycle, and after him, also on a bicycle, Varenka, flushed and exhausted, but gay and high-spirited.

" 'We are going on ahead,' she shouted. 'What lovely weather! Just too lovely!'

"And they both vanished. Belikov turned from green to white, and seemed petrified. He stopped short and stared at me.

" 'Good heavens, what is this?' he asked. 'Can my eyes be deceiving me? Is it proper for high school teachers and ladies to ride bicycles?'

" 'What's improper about it?' I asked. 'Let them ride and may it do them good.'

" 'But you can't mean it,' he cried, amazed at my calm. 'What are you saying?'

"And he was so shocked that he refused to go farther, and returned home.

"Next day he was continually twitching and rubbing his hands nervously, and it was obvious from the expression of his face that he was far from well. And he left before the school day was over, for the first time in his life. And he ate no dinner. Towards evening he wrapped himself up warmly, though it was practically summer weather, and made his way to the Kovalenkos'. Varenka was out; he found only her brother at home.

" 'Please sit down,' Kovalenko said coldly, frowning. He had a sleepy look; he had just taken an after-dinner nap and was in a very bad humor.

"Belikov sat in silence for about ten minutes, and then began, 'I have come to you to relieve my mind. I am very, very much troubled. Some malicious fellow has drawn a caricature of me and of another person who is close to both of us. I regard it as my duty to assure you that I had nothing to do with it. I have given no grounds for such an attack—on the contrary, I have always behaved as a respectable person would.'

"Kovalenko sat there sulking without a word. Belikov waited a while, and then went on in a low, mournful voice; 'And I have something else to say to you. I have been in the service for years, while you have entered it only lately, and I consider it my duty as an older colleague to give you a warning. You ride a bicycle, and that pastime is utterly improper for an educator of youth.'

" 'Why so?' asked Kovalenko in his deep voice.

" 'Surely that needs no explanation, Mihail Savvich—surely it is self-evident! If the teacher rides a bicycle, what can one expect of the pupils? The only thing left them is to walk on their heads! And so long as it is not explicitly permitted, it should not be done. I was horrified yesterday! When I saw your sister, everything went black before my eyes. A lady or a young girl on a bicycle—it's terrible!'

" 'What is it you wish exactly?'

" 'All I wish to do is to warn you, Mihail Savvich. You are a young man, you have a future before you, you must be very, very careful of your behavior, and you are so neglectful, oh, so neglectful! You go about in an embroidered shirt, are constantly seen in the street carrying books, and now the bicycle, too. The principal will learn that you and your sister ride bicycles, and then it will reach the Trustee's ears. No good can come of that.'

" 'It's nobody's business if my sister and I do bicycle,' said Kovalenko, and he turned crimson. 'And whoever meddles in my private affairs can go to the devil!'

"Belikov turned pale and got up.

" 'If you speak to me in that tone, I cannot continue,' he said. 'And I beg you never to express yourself in that manner about our superiors in my presence; you should be respectful to the authorities.'

" 'Have I said anything offensive about the authorities?' asked Kovalenko, looking at him angrily. 'Please leave me in peace. I am an honorable man, and do not care to talk to gentlemen of your stripe. I hate informers!'

"Belikov fidgeted nervously and hurriedly began putting on his coat, with an expression of horror on his face. It was the first time in his life he had been spoken to so rudely.

" 'You can say what you please,' he declared, as he stepped out of the entry onto the staircase landing. 'Only I must warn you: someone may have overheard us, and lest our conversation be misinterpreted and harm come of it, I shall have to inform the principal of the contents of our conversation—in a general way. I am obliged to do so.'

" 'Inform him? Go, make your report and be damned to you!'

"Kovalenko seized him from behind by the collar and gave him a shove, and Belikov rolled noisily downstairs, rubbers and all. The staircase was high and steep, but he arrived at the bottom safely, got up, and felt his nose to see whether his spectacles were intact. But just as he was rolling down the stairs, Varenka came in, accompanied by two ladies; they stood below, staring, and this was more dreadful to Belikov than anything else. I believe he would rather have broken his neck or both legs than have been an object of ridicule. Why, now the whole town would hear of it; it would come to the principal's ears, it would reach the Trustee. Oh, there was no telling what might come of it! There would be another caricature, and it would all end in his being ordered to retire from his post.

"When he got up, Varenka recognized him and, looking at his ludicrous face, his crumpled overcoat, and his rubbers, not grasping the situation and supposing that he had fallen by accident, could not restrain herself and burst into laughter that resounded throughout the house:

" 'Ha-ha-ha!'

"And this reverberant, ringing 'Ha-ha-ha!' put an end to everything: to the expected match and to Belikov's earthly existence. He did not hear what Varenka was saying; he saw nothing. On reaching home, the first thing he did was to remove Varenka's portrait from the table; then he went to bed, and he never got up again.

"Two or three days later Afanasy came to me and asked whether the doctor should not be sent for, as there was something wrong with his master. I went in to see Belikov. He lay silent behind the curtains, covered with a quilt; when you questioned him, he answered 'yes' and 'no' and nothing more. He lay there while Afanasy, gloomy and scowling, hovered about him, sighing heavily and reeking of vodka like a tavern.

"A month later Belikov died. We all went to his funeral— that is, all connected with both high schools and with the theological seminary. Now when he was lying in his coffin his expression was mild, pleasant, even cheerful, as though he were glad that he had at last been put into a case that he would never leave again. Yes, he had attained his ideal! And as though in his honor, it was cloudy, rainy weather on the day of his funeral, and we all wore rubbers and carried umbrellas. Varenka, too, was at the funeral, and when the coffin was lowered into the grave, she dropped a tear. I have noticed that Ukrainian women always laugh or cry—there is no intermediate state for them.

"I confess, it is a great pleasure to bury people like Belikov. As we were returning from the cemetery we wore discreet Lenten faces; no one wanted to display this feeling of pleasure—a feeling like that we had experienced long, long ago as children when the grownups had gone out and we ran about the garden for an hour or two, enjoying complete freedom. Ah, freedom, freedom! A mere hint, the faintest hope of its possibility, gives wings to the soul, isn't that true?

"We returned from the cemetery in good humor. But not more than a week had passed before life dropped into its old rut, and was as gloomy, tiresome, and stupid as before, the sort of life that is not explicitly forbidden, but on the other hand is not fully permitted; things were no better. And, indeed, though we had buried Belikov, how many such men in shells were left, how many more of them there will be!"

"That's the way it is," said Ivan Ivanych, and lit his pipe.

"How many more of them there will be!" repeated Burkin.

The high school teacher came out of the barn. He was a short, stout man, completely bald, with a black beard that nearly reached his waist; two dogs came out with him.

"What a moon!" he said, looking up.

It was already midnight. On the right could be seen the whole village, a long street stretching far away for some three miles. Everything was sunk in deep, silent slumber; not a movement, not a sound; one could hardly believe that nature could be so still. When on a moonlight night you see a wide village street, with its cottages, its haystacks, and its willows that have dropped off to sleep, a feeling of serenity comes over the soul; as it rests thus, hidden from toil, care, and sorrow by the nocturnal shad-

ANTON CHEKHOV

ows, the street is gentle, sad, beautiful, and it seems as though the stars look down upon it kindly and tenderly, and as if there were no more evil on earth, and all were well. On the left, where the village ended, the open country began; the fields could be seen stretching far away to the horizon, and there was no movement, no sound in that whole expanse drenched with moonlight.

"Yes, that's the way it is," repeated Ivan Ivanych; "and isn't our living in the airless, crowded town, our writing useless papers, our playing vint—isn't all that a sort of shell for us? And this spending our lives among pettifogging, idle men and silly, unoccupied women, our talking and our listening to all sorts of poppycock—isn't that a shell, too? If you like, I will tell you a very instructive story."

"No; it's time to turn in," said Burkin. "Tomorrow's another day."

They went into the barn and lay down on the hay. And they were both covered up and had dozed off when suddenly there was the sound of light footsteps—tap, tap. Someone was walking near the barn, walking a little and stopping, and a minute later, tap, tap again. The dogs began to growl.

"That's Mavra," said Burkin.

The footsteps died away.

"To see and hear them lie," said Ivan Ivanych, turning over on the other side, "and to be called a fool for putting up with their lies; to endure insult and humiliation, and not dare say openly that you are on the side of the honest and the free, and to lie and smile yourself, and all for the sake of a crust of bread, for the sake of a warm nook, for the sake of a mean, worthless rank in the service—no, one cannot go on living like that!"

"Come, now, that's a horse of another color, Ivan Ivanych," said the teacher. "Let's go to sleep."

And ten minutes later Burkin was asleep. But Ivan Ivanych kept sighing and turning from one side to the other; then he got up, went outside again, and seating himself near the door, lighted his pipe.

1898

GOOSEBERRIES

The sky had been overcast since early morning; it was a still day, not hot, but tedious, as it usually is when the weather is gray and dull, when clouds have been hanging over the fields for a long time, and you wait for the rain that does not come. Ivan Ivanych, a veterinary, and Burkin, a high school teacher, were already tired with walking, and the plain seemed endless to them. Far ahead were the scarcely visible windmills of the village of Mironositzkoe; to the right lay a range of hills that disappeared in the distance beyond the village, and both of them knew that over there were the river, and fields, green willows, homesteads, and if you stood on one of the hills, you could see from there another vast plain, telegraph poles, and a train that from afar looked like a caterpillar crawling, and in clear weather you could even see the town. Now, when it was still and when nature seemed mild and pensive, Ivan Ivanych and Burkin were filled with love for this plain, and both of them thought what a beautiful land it was.

"Last time when we were in Elder Prokofy's barn," said Burkin, "you were going to tell me a story."

"Yes; I wanted to tell you about my brother."

Ivan Ivanych heaved a slow sigh and lit his pipe before beginning his story, but just then it began to rain. And five minutes later there was a downpour, and it was hard to tell when it would be over. The two men halted, at a loss; the dogs, already wet, stood with their tails between their legs and looked at them feelingly.

"We must find shelter somewhere," said Burkin. "Let's go to Alyohin's; it's quite near."

"Let's."

They turned aside and walked across a mown meadow, now going straight ahead, now bearing to the right, until they reached the road. Soon poplars came into view, a garden, then the red roofs of barns; the river gleamed, and the view opened on a broad expanse of water with a mill and a white bathing-cabin. That was Sofyino, Alyohin's place.

The mill was going, drowning out the sound of the rain; the dam was shaking. Wet horses stood near the carts, their heads drooping, and men were walking about, their heads covered with sacks. It was damp, muddy, dreary; and the water looked cold and unkind. Ivan Ivanych and Burkin felt cold and messy and uncomfortable through and through; their feet were heavy with mud and when, having crossed the dam, they climbed up to the barns, they were silent as though they were cross with each other.

The noise of a winnowing-machine came from one of the barns, the door was open, and clouds of dust were pouring from within. On the threshold stood Alyohin himself, a man of forty, tall and rotund, with long hair, looking more like a professor or an artist than a gentleman farmer. He was wearing a white blouse, badly in need of washing, that was belted with a rope, and drawers, and his high boots were plastered with mud and straw. His eyes and nose were black with dust. He recognized Ivan Ivanych and Burkin and was apparently very glad to see them.

"Please go up to the house, gentlemen," he said, smiling; "I'll be there directly, in a moment."

It was a large structure of two stories. Alyohin lived downstairs in what was formerly the stewards' quarters: two rooms that had arched ceilings and small windows; the furniture was plain, and the place smelled of rye bread, cheap vodka, and harness. He went into the showy rooms upstairs only rarely, when he had guests. Once in the house, the two visitors were met by a chambermaid, a young woman so beautiful that both of them stood still at the same moment and glanced at each other.

"You can't imagine how glad I am to see you, gentlemen," said Alyohin, joining them in the hall. "What a surprise! Pelageya," he said, turning to the chambermaid, "give the guests a change of clothes. And, come to think of it, I will change, too. But I must go and bathe first, I don't think I've had a wash since spring. Don't you want to go into the bathing-cabin? In the meanwhile things will be got ready here."

The beautiful Pelageya, with her soft, delicate air, brought them bath towels and soap, and Alyohin went to the bathing-cabin with his guests.

"Yes, it's a long time since I've bathed," he said, as he undressed. "I've an excellent bathing-cabin, as you see—it was put up by my father—but somehow I never find time to use it." He sat down on the steps and lathered his long hair and neck, and the water around him turned brown.

"I say—" observed Ivan Ivanych significantly, looking at his head.

"I haven't had a good wash for a long time," repeated Alyohin, embarrassed, and soaped himself once more; the water about him turned dark-blue, the color of ink.

Ivan Ivanych came out of the cabin, plunged into the water with a splash and swam in the rain, thrusting his arms out wide; he raised waves on which white lilies swayed. He swam out to the middle of the river and dived and a minute later came up in another spot and swam on and kept diving, trying to touch bottom. "By God!" he kept repeating delightedly, "by God!" He swam to the mill, spoke to the peasants there, and turned back and in the middle of the river lay floating, exposing his face to the rain. Burkin and Alyohin were already dressed and ready to leave, but he kept on swimming and diving. "By God!" he kept exclaiming. "Lord, have mercy on me."

"You've had enough!" Burkin shouted to him.

They returned to the house. And only when the lamp was lit in the big drawing room upstairs, and the two guests, in silk dressing-gowns and warm slippers, were lounging in armchairs, and Alyohin himself, washed and combed, wearing a new jacket, was walking about the room, evidently savoring the warmth, the cleanliness, the dry clothes and light footwear, and when pretty Pelageya, stepping noiselessly across the carpet and smiling softly, brought in a tray with tea and jam, only then did Ivan Ivanych begin his story, and it was as though not only Burkin and Alyohin were listening, but also the ladies, old and young, and the military men who looked down upon them, calmly and severely, from their gold frames.

"We are two brothers," he began, "I, Ivan Ivanych, and my

brother, Nikolay Ivanych, who is two years my junior. I went in for a learned profession and became a veterinary; Nikolay at nineteen began to clerk in a provincial branch of the Treasury. Our father was a *kantonist,*[1] but he rose to be an officer and so a nobleman, a rank that he bequeathed to us together with a small estate. After his death there was a lawsuit and we lost the estate to creditors, but be that as it may, we spent our childhood in the country. Just like peasant children we passed days and nights in the fields and the woods, herded horses, stripped bast from the trees, fished, and so on. And, you know, whoever even once in his life has caught a perch or seen thrushes migrate in the autumn, when on clear, cool days they sweep in flocks over the village, will never really be a townsman and to the day of his death will have a longing for the open. My brother was unhappy in the government office. Years passed, but he went on warming the same seat, scratching away at the same papers, and thinking of one and the same thing: how to get away to the country. And little by little this vague longing turned into a definite desire, into a dream of buying a little property somewhere on the banks of a river or a lake.

"He was a kind and gentle soul and I loved him, but I never sympathized with his desire to shut himself up for the rest of his life on a little property of his own. It is a common saying that a man needs only six feet of earth. But six feet is what a corpse needs, not a man. It is also asserted that if our educated class is drawn to the land and seeks to settle on farms, that's a good thing. But these farms amount to the same six feet of earth. To retire from the city, from the struggle, from the hubbub, to go off and hide on one's own farm—that's not life, it is selfishness, sloth, it is a kind of monasticism, but monasticism without works. Man needs not six feet of earth, not a farm, but the whole globe, all of Nature, where unhindered he can display all the capacities and peculiarities of his free spirit.

"My brother Nikolay, sitting in his office, dreamed of eating his own *shchi,* which would fill the whole farmyard with a deli-

---

[1] The son of a private, registered at birth in the army and trained in a military school.

cious aroma, of picnicking on the green grass, of sleeping in the sun, of sitting for hours on the seat by the gate gazing at field and forest. Books on agriculture and the farming items in almanacs were his joy, the delight of his soul. He liked newspapers too, but the only things he read in them were advertisements of land for sale, so many acres of tillable land and pasture, with house, garden, river, mill, and millpond. And he pictured to himself garden paths, flowers, fruit, birdhouses with starlings in them, crucians in the pond, and all that sort of thing, you know. These imaginary pictures varied with the advertisements he came upon, but somehow gooseberry bushes figured in every one of them. He could not picture to himself a single country-house, a single rustic nook, without gooseberries.

" 'Country life has its advantages,' he used to say. 'You sit on the veranda having tea, and your ducks swim in the pond, and everything smells delicious and—the gooseberries are ripening.'

"He would draw a plan of his estate and invariably it would contain the following features: a) the master's house; b) servants' quarters; c) kitchen-garden; d) a gooseberry patch. He lived meagerly: he deprived himself of food and drink; he dressed God knows how, like a beggar, but he kept on saving and salting money away in the bank. He was terribly stingy. It was painful for me to see it, and I used to give him small sums and send him something on holidays, but he would put that away too. Once a man is possessed by an idea, there is no doing anything with him.

"Years passed. He was transferred to another province, he was already past forty, yet he was still reading newspaper advertisements and saving up money. Then I heard that he was married. Still for the sake of buying a property with a gooseberry patch he married an elderly, homely widow, without a trace of affection for her, but simply because she had money. After marrying her, he went on living parsimoniously, keeping her half-starved, and he put her money in the bank in his own name. She had previously been the wife of a postmaster, who had got her used to pies and cordials. This second husband did not even give her enough black bread. She began to sicken, and some three years later gave up the ghost. And, of course, it never for a moment occurred to my brother that he was to blame for her death. Money, like vodka, can do queer things to a man. Once in our town a merchant lay on his deathbed; before he died, he ordered a plateful of honey and he ate up all his money and lottery tickets with the honey, so that no one should get it. One day when I was inspecting a drove of cattle at a railway station, a cattle dealer fell under a locomotive and it sliced off his leg. We carried him in to the infirmary, the blood was gushing from the wound—a terrible business, but he kept begging us to find his leg and was very anxious about it: he had twenty rubles in the boot that was on that leg, and he was afraid they would be lost."

"That's a tune from another opera," said Burkin.

Ivan Ivanych paused a moment and then continued:

"After his wife's death, my brother began to look around for a property. Of course, you may scout about for five years and in the end make a mistake, and buy something quite different from what you have been dreaming of. Through an agent my brother bought a mortgaged estate of three hundred acres with a house, servants' quarters, a park, but with no orchard, no gooseberry patch, no duck-pond. There was a stream, but the water in it was the color of coffee, for on one of its banks there was a brickyard and on the other a glue factory. But my brother was not at all disconcerted: he ordered a score of gooseberry bushes, planted them, and settled down to the life of a country gentleman.

"Last year I paid him a visit. I thought I would go and see how things were with him. In his letter to me my brother called his estate 'Chumbaroklov Waste, or Himalaiskoe' (our surname was Chimsha-Himalaisky). I reached the place in the afternoon. It was hot. Everywhere there were ditches, fences, hedges, rows of fir trees, and I was at a loss as to how to get to the yard and where to leave my horse. I made my way to the house and was met by a fat dog with reddish hair that looked like a pig. It wanted to bark, but was too lazy. The cook, a fat, barelegged woman, who also looked like a pig, came out of the kitchen and said that the master was resting after dinner. I went in to see my brother, and found him sitting up in bed, with a quilt over his knees. He had grown older, stouter, flabby; his cheeks, his nose, his lips jutted

out: it looked as though he might grunt into the quilt at any
moment.

"We embraced and dropped tears of joy and also of sadness
at the thought that the two of us had once been young, but were
now gray and nearing death. He got dressed and took me out to
show me his estate.

" 'Well, how are you getting on here?' I asked.

" 'Oh, all right, thank God. I am doing very well.'

"He was no longer the poor, timid clerk he used to be but
a real landowner, a gentleman. He had already grown used to his
new manner of living and developed a taste for it. He ate a great
deal, steamed himself in the bathhouse, was growing stout, was
already having a lawsuit with the village commune and the two
factories and was very much offended when the peasants failed to
address him as 'Your Honor.' And he concerned himself with his
soul's welfare too in a substantial, upper-class manner, and performed good deeds not simply, but pompously. And what good
works! He dosed the peasants with bicarbonate and castor oil for
all their ailments and on his name day he had a thanksgiving
service celebrated in the center of the village, and then treated
the villagers to a gallon of vodka, which he thought was the thing
to do. Oh, those horrible gallons of vodka! One day a fat landowner hauls the peasants up before the rural police officer for
trespassing, and the next, to mark a feast day, treats them to a
gallon of vodka, and they drink and shout 'Hurrah' and when
they are drunk bow down at his feet. A higher standard of living,
overeating and idleness develop the most insolent self-conceit in
a Russian. Nikolay Ivanych, who when he was a petty official was
afraid to have opinions of his own even if he kept them to himself,
now uttered nothing but incontrovertible truths and did so in the
tone of a minister of state: 'Education is necessary, but the masses
are not ready for it; corporal punishment is generally harmful, but
in some cases it is useful and nothing else will serve.'

" 'I know the common people, and I know how to deal with
them,' he would say. 'They love me. I only have to raise my little
finger, and they will do anything I want.'

"And all this, mark you, would be said with a smile that

bespoke kindness and intelligence. Twenty times over he repeated: 'We, of the gentry,' 'I, as a member of the gentry.' Apparently he no longer remembered that our grandfather had been a peasant and our father just a private. Even our surname, 'Chimsha-Himalaisky,' which in reality is grotesque, seemed to him sonorous, distinguished, and delightful.

"But I am concerned now not with him, but with me. I want to tell you about the change that took place in me during the few hours that I spent on his estate. In evening when we were having tea, the cook served a plateful of gooseberries. They were not bought, they were his own gooseberries, the first ones picked since the bushes were planted. My brother gave a laugh and for a minute looked at the gooseberries in silence, with tears in his eyes—he could not speak for excitement. Then he put one berry in his mouth, glanced at me with the triumph of a child who has at last been given a toy he was longing for and said: 'How tasty!' And he ate the gooseberries greedily, and kept repeating: 'Ah, how delicious! Do taste them!'

"They were hard and sour, but as Pushkin has it,

> The falsehood that exalts we cherish more
> Than meaner truths that are a thousand strong.

I saw a happy man, one whose cherished dream had so obviously come true, who had attained his goal in life, who had got what he wanted, who was satisfied with his lot and with himself. For some reason an element of sadness had always mingled with my thoughts of human happiness, and now at the sight of a happy man I was assailed by an oppressive feeling bordering on despair. It weighed on me particularly at night. A bed was made up for me in a room next to my brother's bedroom, and I could hear that he was wakeful, and that he would get up again and again, go to the plate of gooseberries and eat one after another. I said to myself: how many contented, happy people there really are! What an overwhelming force they are! Look at life: the insolence and idleness of the strong, the ignorance and brutishness of the weak, horrible poverty everywhere, overcrowding, degeneration, drunkenness, hypocrisy, lying—Yet in all the houses and on all the streets there is peace and quiet; of the fifty thousand people who live in our town there is not one who would cry out, who would vent his indignation aloud. We see the people who go to market, eat by day, sleep by night, who babble nonsense, marry, grow old, good-naturedly drag their dead to the cemetery, but we do not see or hear those who suffer, and what is terrible in life goes on somewhere behind the scenes. Everything is peaceful and quiet and only mute statistics protest: so many people gone out of their minds, so many gallons of vodka drunk, so many children dead from malnutrition—And such a state of things is evidently necessary; obviously the happy man is at ease only because the unhappy ones bear their burdens in silence, and if there were not this silence, happiness would be impossible. It is a general hypnosis. Behind the door of every contented, happy man there ought to be someone standing with a little hammer and continually reminding him with a knock that there are unhappy people, that however happy he may be, life will sooner or later show him its claws, and trouble will come to him—illness, poverty, losses, and then no one will see or hear him, just as now he neither sees nor hears others. But there is no man with a hammer. The happy man lives at his ease, faintly fluttered by small daily cares, like an aspen in the wind—and all is well."

"That night I came to understand that I too had been contented and happy," Ivan Ivanych continued, getting up. "I too over the dinner table or out hunting would hold forth on how to live, what to believe, the right way to govern the people. I too would say that learning was the enemy of darkness, that education was necessary but that for the common people the three R's were sufficient for the time being. Freedom is a boon, I used to say, it is as essential as air, but we must wait awhile. Yes, that's what I used to say, and now I ask: Why must we wait?" said Ivan Ivanych, looking wrathfully at Burkin. "Why must we wait, I ask you? For what reason? I am told that nothing can be done all at once, that every idea is realized gradually, in its own time. But who is it that says so? Where is the proof that it is just? You cite the natural order of things, the law governing all phenomena, but is there law, is there order in the fact that I, a living, thinking man, stand beside a ditch and wait for it to close up of itself or fill up with silt, when I could jump over it or throw a bridge across it? And again, why must we wait? Wait, until we have no strength to live, and yet we have to live and are eager to live!

"I left my brother's place early in the morning, and ever since then it has become intolerable for me to stay in town. I am oppressed by the peace and the quiet, I am afraid to look at the windows, for there is nothing that pains me more than the spectacle of a happy family sitting at table having tea. I am an old man now and unfit for combat, I am not even capable of hating. I can only grieve inwardly, get irritated, worked up, and at night my head is ablaze with the rush of ideas and I cannot sleep. Oh, if I were young!"

Ivan Ivanych paced up and down the room excitedly and repeated, "If I were young!"

He suddenly walked up to Alyohin and began to press now one of his hands, now the other.

"Pavel Konstantinych," he said imploringly, "don't quiet down, don't let yourself be lulled to sleep! As long as you are young, strong, alert, do not cease to do good! There is no happiness and there should be none, and if life has a meaning and a purpose, that meaning and purpose is not our happiness but something greater and more rational. Do good!"

All this Ivan Ivanych said with a pitiful, imploring smile, as though he were asking a personal favor.

Afterwards all three of them sat in armchairs in different corners of the drawing room and were silent. Ivan Ivanych's story satisfied neither Burkin nor Alyohin. With the ladies and generals looking down from the golden frames, seeming alive in the dim light, it was tedious to listen to the story of the poor devil of a clerk who ate gooseberries. One felt like talking about elegant people, about women. And the fact that they were sitting in a drawing room where everything—the chandelier under its cover, the armchairs, the carpets under-foot—testified that the very people who were now looking down from the frames had once moved about here, sat and had tea, and the fact that lovely Pelageya was noiselessly moving about—that was better than any story.

Alyohin was very sleepy; he had gotten up early, before three o'clock in the morning, to get some work done, and now he could hardly keep his eyes open, but he was afraid his visitors might tell an interesting story in his absence, and he would not leave. He did not trouble to ask himself if what Ivan Ivanych had just said was intelligent or right. The guests were not talking about groats, or hay, or tar, but about something that had no direct bearing on his life, and he was glad of it and wanted them to go on.

"However, it's bedtime," said Burkin, rising. "Allow me to wish you good night."

Alyohin took leave of his guests and went downstairs to his own quarters, while they remained upstairs. They were installed for the night in a big room in which stood two old wooden beds decorated with carvings and in the corner was an ivory crucifix. The wide cool beds which had been made by the lovely Pelageya gave off a pleasant smell of clean linen.

Ivan Ivanych undressed silently and got into bed.

"Lord forgive us sinners!" he murmured, and drew the bed-clothes over his head.

His pipe, which lay on the table, smelled strongly of burnt tobacco, and Burkin, who could not sleep for a long time, kept wondering where the unpleasant odor came from.

The rain beat against the window panes all night.

1898

THE DARLING

Olenka Plemyannikova, the daughter of a retired collegiate assessor, was sitting on her porch, which gave on the courtyard; deep in thought. It was hot, the flies were persistent and annoying, and it was pleasant to think that it would soon be evening.

Dark rainclouds were gathering in the east and there was a breath of moisture in the wind that occasionally blew from that direction.

Kukin, a theater manager who ran a summer garden known as The Tivoli and lodged in the wing of the house, was standing in the middle of the courtyard, staring at the sky.

"Again!" he was saying in despair. "It's going to rain again! Rain every day, every day, as if to spite me! It will be the death of me! It's ruin! Such a frightful loss every day!"

He struck his hands together and continued, turning to Olenka:

"There, Olga Semyonovna, that's our life. It's enough to make you weep! You work, you try your utmost, you wear yourself out, you lie awake nights, you rack your brains trying to make a better thing of it, and what's the upshot? In the first place, the public is ignorant, barbarous. I give them the very best operetta, an elaborate spectacle, first-rate vaudeville artists. But do you think they want that? It's all above their heads. All they want is slapstick! Give them trash! And then look at the weather! Rain almost every evening. It started raining on the tenth of May, and it has kept it up all May and June. It's simply terrible! The public doesn't come, but don't I have to pay the rent? Don't I have to pay the artists?"

The next day toward evening the sky would again be overcast and Kukin would say, laughing hysterically:

"Well, go on, rain! Flood the garden, drown me! Bad luck to me in this world and the next! Let the artists sue me! Let them send me to prison—to Siberia—to the scaffold! Ha, ha, ha!"

The next day it was the same thing all over again.

Olenka listened to Kukin silently, gravely, and sometimes tears would come to her eyes. In the end his misfortunes moved her and she fell in love with him. He was a short, thin man with a sallow face, and wore his hair combed down over his temples. He had a thin tenor voice and when he spoke, his mouth twisted, and his face perpetually wore an expression of despair. Nevertheless he aroused a genuine, deep feeling in her. She was always enamored of someone and could not live otherwise. At first it had been her papa, who was now ill and sat in an armchair in a darkened room, breathing with difficulty. Then she had devoted her affections to her aunt, who used to come from Bryansk every other year. Still earlier, when she went to school, she had been in love with her French teacher. She was a quiet, kind, soft-hearted girl, with meek, gentle eyes, and she enjoyed very good health. At the sight of her full pink cheeks, her soft white neck with a dark birthmark on it, and the kind artless smile that came into her face when she listened to anything pleasant, men said to themselves, "Yes, not half bad," and smiled too, while the ladies present could not refrain from suddenly seizing her hand in the middle of the conversation and exclaiming delightedly, "You darling!"

The house in which she lived all her life and which was to be hers by her father's will, was situated on the outskirts of the city on what was known as Gypsy Road, not far from The Tivoli. In the evening and at night she could hear the band play and the skyrockets go off, and it seemed to her that it was Kukin fighting his fate and assaulting his chief enemy, the apathetic public. Her heart contracted sweetly, she had no desire to sleep, and when he returned home at dawn, she would tap softly at her bedroom window and, showing him only her face and one shoulder through the curtain, give him a friendly smile.

He proposed to her, and they were married. And when he had a good look at her neck and her plump firm shoulders, he struck his hands together, and exclaimed, "Darling!"

He was happy, but as it rained on their wedding day and the night that followed, the expression of despair did not leave his face.

As a married couple, they got on well together. She presided over the box office, looked after things in the summer garden, kept accounts and paid salaries; and her rosy cheeks, the radiance of her sweet artless smile showed now in the box office window, now in the wings of the theater, now at the buffet. And she was already telling her friends that the theater was the most remarkable, the most important, and the most essential thing in the world, and that it was only the theater that could give true pleasure and make you a cultivated and humane person.

"But do you suppose the public understands that?" she would ask. "What it wants is slapstick! Yesterday we gave 'Faust Inside Out,' and almost all the boxes were empty, and if Vanichka and I had put on something vulgar, I assure you the theater would have been packed. Tomorrow Vanichka and I are giving 'Orpheus in Hell.' Do come."

And what Kukin said about artists and the theater she would repeat. Like him she despised the public for its ignorance and indifference to art; she took a hand in the rehearsals, correcting the actors, kept an eye on the musicians, and when there was an unfavorable notice in the local paper, she wept and went to see the editor about it.

The actors were fond of her and called her "the darling," and "Vanichka-and-I." She was sorry for them and would lend them small sums, and if they cheated her, she cried in private but did not complain to her husband.

The pair got on just as well together when winter came. They leased the municipal theater for the season and sublet it for short periods to a Ukrainian troupe, a magician, or a local dramatic club. Olenka was gaining weight and beamed with happiness, but Kukin was getting thinner and more sallow and complained of terrible losses, although business was fairly good during the winter. He coughed at night, and she would make him drink an infusion of raspberries and linden blossoms, rub him with eau de Cologne and wrap him in her soft shawls.

"What a sweet thing you are!" she would say quite sincerely, smoothing his hair. "My handsome sweet!"

At Lent he left for Moscow to engage a company of actors for the summer season, and she could not sleep with him away. She sat at the window and watched the stars. It occurred to her that she had something in common with the hens: they too stayed awake all night and were disturbed when the cock was absent from the henhouse. Kukin was detained in Moscow, and wrote that he would return by Easter, and in his letters he sent instructions about The Tivoli. But on the Monday of Passion Week, late in the evening, there was a sudden ominous knock at the gate; someone was banging at the wicket as though it were a barrel—

boom, boom, boom! The sleepy cook, her bare feet splashing through the puddles, ran to open the gate.

"Open, please!" someone on the other side of the gate was saying in a deep voice. "There's a telegram for you."

Olenka had received telegrams from her husband before, but this time for some reason she was numb with fright. With trembling hands she opened the telegram and read the following:

"Ivan Petrovich died suddenly today awaiting prot instructions tuneral Tuesday."

That is exactly how the telegram had it: "tuneral," and there was also the incomprehensible word "prot"; the signature was that of the director of the comic opera company.

"My precious!" Olenka sobbed. "Vanichka, my precious, my sweet! Why did we ever meet! Why did I get to know you and to love you! To whom can your poor unhappy Olenka turn?"

Kukin was buried on Tuesday in the Vagankovo Cemetery in Moscow. Olenka returned home on Wednesday, and no sooner did she enter her room than she sank onto the bed and sobbed so loudly that she could be heard in the street and in the neighboring courtyards.

"The darling!" said the neighbors, crossing themselves. "Darling Olga Semyonovna! How the poor soul takes on!"

Three months later Olenka was returning from Mass one day in deep mourning and very sad. It happened that one of her neighbors, Vasily Andreich Pustovalov, the manager of Babakayev's lumberyard, who was also returning from church, was walking beside her. He was wearing a straw hat and a white waistcoat, with a gold watch-chain, and he looked more like a landowner than a businessman.

"There is order in all things, Olga Semyonovna," he was saying sedately, with a note of sympathy in his voice; "and if one of our dear ones passes on, then it means that this was the will of God, and in that case we must keep ourselves in hand and bear it submissively."

Having seen Olenka to her gate, he took leave of her and went further. All the rest of the day she heard his sedate voice, and as soon as she closed her eyes she had a vision of his dark beard. She liked him very much. And apparently she too had made an impression on him, because a little later a certain elderly lady, whom she scarcely knew, called to have coffee with her, and no sooner was she seated at table than the visitor began to talk about Pustovalov, saying that he was a fine, substantial man, and that any marriageable woman would be glad to go to the altar with him. Three days later Pustovalov himself paid her a visit. He did not stay more than ten minutes and he said little, but Olenka fell in love with him, so deeply that she stayed awake all night burning as with fever, and in the morning she sent for the elderly lady. The match was soon arranged and then came the wedding.

As a married couple Pustovalov and Olenka got on very well together. As a rule he was in the lumberyard till dinnertime, then he went out on business and was replaced by Olenka, who stayed in the office till evening, making out bills and seeing that orders were shipped.

"We pay twenty per cent more for lumber every year," she would say to customers and acquaintances. "Why, we used to deal in local timber, and now Vasichka has to travel to the province of Mogilev for timber regularly. And the freight rates!" she would exclaim, putting her hands to her cheeks in horror. "The freight rates!"

It seemed to her that she had been in the lumber business for ages, that lumber was the most important, the most essential thing in the world, and she found something intimate and touching in the very sound of such words as beam, log, batten, plank, box board, lath, scantling, slab . . .

At night she would dream of whole mountains of boards and planks, of endless caravans of carts hauling lumber out of town to distant points. She would dream that a regiment of beams, 28 feet by 8 inches, standing on end, was marching in the lumber-yard, that beams, logs, and slabs were crashing against each other with the hollow sound of dry wood, that they kept tumbling down and rising again, piling themselves on each other. Olenka would scream in her sleep and Pustovalov would say to her tenderly: "Olenka, what's the matter, darling? Cross yourself!"

Whatever ideas her husband had, she adopted as her own.

If he thought that the room was hot or that business was slow, she thought so too. Her husband did not care for entertainments and on holidays stayed home—so did she.

"You are always at home or in the office," her friends would say. "You ought to go to the theater, darling, or to the circus."

"Vasichka and I have no time for the theater," she would answer sedately. "We are working people, we're not interested in such foolishness. What good are these theaters?"

On Saturdays the two of them would go to evening service, on holidays they attended early Mass, and returning from the church they walked side by side, their faces wearing a softened expression. There was an agreeable aroma about them, and her silk dress rustled pleasantly. At home they had tea with short-bread, and various kinds of jam, and afterwards they ate pie. Every day at noon, in the yard and on the street just outside the gate, there was a delicious smell of *borshch* and roast lamb or duck, and on fast days there was the odor of fish, and one could not pass the Pustovalov gate without one's mouth watering.

In the office the samovar was always boiling and the customers were treated to tea with doughnuts. Once a week the pair went to the baths and returned side by side, both with red faces.

"Yes, everything goes well with us, thank God," Olenka would say to her friends. "I wish everyone were as happy as Vasichka and I."

When Pustovalov went off to the provinces of Mogilev for timber, she missed him badly and lay awake nights, crying. Sometimes, in the evening, a young army veterinary, by the name of Smirnin, who rented the wing of their house, would call on her. He chatted or played cards with her and that diverted her. What interested her most was what he told her about his domestic life. He had been married and had a son, but was separated from his wife because she had been unfaithful to him, and now he hated her; he sent her forty rubles a month for the maintenance of the child. And listening to him, Olenka would sigh and shake her head: she was sorry for him.

"Well, God keep you," she would say to him as she took leave of him, going to the stairs with him, candle in hand. "Thank you for relieving my boredom, and may the Queen of Heaven give you health!"

She always expressed herself in this sedate and reasonable manner, in imitation of her husband. Just as the veterinary would be closing the door behind him, she would recall him and say:

"You know, Vladimir Platonych, you had better make up with your wife. You ought to forgive her, at least for your son's sake! I am sure the little boy understands everything."

And when Pustovalov came back, she would tell him in low tones about the veterinary and his unhappy domestic life, and both of them would sigh and shake their heads and speak of the boy, who was probably missing his father. Then by a strange association of ideas they would both turn to the icons, bow down to the ground before them and pray that the Lord would grant them children.

Thus the Pustovalovs lived in peace and quiet, in love and harmony for six years. But one winter day, right after having hot tea at the office, Vasily Andreich went out without his cap to see about shipping some lumber, caught a chill and was taken sick. He was treated by the best doctors, but the illness had its own way with him, and he died after four months. Olenka was a widow again.

"To whom can I turn now, my darling?" she sobbed when she had buried her husband. "How can I live without you, wretched and unhappy as I am? Pity me, good people, left all alone in the world—"

She wore a black dress with white cuffs and gave up wearing hat and gloves for good. She hardly ever left the house except to go to church or to visit her husband's grave, and at home she lived like a nun. Only at the end of six months did she take off her widow's weeds and open the shutters. Sometimes in the morning she was seen with her cook going to market for provisions, but how she lived now and what went on in her house could only be guessed. People based their guesses on such facts as that they saw her having tea with the veterinary in her little garden, he reading the newspaper aloud to her, and that, meeting an acquaintance at the post office, she would say:

"There is no proper veterinary inspection in our town, and that's why there is so much illness around. So often you hear of people getting ill from the milk or catching infections from horses and cows. When you come down to it, the health of domestic animals must be as well cared for as the health of human beings."

She now repeated the veterinary's words and held the same opinions about everything that he did. It was plain that she could not live even for one year without an attachment and that she had found new happiness in the wing of her house. Another woman would have been condemned for this, but of Olenka no one could think ill: everything about her was so unequivocal. Neither she nor the veterinary mentioned to anyone the change that had occurred in their relations; indeed, they tried to conceal it, but they didn't succeed, because Olenka could not keep a secret. When he had visitors, his regimental colleagues, she, pouring the tea or serving the supper, would begin to talk of the cattle plague, of the pearl disease, of the municipal slaughterhouses. He would be terribly embarrassed and when the guests had gone, he would grasp her by the arms and hiss angrily:

"I've asked you before not to talk about things that you don't understand! When veterinaries speak among themselves, please don't butt in! It's really annoying!"

She would look at him amazed and alarmed and ask, "But Volodichka, what shall I talk about?"

And with tears in her eyes she would hug him and beg him not to be angry, and both of them were happy.

Yet this happiness did not last long. The veterinary left, left forever, with his regiment, which was moved to some remote place, it may have been Siberia. And Olenka remained alone.

Now she was quite alone. Her father had died long ago, and his armchair stood in the attic, covered with dust and minus one leg. She got thinner and lost her looks, and passers-by in the street did not glance at her and smile as they used to. Obviously, her best years were over, were behind her, and now a new kind of life was beginning for her, an unfamiliar kind that did not bear thinking of. In the evening Olenka sat on her porch, and heard the band play at The Tivoli and the rockets go off, but this no longer suggested anything to her mind. She looked apathetically at the empty courtyard, thought of nothing, and later, when night came, she would go to bed and dream of the empty courtyard. She ate and drank as though involuntarily.

Above all, and worst of all, she no longer had any opinions whatever. She saw objects about her and understood what was going on, but she could not form an opinion about anything and did not know what to talk about. And how terrible it is not to have any opinions! You see, for instance, a bottle, or the rain, or a peasant driving in a cart, but what is the bottle for, or the rain, or the peasant, what is the meaning of them, you can't tell, and you couldn't, even if they paid you a thousand rubles. When Kukin was about, or Pustovalov or, later, the veterinary, Olenka could explain it all and give her opinions about anything you like, but now there was the same emptiness in her head and in her heart as in her courtyard. It was weird, and she felt as bitter as if she had been eating wormwood.

Little by little the town was extending in all directions. Gypsy Road was now a regular street, and where The Tivoli had been and the lumberyards, houses had sprung up and lanes had multiplied. How swiftly time passes! Olenka's house had taken on a shabby look, the roof was rusty, the shed sloped, and the whole yard was invaded by burdock and stinging nettles. Olenka herself had aged and grown homely. In the summer she sat on the porch, feeling empty and dreary and bitter, as before; in the winter she sat by the window and stared at the snow. Sometimes at the first breath of spring or when the wind brought her the chime of church bells, memories of the past would overwhelm her, her heart would contract sweetly and her eyes would brim over with tears. But this only lasted a moment, and then there was again emptiness and once more she was possessed by a sense of the futility of life; Trot, the black kitten, rubbed against her and purred softly, but Olenka was not affected by these feline caresses. Is that what she needed? She needed an affection that would take possession of her whole being, her soul, her mind, that would give her ideas, a purpose in life, that would warm her aging blood. And she would shake the kitten off her lap, and say irritably: "Scat! Scat! Don't stick to me!"

And so it went, day after day, year after year, and no joy, no opinion! Whatever Mavra the cook would say, was well enough.

One hot July day, toward evening, when the cattle were being driven home and the yard was filled with clouds of dust, suddenly someone knocked at the gate. Olenka herself went to open it and was dumfounded at what she saw: at the gate stood Smirnin, the veterinary, already gray, and wearing civilian clothes. She suddenly recalled everything and, unable to control herself, burst into tears, silently letting her head drop on his breast. She was so agitated that she scarcely noticed how the two of them entered the house and sat down to tea.

"My dear," she murmured, trembling with joy, "Vladimir Platonych, however did you get here?"

"I have come here for good," he explained. "I have retired from the army and want to see what it's like to be on my own and live a settled life. And besides, my son is ready for high school. I have made up with my wife, you know."

"Where is she?"

"She's at the hotel with the boy, and I'm out looking for lodgings."

"Goodness, Vladimir Platonych, take my house! You don't need to look further! Good Lord, and you can have it free," exclaimed Olenka, all in a flutter and beginning to cry again. "You live here in the house, and the wing will do for me. Heavens, I'm so glad!"

The next day they began painting the roof and whitewashing the walls, and Olenka, her arms akimbo, walked about the yard, giving orders. The old smile had come back to her face, and she was lively and spry, as though she had waked from a long sleep. Presently the veterinary's wife arrived, a thin, homely lady with bobbed hair who looked as if she were given to caprices. With her was the little boy, Sasha, small for his age (he was going on ten), chubby, with clear blue eyes and dimples in his cheeks.

No sooner did he walk into the yard than he began chasing the cat, and immediately his eager, joyous laughter rang out.

"Auntie, is that your cat?" he asked Olenka. "When she has little ones, please give us a kitten. Mama is terribly afraid of mice."

Olenka chatted with him, then gave him tea, and her heart suddenly grew warm and contracted sweetly, as if this little boy were her own son. And in the evening, as he sat in the dining-room doing his homework, she looked at him with pity and tenderness and whispered:

"My darling, my pretty one, my little one! How blond you are, and so clever!"

"An island," he was reciting from the book, "is a body of land entirely surrounded by water."

"An island is a body of land . . ." she repeated and this was the first opinion she expressed with conviction after so many years of silence and mental vacuity.

She now had opinions of her own, and at supper she had a conversation with Sasha's parents, saying that studying in high school was hard on the children, but that nevertheless the classical course was better than the scientific one because a classical education opened all careers to you: you could be either a doctor or an engineer.

Sasha started going to high school. His mother went off to Kharkov to visit her sister and did not come back; every day his father left town to inspect herds and sometimes he stayed away for three days together, and it seemed to Olenka that Sasha was wholly abandoned, that he was unwanted, that he was being starved, and she moved him into the wing with her and settled him in a little room there.

For six months now Sasha has been living in her wing. Every morning Olenka comes into his room; he is fast asleep, his hand under his cheek, breathing quietly. She is sorry to wake him.

"Sashenka," she says sadly, "get up, my sweet! It's time to go to school."

He gets up, dresses, says his prayers, and sits down to his breakfast: he drinks three glasses of tea and eats two large dough-nuts, and half a buttered French roll. He is hardly awake and consequently cross.

"You haven't learned the fable, Sashenka," says Olenka, looking at him as though she were seeing him off on a long journey. "You worry me. You must do your best, darling, study. And pay attention to your teachers."

"Please leave me alone!" says Sasha.

Then he walks down the street to school, a small boy in a big cap, with his books in a rucksack. Olenka follows him noiselessly.

"Sashenka!" she calls after him. He turns around and she thrusts a date or a caramel into his hand. When they turn into the school lane, he feels ashamed at being followed by a tall stout woman; he looks round and says: "You'd better go home, auntie; I can go alone now."

She stands still and stares after him until he disappears at the school entrance. How she loves him! Not one of her former attachments was so deep; never had her soul surrendered itself so unreservedly, so disinterestedly and with such joy as now when her maternal instinct was increasingly asserting itself. For this little boy who was not her own, for the dimples in his cheeks, for his very cap, she would have laid down her life, would have laid it down with joy, with tears of tenderness. Why? But who knows why?

Having seen Sasha off to school, she goes quietly home, contented, tranquil, brimming over with love; her face, grown younger in the last six months, beams with happiness; people meeting her look at her with pleasure and say:

"Good morning, Olga Semyonovna, darling! How are you, darling?"

"They make the children work so hard at high school nowadays," she says, as she does her marketing. "Think of it: yesterday in the first form they had a fable to learn by heart, a Latin translation and a problem for homework. That's entirely too much for a little fellow."

And she talks about the teachers, the lessons, the textbooks— saying just what Sasha says about them.

At three o'clock they have dinner together, in the evening they do the homework together, and cry. When she puts him to bed, she takes a long time making the sign of the cross over him and whispering prayers. Then she goes to bed and thinks of the future, distant and misty, when Sasha, having finished his studies, will become a doctor or an engineer, will have a large house of his own, horses, a carriage, will marry and become a father. She falls asleep and her dreams are of the same thing, and tears flow down her cheeks from her closed eyes. The black kitten lies beside her purring: Purr-purrr-purrr.

Suddenly there is a loud knock at the gate. Olenka wakes up, breathless with fear, her heart palpitating. Half a minute passes, and there is another knock.

"That's a telegram from Kharkov," she thinks, beginning to tremble from head to foot. "Sasha's mother is sending for him from Kharkov—O Lord!"

She is in despair. Her head, her hands, her feet grow chill and it seems to her that she is the most unhappy woman in the whole world. But another minute passes, voices are heard: it's the veterinary returning from the club.

"Well, thank God!" she thinks.

Little by little the load rolls off her heart and she is again at ease; she goes back to bed and thinks of Sasha who is fast asleep in the next room and sometimes shouts in his sleep:

"I'll give it to you! Scram! No fighting!"

1899

THE LADY WITH THE PET DOG

A new person, it was said, had appeared on the esplanade: a lady with a pet dog. Dmitry Dmitrich Gurov, who had spent a fortnight at Yalta and had got used to the place, had also begun to take an interest in new arrivals. As he sat in Vernet's confectionery shop, he saw, walking on the esplanade, a fair-haired young woman of medium height, wearing a beret; a white Pomeranian was trotting behind her.

And afterwards he met her in the public garden and in the

square several times a day. She walked alone, always wearing the same beret and always with the white dog; no one knew who she was and everyone called her simply "the lady with the pet dog."

"If she is here alone without husband or friends," Gurov reflected, "it wouldn't be a bad thing to make her acquaintance."

He was under forty, but he already had a daughter twelve years old, and two sons at school. They had found a wife for him when he was very young, a student in his second year, and by now she seemed half as old again as he. She was a tall, erect woman with dark eyebrows, stately and dignified and, as she said of herself, intellectual. She read a great deal, used simplified spelling in her letters, called her husband, not Dmitry, but Dimitry, while he privately considered her of limited intelligence, narrow-minded, dowdy, was afraid of her, and did not like to be at home. He had begun being unfaithful to her long ago—had been unfaithful to her often and, probably for that reason, almost always spoke ill of women, and when they were talked of in his presence used to call them "the inferior race."

It seemed to him that he had been sufficiently tutored by bitter experience to call them what he pleased, and yet he could not have lived without "the inferior race" for two days together. In the company of men he was bored and ill at ease, he was chilly and uncommunicative with them; but when he was among women he felt free, and knew what to speak to them about and how to comport himself; and even to be silent with them was no strain on him. In his appearance, in his character, in his whole make-up there was something attractive and elusive that disposed women in his favor and allured them. He knew that, and some force seemed to draw him to them, too.

Oft-repeated and really bitter experience had taught him long ago that with decent people—particularly Moscow people—who are irresolute and slow to move, every affair which at first seems a light and charming adventure inevitably grows into a whole problem of extreme complexity, and in the end a painful situation is created. But at every new meeting with an interesting woman this lesson of experience seemed to slip from his memory, and he was eager for life, and everything seemed so simple and diverting.

One evening while he was dining in the public garden the lady in the beret walked up without haste to take the next table. Her expression, her gait, her dress, and the way she did her hair told him that she belonged to the upper class, that she was married, that she was in Yalta for the first time and alone, and that she was bored there. The stories told of the immorality in Yalta are to a great extent untrue; he despised them, and knew that such stories were made up for the most part by persons who would have been glad to sin themselves if they had had the chance; but when the lady sat down at the next table three paces from him, he recalled these stories of easy conquests, of trips to the mountains, and the tempting thought of a swift, fleeting liaison, a romance with an unknown woman of whose very name he was ignorant suddenly took hold of him.

He beckoned invitingly to the Pomeranian, and when the dog approached him, shook his finger at it. The Pomeranian growled; Gurov threatened it again.

The lady glanced at him and at once dropped her eyes.

"He doesn't bite," she said and blushed.

"May I give him a bone?" he asked; and when she nodded he inquired affably, "Have you been in Yalta long?"

"About five days."

"And I am dragging out the second week here."

There was a short silence.

"Time passes quickly, and yet it is so dull here!" she said, not looking at him.

"It's only the fashion to say it's dull here. A provincial will live in Belyov or Zhizdra and not be bored, but when he comes here it's 'Oh, the dullness! Oh, the dust!' One would think he came from Granada."

She laughed. Then both continued eating in silence, like strangers, but after dinner they walked together and there sprang up between them the light banter of people who are free and contented, to whom it does not matter where they go or what they talk about. They walked and talked of the strange light on the sea:

the water was a soft, warm, lilac color, and there was a golden band of moonlight upon it. They talked of how sultry it was after a hot day. Gurov told her that he was a native of Moscow, that he had studied languages and literature at the university, but had a post in a bank; that at one time he had trained to become an opera singer but had given it up, that he owned two houses in Moscow. And he learned from her that she had grown up in Petersburg, but had lived in S—— since her marriage two years previously, that she was going to stay in Yalta for about another month, and that her husband, who needed a rest, too, might perhaps come to fetch her. She was not certain whether her husband was a member of a Government Board or served on a Zemstvo Council, and this amused her. And Gurov learned too that her name was Anna Sergeyevna.

Afterwards in his room at the hotel he thought about her— and was certain that he would meet her the next day. It was bound to happen. Getting into bed he recalled that she had been a schoolgirl only recently, doing lessons like his own daughter; he thought how much timidity and angularity there was still in her laugh and her manner of talking with a stranger. It must have been the first time in her life that she was alone in a setting in which she was followed, looked at, and spoken to for one secret purpose alone, which she could hardly fail to guess. He thought of her slim, delicate throat, her lovely gray eyes.

"There's something pathetic about her, though," he thought, and dropped off.

II

A week had passed since they had struck up an acquaintance. It was a holiday. It was close indoors, while in the street the wind whirled the dust about and blew people's hats off. One was thirsty all day, and Gurov often went into the restaurant and offered Anna Sergeyevna a soft drink or ice cream. One did not know what to do with oneself.

In the evening when the wind had abated they went out on

the pier to watch the steamer come in. There were a great many people walking about the dock; they had come to welcome some-one and they were carrying bunches of flowers. And two peculiarities of a festive Yalta crowd stood out: the elderly ladies were dressed like young ones and there were many generals.

Owing to the choppy sea, the steamer arrived late, after sunset, and it was a long time tacking about before it put in at the pier. Anna Sergeyevna peered at the steamer and the passengers through her lorgnette as though looking for acquaintances, and whenever she turned to Gurov her eyes were shining. She talked a great deal and asked questions jerkily, forgetting the next mo-ment what she had asked; then she lost her lorgnette in the crush.

The festive crowd began to disperse; it was now too dark to see people's faces; there was no wind any more, but Gurov and Anna Sergeyevna still stood as though waiting to see someone else come off the steamer. Anna Sergeyevna was silent now, and sniffed her flowers without looking at Gurov.

"The weather has improved this evening," he said. "Where shall we go now? Shall we drive somewhere?"

She did not reply.

Then he looked at her intently, and suddenly embraced her and kissed her on the lips, and the moist fragrance of her flowers enveloped him; and at once he looked round him anxiously, wondering if anyone had seen them.

"Let us go to your place," he said softly. And they walked off together rapidly.

The air in her room was close and there was the smell of the perfume she had bought at the Japanese shop. Looking at her, Gurov thought: "What encounters life offers!" From the past he preserved the memory of carefree, good-natured women whom love made gay and who were grateful to him for the happiness he gave them, however brief it might be; and of women like his wife who loved without sincerity, with too many words, affected-ly, hysterically, with an expression that it was not love or passion that engaged them but something more significant; and of two or three others, very beautiful, frigid women, across whose faces would suddenly flit a rapacious expression—an obstinate desire to take from life more than it could give, and these were women no longer young, capricious, unreflecting, domineering, unintelligent, and when Gurov grew cold to them their beauty aroused his hatred, and the lace on their lingerie seemed to him to resemble scales.

But here there was the timidity, the angularity of inexperienced youth, a feeling of awkwardness; and there was a sense of embarrassment, as though someone had suddenly knocked at the door. Anna Sergeyevna, "the lady with the pet dog," treated what had happened in a peculiar way, very seriously, as though it were her fall—so it seemed, and this was odd and inappropriate. Her features drooped and faded, and her long hair hung down sadly on either side of her face; she grew pensive and her dejected pose was that of a Magdalene in a picture by an old master.

"It's not right," she said. "You don't respect me now, you first of all."

There was a watermelon on the table. Gurov cut himself a slice and began eating it without haste. They were silent for at least half an hour.

There was something touching about Anna Sergeyevna; she had the purity of a well-bred, naive woman who has seen little of life. The single candle burning on the table barely illumined her face, yet it was clear that she was unhappy.

"Why should I stop respecting you, darling?" asked Gurov. "You don't know what you're saying."

"God forgive me," she said, and her eyes filled with tears. "It's terrible."

"It's as though you were trying to exonerate yourself."

"How can I exonerate myself? No. I am a bad, low woman; I despise myself and I have no thought of exonerating myself. It's not my husband but myself I have deceived. And not only just now; I have been deceiving myself for a long time. My husband may be a good, honest man, but he is a flunkey! I don't know what he does, what his work is, but I know he is a flunkey! I was twenty when I married him. I was tormented by curiosity; I wanted something better. 'There must be a different sort of life,' I said to myself. I wanted to live! To live, to live! Curiosity kept eating at me—you don't understand it, but I swear to God I could no longer control myself; something was going on in me: I could not be held back. I told my husband I was ill, and came here. And here I have been walking about as though in a daze, as though I were mad; and now I have become a vulgar, vile woman whom anyone may despise."

Gurov was already bored with her; he was irritated by her naive tone, by her repentance, so unexpected and so out of place; but for the tears in her eyes he might have thought she was joking or play-acting.

"I don't understand, my dear," he said softly. "What do you want?"

She hid her face on his breast and pressed close to him.

"Believe me, believe me, I beg you," she said, "I love honesty and purity, and sin is loathsome to me; I don't know what I'm doing. Simple people say, 'The Evil One has led me astray.' And I may say of myself now that the Evil One has led me astray."

"Quiet, quiet," he murmured.

He looked into her fixed, frightened eyes, kissed her, spoke to her softly and affectionately, and by degrees she calmed down, and her gaiety returned; both began laughing.

Afterwards when they went out there was not a soul on the esplanade. The town with its cypresses looked quite dead, but the sea was still sounding as it broke upon the beach; a single launch was rocking on the waves and on it a lantern was blinking sleepily.

They found a cab and drove to Oreanda.

"I found out your surname in the hall just now: it was written on the board—von Dideritz," said Gurov. "Is your husband German?"

"No; I believe his grandfather was German, but he is Greek Orthodox himself."

At Oreanda they sat on a bench not far from the church, looked down at the sea, and were silent. Yalta was barely visible through the morning mist; white clouds rested motionlessly on the mountaintops. The leaves did not stir on the trees, cicadas twanged, and the monotonous muffled sound of the sea that rose from below spoke of the peace, the eternal sleep awaiting us. So it rumbled below when there was no Yalta, no Oreanda here; so it rumbles now, and it will rumble as indifferently and as hollowly when we are no more. And in this constancy, in this complete indifference to the life and death of each of us, there lies, perhaps, a pledge of our eternal salvation, of the unceasing advance of life upon earth, of unceasing movement towards perfection. Sitting beside a young woman who in the dawn seemed so lovely, Gurov, soothed and spellbound by these magical surroundings—the sea, the mountains, the clouds, the wide sky—thought how everything is really beautiful in this world when one reflects: everything except what we think or do ourselves when we forget the higher aims of life and our own human dignity.

A man strolled up to them—probably a guard—looked at them and walked away. And this detail, too, seemed so mysterious and beautiful. They saw a steamer arrive from Feodosia, its lights extinguished in the glow of dawn.

"There is dew on the grass," said Anna Sergeyevna, after a silence.

"Yes, it's time to go home."

They returned to the city.

Then they met every day at twelve o'clock on the esplanade, lunched and dined together, took walks, admired the sea. She complained that she slept badly, that she had palpitations, asked the same questions, troubled now by jealousy and now by the fear that he did not respect her sufficiently. And often in the square or the public garden, when there was no one near them, he suddenly drew her to him and kissed her passionately. Complete idleness, these kisses in broad daylight exchanged furtively in dread of someone's seeing them, the heat, the smell of the sea, and the continual flitting before his eyes of idle, well-dressed, well-fed people, worked a complete change in him; he kept telling Anna Sergeyevna how beautiful she was, how seductive, was urgently passionate; he would not move a step away from her, while she was often pensive and continually pressed him to confess that he did not respect her, did not love her in the least, and saw in her nothing but a common woman. Almost every evening rather late they drove somewhere out of town, to Oreanda or to the waterfall; and the excursion was always a success, the scenery invariably impressed them as beautiful and magnificent.

They were expecting her husband, but a letter came from him saying that he had eye-trouble, and begging his wife to return home as soon as possible. Anna Sergeyevna made haste to go.

"It's a good thing I am leaving," she said to Gurov. "It's the hand of Fate!"

She took a carriage to the railway station, and he went with her. They were driving the whole day. When she had taken her place in the express, and when the second bell had rung, she said, "Let me look at you once more—let me look at you again. Like this."

She was not crying but was so sad that she seemed ill, and her face was quivering.

"I shall be thinking of you—remembering you," she said. "God bless you; be happy. Don't remember evil against me. We are parting forever—it has to be, for we ought never to have met. Well, God bless you."

The train moved off rapidly, its lights soon vanished, and a minute later there was no sound of it, as though everything had conspired to end as quickly as possible that sweet trance, that madness. Left alone on the platform, and gazing into the dark distance, Gurov listened to the twang of the grasshoppers and the hum of the telegraph wires, feeling as though he had just waked up. And he reflected, musing, that there had now been another episode or adventure in his life, and it, too, was at an end, and nothing was left of it but a memory. He was moved, sad, and slightly remorseful: this young woman whom he would never meet again had not been happy with him; he had been warm and affectionate with her, but yet in his manner, his tone, and his caresses there had been a shade of light irony, the slightly coarse arrogance of a happy male who was, besides, almost twice her age. She had constantly called him kind, exceptional, high-minded; obviously he had seemed to her different from what he really was, so he had involuntarily deceived her.

Here at the station there was already a scent of autumn in the air; it was a chilly evening.

"It is time for me to go north, too," thought Gurov as he left the platform. "High time!"

III

At home in Moscow the winter routine was already established: the stoves were heated, and in the morning it was still dark when the children were having breakfast and getting ready for school, and the nurse would light the lamp for a short time. There were frosts already. When the first snow falls, on the first day the sleighs are out, it is pleasant to see the white earth, the white roofs; one draws easy, delicious breaths, and the season brings back the days of one's youth. The old limes and birches, white with hoar-frost, have a good-natured look; they are closer to one's heart than cypresses and palms, and near them one no longer wants to think of mountains and the sea.

Gurov, a native of Moscow, arrived there on a fine frosty day, and when he put on his fur coat and warm gloves and took a walk along Petrovka, and when on Saturday night he heard the bells ringing, his recent trip and the places he had visited lost all charm for him. Little by little he became immersed in Moscow life, greedily read three newspapers a day, and declared that he did not read the Moscow papers on principle. He already felt a longing for restaurants, clubs, formal dinners, anniversary celebrations, and it flattered him to entertain distinguished lawyers and actors, and to play cards with a professor at the physicians' club. He could eat a whole portion of meat stewed with pickled cabbage and served in a pan, Moscow style.

A month or so would pass and the image of Anna Sergeyevna, it seemed to him, would become misty in his memory, and only from time to time he would dream of her with her touching smile as he dreamed of others. But more than a month went by, winter came into its own, and everything was still clear in his memory as though he had parted from Anna Sergeyevna only yesterday. And his memories glowed more and more vividly. When in the evening stillness the voices of his children preparing

their lessons reached his study, or when he listened to a song or
to an organ playing in a restaurant, or when the storm howled in
the chimney, suddenly everything would rise up in his memory:
what had happened on the pier and the early morning with the
mist on the mountains, and the steamer coming from Feodosia,
and the kisses. He would pace about his room a long time,
remembering and smiling; then his memories passed into reveries, and in his imagination the past would mingle with what was
to come. He did not dream of Anna Sergeyevna, but she followed
him about everywhere and watched him. When he shut his eyes
he saw her before him as though she were there in the flesh, and
she seemed to him lovelier, younger, tenderer than she had been,
and he imagined himself a finer man than he had been in Yalta.
Of evenings she peered out at him from the bookcase, from the
fireplace, from the corner—he heard her breathing, the caressing
rustle of her clothes. In the street he followed the women with
his eyes, looking for someone who resembled her.

Already he was tormented by a strong desire to share his
memories with someone. But in his home it was impossible to talk
of his love, and he had no one to talk to outside; certainly he could
not confide in his tenants or in anyone at the bank. And what was
there to talk about? He hadn't loved her then, had he? Had there
been anything beautiful, poetical, edifying, or simply interesting
in his relations with Anna Sergeyevna? And he was forced to talk
vaguely of love, of women, and no one guessed what he meant;
only his wife would twitch her black eyebrows and say, "The part
of a philanderer does not suit you at all, Dimitry."

One evening, coming out of the physicians' club with an
official with whom he had been playing cards, he could not resist
saying:

"If you only knew what a fascinating woman I became acquainted with at Yalta!"

The official got into his sledge and was driving away, but
turned suddenly and shouted:

"Dmitry Dmitrich!"

"What is it?"

"You were right this evening: the sturgeon was a bit high."

These words, so commonplace, for some reason moved Gurov to indignation, and struck him as degrading and unclean. What savage manners, what mugs! What stupid nights, what dull, humdrum days! Frenzied gambling, gluttony, drunkenness, continual talk always about the same things! Futile pursuits and conversations always about the same topics take up the better part of one's time, the better part of one's strength, and in the end there is left a life clipped and wingless, an absurd mess, and there is no escaping or getting away from it—just as though one were in a madhouse or a prison.

Gurov, boiling with indignation, did not sleep all night. And he had a headache all the next day. And the following nights too he slept badly; he sat up in bed, thinking, or paced up and down his room. He was fed up with his children, fed up with the bank; he had no desire to go anywhere or to talk of anything.

In December during the holidays he prepared to take a trip and told his wife he was going to Petersburg to do what he could for a young friend—and he set off for S—— What for? He did not know, himself. He wanted to see Anna Sergeyevna and talk with her, to arrange a rendezvous if possible.

He arrived at S—— in the morning, and at the hotel took the best room, in which the floor was covered with gray army cloth, and on the table there was an inkstand, gray with dust and topped by a figure on horseback, its hat in its raised hand and its head broken off. The porter gave him the necessary information: von Dideritz lived in a house of his own on Staro-Goncharnaya Street, not far from the hotel: he was rich and lived well and kept his own horses; everyone in the town knew him. The porter pronounced the name: "Dridiritz."

Without haste Gurov made his way to Staro-Goncharnaya Street and found the house. Directly opposite the house stretched a long gray fence studded with nails.

"A fence like that would make one run away," thought Gurov, looking now at the fence, now at the windows of the house.

He reflected: this was a holiday, and the husband was apt to be at home. And in any case, it would be tactless to go into the

house and disturb her. If he were to send her a note, it might fall
into her husband's hands, and that might spoil everything. The
best thing was to rely on chance. And he kept walking up and
down the street and along the fence, waiting for the chance. He
saw a beggar go in at the gate and heard the dogs attack him; then
an hour later he heard a piano, and the sound came to him faintly
and indistinctly. Probably it was Anna Sergeyevna playing. The
front door opened suddenly, and an old woman came out, followed by the familiar white Pomeranian. Gurov was on the point
of calling to the dog, but his heart began beating violently, and
in his excitement he could not remember the Pomeranian's name.

He kept walking up and down, and hated the gray fence
more and more, and by now he thought irritably that Anna Sergeyevna had forgotten him, and was perhaps already diverting
herself with another man, and that that was very natural in a
young woman who from morning till night had to look at that
damn fence. He went back to his hotel room and sat on the couch
for a long while, not knowing what to do, then he had dinner and
a long nap.

"How stupid and annoying all this is!" he thought when he
woke and looked at the dark windows: it was already evening.
"Here I've had a good sleep for some reason. What am I going
to do at night?"

He sat on the bed, which was covered with a cheap gray
blanket of the kind seen in hospitals, and he twitted himself in his
vexation:

"So there's your lady with the pet dog. There's your adventure. A nice place to cool your heels in."

That morning at the station a playbill in large letters had
caught his eye. *The Geisha* was to be given for the first time. He
thought of this and drove to the theater.

"It's quite possible that she goes to first nights," he thought.

The theater was full. As in all provincial theaters, there was
a haze above the chandelier, the gallery was noisy and restless; in
the front row, before the beginning of the performance the local
dandies were standing with their hands clasped behind their
backs; in the Governor's box the Governor's daughter, wearing

a boa, occupied the front seat, while the Governor himself hid modestly behind the portiere and only his hands were visible; the curtain swayed; the orchestra was a long time tuning up. While the audience were coming in and taking their seats, Gurov scanned the faces eagerly.

Anna Sergeyevna, too, came in. She sat down in the third row, and when Gurov looked at her his heart contracted, and he understood clearly that in the whole world there was no human being so near, so precious, and so important to him; she, this little, undistinguished woman, lost in a provincial crowd, with a vulgar lorgnette in her hand, filled his whole life now, was his sorrow and his joy, the only happiness that he now desired for himself, and to the sounds of the bad orchestra, of the miserable local violins, he thought how lovely she was. He thought and dreamed.

A young man with small side-whiskers, very tall and stooped, came in with Anna Sergeyevna and sat down beside her; he nodded his head at every step and seemed to be bowing continually. Probably this was the husband whom at Yalta, in an access of bitter feeling, she had called a flunkey. And there really was in his lanky figure, his side-whiskers, his small bald patch, something of a flunkey's retiring manner; his smile was mawkish, and in his buttonhole there was an academic badge like a waiter's number.

During the first intermission the husband went out to have a smoke; she remained in her seat. Gurov, who was also sitting in the orchestra, went up to her and said in a shaky voice, with a forced smile:

"Good evening!"

She glanced at him and turned pale, then looked at him again in horror, unable to believe her eyes, and gripped the fan and the lorgnette tightly together in her hands, evidently trying to keep herself from fainting. Both were silent. She was sitting, he was standing, frightened by her distress and not daring to take a seat beside her. The violins and the flute that were being tuned up sang out. He suddenly felt frightened: it seemed as if all the people in the boxes were looking at them. She got up and went hurriedly to the exit; he followed her, and both of them walked

blindly along the corridors and up and down stairs, and figures
in the uniforms prescribed for magistrates, teachers, and officials
of the Department of Crown Lands, all wearing badges, flitted
before their eyes, as did also ladies, and fur coats on hangers; they
were conscious of drafts and the smell of stale tobacco. And
Gurov, whose heart was beating violently, thought:

"Oh, Lord! Why are these people here and this orchestra!"

And at that instant he suddenly recalled how when he had
seen Anna Sergeyevna off at the station he had said to himself that
all was over between them and that they would never meet again.
But how distant the end still was!

On the narrow, gloomy staircase over which it said "To the
Amphitheatre," she stopped.

"How you frightened me!" she said, breathing hard, still
pale and stunned. "Oh, how you frightened me! I am barely alive.
Why did you come? Why?"

"But do understand, Anna, do understand—" he said hurriedly, under his breath. "I implore you, do understand—"

She looked at him with fear, with entreaty, with love; she
looked at him intently, to keep his features more distinctly in her
memory.

"I suffer so," she went on, not listening to him. "All this time
I have been thinking of nothing but you; I live only by the
thought of you. And I wanted to forget, to forget; but why, oh,
why have you come?"

On the landing above them two high school boys were looking down and smoking, but it was all the same to Gurov; he drew
Anna Sergeyevna to him and began kissing her face and her
hands.

"What are you doing, what are you doing!" she was saying
in horror, pushing him away. "We have lost our senses. Go away
today; go away at once—I conjure you by all that is sacred, I
implore you—People are coming this way!"

Someone was walking up the stairs.

"You must leave," Anna Sergeyevna went on in a whisper.
"Do you hear, Dmitry Dmitrich? I will come and see you in
Moscow. I have never been happy; I am unhappy now, and I

never, never shall be happy, never! So don't make me suffer still more! I swear I'll come to Moscow. But now let us part. My dear, good, precious one, let us part!"

She pressed his hand and walked rapidly downstairs, turning to look round at him, and from her eyes he could see that she really was unhappy. Gurov stood for a while, listening, then when all grew quiet, he found his coat and left the theater.

IV

And Anna Sergeyevna began coming to see him in Moscow. Once every two or three months she left S——, telling her husband that she was going to consult a doctor about a woman's ailment from which she was suffering—and her husband did and did not believe her. When she arrived in Moscow she would stop at the Slavyansky Bazar Hotel, and at once send a man in a red cap to Gurov. Gurov came to see her, and no one in Moscow knew of it.

Once he was going to see her in this way on a winter morning (the messenger had come the evening before and not found him in). With him walked his daughter, whom he wanted to take to school: it was on the way. Snow was coming down in big wet flakes.

"It's three degrees above zero, and yet it's snowing," Gurov was saying to his daughter. "But this temperature prevails only on the surface of the earth; in the upper layers of the atmosphere there is quite a different temperature."

"And why doesn't it thunder in winter, papa?"

He explained that, too. He talked, thinking all the while that he was on his way to a rendezvous, and no living soul knew of it, and probably no one would ever know. He had two lives: an open one, seen and known by all who needed to know it, full of conventional truth and conventional falsehood, exactly like the lives of his friends and acquaintances; and another life that went on in secret. And through some strange, perhaps accidental, combination of circumstances, everything that was of interest and importance to him, everything that was essential to him, everything about which he felt sincerely and did not deceive himself, everything that constituted the core of his life, was going on concealed from others; while all that was false, the shell in which he hid to cover the truth—his work at the bank, for instance, his discussions at the club, his references to the "inferior race," his appearances at anniversary celebrations with his wife—all that went on in the open. Judging others by himself, he did not believe what he saw, and always fancied that every man led his real, most interesting life under cover of secrecy as under cover of night. The personal life of every individual is based on secrecy, and perhaps it is partly for that reason that civilized man is so nervously anxious that personal privacy should be respected.

Having taken his daughter to school, Gurov went on to the Slavyansky Bazar Hotel. He took off his fur coat in the lobby, went upstairs, and knocked gently at the door. Anna Sergeyevna, wearing his favorite gray dress, exhausted by the journey and by waiting, had been expecting him since the previous evening. She was pale, and looked at him without a smile, and he had hardly entered when she flung herself on his breast. Their kiss was a long, lingering one, as though they had not seen one another for two years.

"Well, darling, how are you getting on there?" he asked. "What news?"

"Wait; I'll tell you in a moment—I can't speak."

She could not speak; she was crying. She turned away from him, and pressed her handkerchief to her eyes.

"Let her have her cry; meanwhile I'll sit down," he thought, and he seated himself in an armchair.

Then he rang and ordered tea, and while he was having his tea she remained standing at the window with her back to him. She was crying out of sheer agitation, in the sorrowful consciousness that their life was so sad; that they could only see each other in secret and had to hide from people like thieves! Was it not a broken life?

"Come, stop now, dear!" he said.

It was plain to him that this love of theirs would not be over soon, that the end of it was not in sight. Anna Sergeyevna was growing more and more attached to him. She adored him, and it was unthinkable to tell her that their love was bound to come to an end some day; besides, she would not have believed it!

He went up to her and took her by the shoulders, to fondle her and say something diverting, and at that moment he caught sight of himself in the mirror.

His hair was already beginning to turn gray. And it seemed odd to him that he had grown so much older in the last few years, and lost his looks. The shoulders on which his hands rested were warm and heaving. He felt compassion for this life, still so warm and lovely, but probably already about to begin to fade and wither like his own. Why did she love him so much? He always seemed to women different from what he was, and they loved in him not himself, but the man whom their imagination created and whom they had been eagerly seeking all their lives; and afterwards, when they saw their mistake, they loved him nevertheless. And not one of them had been happy with him. In the past he had met women, come together with them, parted from them, but he had never once loved; it was anything you please, but not love. And only now when his head was gray he had fallen in love, really, truly—for the first time in his life.

Anna Sergeyevna and he loved each other as people do who are very close and intimate, like man and wife, like tender friends; it seemed to them that Fate itself had meant them for one another, and they could not understand why he had a wife and she a husband; and it was as though they were a pair of migratory birds, male and female, caught and forced to live in different cages. They forgave each other what they were ashamed of in their past, they forgave everything in the present, and felt that this love of theirs had altered them both.

Formerly in moments of sadness he had soothed himself with whatever logical arguments came into his head, but now he no longer cared for logic; he felt profound compassion, he wanted to be sincere and tender.

"Give it up now, my darling," he said. "You've had your

cry; that's enough. Let us have a talk now, we'll think up something."

Then they spent a long time taking counsel together, they talked of how to avoid the necessity for secrecy, for deception, for living in different cities, and not seeing one another for long stretches of time. How could they free themselves from these intolerable fetters?

"How? How?" he asked, clutching his head. "How?"

And it seemed as though in a little while the solution would be found, and then a new and glorious life would begin; and it was clear to both of them that the end was still far off, and that what was to be most complicated and difficult for them was only just beginning.

1899

ON OFFICIAL BUSINESS

The deputy examining magistrate and the county physician were on their way to an autopsy in the village of Syrnya. En route they were caught in a blizzard; they wasted a great deal of time traveling in circles and arrived at their destination not at midday, as they had intended, but in the evening when it was already dark. They put up for the night at the village headquarters.[1] It was here that the dead body happened to be lying, the corpse of the Zemstvo insurance agent Lesnitzky, who had come to Syrnya three days previously and, after settling in the village headquarters and ordering the samovar, had shot himself, to the complete surprise of everyone; and the fact that he had ended his life under such strange circumstances, with the samovar before him and the food he had brought along laid out on the table, led many to suspect murder; an inquest was in order.

[1] A cottage in which community meetings and sessions of the village elders were held and which was sometimes used as a hostelry.

In the entry the doctor and the examining magistrate stamped their feet to shake off the snow, and near by stood an old man who belonged to the lowest order of rural police: Ilya Loshadin; he was holding a little tin lamp in his hands to give them light. There was a strong smell of kerosene.

"Who are you?" asked the doctor.

"The p'liceman," answered Loshadin.

He used to spell it "pleaceman" when he signed the receipts at the post office.

"And where are the inquest witnesses?"

"They must have gone to have tea, your honor."

To the right was the best room, the travelers' or gentry's room; to the left a room for the lower orders with a big stove and a sleeping platform. The doctor and the examining magistrate, followed by the policeman, holding the lamp high above his head, went into the best room. Here, motionless on the floor, close to the table legs, lay a long body, covered with a white sheet. In the dim light of the lamp, in addition to the white cover, a pair of new rubbers could be clearly seen, and everything about the place was weird and sinister: the dark walls, and the silence, and the rubbers, and the immobility of the dead body. On the table stood a samovar, long since cold; and round it packages, probably containing food.

"To shoot oneself in the village headquarters, how tactless!" said the doctor. "If you do want to put a bullet through your brain, you ought to do it at home, in some shed."

He sank onto a bench, just as he was, in his cap, his fur coat, and his felt boots; his companion, the magistrate, sat down opposite him.

"These hysterical and neurasthenic people are great egoists," the doctor went on bitterly. "If a neurasthenic sleeps in the same room with you, he rustles his newspaper; when he dines with you, he has a row with his wife unrestrained by your presence; and when he feels like shooting himself, he shoots himself in village headquarters, so as to give everybody the greatest amount of trouble. Under all circumstances these gentlemen think only of themselves! That's why elderly people so dislike our 'nervous age.' "

"Elderly people dislike so many things," said the magistrate, yawning. "You ought to point out to the old fellows the difference between the suicides of the past and the suicides of the present. Formerly the so-called gentleman shot himself because he had embezzled Government funds, but nowadays it's because he's fed up with life, depressed. Which is better?"

"Fed up with life, depressed; but you must admit that he might have shot himself somewhere else than at the village headquarters."

"Such aggravation!" said the policeman, "such aggravation! It's a regular punishment. Folks are all upset, your honor; they've not slept these three nights. The children are crying. The cows ought to be milked but the women won't go to the barn—they're scared—that they may see the dead gentleman in the dark. Sure they're foolish women, but some of the men is scared, too. As soon as it's dark they won't pass the place alone, but only in a drove. And the witnesses too—"

Dr. Starchenko, a middle-aged, dark-bearded man in spectacles, and the magistrate Lyzhin, a fair-haired man, still young, who had taken his degree only two years before and looked more like a student than an official, sat in silence, musing. They were annoyed at having been delayed. Now, although it was not yet six o'clock, they had to wait till morning, spending the night here; and they pictured a long evening, a long, dark night, boredom, wretched beds, cockroaches, morning chill; and listening to the storm that howled in the chimney and in the garret, they both thought how unlike all this was the life they would have wished for themselves and of which they had once dreamed, and how far away they both were from their contemporaries, who at that moment were walking about the lighted streets in town without noticing the weather, or getting ready for the theater, or sitting in their studies over a book. Oh, how much they would have given now only to stroll along the Nevsky or along Petrovka in Moscow, to listen to decent singing, to spend an hour or so in a restaurant!

Hoo-oo-oo! sang the storm in the garret, and something outside banged viciously, probably the signboard on the cottage. Hoo-oo-oo!

"You can do as you like, but I don't want to stay here," said Starchenko, getting up. "It's not six yet; it's too early to go to bed; I'll drive somewhere. Von Taunitz lives not far from here, only a couple of miles from Syrnya. I'll drive there and spend the evening with him. Officer, go and tell my coachman not to take the horses out. And what will you do?" he asked Lyzhin.

"I don't know; I'll probably go to sleep."

The doctor wrapped his fur coat round him and went out. He could be heard talking to the coachman and there was the sound of bells shaking on the frozen horses. He drove off.

"It's not right for you, sir, to spend the night in here," said the policeman. "Go into the other room. It's not clean there, but for one night it don't matter. I'll get a samovar from a peasant and heat it directly. I'll pile up some hay for you and then you can go to sleep, and God be with you, your honor."

A little later the magistrate was sitting at a table in the other room, drinking tea, while Loshadin the policeman stood at the door, talking. He was an old man of about sixty, short and very lean, hunched and white-haired, with a naive smile on his face and watery eyes; and he kept smacking his lips as though he were sucking a candy. He was wearing a short sheepskin coat and felt boots, and did not let his stick out of his hands. The magistrate's youth aroused his compassion and that was probably why he addressed him familiarly.

"Fyodor Makarych, the Elder, gave orders that he was to be informed when the police inspector or the examining magistrate came," he said, "so I reckon I must go now. It's nearly three miles to the district office, and the storm's bad, the snowdrifts are a caution—blamed if I'll get there before midnight. Listen to it howl!"

"I don't need the elder," said Lyzhin. "There's nothing for him to do here."

He looked at the old man with curiosity and asked:

"Tell me, grandfather, how many years is it you've been a policeman?"

"Why, about thirty. Five years after the Freedom[2] I got to be policeman, you can figure out for yourself. And I've been on the go every day since. People have holidays, but me, I'm always on the go. When it's Easter and the church bells are ringing and Christ has risen, I keep on trotting, with my bag. To the treasury, to the post office, to the police inspector's lodgings, to the district magistrate, to the tax collector, to the municipal office, to the gentry, to the peasants, to all Orthodox folk. I carry packages, notices, tax blanks, letters, all kinds of forms, reports, and you know, kind sir, your honor, they've got such forms nowadays to write numbers on—yellow, white, red—and every gentleman or priest or well-to-do peasant must write down a dozen times a year how much he has sown or harvested, how many bushels or poods he has of rye, how many of oats, and of hay, and all about the weather, you know, and insects, too, of all kinds. Of course you can write what you like, it's only a rule, but you must go and hand out the papers and then go and collect 'em again. Here, for instance, there's no call to cut open the gentleman; you know yourself it's all foolishness, you only dirty your hands, but here you've gone to the trouble, your honor, you've come because it's the rule, there's no getting round it. For thirty years I've been walking my legs off according to rule. In summer it's all right, it is warm and dry; but in winter and fall it puts you out. There were times I was drowning and times I was near froze to death; all kinds of things happened to me—wicked people in the woods took my bag away; I've got it in the neck and I've been brought to law."

"What for?"

"Fraud."

"What do you mean, fraud?"

"Why, you see, Khrisanf Grigoryev, the clerk, sold the contractor some boards as didn't belong to him—cheated him, that is. I was mixed up in it. They sent me to the tavern for vodka; well, the clerk didn't go shares with me—didn't even stand me

---

[2] The emancipation of the serfs, proclaimed in 1861.

a drink; but seeing as I'm a poor man, and so a no-account person, not to be relied on—to look at, that is—we were both brought to trial; he was sent to prison, but, praise God! I was acquitted on all counts. They read a paper, you know, in the court, about it. And they were all in uniform—in the court, I mean. I can tell you, your honor, for anyone not used to 'em, my duties are a caution, Lord keep you from them; but me, I don't mind it. Matter of fact, when I'm not on the go, my feet hurt. And at home it's worse for me. At home you have to light the stove for the clerk in the district office, to fetch water for him, to clean his boots.''

"And what's your salary?'' Lyzhin asked.

"Eighty-four rubles a year.''

"I'll bet there are other little sums coming in. There are, aren't there?''

"Other little sums? No, indeed! Gentlemen nowadays don't often give tips. Gentlemen is strict nowadays, they take offense easy. If you bring him a paper, he's offended, if you take off your cap to him, he's offended. 'You used the wrong entrance,' he says. 'You're a drunkard,' he says. 'You smell of onion; you're a blockhead,' he says; 'you're the son of a bitch.' There are some as is decent, of course; but what does it get you? They only laugh at you and call you names. Take Squire Altuhin, for instance, he's good-natured; and to look at him, he's sober and in his right mind, but as soon as he lays eyes on me he shouts God knows what. The name he calls me! 'You—' says he.''

The policeman pronounced some word but in such a low voice that it was impossible to make out what he said.

"What?'' asked Lyzhin. "Say it again.''

" 'Administration,' '' the policeman repeated aloud. "He's been calling me that for a long time, for maybe six years. 'Hello, Administration!' But I don't mind; let him, God bless him! A lady will send you a glass of vodka and a piece of pie sometimes, and you drink her health. But it's mostly the peasants that give me something; peasants are more warm-hearted, they fear God: one will give you a piece of bread, another some cabbage soup, and there's some as stand you a glass. The village Elders treat you to tea in the tavern. Here the inquest witnesses have gone to drink tea. 'Loshadin,' they says, 'you stay here and keep watch for us,' and each of 'em gives me a kopeck. They're scared, not being used to it, and yesterday they gave me fifteen kopecks and stood me a glass."

"And you, aren't you scared?"

"I am, sir; but of course it's all in the line of duty, there's no getting round it. Last year I was taking an arrested man into town and he laced into me and took it out of my hide! And all around us—fields, woods—how could I get away from him? And that's how it is here. I remember the gentleman, this Lesnitzky, when he was that high, and I knew his father and his mama. I am from the village of Nedoshchotova, and the Lesnitzkys, they weren't more than two thirds of a mile from us and even less, their land bordered on ours, and the old master, Lesnitzky, he had a sister, a God-fearing, charitable maiden lady. God rest the soul of Thy servant, Yulia, of sainted memory! She never married, and when she was dying she divided up all her property; she left two hundred and fifty acres to the monastery, and five hundred to our village commune for her soul's sake; but her brother, I mean the master, he hid the paper, they say he burnt it in the stove, and took all this land for himself. To be sure, he thought it would be to his benefit; but no, wait, you can't get on in the world by wrongdoing, brother. For twenty years the master didn't go to confession. There was something as kept him from church, you see, and he died without the sacrament. He busted. He was as fat as they come. He busted lengthwise. Then everything was taken away from Seryozha, the young master, I mean, to pay the debts—every last thing. Well, he hadn't got very far with his book learning, he couldn't do anything, and the president of the Zemstvo Board, his uncle, he says to himself: 'I'll take him'—Seryozha, I mean—'to be our agent; let him insure people, that's easy work.' And the gentleman was young and proud, he wanted to live in better style, on a grander scale, and have things his way; to be sure, it hurt his feelings to be jolting about the county in a trashy cart and talking to the peasants; he would walk and keep looking on the ground, looking on the ground and saying nothing; if you called him right in his ear, 'Sergey Sergeyich!' he would look round like this, 'Eh?' and stare at the ground again; and now you see he's laid hands on himself. It don't fit, your honor, it's wrong, this thing, and there's no understanding what goes on in the world, merciful Lord! Say your father was rich and you're poor; it's eating humble pie, no denying it, but there, you've got to put up with it. I used to live well, too, your honor; I had two horses, three cows, I used to keep twenty head of sheep; but that time's past, and here I am with nothing but a bag, and even that's not mine, it's the Government's. And now in our village, if the truth be told, my house is the worst of the lot. Mokey had four footmen to scrape and bow, Mokey is a footman himself now; Petrak had four workmen to dig and delve, and now Petrak is a workman himself."

"And how was it you came down in the world?" asked the magistrate.

"My sons are terrible boozers. They get so soused, so soused there's no saying what it's like, you wouldn't believe me."

Lyzhin listened and thought how he, Lyzhin, would go back to Moscow sooner or later, while this old man would stay here forever and would always be on the go. And how many times in his life he would come across such battered, unkempt, "no-account" old men, whose souls cherished equally the fifteen kopeck piece, the glass of vodka, and the profound belief that you can't get along in this world by wrongdoing.

Then he grew tired of listening, and told the old man to bring him some hay for his bed. In the traveler's room there was an iron bedstead with a pillow and a quilt, and it could have been brought in; but the deceased had been lying beside it for nearly three days (and he may have been sitting on it just before his death), and now it would be disagreeable to sleep on it.

"It's only half past seven," thought Lyzhin, glancing at his watch. "How awful!"

He was not sleepy, but having no means of passing the time, he lay down and covered himself with a plaid. Loshadin went in and out several times, clearing away the dishes; smacking his lips and sighing, he kept stomping about the table; at last he took his little lamp and went out, and looking at his long gray hair and bent body from behind, Lyzhin reflected: "Just like a magician in an opera."

It grew dark. The moon must have been behind the clouds, as the windows and the snow on the window-frames could be seen distinctly.

"Hoo-oo-oo!" sang the storm. "Hoo-oo-oo!"

"He-e-e-lp!" shrieked a woman in the garret, or so it sounded. "He-e-e-lp!"

Thump! something outside banged against the wall. Bang!

The magistrate listened; there was no woman up there, it was the wind wailing. It was chilly, and he put his fur coat over his plaid. As he got warm, he thought how all this—the blizzard, and the cottage, and the old man, and the dead body lying in the next room—how all this was remote from the life he desired for himself, and how alien it all was to him, how petty, uninteresting. If this man had killed himself in Moscow or somewhere near the city, and he had had to hold an inquest on him there, it would have been interesting, important, and perhaps it would have seemed terrible to sleep in the room next to that in which the corpse lay. Here, hundreds of miles from Moscow, all this appeared somehow in a different light; it was not life, not human beings, but something that existed "according to rule," as Loshadin said; it would not leave the faintest trace in the memory and would be forgotten as soon as he, Lyzhin, drove away from Syrnya. The fatherland, the real Russia, was Moscow, Petersburg; but these were the provinces, the colonies. When you dream of playing a part, of becoming known, of being, for instance, examining magistrate in important cases or prosecutor in a circuit court, of being a social lion, you inevitably think of Moscow. If you are to live, then it must be in Moscow; here, nothing matters to you; you get reconciled readily to your insignificant role, and only look for one thing in life—to get away, to get away as quickly as possible. And in his mind Lyzhin hurried through the Moscow streets, called on acquaintances, met relatives, colleagues, and his heart contracted sweetly at the thought that he was only twenty-six, and that if in five or ten years he could break away from here and get to Moscow, even then it would not be too late and he would still have a whole life ahead of him. And as he began to doze off, and as his thoughts became confused, he imagined the long corridors of the Moscow court, himself delivering a speech, his sisters, the orchestra which for some reason kept droning: Hoo-oo-oo! Hoo-oo-oo!

Thump! Bang! sounded again. Thump!

And he suddenly recalled how one day, when he was talking to the bookkeeper at the Zemstvo office, a thin pale gentleman with dark eyes and black hair came up to the counter; he had a disagreeable look in his eyes such as one sees in people who have slept too long after dinner, and it marred his delicate, intelligent profile; and the high boots that he was wearing did not suit him, they looked clumsy. The bookkeeper had introduced him: "This is our Zemstvo agent."

"So that was Lesnitzky—this very man," it now occurred to Lyzhin.

He recalled Lesnitzky's low voice, called to mind his gait, and it seemed to him that someone was walking beside him now with a step like Lesnitzky's.

All at once he was terrified, his head felt cold.

"Who's there?" he asked fearfully.

"The p'liceman!"

"What do you want here?"

"I've come to ask, your honor—You said this evening as the elder wasn't needed, but I'm afraid he'll be angry. He told me to let him know. Shouldn't I go?"

"The deuce, I'm fed up with you," said Lyzhin with vexation, and covered himself up again.

"Maybe he'll be angry. I'll go, your honor. I hope you'll be all right here."

And Loshadin went out. There was coughing and whispering in the entry. The inquest witnesses must have returned.

"We'll let these poor devils get off as early as possible tomorrow—" thought the examining magistrate; "we'll do the autopsy as soon as it's light."

He began to doze off when suddenly he again became conscious of steps, not timid this time, but quick and noisy. A door slammed, voices were heard, the scratching of a match. . . .

"Are you asleep? Are you asleep?" Dr. Starchenko asked hurriedly and crossly as he lit one match after another. He was covered with snow from head to foot and he had brought cold air in with him. "Are you asleep? Get up! Let's go to von Taunitz's. He's sent his horses to fetch you. Let's go. There you will have supper, at least, and sleep decently. You see I've come for you myself. The horses are excellent, we'll get there in twenty minutes."

"What time is it now?"

"Quarter past ten."

Lyzhin, sleepy and out of sorts, put on his felt boots, his fur coat, cap and hood, and went out with the doctor. The frost had abated, but a strong, piercing wind was blowing and chasing down the street clouds of snow that seemed to flee in terror; high drifts had already piled up against fences and on door-steps. The doctor and the magistrate got into the sleigh, and the white coachman bent over them to button up the apron. They were both hot.

"Go ahead!"

They drove through the village. "Cutting a fluffy furrow there," the magistrate quoted the poet to himself, as he listlessly watched the working of the outrunner's legs. There were lights in all the cabins, as though it were the eve of a high holiday: the peasants had stayed up because they were afraid of the dead man. The coachman sullenly held his peace, he must have turned glum while he was waiting at the village headquarters, and now he too was thinking of the deceased.

"When they found out at von Taunitz's," said Starchenko, "that you were spending the night in the village, they all attacked me for not having brought you along with me."

At the turning, as they left the village behind them, the coachman suddenly shouted at the top of his voice: "Get off the road!"

A man flashed by: he was standing in the snow up to his knees, having moved off the road, and was staring at the troika.

The magistrate caught sight of a hooked staff, a beard, and a bag slung sideways, and it seemed to him that it was Loshadin, and he even fancied that the man was smiling. He flashed by and vanished.

The road at first skirted the forest, then, broadening, cut through it; old pines and a young birch grove shot past, as well as tall, gnarled young oaks standing singly in the clearings where the wood had recently been cut; but soon everything was lost in clouds of snow; the coachman said that he could see the forest, but the magistrate could see nothing but the outrunner. The wind blew at their backs.

Suddenly the horses stopped.

"Well, what now?" asked Starchenko crossly.

Without a word the coachman climbed down from the box and began to run around the sleigh on his heels; he made larger and larger circles, getting further and further away from the sleigh, and it looked as though he were dancing; finally he returned and began turning off to the right.

"You've lost your way, eh?" asked Starchenko.

"No ma-a-atter—"

They came to a hamlet with not a light in it. Then again, forest and fields. And again they lost their way, and the coachman climbed down from the box and performed his dance. The troika flew along a dark road under overarching trees, flew swiftly, and the hooves of the fiery outrunner knocked against the dashboard. Here the trees roared fearfully and resonantly, and it was pitch dark, so that those in the sleigh felt as though they were rushing into an abyss. Suddenly bright light from an entrance and windows flashed upon their eyes, and they heard the friendly, steady barking of dogs and the sound of voices. They had arrived.

While they were taking off their fur coats and felt boots downstairs in the entry, *"Un petit verre de Clicquot"* was being played on the piano upstairs, and the stamping of children's feet was heard. Immediately they were enveloped in the genial warmth and the smell peculiar to an old mansion where, whatever the weather, it is warm and clean and comfortable.

"That's splendid!" said von Taunitz, a fat man with an incredibly broad neck and sidewhiskers, pressing the magistrate's hand. "That's splendid! Glad to see you here, delighted to make your acquaintance. We're by way of being colleagues, you know. At one time I served as assistant prosecutor, but not for long, only two years. I came here to see to the estate, and I have grown old here—in a word, I'm an old fogey. Glad to see you here," he continued, obviously controlling his voice so as not to speak loudly; he and his guests were on their way upstairs. "I have no wife. She died. But here are my daughters, let me introduce you," and turning round, he shouted downstairs in a stentorian voice, "Tell Ignat to have the sleigh ready by eight o'clock tomorrow!"

In the drawing room were his four daughters, young, pretty girls, all in gray dresses and with their hair done in the same style, and their cousin, also young and attractive, with her children. Starchenko, who was already acquainted with them, at once began begging them to sing something, and two of the young ladies kept on declaring that they could not sing and had no music; then the cousin sat down at the piano and with quavering voices they sang a duet from "The Queen of Spades." Again *Un petit verre de Clicquot* was played, and the children danced about, stamping their feet in time. And Starchenko pranced about, too. Everybody laughed.

Then the children said good night and went off to bed. The magistrate laughed, danced a quadrille, paid court to the ladies, and kept wondering whether it were not all a dream. The wretched room at the village headquarters, the pile of hay in the corner, the rustle of the cockroaches, the disgusting, poverty-stricken setting, the voices of the inquest witnesses, the wind, the blizzard, the danger of getting lost; and suddenly these magnificent, bright rooms, the sound of the piano, the beautiful girls, the curly-headed children, the gay, happy laughter—such a transformation seemed to him like what happens in a fairy tale, and it seemed incredible that such transformations were possible within a distance of two miles in the course of a single hour. And dismal thoughts prevented him from enjoying himself, and he kept thinking that all about him was not life but scraps of life, fragments, that everything here was accidental, that one could draw no conclusion from it; and he even felt sorry for these girls, who were living and would die here in the wilds, in the provinces, far away from civilization where nothing is accidental, but everything is rational and governed by law, and where, for example, every suicide is intelligible, and it is possible to explain its why and wherefore and its significance in the general scheme of things. It occurred to him that since the life about him here in the wilds was unintelligible to him, and since he did not see it, it meant that it was non-existent.

At supper the talk was of Lesnitzky.

"He left a wife and child," said Starchenko. "I would forbid marriage to neurasthenics and people with a deranged nervous system, I would deprive them of the right and the capacity to have offspring. To bring neurasthenic children into the world is a crime."

"The unfortunate young man," said von Taunitz, sighing gently and shaking his head. "How much thinking you must do, how much suffering you must go through before you decide to take your own life—a young life! A misfortune like that can happen in any family, and that's terrible. It's hard to bear it, intolerable."

All the girls listened silently, with grave faces, looking at their father. On his part, Lyzhin felt that he ought to say something, but he couldn't think of anything, and merely observed:

"Yes, suicide is an undesirable phenomenon."

He slept in a warm room, in a soft bed, covered with a blanket, under which was a fine clean sheet, but for some reason did not feel comfortable; perhaps it was because the doctor and von Taunitz were talking for a long time in the next room, and overhead, in the attic and in the chimney, the wind was roaring just as it did at the village headquarters and howling as plaintively: Hoo-oo-oo-oo!

Von Taunitz's wife had died two years previously, and he had not yet reconciled himself to the fact, and no matter what he talked about, he always referred to his wife; and there was nothing about him to suggest the public prosecutor any more.

"Is it possible that I may get into such a state some day?"

thought Lyzhin, as he was falling asleep and as he listened through
the wall to his host's subdued and, as it were, orphaned voice.

The magistrate's sleep was restless. He was hot and uncomfortable, and he dreamed that he was not at von Taunitz's, not in
the soft clean bed, but still at the village headquarters, lying on
the hay, and hearing the low voices of the witnesses; he imagined
that Lesnitzky was near by, fifteen paces away. In his dream he
recalled how the insurance agent, black-haired, pale, wearing
high, dusty boots, had approached the bookkeeper's counter.
"This is our insurance agent—" Then he dreamed that Lesnitzky
and Loshadin the policeman were walking through the open
country in the snow, side by side, supporting each other; the
blizzard was eddying above them, and the wind was blowing at
their backs, but they walked on, chanting, "We go on, go on, go
on. . . ."

The old man looked like a magician in an opera, and indeed
both of them looked as though they were performing in a theater:

"We go on, go on, go on! You are where it is warm and
bright and cozy, but we go on in the cold, in the storm, through
deep snow. We know nothing of rest, we know nothing of joy.
We carry the whole burden of this life, of ours and yours. Hoo-
oo-oo! We go on, go on, go on . . ."

Lyzhin woke and sat up in bed. What a muddled, bad dream!
And why did he couple the policeman and the agent in his dream?
What nonsense! And now, as Lyzhin sat up in bed, clasping his
head in his hands, his heart beating wildly, it seemed that indeed
the lives of the policeman and the insurance agent had something
in common. Didn't they go through life side by side, holding on
to one another? Some tie, invisible yet significant and essential,
existed between the two of them, even between them and von
Taunitz, and among all, all; in this life, even in these wilds,
nothing is accidental, everything is filled with one common idea,
everything has one soul, one aim, and to understand it, it is not
enough to think, to reason, perhaps one must also have the gift
of insight into life, a gift which evidently is not vouchsafed to all.
And the unhappy "neurasthenic"—as the doctor called him—
who had broken down and killed himself, as well as the old

peasant who spent his whole life trotting from one man to another every day, were accidents, fragments of life, only for him who thought of his own life as accidental, but were parts of one marvelous and rational organism for one who regarded his own life as part of that common whole, and had a penetrating insight into that fact. So Lyzhin thought, and it was a thought that he had long secretly harbored and that only now unfolded fully and distinctly in his consciousness.

He lay down and began to drop off; and suddenly they were again walking along together and chanting: "We go on, go on, go on. . . . We take from life all that it holds of what is most bitter and burdensome, and we leave to you what is easy and joyous; and sitting at supper, you can discuss coldly and reasonably why we suffer and perish, and why we are not as healthy and contented as you."

What they were chanting had occurred to him before, but this thought crouched somewhere in the background behind other thoughts and flickered timidly like a distant light in misty weather. And he felt that this suicide and the peasant's misery lay on his conscience, too; to be reconciled to the fact that these people, submitting to their fate, shouldered all that was darkest and most burdensome in life—how terrible that was! To be reconciled to this, and to wish for oneself a bright and active life among happy, contented people, and constantly to dream of such a life, that meant dreaming of new suicides of men crushed by toil and care, or of weak, forgotten men of whom people only talk sometimes at supper with vexation or sneers, but to whom no help is offered. And again:

"We go on, go on, go on. . . ."

As though someone were knocking with a little hammer on his temples.

He woke early in the morning with a headache, roused by a noise; in the next room von Taunitz was saying to the doctor in a loud voice:

"You can't leave now. Look at what's doing outdoors. Don't argue, but just ask the coachman: he won't drive you in such weather if you pay him a million."

"But it's only two miles," the doctor was saying in an imploring voice.

"But even if it were a quarter of a mile. If you can't, you can't. As soon as you drive out of the gates, it will be just hell, you will lose your way in a minute. I won't let you go, no matter what you say."

"By evening it's bound to quiet down," said the peasant who was lighting the stove.

In the next room the doctor began talking of the severe climate that influences the Russian character, of the long winters that, restricting freedom of movement, interfere with the intellectual growth of the people; and Lyzhin heard these pronouncements with vexation, looked out of the window at the drifts that had piled up against the fence, stared at the white dust that filled all visible space, at the trees that bent despairing now to the right, now to the left, listened to the howling and the banging, and thought gloomily:

"Well, what moral can you draw from all this? It's a blizzard, and that's all there is to it . . . ."

They lunched at noon, then wandered aimlessly about the house; they stood at the windows.

"And Lesnitzky is lying there," thought Lyzhin, as he watched the snow eddies furiously circling above the drifts. "Lesnitzky is lying there, and the inquest witnesses are waiting—"

They spoke of the weather, remarking that the snowstorm usually lasted two days and two nights, rarely longer. At six they dined, then they played cards, sang, danced; finally they had supper. The day was over, they went to bed.

In the small hours of the morning everything quieted down. When they got up and looked out of the windows, the naked willows with their weakly drooping branches were standing quite motionless; the sky was overcast and the air was still, as though nature were now ashamed of its orgy, its mad nights, and the free rein it had given its passions. The horses, harnessed tandem, had been waiting at the steps since five o'clock in the morning. When it was fully light the doctor and the magistrate put on their fur coats and felt boots, and taking leave of their host, went out.